THIS FAR WEST

Melissa —
Since you're
way smarter than J
am, J'd really
appreciate you letting
me know what you
think. If you love it,
tell everyone. otherwise... well,
let's just keep it
between us.

THIS FAR WEST

Doug Williams

Writer's Showcase
San Jose New York Lincoln Shanghai

This Far West

Writer's Showcase
an imprint of iUniverse.com, Inc.

For information address:
iUniverse.com, Inc.
5220 S 16th, Ste. 200
Lincoln, NE 68512
www.iuniverse.com

ISBN: 0-595-15864-1

Printed in the United States of America

To my parents, who are nothing like the people in this book and who—despite what they had to work with—still did a hell of a job. And to my wife Shari, who agrees with all that but still looks at me sometimes and shakes her head.

Acknowledgements

This could not have been written without the assistance of many contributors—some seen, some unseen.

If I were to footnote the story, three books would have the large majority of citations. *The Agency: The Rise and Fall of the CIA* by John Ranleigh, provided the historical context for those events that led to the establishment of Arabaq. *Shoot the Women First*, by Eileen MacDonald, was instrumental not only in helping to create the backstory involving Arabaqi women, but also in the development of certain characters in the novel. And Ronald Eriksen's wonderful little volume, *How To Find Missing Persons*, birthed many of Maxie McQueen's investigatory practices. Background on the history of chemical warfare and chemical agents—all of which is true, including the December 1974 U.S. Senate vote that drives the plot—was drawn from hundreds of sources located on Internet databases.

To my knowledge, there is no computer program that works in exactly the same way as the fictional Felon Find. It is an invention drawn from a number of products, most notably Crime Lab image enhancement software and Face ID facial recognition software. The photo enhancement system described in the book is based on PhotoStudio from ArcSoft and a high-tech surveillance system provided by U.S. Public Technologies that was written about at some length in the Jan. 27, 1999, *San Diego Union-Tribune*.

While there is a Stones River near Nashville, there is no Stones River State Prison. Much of the description of the facility—and the treatment of psychotic patients—has its roots in a Nov. 8, 1998, article in *The New York Times* magazine written by Bruce Porter. Similarly, although Paramount's Carowinds does exist, it does not offer an attraction called

The Millennium Plunge. There is a ride at the park called Thunder Road that is located where The Plunge is depicted in the book. It, too, is awfully scary.

I'd also like to thank M. Clark Parker for his help educating me on North Carolina's child-custody laws; members of the Charlotte-Mecklenburg Police Department and the FBI for their assistance in discussing how, when and where ballistics tests are undertaken (for obvious reasons, they shall remain anonymous); Jennifer Warren for typing and valuable research help; Wade Wingard for explaining how to make a bad photo image better; and finally, to the faceless guy on the Internet who answered all my inquiries about sniper rifles, but whose name got zapped when I switched ISPs. All I can say is that he was better than any book.

Any errors or misinterpretations are the sole responsibility of the author.

Doug Williams, Houston, May 21, 2001

Chapter 1

Kevin Columbus stared at the stack of $100 bills, and watched his life fade to gray. Two thick inches of the great American currency, more like two and a half or maybe even three, amazing what the eyes could calculate when the IOEverybodies were going up faster than the space shuttle. Maybe not enough to make him a finalist on *Who Wants To Be A Millionaire*, but good enough for a spot on *Let's Make A Deal*, which was more or less what was going on, what he was considering. A deal. All he had to do was decide whether he could absorb the body shot to his conscience, and if so, what that said about how far and in what direction life had taken him.

"I know what you're thinking," the man across the desk said. A smile, thin and easy, way too self-important, crept onto his round face, the pulpy façade of a head that was two sizes too big. At its center was a nose that alcohol had painted emergency-light red, earning him the nickname Rudolph and ensuring that every Halloween he graced the political costume party circuit in his wide-cut Hugo Boss suits accessorized by strap-on reindeer antlers.

Kevin blinked hard, slamming his lids shut in the hope that when they reopened, he'd see things a little more clearly. No luck. He looked briefly at the man, not willing to engage him in a stare, almost afraid, like there was guilt—or at least collusion—in the mere act of eye contact. "Do you?" he asked finally. Although everything that was still right about Kevin Columbus told him to forget the cash and just get up, walk out, ignore the solutions that had shape-shifted into crisp green C-notes, it wasn't that easy. Little things got in the way, you know, like rent and lease payments on the car and maxed-out credit cards that were bordering on criminally overdue. Dry cleaning'd be nice, too, he thought, looking down at off-white khaki pants and a lightweight denim shirt, both spider-webbed with wrinkles, evidence of an ongoing allergy to simple domestic chores.

"Yes, son, yes I do." The man picked up a fat, half-smoked cigar from a jade-green marble ashtray shaped like a long, narrow ukulele, fired it up with a mini-blowtorch lighter, Kevin flinching at the blue flame, the thing looking like it could weld steel. He leaned back in the executive leather chair, stuck a couple of Bally-shoed feet up on the desk, folded his hands over a gut that probably had its own zip code. "You're thinking, What is this world coming to? What kind of place is it where the most powerful person in this state—with due respect to the Governor—sits in a meeting with a private consultant and offers him money to protect what could, *could*, I want to emphasize, be construed as a criminal act?" He blew a fluffy cumulus cloud of grayish smoke into the air above him. It hung there like a thunderhead in waiting.

The guy wasn't even close to being right, Kevin not thinking about anything so cosmic. No, he was thinking about his old man, 25 years dead, always counseling him to follow his internal compass. "Keep it pointed up," Jon Columbus said, "straight up, focused, aiming north. It'll always get you out of the woods." Which sounded good when you're 12, but gee, Dad, what happens when time is running short, the forest has all of a sudden gotten dark as a grave and the smiling predators are sharpening their eating utensils?

Kevin didn't mention any of this, though, the dilemma being personal and the wad of cash hitting the Mute Button on his moral outrage. He didn't say anything actually, not wanting to send a message that he was overly interested or eager to consider the offer, and not real hot about the idea of confronting what any such contemplation would imply—imply, hell, what it would *say*—about the current direction of the Columbus Compass. So he forced his attention elsewhere. To one wall, whose framed certificates announced that Wayne Earl Wiley had graduated from the University of North Carolina Law School, and could practice before the State Supreme Court, the U.S. Federal District Court, the 4th Circuit Court of Appeals and the Supreme Court of the United States. To the mantel over a fireplace that dominated one wall of the square, cavernous, strangely empty-feeling office, where plaques mounted on glass holders recognized Wayne Earl Wiley as Most Valuable Legislator, Education's Man of the Year and a Friend of Children. And finally, to the credenza behind the desk, and its photos of a proud husband and father, a wife whose pasted-on smile said she knew more than she'd ever tell, two beautiful blonde little girls and a Golden Retriever.

The Ideal Public Servant. The Perfect Family Man.

"And the answer to that question is pretty damned simple," State Sen. Wayne Earl Wiley said, grin spreading like an oil spill. "The answer is, I don't much care. Because we, you and me, we didn't make this world. We are products of it. So what this world is, what other folks have turned it into—that ain't my problem. My problem is living in it the best way I can." He took another draw on the cigar, exhaled slowly. "I hear that is not inconsistent with your problem, either."

Kevin's first instinct was to fire back, tell this pompous prick to go to hell, that other than having two arms and two legs, they were nothing alike, and whatever problems he had were *very* inconsistent with those that had been rusting the good senator's ethical center for decades. Problem was, the pompous prick was in charge—aren't they always?—and he'd put the money on the table. So Kevin swallowed his self-righteousness, looked up at Wiley, and asked simply: "Why me?"

"You come highly recommended."

"I'm good at what I do."

"Maybe the best, I'm told."

Kevin shrugged, getting a tan from the praise, forgetting for a second he was being hustled. "Maybe."

"But you lost your job." Wiley's smile reminding him of life's lesson, the one that went, Doesn't matter how good you are, just who's on top, which you ain't, PR-boy. "Now why is that? Why is it that a fella, all your skills, why is it he just can't catch a break?"

Kevin wished he had an Uzi because man, couldn't he do some good for the people of North Carolina right about now? "I do okay, senator." Stupid answer, both of them knowing if *that* was true, they wouldn't be here.

Wiley smiled, eyes twinkling like some Santa who was skimming from the top of the gift bag, then nodded with pseudo insight, a weary survivor who'd taken one or two at-bats against life, and had ripped more than a few curve balls into the cheap seats. Which was a joke, because the Wayne Earl Wileys of the world always got a free pass, an intentional walk, and it had nothing to do with anything except the fact that if you challenged them, they'd figure out a way to get back at you, and it would not be pleasant. "Tough world out there," Wiley said, mock-somber.

Kevin considered that, answering after a second: "It is what it is."

Which made Wiley go, literally, ho-ho-ho. "Lucky for me."

Too bad about the people, though, Kevin thought, wisely keeping the commentary to himself, all that money being on the table. "Who gave you my name?"

"Beau LaLonde."

Blister, Kevin thought, now *really* wishing he had a gun. "And what did Beau say?" Absently running his hands through brown hair that framed a somewhat boyish face, hair that had gone too long without a trim, and that at age 37 was only now starting to show the silvery streaks of "maturity."

Wiley shrugged. He had large, broad shoulders, hinting that some-where under the fat suit was an athlete long dead. "He told me you were smart and could spin shit real good."

"I strategically rearrange the truth."

"See there!" Wiley whooped in phony admiration. "Just like I said. You just called yourself a goddamned liar, but made it sound more honorable than the Queen of England. Beau was right."

"Did he also tell you I'm smarter and better at it than he is?" Way too much pride in his tone, way too much anger. Way dumb, too, the rule being: Never let anyone know what you're really thinking.

"Hell, that sofa there is smarter than Beau." He gestured to his right, to a dark love seat in deep brown, slightly distressed leather, and half-chuckled. "But the difference is that Beau'll cut your heart out to get ahead. That sofa doesn't want to get ahead. It just sits there, real quiet, and puts up with whatever assholes come its way."

"I know."

"I'm told you do. Hell, you put up with ol' Beau—who's an asshole of monumental proportions—and look what happened. He got you fired, took your job. Hell, I hear he's even banging your secretary."

Don't show him a thing, Kevin warned his rage. Betray nothing. "I wasn't fired," he answered, looking at Wiley dead-on, eye to eye, letting him know this was only about setting the record straight, no more, no less. "My job was eliminated. I was downsized."

"Fine, if it makes you feel better—"

"What else have you been told about me?" Quickly changing directions, veering out of the personal history lane, not even a little interested in talking about the power company or the process that had left him abandoned after 15 years of blind loyalty.

"That you need work, and could use some money. Well"—hands extended, Ta-Da!—"there it is."

Which brought Kevin's focus back to the stack of bills on Wiley's desk. Had to be, what, five grand there? Six? That was a lot of antiseptic, a pile of cure-all for whatever ethical qualms could make a mere man all feverish. "Tell me more about the job."

Wiley leaned forward, and laced his fingers on top of a large leather-rimmed desk calendar, a gift from one of the insurance companies his

Senate committee regulated. If the empty date blocks told a story, it was that the senator didn't have a single appointment scheduled for the entire month, meaning maybe the public was halfway safe, at least in the short run. "The job is to buy time for a corporate associate of mine. Company called American Environmental Security. You heard of them?" Kevin said he hadn't. "Local waste management outfit, and not bad people, that business being what it is."

"What's their problem?"

"Seems that they took a couple dozen barrels of pretty nasty stuff from somebody who was looking to beat the government and save a dime or two, and buried them in an empty field 20 or so miles north of here. Unfortunately, they have now discovered that their dump site is right on top of an aquifer that's the source of drinking water for a little town of about 800 folks around there." His face transmuted to sadness that was too obvious to be genuine. "And they think the barrels have started to leak."

"So their problem is, they're poisoning people."

Wiley hooked Kevin's eyes, wouldn't let go. "Some folks might say that." Paused, readied the set-up, which sounded like this: "Course, we wouldn't be paying them $10,000 to do it."

On cue, Kevin's attention went straight to the cash. Ten Grand. A *really* big pile of cure-all.

"Now before those people start running around," the senator continued, Kevin's reaction not lost on him, "scaring the daylights out of everybody and their hunting dog, we need a little time."

"For tests?"

Wiley let loose a big guffaw, like that was the stupidest thing he'd ever heard. "Yeah. For tests."

"Maybe they should have thought about the consequences before they did what they did."

"They did, and they earned a shitload of money, which pretty much made any other consequence acceptable."

"What about the people who are drinking that stuff?"

Wiley jabbed a pudgy finger at him. "Listen up, son. I ain't offering you $10,000 to be their voice. This is a democracy. The process gives them a voice. I'm offering you $10,000 to make sure the company's voice gets heard if and when this hits the papers."

"What's your job?"

"To make sure that doesn't happen."

"And if it does?"

He shrugged. "Like I said. You buy me some time, I buy me some judges and regulators, everybody wins." Sounding like it was real simple, no big deal, the way things get done in a free society. "Now, I want you to know something else, son. There's lots more money where this came from—and a lot of juice behind it—and the combination of power and money can buy a lot of consequences."

With enough left over for a hefty down payment on deliverance, Kevin thought.

"I know that, being an honorable sort of boy and all, you don't want to act rashly," Wiley continued. "I respect that. But the choice you got ain't all that complicated: You do what's good for you, or you do what's good for everybody else. Look at what's come of Beau." Pause. "Then take a look in the mirror."

Cheap shot, but it landed deep enough under Kevin's skin to pierce an inner truth. "I want to think it over."

"You got two weeks," he said, oddly efficient, reaching for a dime-store spiral notebook and ballpoint pen. He jotted down some names and phone numbers, handed them to Kevin with the knowing smirk of a career confidence man, a role he'd elevated to high art after a lifetime in politics. "Like any good public official, I want you to make an informed decision. So feel free to contact these folks. They'll tell you the whole story."

A politician offering the whole story, Kevin thought. What's wrong with *this* picture?

He stood to leave, had one hand on the doorknob to let himself out when Wiley called, "I probably don't need to say it, but this little session was off the record. If any word should leak out, for whatever reason, I'll deny it, I'll deny knowing you, and I'll produce 30 people who will swear they were with me when this meeting allegedly occurred." Wiley stopped briefly, for effect. "And, of course, there would in all likelihood be, well, unintended...*consequences*...to that disclosure." A low, menacing laugh followed, Kevin seeing in his mind Wiley twirling a moustache, which was appropriate, him feeling like he was tied to the tracks, the Runaway Express gaining steam, not a hero in sight.

But he didn't turn, not about to give the man the satisfaction of Threat Received. Just walked through the door into a wide hallway that passed two other offices and the receptionist's desk, and then down a short flight of steps to the downtown Charlotte streets. Outside, the early afternoon skies sobbed with rain. Kevin stood under a copper-colored awning that read Wayne Wiley & Associates, P.A., watching the stormwaters get sucked into the gutter, thinking, There go the night's profits.

Rain on Tuesdays was a problem. It kept people at home, meaning they weren't at the southside bar asking his friend Maxie McQueen to find their lost loves, meaning Kevin paid the price. Literally. Because even if he didn't pull a lot of cash from the bar gig, every little bit helped, Slow Flow being preferred to No Flow as a financial position.

He glanced at his watch, a $13 Timex from Wal-Mart that seemed like a cool thing to wear when he was pulling down 85K, but in the past few years had become an unintended reflection of his new economic status. Just after two, still early, all kinds of time for things to clear up. Staring into the low-slung clouds, he wondered if a small prayer would do any good. Nothing major. No pleas for personal gain because that just wasn't right (although if you *are* listening up there, any celestial favor would be greatly appreciated). Just a small request for guidance or direction, some celestial roadmap to whatever destination the Fates had chosen, a sense of purpose, anything that would give shape to the future, connect some of life's dots.

Kevin closed his eyes, wondering if anybody who could make a difference was paying any attention, and if they were, would they care? He hadn't counted on hearing a voice, kind of like an angel with a hangover, sandpaper for vocal cords, posing a dilemma that he was in no mood to ponder, not now, not with things being what they were:

"You figure this is the beginning, or did we miss the chance?"

A white guy standing there, outside the awning, rain streaming down a thin face that—along with his hair—needed some serious mowing. Jeans, green Army surplus jacket, basketball shoes that were white gone-to-street, no laces. Call Central Casting, say Give me somebody homeless, he'd be the one sent over. "Excuse me?" Kevin said, tightening up, feeling that wave of revulsion and anxiety everyone gets when confronted by somebody who puts a welcome mat outside a refrigerator box.

"This debate over the millennium," the guy said, looking at him with a weird depth and clarity, like he saw and understood things really important that weren't exactly there. "Was the year 2000 the beginning of the millennium, and did we miss our chance for renewal? Or is it 2001, and is there still hope?" Smacking his lips, chewing invisible gum, looking intently at Kevin as if the future of the world hung in the balance.

"I, uh, never much thought about it," he said, not sure if he was concluding or inviting the discussion.

The bum nodded slowly, like Kevin was either Einstein and had just explained the universe or was the biggest fool in the history of the galaxy. "That's what they want." Head bobbing up and down. "They're counting on it." Bob-bob-bob. "As long as you don't know which is which, too late or still hope, too late or still hope, take your pick, then they've got control."

Before Kevin could say anything, the guy tossed him a wink that doubled as a facial tic, and shuffled off into the storm, bringing their personal *X-Files* moment to a sudden end and returning Kevin to a world whose only issue at the moment was whether there was any way to redefine Wayne Earl Wiley's offer, justifying it more as a resource for personal salvation and less as hush money. And as he thought about that, and whether taking the deal amounted to a second chance or simple surrender, he again closed his eyes, hoping that in the personal darkness he'd find something resembling divine relief.

A hearty, deep, thunderous laugh roared from above. Kevin smiled wryly, shook his head. "Sorry to interrupt," he said half-aloud, stepping from under the protective awning into the downpour, no umbrella, no raincoat, no defense from the forces of nature, which pretty much signaled the rain to come down even harder. "It's just me, looking for a clue, some answers, whatever off-the-rack wisdom the keepers of knowledge are dispensing today."

Another crack of thunder, this one shorter, sharper, taunting, seeming to say:

Excuse us, but who are you again, and why should we care?

Kevin Columbus just plodded on, not answering. Why bother? The Powers Above, whoever they were, they had all the answers. And judging from the way things were shaping up, they weren't talking.

•

When Gary Devereaux asked his doctor, simply, "Is it the Big Casino?"—stealing the line from an old Sinatra movie—he already knew. The operative question at the moment was how long, and even though the prognosis of three months had an impact, it was fleeting. Devereaux had already begun to focus on a more immediate task at hand:

How to keep them from murdering Kevin Columbus after he was gone.

Gary Devereaux had been fighting wars—some of them in plain sight, most not—since he lied about his age to enlist in the Army Air Corps in 1944. And he had long ago learned that for all the brains and courage and insanity that intelligence work required, there was one quality that mattered above all else:

Not caring.

Friends died. Enemies died. Colleagues became traitors. Traitors became colleagues. In the so-called intelligence "family," there was no loyalty. It was a world defined only by ambiguity, and those who dwelled in it had to accept the fact that getting killed or betrayed was as common in his job as punching the time clock was to an honest job. You did what the higher-ups commanded, and if you died because of the unexpected treachery of the person next to you, the guy who was just like a brother, so be it. At least you entered death's doors with eyes wide open, hand-in-hand with the misty knowledge that you went down for something that resembled a good cause.

So he didn't much care about dying. It was an occupational hazard, and at age 72, Gary Devereaux had avoided a premature end on more occasions than he deserved. No, what he cared about now was protecting Kevin from the lethal fallout of the past quarter century, and the murders, lies and deceit that had delivered them to the start of a new American century.

Devereaux walked out of the medical complex onto Doctor's Plaza, a row of flat-roofed pink and mauve colored specialty shops—wheelchairs, crutches, prosthetics, you name it—that had sprouted to serve the sprawling and ever-expanding new industry known simply as Health Care. It was hot, not uncommon for the Gulf Coast of South Florida this time of year, and the day—his doctor's pronouncement aside—seemed brighter than usual. He stood for a moment in the sun, 6-foot frame barrel-solid and still carrying the weight he'd put on more than two decades ago in the "transformation," white linen pants cut just right—breaking exactly where they were supposed to break atop the tan hurackes—eyes squinting even behind the classic aviator shades. The light made his curly silver mane, added in later years to further separate who he was now from who he'd been in the past, glisten more than usual. Likewise the tufts of hair that peeked over the top of his short-sleeved silk shirt, cream-colored with brown drawings of C-47s, Gooney Birds, all over it.

Death aside, Devereaux decided he wanted a cigar.

He meandered down the bleached-white sidewalk, occasionally finding a patch of shade where the palm trees along the street trumped the sun. There was a little wine bar at the corner. Service was dreadful, but it was the only place in the city where he could buy his favorite cigar, a Montecristo No. 2, which after sitting down at one of the outside tables he ordered and asked an indifferent waiter in a black T-shirt and jeans to snip its tapered end for him. When the kid came back with the 6 1/8th inch Figurado, Devereaux ordered a triple shot of Bushmill's, a bottle of Pilsner Urquell as a chaser. Screw it, he thought. It's not the liver that's killing me. It's the pancreas.

Using one of the long-stemmed wooden matches that came with the cigar, Devereaux fired up and drew deeply. The rich taste, tinged with cinnamon and chocolate and a touch of leather, filled his mouth. He savored the smoke, swirled it around his palate, exhaled some, took a bit into the lungs. Strong, full-bodied.

Across the street, an attractive woman with long tanned legs and a white tennis outfit climbed agilely out of a red Mercedes coup, and walked into the upscale grocery store that sat opposite the wine bar. She reminded Devereaux of Kevin's mother. Meredith. Quickly, as quickly as age and longing would allow, he pushed the memory away, closing his eyes as much to the intense sun above as to the image of Meredith Whitney Wade, the one true love of his life.

A Jeep Wrangler pulled into one of the angle parking places in front of him, top down, three high school kids on holiday, radio blaring a Top 40 song that quickly segued into the day's lead news story:

"White House officials were cautiously optimistic about the stunning report out of Arabaq today that General Fakhir Azid has announced his regime's unilateral decision to stop the production of chemical and biological warfare agents."

"I'll be goddamned," Devereaux said to himself. Almost at once, another voice began to steal its way into his thoughts. A voice both distant and contemporary, whose owner was as responsible as anyone else for everything Gary Devereaux had done in his life—good or bad, depending on one's perspective—and everything he would have to do in the short time that remained…

"Gary? Did you hear me? The Royal Family has been overthrown."

"I heard you."

"We missed it. The Company was asleep at the goddamned switch, and that lunatic Azid is in control!"

"These things happen."

"Yeah, well, it wasn't supposed to happen. Not to us, not to me and you and Bart, and I wanna know what we're gonna do!"

"Calm down." A pause, thinking. "Did any of our people get out?"

"No. Azid's Imperial Guards slaughtered everyone when they took over the facilities."

"Good."

"Good? Are you fucking nuts?"

"No. I'm pragmatic. And my pragmatism tells me that we're fortunate."

"What is so damned fortunate about it? The plants are in his control, Gary. Azid has the secrets!"

"There aren't any secrets. Not officially."

"But—"

"No one knows these sites exist. So anyone who died for their role in this matter never existed, either."

There was a long pause at the other end of the line. Then: "One of them did, Gary. Let's not forget that. One of them did."

As the breathless reporter went on about the global impact of the announcement from Arabaq, Gary Devereaux didn't know whether to feel surprised or vindicated. Failing at both, or probably just not caring one way or the other, he decided he was just tired. The strange trip that was his life—made even stranger by this Azid thing, coming as it did on the day he learned he was going to die for yet a second time, this time for real—was drawing to a close. Devereaux rubbed his eyes behind the green-black shades, pulled a $20 bill from inside the beige sock on his left foot, and signaled for the check. Time to go home. Back to the beach house. To plot his next, and likely final, move: To save Kevin Columbus.

He had to move fast. Because even though he was going to die soon, he couldn't shake the feeling that the end was going to come even sooner.

●

"Cash. Now. All of it."

Homer St. John looked at her face, and wondered if the whole thing had been a scam. Here was this good-looking black girl, said she was a private eye, demanding payment before she delivered. Maybe she was a hooker! Imagine that. A hooker. Right here in the front office of Homer's Superior Cleaners, creator of Three Shirts For A Dollar Thursdays, specializing in stains. Homer, that is. Specializing. Not the hooker.

"But I thought you said 50 percent now, that's 200 bucks—"

"I can add."

She wasn't smiling, but at least she wasn't going for her gun. St. John figured that was a good sign. He smoothed out his tie—orange paisley, made her want to gag—and fiddled with the top button of his one-size-fits-small white shirt with the fraying short sleeves. "I didn't mean to suggest, uh, it's just that—"

"What it's *just that*, Homey, is *just that* my lawyer called me this morning, and said if I don't have $400 in his hands by tomorrow morning, my gloriously sexy Nubian ass is gonna have to find different legal representation. Which, I hasten to add, I am not inclined to do 16 and one-half months into my case."

What little color remained in Homer St. John's pudgy face evaporated. Talking about her butt like that, even though it was a nice one, especially in those painted-on jeans, not that he'd noticed. "Do you, um, have...legal problems?"

"No," she snapped. "Do you?"

"Well, as we discussed, my, uh, former business partner has, well—"

"He made like an egg and beat it, Homes. Took nine grand of your hard-earned dry-cleaning profits, and blazed off to his ex-wife in Gastonia. His ex-wife, that is, with an unlisted phone number and a post office box, the combination of which disables your attempts to track him down and reacquire what is rightfully yours."

Homer St. John shuffled. Even though he was sitting behind a cheap metal desk, she could see his feet moving around on the floor, forward and back and forward and back, like he was going nowhere in baby steps. "Ninety-three hundred, actually."

"Four point three percent of which is $400."

"How do you know that?"

"I can divide. Multiply. I am just a math-uh-matical wizard, Homes, and the figures I am currently obsessed with are, in order, Four Oh Oh. Which I want. Now. In cash."

He looked squarely into her dark brown eyes, trying to summon the nerve to say something truly manly. Nothing that wouldn't get him shot came to mind. The girl—34, 35, he thought, give or take—leaned back into the standard-issue, plastic-molded waiting room chair, crossed her long legs and let loose the kind of sigh that Homer St. John always thought tended to make ladies' breasts heave. As he lost his mental place wondering about those lovely breasts all a-heave under that rough-girl black denim shirt, he resolved to get control of the situation. He was, after all, the client, the meal ticket, and if her breasts were—

"Am I gonna have to kill you, Homes?" Her voice took the starch out of more than just his resolve. "Because it's gonna cost you a lot more than four hundred, you keep staring at my chest like that."

An invisible hook seemed to jerk Homer St. John back into his faux animal-hide chair. "I'm sorry," he mumbled, "I didn't mean, I just—oh, mercy, I can be such a boob sometime."

She cocked one eyebrow, gave him a lopsided grin. "Excuse me?"

"I said—"

St. John caught himself, went red as Lenin's blood. "Omigod."

Jesus, she thought, when this guy fell out of the stupid tree he caught every branch on the way down. She leaned forward, put her elbows on the desk, locked her fingers into a "here's the church, here's the steeple" position, except without the steeple. Rested her face lightly on the clasped hands. Grinned wearily. "Homes. Listen: Give me the $400, I'll make the call from right here, we get the address, your lawyers serve the papers. You win, dry cleaners rule, blah blah blah."

"What if it doesn't work. Do I get my money back?"

"No. You get to sleep with me."

Homer St. John couldn't get the money on the desk fast enough. Men, she thought. Predictable as a dog's footprints in the mud.

He counted out four $100 bills. Not once. Not twice. Three times. "You're sure it's all there, Homes?" she asked. He counted it again, blind to the You Are A Disgusting Pig subtext that spiked her tone.

She picked up the phone and dialed. Homer was looking at the only thing hanging on the wall, a high school band calendar. She couldn't tell if he was trying to schedule their tryst, or was only now grasping the fact that it was still 1996 staring back at him. Whichever, he was transfixed.

So when the monkey sounds started, Homer St. John tumbled ass over teakettle out of his chair. "What's that?" he screamed, peering over the top of his desk like some nerdy Kilroy Was Here, eyes cutting to one side of the 14- by 14-foot office and then to the other, keeping a sharp lookout for the impending primate stampede.

She held up a cassette player, to which she'd attached a pair of mini-speakers, out of which came lots of monkey sounds. Loud monkey sounds. With the hand that wasn't holding the phone, she gestured for him to chill out, and go into an adjoining room and listen on another line. He did as ordered. In a second the show began.

"Gastonia Post Office, this is Mike." A bored voice.

"Yo, Mike, it's Viola Chestnutt from downtown. How you all doing out there in the booming metropolis of Gastonia."

"Fine."

Ah, postal workers, she thought. Got to love their economy of expression. "Yeah, well, listen, I got me one major-domo-sized problem here—"

"Where are you? In a jungle? You sound like you're in the jungle."

"That's my problem, Mike. I got three crates of monkeys sitting not 10 feet from me."

"Monkeys?" Mike didn't sound happy. On the other hand, Homer St. John looked for the first time like he was intrigued by something besides one of her body parts.

"Of the ring-tailed variety. I'm supposed to ship 'em to a woman over there, but all I got is a P.O. box. How 'bout checking the 10-93, and getting me a street address?"

"I can't do that," Mike said, indignant. "It's not public information."

She cranked up the volume on the tape player, and moved the phone closer to one of the speakers. "For crissakes!" she screamed. "Will you all shut your damned banana holes?" Back into the phone: "Sorry, Mike. You ever seen a hungry ring-tailed monkey?"

"Uh, no. Can't say as I have."

"These are my first, Mike. I'm never going back to the zoo. Ever." She waited for a response, got nothing, moved on. "Mike. Man. Talk to me."

"I told you, Winona"—for some weird reason, calling her the wrong name just cracked Homer St. John up—"I can't give you the address."

"Then we got us a sitchy-ation, Miguel, 'cause I'm lookin' at a slew o' monkeys with no place to go. You guys got a place for live animals there?"

"What? There's no way—"

She heard the sudden panic in his voice, thinking I Own You. "Better find something, then, 'cause these critters are on the next truck outta here, coming directly to you, Live from Gastonia, Hey, Hey, it's the Monkeeeeees!"

"No! Wait!"

"Wait, hell. You think I want these smelly, starving, vine-swinging little apes hanging around here, making all this racket, stinking up *my* office with their monkey do-do? There's no way in the world—"

"Okay, okay, okay."

She grinned at St. John and winked. "I'm sorry, Mike. What was that again?" Ah, sweet victory.

"The name. What name do you want?"

"Mabel Lloyd."

"Hang on." About 20 seconds later, Mike was back on the line. "I got a Mabel H. Lloyd, a Mabel T. Lloyd and an M.L. Lloyd." She shot a look at Homer, who clenched the phone between his neck and shoulder while giving her the sign of a T. Then he promptly dropped the damned thing. "What was that?" Mike asked. "Somebody on another phone?"

"Uh, Rhoda knocked an ashtray off the desk."

"Rhoda? One of the monkeys is named Rhoda?"

"No, Mike, Rhoda ain't no monkey. She's one of ours. Though I got to tell you, she's got some hair on her—"

"That's more than I care to know about Rhoda, thank you."

"Okay, then. It's Mabel T. Lloyd at…"

"At 1404 Emerson Way."

"Mike, you don't know how many people will unknowingly applaud this random act of courage."

She hung up before he could answer, and shut off the tape recorder. The little room was silent except for the sound of Homer St. John's accelerated breathing. "Oh, wow, that was just the best thing I have ever seen."

She took the four bills, stuffed them into her jeans pocket, put on a black L.A. Raiders baseball hat—backward—and smiled at him. "That's only 'cause you ain't ever seen me butt nekkid, Homey."

With that, she spun on the heel of her right python boot and walked triumphantly into the rain, calling out over her shoulder, "And don't be chokin' no chickens thinking about it either, Homes, or I may be forced to kill you."

Homer St. John called out something to her, but the words landed unheard on the back of his door. Maxie McQueen, former police detective and now private investigator, had left the building. And as was her habit since nearly beating a fellow cop to death the year before, she never looked back.

●

Gary Devereaux's beach house was modest by most standards. One large room doubled as a kitchen and den; a terrazzo floor segued into some all-purpose carpet, signaling the end of the former and the beginning of the latter. The walls were painted off-white, and graced with the usual coastal artwork: paintings of salt-marsh beach-scapes and sea birds and ocean sunsets and fish. A broken-down leather recliner sat in one corner. In another was a dark walnut entertainment center, floor to ceiling, that had a television set lodged on its center shelf and held a lot of glass knick-knacks that looked like they could have belonged to anyone but Devereaux. Against a large picture window that opened onto the neighbor's rain forest of a side yard was a plush sofa that had not graced Devereaux's frame in as long as he could remember; there was a turquoise and black, Southwestern-looking blanket draped over it that fit with nothing else in the room. An anonymous gift from Meredith, he'd always assumed. Sliding Japanese screens could be pulled out to mask all the windows in the place, and exclude the world from any knowledge of what was going on inside. He liked that, putting the screens to optimum use. Only at night would he expose himself to the Gulf of Mexico that, at high tide, rolled to within 50 feet of his cracked concrete rear patio.

The air of unintended and detached eclecticism—Asia meets Arizona meets Traditional Beach—gave the place a feeling of domestic fraud, like it was a poorly assembled showroom model disguised as somebody's idea of the real thing. This was not so much a home as it was a permanent stopover. Given that he'd been leasing it on a year-to-year basis for 15 or so years—never complaining when Liz Fletcher, the realtor, boosted the rent "just to cover my costs, you understand"— Devereaux had never felt much attachment to his "on-paper" life. Recently, he'd felt it even less, spending most of his time in the massive bedroom, at a large printer's desk that made him feel more secure than anyplace else under the roof. Beneath the desk was perhaps the only clue to Devereaux's true past, a reinforced titanium safe so strong it would take three sidewinders to knock it out—but even more important, strong enough to hold and protect the secrets.

Back from the wine bar, he went directly to the safe, punched the complex combination into a computer-operated keypad on the front of the box, withdrew three items. A scrapbook. A No. 10 envelope, white but slightly yellowed with age. An old snapshot. From the main drawer of the desk, he produced two 5-by-7 manila clasp mailing folders, another white business-size envelope, and a little pair of scissors, like the kind children use in elementary school art classes.

He'd cracked out a plan while returning to the island. It was really pretty basic: Put the evidence in the possession of those it could help the most, and those it could destroy, and let the threat remain real if unspoken.

Large, unmade bed behind him—flanked by rattan nightstands stacked with foreign policy magazines and painkillers—Gary Devereaux worked intently. With remarkably steady hands, he removed a strip of film negatives from the yellowing envelope he'd taken from the safe. Slowly, he counted the frames, each of which had a small number in the upper right-hand corner. He began at 208; at 213, he stopped, and sliced that portion of the film away from the next image. One more stroke of the mini-scissors, and the next frame, Frame 214, was alone. Devereaux put it in the white envelope, and replaced the remaining frames in the other.

Then there was the snapshot.

He squinted at it under the brass desk lamp, whose green horizontal shade threw an eerie light on the wall behind him. Twenty-five years ago, the three of them standing there at the lake resort. They could have been any three Americans off on a Swiss holiday, seemingly without a care in the world. Devereaux smiled, not without regret. Thinking: How images can deceive so thoroughly.

He tore the photo in two pieces. Not in half. Two-thirds and one-third. Just like the three people in the picture. Only different.

The two-thirds portion was added to the envelope that contained Frame 214. Devereaux packaged the other part with the remaining negatives, put them into one of the 5-by-7 mailers and sealed it without including a note or letter. On the front, he scribbled an address that was unfamiliar to most of America, but known widely to those handful of people who ran it.

That done, he considered the second package. What to say, what to say?

No time for melancholy. Not after all these years. Just be honest. For once in your life, be honest. He was. Brief, straight to the point, no drippy emotion.

Devereaux quickly wrote out a note, added it to the envelope with Frame 214 and the rest of the torn photo, sealed everything in the second manila mailer, addressed it and walked up to the little postal station tucked away in the corner of a strip shopping center a half mile or so from the beach house. Satisfied that both packages would arrive if not the next day, at least the day after, he paid 52 cents for each and returned home to finish the job.

There was a moment when he considered making the call from a pay phone. But he wasn't up for the aggravation. Home was easier, anyway, and when you're about to die, there is added value to convenience.

Using the princess phone in his bedroom, Devereaux dialed directory assistance, got the number, placed the call. When the operator picked up, he said he needed to talk to his cousin. Their great aunt had suffered a heart attack, and was going to die. The operator said she understood, but there was policy, and the policy was that his cousin would have to call back collect. Devereaux figured as much, and said that was fine. He went to the kitchen and poured himself a shot of Bushmill's—which he drank over ice, in a black coffee cup emblazoned with white starfish—and waited.

Ten minutes later, the call came.

Devereaux picked it up on the second ring, agreed to accept the charges. "Do you know who this is?" he asked evenly after a moment.

"Yeah." There was a touch of anxiety in the voice, but it seemed tempered by an odd resignation.

"I thought you might want to know that you're the last of a dying breed." There was silence. "Do you understand me?"

"Yeah." Voice flatter this time. No emotion.

Without another word, Gary Devereaux replaced the phone. Retrieving the scrapbook—something fell out, an old news clipping, but he didn't notice—he went back to the kitchen and refilled the cup, then to a drawer in the scarred wooden credenza in the den where he pulled out an ivory-handled pistol, just like Patton had in North Africa.

He sat down in the broken leather chair and hit the television remote. One of those sleazy afternoon talk shows was on, this one about deadbeat dads who continue carrying on affairs with their ex-wives because neither wanted the responsibility of raising the kids. Most people watching in perverse fascination were probably thinking, Good God, are there really people like that in this world? Sadly, there were. Gary Devereaux knew them.

Gun at his side, he began to read the scrapbook, again, as he had done so many times in the past quarter century. And he waited. Not to die, for death was now a certainty. No, he waited to see who they would send.

•

It took less than 45 seconds.

Inside the small, one-story brick building outside of Falls Church, Virginia, the monitoring system captured the calls, ran them at hyperspeed through phone records from every country in the world that was wired for talk. Not only was it quick. It was puzzling to the technician staring at his computer screen.

For going on 15 years, this little non-descript operation—DDI Industries, according to the block letters above the front door—had been intercepting calls to and from the number in South Florida. There had been thousands, literally, to almost any location on the planet, none of them adding up to much of anything. Nothing, anyway, that raised any red flags with the consortium of business people who scuttlebutt had it were bankrolling DDI. And he'd been here watching this number, and a whole lot more, from the get-go, in the process making a ton more money—legal or illegal—than he'd ever pulled down during his days with The Company.

If what the computer was telling him was right, the guy in South Florida had been on the horn to a state prison in Tennessee. What was weird was that in all the years he'd been eye-balling this cat on the beach, the man had never called or received a call from this particular number. Just for the hell of it, he cross-referenced all Tennessee numbers against the guy's phone history. Nada.

The technician thought it over, wondering if he should save it for the weekly report, due day after tomorrow, or call it in immediately. Deciding a first-time abnormality merited on-the-spot action, he picked up the secure phone in his office, dialed a private number. When the crackling static ended, signifying that the line was secure, he related the discovery. And when the weary voice at the other end said only "Oh, Christ" before breaking the connection, the technician began wondering if he'd done the right thing.

Chapter 2

If Oliver Stone, Leslie Stahl and Bill Gates ever had an illicit *menage a trois,* Rollie Merke was reasonably sure he'd have been their collective love child: A dogged conspiracy monger slash journalist born for the computer age.

From his basement apartment in Alexandria, Virginia, he published an Internet magazine called *Merkey Waters,* which his web site said was devoted to "Sniffing Out the Stench of Secret Schemes." Befitting such a character, the one-room living area—his cyber newsroom—was lit by little more than two computer screens and the three television sets that delivered news shows from around the world, thanks to a friend who was expert at stealing satellite signals from the local cable company. The dull monitor-glow-as-lighting was probably for the best anyway, as illumination of any sort would have been hostile to Rollie, whose gaunt frame, pallid skin, bowl haircut and wispy blond chin-whiskers—he looked like the twisted twin of Scoobie Doo's owner in the Saturday morning cartoon show—had been known to make babies cry and dogs bark.

Even if the place had been bathed in spotlights, it would not have been pretty. Battered metal file cabinets, choked with reports of fiendish worldwide plots. A green couch, Salvation Army vintage, that had a second job as Merke's bed. Two wooden Jack Daniel's crates, end to end, a very '60s, very Boheme coffee table. Mud-colored shag carpet. Standard movie poster collection: *The Parallax View, JFK, Executive Action.* In one corner was a hat rack that held an array of floppy canvas surf hats. "Web surfer, get it?" he'd ask anyone who looked at them, and at Rollie, and figured this was a guy who couldn't catch a wave with a baseball glove the size of Wyoming.

Like so many of his fellow conspiracy travelers, Merke had started with the usual suspects—Oswald, Ruby, Sirhan, James Earl Ray, Arthur Bremer, that crowd—creating a crude web site from a cookie-cutter, do-it-yourself package he picked up on Buy.Com. Ignoring the fact that there were more than a billion pages on the Net, Rollie couldn't understand why he wasn't getting any hits, not even on his biggie—a 2,214-word piece that "confirmed" it was Lyndon Johnson, not Oswald, who was on the 6th floor of the book depository in Dallas. The story was that LBJ had been brainwashed by the Mafia to kill Kennedy, a la *The Manchurian Candidate*. The guy portraying LBJ in the motorcade was really the head of a monolithic defense company who was there to provide plausible deniability in the event Johnson was linked to the conspiracy, which revolved around an affair between Castro and Marilyn Monroe that was in reality the true cause of the Cuban Missile Crisis.

Then one day, he got an anonymous email from somebody known only as CABALGUY, suggesting that maybe he ought to quit riding those tired old nags and climb on a new horse: U.S. Senator Richard Worth, who was assassinated on the streets of New York City, July 6, 1975, by a right-wing crazy named Rayfield Buskin. And faster than the Warren Commission could say Single Bullet Theory, Merke started getting a never-ending stream of scoops that left the dedicated shadow-chaser no choice but to take up the challenge.

Never mind that personal diaries showed Buskin's rage over Worth's emergence as a serious contender for the presidency in 1976. Or that Buskin had written threatening letters to the senator, or that photo archives showed him at no less than a dozen Worth events in May and June. Or that Buskin had denounced Worth on a radio call-in show for being weak on communism and for failing to recognize that pre-marital sex in Third World countries was the greatest moral crisis of the day. Or that the five-member Knight Commission, headed by a respected

Harvard professor, had ruled that Rayfield Buskin—an expert marks-man, by the way, who'd taught himself to shoot after his home was robbed by two black men—alone was responsible for firing two bullets into Worth's head as the senator walked into *The New York Times* build-ing for an editorial board meeting.

Details, Rollie Merke sneered. Details.

Following the age-old media dictum that only living people can refute a lie—Worth was dead, and Buskin was shot to death by a body-guard whose bad heart, an autopsy showed, stopped pumping in the excitement of the moment—Merke's monthly net-zine spun into over-drive. There were wild tales of drug dealers in Marseilles who dealt coke to U.S. politicians—Worth included. Rogue Green Berets who felt Worth's opposition to chemical warfare in the jungle was tantamount to treason. Self-described mercenaries who related in great detail how a team of killers was recruited out of Angola by white supremacists to murder Worth over his liberal civil rights position. Nothing was too bizarre. Especially when it involved dead people who couldn't sue.

The leads continued, too, many of them written in such perfect Merke Speak that all he had to do was slap on a headline and byline, and go for the glory. CABALGUY never wrote anything, though. He was more of a tipster, a cyber-source whose information could have come from J. Edgar Hoover's ghost for all Merke cared, just so long as it found its way into the *Merkey Waters* email box, enabling Rollie to keep issuing FLASH reports, like the one he was polishing up right now, the one'd he'd gotten not 10 minutes ago:

Worth Conspirator Devereaux To Go Public In Florida!
Is 25-Year Stench Of Senator's Death About To Lift?

Rollie Merke sat in the semi-darkness, reread the 150-word item, and then the headline. He smiled at the bold, black, dense type that filled the Sony Trinitron monitor, and moved the mouse over the Apply box on the menu. Clicked once. In a few minutes, the word would be out, and

Rollie Merke would be the hero of hundreds, thousands—millions!—
for unraveling the last great conspiracy of the 20th century.

Or, if everything continued to go as planned, preserving it.

•

More than a thousand miles to the southwest, in the Hill Country of
Central Texas just outside of Austin, Taylor Shepard powered up her
laptop, a high-end notebook from Rodale Technologies. It was gorgeous
outside, and she'd opened every window in the anonymous, sparsely
furnished efficiency apartment that sat in one corner of a complex just
off Interstate 35, about 20 minutes north of the state capital.

As was the routine every day before she started making her calls, the
32-year-old freelance writer sat at the glass-topped table in her tiny
kitchen—wearing only a bright orange University of Texas sleep shirt
that stopped halfway down her long legs, blonde hair pulled through
the back of a Gap baseball hat—and logged onto her Internet provider.
She waited for the connection, took a sip of coffee from her Don't Mess
with Texas cup—great theme, she'd always thought, part of a statewide
anti-litter campaign—saw a tiny exclamation mark next to the envelope
icon in the lower right-hand corner of the screen.

You've got mail.

She moved the cursor to the icon, clicked on it. Twelve new messages.

The first was from an underground magazine in Seattle stating they
were considering her piece on the rise of satanic cult activities in high
schools, and would get back to her quickly. Another from an alternative
weekly in L.A., promising careful review of her proposal for a story on
the rise of white slave rings in upscale suburban neighborhoods. A third
from her publication of last resort, *Eye in the Keyhole*, a checkout-line
tabloid that was gaga over her 99 percent fictitious report that Michael
Jackson was undergoing cosmetic surgery to make himself look like
Elvis. They promised her that a coming week's front page would

scream: "Will King of Pop Be Satisfied Being Just King? Will Gloved One Drop Pop?" Payment would be wired, per her typical instructions.

All that, and nine rejections.

"Goddammit," she muttered, rubbing her green eyes under the Kazuo Kawasaki designer glasses, tinted slightly blue. They go for the cults, and white slavery in the suburbs, and anything that has Elvis in the first sentence. But they're not even slightly interested in the greatest single mystery of our time:

Who killed Richard Worth?

Well, maybe in its own weird way this isn't so bad, she rationalized, deleting the rejections one by one from her mailbox. After all, the lack of interest gave her some cover, some protection. The fewer people out there chasing the story, the better for her. She could operate quietly, in the shadows, out of the glare, without any snooping little reporters getting in the way. Better yet, she more or less owned the story, which meant she could bend it, shape it, *create* it in any way that suited her. All things being equal, that wasn't necessarily bad.

But it wasn't exactly aces, either. The new media millennium didn't look a whole lot like the one that has just passed, so if a story didn't reek of bimbos and blowjobs and generate a whole new batch of Woodward and Bernstein wannabes—committed to winning a Pulitzer, taking down a president and selling the rights for seven figures—then conventional wisdom held that there was nothing there to write. Worth's death hadn't generated much of anything, other than a blanket acceptance of the Knight Commission's conclusions, a handful of quickly dismissed books and some "educational" software that went for $29.95 at Best Buy. Periodically, there would be a lone uptick in fascination with political murders—release of classified documents about the JFK killing, for example—and she'd place a story, usually in a Web e-zine or maybe *The Keyhole*, that would be immediately debunked as madness, plunging the flame of intrigue into an Arctic lake of ridicule and disbelief and reaffirming everyone's belief that everything about Worth's murder was exactly as it seemed.

So after a freelance career that had begun when she returned from backpacking in the Middle East and graduated from Northwestern, all her Worth File contained was a stack of clips that seemed to just bury the story deeper and an address book full of loonies who'd taken one too many hits off the conspiracy bong.

Speaking of which.

Taylor put the cursor over Bookmarks on the Internet tool bar, and clicked once. Thirty-three web sites turned up, ranging from *USA Today* to CNN to a newsletter about JFK's murder called *The Grassy Knoll*. Pressing the Down arrow, she brought the cursor where she wanted it, hit Enter and watched as *Merkey Waters* began to fill her screen.

The first image was a large pencil drawing of Merke, lines without detail, that had the amateur feel of a child's self-portrait. Next to that, along the right edge of the screen, was a narrow strip of headlines under a bright yellow box whose large black letters howled: *Today's Stink*. Beneath the banner were the usual outrages:

SECOND GUNMAN BELIEVED SIGHTED IN AMSTERDAM SEX VIDEO.

JOE CAMEL AT WORTH DEATH SCENE?

JULY 6, 1975: WHERE WAS TONY ORLANDO?

My God, Taylor Shepard thought, not bothering to give any of them so much as a glance. What kind of world offers a fool like this a soapbox and a megaphone, and pays for the privilege of listening? This one, she thought. This one.

Suddenly, the screen went blank.

There was a noise—it sounded like a small explosion, maybe a muffled gunshot—and *The Merke Report* disappeared into a sea of blood red.

A second explosion blew the red away.

Replaced it with a word—

FLASH!!!

— and then a headline—

Worth Conspirator Devereaux To Go Public In Florida.
Is 25-Year Stench Of Senator's Death About To Lift?

A thick black bar beneath the second line invited readers to Click Here for The Inside Story.

"Devereaux," she said softly. "Devereaux."

Taylor Shepard smiled cryptically. After a moment, as if on cue, she began to write.

●

"Yo. Kevin. Amigo. *Que pasa?*"

Maxie McQueen looked at the short, Armani-suited 30-something guy with slicked-back jet-black hair who'd just sauntered up to her at Score, a south Charlotte sports bar. He caught her gaze, flashed a smile so unnaturally white it looked digitally enhanced, and winked. Maxie beat back the urge to grab an icepack and plunge it through the offending eye. Instead, she looked at Kevin Columbus, standing next to her, sipping a Miller Lite. "Friend of yours?" she asked, skeptically.

"Former associate," he answered, uncomfortable with the surprise encounter. "Max, this is Beau LaLonde."

Maxie drained the club soda, her drink of choice since the nasty little incident affectionately known as The Fesperman Christening, "You French, or just affected?" she asked.

LaLonde gave her an autopilot smile. "Cajun. My daddy's from Louisiana."

"Ah," she nodded, doing her best imitation of bored. "So you're a crook."

The smile widened. "And I'd just love to steal that heart of yours, girl."

Maxie stared a light saber at him. "You see a girl, you paint her house. Otherwise, you can call me Ms. McQueen or shut the hell up."

"Whoa, Kev, dude, you better try to tame this one before getting back in the saddle," he roared, way too loud, saying it in a way that made the sexual connotation clear, eyes sparkling like a $14 diamond. "She's a lit-tle vixen."

"No," Kevin deadpanned. "Vixen is a reindeer. Does heavy lifting for a fat white guy."

Maxie picked it up from there. "I, on the other hand, carry a gun, and know how to turn PMS into a legal defense."

LaLonde's glance ping-ponged from one of them to the other and back, expression lathered in confusion, like he didn't know if she was being serious, or if it was a joke—and if it was, who it was on. After an uncertain pause, he asked, "So, uh, what're you saying?" cocky grin frozen somewhere between self-styled cool and calling 9-1-1.

A sharp knock bounced off the top of the bar, Maxie slamming her glass down, followed by a question that came out of nowhere: "Your mama and daddy weight-lifters?"

Beau LaLonde looked even more confused now, like a duck someone had smacked in the head. "Uh, what do you—"

"It's not a trick question, skippy. And I ask it only because I have this feeling they were major league Mr. and Ms. Universes."

"Huh?" Really lost now, three dimensions beyond The Twilight Zone.

"I figure that's the only way they coulda raised an all-world dumbbell like yourself." She smiled, not meaning a muscle of it, informed them she was off to powder her nose.

"Ouch," LaLonde said, watching her disappear through a door that said Ladies' Locker Room. "She's a piece of work."

Kevin nodded. "That she is."

Beau caught one of the server's attention, ordered a margarita and pulled up a barstool. "So, Kev, how you doing, man? Good? I hear things. I mean, this detective scam"—gesturing to a sign over the door that said, Find Your Lost Love—"what a stunt. Mondo perfecto. Wish it was my idea."

"It would've died from loneliness if it had been." Smiling, tossing the line off, a joke between a couple of old buddies, except there was no hiding the fact that Kevin meant every syllable, him holding Beau LaLonde in a regard typically reserved for, say, a nest of spiders—apologies to the spiders.

"Hey, you're not pissed about the job thing." Looking genuinely hurt, even surprised, like How Could You?

The *job thing*? What an asshole. "I'm not pissed about anything. Life's too short."

"Because, you know, I went to bat for you. With the beancounters." Beau greeted the arrival of his margarita—rocks, no salt—like it was the Second Coming. He took a long sip, tried to gauge what was kicking around in Kevin's head so he could measure his own response.

Kevin on the other hand was desperately trying not to launch this guy into Y3K. "And don't think I don't appreciate it." His tone saying, Not too damned likely.

LaLonde fiddled with his watch. A Rolex. "I didn't sell you out, amigo." He put a hand on Kevin's shoulder, squeezed, got serious. "What they did to you was a crime. If it was me making the decisions, no way you'd be outta there."

"If it was you making the decisions, I'd've left of my own free will." Kevin's arms were glued to his side, hands going from clenched fist to full extension, eventually finding a rest area in the pockets of his jeans.

"Now hang on there, partner—"

"They had a layoff list, Beau. My name wasn't on it. Yours was. That little girl you were screwing in Human Resources showed it to you. My name suddenly appears, yours suddenly disappears. A blind man could put that puzzle together."

"Then why'd I tell Wayne Earl Wiley about you?" Saying it in a haughty tone, like Oh, Yeah? So There.

Kevin took a long tug from the beer and glanced at one of the big-screen TVs on the wall. Astros-Cards, 'Stros up 7-1 in the eighth. "The good senator enlighten you as to what the job is?" Eyes wandering edgily over the dark room, most of the wooden booths full—each had its own mini-TV for sports viewing—most of the tables empty. Refusing to look at LaLonde. Choking the life out of the Miller bottle.

Beau LaLonde tried not to seem clueless, wanting to appear to be In The Know, but still looking as if Kevin had just pop-quizzed him on the formula for cold fusion. Took a sip of the drink, like there was insight to be found in margarita mix. Flicked a piece of non-existent lint from the charcoal gray Armani suit jacket. Lightly patted hair that seemed lacquered to the top of a face Kevin always thought was just a moustache and glasses away from looking like Mr. Potato Head's corporate twin. Rolled the chunky gold bracelet around on his right wrist. Smiled emptily at a bored waitress who responded by staring right through him. "I know the story. More or less."

Which broke Kevin up. "Jesus, Beau, how do you make it in the business world? Being allergic to the truth is one thing. But you can't even lie convincingly. And if you can't do that, you can't play the game."

"What do you know about playing the game?" Answering sharply, seeing a chance to retake control of the conversation. "If you played the game, you wouldn't be here."

"That wasn't my job."

"It's the only job that matters," LaLonde snorted, stepping back, eyeing Kevin like he was an auction item, assessing the goods before making a bid. "You know something? Everybody at the power company respected you, but nobody really liked you. You never partied with them. Never ate with them. Never chased women with them." Smiled sadly, and falsely, shook his head. "I mean, what were you thinking? Did you really believe business was about how good you were at your *job*? Please." He pulled a flat engraved silver case from inside the Armani coat, removed a cigarette—brown, English, how utterly Beau—and fired it up. "It's a new world, my friend, and it's got nothing to do with substance or skill."

"Then tell me what it is about, oh sage one." Grip getting tighter on the longneck.

"It's all about what you can do for me. You did your job, and you did it well—"

"I don't need a review from you."

"Yeah, fine, whatever." LaLonde waved his hands dismissively, took another hit from the cigarette, which had the sweet-bitter smell of cloves. "You did your job, and that's good. But I cultivated people who mattered. And that's better." Kevin leaned back against the bar, taking everything in without seeing it, wishing he could reach inside himself, find the razors that were carving up his guts and use them to fillet this arrogant sonofabitch. "You got to start thinking about *you*, man. What's in it for *you*. What *you* want."

At that moment, Kevin knew exactly what he wanted, and when Beau added—

"Victim or victimizer, man, take your pick."

— he acted on it.

With one fast, fluid motion, the beer bottle was off the bar, long neck in Kevin's hold, starting an arc that was unmistakably destined for Beau LaLonde's head.

Just as fast, so quick that no one other than the combatants had any idea what was about to happen, it stopped.

Not by Kevin's will, which at that moment was off the scope, beyond his control, but by a dark, slender hand that cuffed his wrist barely an instant after the bottle lifted off. "Don't do it," Maxie said. "I speak from experience."

Without emotion or protest, Kevin set the bottle down. In the few seconds that followed, Beau LaLonde thawed from the stark realization that his head had nearly gone into orbit. "You need to do the world a favor and put a lid on that temper, man," he said at last, trying mightily to put himself back together, the effort sabotaged by a voice that didn't believe its own words and a sudden flop sweat that threatened to drown his crisp hairline. "One of these days, you're gonna kill somebody."

"And if there is a God, it'll be you," Maxie smiled sweetly. "So why don't you do us all a favor, make like a cow patty and hit the trail"—pause for effect—"uh-mee-go."

Beau stubbed the cigarette out in an ashtray, hands shaking slightly. Trying the macho bravado act, he made a big deal of letting his eyes take a stroll up and down Maxie, who was still arrayed in the black Mean Ass Denim Chic she'd worn while charming Homer St. John earlier in the day. "When you want to be with a real man, you call me."

"When I want to be with a real man, I'll watch a Wesley Snipes movie." LaLonde stood, started to say something. Maxie cut him off in mid-syllable. "Beat it, skippy. You're bad for business." He said nothing, just smiled—smirked, really—shook his head slowly, like You Are Such Losers, and moved to another end of the bar.

Maxie watched him with not a little scorn before turning to Kevin. "You know, if it wasn't for him, I'd say you were the stupidest white person I'd ever met."

"What?" Saying it half-heartedly, knowing where all this was going.

"That Raging Bull with a bottle number, which I need not say could've cost us this gig." Kevin nodded, shook his head, a silent admission she was right. "Which would divert money from The Maxie McQueen Legal Fund. Which would mean I'd probably have to kill you."

Kevin blew out a lung full of air. "Sorry. I worked with Blister—actually, he worked for me—at the power company."

"Blister?"

"He always showed up after the work was over." Maxie nodded, the name making perfect sense, and ordered a double scotch and soda, hold the scotch. "I hired him and after I got laid off, he got my job."

She ran that through her mental processor. "Lemme get this straight. You work for this company what 12, 15 years, they let you go and keep that moe-ron?"

Kevin nodded. "He had friends in high places. I didn't."

"Story of our lives." He got her subtext immediately, Maxie's Christening of the Good Ship Fesperman striking too many of the aforementioned highly placed people in the wrong way, no pun intended, and her paying the price.

"We probably ought to mosey on back to the workplace," Kevin suggested, trying to change the subject, motioning to the promotional table display set up next to the bathrooms—photo of Maxie, looking like an inner-city Mrs. Peel, from the old *Avengers* television series, black jeans, leather jacket, Raiders cap, what the papers called The Full Maxie. "Who knows what lost loves are just waiting to be found."

As he started to move, she planted a hand in his breastplate. "I don't mosey, junior. I sashay."

And she did, accompanied by every eye in the place. Men wanting her, women envying her, everybody wondering what in God's name she was doing hanging out with a goofy white guy like Kevin Columbus, looked like an unmade bed.

It was simple. When he was head of corporate communications for a large regional utility company, she'd been the police department's liaison to the business community. Maxie, naturally, thought it was a lot of see-through PR—black, woman, progressive cop shop, aren't we enlightened?—but tolerated the assignment, her being no dummy, knowing full well it would keep her star pointed in the right direction. They'd wound up on a community relations committee together, and after a couple of meetings found more than a few connect points. Both loved their jobs, were good at what they did, didn't much care for office politics. Both had earned a "someone to keep an eye on" label early in their careers. Both were ambitious, but unlike almost everyone else in their respective professions, it was ambition with a purpose.

All of which was pretty impressive, except it didn't account for a thing when their respective roofs collapsed.

After 15 years with the utility—he'd gone there straight from college, and risen through the proverbial ranks—Kevin Columbus was reclassified as Dead Wood and terminated. Competitive climate, the fat-assed human resources hatchet man said, got to cut costs, tough decision but we got to think about the shareholders, yada yada yada. All of which was true, and Kevin knew it, but come on. Blister's machinations aside, didn't loyalty have any place in the corporate equation? He'd had three offers over the years, each one for more money than the last, and he'd rejected them all. The job, his job, *that* job, was the only thing that ever mattered, and if you'd asked him to make a decision between his personal and professional life, don't hold your breath because work was going to win. Every time. In the absence of relationships that lasted any more than a few months—and with the death of his father in 1975 and his mother's weird but in-character decision to abruptly remarry and run off to operate a bed and breakfast in Arizona—the power company had become his only family, his sole investment. There was a contract of sorts between them, he believed, and he felt a duty to respect that.

Clearly, the corporate parent felt no such compulsion.

He'd been out on his own for about 18 months, doing freelance writing and consulting work, getting by if not necessarily ahead, when Maxie called. Out of the blue, just like that, saying, "I'm off the force. Don't believe anything you hear. I wasn't really trying to kill him. I might've if they hadn't pulled me off, but they did, so who cares? Let's do some business."

Her business was Max McQueen, Private Investigations, and she wanted Kevin to help generate some client traffic. Off the top of his head, he suggested they go to local singles bars one night a week and offer to find lost loves. She said that was the craziest thing she'd ever heard, he said fine and hung up, she called back in 30 seconds saying she still thought the idea was dumb as a bag of hammers but what the hell, money was money. Except at first, there wasn't a whole lot of that either, Kevin explaining to her they had to get a following, win some free publicity, Maxie explaining to *him* how grocery stores had this new policy, maybe he'd heard of it, the one that says We Only Take Money Not Free Publicity For Food.

Then they struck gold. Using a special locator software package that an unnamed supporter inside the police department had pilfered for her, Maxie broke a big one. A young bride-to-be, the daughter of a man who owned one of the few remaining independent banks in the city, got stood up at the altar before God and a whole lot of Daddy's friends, the runaway groom last seen slinking out of the back of the church, crying like a little baby.

One night, barely two months after the incident, the jiltee came into Score. Egged on by a couple of friends and six Jell-O shots, she went to Maxie's table, sobbed her story. For some reason—probably because the kid was in one way kind of like Maxie, who also thought she'd found The One, had his child, and then watched as the sonofabitch ran from his responsibility "like I had the Ebola virus"—she took a special interest in the banker's daughter. Three weeks later, she'd found the fleeing fiancée who, as it turned out, left because he thought he'd fallen in love with the stripper at his bachelor party. "I needed some time to get right," the young man told her after the software revealed he'd just gotten a chauffeur's license to drive food supply trucks in Omaha. "There had never been anybody else, and suddenly there was, and I didn't know what else to do. So I ran."

"Don't apologize," Maxie had said. "You're a man. It's in your blood."

She dragged him back to Charlotte, reunited him with the jiltee—cold feet, not a hot stripper, being the excuse, never mentioning the purloined software, the possession of which probably broke more than a few laws. Kevin called *The Observer*, which gave it a ride on the front page. All of a sudden, Maxie was The Love Detective. She cut a solo deal with Score, the bar, guaranteeing 10 percent of the cover, and half of everything the bar sold above $500. Drawing as many as 200 people, she could make upwards of six, seven hundred on a good night—a third of which she shared with her "white devil agent." And every Tuesday, they sat at their little display table, asked the lovelorn a few questions, took some notes, looked concerned. Maxie did her thing, found a wayward guy or girl on occasion, Kevin made a couple of phone calls to the local media, somebody reported something, people cooed and said Isn't That Nice, the legend continued.

Although on this Tuesday night, the legend was not exactly hitting on all cylinders.

As Kevin feared, the rain had crippled the evening traffic. They'd gotten their inquiries; there just weren't a whole lot of people at the place. Populations at the booths and tables were dropping. Six drinkers sat at a long S-shaped bar. Only two of 12 pool tables were getting any action. The high point of the evening was when some college kid walked in with a live python wrapped around his neck, said, "My friend here needs some help." Maxie pulled out her Swiss Army knife, motioned to Kevin. "My friend here needs some snakeskin boots." The college kid left.

Back in their respective places at the Love Table, Kevin nodded and smiled at a couple of professional-looking women—best guess, legal secretaries, one finishing off a soft drink through a straw, the other a gin and tonic—who were making eye contact with him as they rose from a booth across the room. The one with the Coke was pregnant. Kevin quickly closed his eyes, opened them after a moment, seeing Maxie staring at him like he was some freak. "What is that?" she asked.

"What is what?"

"Every time you see a woman 'with child' you close your eyes and mumble."

"I don't mumble."

"Don't give me that. I can see your thin little white-boy lips moving. Now what does it mean?"

She'd fixed those killer eyes on him, started to move her head back and forth, slightly, like If you don't answer me, pain is in your future, so you might just as well admit it, ain't no way out of this. "I see a pregnant woman, and I just, uh, I say a little prayer. You know. A silent little prayer. That she'll have a happy and a healthy kid. No big thing." He smiled again at the pregnant woman and her friend as they left.

"You ever pray for me and J.J.?" Meaning her 8-year-old boy, Jamal Jackson, who Maxie had been raising alone and who was now the subject of a long, mean, expensive custody fight—not between Maxie and the father, who to this day she hadn't identified, but between Maxie and her sister Carmella.

"All the time."

"Then how 'bout you ring up whoever it is you have these discussions with, and figure out a way to get him back with me?"

Kevin closed his eyes, massaged his forehead, kicked himself for bringing up *that* issue, thinking Good Lord, when God was handing out brains, did you think He said Trains and put in a special request for one that goes backward? At that moment, all he wanted to do was crawl under the table or slink out or vaporize, anything that would save him from diving any deeper into the fool pool.

"Excuse me. I know the sign says Love Detective. But do you look for people that other people love, even if those people aren't, like, lovers?"

Kevin opened his eyes, saved by the voice. It belonged to a smallish, mousy-looking woman, 30s, not unattractive, with wavy black hair to just above her shoulders. She wore a simple blue dress, white daisy print pattern. Her left hand was loosely wrapped around something.

To Kevin, she looked lost. To Maxie, she looked terrified.

"Who are you looking for?" Maxie asked with a gentleness whose occasional sudden arrival never ceased to amaze Kevin.

"My brother," she said. "Older brother, I mean. Henry Lee."

Maxie smiled, still being all warm and nice, still amazing Kevin. She gestured for the girl to sit down at the chair opposite them. "You know, Miss—"

"Hubbard." The name seemed a reluctant escapee from her lips. "Donna Hubbard."

"Okay, Donna. What I wanted to say was that after 48 hours, you can file a missing persons report with—"

"Oh, it's been longer than 48 hours. It's been 25 years." Maxie shot a look at Kevin, both of them thinking this could get real strange real fast. "I need to know if he's alive. That's all. Really. Um. Whether my uh, brother, Henry Lee, my brother Henry Lee…whether he's alive. Or, um, dead." Biting her lower lip, trying to beat back tears.

"Okay…" Maxie ventured.

"Because if he is…" A single sob racked her, and she took a breath so deep it sounded like she was trying to suck all the air from the room. As if not knowing what else to do, she opened her left hand to reveal a yellowed newspaper wirephoto. Eight people, standing on a street in some concrete canyon of a metropolis, all pointing in various directions at something—the conspiracy freaks had all said some*one*—off the frame.

What is *this* all about, Kevin thought, recognizing the photo instantly.

Hesitantly, with a quivering index finger, the girl touched the image of a small child hanging on to an older man, most likely her father, his free hand and arm jutting left and skyward. The child wasn't pointing. Instead, her head was bent far back, attention focused on something above, and in the opposite direction, the other side of the street. "That's me." She stopped suddenly, clipping her words, almost as if she didn't want to say too much, afraid of what these two strangers might do with the knowledge.

"Take your time, honey," Maxie said, patting the girl's hand, leaning closer, caressing her with a voice that promised I'm Going To Take Care Of You. "Just tell me what's got you so upset."

This time, the words didn't have to fight their way from Donna Hubbard's mouth. They simply tumbled out, like heavy stones over a cliff of uncertain height and peril:

"If he's dead, I'm the only one left for them to kill."

Chapter 3

Marvin "Huck" Finn, Attorney at Law, leaned back in his pricey-looking leather executive's chair, idly scratched the top of his shaved head and pushed up the sleeves of his ice-blue Fila warmup jacket to the elbows. "Detective," he said, tone and expression taking a turn for the somber, "there has been a complication. Two complications, actually."

Maxie McQueen instantly wished she had the four bills back, the ones she'd earned the day before from Homer the Dry Cleaner and had just handed over to her lawyer. "That doesn't sound real good, counselor," she said, eyeing him, asking herself once more why in God's name she'd picked an attorney who advertised in the newspaper's Sunday TV section, whose phone number was 1-800-CASH NOW and whose office was between a yogurt shop and bail bondsman in a strip shopping center he affectionately called Health and Wealth Mall. Getting the same answer: Because he's the only one she could afford.

"It's not, I'm afraid." Huck smiled, sadly, which was out of character. He was a good guy, a shyster, sure, but he was her shyster, and she'd genuinely come to like him in the 16 or so months he'd represented her in the fight to pry J.J. from Carmella's wannabe mommy talons. How could she not like someone who, when they first met, asked: "You know why an apple and a lawyer are alike? They both look good hanging from a tree." Then he laughed that squeaky laugh of his, made him sound like a gerbil on helium.

But the Huck that sat opposite her now, framed on three sides by self-assembled pressed-wood bookcases that held dusty copies of the North Carolina statutes, wasn't the guy who'd amused and entertained her, or who at times had actually given her hope. This Huck seemed down, resigned, even pensive. "Part of the problem is, of course, unrelated to you," he continued. "It is a business matter, revolving purely around the firm and its financial practices." *Firm* being a euphemism for the one-room storefront office, battered wooden desk and crammed metal file folders that technically served as his place of work.

Great, Maxie thought. "Let me guess: Internal Revenue."

He shrugged. "Suffice it to say that I may be forced to pursue my career from a more, how shall I put it...*tropical* setting."

"Huck, man, listen to me, you can't back out, we're too far down the road—"

"Detective, please." He cut her off with a cross-handed gesture, like a miniature version of a baseball umpire's Safe signal. "That's my problem. Not yours."

Oh, God. "What's my problem, then?"

"The Witch." His name for her Carmella. "She and Speedo"—his name for Theo, her husband and co-conspirator—"are asking the court to terminate parental rights."

Maxie felt her body go hot and limp at once, like melted lead. "She can't do, I mean, how can she—"

"Her lawyers will attempt to portray you as Mommie Dearest with a gun and a violent temper."

"That's nuts, and you damned well know it!" She rose from her chair—it looked like a dinette set remainder—and started pacing. Huck's office being barely big enough for the lawyer himself, she was basically meeting herself coming back. "I'm an all-world mother. Hell, I even took an apartment I can't afford, just so J.J. could have his own room. There's not a weekend goes by we're not at the mall, or the movies, Carowinds, go-carts—"

"Detective—"

"Hell, the kid has more Nikes than Michael Jordan—"

"Detective—"

"And before that bitch stole him from me, he was doing great with his piano lessons, man, gonna be bigger than Stevie Wonder—"

"Detective—"

Stopping suddenly, right in Huck's face: "He's my son, goddammit! *Mine!*"

The lawyer didn't so much as twitch, having seen and heard all this before. "You might even prepare yourself for allegations of endangerment. And I'm afraid that, given the rather extreme position the judge has taken to date, a juvenile court may not be willing to see things much differently."

Maxie collapsed back into the chair, energy replaced by a sudden exhaustion deep enough to drown in. "One mistake." Shaking her head slowly, looking up at him. "One stupid mistake, and now I've got to go to court and fight for the legal right to be my child's parent?" Huck nodded. "This isn't right. Not even a little."

"The law is not about who's right and who's wrong," he said softly. "It's about who wins."

"Yeah. Right. And what are my chances of winning?"

Huck arched an eyebrow. "On a scale of one to 10?"

Her irritation flashed. "Just gimme a damned answer."

"About minus five."

"What's it gonna take to keep from losing my son?" Trying to think it through, latch onto anything that didn't look, feel or sound like surrender.

"Another lawyer."

"That's a given, Huck. What else?"

"A great deal of money. And a lot of pull."

Neither of which, they both knew, Maxie possessed.

It all started with a murder that defied logic.

Then-Homicide Detective Maxine Arliss McQueen had spent most of the day at a barber shop in Hampshire Hills, a quiet neighborhood in northeast Charlotte that over the past two decades had gone from nearly all white to 75 percent black. A 17-year-old-kid casually walked into the place, smiled at Herman the barber, and shot him twice in the face with an Undercover .38. Before the customer in the chair could move, he was dead from a single bullet in the forehead. A third victim, an old guy who just hung out at the shop to escape the heat and read back issues of *Jet* magazine, was wounded in the chest, and not expected to live. Then, just as casually as he had walked into the place, the boy put the gun in his mouth and with the fifth of the five-shot .38 blew his brains all over the mirror behind the shop's two cracked leather chairs.

Three dead, one dying, no motive. Wasn't a robbery. No gang fingerprints. While they'd have to wait for the coroner's report to see if the kid was on drugs, nothing suggested he was a junkie. Nothing suggested anything, which was what made it all so unnerving. Here was a nice-looking boy, draped in Hilfiger, looked like he could have been an extra in *The Cosby Show,* who for reasons they'd probably never know just decided to check out in a way that guaranteed 15 minutes of fame as the local news lead.

The incident had left Maxie shaken. It was one of those rare moments when she wondered about the world she'd chosen to bring J.J. into. Carmella—fat and happy in that upscale North Charlotte neighborhood, married to an assistant to the assistant to the assistant vice president for something at Bank of America, the two whitest black people she'd ever met—had warned her, even argued for an abortion. Maxie told her in no uncertain terms that wasn't going to happen. It had nothing to do with philosophies or religion, anything like that. She just wanted a kid. Besides, she suspected that what really griped Sis was how having an unwed mother in the family might affect the rise of her corporate-climbing husband.

"This can be a bad place," Carmella had sermonized, especially annoyed that Maxie would not tell her who the father was, "and a child without a family, a whole family, will be its surest, most innocent victim."

At the time, Maxie just chuckled, telling her to save it for church. The day of the murder, though, Carmella's words had the ring of truth rather than pulpit preaching.

She'd worked late on the case, trying to track down the shooter's family and friends. The lack of success in finding anyone who could illuminate the crime had served only to ratchet up her frustrations and fears. J.J. was at a sleepover party with some of his friends—Carmella and Theo, childless themselves, had volunteered to serve as chaperones, part of what Sis had called their Pilot Parents program, like J.J. was some test serum from the Centers for Disease Control—and as much as Maxie wanted, needed, to see her son, she concluded that her anxiety was a burden better left unborne by the boy. So when a former partner, Carlton Grigsby, suggested they grab a drink at the local cop bar after work, it sounded like a good idea.

At the time, anyway.

They arrived late, and there had obviously been some serious imbibing going on. Maxie threw back three quick tequilas to file down her nerve endings, and was on Red Stripe number two when some rookie cop named Fesperman, a white kid with close-cropped hair and the look of a Montana militia man, started talking about the barber shop shooting. He went on a beer-fueled rant about the likely identity of the shooter. "I'll bet you a dollar to a donut," he brayed, pushing aside nervous whispered warnings to shut up, "that he ain't got a daddy, and his mama's on welfare." It was at that point that he half-turned and sneered, over his shoulder, in Maxie's direction. "Proof that what this city don't need is another unwed mother with a baby gonna grow up a murderer."

At which point Maxie grabbed a half-full bottle of Absolut Citron by the throat, and christened the good ship Fesperman with a vicious crack to the head. After he dropped like an anchor, half-conscious and bleeding from a gash that later required 18 stitches, Maxie climbed on top of him, pinned his arms with her knees and held the jagged glass neck of the bottle under his chin. "Some children of unwed mothers grow to avoid the trap of murder," she said, slowly, hissing through clenched teeth. "The same, however, cannot be said for their mothers."

Nobody knew for certain if Maxie was going to slash the rookie cop's carotid artery. She said she wasn't. Anyway, before she even had a chance, three of her colleagues had yanked her off Fesperman, who quickly passed out from a fear cocktail chased by a bloody hole on his scalp.

It was a dumb thing to do, Maxie knew that, dumb, dumb, dumb. And yeah, the higher-ups at Charlotte-Mecklenburg PD would no doubt have to do something to her. Worst case, she figured, a reprimand, administrative duty for 90 days. There were extenuating circumstances, after all, and everybody in the place knew it.

Except that the rookie cop's father was the largest single contributor to the speaker of the North Carolina House of Representatives, who happened to represent Mecklenburg County in the state legislature. In the eight hours that followed the incident, a lot of phone calls were made, some of which no doubt explained why, at 6:20 the next morning, two uniformed officers were at the front door of her apartment saying she was being charged with attempted murder.

Dazed by the warrant, she remembered very little of what happened between that moment and the meeting, 90 minutes later, with the deputy police chief and a toady from the mayor's office. The meeting, though, she could recite just about every word of that.

"You are in a lot of trouble, Detective McQueen," the toady said. "You have placed the mayor, the city and the department in a precarious position. The question now is, are you willing to extricate yourself—all of us—from this mess you have created?"

Sure, Maxie said. Whatever it takes to make this go away.

The toady smiled. "The mayor appreciates your cooperation."

He slid a piece of paper toward her, asking for a signature at the bottom, in the space between RESPECTFULLY SUBMITTED and MAXINE ARLISS MCQUEEN. A resignation letter.

She came out of the chair like a bottle rocket, rudely pushing the table into the toady's midsection, sending a spray of black coffee all over his starched pink Ralph Lauren dress shirt, yelling, "You tell the mayor Maxie McQueen said go to hell, you little two-bit, political hack blowboy!" She looked at the deputy chief. "Right, chief?"

The deputy chief said nothing. "Detective," the toady continued, evenly, "if you refuse, the following sequence of events will occur: You will be fired. You will be indicted. You will be tried and convicted. You will be put away for a long time, a very long time, I assure you. And your child will become the custody of the state, spend his formative years learning the lessons of juvenile crime, preparing for a life that will in all likelihood end in a crumbling public housing project, with a drug-deal gone bad." He straightened himself up, went to the refrigerator in the room where they were meeting, pulled out a bottle of seltzer water and poured a little bit of it on the coffee splotch on his shirt. "And if you act now, I won't bill you for the dry-cleaning costs."

He'd bagged her. They both knew it.

With the powers-that-be so arrayed, Maxie knew there was no future in arguing or threatening to sue, and she sure as hell wasn't going to plead for their forgiveness, their understanding and a second chance. Shooting a look at the chief that managed to send him a message of rage and betrayal and disappointment all at once, she signed the papers and walked out, head held high, not averting a single glance that came her way. Only got weak once, and then just for a millisecond, when she saw Carl Grigsby, her old partner, standing at the coffee machine, looking broken, not even able to flash her his famous wink, the one that was shorthand for Everything Is Gonna Be Okay.

She went straight to Carmella's home to get J.J. from the sleepover. What she found instead was a restraining order preventing her from getting within 50 feet of her child. Signed by a judge who, no surprise, was a former law partner of the House speaker. Defiant, standing by the door frame garbed in a pink nightgown and bunny feet slippers, preventing Maxie from coming in, Carmella coolly informed her: "We are asking for an emergency hearing."

She could've been speaking Hindu, all the sense it made. "What?"

"For custody of J.J."

Maxie just stared at her, unbelieving. "Are you on drugs, woman?"

"Our lawyer says the boy will be ill-served by a mother of questionable moral standing. Sex out of wedlock. No father. Binge drinking. Attempted murder. We expect to be heard the day after tomorrow."

There were words, Maxie accusing Carmella and Theo of legitimized kidnap, Carmella responding that a child should not be raised in a home where there were guns, by "a woman of violence." This went on for 10 minutes, right there on the front steps, Carmella finally trying another tack in an effort to douse the fire. "I understand your feelings," she said, looking all concerned, Maxie knowing there wasn't a shred of genuineness to the performance. "But listen: You have no income. You have no insurance. You are without any means of support. So tell me, sister, just how do you expect to care for your son?"

She knew everything, Maxie thought. Somebody had wired this deal from top to bottom.

"You always spoke of the child," Carmella continued. "I'm thinking of J.J. You have to understand that. Please, don't get mad."

"I don't get mad, Sis. I get even."

Which caused Carmella to stand a little more rigid, and invited a resumption of fire. In a moment, it passed, replaced by a knowing chilliness Carmella seemed to have patented. "I'll be sure to tell them that at the custody hearing," she said, slamming the door in Maxie's face.

The search for lawyers had started at that moment, ending in a comic-tragic kind of way with The Huckster.

At the emergency hearing, they'd drawn a hard-liner who by reputation and record was not likely to rule in Maxie's favor, regardless of the fact that she was the natural birth mother. He didn't, granting Carmella and Theo temporary custody and scheduling a hearing two months later, at which he again presided while Carmella and Theo and a cast of thousands chanted the same mantra—no father, no job, no money, violent tendencies, guns in the home—contrasted with the gingerbread house in white suburban Charlotte whose benefits J.J. technically enjoyed. Seeing nothing to reverse his initial decision, and conveniently ignoring the fact there was no evidence to support any charge other than Maxie was a loving, caring mother, the judge granted aunt and uncle permanent custody. While Maxie could seek a re-hearing, she would have to present evidence that circumstances had changed. So she quit drinking altogether, and started working to aggressively build her detective business. Income and sobriety followed, but a change of heart by the judge didn't:

Six months later, he reaffirmed his earlier decision.

And now, less than a year later, Huck's latest announcement seemed to suggest Maxie's losing streak was about to continue unbroken.

●

Gary Devereaux spent half the night reading and rereading the articles he'd kept in the album, stolen and secret memories, some not even true. A little after two in the morning, he placed the leather-bound book in a small metal garbage can, doused it to near saturation with lighter fluid, and watched as his personal history vanished once more, this time sanitized by flames rather than experts in the art of human transformation. The evidence suitably destroyed—he buried the ashes in the side yard—Devereaux returned to the broken recliner, which had been turned into something of a fortress. Tucked between the seat cushion and the side that was intact was the bottle of Irish whiskey, now empty, and the television remote. Tucked into the other side was the .45. On his lap was the Southwestern blanket, pulled from the rarely sat-on sofa, and a couple of pillows, beige with seahorses stitched into them. Domestic sandbags. The knowledge of what was coming hot-wired his brain cells, making sleep impossible, leaving him staring at but not watching an endless line of television shows, the 9 a.m. edition of which had Regis and Joy interviewing the young star of a new teen-friendly drama from Fox.

But that was the plan: Sit there and wait, and when they arrived, reveal nothing until they made the first play.

Whoever *they* turned out to be.

At 10:29 a.m., the day after he'd made the call that could end more than just his life, someone rang the doorbell, knocking Devereaux out of a haze that was induced as much by exhaustion as alcohol. "Federal Express for Mister Gary, uh, Dever-awks?" a puzzled but eager voice chirped from the other side of his door.

"Leave it," he mumbled, loud enough to be heard, not wanting to cross the room and open the door. His right hand found the .45.

"No can do, sir. Need a signature."

Persistent. "Then leave a pickup notice. I'll get it later." Gripping the gun tighter.

"It's not ticking or anything," the delivery person laughed, trying to make a joke.

"Then your truck and your warehouse are safe." The booze had deadened his senses, but not his irritation at stupid chitchat. "Leave it, and be on your way."

"Whatever you say, sir."

Devereaux heard a notebook scraping on something, followed by the sound of the screen door pressing against the main door when the notice was taped to it. Feet walking away. An engine cranking up. A vehicle driving off.

He waited, listening for the sounds of a return, hearing nothing.

Funny, he thought. Here you are, going to be dead for sure in a few months. But still, you're afraid someone is going to steal what little remains of the rest of your life. Paranoid old fool.

Tossing aside the pillows, Devereaux struggled to his feet and staggered uncertainly to the door, remembering the days when he could kill a fifth of Seagram's and still do what had to be done. That was the problem with age, he mused. It came with too many memories.

When he opened the door, one of them, born a quarter century before in Nashville, was resurrected—

"You can't do it," the shorter of the two men—blondish, reed-thin— said, sneering, putting him squarely in the crosshairs of a glare so filled with hate and derogation that it was as if pure evil had settled upon them all. "You know why?" The eyes now dripping with superiority. "Because you're a child, a fucking ch—"

—and he could have sworn he was looking into those same eyes, again, after all this time, eyes made even clearer and, yes, even deader, by the brilliance of the morning Florida sun.

"Sonofabitch," Gary Devereaux said, in an odd way happy that in the waning moments of his life, he could enjoy a final revelation.

"Let's go inside." The FedEx chirpiness was gone, replaced by a .45 that looked remarkably similar to the Colt Devereaux had used years ago to commit the only murder he'd ever been directly responsible for.

"I don't have them," he said, backing away from the door, into the room, answering a question that had yet to be posed. "In my current state, life insurance has little value."

"No truer words were ever spoken, Gary." There was a thin smile, joyless, and a sad shake of the head. Devereaux saw it, and recalled Nashville once more.

Chapter 4

Maxie wished she and Kevin had persuaded Donna Hubbard to background them the night before, at the bar, because after taking the one-two combo from Huck that morning, she wasn't even slightly up for chasing down a long-lost brother—all that conspiracy nonsense aside—when her kid was slipping further away. But the girl had said she wasn't ready to meet just then, needed some time to get herself and some history together. And there was no way Maxie could pass this child along to Kevin, who was more or less along for the ride.

Besides, Donna said she could pay, cash to boot, which had a prioritizing effect on Maxie, basically pushing everything else to the back burner. No mention of how much, but so what? If it could be spent, and God knows if anybody could spend it, a lawyer could, that was cool with her. Make a few calls, bank a few bills, get a new attorney—already had three names from the Bar Association's referral service in Raleigh. Who knows, money left over, maybe she'd hire a hit man for Speedo and the Witch, or do it herself if the cash well was dry.

Not that she'd thought about it, murder that is, not seriously. But there had been visions of kidnapping, threats of bodily harm, begging and pleading, hostage-taking—the whole made-for-TV-movie thing. But for all the swirling anger and hatred and fear, Maxie at least had the sense to understand that any fool thing she did would only make matters worse. So she'd play by the rules, at least for now. And if fate took a pass on helping her out, and all the decent, law-abiding options vanished like steam, well, hell, she'd just have to go on and take the plunge, whack Speedo and the Witch, steal her child back, give J.J. a life on the lam, free of all the things that make a little kid's young life worth remembering.

Lucky boy, she though grimly. Lucky, lucky boy.

●

"Everybody in the picture's dead," Donna Hubbard said bluntly, gesturing to the newsphoto on a low, glass-topped coffee table in Maxie's living room. Donna and Kevin sat on a non-descript gray sofa, which other than a black beanbag chair was the only place to park. Maxie was opposite them, cross-legged on the floor.

"My dad, his name was Wilmer, was shot in a hunting accident later that year, 1975," she continued in a soft, respectful voice that was touched by the Old South, reciting the events almost by rote, as if reading from a history book rather than recounting a collection of family tragedies. Putting her finger over the image of each person as she spoke. "My mom had a heart attack in 1976. My sister Gretchen and her little boy got caught in the middle of a convenience store robbery two years after that. There was a shootout. They both died. This is Ricky. He was a year younger than Henry Lee. Leukemia took him in 1988. My mom's brother, Tommy, he got stabbed to death in a poker game in New Orleans. It was 1992. Then Darlene. Last week. In the car accident." Feebly, Donna added: "My family's all gone."

Maxie instinctively looked at the mantel over her pretend fireplace, propane-engineered logs, which she never used for fear of blowing the apartment up. Pictures of J.J. Lots of them.

Kevin stared at the photo on the coffee table. Ever since Richard Worth's murder 25 years before, it had become one focal point of an ever-sputtering effort to show that someone other than Rayfield Buskin had been involved in the senator's shooting. All these people, standing on 43rd Street in New York, right by *The Times,* staring and pointing every which way, their faces masked with confused horror.

All except the little girl.

Donna took a sip of decaf Diet Pepsi, the strongest thing Maxie had in the house these days. "Henry Lee was looking for a bathroom," she continued. "There was no place to go; we tried a little walk-in restaurant or something, but they said we couldn't use it unless we bought something. And Daddy said for that kind of money, Henry Lee could just hold it in." She flashed a slight, girlish smile that memory quickly extinguished.

"And that was the last time you saw him?" Maxie asked.

"Yes, ma'am. When he went into that building down the street from where Senator Worth was shot."

"How long was he gone?"

"Before the shooting? Maybe 10 minutes."

Maxie considered that for a moment. "Why were you in New York?"

The girl brightened. "Oh, Henry Lee paid for all of us to come up. It was a family vacation." Maxie and Kevin exchanged looks, Donna catching their doubting expression and explaining, "Oh, that's just the way he is. Generous and all." The brightness dissolved. "The way I hope he still is, anyway."

"He just turned up one day, and said you were going to New York?"

"Yes, ma'am. Him and an Army buddy who spent the night before carrying us all to the train station the next morning."

Kevin stared at the child in the photo. "You look pretty calm."

"I'm not really sure I knew what was happening." She hesitated. "I'm not sure I know now."

"Why don't you tell us what you think happened, what you saw, what you can remember," Maxie suggested.

Donna Hubbard closed her eyes, as if the story was somehow etched in the darkness of her mind. "It was Sunday, and we were just walking—"

— through Times Square. It was a little after noon, and the day was a scorcher, up around 90, which they knew because there was a sign or billboard on top of one building that gave the time and temperature.

They'd eaten at the Howard Johnson's, and were headed south down Broadway, going nowhere in particular, country-come-to-the-city, taking it all in. At 43rd Street, Henry Lee decided he had to go to the bathroom. Some good-natured ragging followed—Wilmer Hubbard announcing, "Son, I swear to God, you pee more'n any woman I ever met. More'n your grandmama, even, and she pissed like a thoroughbred"—but Henry Lee just said when you got to go, you got to go. He ducked into a stand-up diner, only to return with news that the restroom was off limits to everyone but paying customers, whereupon Wilmer Hubbard said he'd be damned if he was going to pay for the boy to take a leak. So Henry Lee told them all to just hang on, he'd run into this place on the other side of *The Times*, and see if they'd let him use the can. He headed toward 8th Avenue, and disappeared into the building at the corner.

Not expecting an especially long wait, the Hubbard family just meandered along the sidewalk—walking in a pack, all too aware of the horror stories about what happened to out-of-towners in the big bad city—up the block and then back, glancing into windows, averting the eyes of passersby, watching the Sunday matinee theatergoers arrive for a pre-show brunch.

Five minutes passed. Then six. Seven. Eight. No sign of Henry Lee.

Just before 12:30, a black car pulled up. Big, not a limo, but impressive anyway. Two men in the back seat, one in the front, all of them sitting there for a few seconds before finally getting out. The driver first, looking up at the buildings, then along the street. Then the two in the back, one of them shorter than the other, wiry and intense, early 40s, black-framed glasses. The other was taller and more thickly built, wearing a bow tie—"one you tied yourself, not a clip-on"—and toting a brown leather briefcase whose gold buckle fasteners caught the sun as he passed behind the car. All in dark suits. The two men from the back seat moved quickly along the sidewalk and up the steps to *The Times*. The third man, the driver, lingered behind. Then the man in the glasses stopped right before going in, and said something first to the one in the bow tie, and the two of them froze, right there on the steps, and then to the driver, who started doing something funny with his arm, "like it was trying to take off from the rest of his body," and then just like that—

"The shooting started," Donna continued. "We heard these pops—they sounded almost like a car backfire—and everybody started pointing, and then there were some more pops, and we all dropped to the sidewalk, scared out of our minds. None of us moved, nobody said a word except Daddy, who kept saying The Lord's Prayer. Anybody watching would've thought we were the ones that'd been hit." She stopped for a moment, but her composure was no where near cracking. "We didn't know then it was Senator Worth who'd been killed."

Both Kevin and Maxie were struck by her detached, oddly impassive narrative. It seemed that more than just the years alone now separated Donna Hubbard from that day on the street.

"These pops you heard," Kevin prodded, cautiously, not knowing how far to push. "Where did they come from?"

"Everywhere, it felt like. That's why we're pointing all over the place."

Which was not inconsistent with the Knight Commission report, Kevin knew. The assassin on the left side of the street, across from *The Times*, shooting Worth; the private security man on the 16th floor of a building opposite, taking out the assassin. "Do you remember what you're looking at up there?" he asked, again tapping her then 8-year-old image on the photograph. "Was it the private security guard?"

Donna shook her head. "No, sir. I never saw him."

"Well, you sure got a lot of interest in something," Maxie smiled.

"A man in the window."

That surprised Kevin a little bit. He didn't know a lot about Worth's murder, and most of his thin knowledge had come in the past few hours via Internet searches. And for all the half-baked conspiracy theories he'd discovered, not even the most ridiculous mentioned any man in any window other than the principals—all of whom history and death had accounted for. He looked over at Maxie, who raised her eyebrows a bit and almost imperceptibly hunched her shoulders, inviting him to take over.

"And this man you saw, he wasn't Henry Lee?"

"No," she answered, then shrugged. "I just thought he was someone who lived there. I don't know. But I think he was as scared as the rest of us, because his hands were over his face, covering it, like he was crying or in pain, something like that."

"And this was on the same floor as the security guard?"

"The 16th. Yes, sir."

Kevin considered that for a moment before asking: "You're familiar with the Knight Commission, right?" She said she was. "Did you tell any of this to the investigators?"

"Yes, sir. I told them just what I told you."

"What did they say?"

"That I must've been mistaken. He said they had already run a check or something on all the rooms, and nobody was in the one where I saw the man. There was somebody in the room just below it, though, on the 15th floor, and they told me—the people who talked to me, I mean—they said when the shooting started, he went to the window to see what all the fuss was about." She took a little breath. "They told me that's what I saw."

"Was it?" Maxie asked.

Donna smiled unsteadily. "That was a long time ago, Miss McQueen. I was 8 years old. At that age, anything is possible."

Kevin: "Did you talk to the Knight Commission about Henry Lee?"

"I didn't. But Daddy told them why we were there, and a little bit about Henry Lee. They didn't seem too concerned."

Maxie could barely contain her disbelief, trying to drain the skepticism from her voice. "You mean to tell me that your brother goes into the building where shots are fired, then disappears, and it doesn't raise any red flags with the investigators?"

"He was on the side of the angels, ma'am, where the good guys were. The man who killed Senator Worth was across the way." Pointing again to the picture.

It didn't feel exactly right, but Maxie couldn't argue with the logic, at least not now. "What did you do when he didn't show back up?" she asked, edging back into the moment. "Did you think that was a little strange?"

Donna Hubbard bit her lower lip. "Yes and no. Henry Lee sometimes would just do that. Up and disappear." She paused, squirmed, straightened out her denim shift. "You have to understand. Henry Lee was kind of, well…unstable." Kevin and Maxie locked eyes again, and he could see what was flashing through her mind: Great. A disappearing nut. Just wonderful. "It was Vietnam. I think it made him loony tunes."

Maxie: "So you though this was just another one of his vanishing acts?"

She nodded. "Pretty much. Truth is, we hadn't heard from him in six, maybe nine months—hadn't seen him for more than a year—when he just turned up at our front door with his friend and announced we were going to New York City."

"Why do you think he left this time?"

"After the shooting? He was scared, I guess. All the hullabaloo." She paused. "We also wondered if, well, you know…the money…"

"What money?" Maxie asked, more sharply than she intended.

"To take us to New York. See, Henry Lee never had much. Truth be told, none of us did. Daddy provided for us and all, and we didn't want for much of anything. But we were never what you'd call well-off. Then Henry Lee takes us on a vacation and pays cash for the whole deal."

"So you wondered where it came from?"

"Yes, ma'am."

Maxie smiled softly. "Any ideas?"

"No, ma'am. I was taught not to ask about things like that."

"How about your mother and daddy? Do you think they might have asked?" Donna said she didn't know, but that the subject never came up as far as she knew. Maxie considered her next question long and hard before finally asking: "Donna, do you have any idea about why someone might, uh, not want everyone in your family to stay…healthy?"

This, obviously, was something the girl had thought about. "At first, I didn't. At first I just figured we were unlucky, that God needed their souls for someone else."

"But you don't think that anymore?"

"I don't know what to think, Miss McQueen. I keep hearing that the government can do whatever it wants to people. And I started to wonder, well, hey, maybe they do kill other Americans. Maybe there is something to all this talk about conspiracies, and maybe something did happen in New York that day that we weren't supposed to see."

Maxie's gentle, out-of-nowhere smile grew. "Is that what you really think?"

"How else would you explain what happened?"

"It's a funny world, Donna, full of chaos and confusion. Strange things, unexplained things—they happen all the time."

The girl nodded. "With all respect, Miss McQueen, I think that's half right. I agree that strange things happen. But I also think they can all be explained. It's just that the people who can explain 'em, well, they don't seem real interested in letting any of us in on their little secrets." Coming from Donna Hubbard, the comment sounded more plaintive than paranoid. The girl reached into her purse, and pulled out a three-by-five dime-store portrait of her brother, full-dressed in his Army uniform. "But I guess that's why we're here, right?" She smiled tightly and handed the photo to Maxie.

Nice-looking boy. Pretty blue eyes. Dark hair, not close-cropped military style, but just long enough to have a part on the right side. Narrow face that emphasized a firm jaw line and high cheekbones. Little ears that stuck out in a way that drew attention from his otherwise attractive appearance. Put the kid in a white suit, he'd be a dead ringer for one of those 1940's crooners. "This is how he looked the last time you saw him?" Maxie asked, passing the photo to Kevin.

"Pretty much, yes, ma'am."

"Anything the picture doesn't show?"

Donna's eyes narrowed in puzzlement. "How do you mean?"

"Tattoo. Birth mark. Scar. Something that separates him from everybody else?"

"No," she said after a moment, shaking her head slowly. "I suppose the only thing different about Henry Lee was his little finger." Donna held her right hand up, palm forward, fingers splayed, wiggling the pinkie. "When he was a kid, Henry Lee and a friend were out fishing on a lake. When they were tying the bass boat up, his hand got smashed against the dock. He lost the last joint on his finger." Waving the pinkie again.

Well, Maxie thought, it's something. She stood. "Okay, let's see if we can beam up Henry Lee Hubbard from cyberspace."

What passed as Maxie's "office" was the smaller of the apartment's two bedrooms. On one desk—which was, in fact, a 6-foot-long metal table with folding legs—was an in-basket stacked with what looked like eight years of reading material. Some of it about contemporary investigative practices, some about competitive intelligence, but most of it involving the rights of children and parental custody. Along one wall was a wide, five-drawer filing cabinet she'd picked up for a fire-sale price from a 42-year-old family business, a hardware store, that had gone bankrupt. Five bucks. At that price, she didn't even bother to strip away the masking tape that was blackening along one side.

The only other piece in the room was a basic card table—Maxie's other "desk"—where the real work was done. On it was a fax/copier, a phone, answering machine, mid-range color printer and photo scanner, and an IBM personal computer that, while temperamental, acted well enough often enough to perform its most important function:

Run Felon Find, a software program designed to help law enforcers—public and private—locate and apprehend everything from serial killers to runaway grooms-to-be.

"What I'm going to do," Maxie explained to Donna, pulling up another chair next to hers, both facing the terminal, motioning for the girl to sit, "is transfer the picture of Henry Lee into the hard drive." Which she did. It took next to no time for the scanner to electronically read the photo and put it in the computer's memory; as it did, the image of Henry Lee appeared on her terminal, and then vanished altogether once she'd saved it in the appropriate file. A dozen or so icons were still visible against a blue desktop background. Maxie put the cursor over one of them and logged on to the Internet. When the connection was made, she double-clicked on another, a badge symbol that said Run Felon Find 3.0.

"This thing will read the picture based on physical characteristics," she continued, hitting the keys so fast that Donna was dazed watching the parade of ears and eyes and noses flash momentarily on the screen. None of this was new to Kevin—it was standard fare in the search for lost loves—so he was standing behind them, not paying much attention, flipping through Maxie's latest *Newsweek*. "I'm using the male Caucasian database. It has 72 different hairstyles, 29 sets of eyes, 122 mouth types, 90 chins, 44 different variations of facial hair, 37 shapes and styles of glasses, 112 scars or tattoos." More typing, more screens. "The software reads the digital photo of your brother, and finds which one of those physical characteristics match it in some way." On the monitor, images kept flying past. "Then it cross-references the results against the contents of a half-dozen databases that we've accessed on the Internet—licenses, mug shots, newspaper photos, that kind of thing. When it's done, the program pulls out any possible match-ups and ranks them according to the likelihood of a positive ID."

The screen froze. Everything stopped. Those thousands of images had been reduced to four words: You have six matches.

Maxie brought the first one up. It was a wire service picture of a fire-man in Beaumont, Texas, who was smiling and holding a less-than-enthused cat he had just pulled from a tree, dated October 1975. There was a 12 percent chance of a match. Donna peered at the grainy black-and-white on the monitor. "No," she said, not having to say what her voice shouted: If this was the best shot, we're not getting anywhere.

They didn't. The only other possibilities were a couple of major league baseball players—despite herself, Donna chuckled at that one—a drifter doing time for murder, a state senator from Utah and a skin-care guru selling hope in a bottle out of Southern California. So much for high-tech sleuthing, Maxie thought, shutting down the machine.

"What do we do now?" Donna asked when they had returned to their respective places in Maxie's living room.

"Missing persons is a time-intensive kind of thing," Maxie said, try-ing to soften the blow she was about to deliver. "It can go on for weeks. Months, even."

The girl nodded. "When can you start?"

Kevin and Maxie exchanged quick glances. "What I mean is that the longer the investigation, the more, uh, expensive it's going to be. And to be truthful with you—"

"I have money," Donna interrupted, not proudly or defensively, more like a plea.

"I'm sure you do. But Henry Lee's been gone for what, 25 years? That's a long time. If your brother is still alive, my guess is he's become somebody else, got himself a whole new identity. Whatever you tell me about him would probably be useless. You'd be asking me to start from ground zero. As I said, it would take a lot of time."

"I have a lot of money." Donna Hubbard's innocent voice went stiff.

Kevin felt it, too. "What Maxie's trying to say is—"

"Excuse me for interrupting, Mr. Columbus, but everyone in my family is dead." Voice still firm, but now taking on a bit of impatience. "I don't think I'm a nut, and I also don't think what's happened to my family is a coincidence, either." She turned to Maxie. "I don't want to die. But I don't want to spend the rest of my life scared of my own shadow. So"—reaching into her canvas satchel, pulling out a brown paper bag—"I'll pay you two hundred dollars a day, plus expenses, if you can find anything that might keep either of those things from happening." She took a wad of crumpled bills from the bag, counted out $1,000, stacked it on the glass table, pushing the edges together, making it look all nice and orderly. "There's a down payment."

Kevin feeling a weird déjà vu, thinking about Wayne Earl Wiley.

Maxie wishing she was a better person, wanting to empathize with this soft, lost, confused child, willing herself to focus on the girl's grief and act with integrity, but losing the fight, thinking only of her son, and the legal battle that loomed, and how much it was going to cost, and when she looked at Donna Hubbard, she didn't see a victim but a savior. That was bad, but that was life.

"It could take a long time," Maxie said again, making one last effort to do the honorable thing, and convince this girl that there were better, smarter ways to burn her cash, but not trying too hard to convince.

"I don't care how many days or weeks or months it takes. I have more money. It's in a safe-deposit box down at the bank. I'll show it to you—"

Maxie hearing herself mutter, "That won't be necessary"—

Donna continuing anyway: "It's been in the family for years"—

Kevin, sensing something, fishing, asking, "How many years?"—

Donna, wide-eyed and unknowing, saying, "Twenty-five"—

Maxie not hearing anything but the sound of her little boy's voice—

Kevin, never a big believer in coincidences, wondering if there was anything significant to the timing, just before Richard Worth was murdered—

Maxie, thinking of nothing but family, hopeful at last.

Chapter 5

"Is this Kevin Alexander Columbus?"

Kevin Alexander? A blast from the past, nobody calling him that since grade school. "Yes, it is." Phone scrunched between his head and shoulder while he juggled coffee-making components in the dollhouse-sized kitchen.

"This is Detective Ty Roper, Island City PD. Florida."

"Okay." Five scoops of Maxwell House in the coffee filter—half of the fifth one ending up on the countertop, naturally.

"I am inquiring as to your relationship with a Mr. Gary Devereaux."

"Who?" Filling the pot up to the line that indicated you were making 10 cups, and pouring the water into the wide mouth at the top of the black machine.

He heard the cop sigh wearily. "Gary Devereaux. White male. About 70. Gray curly hair. Six one or two. Strong build. Ran some outfit, a think tank—whatever the hell *those* are—called Americans for America."

An image creased Kevin's mind, which other than bringing a tall Norman Mailer to mind meant nothing. "Sorry. I don't know him. Why?"

"Shot himself yesterday. With a pearl-handled .45. Just like Patton's."

"Ivory-handled. Patton's was ivory-handled."

A jolt of hope in Detective Roper's voice: "So you know the gun?"

"Saw the movie." The coffee was starting to trickle into the pot. Kevin pulled a mug from the cupboard—it had an M. C. Escher painting on it, the one where you follow the stairs up and over and around, and end up nowhere, or at least right where you started—wiped it out with his green Nike T-shirt, poured in some morning jet fuel.

"You go to Oak Street Elementary School?"

"Yeah," he said, interested now, listening a lot more closely, wondering why the hell a cop in Florida was calling him, first of all, and second trying to figure out how he knew Kevin had been a kid in—

"Upstate New York, isn't it?"

"Yeah," he repeated, a bit more slowly. "We were stationed there when my dad was in the Air Force. It's where I went to fourth, fifth and sixth grade."

"What's your dad's name?"

"It's not Devereaux." Another weary wheeze from Florida, Kevin quickly apologizing, not meaning it but also not wanting to irritate someone who seemed to know something about him, especially with that guy being a cop. "His name was Jonathan. Major Jonathan Alan Columbus."

Which seemed to drain some of the irritation from Roper's voice. "You ever hear him mention that name, maybe, Devereaux? Like a friend, somebody he knew in the service, neighbor, that kind of thing?"

"Never."

"Then how do you figure he knew you?"

That stopped him. "How do you know he did?"

Roper started to say something, then caught himself. "'Love it or leave it.' You ever heard that phrase?"

Really interested now. "Yeah." He poured some milk into his coffee, and wandered into the dining area of the apartment, just off the kitchen—it was really the far end of a rectangular living room—and sat at one of the stool-height chairs that accompanied a tall, round breakfast table, at the center of which was a glass globe filled with desert sand and rocks. A gift of desolation from his absent mother.

"Ever use it?" Roper prodded. "That phrase?"

"I might have." Alert, seeing that all this had some destination in the cop's mind, preferring to get there first if at all possible.

"The reason I ask is, I'm holding this little article, like a newspaper article, that's from a school paper, the Oak Street *Star*. Student paper, I'm guessing. There's this headline on it, says "Love it or Leave it," and I was just wondering what some guy who you never knew or met, what he's doing with a clipping that goes—"

"America is a great place. The president is a great man, and we should trust him. One reason America is so good is that we are free to say what we want, even if that isn't what some people want to hear. But I think there are times when the people who are free to say bad things about our country should just shut up and get behind the president. I don't like war any more than the next person. I go to bed every night and pray I won't wake up the next morning with a giant A-bomb in my back yard. But I trust the president. If he thinks we ought to be in this war, then we should support him. That is the price of freedom. You trust the people who are in charge to do the right thing. If all of those long-haired hippies can't do that, then maybe they ought to just get in their vans and go to Russia or China or someplace where it's okay to hate America. But I love America, and I am sick of people burning the flag and saying we're killers. We're not killers. We're Americans. I think President Nixon is a great president."

"—signed by none other than Kevin Alexander Columbus?"

Kevin stared at his coffee cup, silently asking himself the same question Roper had raised: Whoever Devereaux was, what was he doing with a child's blind patriotic ramblings that were more than 25 years old? "I couldn't tell you."

A weary sigh. "Listen, Mr. Columbus, it is about 110 in the shade down here in paradise, making it just a tad hotter than hell. I'm already sweating more than a virgin on prom night, and if you keep dancing with me, it's just gonna make me hotter, and sweatier, and eat up what little patience is left in this going-to-donuts, 55-year-old body. So let's just cut the doo-dah. You know what this thing, this article, is. What I wanna know is why it was at the home of a fella whose brain matter is all over a painting of a fish right now."

"I don't have a clue. I swear." Kevin, shaking his head, as if the cop could see it and that would make the words more believable.

"But you did write it."

"I was 10 or 11 years old. When I was a child, I spoke as a child."

"Jesus. You sounded like chairman of Young Fascists for Nixon." Despite himself, Kevin laughed. "Must've thrilled the shit outta your old man, though. Hell, if I wrote that, my old man'd be sitting at the corner bar, crowing about how he was raising a true red-white-and-blue kid."

"Your dad a military guy?"

"A fucking warrior. Survived Omaha Beach, 6th of June, '44. Died last year."

"I'm sorry." He wasn't, but he felt it was something he needed to say.

"So, was he proud of you? Your old man?"

Kevin knew the drill. Roper was changing the flow of the questioning in mid-stream, acting like they were all buddy-buddy, hoping Kevin would trap himself in a lie. But since there was no way he was lying, there was no way he was going to get trapped. "Yeah," Kevin said. "The day he saw the article, he'd just come in from Morocco or some other far-away place that smacked of intrigue. He blew into the kitchen like he always did, decked out in that green flight suit, dropped his B-4 bag in the middle of the floor, and hauled me up into his arms—"

"Little Buddy, that article you wrote was the best thing I ever read."

"I meant it, dad."

"I know you did."

"It's what you taught me. It's the way you taught me to be."

"And you deserve a commendation."

"A medal?"

"Nosireebob. We're going out, and I'm gonna buy you anything you want."

"Anything? No matter what it costs?"

"Nothing's too expensive for my All-American kid."

" Bought me a Buddy Rich LP. *Time Being*, I think it was."

"You a drummer?"

"Hardly. My dad was a jazz junkie, and there was a lot of Buddy Rich stuff in the record racks. Every time he'd put something on, I'd start banging the hell out of everything in sight. Finally, we put together this makeshift drum set in my bedroom. Hung a pie plate from the top bunk bed—that was the cymbal. White plastic ottoman was one drum. He stretched some canvas over a piece of plywood for a snare, and gave me a cheese grater—"

"What the hell did you use a cheese grater for?"

"To make noise." Which got a laugh out of Roper. "He called me Little Buddy, said that if I grew up to be like Rich, I'd turn out okay, because Rich was who he was. No pretense or phoniness. What you heard, what you saw—that was it. Period."

"Where's your dad now?"

"Dead. Went down in Vietnam, April of '75, about two weeks before Saigon fell."

"I'm sorry." Unlike Kevin, Roper sounded as if he actually meant it. "You get him back? His body, I mean?"

"Not for three months. He was officially listed as MIA until July, when my mother went to Switzerland to recover the body. He's buried in Arlington. It was his dream. He always said he was proud to be among heroes in life, and he'd be prouder still to be among heroes in death."

"Warriors, huh?" Roper said after a second.

"Yeah," Kevin smiled, equal parts sadness and fondness. "Warriors."

Another moment or two passed during which Roper evidently decided there was nothing else to pursue here. "Aren't you even the slightest bit interested in why this guy had some ancient newspaper clipping you wrote a hundred years ago?"

"Those are days of yore, detective. Another life." Not going so far as to say it was a better one, but at least his father had been alive, his mother hadn't taken a back flip off the deep end and he'd arisen every morning with the certainty that nothing was beyond his grasp. "Who knows," he added after a moment, offhand, "maybe the guy was looking for recruits."

"For what?"

"Americans for America. Maybe he saw my potential at an early age, and was tracking my progress. Maybe that was his job: Recruiting for the national future." His voice put quote marks around the last three words.

"So he shot himself because the recruit well ran dry, huh?"

"It's an explanation."

"So is El Nino." Roper laughed slightly at his own joke. "Anyway, if you're banging the shit outta that jerry-rigged drum kit in the next day or so, and something comes to mind about Devereaux or any of this, give me a call, okay?"

"Sorry. Can't do it."

Roper's seen-it-all, heard-it-all tone got edgy. "Perhaps you didn't hear me, son—"

"I don't have the drum kit anymore. I put away childish things."

"Maybe you ought to think about rebuilding it, you know? Help you remember stuff."

"I remember things just fine, detective. Just fine."

●

Roscoe Chatham sat on the bottom bunk in his prison cell, staring at the two cellophane-wrapped Puros Indios, trying to figure out the right thing to do.

For the past three years, he and his roommate Ordell had this thing going. Every Tuesday, Roscoe's girlfriend Bev—a hooker he'd met by way of the Internet—would deliver a pair of cigars to him during weekly visitation. Later in the day, he and Rooms would fire those babies up, talk trash about what they'd do if they ever returned to the world—chances of that being less than zero, Ordell being a confessed murderer—and enjoy a moment of civilized pleasure in this barbed-wired heart of human darkness.

Problem was, Ordell had taken the off-ramp into Loony Town two days ago. He did that sometimes, went wacko batshit crazy, and when it happened, the powers-on-high tossed him into the rubber hole for an extended stay, leaving Roscoe all by his lonesome in the cell. Which was usually fine, Roscoe kind of liking the occasional privacy, except this time it left him with a pair of primo stogies and a dilemma: Should he wait for Rooms to beam back to Earth, or just go ahead and smoke these bad boys *el solo*?

To Roscoe, the issue was all about routine. In the joint, routine was what got you through. Every day that passed into the next one without incident, well, that was one to chalk up in the Win column. Made things easier, routine did, and a hell of a lot more predictable. When you're just trying to get through, knowing what lies around the corner isn't such a bad thing. And their routine, his and Ordell's, had been to smoke a cigar together every Wednesday.

Of course, the routine had already been thrown off some. Just a little, anyway. Bev had gotten pinched a couple days back, which was why the punk rock-looking chick, her name was Gina, it was why Gina had brought the smokes. They'd sat there in the prison's common room, an ill-ventilated space about the size of a high school gym with yellow walls, an antiseptic smell and dozens of cafeteria-style metal tables, and made small talk. Roscoe interested in whether Bev was going to get out of her jam, Gina telling him not to worry, everything was cool. Her asking him if there was anything else he needed, meaning sex under the table but not saying it, telling him Bev said it was okay, whatever he wanted. Roscoe smiling thinly, saying he'd pass but thanks all the same.

She shrugged and said she understood, but Roscoe thought that was bullshit. Girl like her, not bad to look at even with a spiky hairdo that looked more wig than real, she wasn't used to being refused. But she didn't get all snotty about it. Just picked up her cheesy beaded pocketbook, pranced off on a pair of skyscraper heels, really nice butt moving in slow motion, as if to remind Roscoe of what he was missing and what a dope he was for saying no. Out the door. Gone.

Leaving him with the two Puros Indios, and a decision.

On the one hand, he could wait for Ordell to make an appearance on Reality Road. They'd smoke 'em together, lie to each other about their dreams, just like old times. But that would mean no cigar for a week, which would wreck his routine, Roscoe's, waiting for Roomie to come out of storage. And hell, a guy as Daffy Duck as Ordell, who knows whether one week wouldn't turn into another, and then another, and then another, and what about the routine then, huh? On the other hand, he could just fire both those babies up now, tell Ordell half the truth—Bev got hauled in, missed a trip, end of story—and that's the name of that tune.

Man, when you put it that way, ain't no choice at all.

Roscoe pulled one of the cigars from the breast pocket of his blue prison jumpsuit, unwrapped it, bit off the tip, peeled away the green band with the red border at the top, something he'd taught Ordell to do, because only yo-yos smoked with the band still on. Fired it up. Took a long deep drag, inhaling just a bit.

Whoa, mama. This thing is hot, baby, hot hot hot.

He pulled another mouthful of smoke out of it. Did it again. Two, three, four times. He'd never had one of these, and figured it was an acquired taste.

Hotter still. Dry, too. Make a man thirsty as the moon.

Roscoe Chatham stood to go over to the sink, get a hit of water from the faucet.

Everything went blurry. He collapsed.

Tried to cry out, say something, but his throat wouldn't let him.

Closing his eyes, trying to get his shit together, opening them to a searing pain from the light that reflected off his stainless steel commode, the sun's high beams passing unshielded through involuntarily dilated pupils.

Stiffening. Muscles and joints, anything that was supposed to move was starting to freeze up, except lying there, it wasn't cold, it was boiling hot, like the concrete floor was really a range, and all the burners were cranked up to High.

Couldn't swallow at all, now.

Or see.

Or move.

The only thing that seemed to be working was his heart.

It was in overdrive. Running about 90 miles an hour. Going like there was no tomorrow.

Which for Roscoe Chatham, there wasn't.

Chapter 6

Kevin Columbus discovered early on that one of the unexpected pleasures of being an independent contractor was that every day was a potential pay day. None of this first and the 15th stuff, no waiting for the office secretary to drop your check by, scrambling to the bank before 2, none of that. Checks could arrive any day, Monday through Friday, even Saturday, creating a never-ending anticipation rare in the nine-to-five world, an ongoing sense that economic salvation was never more than a day away. Of course, the trade-off was you never knew where your next meal was coming from, and if you did, there was always some lingering doubt as to how you were going to pay for it, and if you could, whether it'd be your last for a little while.

Which explained why, after Kevin had hung up from Detective Roper—puzzled, sure, maybe intrigued—he started focusing on things that really mattered, starting with how long he had to live.

As was the routine a couple times a week, more during leaner periods, he called the bank's 800 line, punched in his checking account number, got the balance, did the same with his savings (such that it was), added up the two. Barely $400, including the take from Score a couple of nights before, not good. Next was a quick mental check of all the invoices that were still out, which included $500 from a loan outfit he'd written direct mail letters for, promoting "limited time only" interest rates of 24 percent; a couple hundred bucks from the local health food store for his work publicizing Tofu Tuesdays; another hundred or so from Captain Congrats, the goofball who delivered singing telegrams to recipients who were more embarrassed than moved by Kevin

Columbus's rhyming little ditties, and 50 or 75 here and there for radio ads for Dogman's, a local dance club.

Not quite a thousand dollars.

Throw in the $400 or so on hand, and divide by $2,450—the minimum he needed to live every month, almost half of it going to rent and the payment on the Explorer that had once been covered by a car allowance—and it added up to:

Wayne Earl Wiley.

Kevin eased over to the window of his seen-better-days brick apartment, looking vacantly through worn drapes onto a South Charlotte thoroughfare so choked with traffic it could pass for a parking lot. Why couldn't he be more like Maxie? She didn't believe there was anything strange about the death of Donna Hubbard's sister, told him as much the day before, after they'd met with the girl, not even trying to fake a justification. And the stuff about Worth's murder—even the interesting stuff, like Henry Lee turning up with money just a few days before taking his family to New York, or Henry Lee going to take a leak in the building where shots were fired, or Donna's family getting a bag full of cash a week later—that all sailed right over her head, too. Her only rationale for taking the case was honest economic gain: "I need money, and she's willing to give it to me."

No hand-wringing, second thoughts, searing guilt or fear that God might think twice about admitting her inside the Pearly Gates because she'd bartered her moral values for a few pieces of silver. Decision made, move on.

Sure, Maxie had just cause—getting J.J. back—and you could argue that it changed the ethical playing field. Kevin's only crusade was defending himself from the bill collectors, which didn't rank real high in the scheme of honorable things. Jon Columbus had taught him responsibility at an early age, refusing to give him money when the allowance had run dry, and encouraging him to open a savings account at the tender age of 10. "Life is full of rainy days, Little Buddy," he said the day they walked into the bank. "And the brown stuff that comes pouring down from the sky doesn't smell like pennies from heaven." Wonder what he'd say now, seeing the stack of unpaid bills in the kitchen drawers, the threatening letters from someplace in Houston warning that people were standing by to repossess half his life if payments weren't forthcoming, or if he heard the well-rehearsed lies to the landlady, tales of a non-existent sister needing money for an abortion, Gee Mrs. Wright, could you float me for a month?

He recalled a conversation they'd had, August 1974, sitting on a low-slung blue and black checked sofa, watching Richard Nixon's resignation speech on television. "What do you think about Nixon, dad? Was he wrong?" Kevin asked, his eyes not moving from the image of the president—dark and pale at once—that filled the color console set in their living room. Jon Columbus didn't answer at first. When Kevin finally turned to him, and said, "Dad?" the Major didn't talk about good and evil, or serve up warmed-over platitudes that could pass for a civics lecture. Rather, he said what sounded to be exactly what he believed:

"You pays your money, you takes your chances."

It was an old military saying, one Kevin had heard before. The gist was, in any game of chance—and what was life, if not the biggest such game in the world?—there had to be an ante of some sort, and you had to be willing to pay up, and when you did there was no point worrying, because worrying wasn't going to change the odds of things going very right or very wrong. Once you were in, you were in. Justify, sure. Rationalize, if it made you feel better. But never forget it was your call, you made it with eyes wide open, so shuttup and live with it.

So, dad, Kevin said to himself, going into the kitchen for another cup of coffee, what's the call? Should I grab Wayne Earl Wiley's money—the ante—and everything that implies, solve all my fiscal problems, never look back? Keep plugging honestly away, waiting for something good to happen along a high road that could very well lead nowhere? Or maybe just sit it out, decide not to decide, aware but never admitting that doing nothing meant turning the title of your life over to those who never hesitated, not for a second, to go for anything that was up for grabs?

He could hear the old man's voice clear as if Jon Columbus was standing there sipping coffee with him: "For crissakes, quit pissing and moaning and do something—even if it's wrong."

Which made Kevin smile to himself, muttering, "Let's not elevate this to the status of Greek tragedy," adding with a self-deprecating laugh, "at least not yet." No decisions had to be made at the moment. In a few hours, he'd be meeting with one of the people whose names Wiley had given him, a state regulator, and would take whatever he learned there, add it to the decision-making mix, see what happened.

The dilemmas of the moment safely delayed, Kevin got some more coffee and started working on television ads for a company called Wreckless Driving, which specialized in the sale of used—excuse us, *experienced*—automobiles. The work was ultra low end. One month, a guy was screaming about cars from atop an elephant ("Don't be a dumbo, come catch our sale, it's a jumbo!"), the next from a Shetland Pony ("I've told so many people about this sale, I've gotten a little horse!"), and now Kevin had him pointing to an ostrich on a leash, frothing: "Our deals are so great, we even got this fella to get his head out of the sand!" Dumber than a box of birds, to maintain the animal motif, but traffic on the lot was up 18 percent, and the general manager of the place thought Kevin Columbus was a P.T. Barnum for the new millennium.

He worked for a couple hours, to 11:30, then was up pacing. Mail time was near.

Kevin walked his usual pre-delivery L-shaped path: From the front door, down a short entrance/hallway and around the corner to the main room of the apartment, which he'd taken in an effort to shave costs after the layoff. Past the entertainment center that held a TV, 30-inch screen, VCR, and an upper-range CD player and Klipsch bookshelf speakers—all reminders of the good days, the better days—complemented by various books about starting your own business, making your first million, blah blah blah, none of them read. Then to the eating area, where the tall table and stools were. If he wanted to break the monotony of the walk, he'd drop down into the comfortable burnt-orange chair he'd picked up for $50, or maybe the fold-out tan sofa where he slept since turning the single bedroom into an office.

Back and forth, back and forth, 11:35, then 11:37, then 11:40, then—

Metal clacking outside his front door. Feet shuffling. Papers rustling. Sounds that were as clear and assured as any cash register.

Kevin waited a moment for the postman to leave, and got the mail. Thick stack today, oh what treasures await?

Lots, as it turned out.

He quickly put aside the "you have been pre-approved" credit card application that promised a 4.9 percent rate, and the blue-and-white coupon asking Have You Seen This Child? There was the latest bribe from some new long-distance company; Kevin had a standing rule to ignore them until they promised three figures to switch. Tearing this one open, he saw the offer had hit $100. Sold.

Then came the checks. From the mortgage people. The tofu crowd. Even Dogman's. He had cash flow. Well, cash trickle. But it was something.

There was the latest *Entertainment Weekly*, and *Time*, and *Fortune*, and *Business Week*—even that damned pesky *New Republic*, which even though it was addressed to someone else, kept turning up in his mailbox.

There was a manila mailing envelope, no return address, Kevin's name printed neatly on the front, postmarked from—

Island City, Florida?

Carefully—he didn't know why, but care seemed in order—Kevin lifted the end flap of the mailer, emptied the contents onto his dining room table, a white standard business-sized envelope falling out. He unsealed it, found three things inside.

There was a photo negative, real mushy, just a couple of blobs hanging out of what looked like windows in a building. They appeared to be holding something, a fishing pole being the first thing that came to mind, one of them casting it almost straight up, the other toward the right corner. A reddish-yellow number identified the photo as 214.

Next was a note, written in the same hand as the address. Brief, on a sheet of plain stationery: "Little Buddy. These protected me throughout my life. They will protect you in my death."

Little Buddy? Kevin's heart rate took off like an Olympic sprinter.

Then a picture, torn at one side, taken at some lake resort, snow-capped mountains in the background, Switzerland, maybe, and the Alps. Two people in the shot. Major and Mrs. Jonathan Columbus. His dad looking concerned, as if the weight of the world had taken up residence on his shoulders. Mother Meredith looking almost put-out, gazing at whoever sat unseen on the other side of the tear, a tatooed arm barely visible around her shoulders.

Kevin turned the picture over, saw these words—

Developed by Hans Juergen, Precision Photo Works, Geneva—

And then these—

On this day—

And then the date—

10 July 1975.

No, Kevin thought, sweat starting to cling like a wetsuit, this cannot be true.

Quickly, he flipped the photo back over, looked at the man's image again. Even though the eyes were buried under aviator's sunglasses and the mouth stretched into a tight line that was continents away from the smile he remembered, Kevin Columbus knew that face, those features. It was his dad, looking exactly as he had the last time they'd been together, right before Major Jonathan Columbus's last tour in Vietnam, where the United States government said he died in a plane crash on April 12, 1975.

•

Walter Frost stared at the contents of the manila mailing envelope, postmarked Island City, Florida, that sat, quietly, explosively, on the desk in the study of his Georgetown home. Outside, official Washington was purring with motion, some of it progress, most just activity. But here, in the elegant townhouse just a few blocks from the bustle of M Street and its shops and restaurants, everything had stopped. And what Walter Frost did during the next week or 10 days would determine if that standstill and its inevitable aftermath would wend its way downtown, to Constitution Avenue, to Pennsylvania Avenue, to God knows where else.

At age 72, Walter Frost was still a marquee name at Frost & Winston, one of the district's top lawyer-lobbying firms, a K Street legend that The Washington *Post* said had "more day-to-day connections than the entire airline industry." He didn't practice law, hadn't set foot in a courtroom for years. Didn't prowl the halls of Congress on behalf of the firm's clients, a roster that reflected his own personal eclecticism, ranging from Fortune 500 companies to world hunger organizations to three non-warring royal families in the Middle East. Didn't sit on a lot of boards, drawing tens of thousands of dollars as high-priced window dressing for the corporate nobility.

All of which made him something of an abnormality in a city where everyone wanted to be king of his or her domain. And that was fine with Walter Frost. He couldn't have cared less about being a king. Kings died, or were overthrown, or stumbled and crashed onto the rocks of their own vanity. But the ones who made those kings—they were the ones who survived. And that's what Walter Frost did: He created dominance.

Unlike the talking heads in the press and the political consultants and the media advisors who saw power in their own terms—getting stories, winning elections, securing a regular spot on a CNN gabfest, all of it transient—Frost understood that power was not about governance or popularity or ratings or visibility. It was about endurance. Being not only the last man standing, but in the rarified air of politics, the only man standing.

His supreme talent was knowing the right people, the people who made things happen. He could kill a story in a major newspaper with a single phone call. He could put a strong but convivial arm on just about anyone who mattered in the executive or legislative branch—a sitting member of the House or Senate, an agency head, a committee staff chief, anyone. There were even whispers that he could do the same, had done it, with the Supreme Court, an accusation that Frost dismissed without denying, reinforcing the perception of his power and, thus, the fact of it as well. He could raise millions for this cause or that one—he had a weakness for cancer-stricken children—and millions more for candidates of both parties and virtually every ideological stripe, drawing the line only at the extreme Republican right, whose social positions he sometimes accepted but whose tactics too often repulsed him.

He made good things happen, and bad things go away. He was a fixer. And on this day, at this hour, fate had delivered him one hell of a problem to fix.

No, not fate. Not really. He'd done what he did, all of them had, knowing full well what they were getting into. And Walter Frost also knew that this day would eventually arrive. What had eluded him was how it would appear. Now he knew:

A torn photograph, Switzerland in the background. Once a paradise, now a mere memory. A man, his face familiar, arm around a woman Frost knew all too well, a woman who wasn't there, her image—and that of the father who never was—ripped from the picture. Images that, he could only assume, had found their way to the boy, the son, in North Carolina.

Negatives. Sequentially numbered, starting at 210, stopping at 213, resuming at 215. One missing. He looked at the blurred shadows in each, pinned in one dimension against the brick face of the building, remembering instantly the moment, and knowing full well that for all the dark secrets that were born that day, the darkest was on the missing frame, Frame 214, which he also assumed was in the hands of the son.

On the portable color television set tucked among the books that otherwise occupied three of the four walls in his window-less study, a White House reporter came into view. She was attractive, mid-30's, and if Walter Frost had been one to court the spotlight rather than shun it, he would have liked to take her out. But his chosen place was in the background. Besides, even after a dozen years of being alone, he did not have the desire, need or conscience to share his life with anyone other than the late Claire Frost.

"Tom," she gushed with a sense of omniscience that irritated Walter Frost enormously, reporters knowing the least about how government really works, "it appears the cautious optimism about General Azid's decision to stop all chemical and biological weapons production is strengthening by the day. Sources tell us that U.S. officials have flown to Arabaq, and treaty negotiations are about to commence."

For the first time in as long as he could remember, Walter Frost felt older than his years. He closed his eyes and took a deep breath, hoping it might make what was about to follow somewhat easier. It didn't. So he poured himself a snifter of very good brandy from the crystal decanter on the desk, turning to marvel as he so often did at the Impressionist painting that occupied the only wall unhidden by shelved books. He admired the mind and the hand that could apply little dots and dashes of color in a way that created a unified whole whose fine touch was invisible to the eye's logic.

Walter Frost took one sip of the brandy, and then another, steeling himself to make the phone call he had dreaded most of his later life. He dialed the private number, pressed the mute button on the TV remote, silencing a self-styled expert from one of Washington's countless interest groups who was blathering cluelessly about the pending treaty with Arabaq. As the phone at the other end rang, he smiled ruefully at fate's perverse sense of humor.

No, he reminded himself again. Not fate. Everyone knew what they were doing back then. Everyone. Things were going in one direction. They thought it was the wrong one, they forced a turn. Maybe it was the right turn, maybe the wrong one. But it didn't matter. Not now. Not anymore. All that mattered was that they took the turn. And after that, they had no choice but to keep going.

Chapter 7

As he always did when returning from the Capitol, Richard Francis Worth sat alone on the subway—an elongated golf cart on rails, really, whose only destinations were the Rotunda and the Senate offices, a direct line between the people who had power and the place where it was exercised. Striding quickly to his Russell Building Office, he kept his eyes on the floor, watching his next step, ignoring the hopeful gaze of anyone who might want more than a smile and an acknowledgement from him.

There were calls of "Congratulations, senator" and "Way to go, senator." One or two even suggested that he had somehow managed to save the world. Richard Worth—short, wiry and intense, whose shyness was odd for a politician, but masked an extraordinary focus—didn't hear them. He was thinking about history, and why it had taken the Senate so goddamned long to do the right thing.

This fight dated back to 1907 with The Hague Convention, which was an early attempt to ban the use of weapons containing poison. Most of Europe signed on. But the demands of the battlefield proved stronger than the moral imperatives of a piece of paper. The Germans released 5,700 cylinders of chlorine at the second battle of Ypres in 1915; the olive green cloud that rolled over the battlefield, following the contour of the ground because it was heavier than air, left untold numbers dead in its wake. By war's end, Russia's ill-prepared troops had suffered more chemical warfare fatalities than any other nation, and 50 times the fatalities of America.

In an attempt to rid the world of this terror, more than 100 countries were signatories to the 1925 Geneva Protocol, which prohibited the use of biological and chemical weapons in war—though not their development, production or stockpiling. The United States was one of them. All that remained was Senate ratification.

Which had not happened until this day, December 16, 1974.

There were issues, the critics charged. No specific punishment for violators. No procedures for proving allegations that chemical or biological weapons had been used. Some saw the 1925 ban as absolute, others as a "no first use" accord in which participants agreed not to use the weapons so long as the weapons weren't first used against them. That was the crux of the U.S. position; the treaty would not be binding if America were attacked first.

So the Senate fiddled around. Meanwhile, in 1956 a U.S. Army manual stated that biochemical warfare was not banned. A 1959 House resolution against first use of biochemical weapons was defeated. In 1962, chemical weapons were actually loaded on American warplanes for use during the Cuban missile crisis. It wasn't until 1969 that Richard Nixon—*Nixon*, Worth reminded his colleagues repeatedly during the floor fight—unilaterally rejected the first use of chemical warfare and announced that the U.S. was dismantling its offensive biological warfare program. He further ordered that all production of chemical weapons stop. By the early 1970's, there was not a single American facility producing toxic chemical weapons.

Richard Worth hated war in any form. And while the rest of the world focused on the nuclear peril, he was convinced that, in the end, rational men would never utilize their arsenals to facilitate Armageddon. The true risk, he told anyone who would listen, was chemical warfare. Because chemical warfare could be undertaken by any rogue regime, any renegade nation, any murderous leader who had risen to power on a jet pack of nationalist fervor. This was the next great arms race. Richard Worth wanted to stop it.

He worked behind the scenes to pave the way for Nixon's decision to include toxins—chemical weapons produced by biological processes—in the 1969 ban on biological weaponry. He backed the 1971 policy to end direct use of herbicides such as Agent Orange. He was an eloquent and forceful American voice behind a 1972 United Nations convention banning development, use and stockpiling of biological weapons. When the defense establishment wanted to increase spending on defense against biological weapons, he fought it, charging that if the country "acts as if biochemical warfare is a fact of life, we will be doomed to validating its existence in perpetuity." He lost the fight, but made the point.

Then, in 1974, in the aftermath of Watergate, he led the effort to finish what the now-deposed Nixon had started years before: Ratify the Geneva Protocol. Although there were still concerns over verification language, and charges from the extreme right that in the absence of U.S. production, the Soviets—so devastated by gas warfare in World War I—had managed to create a chemical inventory that dwarfed that of America, Worth pursued. He nudged, cajoled and even threatened his colleagues. It wasn't easy. His standoffish demeanor and refusal to engage in the Senate's backslapping, deal-making tradition had made him few friends. Older senators resented what one called his "self-created nobility." Others simply detested what they saw as a holier-than-thou attitude from a snotty little kid—he was only 43, after all—who was more interested in imposing his personal values on the country than he was in their vision of the national good.

Then came The Speech, followed by the *Time* magazine cover story.

A few weeks before the December 16 vote, Worth made an impromptu, impassioned plea to his colleagues. Speaking without notes to a Senate chamber made nearly empty by holiday receptions, he said: "God has bestowed upon us the rarest of gifts: The capacity to make a decision. And for all the rhetoric about military advantages, and chemical stockpiles, and microscopic particles that have the ability to end a human life, what this debate truly comes down to is something far removed from matters of strategic and tactical importance. It comes down to our children.

"Are we going to leave them a world that is more terrifying than that into which we, as presumed leaders, were born? Are we going to let them constitute our eternity, as they should, or are we going to damn them to infinite emptiness for the sake of political expedience? When they look at us in five years or 10 years or 20 years, and ask, Who am I, and what have I become? will the only honest answer be, You are the child of a horrible, horrible union between terror and politics?

"Childhood is a kingdom where no one dies. If you do not put this great nation on record as opposing the cataclysm that chemical warfare represents, you will be leading the rebellion which topples that kingdom. This, in the end, is our choice: Sustain the kingdom of childhood, or destroy it. God has indeed granted us the capacity to decide. I pray that we have the good sense to use it wisely."

A correspondent from *Time* heard Worth's speech, and within a week it was translated into a cover story headlined, "The New Father for a New America." Worth initially had his office try to sidetrack the piece, but his press secretary did not take the directive to heart. After all, publicity like this—glowing, admiring and unsolicited—was gold in a city whose most essential product was perception.

So the story came, and it included an interview with an "uncomfortable" Richard Worth ("My job is to do what I think is right," he was quoted. "I don't exactly understand why that should be so exalted.") There were praising quotes from colleagues who privately detested him but were not about to openly criticize a media-anointed star. With the exception of one or two shots from sources who "spoke only on the condition of anonymity," even a casual reader could not avoid the impression that the senator from New York was America's last best hope. When the Senate finally ratified the treaty, that sense was only heightened, which made Worth a bit uneasy and further strengthened his resolve not to provide the well-wishers he now passed in the corridors any access to him as he returned to his office after the final vote.

Leaving the sixth-floor elevator and starting down the marble floors, he heard a familiar voice call out. It was his administrative assistant, Dan Goggins, followed by Worth's staff person on the Armed Services Committee. Goggins, bow-tied and as political an animal as Worth was not, looked unnerved, edgy. "We got a problem, boss." Without a word, the three of them entered Worth's office through an impressive, unmarked door that enabled them to avoid the reception area, which at that the time was filled with high school carolers from Liberty, about 90 miles north of New York City.

Worth, as was his habit, ignored his desk and sat instead on a deep brownish-red leather sofa that faced the fireplace; Goggins and the committee aide took their places in high-backed chairs—a matched set with the sofa—on opposite sides of a low, cherry-wood table on which the senator's stocking feet were resting. "Go on," was all Richard Worth said. He looked more rumpled than his ill-fitting dark gray suit.

Goggins looked at the staff aide, then at the senator. "We've come across some information that, uh, is unsettling, to say the least. If it's true, it could destroy everything you've worked for. On this treaty, and on this issue." Worth said nothing. He rose, went into the private bathroom a few steps from his desk and drew a glass of water from the faucet. Taking off his suit jacket and dropping it on the sofa next to him, he sat back down and asked Goggins to explain. "Nixon banned the production of chemical warfare agents in 1969. Theoretically, we stopped making the stuff."

"Theoretically?" Worth asked, raising an eyebrow, the glass of water stopping halfway to his mouth. He looked to the Armed Services staffer, who sat still and unblinking.

"Yes, sir," Goggins said. "Intelligence sources have apprised us of the possibility—I want to emphasize that, the *possibility*—the ban was not implemented in good faith."

"What the hell does that mean?" Worth flared, despising the convolution of cover-your-ass language.

Goggins swallowed hard. "That's just it, sir, we don't know. Not exactly."

"What *do* you know?" The exhaustion had evaporated from the senator's voice, which was now as cold and focused as a nuclear warhead.

"We've been led to believe that a covert operation has been in place since 1969 to, uh, produce chemical weapons on America's behalf in a friendly Middle East country."

"Which one?"

"Arabaq."

"Is the government aware of this *possibility*?" Worth had drifted into his prosecutorial mode, and Goggins felt its sting. The two aides exchanged a look, Goggins appearing far more ill at ease than the more stoic Armed Services staffer. "Dan?"

"Well, sir, it seems the government may be the, uh, originator of the operation."

They braced for the coming explosion. Worth for all his sober humanity, had a temper that could ignite with the speed and heat of a wildfire. But there was no eruption. Instead, the senator leaned back, rubbed his eyes in exhaustion—eyeglasses rolling up and down with the motion—and simply muttered, "My God, what are we allowing to happen in this country?" A full minute of silence followed before the senator opened his eyes and fired his gaze directly at the Armed Services staff member. "Were you aware of this?"

The aide shook his head. "No, sir."

"Should you have been?" The staffer's connections to the intelligence community were strong, and there was more than a tinge of Why Didn't You in Worth's voice.

The aide, 47, a longtime Washington player sometimes called The Prince of Darkness for his strong anti-Communist beliefs, caught the subtext. "Whether I should have or shouldn't have is immaterial, senator. What matters is that it happened on my watch. That makes it my failure."

The admission seemed to take some edge off Worth's anger. He was known as someone who hated yes-men only slightly less than he hated people who refused or denied responsibility for their screw-ups.

"All right," the senator said after another moment, looking at the committee aide, "here's what you're going to do. You're going to use every back channel you have. You're going to find and open every secret door that you know exists in government. You're going to unlock the secrets." Pause. "And you're going to get me some goddamned answers."

Goggins tried to jump in. "Senator, as a I said, we're not—"

"Dan, please," Worth cut him off, turning back to the committee aide. "You'd be wise not to fall asleep on this particular watch."

Walter Frost nodded and said nothing. He'd learned long ago the value of silence as a weapon against those who blindly followed their moral compass in a direction that was as unknown as it was inevitable.

Chapter 8

Meredith Whitney Wade had gone to extraordinary lengths to transform the Qaletaqa Inn from a basic bed and breakfast into a home for people she didn't know.

There were the meals, served family style at three wooden tables that, despite their size, were still swallowed by the Sedona, Arizona, hotel's cavernous, rock-walled dining room. Meredith's Southwestern menu included recipes that for the past 15 years had won blue ribbons at the Cococino County Fair, everything from Spanish meatball soup to pinon chicken, duck marinated in chilis to cornish game hen. Then there was breakfast. When her late husband Barry first purchased the Qaletaqa, the house specialty had been traditional huevos rancheros. But Meredith quickly realized that guests passing through on their way to somewhere else would probably appreciate a heartier morning fare, one that propelled them further into the day. Beyond that, she knew that it was the feast at sunrise that would capture the attention of the Eastern travel writers whose praises would justify in-season rates that hovered around $300 a night.

It paid off.

"The breakfast enchiladas are like nothing one has ever experienced," wrote Edward Van Parkes, a notoriously fussy critic who often reviewed for *The New York Times,* during an eight-day tour of Southwestern inns in the mid-1980's. "Lightly grilled tortillas, stuffed beyond capacity with cheeses, green-peppered scrambled eggs and black beans, topped off with fresh chilis and tomato sauce that will result in the best, laziest, mid-morning nap you have ever taken."

With this and ongoing endorsements from Van Parkes, the Qaletaqa—it meant "guardian of the people" in Hopi—became a must-stay for everyone on the Arizona-New Mexico travel circuit. They came for the food, certainly, but also for the ambiance. In keeping with her concept of inn-as-home, Meredith turned the reception area into something of a living room, with Navajo rugs, comfortable black and turquoise sofa-chair sets and enormous dream-catchers dotting the walls, which were high, craggy and slate-colored, just like those in the dining area. On every table—some of them Spanish-looking black wrought iron, others more ranch-styled, low-slung and dark-wooded—was locally fired pottery, and an occasional bronze metal sculpture. The guest rooms were worthy of any loving mother, appointed with fresh-cut pansies, petunias and geraniums plucked from the inn grounds ("I just put down seeds and they grow," Meredith told a reporter for a Tucson paper). There were king-sized canopy beds and actual wood-burning fireplaces. Rather than use the typical "Do Not Disturb" signs, guests seeking privacy could simply hang a small scented brick—encased in black netting—from their door handle. And unlike just about every hotel everywhere, the Qaletaqa gave keys. Large, oversized keys that looked as if they unlocked dungeon doors. Just like home.

Which it may have been for the temporary brothers and sisters, sons and daughters, mothers and fathers, who paid Meredith for the right to be her one-night-stand family. But for the proprietor herself, the Qaletaqa was a prison of guilt, each day starting as this one had: Meredith, sitting alone in her office, scrawling the same words on personalized stationery whose sand tones, red lettering and Indian motif matched the inn's décor:

What is a mother's betrayal?

It was a question that had haunted her for 37 years now. Twelve as Kevin's mother, 25 as his deceiver. As far as her son was concerned, it had all begun the day she simply vanished with Barry Wade, a wealthy Prescott businessman who died four years to the day after their wedding.

Meredith never told her son of the impending marriage, and there was no ceremony to speak of. Kevin simply came home from college one day, junior year, walked into his house and discovered two nice parents, a handsome little boy and pretty little girl, a Dalmatian named Dotty— none of whom he'd ever seen in his life. There were phone calls, heated arguments and words whose hurtful rage burned off the possibility of reconciliation. Then nothing. Kevin simply wrote his mother out of the book of his life, and moved on.

In truth, though, the betrayal had begun long before Meredith abandoned her son and embarked on an empty existence whose deep regret was marinated by liquor and dulled by pharmaceuticals. It had begun before he was even born, on the day Meredith first began to realize that in the minds of the elite, her life and that of the child she carried were less important, less vital, than those of the golden few.

You have to understand, they said.

You'll be taken care of, they promised.

You have to remember the national interest, they demanded.

Occasionally, a fond memory, welcome as a spring thaw, would deliver some momentary relief. When she allowed her mental photo album to flip from page to page—from the time of Kevin's birth, up until Jon's death—Meredith's heart could not help but smile at the pictures of the perfect father. Jon and Kevin playing touch football on the side yard of their brick Air Force base duplex. Kevin as an inept Cub Scout to Jon's patient whittling instructor. Jon explaining to his budding big-league shortstop the art of lightly touching second base before firing to first to complete the double play. Working together on a project for the Oak Street Science Fair, something about rockets and space travel. Tossing a tennis ball in a crowded hotel swimming pool, much to the dismay of a fat woman in a flowered bathing cap they kept beaning. Banging on that damned drum kit they'd rigged in Kevin's room.

Yet like all seemingly perfect things, it was a fraud. As much as she'd tried to play the role they assigned her and be a mother—and no matter what Kevin or anyone else thought, she'd done her best, which was asking a lot under the circumstances—things just didn't work out as planned. Yes, Kevin had made a life for himself independent of the truth, maturing into a man of dignity despite growing up in a landscape of lies, a fact that spoke volumes about his character. But the secrets remained. And a day did not pass that Meredith Wade did not resent the people, herself included, who had so artfully created a world for her son that was utterly devoid of sincerity. All in the name of—

"The national interest. You have to remember the national interest."

Meredith laughed grimly, took a long sip from a tall glass of vodka and orange juice, her own personal breakfast of champions. Underneath the first question, What's a mother's betrayal?—which stared back at her from the page, unanswered, as it had for years—she wrote, The national interest?

That one she could answer. There were no national interests. There were just the interests of men, and ambition, and the so-called national interest existed only to the degree that it merged with those. Anything else was just a party mask, designed to conceal the true intentions of the plotters.

Of which Meredith Wade was one. In her own way, maybe the worst of them all.

She looked at her watch, a diamond-studded Gucci, a gift from Barry. It was already 10:30, and the lunch crowd would soon be arriving. My God, what happens to time? she thought, reaching into a drawer in the antique roll-top desk—more Wall Street than Arizona, but that was Barry—and pulling out a small wooden mirror with turquoise and onyx inlays on the handle. Gazing at her reflection, Meredith took some solace in the fact that the reflected image was not unattractive: Light hair, more ash than blonde, pulled back and held in place with a Navajo-designed pin. Face lightly tanned, thin without being gaunt, no sags or folds. Blue eyes that at some moments were clear as a Canadian lake, at others just as cold. Smooth skin that had triumphed over the vagaries of age thanks in no small part to the miracles of modern science. An inviting smile that at full throttle more than compensated for lips she'd always felt were too thin to be seductive. A well-toned body, thanks to a rigorous thrice-weekly regimen with a personal trainer, arrayed in a gauze dress—the national uniform of the Southwest—drawn at the front by a fringed leather belt whose sterling silver buckle was gently etched with a desert sunrise.

Meredith never had a problem with that image. But the person beneath it tormented her.

She took two Valiums from her small brown leather purse, downing them with another long sip from the fortified orange juice. Time to get ready. The families would be coming soon.

•

There was nothing about Jim Odom that suggested Government Bureaucrat. Not the suit, a high-end Joseph Aboud over a cream-colored shirt, set of matching MontBlancs in the pocket, and brown tie. Nor the watch, a Tag Heuer that was a 3K investment, easy, or the ring on his left little finger, a garnet the size of Argentina framed in diamonds, probably cost twice as much. Not even the hair, which was full, thick and reddish-blonde, looked like it was styled by a Frenchman with one name. If this guy was making it on the salary of a mere public servant, which Kevin figured was 60 grand, 70 tops, he was wearing it all right now.

"You're with the state, right?" Kevin asked, looking at Odom's business card, trying to square it with the figure before him, the process tangled by his brain-scrambling blasts from the past—Roper's call and the package from Island City.

"I head the water division, actually," Odom nodded, a casual over-the-shoulder toss of the arm, aimed at a wall of bookshelves that was packed with white and blue binders and official-looking bound volumes containing North Carolina's environmental laws. They were in the conference room of Wayne Earl Wiley's law firm, which Odom, who worked out of Raleigh, had insisted upon, not saying why, Kevin imagining the senator had a secret camera—that's a *nanny cam*, son, which are perfectly legal—installed somewhere, the better to keep an eye on his investments.

"But you're a consultant to American Environmental Security?"

Odom laughed, peered at Kevin over the top of thin, half-frame reading glasses. "Hardly." He had the manner of a rich man, and three times the smugness. "That would mean I was being paid by a company I regulate, which would taint the process, I believe, and likely run afoul of the law."

Taint the process? Run afoul of the law? Not the kind of phrases that usually roll off the tongue of a government wage slave. "Then what's the connection?"

"Wayne Earl represents American Environmental on this matter, and I am investigating this case." There was a hint of Old Charleston in his voice, superior and regal, but just a hint, making it unclear whether the accent was acquired or contrived.

"So there's no official connection between you and Wiley."

"My company is a client."

"Your company?"

"The True Green Company. We're environmental consultants." He leaned back into the maroon fabric chair, stretched and plopped what had to be Size 14s on the table. The man was tall, maybe 6-4, thin-framed and muscular, Kevin thinking he probably played some hoops in college. "Some years ago, I approached the senator with the thought that, as an expert in environmental matters, True Green might be of some benefit to his corporate clients. Permitting matters, mostly. Assisting in court proceedings and public hearings. Taking a machete to the red tape. That sort of thing."

"And that's not illegal or unethical?" Kevin asked, amazed, like Are You Kidding Me?

"It's a family business. My name is not on any of the papers."

"So? Isn't there some law—"

"We get the laws we accept," Odom shrugged, not answering the question, his scrunching shoulders saying he didn't think it was much of a big deal, either *our* laws or *his* evasion. "On this particular matter, Wayne Earl has engaged my company to assist American Environmental through this little problem."

"Poisoning drinking water doesn't sound like a *little* problem to me."

Another smile came to Jim Odom's face. It was about as good-humored as a plane crash. "Do you have any idea who runs American Environmental Security?" he asked, avoiding a direct response once more. "James Sayyad. He's an Arab, a Saudi. Single biggest political contributor in the state of North Carolina. He also bankrolls the symphony and the ballet, paid to put computers in every orphanage in this county and covered the entire cost to relocate a homeless shelter after the city decided to raze the former site and put up a parking lot. And that's just the first line of his resume as a corporate citizen." He paused. "To put it mildly, Mr. Sayyad is not a person to fuck with."

"I appreciate that," Kevin nodded, not sure if he was being enlightened or warned. "But did this Mr. Sayyad poison those people?"

Another non-answer answer: "Mr. Sayyad is a good man. We only want to ensure he gets the fairest possible hearing on this matter."

"You like him so much, why don't you work for him, get out of the public service racket?" Stupid comeback, Kevin knowing it instantly, knowing he sounded like a whining kid on the playground, Yeah, Well, Your Mother Wears Combat Boots, that kind of thing.

"Because I am more valuable in my current capacity." Said it flat-out, just like that, strange how honesty comes at the most unexpected times, like when you're talking about probably illegal activities. "You might want to consider that before taking your bullshit attitude another step."

Kevin just gaped at him, heart rate spiking at the unstated threat. "What's that supposed to mean?" he asked, finally.

"Mr. Sayyad has many friends. And he takes care of those who take care of him. Look at this." Odom pulled a checkbook-shaped, eel-skin wallet from the Aboud coat, took out a photo and passed it to Kevin. "That's my company's place in Aspen," he explained, referencing the chalet that was cut into the Colorado mountains. "When Mr. Sayyad wanted to expand his operation, we short-circuited the approval process—got it done in three months as opposed to three years—and he gave it to us. A little bonus. And this"—Odom produced a second photo, of a 700 series BMW—"this is our company car. One of our company cars, actually. Mr. Sayyad leased them to us after the state denied a competitor's permit request. Those folks, the company we rejected, they were bad actors. Lots of fines and violations. So we just said no. Best thing we could've done for the people of this state, too. Our job is to protect their health and well-being, and we did it. That's all we're asking you to do: Help us to keep standing up for them."

No trace of irony in Odom's voice, which had elevated false sincerity to high art. Even if there had been, it would've been lost on Kevin, whose glance caromed from one photo to the other, seeing only what was on the paper, and nothing of what was true. "So this is how things work?"

"Let me tell you exactly how things work." The regulator took his feet from the large table, sitting up and moving his chair closer to Kevin, getting almost nose-to-nose, whispering in a hushed voice, mock-conspiratorial: "You had the world on a string. Somebody cut it. You're trying to tie it back together, but the knot just won't hold. Now you can spend the rest of your life tying and re-tying that knot. Or"—pointing to the photos—"you can get a new string."

Kevin again thinking of Maxie, her taking Donna Hubbard's money on a case she knew was going nowhere, not giving it a second or third or fourth thought, not looking back, just doing what had to be done, period.

"So, are you wid' us or agin' us?" Charleston accent gone, replaced by the twang of a dumb old country boy, Jim Odom being anything but. Before Kevin could utter a word, the door to the conference room flew open to reveal a suspendered Wayne Earl Wiley. Odom smiled. "This boy's got some issues we may have to negotiate, senator."

"Well, hell, you better do it quick. That stack of money sittin' on my desk is about to burn a hole in the taxman's pocket, and I'd rather pay for personal services than government services any ol' day of the week."

Odom laughed. "Don't you worry. I believe we're close to reaching an understanding here, don't you, son?"

Kevin looked at him, silent as a church mouse in a python cage, understanding nothing, thinking only of the money and the guy on the street, the homeless guy, the one who asked whether we'd lost the chance for renewal, further than ever from an answer.

•

Maxie McQueen lived for days like this.

South Park Mall. Overflowing bags from The Gap, Abercrombie & Fitch, Banana Republic. A Chicago Dog at J.J.'s favorite, Frank & Stein, which she suspected he liked more for the name than the food, much of which—mustard, onions, relish, tomatoes, peppers—ended up all over his face. CDs from Wherehouse Music, but none of that gangsta crap Maxie thought was polluting the soul of young black America. Although she did like Public Enemy, especially the soundtrack from *He Got Game*, but that may have been because she dreamed of getting Denzel Washington in an empty broom closet for five or 10 minutes, make him see Allah.

But what she loved more than anything else was the smile. J.J.'s smile. My, how she did live for that. And she died a little bit whenever her son's grin was not the first sight of the morning, the last of the evening, and the torch that lit up days darkened by Speedo and the Witch and their plot to legally kidnap the child.

The days at the mall were what passed for supervised visitation. The Witch would drop J.J. at South Park, and mother and son would then do the store-to-store waltz, Maxie trying to talk to the boy, see what was going on in his life, what effect living with Speedo and the Witch was having on him—and, not incidentally, on them, her and J.J. As much as she loved that little kid, their hours together were as much about Maxie as they were about him. She'd heard stories about parents who eventually became immune to the dull ache of separation. No way Maxie McQueen was going to take that route. J.J. kept her sane, gave her hope. He was her life, plain and simple, and the thought that someone, anyone, would deny the sunrise that his goofy grin delivered was simply not acceptable.

They were parked on a wooden bench in their usual place in the mall. Behind them, water danced soothingly from a fountain that was bordered by low trees and shrubs, making the whole thing feel like an oasis in the commercial desert. The real secret to this particular place was its strategic location, which let J.J. keep an eye on the Godiva chocolate shop to their right. At the moment, the boy was working on a Rocky Road cone, careful not to dribble it all over the Bulls jersey they'd just picked up at Champs, but still monitoring activity in the designer candy store, dreaming of the confection that would next service his sweet tooth.

Maxie just stared at him. Couldn't help it. He was at once entertaining and adorable, and it took every ounce of self-control to keep from wrapping herself around him like a protective bubble. But he'd have none of that. Sure, he loved her, never had a problem saying as much. "Just don't get physical about it," he'd add quickly, allowing her a soft, quick peck on the cheek, but that's it, playfully pushing her aside, babbling some nonsense about "my posse" thinking he was a mama's boy.

Posse. She always grimaced at the word. Used to be that *posse* meant something good, a group of folks who set out to right some wrong, deliver justice, haul the bad guys in. Now it was just a euphemism for a gang of baby criminals, kids whose lives too often were nothing more than rough drafts of short, tragic stories. And whenever he said it, or uttered any of the other bits of slang he spoke without understanding their meaning, Maxie always reined in her anger at the world, replacing it with a one simple thought:

This child will not be that way. This one will be different. This one will win.

Maxie looked at him for another moment. "So. How's school?"

"Okay." Not looking up, intent on licking circular swirls around the ice cream cone, keeping it nice and neat and orderly.

She peered under the bill of the Detroit Tigers cap. "Anything cool going on?"

He wrinkled his nose in a kid-sneer that was a lot more kid than sneer. "At school?" Shaking his head, like Mom, You Are So Out Of It. At least, she hoped that was what he was thinking. Mom.

"Getting any better at spelling?"

"Y-E-S." A giggle, an upward turn of the face—darker than hers, the only reminder of his father—a smile whose luster was barely dulled by the absence of one front tooth. Maxie yanked the bill of the cap down over his eyes, which elicited a shriek of laughter and a respond-in-kind attempt on her Raiders cap. She put up some token resistance, ratcheting up J.J.'s laugh and making it more sustained, before finally surrendering. Victory achieved, he went back to work on the ice cream cone.

Maxie eyed him warmly for another second or two, then leaned back on the bench, watching the parade of people wandering in and out of stores, knocked totally off stride when J.J. uttered three words that froze her: "You coming tomorrow?"

Tomorrow? her brain screamed. What's tomorrow? Did I know and forget? What have I—

"It's parents' day at school," he explained, not looking at her, like he already knew the answer but couldn't resist giving it one more try.

She felt the moment turn to rust. "Baby, I, uh—"

"S'okay, Maxie. I understand."

Maxie?

Hearing her name from his voice was like getting slapped, made her speechless, as much because she couldn't talk as she couldn't think of what to say. All she could do was get out "Maxie," nodding her head slowly, crossing and uncrossing her legs, trying not to show any of the concern, anxiety and fear that was showering her like battery acid. She looked at him, and then away, and then back at him. "Why so formal, pal?" Working overtime to sound casual, not succeeding too well.

J.J. just shrugged, kept silent.

She draped her arm over his shoulder, leaned her head close in to his. "Talk to me, man. Whassup?"

"Nothin'."

"Hey. This is me. We got no secrets. Right?" Another shrug. "Then give it up."

The boy took a deep breath, which might have been a sigh. "I just wanted to see how it sounded."

"How what sounded?"

"Me calling you Maxie instead of mom."

Maxie's rage at Carmella, never too far from home on a good day, instantly surged, and it took every ounce of strength and some deep dipping into her personal reserves to beat it back. "Why would you want to do that, sweetheart?" But she knew.

"Carmella said she was gonna be my mom now." Finally, he looked up at her. No tears, which made Maxie feel both sad and proud. Sad, because there was a part of her that wanted this child to need her so deeply that the thought of loss would devastate him. Proud, because this kid had the strength to cope with whatever uncertainties the future tossed at him. "Is that true?" Honesty. That's all the child wanted. A straight answer.

Fair enough, Maxie thought. "Let me tell you a little something about Aunt Carmella." Putting an emphasis on *aunt*, making it very clear that the Witch was not, nor would she ever be, a mother.

They had never really had this talk before. About what she'd done, and how it affected her son, Maxie always thinking he was too young to understand. Like most adults, she underestimated her kid's ability to see through all the crap. "Your mom did something stupid. Really stupid."

"Aunt Carmella said you got drunk and tried to kill a cop." There was a somber tone of say-it-ain't-so in his voice.

Careful, she warned herself. "J.J., there was a man, a police officer, and he said some things about me—and kind of about you—that I didn't think he should have."

"So you didn't try to kill him?"

She thought about choosing some weasel words, lawyer words, technically correct and honestly misleading. But the last thing she wanted to do, especially now, at this moment, was hustle her own kid. "Yeah," she said, exhaling deeply. "Maybe I did. I don't know. But I do know this: I would never have killed that man. I'd never have gone through with it. You have to believe that, sweetheart. You *have* to." She wasn't entirely sure she believed it, but she wanted to, ached to. Sometimes, it's the best you can do.

He glanced up, stared deeply into her eyes, Maxie thinking she'd give an arm to get in the boy's mind, see what he was thinking. "Then how come they fired you?"

She considered explaining the difference between a firing and a forced resignation, deciding it was just too convoluted. "Honey, there are two kinds of people in this world. There's the kind with power, and the kind without it. The reason I lost my job"—not fired, not conceding anything—"was because I made some people who had power mad."

"Do you have power?" Another innocent plea for honesty.

For some reason, it was the simplest question she'd ever been asked, and she responded with a suddenness of ease that surprised even her: "I have the power of you. And no matter what kinda noise that old Carmella starts making about me, she ain't ever gonna get that power. So she might just as well give it up, 'cause me and you, man, we're gonna give her a whuppin'!" She stuck a finger in his rib cage, ran it into the armpit. J.J. cracked up. He was a tough little guy, but defenseless against the common tickle.

As J.J. was getting control of his giggle reflex, a security guard—white shirt, black pants, walkie-talkie on his right shoulder, arm patch, badge and no visible means of defense—strolled by. He flashed them a look that was too close to suspicious for Maxie's liking, a look that equated Black Person with Trouble. Maxie's initial reaction was to get in the guy's face. But being on a 12 step program toward civility, she just smiled and nodded, reminding herself that, after all, she was still doing time in Jesse Helms country.

"Then what do I do about parents' day?" J.J. asked, "'Cause if you don't go, I'll hafta go with Speedo and—"

"Speedo?" Trying to look stern, not succeeding.

"Oops." Another little giggle.

"It's Uncle Theo." Maxie said without a hint of reproach. "At least to his face."

"His butt-ugly face."

"Jamal Jackson McQueen!" she roared, and both dissolved into laughter, so loud it caused a family of passersby to stop, the little girl pointing at J.J. and Maxie as if to say they were the two worst-behaved people in the history of the world.

J.J. ignored them, his good humor veering slightly toward defiance. "And I don't wanna take that butt-ugly face with me to school, 'cause he ain't my daddy."

Choices, she thought, staring into his eyes. Choices. Do I tell Donna Hubbard I've reconsidered and risk losing the money she's willing to send my way—money that, not incidentally, is my only weapon in the war of attrition with Carmella? Or do I explain the conflict and pray that this child who so often seems wise beyond his years can understand? "Baby," she said at last, "I have to be out of town. I have a job that's really important to you and me, and I need to be somewhere tomorrow, and maybe a couple days after that."

"Can't you call it off?" Sad, but not kid-moaning.

"If there was any way, you know I would," Maxie answered, gently.

"Oh-kay." This kid took a licking, she thought, kept right on ticking. "Mom?" he offered after another pause—*Mom*, thank you, God—"I don't feel so good."

Maxie leaned down to look him in the eye, and put her hand on his forehead, checking for a fever. "What's wrong?"

J.J., not returning her gaze, twisting his head down and to one side, so she couldn't get a full facial shot. "I'm feelin' real bad. Like I got a brain tumor."

"A brain tumor?" Suppressing a grin that was fighting to break out.

"Yes, ma'am." Uh-oh. Being polite. Angling for something.

"That's serious." Nodding slowly.

"I don't think it'll last long." Looking up now, seeing if she'd caught the scam.

"Oh?"

"Nah. Just a day." Hope in his voice, hope she'd play along. "Then I'll be okay."

"Gee, that means you'll probably have to miss school tomorrow." He shrugged, like Life Is Full Of Such Sacrifices. "And Parents' Day."

He shrugged again, a big one this time, Life Is Full Of *Really Large* Sacrifices.

Maxie sat back, as if she was giving this whole situation some deep serious thought. "Well, son, I'm afraid a brain tumor ain't gonna cut it."

"Mo-om." Stretching the word into two syllables, bordering on a whine.

"But a stomach ache," Maxie said, slowly, pretending the idea was just now percolating in her mind, "a stomach ache works every time." She looked at her son. "See, they can't tell. It's your word against theirs."

"You mean Speedo and the Witch."

"That's exactly who I mean. And if they don't believe you—"

"I'll just tell 'em moms and dads would never treat their kid like that, and that if they really want to be my parents, they better start acting like it."

Scary. This kid was scary. "Where'd you learn to hustle somebody like that?"

J.J. gestured for her to lean close. When she did, he put his face in her ear and whispered, "My mom taught me," and before she could pull back and tell him how much she loved him, he added, "My *only* mom," and she realized that while things in general could be better, there was really nothing she could say or do that could make this particular moment more perfect.

Chapter 9

"Gimme something. Gimme anything."

Detective Ty Roper stared at the beautiful blonde sitting across from him in the bullpen of the Island City Police Department and allowed his mind to race through a whole lot of suggested—and suggestive—answers. There were a ton of possibilities.

The woman persisted: "I know you probably think I'm nuts—"

He smiled, leaning back in the chair, taking a sip of tepid coffee from his Tampa Bay Bucs cup. "I think you're more screwed up than the dubbing on a bad Jap monster movie. But, hey, that's just my opinion. I could be wrong."

Well, Taylor Shepard thought, at least he's not hitting on me. Which was a good news, bad news deal. The good news: she wouldn't have to play any of those boy-girl games with him. The bad news: those boy-girl games she could play so well weren't going to work on this guy. "You do know who Gary Devereaux is, right?" Crossing her legs, allowing the off-white linen dress to wander up the thigh, hoping for maybe a last dance with Roper.

"Yeah. He's an artist."

"A what?"

"An artist. Uses a .45 for a brush, paints a nice mushroom-shaped picture in blood all over the wall at his beach house. Add a few pieces of brain to the mix, and you got—what do you call it? Multi-media."

So much for the last dance.

Taylor groaned, lit a cigarette, bounced a series of stray glances off the place. Other than the fact that the cop shop occupied the first floor of an 11-story former hotel that was once the spring headquarters of a big-league baseball team, it was pretty much standard issue. Wide-open room. Big, vertical windows letting in enough sunshine to kill off the effects of green-yellow fluorescents that stretched like rail tracks over the length of the ceiling. Batteries of desks, some positioned front to front, others pushed flush against the wall, providing an up-close-and-personal look at bulletin boards covered with everything from mugshots to an alert about "hot" lobsters taken illegally on nearby Mirage Key. An interrogation room along one wall, its shaded rectangular window a less-than-conspicuous two-way mirror. Glass-enclosed office in one corner, no doubt where the Man in Charge hung his trenchcoat. Couple of guys in another corner, talking to each other, laughing quietly, every so often throwing her a look.

And then there was this smug, grinning fool Roper, who she'd been grilling for 20 minutes now, trying to get to first base on the subject of Devereaux's death.

"Honey," he said, drawing her attention from a large poster of a woman, smack-head probably, that said, *I used to be somebody, too,* "I told you everything I know."

"That it was a simple suicide."

"Case closed." Smug, self-satisfied grin.

"Show me the note," she prodded, not letting go. "Where's the note?"

"The empty bottle did his talking for him."

"There's no proof of that."

Roper sighed, rolled his eyes more pointedly than necessary. Reporters. Jesus. Can't live with 'em. Can't feed 'em to sharks. "Well, let's see. The gun was in his hand," he droned, miming the act. "It was a contact wound on his head. There was only one shot. There was no evidence of a struggle. Powder residue on his hands. Ballistics looked at the bullet we pulled out of the wall behind him, checked out the marking on the base and nose, matched it to the gun he was holding." He returned his eyes to her. "How'm I doing so far?"

"Not good enough. You ever heard of Richard Worth?"

The out-of-nowhere question stopped Roper, but not out of shock, more like What's this got to do with the price of fish in Seattle? "Yeah. Some nutcase shot him 20, 25 years ago."

"You check Devereaux's connection to him?"

"To the nutcase or Worth?" Trying to be a pain in the ass, scoring a perfect 10.

Taylor started tapping her foot on the gray tile floor. "Worth."

The detective squinted at her, but she could see he was playacting, and wondered how this guy ever managed in an interrogation room, unless it was smart cop/stupid cop. But when he said, "Yeah, we did actually," she dropped her own irritation routine, suddenly all professional, asked him what he found out. "Off the books, right?" he asked. She told him yeah. "Okay. Now, just between you and me, I figured it was Lee Harvey Oswald did Worth *and* Devereaux—"

"Fuck you, Roper."

"Seriously. He ain't really dead, you know. Lee Harvey. After Dallas, the CIA gave him a makeover, turned him into a chick assassin, like on that TV show, that *La Femme Nikita* thing." He gestured for her to come closer. Against her better judgment, she did. "Word is, she's really Marla Maples. That's why The Donald sacked her. Her gun was bigger'n his, you get my drift." Leaning back fast, palms facing her, a fake defense posture. "But, hey, you didn't hear that from me."

"I haven't heard a goddamned thing from you."

"Just the facts as I know 'em." Hands now folded primly over the top of his belt, which Taylor noticed used to be a notch or two tighter than it was now.

"Did your facts tell you who Devereaux was? That he—"

"Ran some special interest group, yeah. Him and every other hard-on with a passion."

"Did you check it out?"

He looked at her like she'd just beamed in from the third ring of Saturn. "I strike you as somebody who gives a shit about politics?"

"There's a connection there, a connection between Devereaux and Worth and this group. Figure it out, you find the killer." She winked at him. "Trust me."

"Sweetheart, I found the killer." He winked back, exaggerated, mocking. "Trust *me*."

"Fine," she said, settling back, stretching her legs out, her arms up. "I'm not in any hurry. My editors haven't put me on any deadline. When I get the story, they'll run the story. Simple as that. And if I have to stay here all day today, and again tomorrow, and the day after that—"

"Wait a second, hold—"

"—I'll do it. If I have to follow behind while you flatfoot it down the hot Island City pavement, I'll do that, too. If I have to camp outside the little boy's room while you drain the lizard, I will, and if—"

"What do you want from me, lady?" The banter had been kind of fun, but Roper was now tired of the game. "I told you, there's nothing there. I couldn't lead you to water from a sailboat."

"No, it's okay. Really. I can wait." Saying it almost perkily, like she really did have all the time in the world. Which when she pulled out a copy of *Vogue* from her big black leather purse, it appeared she did. After she'd flipped through a couple of pages, she looked up at Roper, smiled brightly, gave a kind of half-wave. "Oh, don't worry about me. Go ahead and do what you do. I'm not going anywhere." The detective had a bad feeling this pushy bitch meant it. When she asked where the ladies' room was—"you know, just in case"—he was sure of it.

Looker or not, he didn't need her in his face for God knows how long. "What's it gonna take to get you outta here."

Taylor loved the sound of surrender. It sounded so *male*. "I already told you, Ty."

Two minutes later, she was gone, Kevin Columbus's name and phone number stashed away in her reporter's notebook, along with a mental note to make a call or two, find out what pushed the kid's buttons.

•

Maxie had flown into Mobile early that morning—nothing was available to Montgomery—rented a car from Budget, and headed north up Interstate 65. The drive was about as exciting as a physics lecture. No towns, factories, life, cows, sheep, nothing. Just a bunch of trees and an occasional cheap-o gas station. By the time she pulled into the sheriff's office about 30 miles south of the state capital, she was happy she'd made it without drifting into a coma.

After an awkward moment when the south Alabama deputy who'd set everything up for her got hold of the fact that she was, gasp, a non-white, the two got along pretty well. His name was Eddie Pratt, and she thought he was good-looking in a farm boy kind of way. Polite—lots of yes ma'ams and no ma'ams dotted the child's sentences—trim and muscled, he looked like the stereotypical Southern cop with none of the baggage.

Pratt had briefed her on the basics of the case while they sipped a Pepsi in the office. It was nothing more than a random act of driver stupidity, as far as he could tell. Darlene Sharpe, Donna's sister, was driving north in the right-hand lane, maybe at a high rate of speed, which may or may not have been a contributing factor. Witnesses said a red pickup roared up behind her, cut left too close in front of Darlene's car, and ran it into an overpass support. The automobile exploded on impact, and spun over and over, coming to rest in the center median about 50 yards down the highway. The townfolks said it was a miracle nobody was killed. Nobody but Darlene, anyway, whose life the miracle chose not to grace.

No one knew who the driver of the pickup was. Without a tag number, it could have belonged to any of about 80 trillion people in

Alabama or the Florida Panhandle or the Redneck Riviera of Gulf Shores and Biloxi.

All of that was consistent with what Donna Hubbard had said. About the only bit of news Maxie learned was that two or three days before the accident, there had been reports of kids up on the overpass, taking pot shots at cars. Pratt said it wouldn't be the first time a local high school jock with too many Buds under his belt had pulled a Winchester off Daddy's gun rack, taken a few hits of dope and mistaken a car for an eight-point buck. But other than a 9-1-1 call to county EMS, from some woman, a tourist who was just passing through and sounded more angry than freaked out, there was no evidence of any shooting of any any kind.

"It was a stupid bonehead move," Eddie Pratt was saying, after they'd gotten out of their respective cars—Maxie always wanting to be mobile, depending on no one—and were surveying the bright, sunlit scene where Darlene Sharpe had died. "A damned tragedy."

The concrete wall of the overpass gave a pretty good picture of the crash. A wide gash-streak was carved out of one side, framed in black, memories of smoke and fire. There were also some bites out of the macadam highway, no doubt courtesy of the car as it flip-flopped its way to incineration, and charred grass and weeds in the center strip where it deep-fried after stopping.

Maxie asked Deputy Eddie a couple of perfunctory questions: How long did it take EMS to get to the scene? ("Faster than usual. They were all pretty excited.") Was there an autopsy? ("Nothin' to autopsy, body was burned so bad. We got the initial ID by running the tags on the car.") Was the automobile checked for funny business, like brake cables that had been cut, open fuel lines, that sort of thing? ("There wasn't much more of the car left than there was of Miz Sharpe.") Of course, without an autopsy report and a good examination of the car, no doors were closed. At the same time, Maxie knew in her gut that there was nothing to queer the official story.

She also knew that in most crime scenes, it wasn't real likely you'd find evidence in the big stuff. Not once had she ever broken a problem case by confining her search to the obvious, things like beds, desks, cabinets, wall safes. It was always the unlikely places. A freezer. Bottle of cologne. Inside an Art Deco clock, or stripped along the frame of a piece of pop art. Once, the case-breaker was nearly buried with a corpse being shipped back to Charlotte for a funeral.

Right now, in the absence of any physical evidence, she figured the only unlikely place to look was 100 or so yards either side of the collision point. She thanked Pratt for his help, said she'd be in touch. Maxie honest-to-God thought he was going to ask her for a date, the way he was saying how nice she looked in all that black denim and digging at the loose dirt with his foot, like shy boys do when they were trying to get up the nerve to make a move, any move. No moves, though. No questions. Pratt just smiled and got in his cruiser. Driving off, he hung out the window and waved before disappearing over a rise in the interstate. Maxie wondered how it would go over, him and her, with the good folks of rural Alabama. Probably like a pregnant pole vaulter.

With that, she turned to the scene. The crime scene, as it were.

•

Kevin had met with Jim Odom thinking he could keep the whole Island City thing on hold in his head, at least for a little while. The thought process that got him there, to the moment of the meeting anyway, was kind of like the one people go through after the grim-faced doctor comes in, holds up the x-rays, points to a dark spot on the liver the size of Denmark, and says Time's Up.

It started with denial, the irrational belief that everything—the photo, the negative, the note, all of it—everything was a perverted hoax, and the silly grade school editorial nothing beyond mere coincidence. Problem with that was the Little Buddy reference in the note, which even he admitted pretty much put a stake through the heart of simple chance. From there, he shifted to a tentative curiosity: If it did mean something, the question was what, and what did it have to do with him? Problems there, too, most of them related to the fact that he didn't have even the beginning of an idea about what was going on, where to start, where to find answers, nothing. Enter fatalism, which was sort of romantic in a wimp-out kind of way, the idea that whatever was happening was already in motion, and he didn't have the power to detour destiny, so why even worry about it? Of course, when life's out of control like that, it can breed terror, which it did, producing a sensation of danger so real he could touch it, an utter fear of events that had come into his life like a virus, silent and unseen. Then, showering, getting ready to see Odom, an odd hope arrived. Maybe Jon Columbus was alive, and for some reason—Kevin had no idea why, par for the course, things taking the turn they had—the old man had lived out his later years in some alternate universe. But then, as it inevitably does, reality hit. Maybe it was the fact that he was on his way to a would-be money meeting, and his own personal situation—which on a good day was tough to put a smiley-face on—tore through the bullshit, exposed his hope for what it was: Wishful thinking, a fantasy. Come on. Say what you will about the photos, the call from Roper, the note and all, but he'd seen his father planted in Arlington, seen the simple white grave marker, run his fingers over the etched-in name. Didn't get any more real than that. Enough said.

Except that after the meeting with Jim Odom, all that changed.

Because by the time he left Wayne Earl Wiley's office, Kevin's brain had become an occupied territory, invaded and taken over by renewed thoughts of the mystery package from Island City, its sender and its implications. Driving back to the apartment, he wondered what caused the change of mind, the sudden return to the curiosity stage, but not tentative now, just the opposite. Maybe it was Odom, a man whose appearance said absolutely nothing about who he really was.

Or avoidance, the fact that he wasn't up for confronting the debate at the core of his sessions with Wiley and Odom, that debate being whether he had what it took to accept their deal and turn his life around, not exactly knowing what that was or what a turned-around life would look or feel like. Who knows, maybe he just wanted an adventure, something to break things up a little, take him somewhere else, let him put his life in cold storage if even just for a day or two.

All Kevin knew was this: What had started with denial had now ended in a throbbing ache for discovery. There were probably all kinds of deep-seated, psycho-babble reasons for it, but at this point he didn't much care, the question of why his mind worked the way it did not being real high on his priority list. At least he had some direction, and that was better than nothing even if where it took him was still a work in progress. All he needed now was a plan to get there.

Roper was a logical jumping-off point, although Kevin sensed the Island City cop had already racked this case up in the Solved column, and wouldn't be inclined to revisit what evidence and circumstance had both affirmed as a suicide. Calling Sedona was always a possibility, even after all these years. Of course, any mother who had neglected to tell her only son about a new husband and sudden relocation—Oops, honey, sorry, the pills make mommy kind of goofy sometimes—was hardly a poster child for family truths. Assuming, that is, she had even a passing acquaintance with such truths. He even considered hiring Maxie, except that he had no money to pay her and she was off in Alabama doing work for someone who did.

Which left only one option: Do it yourself.

Phase I had to kick off with a trip to Florida, finding out what he could about Devereaux. Back at the apartment, he made some reservations on a cheap airfare site on the web, holding his breath when he punched in the number on his credit card—the card he saved for emergencies, which had become all too frequent and all too expensive in recent years—silently praying the charge wouldn't be rejected, which it wasn't, Thank you Lord. He'd get into Island City early the next morning.

Good. The plan was working so far.

After a quick change of clothes—out of the khaki pants, blue shirt and Structure tie that these days passed for the corporate costume, and into jeans, a gray pullover and New Balance running shoes—he kicked off Phase II: Get whatever answers he could about the photo negative, Frame 214. Retrieving the slice of film, he headed to Pronto Photo, a one-hour development shop in a strip center just off I-77, a mile or so from the apartment.

Where the plan hit something of a snag.

Ted, the kid behind the counter, was not especially helpful, staring at the negative through a shot glass-shaped magnifier, muttering, "I dunno, man" in a monotone, like it was a mantra for the brain-dead. His hair was cropped short, dyed purple on the sides and bleached bright white everywhere else, a striking contrast to the black Limp Bizkit T-shirt and baggy, sag-to-the-buttcrack jeans and workboots. Tattoos snaked up arms that looked like human exclamation points. Something that resembled a reddish tumbleweed was growing on his chin. He had a nose ring, and a small silver stud in his eyebrow.

"I dunno, man," Ted muttered again, although this time he finally added some detail: "Looks pretty mushy. Contrast isn't bad. Good blacks and whites. Just not a lot in between." He glanced up from the frame. "I'm not sure you're gonna get much."

"What's the biggest image size you can give me?" Kevin asked, drumming his fingers on the countertop, impatient, tired, not happy that the plan was getting waylaid by a guy who looked like his parents were a couple of punk rock peacocks.

Ted's grin revealed surprisingly white, almost perfect teeth. "Dude. I can take this up to two-and-a-half by like three-and-a-half. Feet! That's no problemo. 'Course, it'll look like a mudslide."

"Then what do you propose?"

Ted's eyes went vacant. "Huh?" Like Kevin was speaking Latin.

"Two questions, okay? Two?" He gave a V sign with his right hand, two fingers, which the kid concentrated on like they held The Answer. "First, what image size do you recommend for the print? Second, is there any way I can make the images clearer?"

"Five by seven," he answered immediately, sounding almost like a human professional. "It'll keep the details as clear as possible." Kevin nodded, said nothing, hoping the silence would remind the kid there was a second part to the equation. The lights started to warm up a little behind Ted's eyes, then hit full glow. "Oh, yeah. Well. Here's what I'd do: Get a good high-res scan of the photo, and take it to some computer guy who's got the software to mess with it."

"Mess with it? Is that a technical term?"

"Yeah. You know. Pull some of the images out. Clean 'em up, make 'em clearer."

Kevin held up the negative. "So you're telling me that with a high-resolution scan, and some computer software, I can get a better look at what's going on in this picture?"

"Correctamundo." While Kevin was signing and dating the paperwork to develop the film, he asked if Ted knew anybody with the technology to clean up the photo. "Yeah, yeah, I do," the kid said, nodding in slow motion. "But you got to promise not to say anything, even if the cops or Bill Gates come in and torture you."

Bill Gates tortures me every time my computer crashes, Kevin thought. "Why is that?" he asked, pushing the signed paper back to Ted.

The clerk cut his eyes one way and then the other, no doubt making sure the store was spy-free. "'Cause it's a secret, man."

Kevin smiled wanly. Great. Just what he needed. Another secret.

•

After browbeating Roper out of Kevin Columbus's name, Taylor Shepard went back to her hotel, pulled out the laptop, made sure it was at 100 percent battery capacity and set up an office on the balcony of her beachfront room, overlooking the water. It was the kind of day tourist brochures were made of. The sun's light was warm and buttery, its intensity dulled by a gentle Gulf breeze that occasionally found the strength to knock off a floppy hat or play havoc with a beach umbrella.

This was the life, she thought, raising her face to the sun, absorbing its energy. One day, maybe even one day soon, it'll be just like this, when everything was over, and the mysteries and conspiracies gone forever. One day.

She logged on to her Internet provider. Waiting for the connection—sometimes it seemed to take forever—she slid out of the dress, throwing on a tank top and cutoff jeans. By the time she returned to the white metal patio table and chair, the computer was telling her that She Had Mail.

Mail. Right. Try crap.

Home-based business opportunities. Offers to watch men have live sex in Denmark. Some holistic remedy guaranteed to cure prostate enlargement. An herbal pill that increased breast size. It never ceased to amaze her. A vehicle as powerful as the Internet, reduced to traveling from cyber-town to cyber-town, selling hope and hype for the millennium from the back of an electronic wagon.

She got an Amstel Light from the in-room service bar, and started shooting through her bookmarked news pages. Other than the impending treaty with Arabaq, there wasn't a lot that interested her. It was more of the same, more crap, just framed in the earnestness of media concern and outrage. A pro-family congressman caught in an affair with a staffer half his age. Questions of whether a rumored Senate candidate had fathered a black child out of wedlock. Lots of huffing and puffing about violence in the movies, television, rap music. Two actresses sniping at each other over a catty reference one made about the other's husband. Meanwhile, back in the real world—the world the media figured no one cared enough about to understand—Social Security and Medicare were going bankrupt. The latest balanced budget had more holes than O.J.'s alibi. Congress was ignoring projections of a revenue slowdown and calling for a billion-dollar tax cut. Drug prices for old people were going through the roof. And campaign finance reform was being debated by the very people who had the most to lose by its passage.

Taylor thought maybe she should just forget the Richard Worth case, pick up her gun, head for Congress, save the Republic from itself.

It was depressing. She needed relief.

From the Bookmark menu on the taskbar, she aimed the cursor at *Merkey Waters*. The screen went blank, before the familiar drawing appeared, and the bright yellow box with black letters announcing *Today's Stink*. Must've been a slow day in the cyber-sleuth business, only one headline dealing with Worth's murder:

SENATOR'S KILLER LIVING AT MICHAEL JACKSON'S NEVER-LAND?

Before she could click to get "the real story," her screen went blank. There was the noise, the gunshot noise. Everything faded to crimson, which itself vanished when the word **FLASH** came up, and the headline:

Devereaux Didn't Take All His Secrets To The Grave.

She stared at the screaming words, and the story that followed, not in disbelief or even with a sense of vindication. More like satisfaction, a feeling that maybe this was all coming to a head, and that she'd soon be able to take her earnings, find a beach not unlike this one—although in a farther-away place—and live the life that had eluded her for the past 20 years. She called U.S. Airways and made reservations for Charlotte, fully intending to get under the skin of one Kevin Columbus, sole surviving acquaintance of Gary Devereaux, and find out what he knew and who he was. It'd probably give more than a few people hives, her stepping off the reservation like that, but she didn't much care. What were they going to do? Shoot her?

Taylor finished the beer, reread the item on Merke's page, smiled.

This was starting to get interesting.

Chapter 10

The crime scene, as it were, gave up nothing.

Maxie had spent close to three hours walking the highway, getting little more than an occasional wolf whistle from good ol' boys in pickups—none of then red, naturally—and the ear-piercing blare of a trucker's horn. She was hot, tired and frustrated, unable to shake the gloomy back-of-the-mind concern that the Hubbard case, while starting slowly, was about to taper off fast. And while a point arrived when she thought it was time to give it up, that this was one of those rare instances where things are what they are, the moment quickly passed. Forget the facts. She had some facts of her own, and they looked like this:

The longer Maxie stayed on this case, the more she was paid; the more she was paid, the more likely she was to put on what passed for a decent fight to hang onto her son. Was she being dishonest, not telling Donna the investigation looked stuck in neutral? No way. The girl was shelling out a lot of cash, and the least Maxie could do was make sure she got an honest day's work in return for an honest day's wage, right?

Right.

The dilemma thus rationalized, Maxie kept trekking up and down the interstate—before, at the point of and after the collision site—looking for anything that would take her somewhere past the reports Eddie Pratt had shown her. Wandered around in the bushes, the scrub pines, the median, the hot macadam. Looking for car parts and clues, finding only 32-ounce beer bottles and fast food containers. A little after 1 in the afternoon, she decided to go back to the beginning, walk the scene one last time.

Which was when she noticed the rock.

It sat off the road, on the approaching side of the overpass, beyond the 100-yard perimeter she'd set for her search. Large and smooth, maybe six feet long, two feet thick, painted grass-green, so it was nearly invisible against the landscape. Seeing it, Maxie felt her excitement surge, more because this was something new than because it was something vital. No matter. It was virgin terrain. It was hope.

Up-close, she could see that the stone wore the thick latex jacket of repeated paintings, inscriptions like GHS Y2K, REBELS RULE and various Greek letters identifying it as a favorite target of high school and college kids, probably a stop along the initiation trail. She peeled the nail file from her Swiss Army knife, scraped away a couple shards of green, found purple and then yellow and then blue, thinking Jesus, this has been painted more times and with more colors than Tammy Faye Baker's face.

Running her hand gently across its surface, as if the thing was some good luck-dispensing Buddha, she was struck by its evenness, it's smoothness. No cracks or ridges or—

Whoa. Wait a second. Back up.

On the left-hand side, near the base, she found an irregularity. The paint had not only been sheared away, but it looked as if someone had taken a hammer and chisel, chipped off a triangular piece, Maxie snap-deciding it had to be from a bullet, not bothering to ask herself what role wishful thinking might have played in the conclusion. She bent down, rubbed the spot lightly, fine white powder attaching itself to her fingers. This had happened recently, she thought, probably the past few days—longer, even, if there hadn't been rain—and maybe, just maybe, as far back as the night Donna Hubbard's sister was killed.

Maxie stood and squinted in the direction of the overpass, trying to see if there was anything resembling a clear sight line. There looked to be, but she wasn't sure. Setting a small hand mirror on the rock, she returned to her car, checked a map and located the overpass road, S.R. 622, then figured out the easiest way to get up there that didn't involve climbing. Ended up driving seven miles to the next exit and doubling back, pulled to a stop on the concrete bridge where Darlene Haggard had died, looked down toward the rock, saw it clearly, the glint of reflected light from the mirror. Oh yeah, a shooter's angle, clear and clean and straight, no doubt about it, no wishful thinking now. The shooter could have positioned himself here, right where she was standing, nailed the rock easy.

Question was, was it the work of a trained professional hitter, a liquored-up schoolboy or a hunter with the eyesight of Mr. Magoo? Somewhere in the South Alabama woods off Interstate 65 was an answer: The bullet. All Maxie had to do was weed through all the trees and bushes and dirt and bugs and wildlife, and find it. Which, thankfully, would take the rest of the day—and, if there was a God and She had some sympathy for Mothers Against Fat-Assed White-Wannabe Bitchy Sisters Trying To Steal Their Kids, maybe even longer.

•

"It's Walter," the call began, "with what I fear is some rather tragic news."

Meredith Whitney Wade stiffened in her upholstered office chair, turquoise with black stripes, and said nothing, knowing full well the real tragedy was not in the news but in its meaning. "Oh?" was all she could manage.

"Gary was diagnosed with cancer. The doctor gave him perhaps three months to live." Pause. "He opted for a premature end, it seems." No sadness in the voice, just a mere statement of fact.

She plumbed her soul for tears. None came.

"There appears to be no evidence to suggest this is anything but a simple suicide," he continued—to which she wanted to scream, *There's no such thing, not in your business.* "But Meredith, there may be a problem."

The tone in Frost's voice, hesitant, searching, told her everything: Gary had given them up. They buried the cocky sonofabitch in life, and now he's going to bury them in death.

"Meredith?" Tension in the voice now, which was odd because Walter Frost had made a career out of hiding what he truly felt.

"I'm here, Walter. I'm just, uh, you know—" not finishing the sentence because she didn't know what she was.

"I understand," he replied, distant and automatic, like he hadn't been paying attention to her and was instead thinking about what he would say next. "Now, Meredith, you must listen to me very carefully. This is vitally important to the national interest."

The national interest. There you go again. "As opposed to mine?" she snapped. "And Kevin's?"

Frost took a moment to let her resentment pass, saying as evenly as possible: "We've been very good to you over the years, Meredith. Both of you."

"Yes, Walter, how nice of you to let us both live." Shakily, she reached for a flask that stayed hidden in the desk for occasions like this one, when the weight of the world needed to be lightened, its pain dulled. Not bothering to find a glass or orange juice, or even drink from the barely-larger-than-a-thimble cap, she swigged the warm liquor straight from the small, flat silver bottle.

Again, Frost refused to rise to her goading. "Meredith, there is a chance that Gary may have placed some rather sensitive materials in some rather unpredictable hands."

"Not mine, Walter. I can assure you of that." Lighting a cigarette, reaching into her purse for a Valium, downing it with another shot of vodka.

"No. Not yours." There was a comforting intimacy in his voice that she knew was as false as a perfect marriage. It was unsettling.

"Kevin's?" Breathless, almost a whisper, like That's Impossible.

"We don't know. We don't even know if anything happened. It could all just be simple paranoia. You know how we are." She could hear him smile. It was just as false, just as unsettling.

"What do you want from me?"

Frost took a deep, audible breath. "If he contacts you, I just need to know if he'd had any communication of any kind with Gary."

"He doesn't even know who Gary Devereaux is."

"Which is why, if there had been contact, he may call you."

Her mind flashed to what Kevin must have felt the moment he walked into a familiar home with an unfamiliar family. "I doubt that."

"Be that as it may, if Kevin does contact you, there could be questions."

"About what?"

"The materials Gary may have have provided him."

She sucked in a lung full of smoke. "What are they?"

"I'd rather not—"

"It's the photo, isn't it." Blurting it right out, just like that, suddenly remembering the moment, 25 years before, and the feeling that had come over her, the sick, sinking feeling that there would come a time when all this would return to destroy—

The three of them, standing by the outside pool at the Park Hotel Nizza, posing for a picture. Lago di Lugano beneath them, the peaks of Monte Bres off in one direction, Monte San Salvatore in another. They'd just come from the modernish silver vinyl and glass bar that overlooked the lake. Next stop was a little basement tavern on Via dei Gorini, La Tinera, which they had more or less adopted as their night life of choice, where they sat on wooden benches with the locals and enjoyed the regional Swiss food, washing it down with wine served in ceramic bowls.

"Is this such a good idea?" she asked just before the photographer, Hans something or other, snapped the photograph.

He didn't answer, wasn't listening.

As Hans smiled and encouraged them to say "Raclette"—a famous cheese made in the canton of Vaud, bordering France to the southwest— she turned and looked at her husband again.

"Isn't this evidence of what happened?"

"No, it's backup protection."

"Protection?" she asked. "From what?"

"His recklessness."

"And why do we need backup? Backup for what?"

He didn't answer.

"Meredith, please. It's best for you if I didn't say. Believe me." Although Frost's words pretended to hug her with consolation, they had an unmistakable finality. "If Kevin does contact you for any reason, you must let me know. Immediately."

She'd tuned him out, thinking instead of escape.

"Listen to me," Frost demanded, suddenly urgent, even angry. "You're part of this. So if you're considering doing something stupid, acting like a mother—"

"That's what I am, goddammit!" The statement was stronger than her resolve, the delivery weak as a sick infant.

"What you are is a co-conspirator," he replied coolly. "You knew everything and did nothing. You're as guilty as the rest of us."

"What are you saying, Walter?" Voice rising, starting to crack, a sure sign she knew just exactly what he was saying, but asking anyway: "Is that, is that some kind—are you threatening me?"

"Not at all," he lied soothingly. "You are in no danger whatsoever. That, I can assure you."

"And Kevin?"

"I believe that to be the case with Kevin as well." No guarantees there. It was as if Kevin's future was beyond the control of Walter Frost. Which while a rarity in Washington—nothing seemed beyond his control, not in the Capital—she knew it was true in this case.

"I'd like some assurances. Can you get them for me? Please?" Give me a sign, any sign, she pleaded silently, that my son will survive whatever is going on.

"You know I can't do that, Meredith."

"Why the hell not!"

"It's not my decision."

"But can't you talk—"

"This is not about me," he interrupted, stern, clearly tired of the discussion. "It is not about you. It's not even about Kevin. It's about America, and whether you are going to allow your son to be put in a position to destroy this government."

"Don't be so melodramatic, Walter," she snorted, the vodka beginning to do her talking. "It doesn't look good on you."

"You abandoned him once, Meredith. Don't do it again."

The killshot Frost fired into her heart felt so real Meredith Wade put a hand over her breastplate, checking for a pulse. By the time she was convinced that some life still pumped through her body, however weakly, the phone line had gone dead.

•

Maxie felt like Long Johnette Silver, 21st Century Pirate.

Red bandana wrapped around her forehead, jeans tucked into the mid-calf-length boots, black tank top that now drew more admiring stares than it did obnoxious commentary, high-tech Oakley shades. Out in some wild unknown place, wilting under the sun, staying in a Red Roof Inn.

Looking for buried treasure.

Armed with a borrowed metal detector delivered personally by her new best friend Eddie Pratt—who also brought along some egg salad sandwiches and sweet tea, still acting like he wanted to take her to the drive-in—Maxie began by studying the probable angle of impact. If it did, in fact, come from a professional hitter shooting from the bridge, the line of fire would have to be pretty clean; that, in turn, would rule out a whole bunch of directions in which the bullet could have ricocheted.

The chipped-out area at the base of the rock was shaped like a narrow, ragged triangle. The impact appeared to be at the tip of the triangle, taking part of the stone surface away as it glanced off. Low trajectory, probably, though not too low. And flat. Probably meant the shot could have sprayed up or down, maybe to the left, maybe the left of center, all depending on the angle. She thought about taking some actual test shots of her own, firing into the rock, seeing where the bullets ended up. But that meant when the metal-detecting began, she was as likely to find the test-fires as the real thing, which seemed sort of stupid. Besides, when she added Black Woman and Gun and Hillbilly Country, it came out to a sequel of *Macon County Line*, which didn't strike her as a two-thumbs-up kind of experience.

So she just started the search, which unearthed an impressive selection of cans—beer, beer, soft-drink, tomato, field peas, string beans; two staplers ("Don't leave home without them," she steamed as the frustration grew); a Yale lock with a bullet hole in it, and a strongbox full of burned documents that looked like they could have been someone's will. When Eddie Pratt stopped back by a little after 5 offering to help, Maxie politely declined. If she found anything, she wanted the chain of knowledge to end with her for the time being. She didn't tell him that, just said it was hot and fruitless and looked like a dead end, him saying she was probably right, but asking for an update if she came up with anything, Maxie lying, saying sure. When he left, they swapped cards, agreed to keep in touch and shook hands, Maxie hanging onto his for just a tad longer than was necessary, more for the fun of it than as a come-on, maybe trying to see if and how he reacted, which he didn't. Instead, the deputy simply dropped her hand, got back into the cruiser and rolled off.

At about 6:30, she figured she'd had about as much fun as a girl had any right to have out here in the wilderness, decided enough was enough, tomorrow was another day, another couple of C-notes. She set the metal detector down without bothering to turn it off, put on her sleeveless black denim shirt. Hands protected by thick gardener's gloves, she gathered all the crap she'd found, put it in a couple of heavy-duty garbage bags Deputy Eddie had given her, tossed them in the trunk of the rented blue Corsica. Pratt had told her there was a trash drop-off an exit behind them, Maxie thinking that was the least she could do. The reminders of her presence removed, Maxie tossed the metal detector over her shoulder, like a rifle whose barrel pointed skyward, and—

Damned if it didn't go off.

She stopped, looked at the thing for some reason—as if she could identify a malfunction by sight, oh, sure—put it back on her shoulder like before.

Same thing.

At first, she was tempted to pass it off as the quirkiness of what she'd spent the afternoon berating as a "cheap-ass, piece-of-shit, Crackerjack-box toy." But as she swept it along the tree line, maybe 15 feet off the interstate shoulder, it kept taunting her. The closer she got to the woods, the louder it got, but only when aimed in one direction, everyplace else generating nothing but low static.

Swiss Army knife in hand, Maxie followed the metal-detecting sonar. It drew her to a cluster of seven trees, scrub pines like every other thing that grew taller than a foot along the interstate, except one of them carried a piece of metal.

Going from tree to tree, scanning up and down, over and around, keeping one eye out for unfriendly locals of both the human and animal sort, she searched every piece of bark she could see. Nothing.

But the machine didn't lie, at least when it was telling her what she wanted to hear, and what she was hearing was the ker-ching ker-ching of racking up those two C-notes a day in an extended investigation.

So, identifying the one tree that seemed to be attracting the most attention, she briefly considered shinnying right up, the idea dying quickly, Maxie not being an expert in things like that, the wilds being as foreign to her as Albania. Besides, the damned thing was way too tall, and didn't have any branches or anything to get a grip on, making it a challenge even for an expert shinnier.

Next to the tree in question were three others that looked as if they had been chainsawed by a hurricane; the top half of one had been sheared off, and rested at about a 45-degree angle against the trunk of the one that was giving the metal detector fits. It didn't provide much of a height boost, maybe 10 feet, but like the $200 she'd banked so far, it was better than nothing. Not trusting her beam-walking abilities, Maxie straddled the broken tree like it was a mechanical bull, inching her way up, feeling the thing sag a little with each movement. But there were no telltale cracks or creaks, like it was giving away, so she kept going. So did the metal detector, which chattered even more maniacally the higher she went.

When she reached the intersection between broken tree and bullet-tree, Maxie took a deep breath, stood unsteadily. Below her feet the dry wood sagged a bit, snap-crackle-and-popping under her weight. She froze, let things settle, scanned the tree's surface. Braced herself with one arm while the other aimed the detector, which was basically obsolete at that moment because Maxie was reasonably sure that pointing it accurately would take two hands, which was impossible unless she wanted to take a 15-foot swan dive into the Alabama dirt below.

Then she saw it. Three feet higher than the top of her head. A chunk of bark had been knocked away, exposing the light wood underneath, and the nesting place of what she was actually starting to believe was her bullet. Maxie tossed the metal detector, unfolded the knife blade, stretched her lean frame toward the spot. Just as she started to carve, the tree again settled under her feet. Maxie stopped, waited for a collapse that didn't come, reached back up to where the bark was missing.

Unable to get a good look at what she was doing, she opted to simply chop at the general vicinity of where she thought the bullet was lodged, looking a little like Norman Bates in *Psycho*, hacking up that blonde in the shower, except Maxie was slashing at a tree hoping it would just unhinge the damned thing, and make it fall to the ground.

And with one final, lunging, stretching thrust, it did.

Followed by Maxie McQueen, who collapsed to earth a second later after a sharp, white-hot pain erupted in her lower back, the feeling unmistakably like someone had put a bullet in her.

Chapter 11

"It's a tragedy," Liz Fletcher said. "Gary was always on time with the rent. Never kicked up a fuss or made a lot of noise. Whenever there was a problem around the place, he took care of it himself. Sometimes he billed me. Sometimes not. The perfect tenant. Just awful." She removed her oversized glasses, and set them on a small white desk that was remarkable for its total chaos, looked back up at Kevin Columbus. "I mean, it was awful that he killed himself, too. He was just—"

"I understand," Kevin said, not wanting to take this any further.

He'd located Liz Fletcher's office within two hours of arriving in Island City that morning. His first stop out of the airport had been the local paper, where he found Devereaux's address in a recent back issue, the brief news item headlined, "Shooting Believed Suicide." But when he arrived at the beach house, there was a local police car parked out front, so he just cruised right by, not wanting to red-flag the cops. A large white truck, emblazoned with the words Calamity Jane's Cleanup Crew, sat on the pocked tar driveway that cut a crescent path through baked brown grass in front of the house. The sanitizers, he figured, getting the brain parts off the wall, scrubbing out the blood stains, making the house a home again.

Stuck into the half-moon of land between the driveway and the road was a sign that life goes on: Available. Weekly or monthly. Liz Fletcher Realty.

From the sign, Kevin got a phone number; from that, a location. As luck would have it, Liz's eager receptionist/junior agent said, Ms. Fletcher was in even though it was a Saturday and would be happy to spend a moment or two remembering Mr. Devereaux—as a man and a client—to any friend of Gary's family. She made the assumption of relationship, which Kevin didn't deny.

"He was an odd man," Liz Fletcher continued, 6 feet of solidly-built peach-colored linen in an early 60-something body, standing behind her desk, gazing through a large picture window that opened onto a bridge to the Gulf beaches.

"How so?" Kevin asked, looking around the office suite, through the door into the receptionist's area, seeing the edge of an orange plastic laundry basket in one corner, a box of Tide sprouting from it. Wash day, he figured.

As she answered, Liz Fletcher's eyes shifted from the window to a framed poster promoting a local film festival, to another poster of a kitten clinging to a tree branch that said Hang in there, Baby. Someone had written something on it, signing with the word Kitty. "He was invisible. An answering machine always picked up his calls—or at least mine. There was no wife or girlfriend or significant other that I am aware of, male or female. He took his mail at the post office over in Mirage Village, at a little strip shopping center." Her eyes finally locked onto his. "But you want to know what I found oddest of all?" Kevin shrugged in silence, or maybe anticipation. "He never offered to buy the place. And it was, is, a great place and one heckuva buy."

The anticipation, if that's what it was, evaporated, Kevin thinking, Is she trying to put a sales move on me? "Why is that so odd?"

Liz Fletcher frowned slightly. "He rented the property for, I don't know, 15 years. That's unheard of on the beach. If people stay in one place that long, and like it that much, they usually make me an offer I can't refuse." A quick shake of the head. "Gary? Not once. Every so often, I'd boost the rent a bit—just to cover my costs, you understand—and he always paid without so much as a peep. I think I could've charged him five grand a month, and he would've done it gladly."

"So he had money?"

She nodded, every strand of silver hair staying in place. "Apparently so. The rent was always here on the first."

"Any idea where it came from?"

"I just assumed it was from that thing, that association he ran. Americans for America. Although I have to tell you, for a political group or whatever it was, they were about as invisible as he was."

"What do you mean?"

"Look at this town. We have what, maybe 100,000 people? A lot of them are retired military, and Republicans, and very, *very* patriotic. This would be, should be, a picture postcard resort for a group like that." She held up a Greetings from Sunny Florida picture postcard in case he missed the point. "But you never heard about it. Never read about it."

"Retired military?" Kevin asked, seeing a link, a connect-point between Jon Columbus and Gary Devereaux. "Was he in the service?"

"Couldn't tell you." The link dissolving, his impression doing a quick fade back to confusion, Liz Fletcher seeing it, feeling a little sorry for him, flashing a smile that glistened with artificial optimism. "But by golly I'll tell you who might." After a brief search, she magically pulled a business card out of the chaos of the small desk and handed it to him.

Thomas Cloud. Attorney at Law.

"You ask me, that sounds like an Indian name," she laughed. Kevin glanced at the card blankly, and then up at her. "Big Chief Cloud apparently has been his lawyer for many, many years. That's where Gary's personal things were sent."

It wasn't much, and lawyers being what they were, it was probably less than that. Still, Kevin asked if he could use her phone to call the man's office. Since it was a Saturday, he doubted Cloud would be anywhere near the law books, but he wanted to at least make the contact. A service picked up on the second ring, as he'd expected, although it was a real person, which was a surprise, who announced he'd reached the offices of Cloud & Associates. "Thomas Cloud, please."

"I'm sorry, but Mr. Cloud is out of town just now." The woman's voice was tinny, almost mechanized, like she was trying to sound like the machine she wasn't.

"Will he be in on Monday?"

"You'd have to ask his secretary."

Jesus. Why were things always harder than they needed to be? "Will *she* be in on Monday?"

"I don't know her schedule."

He took a breath, swallowed his irritation. "Does he call in for messages over the weekend? Mr. Cloud, I mean. Not the secretary."

"Not in my experience."

"And I suppose asking you for a home number—"

"Is out of the question."

Kevin battled the urge to just hang up on this way-too-efficient phone drone, which would make him feel good but not accomplish anything, especially the goal at hand, that being to let Cloud know someone was asking about Devereaux. What *that* would accomplish was a mystery, too, but after a half day in Island City he knew less than when he'd arrived, now figuring what the hell, just throw everything at the wall and see what sticks. So he half-whispered to Liz Fletcher, asking if it was all right to leave this number since he hadn't yet checked into a hotel, her saying fine, Kevin telling the phone drone Cloud could reach him at the realty office or, if it was next week, at his home in Charlotte.

"I'll see that he gets that message," she said, an undercurrent of Don't Hold Your Breath in her voice as she broke the connection.

"You gonna go see him?" Liz Fletcher asked.

"Maybe, maybe not. Depends on if he wants to see me, I guess."

"Well, if you do, could you do me a little favor?" Not waiting for an answer, she walked into the receptionist's area and pointed to the laundry basket Kevin had noticed earlier, him thinking, She wants me to do her laundry? "It's some stuff that the cleaning crew pulled out of Gary's utility room, tucked away in this wooden cabinet, almost like a secret compartment. I know none of this means anything to anybody, but I'm not interested in getting all tangled up in some crazy legal thing, either. So how 'bout you save me a headache, be a dear, and drop these off with Barrister Cloud if and when you go by and see him."

Her finger stayed aimed at the basket like a pointer dog, Kevin finally getting the message that his job was to pick it up. "Sure," he nodded, setting it on one of two salmon-colored chairs that flanked a table and lamp set in the corner. Tossed haphazardly inside were the carton of Tide, neon-yellow rubber gloves still in the package, a half bottle of Clorox, some Bactine, three hardback books and a dark binder note-book. Kevin didn't pay much attention to the books, not at first glance, all of them looking like library vintage, egghead stuff, straightforward socio-academic treatises whose chief function was to bore the living hell out of anyone but the authors. Second glance, though, he checked out the titles—

Family Traditions in Arabaq.
The Role of Family in Arabaqi Society.
Arabaq's Culture of Family.

— and felt that flame of mini-interest spark up again, not unlike when Liz Fletcher had said Devereaux was in the service. Jon Columbus had spent some time in the Middle East during his Air Force days, Kevin fleetingly recalling the old man's tales of Arabs in round boxy hats, long swords and baggy pants—sounded like extras in *Casablanca* to him now—wondering if three books about that part of the world meant anything, getting set to ask Liz Fletcher about that when her phone rang.

She skittered into her office, chirping that "Every call's a customer in waiting," leaving Kevin to thumb through one of the volumes. *The Role of Family in Arabaqi Society.* Various passages were underscored, most of them focusing on how, through history, the bond between fathers and their male children had formed the core of national tradition. "Women have no role in the Arabaqi world other than to produce male offspring," the author wrote. "The father lives in his sons." Not much caring about backward social values in the Middle East, Kevin dropped the tome into the basket, reached for the thick, three-ringed black vinyl notebook, hadn't even cracked it before Liz Fletcher was back with a cordless phone in her hand and a strange look on her face.

"It's Thomas Cloud," she said.

Kevin took the call, leaving the notebook unopened and unread.

•

Stretched out in her hotel room bathtub, head propped up on a towel, two bottles of Motrin and a six-pack of Evian on the floor next to her, Maxie felt like she'd just gone 12 rounds with Ali. But bad as the pain was, and her back felt like it was getting acupunctured with a red-hot railroad spike, it didn't compare to the agony of waiting.

She checked the time on her Casio runner's watch. Five minutes later than it had been when she last looked, which had been 9:54 a.m. Central Time. She closed her eyes, tight, kept them shut, like maybe that would somehow propel her through time, melt away the hours, deliver her from this slow torture.

Dream on, girl.

"Lord, help me," she muttered, half-open eyes revealing that she was, appropriately, right where she had started, in a pre-fab hotel tub the color of off-brand vanilla ice cream, trying not to move because even the smallest stir would trigger another bolt of jagged pain through her back, *Soul Train* on the tube in the other room.

And still no word from Charlotte.

It was shaping up to be a fitting end to what had not been a fun 18 hours.

After her unceremonious fall from grace in the woods courtesy of a muscle spasm or pull or something in her lower back that had been brought on by that one final, slashing lunge for the bullet, Maxie had come to a soft-but-definite stop on the damp ground below. There was a moment of panic, just an instant, when she thought she'd broken her back and was doomed to die right there, watching as bears, owls, buzzards, some other freaks of non-urban nature—damn, she hoped racists weren't cannibals—watching while they sat around and picnicked on her flesh. Then, *duh,* she realized if she felt pain—and she did, big, deep oceans of it—that was better than paralyzed nothingness, though at the moment it was a 50-50 call. So, after she decided she was neither immobile nor somebody's supper, she started a lumbering on-all-fours search for the bullet.

Half hour later, she was en route north on I-65 to Montgomery.

Along the way, she called her sole remaining loyalist at the department in Charlotte, Carlton Grigsby, and wheezed, "I need a ballistics test," every syllable pushing the railroad spike deeper into her back, trying to drive and think and ignore the pain at once, barely managing two out of three at any given moment. "And I don't need anybody asking a lot of questions."

Which, of course, is exactly what Carl Grigsby did, firing Why Don't Yous at her like rounds from an automatic weapon, Maxie taking it until he got to, "Why don't you just come home, forget all the hush-hush stuff, we'll do this thing by the books." Then she got mad.

"You're forgetting Carl, I know how to do it by the books. I've done it by the books. Remember?"

"I didn't mean—"

"And I'm just as good as you, Carl, and better than most, and I don't need the shield to prove it. To you or to myself."

He got the message. Still, he hesitated.

Fine, she thought, we'll do it your way. "You owe me, Carl."

"Ah, Max," he whined. Big strong guy like that, she could almost see him sagging at his desk in the office.

It worked, though, the guilt, Grigsby telling her to ship the friggin' evidence to him at home.

Maxie stopped at an Eckerd's in a strip center south of Montgomery—trying not to reveal her pain, losing the fight, walking slow and stiff like a robot with a corncob up its transistor unit—picked up some packaging and a box of sandwich bags, as well as the Motrin and bottled water. Not wanting to mess with tracking down a FedEx office in some strange city, she found her way to the airport. Along with a one-word note, "Thanks," and her hotel room and phone number, Maxie dropped the bullet into one of the plastic bags, sealed it in a bubble-wrapped manila envelop and shipped the whole thing out air freight, making the 9 p.m. deadline with almost an hour to spare.

After which she returned to the luxurious Red Roof Inn, crawled into the tub and tried to drown the stiffness in her back. The night passed slowly, as nights without sleep do, leaving her to meander restlessly from thought to thought:

What would the tests show? The bullet had been misshapen, which may or may not be a problem. Sometimes even pristine bullets had little or no value unless you had a suspect weapon on-hand for comparison. At minimum, she hoped to get a reading on grooves and twist, which could ID the gun, or at least pare down the possibilities.

What would that tell her? An ever tougher question. She might learn whether the shooter was a pro, or just some drunken yahoo taking his starter rifle out for a test killing. Other than a few weapon-of-choice names, she didn't know a whole lot about precision shooting. But she did know this: Hunting rifles and basic sniper guns are not all that different. With one or two exceptions, the same one that turns a deer into a wall trophy can turn a human into a corpse.

What did that mean? Just this: Unless the ammunition could be traced back to something out-of-the ordinary—a Swiss Sig Sauer SSG 3000, a French FR-F1, an Israeli Galil—chances are she'd be right back where she started, which was that there wasn't a shred of evidence to suggest Darlene Sharpe was murdered, nothing to tell Donna Hubbard, nothing to go on that would buy her another day at two bills per, nothing that would pad the J.J. Rescue Fund.

At about 4 in the morning—the night continuing to produce more questions than answers—she drifted into a sleep whose welcome calm was broken by shivers from the cooled-off tub water. Running a new jet-blast of hot water, she dropped four more Motrin and killed a bottle and a half of Evian, cut some more troubled z's, finally waking to the Saturday *Today Show*, and then *Soul Train*, and then, at 10:04, the shrill ring of her cell phone.

Forgetting her infirmity, Maxie reached for the Nokia portable, and was rudely reminded of the previous day's misadventure. She took a deep breath of recovery, went for the phone again—a more languid motion this time, almost like an arthritic cat stretching—and before she could even say hello, heard Carl Grigsby's deep, intelligent voice barking at her:

"Maxie, what the hell're you into down there?"

"At the moment, a tub." Thinking I don't need this.

Which pissed Carl off, because he was not one to take a lot of lip off anyone, and since Maxie wasn't either, they were looking at a war of serious verbal attrition. "Don't go attitude on me, girl."

She decided very quickly to cut this shit off now. "Don't go playing protector, Carl. You had that chance once, and you faded on me, and there ain't no instant replays in life. What've you got?"

Grigsby let out another whine, this one not amusing Maxie, who told him to shut up, cry on his wife's shoulder, only some other time, finishing him off with another, What Have You Got, making sure he felt each word sting him like a scorpion.

"What I *probably* got is a .308 Winchester," he said, letting his long-distance rage at her chill.

Meant nothing to Maxie. "Something a hunter might use?"

"Yeah." That's all, just a simple agreement, which told her something was up. If it was just a damned hunting gun, Grigsby'd be on her like a swarm of killer bees, raising all kinds of hell about how dumb this whole thing was, and how she needed to get back home now. But he didn't say any of that. He just said Yeah.

"So it's a hunter's rifle? Stray shot, end of story?" Nothing coming from Grigsby, not even a breath. "Carl?"

"Like I said. Probably."

"*Probably*? The hell does that mean, *probably*?"

Even through the line, Maxie could feel Grigsby's impatience. "Max, understand something," he finally answered, evenly, voice maybe flecked with a touch of warning. "To keep this quiet, I couldn't go the full nine yards. I called in a favor or two, but what I got ain't the Gospel." She remained rigid in the tub, told him to go on. "We ran the thing through the computer, and got a list of potential matches. The most likely one is a .308 Winchester."

She didn't care about what was most likely. "What were the others?" Grigsby got real cautious, started backpedaling, qualifying his words, angering her even more with every syllable and, back pain or not, sending her into a full body clench. "For God's sake, Carl, you're not on the witness stand. You don't have to be right. Just tell me what you think you know."

Grigsby paused until he heard her intake of breath, the telltale sign of another Maxie Missile a click away from launch mode, and quickly aborted the strike. "There was only one. Something called an HK PSG-1. It's atypical for America, European made. My guy doesn't think there's a chance in a million your bullet came from this weapon."

"But they're not sure." He said nothing. "Carl?"

"No, Max. They're not. The only way to be sure is to test fire an HK PSG-1 and compare the markings."

"So?" Saying it like this was no big thing, what are you waiting for.

"We don't have the gun here, Max. It's not a, uh…It's not—"

"Get the marbles out of your mouth."

"It's not a run-of-the-mill firearm. It's more, uh—"

"More what?" she snapped.

"Exotic."

"So it's not your basic deer-hunting rifle?"

"Depends on the hunter, I guess."

Maxie ran all this through her mental meat grinder, mind rocking, paying no attention to her back or the rapidly cooling bathwater, thinking only about the case, the cases, Donna Hubbard's and hers, knowing she now had a legitimate reason to stay on the job for at least another day or two. "I need to know where that bullet came from."

"Max, I—"

"What can you do for me?"

"I'd have to go through the FBI—"

"How long will it take?"

"You know the Feds, Max. They only fast-track the high-profile cases, so it could take six or eight months—"

"In six or eight months I won't have my son anymore, Carl, so that is not an acceptable timetable."

"What?" Grigsby's voice was a stunned whisper.

"Figure it out. I'll expect to hear from you first of next week."

•

Thomas Cloud was no Indian. He was probably 50, a five-foot-seven, well-tanned, athletic-looking man, silver hair cut Marine style, decked out in pressed blue jeans and a yellow Ralph Lauren polo shirt, looking at Kevin Columbus with eyes that were a mine shaft into utter darkness.

"I thought lawyer-client privilege ended when the client died," Kevin said, not having a clue what he was talking about. They'd been meeting for 20 minutes, Kevin probing everything from the reasons for Devereaux's suicide to why the dead man had his childhood newspaper clipping at the beach house. He'd held back anything about the books Liz Fletcher had asked him to pass along, thinking maybe they could be used as leverage, which after about three seconds he knew he'd need, the attorney being as talkative as Helen Keller's shadow.

Cloud, sitting behind a large desk, in a large leather chair, in a large office whose large walls contained large photos of him and a lot of leaders of the free world, U.S. and otherwise, didn't even look up from whatever he was writing on a white legal pad. "No."

"You know, if you didn't have any plans to tell me anything, I sure as hell wished you'd said so over the phone, so I wouldn't have come here and wasted my time."

"Which is no doubt valuable," the attorney muttered dryly, still not paying him the respect of eye contact.

"The guy's dead. What difference does it make if you show me his personal stuff. His effects, his estate, whatever."

"Under the law, you have no standing, no right, to make that request."

While Cloud continued writing—longhand, with a gold-nibbed fountain pen—Kevin decided to drop a bomb, see if the aftershock weakened the lawyer's refusals. "What if I'm his son?"

The only thing shocking about the moment that followed was Cloud's sudden laugh, which was deep and friendly, and shot some life into his distant eyes. "Trust me, you're not. I've known Mr. Devereaux since before he arrived in Island City. I'm quite certain of his lack of paternity." But he did quit writing, and his look grew less glowing the more fastened it became to Kevin's face.

Unable to accept the glare for too long, Kevin's eyes worked the room, taking in all the big pictures on the big walls. He wondered what they said about the lawyer's psyche, deciding they probably confirmed the guy was a little prick with a Napoleon complex. There was Cloud with Nixon. Ford. Carter. Ron and Nancy. George Bush. Nothing with the current occupant of 1600 Pennsylvania, which for some reason Kevin thought was odd. Jesus, there were even photos of Cloud with Pat and Bay Buchanan, whom Kevin had always thought were the same person because they looked alike and talked alike and said the same things and he'd never seen them together. Until now. So much for that theory.

The Shah of Iran. Hosni Mubarik. Prince Faud. Anwar Sadat. Netanyahu. Some guy he vaguely recognized—judging from Cloud's appearance, the photo was 25, 30 years old—who was wearing the traditional grand pooh-bah garb of the region, the Middle East region, that is, there being nobody from Germany or France or England up there on those walls, or Asia or Africa. Just the Middle East, making Kevin think about the Arabaq books and wonder.

"Did you represent Americans for America, too?" Kevin asked, trying again to startle Cloud into sending him an unintended signal, swinging and missing, strike two, the attorney not stumbling on one syllable, the single syllable:

"Yes."

"What did you do?"

"I drafted its charter."

"Can I see it?"

"No."

"That's all you did?"

"Yes. Mr. Devereaux maintained total control over all activities."

"What kinds of activities?"

"The kind that only Mr. Devereaux controlled."

"Was it like a political action committee. Charity? Think tank? What kind of group was it?"

Cloud tilted his head upward, ever-so-slightly, peering at him over narrow six-sided glasses, black metal. "A private one." Back to the pad.

"What's going to happen to it now?"

"I have no idea."

"Will it survive?"

A cryptic smirk. "Does anything?"

"My patience is sure dying a slow death, Mr. Cloud."

A pause in the writing. "Then perhaps you should leave before the end arrives."

"But you haven't told me anything."

Looking up now, straight-on, eye-to-eye. "You said you had some information about Mr. Devereaux. I wanted to know what. I have no responsibility, legal or otherwise, to answer any of your questions. Even if I was so authorized, I would decline the opportunity."

"Then let's make a deal."

"A *deal*?" Thin smile, squinting at Kevin like he was an insect, a non-entity, someone who could not conceivably possess anything of value. "And with what does a man with an empty hand and, judging from your appearance, an even emptier wallet, have to deal?"

Kevin let that slide, too, but not before giving his jeans/running shoes/white T shirt/green pullover the once over. "You said you have all Devereaux's personal things, his effects?"

"Yes, yes." Bored, weary, like Get on with it.

"You're wrong."

"Am I?" Dropping the pen not out of shock but irritation. "And what do you have that might complement Mr. Devereaux's existing estate?"

"You show me yours first, counselor." Feeling like he had somehow gained an advantage, but not believing it until Cloud muttered something that sounded like For Christ's Sake, reached into his desk drawer and produced a sheet of paper, single-spaced.

He half-slid, half-threw it at Kevin. "This is what I provided the police, who in turn gave it to the news media."

In large print at the top of the page was FRANCIS GARY DEVEREAUX. Three brief paragraphs followed:

"Francis Gary Devereaux was born in Portsmouth, New Hampshire, April 18, 1928. His father owned a small hardware store, where his mother worked as a bookkeeper. He attended the Georgia Institute of Technology, earning a degree in engineering. A lifelong passion for flying led him to the United States Air Force, where he served from 1951 through his retirement in 1977, during which he served three tours in Vietnam, the first two in combat capacities, the third as a civilian advisor.

"Concerned over the growing rift that the conflict in Vietnam had created, Mr. Devereaux established a private, not-for-profit organization in 1980 called Americans for America. Its role was to promote national unity and patriotism, and to craft strategies that advanced the common good. As the organization's first and only executive director, he counseled numerous governmental, diplomatic and military leaders.

"Responding to his tragic death, Mr. Devereaux's attorney, Thomas Cloud, said, 'Gary was an American who believed profoundly in his country. He did his work quietly, behind the scenes, preferring obscurity to a higher profile. His was a cause we can all share in and be proud of: Restoring and sustaining this nation's greatness. I will miss his friendship. The country will miss his advocacy.'"

Kevin put the paper back on Cloud's desk. "That's all? Three paragraphs?"

The lawyer smiled, and for the first time didn't come across as smug. "He was a man who believed effectiveness could best be achieved outside the glare of notoriety. This was a respectful reflection of who he was."

"Who was he?"

"You read the statement. It's right there. In black and white."

"That's nothing but gray, counselor."

"Sometimes that's all there is, my friend." Kevin started to argue, firing every question he could think of at Cloud, most of them redundant, about Americans for America, why Devereaux would kill himself, what sorts of causes he "advocated" and on and on, the lawyer always elliptical in his answers, revealing nothing, taking it for about two minutes before out of nowhere slamming his hand on the big desk and ordering, "Enough!"

"Fuck you, enough!" Kevin shot back, now angry, tired of the two-step and the attitude. "This guy seems to know things about me that only my father could know, and I want to know how and why, and I'm not giving you anything I've got until I get some goddamned answers!"

The red crept up Thomas Cloud's face like mercury in a thermometer. He drummed the desk slightly with his fingers, one at a time, as if counting to 10 manually, then did it again and again and again, eyes laser-locked on Kevin in a gaze that was more effective than any courtroom strategy, finally speaking after about 60 seconds, his tone measured and tight as a guitar string.

"I don't know who you are, Mr. Columbus. I don't know where, or from whom, you came. Out from under what rock. I don't care, either. I care nothing about you."

Kevin felt the ruthless objectivity in the man's voice start to carve into his determination, but had no intention of backing down. "Then maybe you care about the Arabaq books." It was a Hail Mary play, and he knew it, hoping but not believing for a second they brought any value to the argument.

"I'm sorry?"

It took a moment for Kevin to realize he'd scored a hit on Cloud's attention, and another moment to calm himself down and figure out what to do next. "Three books on Arabaq. The cleaning crew found them at Devereaux's house."

Cloud screwed his mouth into a dismissive smile, shook his head slightly. "Gary had a fascination with the Middle East. He read textbooks on the subject constantly." When Kevin did not challenge the textbook characterization, the lawyer appeared to relax noticeably.

"They must mean something," Kevin sputtered, feeling that his direct hit hadn't even flesh-wounded the lawyer.

"Not to me, and I know everything about Gary Devereaux that matters," Cloud said, rising from the chair, suddenly assuming a magnitude that now matched the big desk and the big walls and the big pictures.

"Do you know if he had a son?" Kevin asked at last, weakly, almost a plea, but refusing to get up, refusing to obey Cloud's unstated demand that he leave.

"I know he had the mumps." The lawyer came around his desk, sitting on its front edge.

"The mumps?"

"As a teenager, yes. Mumps orchitis, actually," he added, as if that explained everything. "Both testicles."

Kevin was starting to get it now, starting to understand, knowing what was about to come, knowing any dream he had that Jon Columbus was alive, no matter how slim, was about to be crushed, seeing the pinlight of hope go out, not sure if that was good or bad, but still feeling devastated about it anyway.

"The man you say was your father was sterile at age 14. There is no clinical, biological or medical way he could have been your father. Anyone's father."

●

Fifteen minutes after Kevin Columbus left his office, Cloud picked up the phone, dialed a private number and a five-digit access code, and waited for the familiar crackling sound to end, signaling the line was secure. "The son was just here," he told Walter Frost.

"And?"

"He says he has some possessions of Gary's."

"Did he reference photographs?"

"No. Books."

Frost paused, then asked slowly: "What sorts of books?"

"Books about Arabaq."

A second pause, this one twice as long. "The notebook?"

"I described them as textbooks. He did not challenge me."

"I want to be very clear about this: The son said nothing to suggest he had the notebook."

"None."

"Nor that he had seen it?"

"No."

"Nor read it?"

"No."

"You're absolutely certain?"

"Absolutely."

"Thank you."

Chapter 12

They had all assembled in the law firm's massive conference room, filling each of the 22 leather chairs that rimmed the oblong, polished dark maple table. Some were businessmen, representing various industries. Chemical, plastics, agricultural, metalworks, energy, construction, defense, technology. Others were ex-diplomats, men who had left the policy and financial constraints of government service to seek more effective and better-paying pursuits. Then there were those about whom no one else at the table asked questions. Shadow warriors, people who knew the unwritten rules by which world order was maintained, and who were capable of executing the will of any superior so long as the directive synchronized with their own personal ideologies.

None of them had won his seat at the table by election or appointment. As such, none were accountable. They were composers of silent music that an unhearing nation, and its leaders, and its people, danced to blindly.

They were neither good men, nor bad, for they advanced a mission whose ultimate ends obliterated the too-easy distinction between black and white. Yes, they had made money in the deal. The industrialists for their know-how. The ex-diplomats for their persuasion and knowledge. The shadow warriors for their stealth and efficiency.

Some were old, in their 70's, having been a member of this small working group since its inception. Others had been targeted later for their knowledge and skill and, in the case of the shadow warriors, their utter devotion to the cause. Different as their ages, backgrounds and proficiencies may have been, however, they all shared one essential trait:

They saw themselves not as business people nor envoys nor operatives. They saw themselves as Americans, people who like Thomas Jefferson said in 1785, would go to hell for their country. They understood that the patriot was indeed scarce, and hated, and scorned, but also brave and necessary. They saw national allegiance not as one brief shining flash of emotion, but rather as the dedication of a lifetime.

And here, on this day, at a table abundant with plates of fresh fruit and pastries, and gleaming silver service sets, they had come to celebrate the victory of a lifetime.

"Gentlemen," Walter Frost said, rising from his chair at the head of the table, toasting them with a fine porcelain tea cup, "I congratulate you on a job well done. Although history will never record your courage and vision, I assure you that your place in the annals of world peace is secured."

There was applause, and a chorus of self-congratulation.

"As I am sure you are aware, General Azid of Arabaq will arrive in Washington one week from this Monday to sign a treaty banning the production of chemical and biological weapons. He is fully prepared to negotiate, on the American behalf, for similar actions by other renegade nations. The president has said that with this one single act, we may have effectively eliminated the threat of a biochemical cold war in the 21st century."

More applause. Smiles everywhere, except among the Shadow Warriors, for whom a job well done was not a reason to celebrate, but a reason to exist.

"Six hundred million dollars," one of the industrialists said. "We managed to save the world for a mere $600 million."

"And make money to boot," another added.

Laughter, which Walter Frost allowed them to enjoy. No, they had not actually done the work. But they certainly deserved a large part of the credit.

"So, Walter, now that we're on a winning streak, who do we go after next?" someone said. "What do we do for an encore? North Korea?"

More laughter and lots of other suggestions all around, most of which disgusted the shadow warriors, who saw these people as simple children, Gucci GIs, playing war, not understanding the demands or the repercussions of global acts that had no place on spread sheets or in annual reports.

Walter Frost smiled broadly, still letting them savor the moment before restoring order with a simple "Please" accompanied by a smile that was not quite as happy as the people in the room thought it should be, given their triumph after nearly 25 years of unsanctioned terrorism.

His look did not go unnoticed. "What's wrong, Walter?" one of them asked.

"We are close," Frost said, his voice soft and strong, eyes settling on each of them for five seconds before moving to the next. "Very, very close."

The room became so silent, it could have been empty. "But we're not there yet," someone said after a moment.

"No," Walter Frost said, almost inaudibly, resigned, with a barely noticeable shake of the head, and a smile conjured by deep regret. "We're not there yet."

The shadow warriors snapped to mental attention.

"Did we miss someone?" the chief financial officer of a large oil company asked, his tone colored by disbelief.

"Yes and no," Frost answered, clearing his throat, sounding as if he was struggling with something. Unusual, many in the room felt.

But not the shadow warriors. They were men of strategies and decisions who cared little about human subtext. Men with a duty. Men of decision. One finally spoke up: "Whose son do we have to terminate, sir?"

Walter Frost didn't answer. Not because he couldn't. But because unlike all the other deaths of all the other sons, the fate of this one rested in hands other than his own.

Chapter 13

Forget it, Kevin Columbus told himself, all of it, every weak-assed little clue.

Roper's call, the kid editorial, the Little Buddy reference, the torn photo. Liz Fletcher's comments about Devereaux's near invisibility and the blurry suggestions of the man's military background. The Arabaq books. Americans for America. Cloud's stonewalling.

Coming back into Charlotte Sunday afternoon—late, naturally, welcome to Airline Deregulation—after a restless beer-sotted night at a Holiday Inn Express near the Island City airport, he'd finally decided to do just that. Put it aside. What was the point? At the tender age of 37, middle age either approaching or already sneakily in place, he needed an identity crisis like Custer needed more Indians, and sure as hell didn't feel any clawing urge to go off on some blind search for self, especially after Cloud dropped his little nuke. Anyway, he'd already done the looking-deep-within thing once, when the power company guillotined him from the corporate head count, and while that personal once-over hadn't delivered him to Frank Capra Land, so what? It was a rough world, rough and unfeeling, drunk with pretended compassion and relentless self-interest, and you either survived it by luck or sheer determination, or it ate you for lunch. And since he hadn't turned up as anybody's Blue Plate Special just yet—forget for a second Wayne Earl Wiley eyeing him like a lumberjack on Slimfast—that said something.

Besides, he knew what he needed to know: Jon Columbus was his father. Jon Columbus died in Southeast Asia. Jon Columbus was buried in Arlington National Cemetery. If that knowledge was in some way partial, if it excluded him from some nether world managed for whatever reason by unseen others, too bad, shit happens. Kevin had his own reality, and it was built on memories that were more truthful than any torn photo, and by God he was not going to let them fade:

Report card day, every A rewarded with a crisp green dollar bill. Calling the old man at the bullpen, on alert, letting him know about a game-winning double he'd cracked off the centerfield fence, two outs, last shot at the plate. Banging on the make-shift drum set as Jon Columbus played air trombone, arms flailing back and forth, exaggerated, reducing the boy to uncontrollable laughter. Air Force Days, Kevin getting lifted into the cockpit of some wondrous craft, messing with the dials and sticks and levers, chasing down Commie MiGs in a treacherous dogfight before blowing them out of the sky while his father mouthed sound effects that were as genuine to the son as the sky above.

Get right down to it, that's all that mattered. His reality, and how he remembered it. So maybe he didn't get the whole picture about who he was. Did anyone? And if they did, he'd bet the farm they spent most of their lives painting over the original, new lines and colors and shapes always turning up on the canvas, an ongoing effort to make the truth into something it wasn't. Well, not him. He had a truth, his truth, and even if it might be incomplete, he had no intention of surrendering it to vague questions of people and places long since passed.

Thinking about all this as he pulled to a stop in front of the mini-warehouse that housed some of his lesser memories, Kevin closed his eyes briefly, mined the mental darkness for a portrait of the old man. It was there in a moment, just like always, in utter focus. Dark, perfectly combed hair. Teeth bright and white and straight as piano keys. Eyes that sparkled like gray diamonds, whose depth held just a hint of intrigue. Broad, carefree smile, and a wit that could cut like a knife without breaking the skin.

That was Kevin's truth. The rest of it was just noise.

Inside his cluttered, chaotic yellow tin storage shed, one of about 200 in a park encircled by razor-wire fence, the air was oven-hot and thick as grape jelly, Kevin starting to sweat through his white T-shirt almost immediately. It never ceased to amaze him, coming to this place north of the city, how much the Storage Condominiums—which was what the owner called them—felt more familiar to him than his own home. There was an antique gramophone he'd picked up at a country auction for $42 at the urging of a girl he was dating. A rowing machine that seemed like a good idea at the time. One box full of certificates and plaques and honors. His college diploma, framed. An engraved silver plate recognizing him as the university's outstanding journalism graduate. A trophy he'd won for finishing first in the 30-35 age group in a 5 kilometer road race, back in the days when he had the time to run for fun and fitness. An award from the Charlotte area Public Relations Society of America for being named Rookie of the Year. Who's Who Among Young American Professionals. Parchment thank-yous from the United Way, the Humane Society and the Children's Hope Fund.

Then there were the ashes of his past, what his mother had simply left in the house after she faded on him. A console stereo and matching television set. The dinette table where Kevin and Jon Columbus would read the sports pages every morning and eat peanut butter and bacon sandwiches for breakfast. An old 100-pound set of weights and a cheap, creaky bench, courtesy of his old man, who before acceding to Kevin's desire to play baseball had tried unsuccessfully to get the boy to bulk up his then-scrawny frame for a shot at football. A mishmash of memorabilia, mostly old family photographs stuffed into oversized envelopes, none of which Kevin had ever explored, tossed into a box designated by red marker, simply, as Family History. His disassembled bunk bed. The 10-speed he'd gotten for Christmas the year a December 24th blizzard kept the family housebound for six days. A blue easy chair where Kevin had read his first book in a single sitting: *Kings of the Home Run*.

Every time he came to the warehouse, his mind traveled momentarily to that late fall day when he came home from college and saw the
unfamiliar faces asking him who he was, and didn't he know Mrs.
Columbus had sold the house, and should they call the Salvation Army
to pick up what she'd left behind? Kevin was first inclined to take it all
and burn it, every last stick of it. But that meant his mother would win,
an unacceptable outcome. So one day, right after New Year's, he and a
friend pulled a rental U-Haul truck up to the garage that had once protected Kevin's bike, his Ping-Pong table and untold other trimmings of
youth, and removed any remaining evidence that this had in fact once
been home. For reasons he either couldn't figure out or wouldn't admit,
he'd carted the stuff with him to Charlotte, kept it here, a tribute to the
bad old days or the good old days, pick one, time turning them into
nearly identical twins.

And so it was today. More contributions to the past—the Arabaq
books—discovered in the present, their meaning unclear, Kevin just
feeling he had to get rid of them like they were bad karma. They were a
mystery he didn't need. If there was some secret link between Jon
Columbus and this shady, suicidal character in South Florida, it didn't
involve him. Devereaux was sterile, couldn't be his father, nothing more
to be found, no need to mark *that* spot with an X. Tossing the books
atop the detritus of his life, in this steamy fabricated little house of
remembrance, seemed like an appropriate epilogue to the short story of
the past few days.

"How ya doin'?"

The voice, coming from behind, startled Kevin so deeply he fell
against a wall of the storehouse, knocking three stacked boxes to the
concrete floor before himself landing on one knee. It was the supervisor, Tom, a friendly man in his 60's who wore a white uniform with a
red star on the left breast pocket, which Kevin always thought made him
look like a Texaco service station guy from the 1950's, or maybe an

aging Communist. "Jesus, you scared the shit outta me," he said, recovering, anxiety pumping even more sweat through his pores.

"Didn't mean no harm, son." The door to the storehouse was wide open, allowing entrance to the late afternoon sun and reducing Tom to a near silhouette. "Just wanted to let you know rent's due on the 15th."

"Thanks." Kevin brushed dust and light grime off his pullover, and cursed silently when he saw a couple of faint black streaks on the knee of the off-white khakis.

"Don't you mention it," Tom said, taking a step back toward the door. "And I hope you have any ol' kind of day you want." With that he was gone.

Kevin again examined his pants. There was a little scrape in the fabric, which meant they might no longer officially qualify as work clothes. "Son of a bitch," he muttered, pronouncing every word clearly, as if in a speech class, punching each with a sharp jab of anger. "Son. Of. A. Bitch!" An uncompromising rage began to scorch his insides, fury growing like a tidal wave, and before he could get his deflector shields in place, it had spun out of control. He began crazily knocking over any other boxes that leaned against the walls, scattering their contents everywhere. Spinning like a helicopter in warp-speed, he swept his arm over the top of the console stereo and dinette table, sending a cheap white plastic radio and a spray of old *Sports Illustrated* magazines to the other side of the warehouse. He found one of the side slats from the bunk bed—the thin wooden planks that kept him from falling out at night—snapped it in two over a knee, took one half, swinging it blind and wild, like a baseball bat, shattering the picture tube on the TV set, and then pummeling the front of the stereo until he'd ripped massive holes into its fabric speaker cover. With one final, lunging swing, he smashed the box of honors and awards, felt a grim satisfaction when he heard the glass from the frames splinter on impact, finally collapsing in a sweaty heap in the center of the little building, amid the ruins of his past.

"Goddammit," he muttered, shifting into a sitting position, kicking at a shoebox that had fallen from the Family History carton, paying no attention as its contents went everywhere. He forced himself to breathe more slowly now, trying to get back in his internal driver's seat, feeling the frustrated anger diminish, replaced by overheated exhaustion. Moments like this, when his temper just went off the leash, scared the hell out of Kevin Columbus. They made him recall the moment when, as a child playing Little League baseball, he'd been pitching to an 11-year-old kid who fouled a pitch into his own right toe. For some reason, the kid just started going off on Kevin, calling him every name in the pre-teen book, all the guys on both teams laughing, Kevin calmly walking to the hitter, jerking the 28-ounce Louisville Slugger from his hands, getting ready to turn his head into meatloaf. The umpire threw him out of the game, the coach reported the incident to his father, Jon Columbus saying only, "Don't let your temper poison your head, son."

That's how he felt right now: Poisoned by an anger that he had allowed himself to drink, like hemlock.

It took a minute or two of stillness and deep, labored breathing and another gallon or two of flop sweat, but everything began to calm down inside of him. His eyes skimmed across the casualties of his assault, lingering for a split second on the overturned boxes, the shards of picture frame glass, the battered stereo—a sight that genuinely saddened him, it being where he first heard Buddy Rich—the little radio, its tubes and wires hanging out like it'd been disemboweled, the photos that'd been in the shoebox he'd just kicked halfway across the floor, the magazines, saved because they had pictures of the Cincinnati Reds on the cover, Jon Columbus's favorite team, the passion for whom he'd passed down to his son—

Wait.

Kevin blinked his eyes, suddenly and rapidly, a vague, ill-formed thought breaking through the weariness, saying Back up, back up, back up, to the pictures, the ones from the shoebox.

Scrambling on all fours—forget the pants, they were ruined already—he retrieved the first photo he could find, stared at the image like it was a corpse, whisper-muttered, "Jesus," quickly found a second and a third, seeing the same thing, sweat starting to run cold despite the sweltering heat, panic surging.

He crawled across the floor to where the shoebox had landed, picked it up, dumped out more photos, looking at them one after another, slowly at first then rapidly, crazily, flipping each aside as if he were tossing cards into an invisible hat, cursing, knowing instinctively he was being dragged back into a place he didn't want to go. And when it was done, when he had gone through every one of them, the final picture remained in his shaking hand, one undeniable fact connecting it to all the others that now lay on the floor like so many dead autumn leaves:

Each contained the images of two people. His mother and father. Jon and Meredith Columbus. Him smiling, her not.

Each torn, as if to eliminate someone or something from the picture.

Each in that way exactly like the photo he'd received in the package from Island City.

Chapter 14

Special Agent Richard Addison had always liked Carl Grigsby. They'd known each other for going on 14 years now, back to the days when Addison worked in the FBI's Charlotte field office and Grisgby was a high-minded street cop who did his work by the numbers. That's what made the detective's urgent Saturday morning request—and the ballistics report he now sat reading at his desk in the FBI's Hoover Building on Monday—all the stranger. It wasn't kosher.

Grigsby was a straight-arrow, someone who knew there were rules—on the job, and in life—and that those rules demanded obedience. It was an attitude that played to his higher instincts, which was important, especially in the world Carlton Grigsby felt he inhabited, a world where every day was a struggle to stay right amid conditions that conspired against it, a world that civility too often seemed to have abandoned. The son of a Methodist minister, Grigsby saw things as either good or bad, black or white, without a lot of room for the in-between. That made him, in Rick Addison's mind, a truly good man. And like everyone else of that ilk, goodness carried with it a cost. In Grigsby's case, it was guilt. Although he viewed the world in clear-cut terms, he also understood the need to sometimes venture into unspoken places. The journey, though necessary, was marked by self-reproach and frequent doubts over the use of imperfect methods to cleanse an imperfect world. He beat back the regret with constant reminders that honorable ends in some way justified un-honorable—not *dis*honorable, *un*-honorable—means.

And Grigsby he did see his role as honorable. To Preserve and Protect. It was a concept that even he sometimes had to admit was dated. Who wouldn't? In a time and place when the front pages dripped with murder and mayhem, people in public office ruined kids half their age, religious fundamentalists preached candy-coated hate and intolerance, and grade schools became shooting galleries—well, one would be hard-pressed not to think that evil had the upper hand, that we were way past preserving and protecting, and the best way to restore balance was to full-throttle root it out. It was a legitimate argument that Carl Grigsby could not totally reject. He simply chose not to practice it, viewing law enforcement as the incremental pursuit of good, a job whose responsibility was shielding storeowners from street thugs, little girls from bad men, kids from drug dealers, classrooms from crime. You did what you could. Eventually, life would get better.

Optimistic? Sure it was. But Carl Grigsby didn't want to dwell on the alternative.

Rick Addison, for his part, was kind of old school, a guy with a wide streak of independence and a decent sense of right and wrong who had little patience for anything, especially the pencil-necked lawyer-accountant geeks the Bureau seemed to be growing in pods at Ivy League schools. Like Grigsby, he too saw the world mostly in black and white, but he'd been around the block a few times and had no problem acknowledging a varying degree of gray. That was part of life, the gray areas, the way things were. Only fanatics, zealots and extremists dwelled on the edges of their own vision of absolute goodness.

Rick Addison had no such vision. The state of things worried him, sure, and he wouldn't take odds against the world going to hell in a handbasket. But he acknowledged that desperate times occasionally called for desperate measures, which he could and would apply. Not that he was a cowboy. In fact, he hated the breed. But he accepted the fact that an altar boy's place was at the altar, and that his place was in a universe that on its best days was morally diverse. So on the one hand, he happily played the Maverick role, dancing to the disco beat in a realm of ballroom bureaucrats, comfortable in the knowledge that there were lines of propriety, and rules of official behavior, and neither were to be broken. On the other, he also knew that periodic lapses—a step over the line here, a bend of the rules there—had tremendous value in an America that urgently needed the eradication of bad things and bad people.

They'd stayed in touch after Addison moved on to Washington, most of their contacts official, though some not. Eight or nine years before, Addison—married with two little girls—had been something of a surrogate priest-confessor for his friend when Grigsby and his wife temporarily separated. It surprised the FBI agent in a way; though friends, neither had ever gotten beyond the basics when sharing their personal lives. But Grigsby said that was just the point: He needed the kind of detachment that could only come from someone who didn't know or share his baggage. Nobody fit that description in the Charlotte-Mecklenburg PD. So they had talked, hours on end over a week-long period, Addison trying to nudge Grigsby toward reconciliation—"Hell, Carl if you can't stick with your family, what good are you?"—the detective seemingly unable to find a reason to continue.

"But what happens when things go bad, Rick, really bad?" Grisgby asked.

"By the time they come to me, they've already gotten there," Addison answered. "I never see the Before. Only the After."

"What if they both look the same?"

"You do what you got to do, I guess, and hope God's in a forgiving mood when you're up for judging."

Grigsby stayed with his wife.

In a weird way, Rick Addison liked the shot of goodness Carl Grigsby gave him. Not that the detective totally pierced Addison's jaded outlook by any stretch of the imagination. But Grigsby was like a single star in the midnight sky, a far-away reminder that maybe, just maybe, there was a better place beyond this one, the kind of place that justified the outlook of people like Carl Grigsby.

That's what it was. Carl Grigsby gave Addison hope. Which was why the Saturday call had set off every one of Rick Addison's internal alarms. This was a good guy, straight-laced and righteous, who'd asked him to do something not entirely above board. Which, Addison being Addison, he'd done, calling in a favor from one of the lab guys over the weekend. But the off-the-books ballistics report he now held damn near burned the flesh from his hand.

Jesus, he thought, reading it again. What in God's name had Carl Grigsby gotten himself into? And what would the Bureau do if and when the government found out what Addison now knew?

•

Donna Hubbard wasn't sure whether to scream or cry or faint. Or maybe just walk out of the coffee shop. "What are you saying? I mean, exactly. Tell me exactly what you are saying." Eyes, hopeful and scared, staring at Maxie, Donna sipping from a coffee cup that clattered from shaking hands when she set it back down on the saucer.

Maxie looked around the diner—a large, noisy retro '50's style place with vintage cars parked in the front lot as a draw—and wished they were anyplace but here. She had returned from Alabama late the previous night, tired and still sore, and would have preferred someplace quiet, out of the glare, like Donna's house. But for some reason the girl was opposed, first blush Maxie figuring Donna feared the neighbors might start asking questions if some Foxy Brown look-alike turned up in what was no doubt a snow white residential area. Not that she thought Donna was a bigot; no, this child was the ultimate innocent, the last remaining sheep in a herd the girl was convinced was being thinned by conspiracy. Donna Hubbard was just scared.

Maxie took a sip of water, which she settled for after the waitress flashed an at-sea look when she ordered her usual club soda with lime. "I'm saying I found a bullet."

"Did it kill my sister?" She clenched and unclenched her hands, laced and unlaced her fingers, as much out of anxiety as to stop the tremors.

"I doubt it. But it may have been fired at her."

Donna Hubbard crumpled into the red, faux leather booth, gazing pitifully out the window into the parking lot. The simple floral-print dress seemed to swallow her thin frame, Maxie thinking the poor girl looked like she'd lost weight in just the few days since they'd met.

For the next couple of minutes, Maxie traced her investigation, starting with the rock and the overpass. The bullet in the tree—professional vanity demanding that she omit the part about busting her ass—getting Carl to do the first test in Charlotte, then persuading him to run it up the pole at Bureau headquarters in Washington—

"The FBI?" Donna gasped, that notion seeming to chill her more than the idea that someone might have murdered her sister and that she might be next.

Maxie reached across the table and took her hand. "It's okay. Nobody's going to know anything except us. Everything's cool."

Donna didn't look quite so sure. "What happens next?"

Good question. The only thing she knew with any certainty was that evidence of an "exotic" rifle at the scene now made this a real investigation, so taking money from Donna was no longer an issue. The issue was how to earn it. "Let's back up for a second, okay?" Donna looked at her with big green eyes, shrugging the shrug of the terminally confused. "As far as you know, your brother is still alive."

"Yes, ma'am. I mean, I don't know whether he's dead or not. Is that the same thing?" Trying to please her, sweet expression asking if that was the right answer.

"That's fine." Gently, wanting to keep this as easy on Donna as possible. "Now, I don't want to suggest anything, and I don't want to upset you. But if—*if*, now—your family was in some way, uh, connected to any of this, can you think of any reason why he might still be alive?"

She considered it briefly. "Maybe they don't know where he is?"

An answer and a question at once, just like everything else, but legitimate anyway. Maxie nodded, started fiddling with the unused silverware in front of her. "Tell me some more about him."

"Henry Lee?" A fresh smile broke out on Donna's face, almost by accident, warming and paining Maxie at once. The merest mention of Henry Lee Hubbard threw the girl back 25 years, to the days of little sister, big brother, when she no doubt looked up at him with adoring love, and he down on her with begrudging affection. It was sad when the good days were the longest gone.

"I was just a little kid," she began, brushing her hair back behind her right ear, the smile fading but still there. "So a lot of it is only memories, stuff like that. And, you know, you kind of remember what you like, what makes you feel good." Maxie said she understood. "When he was young, before the war and all, Henry Lee was, I don't know, a 'man with a plan,' I guess."

"A plan?"

"It was like he always knew where he was going. He was a good student in school, got good grades, big star football player. Worked two jobs so he could help out with expenses around the house—daddy'd get hurt on the job, he was a millworker, and his disability checks didn't go too far."

"Sounds like an All-American kid."

"That's it. That's exactly what he was." Proud like a mother, loving the thought before suddenly darkening. "That's why he went to war, I guess." Looking away, then back at Maxie. "Vietnam, I mean."

Maxie remembered that from their first real interview, waited for Donna to continue, which didn't happen, asking finally if he was drafted, trying to get the narrative back on track.

"Oh, no," she replied quickly, like it was an insult. "Henry Lee enlisted. The day after he graduated, 17th in his class of 212, he went right down to the Army office and signed up. Felt it was his duty, he said, and the country had been good to him and it was time he gave something back."

Great, Maxie thought, I'm tracking Son Of Ollie North.

"He shipped out right after that, first to basic training in South Carolina and then over there."

"When was this?"

"Nixon had just been elected—Henry Lee was big for Nixon, even went door-to-door for him, passing out pamphlets and all that. So I'm gonna guess it was probably 1969. Around then, anyway. He stayed in, too, kept re-enlisting. His cause was America's cause, I suppose." Donna got the waitress's attention and ordered another cup of coffee. "We saw him, I don't know, three times I guess, during all that, and he seemed to be doing pretty well. You know, all things considered." A deeper darkness descended on her once again. "But the last time, he'd changed. A lot."

Wouldn't be the first vet lobotomized by the war, Maxie thought. "Was this when you went to New York?"

"No, ma'am. The time before that."

"How had he changed?"

Donna shook her head slowly. "He was just"—she searched for an appropriate word before settling on "—different. Kind of, I don't know, isolated. He'd always been a friendly boy, but it was like he turned away from people in general."

"Was he angry? Violent?"

A quick, conclusive shake of the head. "Oh, no. Nothing like that. Just apart from us all. Distant." A sad chuckle. "Mama thought it was because he was on drugs, she'd heard all the stories and stuff."

"But it wasn't drugs?"

"No. It was him. Him and the war. Like I said the other day, it made him kind of loony tunes, I think." Another pause. "And maybe it was Tim, too."

Maxie caught the edge in her voice, wondered where this was going. "Tim?"

"Henry Lee's Army buddy. The one who came with him when we went to New York. They were in the same division or unit. Riflemen, I think, or something like that."

"*Riflemen*?" Not even trying to disguise her shock, or her amazement that Donna had failed for whatever reason to mention *that* little bit of information, getting even more mad-bewildered when the girl just nodded her head in response, saying—

"Uh-huh, in the jungle."

— Donna still not picking up on the connection, Maxie thinking For God's sake, the brother was an Army sharpshooter, he goes to the scene of an assassination, and nobody even thinks about putting two and two together?

"Is something wrong?" Donna asked, answering Maxie's question with wide-eyed naivete.

"No, no, no," she shook her head, not wanting to rattle the girl, reminding herself the job was about finding Henry Lee, not solving a 25-year-old murder mystery that according to the official story was no mystery anyway. "Just, uh, thinking." Yeah, thinking about a damned *rifleman*. "Did anyone tell that to the Knight Commission?"

"I didn't. But, you know, it was in his records. And those're public, aren't they?"

Only if the government wants them to be, Maxie thought. "Tell me some more about Tim. Why do you think he had some influence on your brother?"

"His eyes," she answered, almost immediately. "There were Paul Newman eyes. Blue and bright, and they sparkled like a country stream." Despite the words, she clearly didn't relish the memory. "And I always thought it was strange."

"What's that?"

"His eyes. So pretty. But Tim wasn't. He was empty inside, it always seemed to me. I mean, he looked like a serial killer. He did." Another pause for recollection. "And the way he hovered. It was as if he didn't want Henry Lee to have time alone with any of us. Like he was guarding him, or something." A slight shiver. "The guy was creepy. Scary. Oh, and he was the one who had all the money, and paid for us to go to New York." She added the last almost as an afterthought.

"The money?"

Donna nodded. "When they came home that time, before we went to New York. Whenever there was something that needed to be paid for, like our train tickets, Rim Tim Tim was there with the cash."

"Rim what?" This was going way too fast for Maxie, and she didn't need this child talking in tongues.

"Oh, that's what I called him. His last name was Basset or Collie or something. I don't remember. So I gave him a dog's name." A little girl playing games, recalled now without joy.

Maxie nodded, took a sip of water. "When Henry Lee showed up that July, were you expecting him?"

A hesitant, uncertain expression came over Donna's face. "Well, kind of yes, but not exactly." Maxie asked what that meant. "Like I said, we hadn't seen or heard from Henry Lee in forever, and the last time we did, he seemed different. It started to worry mama a good bit. She even tried phoning up the Army once or twice, the Pentagon, wanting them to tell her what Henry Lee was doing and whether he was okay."

"Did they?"

"No, ma'am. They said he was no longer on, whatever they called it, current active duty." She shrugged. "They seemed to be saying he retired but had forgotten to let any of us know about it."

"Wait a second. You're telling me that a kid, an All-American kid, who enlists, re-enlists, loves his country and fights for a cause—you're telling me he just up and walks away?"

"That's what they told us."

"Did you ever think about getting in the car, driving to Washington and demanding to find out what was going on?"

Donna looked at her without comprehension. "Why would we do that? I mean, we thought they were telling us the truth. Why would they lie?"

"It's what they do best," Maxie answered sharply, irritated at this waif's faith-in-the-process jag, thinking maybe she'd underestimated Donna, that the girl was dumb as a box of birds.

"Although, I think Daddy might've agreed with you there, because one afternoon, after he'd been drinking, he got real sad and angry and called up there himself, hollering and screaming, wanting to know where his boy was. Accusing them of brainwashing Henry Lee, and experimenting with him, and doing strange chemical tests on him. Crazy stuff." An embarrassed shake of the head. "They were never real close, Daddy and Henry Lee, and all that time he was over in the war, Daddy never complained, hardly ever even talked about the whole thing. But it was like all at once, he woke up, and found out they'd taken something that was special to him away from him, and he just wasn't gonna stand for it. That's when he started making the calls."

"Calls? There were more than one?"

"Oh, yes ma'am. They went on for days. He even talked to our congressman." She lowered her eyes and voice. "People in the neighborhood were whispering about him."

I bet, Maxie thought. "And after all that, you still got no response?" she asked, knowing the answer, bureaucrats being bureaucrats—

"We sure did." Sweet but firm, her tone saying Damned Right and Good For Daddy. "Two days later, Henry Lee was sitting at our dinner table eating pork chops and rice and gravy."

Maxie thinking this story ain't hitting on all eight cylinders. Government moves slower than the third act of a bad opera. "And this was when you went to New York?"

Donna nodded. "The night before."

"So you're telling me you didn't hear from him or see him for months, and all of a sudden, he and this dog guy, this Tim, they show up out of nowhere?"

"Uh-huh."

"And you think it was your father's phone calls and hell-raising that did the trick, got him back?"

"I can't think of any other reason—"

"This is a very bad idea."

"The old man is jabbering like a fuckin' magpie."

"No. It's too great a risk."

"He talked to a congressman. Tell me about risk."

Silence. Then: "Can we replace him? Is there time?"

"We move in 10 days. You tell me."

He cursed himself for not factoring in a backup. But there had been no options. Fewer people meant fewer loose ends and a cleaner operation. "Is he trustworthy?"

"Henry Lee?"

"Yes."

"He'll keep his mouth shut, if that's what you're asking. He's been good so far. And Tim backs him to the hilt, calls him a real player."

"Tim is an assassin."

"Yeah, and he's still breathing. So we ought to respect his instincts when it comes to his choice of partners."

It was a good point. "All right. But have Tim go with him."

"You're sure that's a good idea. Exposing Tim to civilians like that?"

"It makes no difference. None of you will officially exist after the fact anyway."

"That family will."

A silent assent. "Let me be clear: I don't want those people harmed. This isn't about killing Americans." He caught himself. "Honorable Americans. Patriots."

"Yes."

"But I will do what has to be done. If there is one shred of evidence this thing has been compromised, I'll prune every branch from that family tree."

"I understand."

"What about Henry Lee? Does he want to go, or is he just giving in to the rants of a drunken father?"

"I think he does, yeah. I don't think he's going home to blow the whistle on us. I think he just wants to see his mom and dad."

A moment. "Then who are we to deny a man what amounts to his last request?"

Donna, adding: "I mean, that's the only answer that makes any sense, isn't it?"

Not a grain of it, Maxie thought. "Why New York?"

"We were celebrating," Donna smiled wanly. "Henry Lee really had retired. He'd survived the war, and was home free, and he said he wanted to go to New York and see the fireworks on Independence Day."

Maxie still wasn't buying any of it. "How do you know for sure he retired?"

The question, or its skeptical undertones, threw Donna a little bit. "Well, that's how we, um, I mean—that's how we got the money."

"The money?" Something Donna had said the other day was kicking around way in the back of her head, about money being in the family for years, thinking then it was just, well, *family* money, but not thinking that now.

"His retirement bonus."

A bonus for quitting? "You got a check from the government?"

Donna shook her head. "Cash. We got a package in the mail, a box, full of cash. Daddy went straight down to the bank and put it in their safe."

Which made even less sense. Government did a lot of truly stupid things, but lump-sum cash payouts were unusual for anything except bribes and payoffs. "And you're sure this, uh, bonus came from the government?"

"No. But where else could—"

"Was there a return address?"

"I don't remember."

"Was there a postmark, something that would tell you it came from Washington?"

"I'm sorry, I just don't—"

"Who was it addressed to?" Maxie now squarely in her rapid-fire mode.

"Mama and daddy."

Not to the son. To the parents. "When did you get it?"

"About a week after we got back."

"From New York."

"Uh-huh."

"A week after Henry Lee disappeared."

"Uh-huh."

Maxie thinking but not saying, a week after Senator Richard Worth was murdered on the street.

Chapter 15

February 1975

Dan Goggins was giving the report. But Richard Worth had his eyes on Walter Frost.

He didn't trust the Armed Services aide as far as he could throw the Capitol building. But he kept him around as a sort of pipeline to the other side, a conduit through whom he could contact the sinister forces that Richard Worth believed would subvert the American way of life if given half a chance. Some people might call that effective diplomacy. Others, pure madness. To Worth, though, it was just smart politics, and a prime rule in smart politics—something he'd once said to Frost, jokingly but meaning every word of it—was this: Keep your friends close, but your enemies closer. That way, you might see it coming when they went for your throat.

"We've, uh, we've confirmed that there is a facility in Arabaq," Goggins stumbled, his face a sandwich board for anxiety. "It is producing chemical agents, and it is operating with the approval, um, of the, uh, well, the current regime. The king, I mean."

"How about *this* regime, Dan, *our* regime?" Worth asked, gaze still fixed on Frost, who sat motionless, granite in pinstripes, placid except for the fire he was returning with his own eyes.

Goggins inhaled deeply, looked around the Senate office, brushed a trickle of sweat from his left temple. "There are indications that, uh, that…certain, uh, elements, in this country, have supported this…initiative."

"Elements," Worth said, a caustic smirk creeping over his face, shifting his attention to Goggins, the aide knowing he'd made a major mistake mincing words. "What *kind* of elements, Dan? Hydrogen? Nitrogen? *Are*-gon?"

If only the people could see this Richard Worth, Frost thought. Maybe they'd have second thoughts about his siring the national future.

"We're not sure of that," Goggins answered, trying to restrain his fidgeting, failing completely. "It's not the, uh, the government…per se, I mean. It's not like there was an explicit line item in the budget for something like this." A nervous chuckle that no one shared.

"Then what is it like, *Dan*?" Whenever Worth drifted headlong into sarcasm, he always emphasized his target's name, sneering, making it sound like another way to say You Stupid Piece Of Shit.

Goggins took a moment to compose. He was not Worth's biggest fan either, a confession he'd made to Walter Frost more than once. But the senator was a rising star, and Goggins was more interested in a meal ticket—and the power that follows—than in a best friend. When he resumed, it was straightforward, without hesitation: "There are indications it is a covert operation being financed by U.S. money."

"Is it government money?" The senator's voice thinly disguising an It Better Not Be tone.

"We can't be sure. It's easy to launder cash—grants, contracts, things like that. But we've combed the books, and so far there's nothing. I'd bet it was private."

"From whom?"

"Anyone with a strategic interest in the region, I'm guessing. Oil companies. Defense contractors. Chemical manufacturers."

"Strategic interests, my ass," Worth spit. "These people are making a buck from somewhere. This is about greed."

It's about patriotism, Walter Frost thought.

They were in their assigned spots in Worth's office. The senator on the sofa, coat off, rumpled black suit, glass of tap water on a side table, placed atop a U.S. Senate coaster. Goggins and Frost on the two leather chairs at either end of the low table between them. "Continue," Worth instructed his administrative assistant.

Goggins flipped to a page about halfway through a binder notebook, glanced up briefly at the senator, then down at the notes, then back up again, clearly not knowing what reaction would greet his next words but pushing ahead with unexpected strength. "They're making myco-toxins."

Richard Worth's head slumped backward on the top of the sofa in utter despair. "Mycotoxins. God help us all."

"Specifically a class known as trichothescenes." The senator closed his eyes as if in silent prayer. "Not a whole lot is known about this par-ticular, uh, strain," Goggins added, referring back to technical informa-tion in the notebook. "All we know is they probably cause the death and deterioration of cells in the bone marrow, lymph nodes and intestines, as well as other organs. They also make your blood vessels explode, and can interfere with the blood's ability to clot. This stuff, delivered in a spray, kills anything alive. Nothing survives."

"The Soviets have a years-long familiarity with mycotoxins, senator," Walter Frost interjected without feeling or advocacy. "In World War II, thousands of Soviet citizens died after eating grain that had been improperly harvested. We believe the fungus growing on that grain con-tained trichothescenes."

Worth picked his head off the back at the sofa and stared again at Frost. "Spare me your cold war justifications for genocide, Walter."

"I was simply stating a fact, senator, not making a case." Even, unruf-fled, a lot cooler than Goggins, whose bowels suddenly felt like they were turning to mush at the exchange. He'd warned Frost not to engage Worth on this thing, it was bad enough as is.

"The only fact that matters, *Walter*, is that certain factions in this country, undoubtedly with the tacit approval of the intelligence commu-nity, have contravened the stated policy of the United States government."

Goggins silently prayed that Frost would let it go. No such luck.

"Soviet technical literature contains comprehensive studies of mycotoxins, senator, including how they can be produced on a large scale. The Russians are using them right now, purportedly as insecticides and anti-fungal agents."

"I don't care about Soviet technical literature," Worth shot back, staccato, hitting each T in the last three words like a hammer. "My larger concern is the Constitution of these United States."

Walter Frost nodded and sat back in the leather chair, folded his hands in his lap, said nothing. Fighting with idealists was futile. They didn't own their beliefs; their beliefs owned them.

"Not to make a case one way or the other, senator," Goggins continued, eyes darting between the two other men, "but there is solid evidence to suggest that Laotian and Vietnamese forces, operating under Soviet supervision, have used mycotoxins in Laos, and that the Viet Cong has used them in Cambodia." Now, he looked at Frost for help.

You weak little worm, the committee aide thought, then saying, "That is a violation of the 1972 United Nations convention, senator."

"So that makes this right?" Worth asked, voice going up, face contorted by a derisive, disbelieving smile.

Walter Frost had no intention of giving this sanctimonious prick the satisfaction of a direct answer. "Senator, history has shown quite clearly that no nation with a strong chemical weapons program has ever been the victim of a chemical attack. Only when a nation has been unable or unwilling to threaten retaliation have toxins been used against it."

Worth sat up and leaned toward Frost, a slow boil coming over him. "I don't need a history lecture from you, Walter."

"Those who do not respect history are doomed to repeat it, senator."

"Unlike you, I have a higher respect for human life than for tired parables dispensed with thorough disregard for the American good." He reached for the glass of water. Goggins, who had been looking for a chair to climb under, hoped it might cool him off.

"With all due respect, senator, the image of New Yorkers caught in Times Square under a yellow rain that has them gasping for breath and vomiting blood is hardly a picture of the American good."

Without warning, Worth fired the glass across the room. It shattered against the wall opposite the sofa, leaving a dark trail of water on the blue carpet and knocking off three framed photos of the senator with constituents, causing them to break as well. Goggins braced for the explosion he was sure would follow, watching the senator—wild-eyed, red-faced—and then Frost, who was wearing his trademark mask of indifference. The administrative aide did not know whether to admire Walter's detachment or pity his lack of emotion.

Nothing happened, though. No further explosions. No more ridicule or mockery or, oddly, anger. Dan Goggins had seen it before. So had Frost. With Richard Worth, there was no calm before the storm. It was just the opposite. He'd explode, his fear-inducing temper raging and swelling like waves in a hurricane. Then, just like that, peace. To Goggins, it was that moment of calm that made the sacrifice worthwhile. Because as nutty as Worth could be—and it wasn't unique, as just about every senator he'd worked for had taken a healthy sip from the psychopath's well—serenity meant decision-making time, and Dan Goggins trusted his boss to do the right thing. Always.

"Document everything," Worth said, simply. "I want times, dates, places. Everything. No gaps. No misinterpretations. If you can't pin it down, leave it out."

"Yes, sir," Goggins said, scribbling in the notebook.

"Produce a briefing notebook. One copy."

"Yes, sir."

"For release at the appropriate moment, to the appropriate audience, in an appropriate forum. And I want total secrecy on this, gentlemen. Understood?" Goggins nodded. So, surprisingly, did Frost.

Worth looked at the committee staffer, closely, but without a trace of arrogance or contempt. "Walter, you and I disagree on many matters.

That's one of the reasons I admire you. You have the courage to disagree with me, and to bring another perspective to the debate." Goggins shifted uneasily, knowing he was just the opposite. No one noticed. "You're a brilliant man, and whereas we may differ on this subject, chemical warfare, I truly believe that our common grounds far surpass whatever differences may separate us. But I need a guarantee. Just one guarantee."

"Anything, senator." Not knowing if he meant it, not inclined to have the internal moral debate at the moment.

"I want your personal word that you're with me on this one."

"You have my word, senator. I work for you." Simple, direct, without hesitation.

"People are weakening the foundations of this nation. Powerful people with powerful alliances inside the government. To stop that, we need the element of surprise. We have one chance to do the right thing here."

"I agree, senator," he said.

"We can't reveal ourselves or our intentions to our enemies."

"Yes, sir," Walter Frost nodded, silently beginning to consider his options, wondering how those enemies might do the same.

Chapter 16

That Monday made Kevin feel like a starving man who could chew but not swallow.

Six calls to his mother in Sedona, hoping to get some answers about the torn pictures, or Gary Devereaux, or any other memories that Meredith Whitney Wade hadn't vaporized with booze or pills. Six messages left, none returned, no surprise. All afternoon in the office of Judge Richardson P. Hawkins, the other name or reference, whatever, that Wayne Earl Wiley had given him, a wait that went nowhere endlessly because the judge got hung up in court and couldn't make their 1:15 appointment. Another 45 minutes fighting Charlotte's rush-hour traffic, which he was reasonably sure the dictionary listed as a synonym for Stupid Urban Planning.

And now this.

A blonde, model-beautiful woman, legs that didn't stop for red lights, in Bette Davis sunglasses, red dress that fit like a second skin, sitting on the white Adirondack chair in front of his brick apartment, acting as if she was now the person in charge of his life, the one he went to for everything.

"Nice place," she said, popping open a can of Rolling Rock from the six pack at her feet, making a grand gesture of surveying the flat-roofed, rapidly running-down six-plex whose front doors opened onto a lovely vista of dry brown grass and a cheap auto body repair shop across the street. "Could use a paint job, though. And maybe a scud missile."

About a thousand questions raced each other to be first out of Kevin's mouth as he stood on the cracked, spotted sidewalk that led to his apartment door, but only one made it past his lips: "I'm sorry. Do I know you?"

"Not yet." She crossed and uncrossed her maxi-legs, the red dress seeming to shrink before his eyes, and took another pull from the beer, pouring it down like her insides were on fire. "But you will." After a second marathon guzzle she drained the can, tossed the empty into what passed for his front yard, popped another for herself and offered him one. He didn't accept. "Take it, Kevin," she advised, like there were no real options. "You're gonna need it." She tossed it to him like a challenge.

He fielded the can out of self-defense as much as anything else, opened it, sucked down the exploding fizz, eyed her for a second. "Apparently, there's been some mistake."

"And why is that?"

"I don't use Mary Kay."

"I just sold my last lipstick." Not letting him out of her glare, not backing down.

"Tupperware, either."

"Good, because your neighbor just bought my last microwave-tested, freezer-safe, dishwasher-proof food freshener."

"And you sure don't look like Ed McMahon—"

"If I was holding a $10-million check, Kevin," she said, voice somewhere between a purr and the buzz of an electric chair, standing, walking toward him, body all liquid ease and motion, "I'd've already forged your name and cashed it, and would as we speak be sunning myself in the South of France." Right in front of him now, not six inches from his face, so close he could smell her allure. "Naked, of course."

Of course, he wanted to reply, all suave and James Bond-ish, except a dryness had arrived in his throat without warning, locking up his vocal cords and leaving him to just stand there, looking at her, feeling very stupid, his heart doing something that felt abnormal, like it would run a world record 100-yard dash, rest for a second, then take off again. He wondered which kind of attack it was, anxiety or cardiac, decided it was probably lust.

The smile, which had never left her face, dimmed and chilled to the sub-zero range. "I don't have cosmetics, Kevin. Or plastic kitchen dishes. Or, sadly"—a false, pouty frown—"a pot of gold. My name is Taylor Shepard. And what I have are answers."

Again, he wanted to come back with something casual, off-hand, like To the questions that have plagued mankind for centuries? Or, if she wasn't so gorgeous, maybe even a dismissive, I'm not in the market. But a little unnerved by her coldness, and an intense stare that he felt sure wouldn't be forgotten anytime soon, the best he could manage was, "Answers to what?"

When she said, "Who is Gary Devereaux?" followed by "Give me 10 minutes, and I can tell you," he felt his world go into eclipse. Against every good instinct he ever possessed, Kevin invited her in.

•

"This is ridiculous," Kevin said, pacing back and forth in his tiny kitchen, refusing to even look at the screen on the laptop Taylor was manipulating at the dining room table.

The debate had been going on for more than the agreed-to 10 minutes, pretty much plummeting downhill the moment Taylor told him she sometimes wrote for a supermarket tabloid, her seeing that honesty wasn't always the best policy when the dimmer switch in his eyes went to Off. And even though she'd spent most of her time scrambling back to credibility, Kevin's pain-in-the-butt routine was getting old. "Just read it," she repeated for what felt like the 20th time, "then decide. It's a few seconds out of your life"—pausing to look around his apartment—"which may be a welcome detour."

"Who are you to judge me?" he shot back, having neither the time nor the patience for crackpots and their conspiracy theories. "Shouldn't you be out there making the connection between Walt Disney's frozen brain and JFK Junior's death? Isn't that what inquiring minds want to know?"

Oh, how she wanted to just crunch this little bastard, break him into a thousand little pieces and then stand there and watch while he begged for reassembly. She'd been put down by people a hell of a lot better, and let's not even talk about more worthy, than Kevin Columbus, and she'd be damned if some falling star was going to go superior on her. The problem was, she needed him—or, rather, needed what he knew, which meant playing a role, giving him the perceived upper hand, letting him take his best shots without revealing the urge to kill that mounted with each insult. "I don't care what you think of me," Taylor said slowly, "or about what I do. Judge *me* if you want to, that's fine"—throwing it back in his face—"because it doesn't matter."

"Is that so? Then by all means, tell me what does matter, oh keeper of the Freedom of Speech Flame."

She let that pass, too. "Sit," she said, bordering on a command. "Please." Gesturing to the chair next to her, facing the computer screen. Kevin stopped his back-and-forth, but didn't join her. "Fine." A frustrated, angry smile. "We'll do it your way."

"My way is my way. And it doesn't have anything to do with some gossip-mongering cyber-geek's Internet fantasies." He'd read about Rollie Merke, whose web page Taylor had called up and was struggling to get him to read, and thought the guy was a few programs shy of a hard drive.

She waved one hand at him, in a flicking motion, dismissively, operating the mouse with her other hand, saying, "Just out of curiosity, are you always this big a bastard?"

"It's a gift."

Delivering the zinger: "Your parents must be so proud." The comment muted him just long enough for her to click twice and produce a grainy, black-and-white image on the screen. Half a syllable of something came out of Kevin's mouth before she cut him off with a simple, offhanded, "You know this guy?"

As much as he wanted to ignore her, and go screaming for the hills, away from this woman and her lunatic ideas, Kevin couldn't resist. Still not sitting, he walked over to the table, standing behind her, peered at the screen. Even though it was just a head-and-shoulders shot, he could tell the man in the photo was strong, thick, built like a gray-haired oak tree with arms. Looked to be about 60 or 65. Aviator glasses, which could have come from any mall in any city in the world, and a dark baseball hat, presumably blue, with an old Army Air Corps insignia on it. Kevin remembered that when his dad lied about his age in 1944 and joined the Air Force, it wasn't the Air Force but the Army Air Corps. Meant nothing, though, the hat, just dated the wearer in some way. White open-necked shirt. Not a sense of joy to be found within 100 miles of the picture, either, the look being grim, in some way even burdened, heavy with concern. On the right side of the image was a cloud of smoke. Where or what it came from—cigar, cigarette, forest fire, dry ice—was left to the viewer's imagination.

Kevin searched for reminders, any reminders, of his long-dead father. Nothing registered. "Is that Devereaux?"

She took a slug from what by his count was her third Rolling Rock in less than half an hour. "It's somebody."

"What's that mean?"

"You decide." She pointed and clicked the mouse button, and a full page of type appeared on the screen. "Here. Just sit down and read this."

No hesitation this time. It was as if his doubts, his visceral distrust of this woman, had done a vanishing act under the magic wand of the photo. Kevin did as instructed. The black headline at the top of the page screamed: Does Devereaux's Money Path Lead To The Murderers Of Richard Worth? Then, the explanation:

"Secretive and rank with conspiratorial stink, Gary Devereaux is one of the Worth assassination's most enigmatic figures. Little is known of his smelly exploits other than he created a highly secretive pro-democracy organization called Americans for America, of which he is the only known member. This one-man cabal apparently supports patriotic organizations in the United States and, believes your trusting stink-chaser, abroad as well. But no one knows precisely what Devereaux does and for whom, because his organization is very secret, it has no visible means of support and there are no records of where his feculent funds come from or how they were spent. Smelly rumors refuse to die regarding Devereaux's life, including ones charging he was an ex-CIA operative. Which means his dirty money could have gone where? To topple foreign governments? Subvert the economies of anti-American countries? Covert assassination teams? According to one reliable *Merkey Waters* source, much of the money has been used to finance a conspiracy of silence to thwart probers of the Worth slaying. The money, this source says, paid for professional assassins to murder any living witnesses to the senator's July 6, 1975, shooting in New York. Now tell me if this doesn't stink to high heaven: Eighteen people were interviewed by the New York police or the Knight Commission after it was determined they had seen something that day on the street. All but six are dead. Your trusting foulness finder has scientifically computed the chances of that occurring by coincidence, and concluded they are approximately 80 quadrillion-zillion to one."

Kevin immediately thought of Donna Hubbard, and wished this jackass Merke had included a list of the deceased, or those who had been questioned, or something beyond the warped ramblings of a Net Neurotic. But he hadn't, typical, God forbid the inclusion of facts that might get in the way of publication. The text continued:

"So what it comes down to, fellow stink-seekers, is this: We have a man, Gary Devereaux, who may have raised vast sums of money for rancid activities that have never seen the light of day. We have the biggest secret in the world, Senator Worth's murder, that has been clouded by the fetid air of cover-up. We have at least 12 deaths related to the senator's gun-down that could only be undertaken and committed by a highly paid professional assassin. Devereaux had the secret stinky money. Devereaux had the rancid CIA connections. Devereaux had to be involved. Case closed."

Kevin rubbed his eyes, shook his head and looked up at Taylor Shepard with harsh, angry exhaustion. "I hope you have something more than that to show me," he began, stabbing a finger at the screen, starting to lose it, tired of everybody setting him up for some grand revelation and not delivering a thing. "Because that—*that!*—is the biggest crock of horseshit I have ever read." She nodded, started to explain, but he clipped her fast, getting out of the chair and starting to pace the living room. "That doesn't say anything I basically didn't already know about Devereaux, and those connections to Worth's killing are as bogus as Merke is! Show me one credible fact in there. Show me a link between Devereaux and Worth that didn't come out of this guy's demented mind. Otherwise, get outta my house, go back to covering alien abductions and hooker nuns and three-headed trout, because that's all you're good for—"

"Hey, I don't need a speech on journalism from some has-been, broken-down ex- corporate flack, pal!" Taylor screamed, leaping out of the chair, taking two long strides to confront him face to face, stopping Kevin in mid-step, war declared.

"And I don't need some subterranean pretend Woodward and Bernstein, playing all nice and concerned, probably planning to fuck me before she kills me in that fish-wrapper of hers. Oh, man, I can see it now. There I am, right up there with the Bearded Beauty Queen and the Man With a Thousand Love Handles."

"That'd be a rung up the ladder for you!"

"If that's where the ladder goes, sweetheart, I'll stay where I am, thank you very much. Because this, down here, this is my life, it's what I have, and it may not be *Father Knows Best* or *Leave it to Beaver*, but by God it's better than the swill that consumes you. So why don't you just climb on your broom or your mother ship or whatever it was that dropped you off in my world and go back to the black hole you came from!"

Taylor Shepard's eyes started to blink rapidly, Kevin not being able to tell if she was fighting back tears or the urge to castrate him. "Look," she said, voice surprisingly clear and strong, "I am just trying to help you. That's why—"

"My ass, you want to help. You want the story, and there's nothing you'll stop at, and no one you won't run over, to get it. So let me give you a lead, Deep Throat—and I use the title in the nicest possible way: Somewhere out there is a picture of New York City, July 6, 1975, with a UFO over the Empire State Building—"

"Oh, please." Turning away, going for another hit of Rolling Rock.

"—and I've heard that three homeless guys saw Elvis on Fifth Avenue that day, but he was dressed as a street vendor selling sausage dogs up by Central Park—"

"Go to hell, I'm outta here." Killing another large portion of the beer, still not facing him, slinging stuff in a black leather Kate Spade purse.

"—and I hear, although it's just a theory, that the aliens beamed him down there to draw attention from their plot to kill Worth because the good senator wanted to cut funding for NASA—"

Whirling now, firing at him with hateful eyes. "I hope you die a painful death, Columbus, and your parents turn out to be Rush Limbaugh and Madonna."

"—which pissed off all the ETs because they were planning to hijack the next shuttle mission and threaten to blow up the world if they didn't get the special sauce recipe from Burger King—"

She came at him like a stalker. "It wasn't Elvis they spotted that day, you obnoxious asshole." Before he could say anything, she grabbed his arm, jerking him back toward the laptop with a force so surprising he didn't resist, gluing her right hand to his bicep as she tap-tap-tapped another couple of keys on the computer. Devereaux's page disappeared, replaced by what looked to be a police sketch. "It was him!"

Kevin stared unblinking at the image, which was headlined, Who Was Airport Man?

"Look familiar?" Taylor asked, snide, angry, her tone saying Gotcha.

"What's this?" Suddenly drained of anger, gaze going from the screen to her and back.

"It's a police sketch the cops took from a Swiss Air gate agent at LaGuardia in New York City on July 7, 1975. The man in that picture was just about to get on a plane for Geneva when someone stopped him. The agent didn't hear what was said, but whatever it was, this guy became highly agitated, walked away from that flight, bought a first-class ticket, in cash, for Nashville. The other one, the man who stopped him, went on to Switzerland."

Kevin drilled Taylor with a stare. "Tell me what it means."

"It means he got out, Gary. He's gone."

Disbelieving. Standing at the gate, wondering if the whole thing was going to hell before his eyes. "How?"

"Beats the shit outta me. After he took the shot, he panicked and ran. I'd be willing to bet he knew we were going to take him out next."

"Jesus H. Christ." Two fingers on Devereaux's left hand, index and middle, made up and down scissor motions as he thought. In the background, a speaker announced that his flight was boarding. "Where is he now?"

"Tennessee. Nashville. Shitty little flophouse of a hotel. The Heart of America Inn. Room 6B."

"All right." He thought for another moment, but no more. They did not have the luxury of time. "You go on to Geneva."

"Where are you going?"

"Nashville."

"Let me go with you."

"No. I'll take Tim."

"Tim?"

"*Tim's responsibility was the fire escape. This is his problem more than ours.*" *A black pause.* "*And he's mine.*"

"*You're not thinking of—*"

"*Go. Meredith will follow in a few days. I'll get there when I get there.*"

"*Meredith?*" *Looking genuinely surprised.*

"*To claim the body.*" *Thinking, Jesus, how many times have we gone over this?*

"It's Gary Devereaux," Taylor said simply. "At least, that was the name on the passenger list."

Kevin shook his head slowly, probed the sketch for clues, finding a lot on the surface, but none deeper than the lines on the page. Stared at the drawing, at the dark hair and straight-edge part, the mischievous eyes, and a mouth that he knew, just knew, would turn into an anything-goes smile at the slightest provocation—

"Look familiar?" Taylor asked.

Kevin didn't answer, couldn't answer, just sat there, drowning in a deep-rising sea of confusion, not willing to admit the resemblance, fearing that the mere act of saying it, saying That's My Old Man, would breathe life into what was beginning to feel like a nightmare.

Taylor let the moment linger. He was her target, after all, and in her business, the best strike always came at the point of utter vulnerability. "Kevin, can I ask you a question?" He mumbled something that bordered on consent. "When did your father die?"

"April 12, 1975." Automatic response, burned in his brain.

"When was his body recovered?"

"Early July."

"Senator Worth was killed on July 6, 1975. The next day, July 7, was when Devereaux and this other person were seen at the Swiss Air gate." Kevin shrugged, not knowing what she was driving at. "There's not a single shred of evidence, no record—nothing—that Gary Devereaux existed before July 7."

"So?" he answered feebly, no idea what else to say.

"So don't you find it the least bit odd that within a week of your father's body being recovered—a week, not incidentally, in which a United States senator was murdered—a man who looks surprisingly like the late Major Jonathan Columbus is resurrected as Gary Devereaux?"

Kevin just gaped at her, mouth open, utterly speechless, as lost as he'd ever been in his life, so far gone he didn't have the mental wherewithal to ask just exactly how she'd learned his father's name, or from whom.

Chapter 17

"Who's that?"

Not a How are you? or a You won't believe what I found out. Not even a Hello.

Just a question, more of an accusation really, Maxie's greeting coming across like a gun, drawn and aimed.

Taylor got up from the sofa-bed in Kevin's living room, smoothing the red dress and tugging at the hem, as if trying to make it longer, extending her hand. "Hi, I'm—"

"Wasn't talking to you, Goldie," Maxie interrupted, a healthy hint of threat in her tone. "I'm asking Mr. Columbus here who you are, and what your bony little ass is doing perched on his bed."

"She's a reporter, Max," Kevin said, exhausted, not bothering to stand. Buried in the burnt orange chair that faced his entertainment center, one leg draped over the arm, a glass, nearly drained of a brown liquid that screamed whiskey to the detective's taste buds, sitting on the floor next to him.

At the word *reporter*, Maxie's entire body went rigid, like she'd swallowed a chute of instant-drying cement. Her eyes shot from Kevin to the girl, and back, and then back again, settling onto his face with the fury of a typhoon. "I'm sorry?" she said, finally, outraged and disbelieving.

Taylor felt the tension, but didn't crack. "I'm a freelance writer, magazine work mostly. I've been investigating—"

"From the looks of you, honey, you couldn't find your ass with a heavy-duty flashlight and a map." Turning fire to Kevin. "And you better be telling me the only reason she's here is she lost a bet and had to prove she's a natural blonde—which I doubt, thank you very much—and that this has got nothing to do with nothing of any importance, if you get my drift."

Silence. When Maxie had called, an hour or so earlier, Kevin had warned Taylor things might not go real well.

"For the record," Taylor said, dryly, "I am a natural blonde. And for the time being, Mr. Columbus will just have to accept that on faith."

For the time being? What the hell did that mean? Kevin wondered, for an instant forgetting he was neck-deep in someone else's secret, instead imagining sex with this woman. Just like a guy, he thought, catching himself in the act, though not entirely ready to deep-six the thought quite yet. "Max, listen to me for a second." Getting up, walking toward her.

"You got 60 of them, lover boy," she countered, eyes not leaving Taylor, who was still on her feet and not showing any preference for dancing around a confrontation. The three of them, standing in a trian-gle—Taylor by the sofa, Maxie a few steps to her left at the mouth of the hallway, Kevin next to Maxie—locked in a game of verbal chicken.

"Miss Shepard is—"

"Nice to meet you," she said, full of false pleasance, re-extending a hand to Maxie. "Call me Taylor."

Maxie refused the hand, flashed her a smile that was equaliy counter-feit, adding just in case she didn't get it: "Bite me. *Taylor.*"

Kevin pushed on. "She's been writing about the Worth assassina-tion—"

"You may have heard a little something about it," Taylor said. "Made all the talk shows." An abrupt pause, a strategic frown. "Although I'm not sure if it was ever on Jerry Springer."

Without hesitating, Maxie strode quickly to the dining table, picked up a chair, came charging back at Taylor, aiming it like a lion-tamer, ranting, "No, but sadly for you, I did see the one called Peephole

Reporters and the Bad Black Chicks that Shoved Chairs Up Their Skinny White Asses, and I do feel a rerun coming on!"

Kevin stepped between them. He didn't think for a minute she'd go through with it, but with Maxie's affection for spur-of-the-moment violence, no sense taking any chances. "Time out."

Maxie dropped the chair abruptly. "Time out, my ass, I'm gone." She turned and took three long strides to the front door.

"Max!" It was a mad, confused wail, the cry of someone whose life had been suddenly caught in an unexpected trap whose clamp-down angered him at least as much as it hurt him. Maxie thought she heard a plea in there someplace and stopped a microsecond before turning the doorknob, feeling a bad case of Mother Teresa coming on, wondering if you had to be Catholic to be a saint.

"Get over here," she ordered, grabbing Kevin's arm, hustling him toward the bedroom-turned-office like he was a suspect and they were going into interrogation. Taylor started to say something to Maxie's back, which the detective sensed but had no intention of directly acknowledging, not turning around, instead holding an index finger over her left shoulder in a This Is The One Thing You Need To Know mode, hissing, "If we need you, Goldie, we'll call the escort service. Otherwise, feel free to take a hike." Slamming the office door so hard it knocked a book, *Power and Influence*—unread, naturally—off one of the entertainment center shelves.

In the office, Maxie pinned him against a bare wall, furious. "You are the single stupidest white person I have ever met, do you know that?" It took every fiber of strength she had not to grab his shirt and shake him until he either died, found God or got wisdom. "You're spilling your guts to a damned reporter when you don't have the first idea what, or even if, this is about something. You are dumb as a furball, you know that?"

"Max, please, listen, I haven't told—"

"No. You listen to me. That's your job: To shut your damned mouth while I see if I can jumpstart that dead-ass brain of yours." She was almost on top of him, and he felt the full weight of her anger.

"She knows—"

"You're falling down on your job, junior."

"Look, she may be able to help—"

"I thought I told you to—"

Without warning, Kevin came at Maxie like a shot, shoving her across the small square room, toward a cheap, mostly empty bookcase, getting in her face so fast she didn't have a chance to punch his lights out. "Listen to me, goddammit!" Another wail, this one intense and tortured and frustrated, Maxie thinking for an instant he'd lost it, was about to go Ruby Ridge on him, instinctively reaching for a gun that for better or worse wasn't there. Kevin sensed it too, took a step back, putting his emotions in lock-down for a second, chilling. When he spoke again, the voice and tone seemed distracted, almost calm, but a stressed edge, a sharpness, still colored every word. Maxie thinking he sounded like a factory worker might sound like just before he picked up a shotgun and visited the personnel director who'd denied his request for a couple extra sick days.

"Max, I got something in the mail the other day. I think it was from my father."

"The mail that slow?" Coming back wise because she didn't know what the angle was.

Kevin shook his head, seeming to deny his own words, explaining the conversation with Roper, the package from Island City, his trip to Florida, the meeting with Cloud and the discovery of the torn pictures. "Then this reporter turns up, and in the middle of what sounds to me like a lunatic riff on the Worth assassination, she shows me a drawing on the Internet that, I swear to God, looks like it could've been my dad 25 years ago."

"What'd it have to do with Worth?" she asked, not snappish, feeling a little bit of Kevin's confusion and a lot of pure investigative interest.

He exhaled, rubbed his eyes. "Somebody with the airline, Swiss Air, described him at the gate the day after Worth was shot. According to his passport, he was Devereaux." Maxie said nothing, just taking it all in, no need high-jumping to any conclusions. "For what it's worth, at about that same time my mother was going to Switzerland to recover the old man's body."

"You talk to her about any of this?"

"Tried. No answer." He shook his head, lost and a little sad, looking down at his feet and then back up at her. "Jesus, I feel like somebody or something is taking an egg beater to my identity."

Maxie forged a lean smile. "Then you better brace yourself, Humpty Dumpty, 'cause what I got to say ain't gonna put you back together again." She related her discovery of the bullet in Alabama, the preliminary discussion with Carl Grigsby and the litany of oddities surrounding the Hubbard Family Adventure to New York: Daddy's calls to Washington and Henry Lee's sudden appearance at home. Tim the Dog Man. Bag of cash arriving less than a week after Worth was shot. "And here's the real kicker: Our missing vet was a rifleman in the infantry." Kevin started to say something, but she cut him off. "I know, I know. A trained shooter at the scene, nobody thinks to raise the question, who's on first."

He mulled the converging stories, his about Devereaux and Worth, Maxie's about Henry Lee and Worth, finally asking, "Should we just get out of this now? Walk away from it?"

"Not me. Not at two hundred a day." One firm shake of the head, which transmuted into a sly grin. "Not that this is about the *money*, you understand."

He half-smiled in return. "Perish the thought."

"Besides, I got a feeling you're in this more than you know. Getting out probably isn't an option." He asked what she meant, her smile going into hiding. "Somebody wanted you in. That's the only explanation for the gift-wrapped puzzle from Island City."

"So what do I do?"

"You mean Charlie's Angel out there hasn't given you an idea or two about that?" The grin returned, gentler, Kevin responding in kind, shrugging like a shy virgin on his first trip to a whorehouse, an effect Maxie pretty much A-bombed when she clamped on to the front of his shirt with both hands and jerked him into her. "To start with, you don't go thinking with Little Kevin down there."

"She knows as much about the Worth thing as anyone, and a hell of a lot more than we do. If what's happening—"

"Say it with me, Kevin: I will not tell Satan-Barbie anything."

"But—"

"Kevin?" Yanking him even closer.

"Okay, okay, okay," he agreed, getting out from under her grip and moving across the room, leaning against a wooden dining room table he'd converted to a desk. It sagged in the middle under a Gateway desktop, like a sway-backed nag.

"I'm warning you. If you're thinking about going horizontal with this skank, bad things are gonna happen." He nodded without conviction. "She's a *reporter*, man. She screws people for profit."

"I know, I know. It's just that…" Voice trailing off, Maxie not knowing if he couldn't complete the thought, or just didn't want to.

"It's just that what?"

Kevin looked up, directly into her eyes, the gaze flush with a bafflement as thickly knotted as any she'd ever seen. "If something's going on around me, Max, I'd at least like to know what it is, and why I won the prize." He smiled weakly, followed it with a laugh that was even weaker. "I mean, wouldn't it be something if I turned out to be somebody who matters?"

Maxie thinking Ain't no mystery there, son, you obviously do matter to somebody. The question, though, was to whom, and maybe more to the point, for what reason?

•

Taylor sat at Kevin's dining table seeing the image in her mind, tracing it from memory with a black felt tip on a hotel notepad, The Drake, her favorite.

She knew she should probably be tossing the place while Kevin and Coffee Brown were in the other room having words. But there was no point. What she needed from him wasn't in the kitchen cabinets or the shelves full of unread self-help books. It wasn't stuck behind the cushions in his furniture. And it sure as hell wasn't hidden in the refrigerator, because she'd checked, and it had given up only a half-container of low-fat milk, some Gatorade that had the blue color of a kitchen cleaner and two cans of Miller Lite.

No, what she needed was in his head, and those games had already begun. So instead, she drew.

The lines were bold, confident, each stroke bringing her mental picture more and more into focus. Thick hair, crisply parted. Eyes she managed to fill with intrigue and joy at once. Thin, tighly drawn lips. Nose kind of flat, but not like it had been punched in or broken, and oval, narrow nostrils. Big ears, the shape of conch shells almost, not sticking out but kind of tucked against the side of the head, as if they'd been stapled back. She did some shading here and there, really darkening the hair, scribbling it almost black. Wanted to add some more details, beating back the urge, just like she had the first time, knowing too much was too much, this being a police sketch after all and not a portrait.

Satisfied that she'd reproduced the drawing, Taylor pulled Merke's page back up on the laptop screen, accessed the drawing she'd originally created on the beach-overlooking balcony in Florida, the same drawing she'd sent to Merke and shown Kevin minutes earlier, him drinking it up like a frat boy at a keg party. It was a perfect copy, feature for feature, line for line, the two Jon Columbuses so close they could have been Xeroxed.

Taylor smiled, thought maybe she'd missed her calling, should have been an artist. Then she read the text, the tale of Devereaux she'd whipped together in just a few seconds, back in the Florida hotel as well, and had fired off to Merke, saw how well she mimicked the cyber-screwball's style—he hadn't changed a syllable, just slapped it right in, like always—and quickly rejected the thought. Art was nice. But fiction paid better.

•

"I'm gonna tell you one thing, Goldie, and that's that I'm not gonna tell you nothin'. You got that?"

Taylor, standing in the kitchen and sipping a glass of tap water, nodded silently at Maxie, the recreated drawing now in pieces at the bottom of her purse.

"So having said that, here's the plan." Looking straight at Taylor, like Kevin wasn't even in the room. "Number 1: You don't write anything unless the two of us"—meaning herself and Kevin—"agree to it. Something happens, some accident, some freak of nature thing, and any of this turns up in the paper—or, in your case, the toilet paper—I will be forced to kill you."

Inside, Taylor laughed at the threat. This woman had no idea who she was dealing with. And though her role as reporter required that no such arrangement could ever be made, Taylor wasn't about to let some arcane code of ethics impede the task at hand. "Fine," was all she said.

Which struck Maxie as odd. During her cop days, she'd known more than a few reporters, and not one of them ever resisted the chance to blather about Freedom of the Press, the Public's Right To Know and all that other crap. Not this one, though. This one just passively agreed, which pushed whatever doubts or concerns Maxie had about her even closer to the red zone. "I'm serious as bone cancer, girlie," she added, trying to get a rise out of Taylor, anything that would signal what was going on inside that head of hers.

But Taylor Shepard was too smart, and better at the game than Maxie gave her credit for. "Let me tell you what I'm serious about…*girlie*." With that one sentence, the room temperature dropped about 25 degrees, which was still tropical compared to Taylor's voice. When she spoke again, it was at a clipped pace, empty of anything but the iciest calculation. "I'm serious about breaking this story, and I'm the only one who can do it right because I understand what he's going through." Pointing at Kevin while she reached for her purse, finding her wallet, opening it, extracting a photo. "You see, *girlie*, my dad disappeared in Vietnam, too." Flashing the picture at her, waving it back and forth, the uniformed image registering with Maxie, but only barely. "I don't know where he is, if he's dead or alive, if he's become somebody else, nothing. I don't know a thing about him except he dropped off the edge of the earth without a trace." She cut a glance to Kevin. "Gee, does any of this sound familiar?" He started to answer, but Taylor hurtled on, a cascade of anger, frustration and resent. "And I'm going to tell you something else, *girlie*: If someone came to me with evidence right now that flashed even a micro-dot of light on what happened to my dad, I'd put life on hold in a heartbeat, and go anywhere or do anything to track him down."

She caught her breath, directed the next sentence at Kevin. "That's what's in it for you: The chance to know for sure. Something I have never enjoyed and may never enjoy." Taylor paused to let the comment sink in. Maxie rolled her eyes. Kevin just stared. "But let me be clear about one thing. This is not therapy-by-extension, and just so you won't think me too honorable for helping this poor little sheep, I'll admit there is something in it for me: Respect. Getting out of the supermarket checkout lines and on the front page of *The Washington Post*. I'm dead serious about that, too. I am 32 years old. Solving Richard Worth's death is my best shot, maybe my only one. If this doesn't go anywhere, if it hits a dead end, then I'm going to spend the rest of my life turning out bizarre stories for shitty little rags that do not have so much as a passing acquaintance with the truth, writing for readers who either don't know the difference or just don't care. That is not acceptable to me. It's not an option.

"So I'll play by your rules. For now. But the minute this thing breaks, the minute I have evidence of a conspiracy or that the Knight Commission was wrong—whenever that happens, the rules change. Because I'm going with the story. And if you try to stop me, I will be forced to kill *you*. Now, are we clear on that?" A piercing, challenging stare, bouncing from Kevin to Maxie, as she replaced the photo in her wallet.

"Clear as your bleached roots," Maxie answered.

"Enough," Kevin said, the posturing starting to get on his already-at-the-end nerves.

"Just trying to keep everyone straight," Taylor said.

"Straight, hell, you wouldn't know straight if it bit you on the butt. You are so damned twisted, I bet you got to screw on your undies."

"I don't wear undies."

"That's what I read on the wall at the bus station."

"The bus station? Looking for a one-night husband, were you?"

"Nah. Just saw something scrawled in a bathroom stall that caught my eye: For an average time, call Taylor."

"Funny, most men never forget a night with me."

"Ah, VD: The gift that keeps on giving."

"Why don't you just kill each other now, and end my misery?" Kevin interrupted, shutting them up. He rubbed his eyes harshly, leaving them red and swollen. "Listen to me. Both of you. I am lost here, okay? You two seem to be the only ones who can get me out of the woods. But you better understand one thing: Finding out who Gary Devereaux is and what happened to my old man are all that matter to *me*. Taylor, I don't care about your father or your respectability. Those're your issues. You deal with them. And Max, you may be right, that dealing with her"—motioning to Taylor—"could be the wrong thing to do, stupid beyond belief. I don't know. But I do know that all of a sudden there are a lot of things out there raising a lot of questions about me, and I don't plan on spending the rest of my life thinking about them. For me, *that* is not an option, and if Taylor can find some answers, then I don't care if she's an axe murderer." He dropped back into the orange chair, head in hands, finally looking up, saying: "I just want to know who my father is, and that's hard enough without having to deal with the two of you shaking your asses at each other. So if you don't stop, I'll get a gun and kill the both of you myself."

"Excuse me," Maxie said, dropping her head a bit, cocking an eyebrow, eyes cutting up at him like she was looking over the top of reading glasses, "but do you know who you're talking to?"

"I don't know anything. Nothing. That's why tomorrow, I'm going to initiate my own little investigation. Starting with the VA, the Social Security office, the Air Force—even my wacko mother—anyplace that might have any record of who my old man is." He chuckled, added grimly, "My old *men*," and mumbled something that only had meaning to him. "So, Max, you go your way. Taylor, you go yours. And I'm gonna go mine. If we intersect at some point, great. But until that happens, or even if it doesn't, I would consider it a personal favor if you two took the WWF Texas Death Match routine someplace else."

Maxie grumbled something that sounded like assent, still eyeing Taylor as if she were a fungus. Taylor didn't bother to return the look, just said "Whatever" and stared at the computer screen, the sketch and the text about Gary Devereaux, thinking none of this chitchat really mattered since she'd already mashed Kevin's buttons bigtime, and he'd responded, and she had no intention of stopping now.

•

She didn't like it. Not one bit. And she knew, deep down, that it wouldn't be long before that benchwarmer for the Swedish bikini team had Kevin Columbus dancing like an organ grinder's monkey.

Not my problem, though, Maxie thought, whirling the reconstructed Mustang Mach I—damned thing had more body work than Joan Rivers—whirling it through South Charlotte, getting onto I-77, heading north through the city. Mind in overdrive, car on auto-pilot, cruising right by her exit, Trade Street, the one that took her home.

Not my problem at—

Well, yeah, it is.

Because this thing—conspiracy, missing person case, whatever it was—had gone beyond Kevin and Donna Hubbard and her, now including a reporter, which made for a bad, bad brew. As for Kevin, well, she loved the boy, but he wasn't thinking straight. For all the ups and downs he'd been through—and he was a survivor, put every one of them behind him—this deal about his old man was rearranging his brain cells. A large part of Maxie wondered why, after all these years, he was so suddenly obsessed with this concept of where he came from. What's the point? You are what you are, she wanted to tell him when they were going a few rounds in the bedroom, and you've been that way for a long time, and nothing's going to change that. Maxie wasn't real big on the idea of destiny, though she did think that who you turned out to be was pretty much decided early on. And Kevin's father, or Devereaux, or whoever it was who'd love-seeded his mother, had done a decent job getting the kid ready for a life that had more than its share of detours, dead ends and disappointments. So what did it matter whose blood was in your veins? What was he going to get out of the truth? A transfusion?

Drifting into the right-hand lane on the interstate, just north of downtown, the exit just a couple miles ahead.

And then there's this Taylor person. What was her deal, anyway? Something wasn't right there. For whatever reason, Maxie didn't buy the whole I Wanna Be Somebody performance. It didn't ring true. To start with, the chick was a knockout, no point ignoring that, and Maxie found it ultra hard to believe someone that beautiful hadn't gotten the attention of a big-dog newspaper editor or publisher who was not averse to letting her sleep her way to the top. And caving in like that on the thing about not running with a story unless they all agreed? Real reporters would have laughed at the suggestion. Sure, she came back with that act, I'll play by your rules for the time being. But it had all the honesty of a Chicago election.

Slowing onto the exit ramp. Harris Boulevard. Going right. Just driving. Past the Blackberry Creek condos. University City United Methodist Church.

Oh, and what about that other thing, about *her* father? She's got an old man who disappeared in Vietnam? She refuses to believe he's not dead? Puh-leese. Way too convenient. All of it. Come on. Every school boy's fantasy and suffering from daddy-withdrawal to boot? Woe is me, my ass.

Past two apartment complexes, turning left at the Harris Teeter, onto Mallard Creek Road, past Chesterbrook Academy, Westbrook Business Center, Mallard Crossing Medical Park. Reaching the stone-gated entrance. Taking a left by the sign that says Fine Homes From The Mid-$200's. Somebody yelling at her, Maxie not even bothering to say Huh? or anything like that, just blowing by the clubhouse, the tennis courts, the pool—closed at this hour—all protected by a black wrought-iron fence.

No. Nothing about this girl was in sync with Maxie's knowledge of the world and how it worked. Not a damned thing. She couldn't exactly get her arms around what it was, and that bothered her, too. As a cop, she could feel things. Guy was sitting in an interrogation room, hemming and hawing, flapping his jaws but not giving anything up, she could all of a sudden put the pieces together. Just like that. It wasn't like catching him in a lie, a case where this statement didn't jive with that statement. That was too easy, and mostly happened on TV anyway. It was more like this sudden revelation, an epiphany triggered by nothing more than how he uttered a syllable or when his lips went suddenly thin and white or the way his voice shot up at the wrong time. And things would register.

Past signs that warned Stop, Children at Play.

Jesus, she thought, mind now starting to drift all over the psychological landscape, if only I could do that in life, huh? Wouldn't it be wonderful to be able to assemble all of life's little pieces in a way that turned the puzzle into a nice, comprehensible picture? To instinctively know where the edges were, and stay within them. To realize what fit and what didn't fit, and then have enough sense not to jam things together that had no business being within miles of each other. To look at the hole in the middle of the puzzle, where something really important was supposed to go, and then out of nowhere put your finger on what was missing, and drop it in, and all of a sudden, Bang, everything was right and the picture was clear and it all made sense because you finally understood what was needed to fill that last hole.

Arriving, finally.

It was a nice place, really, a lot nicer than her apartment. Two-story, all-brick, trimmed in white. Bay window almost dead center, a vista into the kitchen. It was a great kitchen, she imagined, full of modern appliances, maybe even one of those islands that sat in the middle where the burners magically appeared when you pressed a button. Porch on one side, wood columns and thigh-high fence, white as well. Perfect lawn, perfectly clipped shrubs. Long driveway—not an oil stain to be found—that flowed into a wide two-car garage that she'd bet had one of those automatic opener deals, a Lexus and some yuppie station wagon inside, probably a damned Volvo. A flag, pale blue with an exaggerated black footprint—Tar Heel, get it?—over the front door, announcing the presence of a University of North Carolina fan. Portable basketball goal at one edge of the driveway, a trampoline in the sloping back yard.

Above the bay window was a large second-floor picture window, with three more smaller ones to the left over the porch and five to the right. Three others at the ground level, on the other side of the front door, one of them revealing a den, she'd bet, a nice one, too, with a big-screen TV and a long L-shaped sofa you could sink into, next to a formal living room where they probably put the tree at Christmas. Then there would be his room. With a soft bed that swallowed him. A little boom box, a good one, not one of those $40 rip-offs, but a Sony or Panasonic or JVC. Desk made out of real wood, strong wood, where he could fight aliens on his computer and learn about the world that awaited him.

Her world.

Jesus. How in God's name could she take her son from that place there, that world where everything was possible, and drop him into the mad uncertainty of her life? Where was the logic to that? Was this about what she wanted or about what was best for the boy, or had she convinced herself that they were the same thing?

Looking at that house, all lit up like a smile, Maxie didn't have any answers. All she knew was that her puzzle was missing a piece at its heart, and it was a little kid who she too often felt she was trying to force fit into her own chaotic picture. A little kid who'd probably have a better shot at everything if she just had the guts to let him go. Hell, she'd let the father go, right? He was a good man, too, and she'd just let him walk away from his responsibilities. Why couldn't she do the same for J.J.? Why couldn't she give the kid the chance he deserved?

Behind her, a white sedan rolled to a stop, blue lights flashing. Maxie wondered who it would be this time? Rob or Leon or the new guy, what was his name? Tom, Dom, something like that.

It was Rob, all decked out in his tan rent-a-cop suit, skinny black clip-on tie, boasting a badge that signified nothing more than a $7-dollar-an-hour job. A graduate student in engineering, he'd told her on their first encounter about six months earlier. "Miss McQueen," he said, coming around to her side of the car, leaning into the window. "This really has to stop."

In the neighborhood, a couple of porch lights flashed on. Somewhere in the darkness, a dog started to bark.

"I'm going, Rob." Not looking at him. Busted.

"They're gonna call the police one of these days. You know that." If Rob had been a bad-ass, it could have been a warning. But he was nice 20-something kid with a smile that would someday serve him well as a father, and he was just trying to help.

"We don't want that to happen, do we?" Turning to him for the first time.

"They think you're gonna kidnap him. Your son, I mean."

Maxie shot him a grin that was more wicked than she felt. "They could be right."

Rob laughed, thinking she really didn't mean it, but not entirely sure. "I have to ask you to leave. We have rules, you know, and I'm just—"

"Doing your job," she recited, nodding, hearing it again for the umpteenth time. He nodded back at her. He was a good-looking boy, reminding her a little bit of Deputy Eddie back in Alabama. The uniform, probably. "Then quit hanging into my car window like some damned gigolo, and I'll let you go back to studying electron fields or magnetic fields or whatever it is that passes for knowledge these days."

"I just try to unlock the secrets of the universe, Miss McQueen." The smile broadened. It was a nice smile, she thought. Warm.

The Mustang coughed its way to ignition. "Well, when you find that key, how 'bout going to the hardware store and running me a copy? I can't seem to figure shit out these days."

Rob laughed. "Happy to do it." He tapped the top of her car twice, like it was a signal she could leave, and Maxie drove off. She glanced into the rear-view mirror once, and saw the front door to that nice big house open, and the silhouette of a little kid standing there, a dark, diminishing shadow against the bright light of the hallway. It took everything in her power not to push the brake pedal through the floor, slam the car into reverse and go back and take him and just be done with it. But no sooner had she seen the image of her son than the light behind him was gone, the door closed, the house suddenly dark, leaving Maxie to wonder if she'd really seen anything at all.

Back on I-77, heading south toward home, she pulled out a lime-green bandana and blew her nose. Must be my sinuses, she told herself. Big girls don't cry.

•

It was a little after two in the morning and Taylor Shepard, no doubt loosened up by the straight vodka she'd been sipping all night, was telling a slightly toasted Kevin Columbus about the one that got away.

"You have to understand," she said, "I didn't have anyone at the time. My father had been gone"—*been gone*, Kevin noticed, not *died* or *disappeared*—"for 10 or 11 years, and my mom had passed away six months earlier. So here I was, alone, looking for companionship—not sex, necessarily, but some antidote to the loneliness. I needed a reason to be. Some, I don't know...some sense of identity. That's when I met Raymond" A pause and a smile that sent a quick stab of stupid jealousy through Kevin. He could see her mind drift off for a moment, the voyage plain in her eyes. "Raymond was a feminist."

"I thought feminists were named Gloria or Susan B. or Phil Donohue."

Taylor laughed. "It wasn't politics, and it wasn't like he was out there marching for women's issues. He was just this compassionate, honorable man who really believed that women had certain rights. Really, *really* believed that. I mean, this guy was like a radical feminist."

"I see." He didn't, but it didn't matter. As the night deepened, and the liquor took the edge of his wariness, Kevin found himself more and more drawn to this woman. After half the bottle of Grey Goose had vanished—Taylor bought it, "expense account item"—so did the reporter in her. So, too, did whatever walls Maxie warned him to build. He couldn't help it. The woman was off-the-charts beautiful, and he hadn't been with anybody who looked that good, even approached it, for what felt like a month longer than forever. Her presence, her smell, her closeness, all of it seemed to give him cover, a momentary break from whatever lurked unseen just off the radar. That's what he wanted, really, a rest or some peace before recommitting himself to the search for his past. Too many weird things were piling up too fast and he had to catch his breath, maybe even forget about it for just a night, one last night.

So he listened, drawn into the web of her tale, the soundtrack from *Grosse Pointe Blank* behind them on the CD player, David Bowie and Queen singing "Under Pressure."

"My dad was a military guy. Traveled a lot. Never with us, though, me and my mom. Always TDYs—temporary duty—30 days here, six months there. Here today, gone tomorrow. That kind of thing." No self-pity in the assessment, no sense of loss, just a statement of fact.

"After he went away"—Kevin catching the euphemism again—"and mom died, I was kind of out of sorts, you know? They were both only children and so was I. When I wanted a family picnic, I would eat a hot dog looking in the mirror." Kevin laughed, but she cut it off with a look that said I'm Serious. Taylor leaned back into the sofa, Kevin sitting cross-legged on the floor opposite her, and took another sip of vodka. "I was scheduled to go off to college." Northwestern, she added, almost parenthetically. "I was looking at four years of living off scholarships and part-time jobs and the dwindling resources of my grandparents. All of a sudden, I said I can't do this. It wasn't as if my life was wrong, or what I was doing was wrong. It was just wrong at the time. Does that make any sense?" She looked at Kevin like he was her shrink, like he had the answers, which he didn't, so he just nodded stupidly, trying without a lot of success to look sage. "That's when I just said to hell with it all, and dropped out of sight, too."

Like father, like daughter, Kevin thought, smart enough not to say it aloud.

"I went to the Middle East. It's where my dad had spent a good part of his career. Morocco. Teheran. Damascus. I was pretty aimless, back-packing, you know, hither and yon, staying at youth hostels, stuff like that. When I needed money, I'd stop wherever I was and work for a few weeks. Then it was off again."

"An American nomad."

She smiled at the thought. "Exactly. Wandering without purpose. That was me."

A thought struck Kevin. "This was when?"

"I don't know, exactly. Around 1985, I think."

"How'd you manage that?"

She took a sip of vodka. "What do you mean?"

"As I recall, the sport of choice in the Middle East around then was burning Reagan dummies."

"Forgive the redundancy." They both laughed lightly. But she quickly turned secret. "I met a guy in Cairo. He turned me into a German." Before Kevin could pose the obvious question, Taylor put up both hands, palms out, saying, "It's illegal, I know, but if you're an American with cash, it's no big thing," resuming the story fast, eliding over any mystery. "Anyway, I'd run out of money—again—and wound up in this women's and children's hospital. There was a mission there, some group called Light in the Tunnel. Kind of a loose mix of peace groups, do-gooders and people who thought they could make a difference."

"American?"

She shook her head. "Hardly. Washington didn't acknowledge their existence. All their money came from charitable contributions."

"Did they?"

"Did they what?"

"Make a difference?"

Taylor Shepard leaned back in the sofa. Kevin could almost see the 15-year-old newsreel flicker in her mind. Expressions bounced around on her face like the ball on a roulette wheel—going from hurt to angry to troubled to betrayed—before settling on what seemed to be nothing more than loss. "You have to understand what it was like," she said, closing her eyes, the empty look giving way to exhaustion.

"What?"

"The hospital. The children. The, the, the…" Groping for words, eyes still shut. "The whole tragedy of it all."

"Of what?"

"El Ashwa."

As if responding to a hypnotist's cue, the pouch beneath Kevin Columbus's right eye—a gift from exhaustion, nerves and a lack of sleep—began to twitch. He heard himself repeat El Ashwa, and watched as Taylor caught his gaze, and held it. "That's where I met Raymond Trotter. In Arabaq."

For the next half hour, she spoke almost non-stop, discussing her brief affair with a committed, idealistic American doctor who sounded like he'd be played by George Clooney in the movie version. It was full of romance, the story of a man who rescued children from the jaws of death and stood up for the women who birthed them—sometimes in the face of his own execution. And, like the best popular cinema, it had an ending both happy and sad, with Raymond Trotter, M.D., finally becoming overwhelmed by the horror of it all, and having to choose between a life of never-ending anguish or his own sanity. He went for sanity, and the film faded out with Raymond in a beat-up Chevy

Impala, driving off into the desert alone, while Taylor stood crying at the outskirts of town wondering where she would go next.

After she'd finished, Taylor looked awful. In the time it had taken to tell the story, her eyes seemed to burrow back into her face. Dark crescent moons underlined both. Her mouth, once glistening with lip gloss, now seemed pale, dull. The strong shoulders—swimmer's shoulders, Kevin thought when he first saw her—had shrunken into her body. Memory had transformed this woman, who seemed so tough and confident and above it all, into One Of Us, a real person, full of frail hopes gone bad and dreams unrealized.

Kevin got off the floor and sat beside her. Without hesitation, she leaned her head against his. They sat back in the sofa for several minutes, saying nothing, before Taylor broke a silence that was more sad than anything else. "I've been lost ever since then, Kevin." Not looking at him. "I've never had a boyfriend. Never even been close to marriage. Lots of casual affairs, older men mostly, which I'm sure the psychiatrists would say stemmed from my search for a father figure and a constant craving for attention." A tiny laugh, full of self-awareness but little else. "I guess that's why I want this story so badly," she went on. "The Worth story."

"For the attention?" Kevin asked, not even thinking.

She punched him lightly. "No, you fool, not for the attention. For the validation."

"The validation of what?"

"Me. You go through life with a dream, you know. Goals. Ambition. And no matter how good you are or think you are, there's always this nagging little squeaky voice in the back of your head, asking, Are you the kind of person who has what it takes to do what has to be done?" She scrunched her shoulders. "I'd sort of like to know the answer, see who I really am, and I think breaking this story will do it."

"I understand." Thinking not about breaking stories, though, but about a stack of cash, 10K, and what deep secret it might first expose and then validate about him.

At last, she turned to him, and their eyes took in each other, and they both knew at that precise moment of connection where the rest of the night was going. "Do you?" she asked, less a question than a plea.

Kevin nodded. Then Taylor Shepard smiled and leaned into him a little more tightly, said it was late, she was tired and didn't have a place to sleep that night. He smiled back and told her he thought something could be arranged, which she said was good, because that's what she wanted.

And Kevin, just as lost and incomplete, held her tightly, saying over and over that everything was going to be okay, just looking forward to the next few hours with her, not caring at that moment if there was an ounce of honesty in anything she'd said. Which was exactly what Taylor Shepard had counted on when shaping a personal history that, while not entirely false, was built upon the truest of lies.

Chapter 18

Arabaq, 1985

The River Thikra lived up to its name. The color and consistency of mud, it was streaked with oil and clotted with human waste. "Not to worry," the water taxi driver said in accented English he'd explained earlier was learned at a time when his fares were rich Americans off on a Persian adventure. "It is cleaner than it looks." For effect, he reached a cupped hand into the abyss and scooped up a handful of the Thikra, drinking it eagerly. A few brownish drops trickled onto his white shirt, joining the yellow and red stains that were already there. If he noticed, he didn't let on. "See?" he smiled, wiping his mouth on the sleeve of his black suit coat. "Clean."

Taylor Shepard held a red bandana over her mouth and nose, trying desperately not to vomit, roasting in the dense, stifling heat, her own perspiration streaking the denim shirt and khaki shorts that were the wanderer's standard uniform.

There had been stories about El Ashwa. She'd heard them everywhere. Syria. Egypt. Jordan. Israel. But nothing had prepared her for the disaster that the city had become since General Azid had overthrown the Royal Family five years earlier and assumed control of this once prosperous nation.

Along the riverbanks, rows and rows of squat, dilapidated buildings the color of rotten pumpkins stood silently. Not one had a full set of unbroken windows. Large crevices spread like vines over most, and about every third structure seemed to be missing one corner, as if it had been sanded off by some force of nature, Human or Mother. There were a handful of balconies still in tact; from each hung a banner of the revolution—an image of Azid, dressed like Fidel Castro, beard and all, wearing a black beret and camouflage greens and pointing two bazookas at an American flag.

The water taxi passed under a bridge. "Sign of progress," the driver said proudly, pointing. He was thin, unshaven, with deep-set eyes and worn, beaten skin. "Rebuilt by Azid after revolution." Taylor vaguely remembered that when Azid's troops moved into the city, they blew up all the bridges to prevent anyone from coming or going. Now they'd built them back. Progress.

On the bridge, and the roads that paralleled the river, retching automobiles dry-heaved black exhaust into the air, accounting for the cloud—darker than smog—that hung over El Ashwa. Most of the cars were American made, but she didn't see a model that post-dated about 1970. The ones that sat dead and abandoned at various points along the Thikra banks looked even older.

Especially striking was the lack of anything green. Trees. Grass. Bushes. Shrubs. There were no gardens or lawns. About all that seemed to rise from the earth were tall power poles that had no purpose other than to remind those who cared that there had been a time, not too far gone, when El Ashwa's utility infrastructure was the envy of the region. Now, though, most of the wires were gone, removed by a government concerned less about the fact that residents were stealing them to hang themselves than the negative PR that accompanied a double-digit suicide rate. What lines did exist sagged low from the poles, buried under overgrown clumps of weeds that flourished everywhere, brown and reedlike and tough, the only form of life stubborn enough and stupid enough to give a damn about surviving the reign of General Azid.

The water taxi began to sputter. Its driver jerked the rudder stick left and said, "No problem," even though Taylor knew full well they were either out of fuel or the rig had joined everything else in this godforsaken place and just given up. In a minute, the metallic stutter evolved into a backfire-like pop that ended when the engine—a grease-laden American outboard motor—coughed three wisps of blue-black smoke into the air and died altogether. "No problem," the driver said again, smiling, too eager to please. "Have backup." He produced a long pole from under the tarp beneath Taylor's feet, stood, and began to propel the craft to shore, like he was cruising along the more civilized waterways of Venice.

Five minutes later, they coasted into the bank. Up a short rise was a two-story concrete building, its color striking her as violated white, no more or less ordinary than any other structure she'd seen since entering the Arabaqi capital.

Except for the sounds coming out of the windows.

Low wails and moans, the unmistakable, unintended lament of the near dead.

Safa Adiva Hospital.

"For the innocent and the gentle," the water taxi driver explained by way of translation. Taylor Shepard wondered how anyone who lived this life, in this city, under this regime, could survive as either.

•

The first time Taylor saw Raymond Trotter, he was crying and holding a woman, maybe 30 or so years old, the body limp and lifeless, dead because he had killed her.

Less than an hour earlier, she'd been brought into the hospital by two members of Azid's elite Sovereign Guards. The revolutionary troops had just murdered her son and husband in another purge of unseen but, according to the general, omnipresent spies. They'd forced her to watch the execution. When she asked permission to kiss her son, they beat her with rifle butts and baseball bats. By the time she arrived in the emergency room, which was already choked with the dead and dying, she was pleading with anyone who would listen to kill her. Raymond

Trotter examined her briefly, stopping after what seemed like a perfunctory once-over. What was the point? She wouldn't survive 24 hours. All he could do was hasten the process and ease her agony, which he did by shooting her full of a secret cache of morphine he kept for that purpose alone.

Watching, Taylor Shepard thought he was like some dark angel in a field of fire. Deeply tanned, good-looking in a male model kind of way, he gently laid the woman down on the cracked ER floor, hollered something in Arabic and stood silently as a young man, barely 14 or 15, quickly arrived to put a sheet over the body. Trotter took a fleeting last look, inhaled deeply, shuddered, and went back to work. As he turned, his sea-green eyes caught Taylor's. She smiled shyly. He just shook his head and disappeared down a half-lit hallway.

Not knowing what else to do, she followed. What she witnessed beyond the double doors that opened into the children's wing of the hospital was at once appalling and horrid—a place of immense and ceaseless suffering.

There were no rooms, just a large common space. The paint on the wall had faded to something between institutional green and institutional yellow, and was peeling and cracking and flaking like dry skin. Beds were everywhere, not organized in any fashion—not rows or lines or anything that resembled a plan. Gurneys sat haphazardly in the midst, some containing archaic-looking medical instruments, most not. All that they shared were smears of blood, fresh and dried, that offered silent testimony to the failure and frustration that roamed the ward with such utter contempt. Equipment, all kinds of equipment— Taylor noticed a dozen infant incubators—lay abandoned and unused between the beds and under the gurneys, broken and useless, stripped for parts, dissected and left for dead like a frog in a high school biology class.

A warehouse-sized nightmare.

But nothing compared to the children.

They were packed on bare mattresses, three to a bed. Squirming restlessly. Crying. As Taylor walked through the ward, dazed, their glassy, bulging eyes shouted to her for help. Legs and arms no thicker than matchsticks. Protruding ribs. Sheets tinged permanent brown, the result of chronic diarrhea that was easily treated anywhere else, but here too often amounted to a death sentence.

She counted three doctors. Two nurses. Forty-seven beds. Hundreds of kids. Infinite misery.

"Welcome to the revolution," a Chicago-sounding voice behind her said. It was the only sign of life in the place.

•

When she and Raymond Trotter walked out of the hospital, it was as if they had entered a deep freeze. Not that it had cooled off outside. But that the inside was so hot.

Heading toward a stone slab covered with weeds and a pile of crumbling bricks—"It's what we call a park here in El Ashwa," Trotter explained—the doctor lit a cigarette and inhaled deeply. "I'm always a little worried about smoking in there," he said, dropping down to sit on the edge of what Taylor guessed was, at some point, the foundation of a doctor's office, maybe a medical supply store. Something hospital-related, anyway.

"The children," was all she could think to say.

Trotter laughed darkly, and took another long draw on the cigarette. It was a Marlboro. "This"—exhaling, cutting his hand through the smoke, almost waving at it—"is better for them than anything they're breathing in the ward. What I worry about is blowing the place up." Taylor asked what he meant. "You smell anything strange in there? Anything out of place?" Not looking at her. Gazing out on the wasteland that was El Ashwa.

Taylor thought. "No."

Trotter took off his dull-white coat, revealing a sweat-soaked gray T-shirt, and handed it to her. "Take a whiff." When she did, her head snapped back in revulsion.

"Gasoline?"

"Diesel," he corrected her. "The whole place stinks of diesel. It may be the only humane thing Azid's crowd ever did for us." Taylor's silence finally drew his gaze to her face. "They banned detergent."

"Detergent?"

He nodded. "We have to clean their clothes with diesel. The upside is, we don't smell the shit and decay and fear as much."

"Why did they ban detergent?"

"Who knows? They banned pencils, too. For the lead, one would imagine. And syringes. So we're using this ancient kind of glass syringe, stuff we used in America 20 years ago. And using 'em. And reusing 'em. And reusing 'em again. They're big into recycling here, you understand. That's why we use the goddamned things 100, 125 times before tossing them."

"Isn't that unhealthy?" she asked, realizing all too late just how ridiculous the question was.

"Not here on Mars." He spit out a piece of tobacco, crushed the cigarette butt underfoot, lit another. "You see, here in Mars, there are no drugs. You can fit the hospital's whole pharmacy into an aspirin bottle. Most patients have started bringing their own. I don't know where they get it. I don't ask. All I know is that a dozen of my patients have to share one single micro-dropper of glucose. And all that does is let them live until tomorrow, which all things being equal is a questionable reward. Sometimes I think it is my get-into-hell free pass."

"What do the other doctors think?"

Trotter looked up at her. The sun halved his face into equal parts light and shade. "What other doctors? The Arabaqi doctors who used to work there took a hike when their pay dropped from $800 a month to $4.50.

They make more money downtown in the bazaars, hawking pistachios and cigarettes."

"So there are no doctors?"

His head sagged. "I lose two kids a day. Malnutrition. Dehydration. Diseases that anyplace other than Mars have a near 100 percent rate of . recovery."

"Then why do you stay?"

A crooked smile. A near invisible shake of the head. "Because it's better than losing five kids a day."

"Doctor Trotter!"

He spun to see one of the orderlies—the same boy who had placed the sheet across the dead woman's body earlier—hanging out of a paneless window, gesturing wildly and shouting in Arabic. "Jesus Christ," Trotter said, getting up.

"What is it?"

"A woman, eight months pregnant. The wall of her apartment collapsed when she was sleeping. A piece of wood cut into her belly. She's dead. But they want me to save the baby. Come on. And pray it's not a girl."

Before she could even ask what that meant, he cryptically explained, talking over his shoulder as she followed.

"You want to know what's really nuts about this place? They have laws, religious laws, that require doctors to kill some children at birth. And when you look at this, the life that awaits those kids—and the death—you'd think that any doctor with an ounce of compassion would do it in the name of mercy. But I insist upon saving as many of them as I can. And I'll tell you something else: My day comes, and Azid's thugs come to the hospital, ready to lord over the ceremony, those bastards're gonna have to get through me before taking that child's life."

"What do you mean," she called, trying to keep up, "require you to kill the children?"

Trotter didn't hear her. He had been consumed into the bowels of the inferno.

Three months later, she got her answer.

•

By that time they had become lovers.

She fell for him on so many levels. He was, she once told him, "the truest believer I have ever met," driven not so much by ideology as by humanity. Azid was committing "high crimes against the undeserving," he said, defining the "undeserving" as women and children, the two segments of Arabaq's male-dominated culture who were controlled by everything and everyone except their own free will.

Then there was what he called his "radical feminism," which he explained one night during a drive into the desert—Raymond had a light green Chevrolet, an Impala, that for some reason always had a full tank of gas—just north of the city. Abortion, he told her, was a crime in Arabaq. The punishment was sterilization and imprisonment. "Can you believe that?" he asked. "I mean, illegal is one thing. Hell, there are people in the States who think we should jail every pregnant 16-year-old, and their doctors, for wanting to opt out of motherhood. But here they want to jail you—for life, now, for life!—and oh, by the way, tie your tubes, too. Just in case you escape, I guess, for a week of sport-fucking, which doesn't matter either, because if they catch you, they kill you."

Taylor turned to him, speaking loudly above the Blondie cassette that was cranked up to its full volume. "Isn't that the eye-for-an-eye thing? Like when you steal something, they chop your hand off?"

"Why don't they clip the guy's pecker, then?" He looked at her with a smile that challenged.

This man *was* different, Taylor thought.

"What you have to understand," he continued, eyes cutting back and forth from her to the wide expanse of nothingness before them, "is that during the revolution that dumped the King, *they* were its strength. The women. They were the backbone. They carried rocks and Molotov cocktails and illegal flags and banners—carried them all past the King's soldiers. The troops never touched them. Never." Admiration in his voice. "*They* planned the riots that went on in the streets. *They* were the intelligence gatherers. *They* were the lookouts, and they'd developed their own kind of sign language for warning their men that the King's soldiers were nearby. One told me that when a small company of troops had taken a dozen or so of their brothers and husbands captive, they swept down on them like 'angry lightning'—that's how she described it, 'angry lightning'—and incited a riot that let the men-folk beat it to safety." He smiled. "And did I tell you three of the troops were beaten to death in the melee?"

"By the women?"

Trotter's smiled grew even wider. "Not officially."

"What's that mean?"

"There was never any inquiry. No finding of guilt or blame. See, the King, for all his flaws—and this place was corrupt, man, more corrupt than you could ever imagine, trust me—the King had the good sense not to take on the women here. He knew they were the power, the Lady MacBeths of the veil set, manipulating these poor weak mere males. More than that, though, he knew how to pick his enemies, and he wisely chose not to fight a fight he had no chance of winning."

The equation didn't add up. "If they're so important, the women, I mean, then why—"

"Context," he answered tersely. "You have to understand the context of Azid's rise."

Trotter explained that Arabaq's drift toward the West under the King brought with it an accompanying affinity for the culture—everything from blue jeans to rock music. There was a significant minority who feared that the Arabaqi essence, "Whatever *that* is," was being contaminated. As more and more people began to worry about losing their cultural identity, the significant minority began to grow even more significantly.

A popular colonel in the King's infantry, Fakhir Azid, recognized the opportunity that public fear represented. Quickly and efficiently—"but above all, quietly," Trotter added—he began to build a base of support within the military. He was in many ways the perfect poster child for a return to traditional values. The father of 12 children, all male, he was a deeply religious man for whom devotion to The Almighty was both a way of life and a justification for the manner in which one lived that life. Playing off the public's uneasy sense that there was something inherently evil about the King's dance with the Corrupt Liberal Satan in Washington, Azid became the voice of opposition. Almost overnight, the simmering resent that Arabaqis held for anyone who strayed from the righteous path, "Whatever *that* is," boiled into revolution. During a single seven-hour period in 1980, Azid—to the thunderous cheers of a populace convinced he represented a return of their values and way of life—had overthrown the King, and executed the entire Royal Family.

"Not too long after that," Trotter continued, "the cheering stopped."

With the King's murder came a complete end to all U.S. aid. The flow of food and medicine simply stopped. Oil, the staple of Arabaqi wealth, sat either in the ground or in barrels at refineries whose technology—imported from the West—was quickly outstripped by other nations in the region. National prosperity plummeted. Except, of course, among Azid and the higher-ups of his regime, who accumulated the wealth necessary to purchase designer clothes from Istanbul and high-end automobiles from the German black market. While there was a growing undercurrent of popular despair, it never saw the light. A careful management of public events—"It made Hitler look like a first-year PR student"—maintained the impression that for all the chaos that had descended upon Arabaq, Azid still had the people's will in his back pocket.

What he also had was a basic understanding that the real danger to his regime was not with the men of Arabaq, who he felt could be intimidated and herded like sheep in whatever direction he chose. No, the problem was the women. Azid had seen their strength and commitment firsthand during his own rise. He knew well that if he was going to stay in power, the woman had to be controlled. So he simply started killing them at birth.

"There's a law, an obscure one—never officially enforced under the King—that requires the attending physician to kill a couple's first-born child if it was not a boy," Trotter explained that night, after they'd driven to a sandy rise that overlooked El Ashwa and stopped to take in the smoggy vista.

It was the first time he'd referenced that "law" since the day they'd met. Now, hearing what it meant, what it was designed to do, she was speechless. In the hush, Trotter heard her revulsion.

"They're big on boys here in Arabaq," he said. "The entire culture is built around fathers and sons. Women are bun ovens." A sudden jolt of anger shot through him like electricity, powering down after a moment into what seemed like basic sympathy. "That's the back-to-traditional-values these people got with Fakhir Azid. A 'kill the women first' strategy for his own survival."

The silence that followed—his somewhat pained, hers perversely fascinated—lingered for a moment. Taylor broke it by asking how the government carried out the law.

"You mean," Trotter shot back, looking at her, green eyes blazing like flaming emeralds, "how they *execute* the people's will?"

Her entire body withdrew deeper into the beige vinyl car seat. "I'm sorry. If you don't—"

But he did.

"They send two people, usually. One of them in a senior capacity. Sometimes a member of Azid's inner circle, sometimes a member of his family. Muscle. A thug. The other is a cleric, a magistrate, some kind of religious official, church elder, something." Leaning back, head resting languidly on the back of the seat. "It's surprisingly simple, really. They have this pillow, this *sacred* pillow, which interestingly enough is called the Sameh." He rolled his head toward her, said, "It's an Arab woman's name, means forgiver," and rolled it back. "The religious guy chants something and hands the Sameh to the doctor who delivered the baby." What followed, the measured delivery, managed to somehow twist detachment, amazement and pure hatred into a single narrative:

"The doctor smothers the child. The religious guy says another prayer. The body is smothered in sacred oil and burned in a sacrificial altar at the parents' house of worship. The boys chant. The women avert their eyes."

He turned to look at her again. But when he spoke, it was surprisingly conversational, as if what he had just recounted was the Mideast version of a campfire story, told more to scare the listeners than to enlighten them. "It makes sense, though."

"What?" Shocked, maybe even outraged.

"Killing the woman. Talk to any anti-terrorist guy in Europe, Asia, here. They'll all tell you the same thing. Women are more committed and fearless than men. Less insecure, too. They're not worried about things like status, how the guys look at them, whether they're gonna get laid that night. They don't have the kind of ego that keeps them from taking a risk for something they believe in. A German intelligence officer told me once that the biggest difference of all is that when a man goes through a door, he hesitates, just for an instant, and then shoots. But a woman goes through the door blasting." He lit a cigarette. "If I was Azid, I'd be scared shitless of women. If I was gonna try and take down Azid, you'd be my first recruit. In a heartbeat."

"Me?" Taylor let loose a small, unintended burst of laughter. The thought made her nervous. Made her wonder if she could do it, too.

Raymond Trotter smiled. It was a nice smile. Not wicked or evil. Not the frustrated smile that masked some inner torture he felt during the

18-hour days at the hospital. Not even the angry, cynical smile he often flashed when throwing off disgusted rants about the hypocrisy and cruelty of Azid's revolution. This smile was kind of cock-eyed, prankish. Like a little-boy con artist who wasn't quite good enough to hide his real objectives, but didn't have the insight, not yet, to realize his transparency.

That's how he came across, anyway.

But Raymond Trotter knew what he was doing. Exactly what he was doing.

He kissed her. They made love right there in the Impala, sliding all over the sweat-slicked vinyl seats, both cracking up in mid-motion when Raymond said, "This fucking car," but barely missing a beat. And when they were spent, they rested, and they did it again. And when they'd finished that second time—it was longer and, impossibly, more erotic than the first time—Raymond grabbed her shoulders and kissed her with a passion and fierceness that she'd only seen in movies, the kind where the underground freedom fighter kisses the unknowing peasant girl the night before his biggest operation.

It frightened her, that intensity. But when Raymond stared deeply into her eyes and said, "Welcome to the insanity, little girl, and Viva la Revolution," her fear simply vanished, burned off by a heat more intense than that of a desert night.

●

They came as planned, as he knew they would.

One in an Armani suit. The other in the sanctioned disguise of a holy man.

How they had learned that Raymond Trotter had just delivered an infant girl was beyond him. But they knew.

The suited one—brown-skinned, with thick black hair and a matching moustache, and eyes that were shallow pools of dull indifference—stood silent, fingering a lapel pin on his coat. A scimitar rising from the desert. Another symbol of the revolution.

The cleric, bad skin, long gray beard and a glassy expression that no doubt signaled communion with some higher existence, was arrayed in ceremonial robes, white, holding the pillow.

The Sameh.

Forgiver.

Murderer.

From the moment they arrived, everything stopped for Raymond Trotter. It was the only time he could remember when he didn't hear the suffering, or see the horror, or feel the damnation of the hospital. It was as if someone had turned the sound off in the delivery room—such that it was—and killed all the lights save for those that illuminated him, the thug, the cleric and the mother.

And the child. The little girl. Who, by some miracle, had actually entered this diseased world healthy but was now going to buy the oasis because of a bad blend of primitive culture and deranged politics.

Raymond Trotter stared down at the mother, soaked with the perspiration of her labor, flimsy gown glued to her spare frame, spotted by the blood of life, emotions walking a thin line between reason—what choice did she have, after all?—and rebellion. Trotter didn't have to go too far under that look to see her trying to grasp the craziness that was hammering at her brain: You force me to have this child under penalty of imprisonment, then you murder her because you fear her strength?

That's what he thought, anyway, asking himself, I wonder how you say *Damned if you do, damned if you don't* in Arabic.

A prayer. He heard the cleric saying a prayer. It was in a dialect that Trotter didn't understand—ancient, probably Bendi—but he didn't have to be a linguist to know it meant the end was near.

And then he was holding the pillow. The sacred pillow. The Sameh.

The old guy nodded. Blessing the act. Eyes glazed with rapture.

The Armani thug folded his arms and looked bored. Another day, another murder.

Beneath Trotter, stretched out on the bed, the thinnest of mattresses separating her from the hard metal support coils, child at her breast, the mother looked past the tray of so-called medical instruments—a scalpel, and a needle and thread, literally, that passed for suturing equipment—and gave him something he thought had long ago departed this godforsaken place:

Understanding.

She knew what had to happen.

And when her lips parted slightly in a tiny, unexpected smile, he saw something else that he absolutely believed did not exist in Arabaq:

Forgiveness.

There were no options. He had to do what he had to do.

Trotter returned a smile that, naturally, she mistook for connection.

He held the sacred pillow in both hands. For the hell of it, he bowed. The holy man, puzzled at the gesture, did the same. The thug pulled on one ear and diddled with his moustache.

Trotter turned to the mother. He bowed again, accidentally banging his head against the tray, the metal tray that held the needle and thread—

And the scalpel—

Knocking the stuff onto the cracking, dirty floor, Raymond not caring, reaching down, like it was automatic, retrieving the instruments, the thug and the cleric thinking this was normal, the young man being a doctor, Raymond standing straight again and in the same motion whipping the scalpel across the thug's throat, slicing the carotid artery with the skill of an assassin, then taking the blade like a kitchen knife and plunging it into the holy man's chest one, two, three, four times and more, red-black blood everywhere, gushing from the thug's neck and the cleric's severed heart like one of those useless oil wells out there in the lifeless desert of Arabaq.

The infant, starting to cry.

The mother, holding her face up and into the spewing blood like it was a shower from heaven, almost basking in the life—however temporary, she had to know—that it delivered to the baby girl.

The thug, flat on his back, looking like a blood fountain.

The holy man, not yet dead but on his way, a sucking noise coming from his chest, eyes that just moments ago were lit with false reverence, starting to dim.

And Raymond Trotter, vanishing.

Forever.

•

Taylor Shepard got the news two hours later.

It was Christmas in the West, but just another dry, dusty day in Arabaq. She was in her room at a local boarding house, one that was populated by non-Arabaqis—mostly Europeans and Asians on contract to El Ashwa companies, or the occasional freelance journalist not on a hefty expense account. The place differed from its native counterparts in that it actually had some furniture, a rarity in a city where people sold anything that wasn't nailed down just to pick up a few more of Arabaq's devalued dollars. She and Raymond shared it with two of his friends, French, a man and a woman, Denis and Agathe, kind of mysterious, both of them scholars, experts in Arabaqi culture and tradition, each long-haired and thin and tightly wound, *very* intense. How Raymond managed to pay for this kind of luxury—not just furniture, but a TV!—was a question that ate at her, but she never asked. People did things to survive. It was part of the American genius. Maybe Raymond did cut a corner or two. But every hour he spent in the hospital made up for it tenfold. That much she did know.

Taylor and the two French nationals were sitting at a small square table, eating a turkey dinner, of all things, sipping some black market wine, celebrating the holiday. It was one of three rooms in the apartment, the other two being bedrooms, the beds being nothing more than mattresses. Still, that was a luxury in El Ashwa. So was indoor plumbing, which they also had. Everyone on the floor used the same bathroom, down the hall, for whose relative cleanliness Taylor took responsibility because, she said after one glance, "it looks likes a chemistry experiment." In one corner, facing a high-backed gray upholstered chair, the black and white television set, reception lousy with the only snow El Ashwa would ever see, propagandized loudly in the background.

Noise. They paid no attention.

Until Raymond's picture came on.

An anchorman, who could have been Azid's twin, was holding a photo of "The Imperialist Satan, Doctor Trotter, CIA"—

CIA? Taylor thought, what the—

Which he suddenly tore in half.

The screen image quickly shifted to a scene of thousands of Arabaqis, waving handmade signs, adorned with scimitars. Frenzied, screaming for blood.

Cut to the Royal Palace, the balcony, a weeping Azid. The crowd now silent. The General, enraged through the tears, looking like a wounded animal caught in a trap, flailing, the crowd getting whipped up again.

"What's going on?" Taylor asked. Agathe motioned her to be quiet.

On the television, Azid was waving a scimitar, the real thing, in one hand. In the other, a silver stake.

"That fool," Denis said, in accented English. Taylor thought he was talking about Azid, when in fact it was Raymond Trotter. He turned to Agathe. "It's time."

"Time to what?" Taylor asked, starting to tremble.

"Leave," Agathe said.

Taylor sat alone at the table, stunned, watching the fuzzy picture on TV, while the other two moved quickly, purposefully, throughout the apartment, picking up the essentials, personal items, anything that would betray them, say who they were, where they had come from and where they were going.

It took less than five minutes.

Somewhere in the back of her head, Taylor thought that this whole thing seemed rehearsed. There was a practiced efficiency about it, like they were '60's anti-war radicals on the run from the FBI, with a routine that automatically kicked in when the Feds got too close.

"Get the car," Denis ordered Agathe.

"The guns?" she answered.

"What guns?" Taylor asked.

"The guns your foolish lover should have used," Agathe said, tersely.

"The car," Denis repeated, ending the conversation. Agathe disappeared.

"What guns?" Taylor repeated.

Denis either didn't hear her, or wasn't listening. He was in their bedroom, his and Agathe's. As dazed as she was puzzled, Taylor followed him, thinking she had never, not once, been on the other side of their door, which had always been closed to her. Denis was on his knees, pulling up floorboards that she thought were coming unattached way too easily. "What are you doing?" she half-asked, half-mumbled.

"Get your things. Quickly." Denis did not look at her.

"My things? But—"

"Do you want to die?" Still not looking at her. Focusing on getting the boards off. "Because that is what is going to happen. They are going to come here, and find you, and kill you."

Taylor was too shocked, too disoriented, to say anything but "Why?"

Denis stopped for a moment, exhaled deeply, sounding frustrated, impatient and resigned all at once. "Because they can." Then he reached into the floor and produced what appeared to be a guitar case, long and thin, and two rolled-up rugs. Noticing that she had not moved, he demanded again that she collect anything that anyone could use to identify her.

Although things were going way too fast to comprehend, she seized on the central idea that her life hinged on doing what Denis said. For the next few minutes, she got her clothes, some things from the bathroom, a couple of English mysteries she'd picked up in Cairo, whatever could identify her. Returning to the main room, where the television was still broadcasting shots of maniacal Arabaqis who miraculously were now waving poster-sized headshots of Raymond, Denis was waiting for her. He held the guitar case in one hand, and had the rolled rugs tucked under an arm. In the other was a bedsheet knotted at one end that held all his worldly possessions.

Taylor looked at him, lost. "Can you tell me what's happening?"

"In the car," Denis said, gesturing for her to leave, and turning to do the same.

"No," Taylor said, voice dead and mechanical, like it came from a robot's corpse. "Now."

Denis froze at her refusal, but decided that getting her to come with him, quickly, was more important to his survival than leaving her to Azid's gangsters. "Raymond killed Azid's son," he said, now facing her. "It is the third son the general has lost since the revolution. Today, he told the masses that Raymond Trotter was responsible for all of them. He has ordered all Arabaqis to extract revenge in his name by slicing off Raymond Trotter's head, and delivering it to the Royal Palace, where it will be publicly displayed on the same silver stake that once held the severed head of the King."

Taylor couldn't move.

"If they can't find him," Denis continued, patiently, "they will seek out anyone who was associated with him, and execute them as conspirators. That is me, and Agathe, and you. If we do not leave now, this moment, they will come here for us. You must understand: It is not

Raymond they want, necessarily. It is blood. Ours will do. Now, please, we must go."

"But go where?"

"To Raymond," Denis replied, softening, now sounding almost sad.

She brightened as much as circumstance would allow. "Raymond?" He nodded, and told her to come along. Following as if in a dream, Taylor asked, "Did he do it? Kill the son?"

"Yes," Denis said simply, ushering her down the hall, past the once-hazardous bathroom she had rescued, to a door that opened onto a flight of iron stairs leading down to a back alley, where Agathe waited in the car.

A green Impala.

Raymond's.

For some reason, the thought of Raymond-as-killer did not bother her as much as it should have, as much as it would have if they'd been in a civilized nation ruled by reason. "Did he kill the other two?"

Denis held her by the elbow, negotiating the way down the fire escape and into the Chevy's back seat. "No," he said, climbing into the passenger side and lighting a cigarette as Agathe put the car in drive and guided it slowly, unobtrusively, out of the alley and into the dead bustle of El Ashwa. "Agathe and I did."

With that admission, Taylor finally grasped that something was going on around her, something she knew nothing about, and that Raymond was at or near its center. That recognition generated a fear in her that was so cold it sent everything about Taylor Shepard—voice, expression, body language—into dead neutral. She could only mutter what her mind was asking her: "Are we going to die?"

Denis and Agathe looked at each other at almost the same moment. The woman shook her head, ever so slightly, the nearly imperceptible gesture instructing Denis that this was neither the time nor the place for truth. Agathe's glower was fierce and unremitting. It was the same look he had seen that first day, when all this began. The day he had watched with admiration as she crouched motionless for six hours, waiting for Munir, Azid's oldest son, to walk out of the college class where he was studying economics and into the cross hairs of the rifle that was now wrapped in a cheap rug tucked away in the trunk of the Impala.

"No," Denis said, gently.

"Not yet, anyway," Agathe added, much less gently, turning onto the El Ashwa Highway, the pothole-ridden thoroughfare that paralleled the River Thikra and delivered the damned into or out of the city, the car picking up speed and quickly disappearing into the broad desert emptiness.

Chapter 19

Over the years, Carlton Grigsby's ass had been reamed by the best of them. But he had never in his life taken a pounding as withering as the one now being doled out by his supervisor, Lt. Harry Powell.

"Have you forgotten who's in fucking charge around here, Carl?" Powell screamed, face to face with Grigsby, the detective smelling bad station-house coffee on the El-Tee's breath. "Have you somehow confused one Carlton Grigsby, a mere shitmaggot detective, with The Man In Charge? Huh?" Before Grigsby could get out a single utterance in this purported question-and-answer session, Powell had reloaded and was firing again: "An unauthorized contact with the FBI on an unauthorized case? Christ, what were you thinking?"

"I wasn't, sir." Grigsby said it quickly, needing to get out of the box. He'd learned long ago that when Powell went off the deep end like this, it was best to take the heat fast, apologize, tell him you'd screwed up, hope for the best.

"That's the understatement of the fucking century." Powell got up from the small round quasi-conference table that was at one end of his office. The lieutenant was built like a shotgun shell, hair going to silver rather than gray, with dark eyes that at this moment were painted even darker by his near off-the-leash rage. Dressed in a suit that fit him without fitting him, Grigsby often thought, looking like it didn't belong, like it had more business on a store rack than on the man's muscular frame.

Powell was an ex-Marine. To say he did not appreciate standard operating procedures being circumvented was a bit like saying Kennedy had a small problem with Cuba. "Do you have any idea how many phone calls I got this morning? Do you have the faintest fucking idea?" Before Grigsby could say he didn't, Powell, pacing like a caged killer beast, answered himself. "Seven, Carl. Fucking seven! One from the Bureau in Washington, asking me what the fuck one of my people is doing tracing some goddamned mystery bullet. One from the SAC here asking me what the fuck one of my people is doing tracing the afore-mentioned goddamned mystery bullet. Two—count 'em, Carl, two!—from the Justice Department, asking me…Hey, care to take a guess what they were asking me?"

All he could do was look Powell straight in the eye and answer. "What the fuck one of your people was doing tracing—"

"Shut the fuck up, goddammit!" the lieutenant screamed, circling Grigsby now, suggesting none too subtly the image of a vulture waiting for the soon-to-be roadkill below to expire at last. "Let's see, what's that?"

"Sir?"

"How many calls?"

Grigsby tallied in his head. "Four."

"Four! Christ, that's just the beginning. If that's not goddamned fucking enough, I get one from the fucking chief, one from the deputy chief and one from some asshole in IAD who I don't even fucking know who thinks you're part of some international conspiracy." Powell stopped for a half second to catch his breath. "Are you, Carl? Are you part of some, some, some—foreign assassination bureau?"

Grigsby shook his head, which seemed to stop Powell in mid-stride and draw him back into the detective's face.

"Well, that's something. By God, that's the best fucking news I've had all fucking morning! Because if you were, Carl, if you were mixed up in some half-assed, fucking secret-code-ring kind of deal, I swear to Christ, I would be forced to rip your head off and shit down your throat! Are we clear on this?"

"Crystal." Not taking his eyes from Powell's, not so much as suggesting that this hyper-enraged rant was having any effect other than to point out that he had fucked up beyond all repair.

Powell quit circling, stalked back to his desk and dropped into the ergomatic chair he needed for a bad back, looking exhausted. When he spoke again, it was more out of frustration than anger. "Seven calls, Carl, and I hadn't even taken my morning constitutional. My sphincter is so fucking tight, I won't squeeze out a decent turd for days." He shook his head. "I don't need this."

Grigsby nodded his silent understanding.

"Now get the fuck outta here."

Grigsby stood. One of the things he admired most about Powell was the lieutenant's ability to go thermonuclear one minute, and then act like nothing had happened the next. Despite its intensity, Grigsby knew this latest eruption would pass. At least, he hoped the sudden dismissal signaled it would.

As he reached the door from Powell's office into the squad room, the boss called out. "One last thing, detective."

Grigsby cringed. Here it comes. "Yes, sir?"

"It goes without saying that you're going to terminate this little fishing expedition right here, right now. If not, I will set your heart on fire and piss gasoline all over you. Understand?"

"I do." Relieved, the 'last thing' not being what he'd thought it would be.

"I'm going to follow up with the county boys in Alabama, too, and I'm going to check out every detail of your story. And, Carl, I swear to Christ, if the name Maxie McQueen surfaces even once—once, Carl!— I will personally rip your eyeballs out and skull-fuck you until I get some answers or you die. Either way, Carl, it won't be pretty. I guaran-goddamn-tee you it will not be pretty. Now get the fuck out of my office, and start doing what the good citizens of this city pay you to do."

Grigsby hesitated, just for a second, wondering if it would be wise to let Powell know about his conversation with Richard Addison, and what the FBI agent had told him.

"Why are you still here?" Powell asked, not looking up from the stack of papers he was pretending to pore over.

Probably not too wise at all, he decided, and left.

•

The automated information service informed Kevin his call would be answered in six minutes. The delay gave him a chance to reread—for about the 10th time—the handwritten note he'd found on the nightstand that morning.

"Off doing some research. Can't get back to you fast enough. Last night was terrific, Kevin. So are you." No signature. Just a script-like T.

Last night. Terrific. Kevin. He was hard-pressed to remember ever having heard those words in the same sentence.

She had been something. Almost passive-aggressive in the bed, letting him lead at one moment, sometimes seeming to demand that he control her, and then other times taking on the dominant role, just like that. And she loved to watch. Whatever they did, and there was little that went unsampled, she could not take her eyes off him and whatever the performance of the moment was. She insisted that he do the same, too, even making him keep the light on all night. "I want to look into your soul," she said at one point just before the sun rose, and they were on the second hour of a marathon encore. "I want to know everything about you."

In a weird way, the sex made him even more comfortable with her, the theory being that once you've been naked with someone, warts and all, there weren't too many secrets left. And when he'd finally fallen asleep, 6:13 a.m. by the digital clock on his nightstand, the last thing he remembered was thinking not how much he enjoyed the acrobatics, but how much he enjoyed the woman next to him. It felt good.

"This is Mamie. Can I hepya?" The voice, slightly rushed, brought him back to the moment.

"Uh, yeah." It took a second for his mind to get fully reoriented. "I'm trying to find out if someone was ever issued a Social Security card." He sipped a cup of coffee, leaned against the kitchen counter.

"Why? Are you a business?" Whoa, suddenly hostile.

"No, ma'am."

"Then why do you want to know?"

"I'm looking for a relative." It sounded a little lame, sure, but he'd decided before making the first call not to lead with the truth, no matter who he spoke to, no matter what they asked. He had no purpose behind that particular strategy. It wasn't like anyone knew who he was, had any idea what he was doing, and the last time he checked, giving felonious phone didn't exactly qualify as a crime, federal or otherwise.

"I can tell you if and whether the aforementioned person in question is alive or whether that said person is deceased. But that is all I can tell you."

Man, how they do get official the minute you ask for something. "That's fine."

"First name?"

"Mine?"

"That depends upon whether you are the aforementioned person in question and whether we are attempting to determine whether you are alive or deceased."

Kevin laughed, thinking maybe he'd mispegged ol' Mamie, thinking maybe she had a sense of humor after all, some wit, and maybe this was going to be a little simpler than doing open heart surgery on his own pumper. When ol' Mamie didn't laugh back, didn't respond at all, silent as a tuna fish, he forgot about that fast. "Jonathan."

"Middle?"

"Alan."

"Last?"

"Columbus." Bracing for some stale comeback, 'Columbus, as in 1492, the *Nina*, the *Pinta*, the *Santa Maria*, that Columbus?' being one of the more frequent. Mamie was all business, though, showing no interest in such banter, moving quickly beyond names to dates, as in Of Birth, to which Kevin knowingly answered, "Uh…"

"I need a date of birth. I can't do anything without a date of birth." Running both sentences together. Kevin told her. A moment passed. Then: "No record on the computer."

He waited for some kind of explanation, maybe another batch of questions to help fine-tune the search, or your basic I'm Sorry, some commiseration, empathy, suggestions for a Plan B, something, these were after all his tax dollars at work, right?

Well, yes, but the silence that followed signaled that Mamie thought she'd done what her job description required, which seemed to be provide one answer to one question. When the hush reached 30 seconds, Kevin actually thought she'd hung up on him. "Is anybody there?" he asked, finally, less than enthused.

"The United States Government." Mamie said it proudly.

Hide your wallets and women. "Then can the United States Government tell me if Jonathan Alan Columbus is alive or dead?"

"Not without a Social Security number."

"And you can't tell me if he has one?"

"Everybody has one. This is America."

"But you said he's not on your computer."

"I did say that. Yes."

"So if he's not there—"

"If he's not there, you've made some mistake."

"What kind of mistake?"

"You spelled his name wrong."

"No I didn't." Wondering what Mamie looked like, and whether a meat cleaver in the scalp would improve her appearance.

"Then the date of birth was wrong."

Oh, my mistake, all those years giving him presents on the wrong day. "That's not possible, either."

"Something has to be wrong."

For starters, Mamie, it's you and your allergy to personal assistance. "Why is that?"

"Because if the name is correct, and the date of birth is correct, and there is still no record of the aforementioned person for whom you are looking in my database—"

"Yes?"

"Then according to the United States Government, that person is not now, nor has ever been, recognized by this nation."

●

Maxie had slept about as little as Kevin had. The image of J.J., standing against the hallway light of that picture-perfect house, stayed with her like an unwelcome dinner guest. So when the phone rang just before 9, she was in the grip of a death-sleep that was only into its second hour.

Before she could even say hello: "You care to tell me what you have gotten yourself into?"

"Excuse me?" Not the typical *Excuse me?* that uniquely Maxie thing accompanied by arched brows and a threat that may or may not be intended, but more of a genuine *Why are you calling me and what are you talking about?*

"That bullet you were so interested in."

She got alert fast, sat up in the bed. "Talk to me, Carl. What about it?"

"No. You talk to me, first. I took a beating from Powell this morning, Max. The man bored me two new assholes, and I can feel the shit starting to fly. So before I show you mine, you better show me yours."

Maxie let the obvious line pass. "Powell? How'd he know about the bullet?" Grigsby told her about the phone calls, where they'd come from, and the lieutenant's final warning that as bad as the whole deal seemed to be, it would only get worse if the name Maxie McQueen was attached in any way. "What's he care about me?" she asked.

"He doesn't care about you, Max. He's worried about our, uh, history—"

History? Oh, that's rich—

"—and that I might be using department assets to help in a private investigation."

"That's exactly what you're doing, Carl."

Which was true, though not high in the list of things he wanted to hear just now. "Max, I'm serious. What's going on?"

"I told you, Carl—"

"You told me you were on a missing persons case—"

"Yeah. Which started with my client's sister, who as we speak is deep fried, six feet under. During the course of the investigation, I wanted to see if the accidental death ruling was valid. I found something that might enlighten me to that end, and asked a former colleague for some assistance. You don't want to help me, fine. But I got a client who wants me to follow this thing to the end, and I'm going to do it with or without you. So light me up, Carl, or leave me the hell alone."

Even over the line, Maxie could hear Grigsby mutter Shit under his breath. Ah, sweet victory.

"All right, Max. But listen to me: This is it. No more favors. I'm way too far over the line as it is."

"Welcome to the world, Carl." She didn't say it nicely.

His angry silence told Maxie she'd hit the right button. "Remember I told you the bullet could've either come from a basic hunting rifle or something more exotic?"

Maxie sat up straighter in the bed, unconsciously smoothing out the Charlotte Hornets T-shirt she'd slept in. "Which was it?"

Grisgby paused for a second. She could almost hear him collecting his thoughts. "Max, before we go there—"

"We're already there, Carl. Talk to me. Now."

•

A second cup of coffee didn't do a lot to douse Kevin Columbus's slow burn at Mamie of the United States Government and her Non-Help Line. Neither did the Department of Veterans Affairs' automated answering service, which put him through what felt like 600 options, none of which had anything to do with why he was calling, before he finally started pushing numbers on the key pad, just trying to get a voice that didn't sound like it ran on battery power. It took a couple minutes, accompanied by a personal rant about how dehumanized life had become in the Age of Technology, before a genuine living, breathing, flesh-and-blood service unit came onto the line. Kevin explained, as he had to Mamie, that he was looking for a lost relative.

"Do you have any numbers on him?" the human asked. He had identified himself as Arlen and, will wonders never cease, sounded like blood and not electrons ran through his veins.

"Numbers?" Wishing maybe he'd been a little more prepared for the morning excursion, then thinking What for, that's their job, then thinking about Mamie, and then back again to maybe he should've gotten his act together first.

"Social Security. Service number?" Kevin explained that he'd had no luck with Mamie, asked Arlen how to go about tracking down his father's service number. "It depends. In the mid-1970's, we switched over from service numbers—you remember, from the old World War II movies—the number on the dog tags?" Kevin said he did. "Well, we switched from those to Social Security numbers as identifiers."

He kind of liked Arlen. "I don't have either. I don't have anything."

"Then I have to be honest with you. Without those numbers, it's going to be tough. We could do a name search—provided his name's not something like Brown or Smith or Jones."

"It's Columbus."

Arlen's voice seemed to brighten. "Columbus. That's good. It's not too common. Might have some luck. Has he filed for benefits?"

"He's dead."

Arlen didn't react, help rather than sympathy being his primary duty. "Do you know if he ever filed for benefits?"

"No."

"If he didn't, we wouldn't have the records."

"Can you at least run a name search for me?"

"Sure. Hang on, let me get to that screen." Some clicking in the background. "Okay. You say it's Columbus?" Kevin said yeah, spelled it out. "First name?"

"Jonathan."

"J-O-H—"

"Jonathan. J-O-N."

"J-O-N?"

Going off in his head, thinking Jesus, what am I speaking? Bantu? Then quickly remembering this wasn't Mamie, it was Arlen, and Arlen was one of the good guys. "That's right."

"J-H-O—"

"J-O-N."

"Right. Yeah. Got it." Pause. "Nope."

Kevin felt a slight stabbing pain behind his eyes. "What does that mean?"

"I'm getting an insufficient data screen. Means I need something else."

"Like what?"

"Service number'd be nice."

"How do I get that?"

"I can give you DOD. A federal information line."

Kevin took down the number. "What is it you're telling me here? Is it just that you don't have his records, or that he never filed?"

"What I'm telling you is we have no record he was ever in the military."

Kevin clenched his teeth, not out of anger but to beat back the near overwhelming urge to explain that Jon Columbus had been in the military, and there were boxes of medals and ribbons, and framed certificates, and pictures of B-47s and B-52s and wing portraits to prove it. All he said, though, was: "Anything else you can tell me?"

"Truthfully?"

"Yeah."

"We got no record he was ever alive."

But he was, Kevin pleaded silently. He had to be.

•

"It came from an HK PSG-1, which is a very large instrument," Carl Grigsby explained. "It's 4-feet-long, weighs 18, 20 pounds. Not your standard-issue deer rifle."

"Don't tell me what it's not, Carl. Tell me what it is."

"It's a collector's rifle, Max. A target rifle."

"So it could be used in a hunting-type capacity."

"Could."

"You don't sound convinced."

"Rifle costs 10 grand, Max. I'd be surprised as hell if Ross Perot had one. I'll give you heavy odds there isn't a single South Alabama country boy has one of these things hanging on a rack over the fireplace in the den."

"Why not? It's a sporting rifle. Isn't that what you said? A target rifle that—"

"Yeah. It's a target rifle."

"Then what's the problem? Why's everybody crawling up your butt over a high-end pop gun?"

"Because this particular high-end pop gun is used by people for one purpose."

"Which is?"

"To kill other people."

●

The photos were spread all over the kitchen counter, like pieces of a puzzle that just wouldn't come together. Unlike the others, they were whole, untorn, holding no secrets.

Jonathan Columbus in a flight suit, just after he got back from the Philippines, around 1968. And with his flight crew—Bob Bailey, Larry Wetzel and Ben Benjamin. In Washington, father and son standing in front of the statue of Iwo Jima, the boy saluting, the old man looked down at him, proud. That Little League game, the year before his dad died, when Kevin drilled a line drive over the left-field fence in the first extra inning of the playoffs, winning the championship, leaping into Jon's arms the second he passed home plate, the shot getting published in the base paper. The two of them doing a big band number on the homemade drum kit.

Don't tell me the man did not exist, goddammit! Don't tell me he was never there! I have pictures. I have proof. I have—

"We're sorry. Your call cannot be completed as entered," the recorded message informed him.

"Jesus Christ," Kevin nearly screamed, "is there anything in this world that works anymore?" He was shaking, trying not to punch out the phone unit on the wall, or the wall itself, at least having the presence of mind to recognize that both would lead to a repair bill he could ill afford at the moment. So he hung up, hit the federal information number one more time, carefully pressing each of the 11 numbers on the key pad, making sure he didn't dial it wrong again, if he had done so before, which he doubted seriously. After two rings: "Your call cannot be completed as entered."

"That's just great," he said to the unperceiving recorded voice. "The government has a multi-purpose, universal, Holy BatBase directory that promises to answer every one of my questions, solve all my problems, and it's the wrong goddamned number!" He stared at the receiver. "With that kind of performance, you ought to run for office. You'd win in a landslide!"

The federal help line wasn't paying any attention.

Kevin chilled for a second, next dialed 0, waited for the operator. When he got a human voice, first try, miracle of miracles, he patiently explained the problem. The woman put him on hold, returned shortly, said only "AT&T," and before Kevin could say so much as Huh? there was another operator asking if she could help him.

Explanation redux.

"I'll dial that number for you. Have a nice day."

Two rings later: "Your call cannot be completed as entered."

Son of a bitch.

Back to 0, another explanation, but at least this one generated a different response or solution or detour or something: "Please dial 1-800-555-1212. That's the 800 information line."

No shit, he thought, punching each button like it was a 98-pound weakling's breast plate.

"Can I help you?"

The voice was overcaffeinated, way too perky, great, just what he needed. "Federal information number, please."

"Oh, I'm sooo sorry. There's no listing for that." Sounding like the non-listing actually caused her pain.

Which, for Kevin, it actually did, though not of the surgical correction type. "I have a number that the government gave me. Can you check that?"

"Have you called it?"

Snap. "No. This is a test of your responsiveness."

"No need to be snarky, sir. I won the customer service award three straight months."

Kevin took a full 10 seconds to calm down, telling himself that a chipper little comeback, something to the effect of Who came in second place, the dead guy? probably wouldn't get him real far. "I'm sorry. I'm just a little frustrated. The runaround has been kind of intense."

"Oh…well…I have just the thing for that." Voice dropping almost to a purr, Kevin thinking, honest to God, she was going to ask him what he was wearing. "Write this down." He halfway expected to hear: One, Nine-Hundred…

But no. It was the 800 repair service line. Kevin asked if whoever answered would take care of him. "If they can't, no one can." He hung up and frowned. The phone company as white knight. Not a comforting thought.

•

"It's an anti-terrorist rifle. Really accurate at 100 to 600 meters."

Maxie flashed back to the interstate, computing in her head the distance from the overpass to the rock. Hundred twenty five yards. Maybe 350, 375 meters. In range. In perfect range.

"You don't miss with this gun," Grigsby continued. "It's got a Hensoldt scope. Six settings. There are people who'll swear it's the most accurate semi-automatic in the world."

She mulled that for a second. "So if a rifle that accurate misses, it means…?"

"That's the point, Max. It doesn't. If that bullet came from this weapon, something threw the shot off—"

It's happening just like it's supposed to, the intelligence from the wire on the woman's phone solid, the vehicle on the way, there, coming over the rise.

Breathing more deeply now, more slowly, getting to the necessary place, the place where the only things that mattered were the gun and the target.

Aiming, becoming one with the rifle, the trigger, the moment—

And at that second, the one second that only instinct can determine is the perfect instant, squeezing the trigger with an easy firmness, feeling the weapon punch ever-so-slightly against—

What the—

"—something that either broke the shooter's concentration—"

"I can't believe that," Maxie said. "I mean, if this person was a pro, they'd have concentration up the wazoo. Wouldn't you think?"

Grigsby agreed. "Maybe something threw a money wrench in the works. Got in the way of the target."

Of course, Maxie thought. Something like—

Where'd that pickup come from?

Trying to stay cool, aiming again, considering what to do, what what what what what—

Hearing the crash, seeing the rolling fireball, not aiming any more, wondering if there was any way the Sharpe woman could have survived, deciding not. Thinking all that setup work, coming out here the past few nights, creating the story of the little redneck country boys free-firing at moving vehicles, all for nothing.

Well, maybe not. The woman was dead, so what did it matter the shot missed? If you get what you want, does the way you got there matter, really?

"It could be some fool with a new toy, Max, which might explain why that bullet came from a tree instead of a body. I can't say for sure. All I can say is that this is not a common weapon. You don't buy it on the street. It is what they give elite units to murder professional killers."

"How many professional killers you think they got in South Alabama, Carl?"

Which Grigsby said brought him to an even more interesting point.

●

Kevin was getting numb as yet another round of robotic voices asked him to choose from yet another set of options that had absolutely no relevance to his inquiry. So he pushed this button and then that one until he got another disembodied command—"Please. Dial. The. Num. Ber. You. Want. To. Re. Port."—the sounds coming out like an oral ransom note, where you cut syllables from whole words and linked them together to create something that in the current climate passed for communication.

He did as instructed, and seconds later was informed that MCI did not maintain the number in question, but that U.S. Sprint did, quickly giving up that number, which Kevin wrote down and called, and damned if he didn't get a real voice from a real woman after just one ring.

A disinterested voice, and a bit nasal, but so what? It listened to his brief explanation, promised to be back in a moment, kept the promise, and promptly informed him the number was no longer in service. She must have heard the sudden rush of anger that blew out of his mouth, because she said, sweetly, "But you might want to try this one."

"This one" was, indeed, the federal information number, and after being offered touch-tone service on everything from draft status to student loans to IRS help—right, has there ever been a bigger contradiction in terms?—he pushed 0 and an impatient woman came on whose tone suggested total contempt for his intrusion.

"Do you have proof of his passing?" she asked sharply.

"Does a funeral ceremony and a grave at Arlington count?"

"Not officially."

"Then—*officially*—I have no proof."

"Do you have a Social Security number?"

"No."

"Service number?"

"No."

Kevin felt the snowball effect building, sure that her next question would be Do you rent the loft space between your ears? already planning a counterattack when she surprised him with:

"Was he in the military when he passed?"

Goodness. Could help be on the way? "Yes."

"The State Department keeps all records of those who passed while serving the country."

"So I should call State?"

"Was he overseas when he passed?"

"Yes."

"Oh." Her voice screamed Roadblock. "Do you know about when he passed?" Kevin told her the remains were officially recovered in July of 1975. She put him on hold, and when she got back on the line, he could hear the sound of pages turning in the background and her rush-reading something, only picking up "records" and "not at State," which pretty much popped his brief bubble of anticipation. But when she said, "You need to call St. Louis," Kevin heard every word, and for the first time started to sense that he was getting someplace.

●

A paid hitter in the South Alabama woods was tough enough for Maxie to grasp, let alone believe. But it was nothing compared to what Carl Grigsby was about to lay on her.

"Just for the hell of it, Rick Addison ran a computer check. Apparently, there's a central database or something where the Feds can compare striations, see if the same gun was used in multiple crimes. Even Rick told me it was a shot in the dark—"

"So to speak."

Grigsby smiled in spite of himself. "He didn't expect to find any matches. I think it was more of a courtesy than anything else." Then he stopped.

"But he did find something, didn't he?"

"Yeah, Max. He did." Dueling silence followed, Maxie waiting for the bombshell, Grigsby not wanting to drop it for fear of collateral damage.

"Carl?"

He exhaled deeply, the sigh coming out of his mouth like a white flag. "The bullet you sent me matches one that CIA had on file."

"*CIA?*"

"Yeah. He didn't know how it got in the database, who put it there, any of the specifics."

"Just that it was there."

"Yeah. That. And where it came from."

"Where'd it come from, Carl?" Not even waiting for him to give it up, just launching straight-away into the question. He said nothing. "Goddammit, Carl, where'd the bullet come from?"

"Arabaq. It's a country in the Middle—"

"I know what it is."

"They pulled it out of the dictator's son in a hospital there. In the capital city. Place called El Ashwa. We've been at political war with them for 20 years."

This was making less and less sense by the minute. "What the hell is the CIA doing in a hospital in Arabaq?"

"Addison didn't know. But he thought it might be wise if you walked away from this one as fast as your legs'll take you. So do I."

"No can do, Carl. I got a kid to support. Remember?"

She hung up before he could start protesting. In a perfect world, she'd know exactly what to do next. But this wasn't a perfect world, and she didn't have a clue. About what to do. About anything.

Except a direction.

She had a direction. North. From Mobile to someplace that I-65 led to. The question wasn't just Where, it was Why? Why, out of the blue, had Donna Hubbard's sister suddenly climbed into a car, and started an apparently unplanned journey that ended up toasting her? Who was she so hell-bent on going to see?

Good questions. Problem was, only the sister and whoever she was hooking up with had the answers. Maxie thought for a second: How do you find the connection between a dead person and a mystery person? What was it that brought two people, different people, hundreds of miles apart, into the same orbit?

She looked absently around the bedroom, eyes falling only fleetingly on the small wooden corner table that held her makeup and mirror. Cheap-ass wooden cabinet with a 19-inch combo TV-VCR. Framed movie poster, *Jackie Brown*, Pam Grier being one of her favorites. GE phone, something some bank had given her, damn thing never worked, seemed to have a mind—

Of course.

They talked. They must have talked to each other.

She considered how to make whatever needed to happen next happen fast, wondering at the same time if she had any equity at all left with Carl Grigsby, deciding it didn't matter, the sonofabitch would owe her forever.

•

A harried woman took his call at the National Personnel Records Center in St. Louis, and passed him along to someone else the minute she heard Kevin say Air Force. The voice that followed was tranquil; more accurately, tranquilized. Sounded like Carlton Your Doorman on that old TV show, whatever it was.

"I'm just trying to confirm that a long-lost family member did, in fact, serve in the Air Force," Kevin said. The guy told him he'd be happy to help, asked for the name, Social Security number and service number, didn't get all pissy when Kevin told him he didn't have the latter two.

All he said was, "Okay, let me check. Just a minute."

Precisely 60 seconds later he returned, unruffled, still operating at 33 rpm in a 78 world. "I checked under all branches."

He stopped. Kevin jumped into the void: "And?"

"There's no record."

"For the Air Force?"

"And Army, Navy, Marines—any of it."

"What does that mean?"

"It could mean his records were not retired to us."

Kevin shook his head. "No. The people at the Federal Information Center said that since he was killed in action overseas, the records had to be with you."

"Are you sure he was in the service?"

He looked down at the pictures, still spread on the kitchen counter, not really mad now, just getting exhausted, like someone had stuck a needle in him, pulled out all the energy. "Yeah. Positive."

"Not a civilian working for the military?"

Thoughts going beyond the pictures now, to mental snapshots of the Officers' Club, the bullpen, the command post and its blackboards all chalked up with the names of Soviet cities that were going to get atomized when and if The Big One came around. "No. He was in the Air Force. I'm sure of it."

"Not according to the government."

"What does the government say?"

"Let's see. He has no service record. No service number. No Social Security number. Correct?"

Kevin closed his eyes, said it was correct.

"According to the government, this man never existed."

"He never existed officially or unofficially?" Kevin asked, as if the distinction somehow mattered.

"He never existed period."

Chapter 20

Walter Frost had both dreaded and expected the call for 25 years.

"We have a security breach."

While cursing the timing—they were so, so close to reaching the summit after a generation of struggle—he had to admit it was not surprising. That everything had remained secret despite a never-ending stream of post-Watergate media feeding frenzies about this outrage or that was nothing short of a miracle. There had been more than a few occasions over the years when Walter Frost had sat in the morning calm of his townhouse office, sipping coffee and reading about the latest sex scandal—Gary Hart, Bob Packwood, Newt Gingrich, any Kennedy—and given quiet thanks for a press corps that covered only what *it* could understand.

This morning was anything but calm, however.

The initial call had come about 8. It interrupted Frost's morning routine of doing *The Times* and *The Post* crossword puzzles—always in ink, always with a jade green, $450 Aurora rollerball, the matching fountain pen spreading too much on the newsprint—at the kitchenette, still in silk robe and slippers. With the passing of his late wife, he found that the mental challenge, such that it was, enabled him to begin each day with something other than a sense of loss.

Another round of conversations followed that seemed to border on hysteria without actually going over the edge. It took a couple of hours, but Frost finally had settled on the bare bones of what felt like a realistic scenario. With a logical narrative in his own head, he weighed whether this was the time to make a phone call that would, eventually, have to come. He'd contained everything else so far—starting with Devereaux's "insurance" package to the son—and could have contained this if it had remained only with the FBI, and the one agent, Addison. But this was CIA, and even though he still had contacts within the intelligence community, he trusted them even less than he trusted the front page of the paper.

Working from handwritten notes on a pad at his desk, Frost called a secure number and briefly explained what had happened. There was no outburst, no sense of panic. Just a handful of questions that suggested a deeper concern.

"How did this happen?"

Walter Frost said he wasn't entirely sure. "It was late in the operation—"

"How late?"

"Number 11. Four months ago. Our best guess is that it was accidental. Someone with the agency, someone not on the inside, inadvertently entered the records."

It was not the desired response. "There are no inadvertencies in the intelligence world, Walter. You more than anyone else should know that."

"Yes, I do. But I must say that it appears to be the only plausible explanation at the moment."

"I still think it borders dangerously close to the impossible."

Frost drew question marks on his notes with the Aurora. "When you eliminate everything that is possible, all that remains is the impossible."

"And you believe you have eliminated all the possible explanations?"

"Yes."

"So you don't think this was intentional? A move designed to abort the treaty at this late hour?"

That was the real question, Walter Frost knew: Was someone in or out of the government trying to outmaneuver them and, if so, to what end? He'd been running that one over and over in his head from almost the instant he learned of the breach, and had come up empty every time. He was certain no one outside of the "banking committee"—what he called the business people who had supported the operation from the start—and the direct participants knew the details. And if someone else did, someone with any kind of political or electoral or ideological agenda, then there would have been ample opportunities to blow the whistle, especially during the past four years. It hadn't happened. Nothing had happened, in fact, until Devereaux made the last phone call, and that had been addressed quickly, if not 100 percent effectively.

No, he said, there was nothing they knew at this moment to suggest it was anything other than an oversight.

"I assume the record has been purged?"

Frost shook his head. "That's a little beyond my purview."

"Nothing is beyond our power, my friend. Witness the past 25 years." Walter Frost did, saw little but killing and conspiracy. "Hold, please."

The line seemed to go dead. An occasional clicking noise indicated that Frost was on hold. In two or three minutes, the voice returned. "Done."

"Good."

"Now, does the agency in any way know about this agent, what's his name?"

"Addison."

"Are they aware of what he's been doing?" Frost said he had been assured that the only people who knew of the CIA connection—beyond the agency employee who had contacted one of the committee's Shadow Warriors with the information—were Addison and a local detective in Charlotte. "What are we going to do about that, Walter?"

"What do you suggest?" Frost had learned long ago not to offer a suggestion until he knew enough to make the right one. Confident as he was that this was probably just an innocent screw-up, there were still too many unanswered questions.

"This fellow, the one in North Carolina, what do you think he knows?"

"Only what Addison has told him, and we have gone to some length to generate intensive third-party pressure on him and his department. He won't be a problem."

"But Addison will be."

Not a question. A statement. Frost closed his eyes wearily, knowing where this discussion was inevitably headed. "We can't—"

"We have no choice, Walter. We must do what we must do."

"He's on our side. He's an FBI agent, for—"

"And it's his job to die for his country, if that is in the best interests of his country. Now you tell me: Is one more casualty—innocent, I'll grant you, and hopefully the last—is one more casualty in the best interests of America if it in some small way helps us eliminate the greatest threat to humanity in the 21st century?"

Frost wanted to pose the rhetorical question of what could possibly be more threatening to a person than his or her pending death. But he knew better than to ask. Beyond that, he knew that the answer didn't matter. Not when there was this much at stake. The only question he posed was a simple one, grounded only in the moment:

"Do you really think he'll be the last casualty, Bart, innocent or not?"

When Bartholomew Knight did not immediately answer, Frost knew they weren't home yet. Not by a long shot.

•

What is a mother's betrayal?

Meredith Wade sat in her office, nursing a mid-morning orange juice booster, pondering the question again as she stared at the stack of phone messages. Eight in the past hour, all of them saying the caller was Kevin—not Your Son, merely Kevin—on top of the half dozen or so she'd already received. None of them taken, none of them returned.

For years, she had justified the secrets, the deception, her withdrawal, all of it, on a single premise: It was for his own safety. What he didn't know couldn't hurt him. A simple equation, one that reinforced her belief that the years-long conspiracy of silence wasn't a conspiracy at all, but rather the natural course of a mother protecting her child from the evils of life.

Like everything else, though, it was a lie, and in her rare moments of self-awareness, she knew it. The truth was, she had simply caved in to their demands, getting nothing but a life of material comfort in the bargain. One could argue that the others, Kevin's father at the top of the pyramid, had at least made a contribution in some way to the history books. She couldn't deny their impact on the latter half of the 20th century. So what if the dead were still dead, and the living were still lying? The country was still running—either because of them or despite them—its people unaware of the schemes that had been quietly driving events all this time. She'd had no such importance. All she had done, her only part, was supporting the conspiracy. That Kevin had become a good and honorable man, especially in this day and time, was an undeniable accomplishment that salved her guilt without ever healing it. But he was still a child of dishonor. For that, she could never forgive herself.

And now, with Gary's death, Kevin had knowledge that could expose the dishonor. The fact that he was unaware of its power meant nothing. Walter Frost had admitted as much when he called, saying he *believed* Kevin would be safe. But the absence of any guarantees told her that if his continued well-being threatened to unravel 25 years of duplicity— what was it Walter had said, Kevin was in a position to "destroy this government"?—the sonofabitch who gave the order wouldn't think twice about putting her son to death.

Which brought her back, again, to the question:

What is a mother's betrayal? What is it that a mother owes her child?

Tolerance? Understanding? She thought not. Those developed from something else, something deeper.

Values? Morals? Important, certainly. But once again, the product of a higher force.

Strength? Support? By all means, though traits like that were not simply passed along from parent to child. Rather, they grew from a foundation, steeped in something—what in God's name was it?—that determined the child's direction and, by extension, the child's life.

What is a mother's betrayal? she wrote once more in her oddly confident, A-student penmanship.

It wasn't, she decided, what a mother teaches or hands down or gives to a child. No. It was what she withholds.

She stared at the stack of message slips again. Tears followed. She wanted to pick up the phone, call him right there on the spot, tell him everything, pleading with him, crying, It wasn't me who betrayed you! And then, after explaining it all, having to listen in silence when he asked, smart boy that he was, How can people who tell us they love their country and would do anything in their power to provide security for their country, how can they deny that to their own son?

That was it. That was a mother's betrayal.

The denial of love. The denial of security.

Love, she printed in big block letters. Followed by, Security. Slowly, with a growing ferocity, she obliterated both words under the fierce scribbling of a tormented child. Then she picked up the phone. After three rings, a distant but familiar voice said hello.

"Kevin? It's me."

"Who's Gary Devereaux?"

Meredith smiled. Ah, Kevin. Never one to mince words. No pretend grace. No spurious niceties. No contrived small talk, How have you been, Long time no see. Straight to the heart of the matter. "Who?" She lit a cigarette, buying time, trying to decide how much he really did know, and what if anything she should tell him.

"Gary. Devereaux." Speaking the name slowly, almost phonetically, like she was from another country and didn't understand the language.

"I don't know? Who is he? You sound upset?" Dusting off the role of Caring Mother.

"You're damned right, I am." Despite the chill, the mere sound of his voice, silent to her for all these years, had a warming effect. "I've been trying to reach you for days. Didn't you get any of the messages?"

"I was in Sante Fe on a buying trip. We're refurnishing some of the rooms, and—"

"Save it for the critics, Meredith, I don't care. Now who's Gary Devereaux?"

Meredith. Her hands began to tremble. She tried to prevent her voice from doing the same. "I'm afraid I have no idea."

"Then maybe you have some idea why he had something I'd written when I was a kid, and why a cop called me after he killed himself, and why he sent me a picture of you and dad in Switzerland?"

Switzerland. Fear bubbled in the back of Meredith's throat like bile. That old fool, she thought. That crazy old fool. He did send the photograph. What was he *thinking*? "Photograph?"

"You're looking at Dad, but someone else's arm is around you."

Someone else. Meredith held her breath. This was the moment that could well determine whether her son lived or died. Cautiously: "I have no idea who that could be. What did he look like?"

"I don't know. The picture was torn."

Meredith said a silent prayer of thanks. "I see. Well, your father often traveled to Switzerland. The other man was a friend of his, as I recall, a pilot who had been grounded because of high blood pressure."

"So you knew him?"

"Casually, I suppose."

"Funny, five seconds ago, you said you didn't know who it was—"

Goddammit, Meredith, if you're going to lie, at least get your wits about you—

"—and I never said it was a man."

"I just, well, assumed. You said, uh, an arm, his arm, was around—"

"Do I assume he's the one in the other pictures?"

She felt like a fish hook had snagged her throat. "What, uh, what other ones?" No idea where this was going, other than it was someplace bad.

"The box of them I found in storage. You and dad. All torn in the same way."

Despite her growing fear, Meredith managed to summon a spasm of anger at herself. Why hadn't she destroyed them, like she had destroyed everything else? What had *she* been thinking?

"And by the way, the picture in Switzerland, the one of you and dad where you're holding the hand of someone you didn't know, but only casually? It was dated three months after dad died in Vietnam." He stopped for a moment, and she heard him take a deep breath. When he continued, the words were flat, even and grinding with impatient anger. "Now I want you to get your head out of the haze of alcohol, and Quaaludes, and valium, and peyote—whatever happens to be the substance of choice in that New Age hell you call home—and tell me what is going on."

She had to tell him. What is a mother's betrayal?

"Who is Gary Devereaux, and what does he have to do with me?"

Even at a distance, she could tell he was three seconds from detonating, but felt incapable of preventing it. Why had she even called? "Sweetheart, listen—"

"Goddammit," he exploded, so loud and intense she pulled the receiver from her ear. "Tell me what is going on!"

"Kevin, please, don't shout at—"

"Read my lips: I want answers, and if you've got any, now's the time to give 'em up, because I feel like I'm drowning in somebody else's gene pool, and trust me, I'm not going down alone!"

Not going down alone? "What do you mean?"

"There apparently are some larger issues involved here, Meredith." Was that a *threat*? She shifted her chair back, away from the desk, and bent forward at the waist, severely, like someone had knifed her. "Now, is Gary Devereaux my father?"

"No." Rocking back and forth, gripping her midsection, as if trying to keep the vital organs from escaping.

"Who is?"

"Yes."

"Goddammit—"

"Jonathan Alan Columbus, Major, United States Air—"

"Then what's he doing in this picture?"

Tightening the grip on her waist, trying to squeeze out the agony. "Mistake, had to be—"

"The Swiss make clocks, not mistakes."

"I don't—"

His questions started to hit her like slaps in the face, fast and sharp and stinging. "Is Dad alive?"

"Kevin—"

"Because according to the government, he never existed."

That's because the records were purged, she wanted to cry out. "Listen—"

"Is he dead?"

"I—"

"Is he?"

What's a mother's betrayal? Lies that protect or truth that destroys? "Yes."

"How did he die?"

"You know—"

"Tell me again!"

"Plane crash—"

"When?"

"No."

"No, what?"

"Gary—"

"Is that Devereaux in the picture?"

"Yes."

"Is he the other one, the one who was torn off?"

"I don't remember—"

"Then think, goddammit. Think!"

"He's in the picture, yes, that's all—"

"You're not making any sense. This isn't—"

"No, he's not your father, he's—"

"What?"

"Yes, he is."

"Jesus Christ, have you lost your mind?!? This is important, goddammit. Don't betray me! Not again!"

At his final, screaming outburst, she slammed the receiver down, staring at it for a moment, seized with fear and anger and sobs and self-loathing, still bent over and rocking, muttering over and over, "What have I done? What have I done?" not even knowing if she was talking about the call to Kevin or the fiction of a life she had created for him, just wanting it all to go away.

But it didn't go away. Especially the words.

Don't betray me. Not again.

They left a wound, deep and jagged, one that would likely remain fresh for some time, and fester even longer.

They also left something else, something unexpected: Rage.

Who it was targeted at—herself for the lies, the others for the treachery, everyone for what they had all allowed to happen—didn't matter. What mattered was that she suddenly felt something besides the ever-present fear and regret, a purpose almost, whose arrival was hastened by neither alcohol nor drugs. A feeling she had to act on, now, knowing all too well how quickly and easily human resolve could be snuffed out.

She picked up the phone.

Hate me if you must, Kevin. But I won't betray you. Not any more.

She dialed.

•

First the FBI. Then the CIA. Now this.

"Meredith, how nice to hear from you." He was lying. They both knew it. On a good day, a call from Meredith Wade kindled a mix of aggravation, impatience and anxiety in Walter Frost. Today, moments after learning he'd have to orchestrate the elimination of an FBI agent, the sound of her voice made him wonder if he could get a two-for-one deal on the contract.

"I just spoke with my son, Walter. It seems he is attempting to climb to the top of the family tree."

Her voice was shaky, which concerned him more than usual. Meredith's instability had always been a manageable irritant. But with events moving at their current pace, and with this woman possessing enough knowledge to destroy everything they had worked for, the prospect of her choosing this particular moment in history to take a final dive over the edge was not comforting. "What does he know?"

Meredith felt as if she had prepared her entire life for this one moment, and would be judged on her success in pulling it off. "Nothing."

He tried to keep even the slightest hint of anxiety out of his voice, proceeding in the straight-ahead manner of a lawyer questioning a friendly witness. "Did he reference a mailing from Gary?"

"No." Lying almost automatically, silently beating herself up for becoming so good at it.

"Did he reference Gary at all?"

"He asked who he was. A local policeman called him after Gary's, uh…suicide." Letting him know she didn't believe the cover story.

Frost didn't care what she believed, only what she had learned. "You're sure?"

"Yes."

"Did he say anything else of any relevance?"

"No. It was a short conversation. I hung up when he started yelling at me."

That red-flagged Walter Frost. "Are you saying he was irrational?"

"He's just confused."

"Meaning?"

"Meaning he's asking a lot of questions, and not getting any answers."

"Then as I told you, Meredith, you have nothing to worry about."

A small, hesitant laugh. "It's not me, Walter, not me who has to worry." Her wan attempt at taking charge was robbed of any impact by a shivering, uncertain tone. Frost, still home, at his desk, still in his robe and slippers despite the late morning hour, could almost see her lips tremble through a false smile. He wrote *Why Me?* on the legal pad. "But you know that. We both know that." A pause, which hit Frost as being a Should I or Shouldn't I Say It hesitation. Then: "All three of us know that."

He looked at his cup of tea on the desk, cold, and frowned. Better to play along, he decided, leaning back in the leather chair. See where she's going with this. "I understand."

"Do you?" Meredith's voice rose, almost as if it had a will of its own, once more conspiring against any sense of threat or challenge she hoped to communicate.

"Yes."

"Good. That's very good, Walter. Because I want you to know something."

What now? he wondered. "I'm listening, Meredith." Soothing, sounding like a psychiatrist.

"I'm his mother, you know."

He thought he heard a slight sob. "I know that. And I know you've been through a lot in that capacity."

You don't know the half of it, she thought, instantly recalling the conversation, in the early 1960's—

"Meredith, you have to understand—"

"I'm sorry, but he made his bed, as it were. All I'm asking is that he lie in it. With me."

"You know that is not possible."

"Why?"

"It would destroy his future."

"And my future? What about my future?"

"You'll be taken care of."

"Taken care of. How admirable."

"Meredith, we have made a tremendous investment in this man. He is among the best and the brightest of his generation. In a world such as ours, he might well be America's only hope."

"For what, Bart? Only hope for what?"

"For the future."

"Where's the hope for my future? And this child's? This child that everyone says I'm going to have, but no one wants the responsibility for? What about that future?"

"And we appreciate it, more than we can ever express. You have been an exemplary mother, and you should be proud—"

"Oh, spare me the horseshit, Walter." The comeback was so un-Meredith that Frost turned and actually stared at the phone, not believing she had said what she did, or he had heard it.

It was also at that moment he began to think hard about whether—or, better stated, what—to do with this woman. "Meredith, there's no need—"

"Listen to me." A brief silence, which Frost chose not to fill. "Are you listening to me?"

"I am."

"Your platitudes aside, I have been an awful mother. I have lied and deceived. I have knowingly participated in a murder and its cover-up—"

"Meredith. Please." Thanking God she'd had the sense to call on a secure line.

"—and I want you to know that the burden of that treachery is growing heavier with each day, Walter, more so given the current turn of events—"

"Enough!" Secure phone or not, he was not going to engage this woman in a conversation whose implications she couldn't begin to imagine.

"You're wrong about that."

A sudden steeliness in her voice, with an attendant cold that sent chills running up his spine like skittering rats. For the first time, Walter Frost felt she was not to be taken lightly. Whatever abstract risk she had always posed to them now seemed to be slipping toward reality, and fast. "What am I wrong about, Meredith?" Careful not to rattle or alarm her, needing to know what she intended to do before launching a pre-emptive strike.

"That this is enough. Because it's not enough. It will only be enough when I say so."

In a balanced person, the comment would have been intentionally cryptic, leaving Frost mute with questions of underlying meaning. From this woman, however, it just sounded deranged. He bit the inside of his cheek to prevent saying as much. "What do you mean, Meredith? Exactly."

She responded quickly, confidently. "It means that with Gary's death, Kevin's safety is now my responsibility."

"It's a responsibility shared by us all."

"But to me, Walter, to me it is a paramount responsibility. Can you say the same? Can any of you?"

He wanted to tell her that now was a bit late in the process to find her Mother Gene, but thought better of it. "I have told you, Meredith, and I can only repeat what I have said: Your son is in no danger."

"That depends, Walter."

"Depends on what?"

"On how much the truth scares you."

This was a bad time for this woman to be talking about truth, Frost thought, and an even worse time to be coming to her senses. "What are you saying now, Meredith? What's the purpose of this conversation." Trying to infuse a hint of shortness in his tone, send her a message that he had limits, and she was starting to push him in their direction.

"The purpose, Walter, is to say that *I've* had enough."

"Enough of what?" Snappish, but attentive. Very attentive. He sat up in the chair, started doodling once again on the yellow legal pad.

"Everything."

Frost considered his next words with prudence. It was clear she had not absorbed the nuance in his voice, hadn't gotten the message. Part of him said turn up the heat, and wait for the woman to come apart, like she had done every other time—and there had been many of them, too many to recount—in the past. But another part said that this born-again strength she seemed to be exhibiting posed a genuine risk, and that the wiser course was to tread lightly. It was a 51-49 call, the majority switching from one position to the other with every passing second. Either way, Frost didn't like the numbers. "What do you want?" he asked, finally, thinking at minimum that if he could get inside her head, maybe he could find some mind map that would lead him to a solution for this little crisis.

"I want a guarantee."

"I told you, Meredith. Kevin is—"

"Not from you, Walter." Frost considered the comment, knowing full well what she meant, puzzling over how real the implied threat actually was. "You took my husband from me," she continued, "and I swear to God, if you—any of you!—take my son, there will be no more secrets."

All right, Frost thought, the threat is on the table. That was a first step. "Meredith, do you honestly think—"

"Don't insult my intelligence, Walter. I believe you people are capable of anything."

Serious, he jotted down on the legal pad. "So you're saying—"

"What I am saying, Walter, is this: Kevin's safety for your treaty."

For one of the few times in his life, Walter Frost was caught off guard. Did this pill-popping woman, this accidental parent, actually think she had the power to determine how his government operated? *His* government? "Excuse me?"

"That's the guarantee I want. Oh, and Walter—"

Very real, he wrote, as in, This has gone way past being a minor annoyance. It was a real threat. Very real.

"—and I want that guarantee to come from his father."

Under normal circumstances, Walter Frost would have reminded this disturbed, troubled woman that Kevin Columbus's father was dead, explaining in soothing tones that the man was yet another casualty in a war whose searing pain had yet to totally release the nation from its grip. He would have tried to give her solace, and empathy, showing that he understood her sense of loss. He would have even suggested ways to help her cope, referring gently to her delusions, suggesting that there were professionals trained to work with people whose inability to forget the past and its demons made the present an intolerable psychological hell.

But no. These circumstances were anything but normal, and they compelled a response that went beyond his traditional boiler-plate concern. That much was clear. So while he could buy himself a little time with a simple promise, Walter Frost knew full well it was a temporary fix, a Band-Aid that would come unstuck the next time she came unglued. He needed something longer-term, permanent, and he'd be damned if this woman was ever again going to blackmail him with her feelings of guilt and maternal inadequacy.

"I'll take care of it," he said.

When she thanked him, he detected an almost instant relief in her voice, as if she felt they had gone eyeball to eyeball, and the famed and feared Walter Frost had blinked.

Which was complete folly. Walter Frost hadn't risen to absolute power by earning a B when someone engaged him in a political test of wills. He'd done it because he was better at the game than anyone alive, and had no rival in the business of shaping strategies that protected the concerns of those people whose continued standing profited him.

Meredith Wade was not among those people. That made the strategy easy, reducing it to an approach even simpler than the false promise he'd served up just moments before:

Get her, he wrote on the legal pad, adding pointedly, in all capital letters, underlined three times:

Now.

●

After his mother broke the connection, Kevin had thrown the phone halfway out of the kitchen, nearly jerking its wire from the wall, thinking Goddammit, if she would stay off the fucking drugs and depressants and liquor, maybe she could reach back through the mist that's filled her head and heart, come up with something that resembled a straight answer. Who knows, maybe she'd even remember, just for a second, that she was—surprise!—his mother, and that the least she could do after all these years was bore a hole or two into the wall that separated them, you know, see if some honesty broke through.

Not likely. After a lifetime of "maybes" with this woman—maybe she forgot to tell me about remarrying, maybe she forgot to drop me a note about moving, maybe she this, maybe she that—he'd gotten off that bus. The hand-scrawling had been on the wall when she didn't even keep the family name, Columbus, just lopping it right off, went back to being a Whitney and then taking on Wade, new husband's name, how truly fucked was that, anyway? So forget about her. He'd made the call, which he had to do, combat duty, and it was done, over, and realistically speaking, if he'd expected any insight from her, a woman who had the emotional depth of a mirror image, well, it was welcome to playland, kiddo. From this point on, he was going to do this his way, not depend on anyone else, take it all step by step, fact by fact, no more of this scatter-gunning around. Play the cards he had, or in this case, the photo, Frame 214, head down to see Ted, check out what if anything they'd done with the picture, start digging his way to the bottom of this pit, wherever it went, ignore everything else, focus on solving the damned puzzle, not weeding through the distractions.

Sounded like a strategy.

Kevin took a deep breath then let it go, like he was expelling the black air of Meredith Whitney Wade out of his body, wondering How many times have I done this before, scrubbed thoughts of her from memory, only to have them come back, like a terminal illness that won't go into remission?

Not this time, man. This time it's mondo finito, sayonara to Ms. Whitney Wade Columbus Wacko and her band of demons.

Then the phone rang, Kevin picking it up fast, wishing it was Taylor, needing the sound of her voice, not even slightly happy to hear his plan take a hit at the words, "Kevin, sweetheart? It's your mother," thinking God is there no end to this?

"You must be looking for somebody else," keeping any semblance of life out of his voice, sending her a message, "because I just went through this mommy thing with a crazy old woman a minute ago who said the same thing, and—"

"Stop it!" Firmness in her voice. Uncharacteristic. "Don't let me ever—ever!—hear you suggest that I am not your mother." The sudden intensity shook him. She sounded like someone whose life was on a timer, and things were ticking down fast. It had the effect of gagging his comeback reflex, got him to shut up and listen. "No matter what happens, no matter what you learn about me, or about your father, or"—her voice caught, as if she were gargling glass—"or anybody else, just don't you ever forget that I am your mother!"

He felt strangely like she *was* being a mother, scolding him almost. In his head, a black-and-white image popped up, a reminder of the only time his father ever struck him, for saying "I hate you" to his mother—something about a birthday present he didn't like, him being a brat—recalling he'd never felt worse in his life than at that moment. Not from the welts on his butt, but from the guilt, which was what he was feeling now, and it was pissing him off because this woman surrendered the right to make him feel bad a long time ago, and there were no rain checks.

"Then you listen to me," he began, crisp and cold, trying to put it all behind him, if even for a few seconds. "There was something else in that package from Devereaux." She drew in her breath, and he heard it. "A note."

"What sort of, uh, note?" The firm voice of a moment before giving way to dread.

"It said that what he sent me—the picture, and some negative, I don't know what it is—it said they were going to protect me after he died. And he called me Little Buddy. In the note. Just like Dad did."

At the other end of the line, Kevin could hear his mother's soft, feathery sobs, tempting him to hang up, pretty sure he wasn't going to get anything more out of this conversation. Then, as she had only now gotten into the habit of doing, she surprised him, telling him, almost growling: "Destroy it all, Kevin. The note. The photo. Everything."

"Why?"

"Just do it, sweetie. Don't ask any more questions."

"What good will that do?"

She almost told him it would save his life—the statement threatening to leap from her soul—but said nothing. After a brief silence, she asked: "Do you know that saying, The truth will set you free?"

"Yeah."

"It's a lie."

For the second time in less than 10 minutes, Kevin Columbus's mother hung up on him.

Chapter 21

June 1975

From the moment Richard Francis Worth had directed them to prepare the backgrounder on chemical weapons activity in Arabaq, Walter Frost and Dan Goggins had been at war. They'd gone at it for nearly a month. The senator's administrative assistant calling in every favor he'd accumulated in 30 years of work on The Hill; Frost doing the same, trying to abort the launch of what he feared would rapidly turn into an out-of-control missile. Still, as they neared the day when the report was to be delivered to Worth, Frost had to concede that Goggins had the momentum.

What bothered him most wasn't the fact that he was getting outflanked. After all, this was just the first skirmish in a fight that would, eventually, be determined on another battlefield. He was, in many ways, just a spy. An information-accumulator and conduit. A stalking horse for others who, at the appropriate time, would manipulate this string or that one, and make the nation dance.

No, what bothered him, ate at his brain, was that it was happening at the hands of a power-seeking little weasel like Goggins, a lifelong hack with the spine of a French pastry. The man was a bureaucrat, out only for himself, allergic to any risk that might run The Good Ship Career aground. Larger issues—the fate of the nation among them—were of little concern to people like him. What mattered was where he would be in a year, two years, three years. At least Frost had a more global perspective. Criticize me if you will, he often thought—and many did, many times—but at least I have a vision for America, and it is one that embraces practical realities, and evolves from my ideas, not my ambitions.

That particular conflict—Goggins's pursuit of his own selfish future versus Frost's self-styled pragmatism—was hardly new. It formed the core of their current debate and, indeed, that of their professional relationship. But what set this latest set-to apart from all the others, and puzzled Frost to no end, was the focus with which Goggins was pursuing the assignment.

In years past, the two of them, not necessarily polar opposites but rarely on the same ideological page, had always managed to reach a middle ground on matters that divided them. Their success at compromise was an important factor in Worth's ability to draw from the moderate right and the moderate left. Frost had grown accustomed to that give-and-take—too accustomed, apparently, given Goggins's solo act on uncovering evidence of the Arabaq operation. Even though that one had caught him off-guard, Frost more or less assumed he could clean it up after the fact. That was a special talent of his. In an arena like politics, where sanitizing the truth was critical to a functioning Republic, the skill made him a vital commodity.

For some reason, however, Goggins wasn't playing ball on this one, and his intensity suggested more than just a typical lapdog need to service the boss and survive unscathed. He'd enlisted Frost's support only sporadically, and appeared never to follow up on the committee aide's recommendations. There were no personal briefings. No paper trails. While Frost got periodic updates from his own sources inside the government, they were never complete, often raising as many questions as they answered. That Goggins was getting more and more face time with Worth—alone, in the senator's office—made Frost all the more uncertain of where this was going. And until he had some feel for the destination, he was not going to take this any higher on his ladder of sources.

But the window of opportunity for making that discovery was drawing short, and Frost still didn't know, exactly, what Goggins had discovered. Yes, he knew there was some private sector involvement, and generally what industries they represented. And yes, he knew they were making chemical weapons. The question, though, was did he know who orchestrated the operation, and the degree to which the government—clandestinely—was involved. In the end, that would drive the response. So what Walter Frost needed to do, was trying to do, two days before the briefing with Worth, was buy some time to get the answers he needed.

When the answer came, it was entirely unexpected.

"Why are you fighting us on this, Walter?" Goggins asked over a drink at The Monocle, a legendary hangout for senators, representatives and lobbyists just off Capitol Hill. Frost caught the use of *Us*, which automatically positioned him as *Them*. "He's made up his mind. And even if he hadn't, you know the guy. He's a true believer."

"So am I," Frost said. "And I believe he's wrong."

Goggins snorted. "Right. I want to be there when you have *that* conversation."

"We can avoid *that* conversation, you know. All you have to do is say you've uncovered no evidence so far, that you need more time to—"

"But I have, Walter. It's there. It exists, and I'm not about to tell Worth it doesn't."

Frost shrugged, sipped his double martini. Bombay gin. "Then let me see it, Dan."

"No can do, Walter. You know that. We've been over it—"

"Repeatedly. Yes, I know. But I want you to consider one thing." Goggins took a sip of his own martini, Beefeater, said nothing. "My sources are at least as good as yours"—they were better, and both knew it, but Frost was in no position to gloat—"and they can at least tell you if and where you're off track."

"I'm not."

"How can you be sure?"

Goggins mulled the question longer than seemed necessary, making Frost believe that there was something else at work here, something deeper, something beyond typical ulterior motives. "Let me just say, Walter, that I know what he wants to know, and I have it for him."

Frost frowned and shook his head. But he didn't let up, reverting to some of the arguments he'd been pummeling Goggins with for most of the previous month. "We both recognize the global threat that chemical weapons represent. We both know that the Soviets and their surrogates are using them. We both know, as I told Worth, that history has demonstrated quite clearly the only deterrent to a chemical attack is an effective response capability, and that any nation devoid of such a capability is more likely to be targeted. Will you at least stipulate to that?"

Goggins said nothing. He'd long quit arguing the facts of this case. They had become irrelevant.

"I'll take your silence as assent." Hoping to draw something out of Goggins, getting nothing, continuing anyway. "Given that agreement, don't you have a responsibility—as a senior advisor, and as a public servant—to at least fight for your position? To at least make the people's case?"

"The *people's* case?" Goggins arched an eyebrow. His mouth twisted into a sarcastic grin. "Come on."

Frost took another tack. "You believe in polls, right?"

"Who doesn't?"

"All right. If we took a survey tomorrow of the American people, and asked them if they believed it was important to possess a credible chemical arsenal as a counter-threat to terrorist activities, what do you think they would say?"

"It doesn't matter."

"What do you mean, it doesn't matter? You just said—"

"I said he's made up his mind, so—"

"So, what? You're going to conform the facts to suit his position?"

"That hasn't been necessary so far."

"How do you know? How do you know that what you've collected isn't disinformation, or contaminated, or—"

"It's not."

"So you're going to let this man go out on a limb—"

"He's already out there, Walter," Goggins shot back, his voice sharp and harsh, clearly tiring of being bullied, "and it's not my job to saw that limb off behind him."

"Then what is your job?"

Dan Goggins slammed a fat hand down on the small, square table. "My job is to get him elected, goddammit," he hissed in an angry whisper. "This issue is his ticket, and mine, and I'm not gonna screw it up. For him, or me."

Inside Walter Frost, every sort of warning bell began to beep wildly.

Almost immediately, Goggins realized he'd said too much and began a less-than-strategic retreat. "Walter, it, uh, it…doesn't, uh, matter what I think." He took a shaky sip of the martini, using the opportunity to collect his thoughts. "It doesn't matter what you think. It doesn't matter what the people think." He pulled the plastic toothpick out of his drink, took the cocktail onion off with his teeth, chewed it anxiously. "Because right now, at this moment in time, at this point in history, it only matters what Richard Worth thinks. And what he thinks, I think."

Walter Frost knew that if Dan Goggins could have had anything in the world at that moment, it would be the chance to take back what he had just said. Too late. "Elected to what, Dan?"

Goggins's eyes shut, like he was in pain. "Shit."

"Dan?"

"Nothing." Eyes still closed, as if the solution to this problem was etched behind the lids.

Frost let him stew for a minute before stating the obvious: "He's not up for re-election until 1978. That's three years off. The man's not even raising any money right now." In the pause that followed, Goggins heard the invisible gun at his head cock, which was exactly what Frost intended. "What are you saying, Dan? That he's running for president?"

Buying time, still, Goggins motioned for a waiter and ordered another round. Nothing was said until the drinks were served. Effective interrogations depended upon the patience of the questioner, Frost knew. Guilty people could not stomach silence. It made them think. "I'd appreciate it if you'd give me a pass on this one, Walter," Goggins said, finally. "I'd consider it a personal favor." Not looking at him, more than aware that he was asking the impossible.

"I can find out, Danny." *Danny.* Getting real familiar. A clear sign of superiority. "You know I can. You know I will."

Goggins put his hand over his mouth, as if physically trying to keep the words in. It slid to the chin, which the index finger and thumb began to stroke, trying to give the impression of sagacity, done in by the trickle of sweat making its way south from his left temple. The man was total discomfort in a three-piece suit. "You didn't hear this from me. Are we clear on—"

"Absolutely," Frost answered quickly, not caring that Goggins knew him well enough to realize he'd use the information in whatever way best suited his ends.

Goggins reached over and locked onto Frost's forearm like it was a life jacket. "I mean it, Walter. There's a lot riding on this. For Worth. And for me. Maybe even for you."

Bullshit, Walter Frost thought.

Then he said: "Let's make a deal, Danny."

•

Bartholomew Knight, professor of Middle Eastern Studies, sat still in his Harvard office, listening intently to the pending disaster his acolyte was describing over the line that only the two of them knew was secure.

"The report pretty much has everything, sir. It lists the processes being undertaken in the Arabaq facility, the chemical agents being produced, and the prescribed uses for those agents. It does not take a quantum leap in logic to recognize the true purpose of the plant."

Knight said he understood, and instructed the young man—*young*, of course, being a relative term, as Frost was but 15 years the professor's junior—to continue.

"He also has a list of the companies supporting the operation."

"How did he acquire that information?" Probing, not irritated.

"He said he did the work on his own, but assured me it had been undertaken in a way that would not reveal his true intent, nor the subject of the probe."

"And you believe him?"

"Dan Goggins is an honorable man. Weak, but honorable. Once he began to tell the story, it flooded out. He didn't have time to create a fiction on the fly. He's not that good. So yes, I believe him."

"I see. Do you have any feelings as to how he acquired this information?"

"My gut tells me that with all the shakeups in The Company—Watergate, the investigations, all of that—there are enough people who either share Worth's misguided idealism, or would see this as a way to protect their own interests in the event he's elected."

"Elected. Yes. And therein lies our current problem. You say he is going to *The Times*?"

"That's the discussion at this point, yes."

"What do you think the press will make of these so-called Worth Papers when he takes them to the editors?"

"They are devotees of Senator Worth. I can only assume they'll give the charges a great deal of attention."

"That is probably not in the best interests of any of the concerned parties."

"Except the senator's."

"Whose planned campaign for the presidency will be built on this revelation."

"Yes, sir."

"Men of vision," Knight sighed. "When will they learn?"

"This one never will." Referring to Worth.

"Then what do you propose we do now?" Knight smiled, wondering how his charge would respond to the pop test.

"We have to make sure the meeting never happens, and the report never sees the light of day." A confident response, delivered without hesitation.

"How do you propose accomplishing that?"

"There are only three of us who know of its existence. Four including yourself."

"What about those who wittingly or unwittingly provided intelligence to Mr. Goggins?"

"I'm reasonably confident that a sufficient response will, uh, encourage them to keep their secrets to themselves." Confident *and* cool. Knight remained impressed.

"Define '*sufficient*.'"

There was a time in every intelligence officer's life, Bartholomew Knight knew, when his investment in the cause—whatever issue it was that drove him—was measured along a continuum that separated surprisingly weak and surprisingly strong. He had seen hand-picked men, men of tremendous potential, take the former course to dead-end jobs in areas of low visibility and even lower promise. Conversely, he had witnessed others who on the surface seemed to possess neither courage nor wile, but who took actions so properly severe that it rattled his own faith in his ability to judge people.

This was that moment for Walter Frost.

And after hearing what he had to say, Bartholomew Knight knew that, in this instance anyway, his judgment had been right. Hanging up, he took a moment to reflect upon how lucky he had been not only to spot the man all those years ago, but also to get him placed so well, and so highly, in the Senate. The conversation just ended was partial payment for his faith. The remainder would come when he monitored Frost's plan to a successful completion. That would enable Bart Knight to fulfill the last unfulfilled dream of his shadowy life, and protect his true star pupil, the one for whom Congress would be a mere stopover on the road to far greater things.

•

Richard Worth's eyes marched, long and angry, over every page, as he recited what amounted to a Who's Who of American Commerce.

"Forrester Chemical. Trannsco. Rodale Technologies. J.B. Rodgers Engineering. Grayson Mining. Hydrogcologica Corporation. Excelsior Oil." He paused, looked up at his bow-tied, agitated administrative aide. "My God," he asked Dan Goggins, staring at him with smoldering contempt, "can this be true?"

Goggins shifted in his chair, one of only two places for guests to sit in Worth's hideaway Senate office. Unlike a lot of his colleagues, who took advantage of these unadorned, unmarked rooms for sexual trysts, card games and drinking binges, Worth used his for the purpose officially designed by the Senate—the people's business. It was anything but ornate, assuming the rumpled persona of its occupant. Cramped and cluttered with paperwork of all origins, the 14 by 14 room contained five pieces of what looked liked consignment furniture: A beat-up desk and creaking chair; a long leather sofa, which Worth was at the moment sharing with scattered papers and a week's worth of *The Washington Star*, unread; a straight-backed, official-looking chair, leather as well, that faced the sofa, where Goggins was sitting, and a long, low walnut table between them. Reports, research and official documents were everywhere, sometimes stacked, sometimes not. Against a wall that stood opposite the one door was a sink and mini-refrigerator that doubled as makeshift bookshelves, housing a dozen or so volumes related to Arabaq and its customs.

"Is this true, Dan?" Worth repeated, his tone screaming with unfettered clarity that he did not like to ask twice.

Goggins squirmed again. Walter Frost, standing by the sink, stoic, thought the administrative assistant looked like he had hemorrhoids.

"You, uh, you said to include only those facts we could, uh, prove," Goggins stammered under the senator's searing gaze.

Worth's attention returned to the document. His lips moved ever so slightly as he silently read the remainder of the names on the list. With each entry, his head seemed to shake a little more forcefully, and with good reason. In addition to the seven he had just named, there were 11 others; of the total of 18, more than three-fourths were Fortune 500 companies, marquee names in the global economy.

The senator's gaze shifted to Walter Frost. "Do any of these"—he seemed to search for the appropriate word, one he could spit out—"*institutions* know that this report exists, or that we are aware of their illicit, immoral, corrupt activities?"

Frost wanted to say that it was the institution of Congress—not these patriotic enterprises—that had pursued the illicit, immoral, corrupt policy of eliminating the American chemical weapon counter-threat. That argument, however, had no standing in this room, especially now that this contemporary Caesar had crossed his own political Rubicon. "I have not been made privy to any of the findings, senator."

"To your *knowledge*, then, have any of these companies been made aware of our investigation?"

"I resent the inference, sir."

Dan Goggins began blinking fast, uncontrollably, sinking as deeply into the chair as physics would allow.

"What inference is that?" Worth asked.

"The inference that I would for whatever reason leak this information."

"I never inferred that, Walter." Smiling, liking the idea that he'd pierced Frost's widely admired remoteness. "I think I made that concern quite clear with your near exclusion from the fact-finding process." When Frost surrendered nothing, Worth's look of mean glee shifted to one of sneering mockery, his specialty. "Well, what *do* you know, Walter?" he asked, leaning back on the sofa, the Arabaq report open in his lap, body language saying, Show Me.

"Only what I've been told is in the document."

The senator's focus turned to Goggins, who he knew was the weaker of the two men, the one who would fold under pressure. "Is that true, Dan? Is that all Walter here knows?"

The question hit Goggins like a sucker punch to the jaw, coming out of nowhere, startling him. "I, uh…I mean, we, we, we…worked on this, uh, independently, to, uh, some degree, and uh—"

"And I passed along all my information, senator, per his instructions, to do with as he deemed appropriate. My findings were divided into two categories—what I believed to be true, and what I could not confirm—and included detailed explanations as to why I accepted or doubted their veracity."

Worth's attention worked its way back to Goggins, whose momentary lapse in confidence had melted away in the wake of Frost's unexpected support, despite the fact that no such findings or explanations existed. "Dan?"

"It's just like he said, senator."

"Dan, I want to know just what *you* say because, quite frankly, I never know whether to believe Walter." Worth smiled, smugly, looking from his administrative assistant to the committee aide.

"Then why do you keep me on, senator?" Frost asked. Goggins felt another panic attack coming in.

Worth's conceited smile widened. "Because one of my endless entertainments is wondering from which direction you will come at me from one day to the next. Friend or foe."

"I've never been disloyal to you, senator."

"I didn't say you were. I was just asking, albeit idly, if you were my friend or my foe. Let's see, if this is Thursday, you must be…what? Friend?"

There it was. The bait. Dangling right in front of him.

"Thursday, you say?" Frost answered, easily. "I think you're right, senator. I think Thursdays are Friend days."

Worth let out a comfortable chuckle, and turned to a breathless Dan Goggins. "You can learn a lot from this man," he said, gesturing to Frost. "He has the wisdom and strength not to fall captive to my goading."

Walter Frost smiled, and said nothing. What was the point? This would all be over in a few weeks anyway.

Chapter 22

Kevin stared at the 5-by-7 photograph, speechless, while Ted the tat-tooed stick boy at Pronto Photo reminded him of their previous conversation. "I told you, man. Mud. Mudslide Slim. Muddy Waters. Mudpud—"

"I get your point." Barely looking up, with absolutely no patience.

"Dude." Freak-speak for Chill Out.

"You're telling me this is the best you could do?"

Which appeared to upset Ted's sense of professional pride. "Yo. Dude. The picture sucks, the print sucks. I am not Houdini. I cannot turn a silk ear into a pig's purse."

The car wreck of a malapropism flew past Kevin, who was now more interested in finding a Plan B. "What was it you told me when I came in the first time? Something about computer enhancement?"

The lights in Ted's eyes came up, just as they'd done at a similar point in their conversation the other day. "Yeah. Get a high-res scan. Find somebody who's got the software to clean it up."

"You said your brother could do that?"

Ted's expression went to full-bulb, like he was hearing this for the first time. "Yeah. My bro. He be the man."

It was a thought that Kevin was mumbling to himself—*Ted's bro be his man*, isn't that ultra cool—as he wandered out of the photo shop and dropped onto a concrete bench fronting a parking lot, family sedans and SUVs blazing around, horns blaring, the whole scene just a pace car and checkered flag shy of Indy. Still staring at the picture, the picture staring right back, not giving up a thing, no insight, enlightenment, clues, nothing.

"Looks like hell." A woman, uninvited, had settled onto the bench next to him, sticking her nose into his world. Waiting either for a bus or a handout, he figured, but serving her social responsibility as an art critic in the meantime. She was probably 40, looked 80, wore the grim clothes and expression of the perpetually lost. Her pronouncement having been made clear, she sucked on her teeth, rose from the bench and ambled off, a slight lilt to her walk, doing the another-day-in-paradise shuffle.

He had to admit she was right, though. The picture did look like hell.

Dreadfully out of focus to start with, a mini-portrait of fuzzy, nonexistent detail, taken from an odd perspective. From what he could tell, the photographer was opposite and higher than whatever he was shooting. The image that resulted provided a warped, almost twisting point of view. Kevin could see that the dominant element was the front of a building, maybe an apartment building, maybe offices. Urban, anyway. The two shapes he had seen, the ones that looked like fishermen, were just below the center of the frame. They still looked like they were casting a line, or maybe pointing at something, the one on left aiming and up, the other to the lower right. The second one, the one pointing right, almost looked as if he was playing a trombone, which was ridiculous, which put it in the category of Making As Much Sense As Anything Else at the moment. Above the shapes were two rows of brightly contrasted rectangles, vertical, that he assumed were windows; part of a single row was below them. Other than a shard of darkness along what he assumed was the bare arm of one of the images hanging out the window—the trombone player, right arm extended with the slide—there was nothing special, nothing distinguishing about either figure. They were just shadows.

Occupying the lower left-hand corner, next to the big building, was a smaller structure. Shorter, the top of it coming to a level just above the edge of the photo. There was some kind of signage on top of it, like a billboard, though Kevin couldn't make out what it advertised. Just a rectangle with a series of barely discernible letters on it, for some reason reminding him of all those signs he'd seen, the ones that kept an automated running countdown of how many months, weeks, days, hours, minutes and seconds until the end of the 20th century. To one side of it were three pipes or tubes, air vents most likely, perfectly normal for an inner-city rooftop.

"Hell," a vaguely familiar voice said.

Hovering over him was the same woman who moments ago had offered an identical commentary. "It's all I got," he said, halfway to himself, halfway to her.

"Sounds like a personal problem to me," she said, looking at him hard, making him just a bit uneasy. "Get a life."

"I had one," he heard himself say.

"Didn't we all?" With a face that was erased of expression, she gave him a final look and wandered off once more. As she drifted into the parking lot, he heard her mutter "Hell" again, wondering whether she was confirming her impression of the picture, describing his life or simply making a comment about the world in general. At that point, any one of the three seemed valid.

•

Rollie Merke was gleeful. CABALGUY had come through again, and this one was a mega-biggie:

FBI Connected To Worth Assassination!!!

A Second Magic Bullet? A Second Grassy Knoll?

Wasn't just a headline, either, the sound-bite creation of some kook who'd had one too many Jolt colas. Uh-uh, no way. CABALGUY was The Man, The Postman, and boy had he delivered on this one. Guy had details, the kind of details that said he was well placed, knew what he was talking about. No whiskey-soaked charges that Nancy Reagan and Jack Ruby had been lovers, or purported pictures of Sirhan Sirhan and Mao meeting secretly at Disneyland. None of that. This was the real cyber-deal, the down and dirty, the one true thing. If the guy was a nut job, Merke couldn't tell from reading the email:

"Listen closely. The FBI has in its possession a ballistics test on a bullet that has been connected to the murder of Richard Worth. It was removed from a wooded area in the American South, and has the potential to point investigators in the direction of the senator's real killers. The Bureau is concerned that if this information goes beyond the one agent who sanctioned the test, Richard Addison, the wide-ranging conspiracy could begin to collapse. Do this right and more will follow."

Turning quickly to the keyboard while the email was still fresh in his mind—Merke never printed anything out, not wanting any records that might be stolen by the National Security Agency, not even trusting a shredder, because if they could shred something they could unshred it, too—he began typing away. One of the TV sets in the otherwise dark apartment was broadcasting a press briefing from the State Department on the pending Arabaq treaty, C-SPAN airing it live. Merke paid no attention as he hammered out the latest tale of deceit:

"The rancid stink of governmental conspiracy has risen from the reeking grave of Richard Francis Worth. Your faithful finder of foul facts has learned that Richard Addison, an agent with the Fetid Bureau of Investigation—that's the FBI to you non-stinkmeisters—has in his possession new evidence in the late senator's murder: A magic bullet, retrieved from a grassy knoll somewhere in the South—a link to the infamous grassy knoll in Dallas, and another great unsolved mystery, hmmmmmm?—that the Feebs are trying to put under a six-foot mound of malodorous muck…the better to lie to you, my friends. But fear not! Your loyal prober of putridity will not let them get away with this continuing assault on the national nostrils. Conspirators beware: The garbologist of good is on the case!"

Merke pulled a toothbrush from the pencil holder on his desk—an Oral-B, hard bristles—and started working away as he reread the story. Didn't have to change a word. It was that good. No, it was perfect. This was the one, he thought, that would break the story wide open. The Feds involved in Worth's killing? Man, that made the fake autopsies of JFK look white-bread by comparison, and it was light years better than all that talk about how someone had taken off with the dead president's brain and sold it to Nazi doctors in Bolivia who had frozen it cryogenically for insertion into Hitler's cranial cavity.

Oh, yeah, CABALGUY was the real cyber-deal, he thought again, moving the mouse over the Apply box on the menu, brushing avidly. This one actually did reek of the truth. He clicked once, and sat back to await the outrage that was sure to follow as hundreds, thousands—no, millions!—of unsuspecting Americans learned just how duplicitous their government could really be.

●

In Falls Church, the computers at DDI Industries were programmed to capture, read and assess any Internet item containing 67 different words or phrases.

Anything traveling through cyberspace that included one or more of them was automatically flagged and quarantined. An advanced cookie built into the system—a program that seized information about the source of the material—immediately identified the sender. Wire reports and stories from newspaper web pages were scanned briefly for content and then released. Chat rooms and newsgroups were regularly monitored, and their content analyzed. Anonymous screen identities were attached to living, breathing people and fed into a larger database that coded them according to special interest, with an emphasis on the conspiracy enthusiasts, and their every moment online was electronically watched.

With all of this knowledge, the computer—unencumbered by human unpredictability—made one of three decisions: Allow the item access to the Information Highway. Make sure it got lost in cyber-space. Or redirect it for further action.

CABALGUY knew all 67 words and phrases that triggered the process.

One of them was *Worth*. Another was *Merkey Waters*.

When the self-styled garbologist of good sent his Worth-related reports across the modem, the DDI computers intercepted them within two seconds. Most were thrown back into the e-waters. A few were conveniently erased—remaining on Merke's computer, for his own edification, but visible nowhere else. The others, and there were just a few, were automatically rerouted to a single unit that was rarely in the same place twice. That's where they stayed, to be viewed by one user only.

The equipment that enabled all this to occur was a one-of-a-kind system developed by Rodale Technologies. It cost $22.4 million to design, a sum that shareholders never saw because it was buried under layers of R&D expenditures, and was part of Rodale's contribution to the cause. The others gave money. Rodale gave intelligence, and received a lot of government contracts in return, including a sole source Department of Energy deal that generated seven figures annually and had been doing so for the past few years. But unlike the cash that all the others had given, which had been channeled into a secret fund for the sole purpose of killing more than a dozen people, Rodale hadn't been directly responsible for a single death.

With Rollie Merke's latest "scoop," however, all that was about to change.

Chapter 23

All Richard Addison wanted was a cup of black coffee.

"Can I steam some milk in that for you?" the too-eager child behind the counter asked. He was in the standard green and light brown uniform—matching hat, naturally—with a too-wide smile and an embroidered patch on his shirt that said Cubby. Like the Mouseketeer.

"No, thank you," Addison said. "Black will be fine."

"Cinnamon stick?"

Addison wondered what the world was coming to. You could pollute air and water. An argument could be made that television polluted minds, though Addison wasn't one of those people who believed that good kids watched the evening news and went out and shot up a school district. And he was relatively sure that rock music polluted the senses. But that was the beauty of diversity, the reward of America: Anybody could fuck up anything.

Except coffee.

Coffee was the last pure thing, and one of the true joys of Rick Addison's life. No big secret why. He'd been weaned on it. Unlike a lot of the new FBI pod people, he came up in law enforcement. That mindset didn't change once he got to the Bureau, either. So he didn't squawk about spending a lot of days and nights camped in non-descript cars or vans, or in little rooms listening to tape-recorded conversations, or in nasty hotels with cameras aimed at the sidewalk below, waiting to capture the right guy going into the wrong place. All he asked for, all he ever needed to get through those hours—more gruntwork than glory, he knew and he accepted—was a cup of coffee. Didn't have to be good. Just black.

"Chicory?" Cubbie, who was probably 16 or 17, was holding up something that looked like a miniature tree branch, which he was suggesting be inserted into Rick Addison's cup. The agent had some other options for insertion, but wasn't sure the young man would appreciate them.

"No, thank you."

"I have some new chocolate flavoring that's really awesome."

Christ, this kid was unrelenting. Addison would have loved to stretch his arms just to the point that it would open his dark suit coat, give John-Boy here a glimpse of the shoulder holster and its occupant. Except he was unarmed. "Black'll be fine."

"You're sure?" Still smiling, way too friendly, Addison wondering if the little prick was coming on to him.

Looking around the place—all light-colored wood tables and green leather-topped stools, matching the uniform motif, nobody else there but a pretty blonde girl in a Georgetown Law sweatshirt, poring over a tort book—the FBI agent was thinking he didn't need this crap. Not tonight. Not after four Crown and gingers at a bar up the street. Not from some high school kid in one of those frou-frou coffee places that seemed to multiply like flies on a shit stack. Not after a day like this one.

And it had been a day.

He'd been yanked off a missing persons/kidnap case that had consumed him for most of the past two weeks. Seems the father, a guy he'd met exactly once, for about 10 seconds, not a word passing between them, all of a sudden decided he didn't like Addison. The agent, he was informed upon learning of his removal, reminded the man of a playground bully who used to beat him up and steal his lunch money in grade school. Addison had fought to stay on the case, at one point asking his supervisor, "Who's running this goddamned nuthouse anyway? Us or the inmates?" At which point he was reminded that it might be wise to curb his attitude, things being what they were.

Addison didn't have to ask what *that* meant.

Amazing thing about the Bureau. Take the politicians out of the mix—the director, his cronies, the wannabes, anybody with an agenda—and these people could be as quiet as an offshore banker. But let somebody get his or her ass chewed, and the Hoover Building turned into Gossip Central. So it took just under two minutes or so for word of his major-league ass-chewing on the Grisgby thing to make the rounds, and just slightly longer for the in-house positioning to begin. Friends were friends, and foes were foes, he'd learned from office politics, and they could shift like the weather. Self-interest, on the other hand, was forever.

"Would you like some whipped cream on that?"

Addison stared hard at the kid, noticing for the first time he wore braces, the flesh-colored kind that were almost invisible. "No."

Maybe it was a sign, getting his head handed to him on a platter like that, a sign the time had come to take a hike. His boss hadn't ruled out the possibility of disciplinary action, punching the words "North Da-Fucking-Kota" with purpose, the threat obvious as a Macy's Thanksgiving parade. Here he'd busted his hump for the country and the Bureau for 11 years, and they're racking his balls over a stupid favor he'd done for a onetime friend in the boonies somewhere. Agents did that shit all the time. You kept a favor bank with everybody—cops, doctors, lawyers, locals, legislative staff, the world—because you never knew when withdrawal time might roll around, and when it did, you had to be damned sure there was a balance.

Addison had done it. Carl Grigsby was as asset on his balance sheet, and now they were telling him to close that account. Made no sense to Addison, none at all, that everyone was getting the red ass over some off-the-books ballistics test. Sure, the gun was unusual. And yeah, if they found out about the CIA hit on the computer there'd be even more hell to pay. And in retrospect, he probably should've have run the whole thing up the flagpole first. But Grigsby asked him to hold off for at least a day or two, and Addison said fine, no big thing. He was happy to let Carl do the legwork and besides, what could happen in 48 hours anyway?

"Chocolate sprinkles?"

Which brought Addison back to the moment. "In my coffee?"

"Yes, sir," Cubbie nodded professionally.

"I thought you put chocolate sprinkles on doughnuts."

"We don't carry doughnuts, sir. Not here at Coffee Nation." He reached over the countertop, pointing to a glass display case that contained a tray of what to Addison looked like small breaded bricks. "Would you like to try a biscotti?"

"I'm not eating anything that sounds like a foreign car."

"They're a delight." Beaming.

The agent smiled tightly. "I'm sure they are. But I don't want one. What I want is a cup of coffee. Black coffee. The only thing I want in it is caffeine. Not sprinkles or milk or anything else, although I am not opposed to artificial additives that might cause cancer. I would like it hot. I would like it in a cup. A large cup. A cup I can take with me."

Cubby's expression began with devastation, devolving quickly to condescension, like You Heathen. "It will be a few minutes, sir."

All this was making Rick Addison more and more hostile. "Hold on. This is a coffee shop—"

"Coffee *bar*," Cubbie snapped, leaving out the *thank you very much.*

"—and you're telling me you don't have coffee ready, all the time?"

"Good things come to those who wait." He moved swiftly over to a battery of stainless steel gadgets, pushing a button here, throwing a lever there, muttering, "And at Coffee Nation, our warm beverages are worth it," as if that was some training mantra the staff was supposed to dish out when a customer got irritated because there was no available coffee.

"Where's the head?" he asked. Cubbie stopped, like the question amounted to some big imposition, and jabbed a finger in the direction of a sign that said Restrooms. He returned to what he was doing.

Growing the goddamned beans, Addison thought, pushing open the door into the john.

The front page of the day's *Post* was on the wall over the urinal, framed in a thin plastic protective box. Addison looked at it, wondering who took a pee that lasted long enough to read some arcane story about foreign affairs or politics or government. Washington had inoculated him against what he read in the paper. He'd learned that nothing happens unless someone wants it to happen, and that whoever wants it to happen always has some larger purpose, and it usually has nothing to do with the so-called greater good, whatever that was. No, he truly believed that there was no such thing as spontaneity or fate, not in this town. Everything had a reason, and the only people who knew the reason were the ones with an interest in keeping it quiet. Unless, of course, it was in their interest to leak it. But that was a whole other can of worms.

Rick Addison zipped up, rinsed his hands and looked around for some paper towels. No luck. Dispenser was empty. Typical. "Fuck me," he grumbled, drying off on his pants, wondering if that goofy Gen X Juan Valdez in there had gotten around to brewing his coffee.

He pushed through the door, looked to see where Cubbie was in the process, bracing himself for some more snippy comments, summoning as much patience as he could.

But the kid was nowhere. Literally.

Addison's brain started to pound. He stopped. Cut his narrowing eyes from the counter where the kid should have been, to the front entrance, then back, taking in every detail as he did, looking for whatever it was that made this feel not quite right.

A voice started screaming Get your weapon. Addison automatically reached for a .38 that wasn't there.

"Where's my coffee?" he called. Still looking around, seeing nothing, but knowing something was up, and it wasn't good—

Walking slowly, gingerly even, around to the other side of the counter—

Seeing it then, the trickle of syrup, dark and thick—

Chocolate or cherry, something—

Coming from nowhere, though, no overturned jugs or bottles of stuff—

No containers, no cartons—

Just the body, Cubbie's, which he saw now, halfway against a metal refrigeration unit, bent at the waist, head resting on the floor—

Top of it gone, leaking blood—

"Jesus Christ," Richard Addison half-snarled, wondering what the fuck he'd walked into—

Looking up, trying to see if the shooter had booked—

Staring into a goddamned Makarov of all things, terrorist pistol, Middle East, Western Europe—

Suppressor—

Shit—

Addison saying, "FBI," but not bothering to go for his ID—

The shooter saying, "I know"—

Being the last two words Rick Addison ever heard.

Chapter 24

"Anybody there?"

It was 7 in the morning, and the rest of the world was up and running. This girl should be, too. She banged on the door again, a brass knocker that had seen better days, called the woman's name for the fifth time.

Nothing.

She peered through the peephole, feeling just like that blonde tabloid reporter, trying to get a glimpse, a hint, a clue that might suggest something besides dead, stagnant air lived inside.

Couldn't see a thing.

Holding the glass storm door open wider now, down on her knees, looking through the mail slot, not caring one iota if some nosy neighbor called the cops to report a Peeping Thomasina.

Still nothing.

Wait. A kneecap, partially covered by a simple white cotton nightie, with prints of sheep jumping over fences. She tried to get up fast, maintain some sense of dignity. The door opened too quickly.

"Miss McQueen?" Donna Hubbard seemed genuinely surprised that the woman she'd hired to investigate her sister's death would be conducting this kind of surveillance.

At this point, Maxie didn't much care what Donna or any-damned-body else felt. She'd been at war with Carl Grigsby since yesterday about the friggin' phone records, and while he'd finally given them up 15 minutes ago in the parking lot of an IHOP, he hadn't missed the chance to put her through the ringer—pissing and moaning about how she'd gotten him into deep shit, Right Carl, you wanna talk about deep shit, let's talk about *deep shit*—and she'd be damned if this little woman-child was gonna pass judgment on her, Maxie McQueen, no matter how fat the payday was, so—

Yo, girl, chill.

"I'm sorry to bother you at this hour, Donna, and I apologize for any inconvenience. But this is important." Said it pleasantly, sweet as pie.

Standing at the door, the girl smiled sleepily. "It's no inconvenience, Miss McQueen. And it must be important if you came all the way out here this early." She rubbed her eyes and yawned. "I'm just sorry I made you wait. Please, come in."

Maxie said nothing except "Thank you," and walked into Donna Hubbard's sparse living room, reminding herself that some people were capable of goodness, even in this world.

●

"Whoa, man. This is going to be some mighty adventure."

Mike Farmer, Ted from the photo shop's slightly older brother, stared closely at the picture he'd just called up on the computer screen. Even at 1200 dpi—which was seriously high resolution, probably cost that guy Kevin $50, $80 bucks for the scan—the thing looked like someone had ground dirt clods into it. Hardly any detail at all, just a lot of images that appeared to be something. Buildings, with a couple of blobs in the middle that looked to Mike Farmer like Rorschach tests. That thing in the lower left-hand corner, which Kevin said he thought could be a sign, was kind of interesting. Maybe more different than interesting. But at least it was something to play with.

Which was what Mike Farmer had been doing since about 5 in the a.m., sitting at the desk in his bedroom, parents racked out down the hall, Trevor and Judy resting up for another tough one in the work-a-day world. Playing. That, and earning a hundred bucks from Kevin

Columbus. Well, seventy five bucks, actually, after he kicked back a quarter of the bill to Ted, who insisted on the commission for his referral when the guy said he needed some photo manipulation. If Mike had known the shot was going to be this bad, though, he'd have asked for another hundred.

He leaned into the screen, trying to figure out where to go next. Looking down from above the computer, lit only by the terminal's dull light, was Bill Gates, his posterized image magic-markered with thick nose hair, devil horns and a blackened front tooth. Curtains drawn, making it so dark the *Spawn* poster next to it was just about invisible. So were the ones with Metallica, Danzig, Ozzy, Henry Rollins (whose tattoos were the inspiration for Ted's, but Mike always thought something got lost in translation). Rolled up on his unmade bed—Judy wasn't real big on cleaning his room, with Mike being 24, employed at an alternative record store, not putting his engineering and art dual major to any meaningful use—was a poster of Marilyn Manson that somebody at work had given him. It'd stay that way, too, rolled up, Mike not being real hot over panty-wearing weirdos even if they were married to that chick who was in *Jawbreaker*.

He zoomed in on the Rorschach tests in the lower center of the shot, the close-up just making everything fuzzier. Hit a couple of keys, pulled back, knocking the entire image down to 80 percent of original size. A little better. Then down to 75 percent, which got him some more clarity with the image in the lower left-hand corner, the alleged sign, but collapsed just about everything else into darkness. Trying it at 50, the whole thing just about went to black, so he notched up in 5 percent intervals, searching for the point where he got the best detail and contrast before it all went to mush. At 75, he ticked it up one percent at a time, finally deciding that 78 would be the ideal.

Mike Farmer pulled on his headset, and hit the CD remote, sending Guns 'n' Roses blasting into his brain. He saved the image, cleared the screen, doubled-clicked on a skull-and-crossbones icon of his own creation that said Pirate's Treasure. An image of a schooner bobbing on the bounding main popped up onto the screen, a list of 11 functions along the left side. Mike dropped the cursor to the third one, Photo Manipulation, and clicked the mouse.

"Doctor Farmer to ER, Doctor Farmer to ER," he said to himself, adding: "No need to intubate, Nurse Pamela Lee. We're going straight to surgery."

Frame 214 came to the screen. Doctor Farmer started operating.

•

Donna Hubbard stared again at the printout of phone numbers. They meant nothing to her, hadn't meant anything for the past 10 minutes when she'd been trying to figure out why her sister had made nine calls to area code 615 the day before she died.

"It's Nashville," Maxie explained, again, hoping that the repetition of facts might shake loose something beside lint in Donna's mind, four cups of coffee quickly replacing her patience with a set of nerves that were three steps from high jumping through her skin. "Nashville, Tennessee." Saying *Tennessee* like it was some great clarifier, like there was a Nashville, Oregon, it could be confused with.

"I'm sorry," Donna said, a splash of frustration in her voice, sensing Maxie's annoyance, shaking her head faster than she had before. "It just doesn't mean anything. I've never been there. I don't know anything about it except that's where The Grand Ole Opry is."

A tight wire of a smile came to Maxie's face. "You have no relatives in Tennessee, then?"

Donna looked down at her fuzzy-slippered feet. "Miss McQueen, I may not have any relatives at all."

This was all going down the investigative toilet in a very big way. "I meant—"

"I know what you meant." The girl smiled at her, sleepy, exhausted. "I just don't have any idea why my sister would have called all those people, or why she would have been going to Tennessee."

Maxie got up from the floral-designed sofa—lots of red flowers on it, long, bright red flowers—and asked, "Where's the phone?"

Donna stood as well. "I'm sorry?"

"The phone. I'm going to call these numbers."

"*All* of them?" She looked down at the list as if calling them would be like calling the entire Manhattan phone book. Maxie nodded. "But if we don't have family, or friends, or—"

"Donna, we have to approach this with the assumption that we don't know everything."

"But what if—"

"What if what?"

"I mean, it's kind of early, isn't it?"

Something was bothering the girl. Maxie knew it instantly. The body language, the refusal to meet her gaze, the hesitant voice. If this child had been charged with a crime, and they were sitting in a room at the precinct, Maxie would have put the hammer down on her, just gone full-bore, non-stop, pounding her like a meat patty, just—

"What if she had a secret, Miss McQueen?"

The purity of the question brought Maxie up short. "Did she?"

"I don't know." Hitching her shoulders like an uncertain child.

"What if she did, and that secret was somehow responsible for her death?"

"Is that what you think?" All wide-eyed, genuinely wanting an answer.

"What I think, honey, is that we have no choice but to go down every street."

"My sister was unhappy." The words came out of nowhere, and were so blunt and terse and pent-up that Maxie felt she was the first person to ever hear them.

One eyebrow went north, all this starting to feel not too good. "Unhappy, how?"

Donna wet her lips in a little-girl way, nervous and unsure. "In her marriage."

The only sign of Maxie's rage was an extended clenching of each hand into a tight fist, like she was squeezing an invisible rubber ball. She hated surprises, and if the surprise of the day turned out to be that this was nothing more than some goddamned *domestic*—

"I don't think it had anything to do, you know, with what happened," Donna added quickly, unaware she'd done or said anything to ignite Maxie's afterburners.

The detective rose and stood straight up, rigid, like her erect body was the last bastion of patience, the only thing holding back a rising anger that threatened to pour over this little lost waif and drown her in a mega-dose of Total Maxie. "We'll just see what we see. Now, where's the phone?"

"You're sure this is—"

"The phone, Donna." Her tone saying pretty clearly that enough was enough, somebody had to be in charge, and guess what, child, it ain't you. Donna pointed to a white princess phone that sat on a serving counter separating the kitchen from the dining room. Not cordless, which for some reason didn't surprise Maxie, this girl not striking her as a walker-talker.

She put the printout on the counter and dialed the first number, looking disinterestedly into the kitchen. A big round cookie jar with a cat's face painted on it sat next to a prehistoric Mr. Coffee machine. On top, a grinning ceramic mouse doubled as the handle of the cookie jar, Maxie guessing it was somebody's idea of cute, the mouse being over the cat. But who's got the cookies, rodent? Huh? The fat cat. Anybody wants a cookie, all they got to do is pick your vermin ass off the top, anyway, so what the hell're you smiling at, mousy little son of a—

"Days Inn. Can I help you?"

Maxie hung up.

Back seated on her floral sofa, Donna Hubbard looked over and asked tentatively, "Any luck?"

"Disconnected," she lied. Dialed again.

"Comfort Inn."

And again.

"Hampton Inn."

And again, Roadway Inn, and again, Quality Inn, and again, Ramada Inn, and again and again—

Getting the same answers that kept taking her to the same place—

Thinking Donna Hubbard's sister was killed driving to meet up with some guy she was banging whose name wasn't on the marriage certificate—

Then thinking this gravy train was about to reach its final destination—

And then about what the fees for the job would end up being, adding them up in her head, computing what they'd mean to the court fight, and whatever chance she had of keeping J.J.—

Thinking about all that until the seventh call went through, when whoever was at the other end picked up and said—

"Stones River State Prison"—

And then thinking back to one of the pictures she'd pulled off Felon Find, the criminal ID program, on day one of this journey, Donna and Kevin at her place—

Marveling about how good she was at what she did, and at how fast she could put one and one together—

Marveling even more about how this time, it might even add up to something.

•

The program Mike Farmer was using on Frame 214 actually came from Germany, where some company had come up with a system that let cops give out tickets for traffic violations by mail. It worked like this:

High-speed, 35mm cameras were put inside boxes that were then attached to power poles at intersections where the police thought drivers might not be coming to the legally required full halt. Sensors were hidden in a thin, invisible-to-the-eye wire that stretched across the road, and when they picked up a continuing cruise as opposed to a complete stop, they triggered the camera, which started snapping away, getting shots of the front, side and back of the car. Specially designed software and scanners allowed the cops to click on certain images within the photo—license tag, driver's side window—and get clear close-ups of the plate number and the person behind the wheel.

It performed great in Europe, raising local fine-related revenues and cutting driving incidents in some places by more than 80 percent. So, thanks to a federal highway safety grant, it was exported to the United States for a trial run in California. A buddy of Mike's in Palo Alto worked with the company that fine-tuned the software, making it more compatible with the system used by a small police force outside of San Francisco that would test it. But it smacked a little too much of Big Brotherism to this guy, so he downloaded a trial version of the program on disk and sent it to Mike as a kind of high-tech protest. All Mike had to do was find the serial number—which he did, on a crack software website that was later shut down for illegally providing such things—and everything was good to go.

More into capitalism and entertainment than revolution, Mike Farmer took the program and put it to work, wedding it with a high-end photo enhancement and editing package another friend had pirated for him. This one let him use simple point-and-click tools to do just about anything to any image. Want to change a color? No sweat. Take a thumbnail, blow it up, airbrush a rough spot? Piece of cake. He could make it lighter, darker, sharper, smoother. He could look at it through various kinds of lenses, from fisheyes to telescopic. He could introduce special effects—ripples, wrinkles, blurs, waves, ribbons, smudges, grain.

And when he merged the two programs—the traffic package for its ability to turn sometimes cloudy images into fine detail and then enlarge them, the photo edit package to let him play with the images once he got them—Mike Farmer had a gold mine on his hands. Except he had acquired both programs illegally, which limited the opportunities for mass commercialization. Still, he had a pretty decent black market business going on, mostly from ad agencies whose photo shoots hadn't turned out exactly like the client wanted. Those, and the occasional professional reference from Ted.

Like the guy Kevin, and this piece-of-crap picture.

Mike started the operation with what looked like the front of the building. It was the largest image in the frame, and had the best contrast. Bright façade, plain, vertical rectangles, probably windows. He wouldn't get much from the two Rorschach tests, pointing at whatever they were pointing at, but he'd worry about them later. Same with what Kevin thought was a sign in the lower left-hand side.

He brought the cursor to a top corner of the building and clicked once, enabling him to draw a dotted-line box around the image. On the menu, he hit a command that said Explode, which brought the boxed image full frame on the computer screen. Another command, one that said Modify Contrast, and the makeover began. Beginning at the top, Mike watched as line by line, the image self-adjusted. What had been almost solely black and white now began to show some lighter midrange tones as the adjustment worked its way to the bottom of the screen. The building itself emerged not quite so stark and bright, more like it was tan, he thought. Inside some of those vertical rectangles, which he was now sure were windows, he saw softer, irregular shapes that had to be curtains. No ledges or balconies, anything that suggested somebody lived there, Mike thinking the place was more like a hotel or a boarding house, maybe an office building. Even the Rorschach tests, blobby as they were, got a bit clearer, which was a little like saying the Pacific was an inch shallower.

Satisfied at the first pass, he decided to put this part of the photo through one more run, Clear Correct, deliver some more detail. As it had moments before, the image reconformed itself, as if the computer was peeling away a thin sheen of obscurity line by line. Since the biggest improvement always came with the initial run-through, the second trip didn't reveal as much. Mike did see some fine lines running horizontally and vertically through the building, thinking bricks and that the place had a kind of old industrial feel, not from the so-called New South, more likely the Old North.

He directed the computer to print a copy of the screen image, and moved on to the Rorschach tests.

There were two of them, positioned almost identically. Well, almost identically. Blob No. 1, the one on the left, was pointing or gesturing or aiming or fishing, whatever, almost straight up. The other one, Blob No. 2, was hunched into a kind of ball in the next window, pointing down, off-frame, toward the right corner.

Mike drew another dotted-line box, this one horizontal, around the two blobs, brought it up full screen, ran the contrast program, watched again as the screen image corrected itself, seeing about halfway through that this one was going to be tougher. With the building, the image was larger, and some of the tones were clearly different. But these two really were ink spots. If he was going to get anything at all, he needed to climb deeply into their dark little forms.

Separating the image that was aiming upward, he saved it to another file. Then he opened the Fight The Power Drive program— what his friend had dubbed the German traffic-monitoring software—and moved the saved image into a folder called Peep Show. When he inserted the photo into Peep Show, it reappeared under a maze of horizontal and vertical lines that broke it into a grid of 72 blocks, six across and 12 down.

The major problem with Peep Show, other than when you clicked there was a dancing nude woman rather than an hourglass or timer, how totally non-technical, was that it laid the grid arbitrarily over the photo. So larger images, like a person, could be chopped into more than one block, which was what happened here, almost slicing Blob No. 1 horizontally at the waist and vertically so that the left and right arms were in two different areas.

Where to start, where to start?

There were only two questions that mattered, really: Who was this guy, assuming it was a human, and what was he pointing? What he was pointing *at* was irrelevant because it was totally off the scope.

Mike moved the cursor to the grid that contained what looked to be Blob No. 1's torso, from the waist up, and the left arm. He clicked once. The nudie icon popped up and started shaking grossly exaggerated breasts while the processor went to work analyzing every bit of information contained in the digital scan. As the software made conclusions—this is a nose, this is a mouth, this is a scar over the right eye—it blended that information with a self-contained cyber-dictionary of images to reconstruct the photo with as much detail as possible.

The whole process took about three minutes, long enough for Mike Farmer to pop downstairs, grab some grape juice, stick an old Ramones CD in the player and get back to business.

"Whoa, dude," he said, sitting back down, looking at the vastly clarified image on the screen. "You must be in monster pain."

In fact, the object in the photo looked to be in utter agony.

The cleaned-up section of the frame revealed a somewhat shadowy profile dominated by a large nose and dark horn-rimmed glasses. He—Mike being pretty sure the subject was a guy, girls not being real cool on geek glasses unless they read poetry at wine bars—looked to be wearing a short-sleeved, dark-colored shirt. Not quite black, Mike figured, but a deep primary color, probably red or blue. The head was bent back at the neck and to the left. There was a rough, uneven spot at the front, and above that a gray blur hovered like a light mist. The man's left arm was stretched out and pointed backward, as if he was gesturing to someone standing behind him.

"Pretty friggin' weird," Mike Farmer whispered, starting to wonder just what kind of creepy shit this guy Kevin was into.

He printed the image out, returned to the full frame, and isolated a second grid.

In this one, the man's right arm was extended skyward, like he was making some weird sign to God. But what was really kind of freaky deaky was that the arm looked seriously longer than the other, half again as long or maybe more, as if there was something attached to it, like a stilt. Dark against the light of bare skin, this stilt seemed to begin at the elbow, where it was fatter, and go straight out before narrowing to a tapered point. He tried to zoom in to see if he could get a better look, but it was no go. The close-up turned everything to tiny rectangles of black and white and gray.

Mike added that image to his print stack, and turned to the other Rorschach test. Blob No. 2.

Although he had a pretty self-contained image on the grid—the positioning of the shape put just about all of it in a single box—it only took Mike about five seconds to see that this one would be a wash.

The figure was hunched over, head down and twisted into his arm, almost like he was listening closely to what his right bicep had to say. No face, no chance for a profile, no way to know what the guy looked like except for dark hair, big deal, welcome to the entire population of China. Whatever he was wearing had the same tone as the building, making him blend in almost perfectly against the surroundings, camouflaging him pretty well. Not like Blob No. 1, whose dark shirt had to stand out against everything around and made him as easy to see as a sorority girl at a Black Sabbath concert.

This one had something coming out of his lumpy form, too, but he was in charge of it. Blob No. 1 looked like he was losing his, tossing it in the air or something. But Blob No. 2 was in total control. Truth was, whatever was coming out of him looked strapped on. About the only image of any significance was a mark of some kind on the underside of what Mike assumed was No. 2's right arm, a birthmark, maybe, shaped sort of like an arrow, that ran parallel to the line of whatever it was the guy was holding and pointing.

Mike knew he could spend the next seven years of his life poring over this one, and not get one additional piece of useful information. Just for the hell of it, he isolated the grid image, blew it up 15 percent, printed a copy and returned to the Big Picture.

From the outset, he'd been pretty sure that the only chance for any real detail was going to come out of the sign thing, or whatever it was in the lower left-hand corner of the frame. As bad as the original photo was, the sign looked to be individual light images against a black backdrop, which was good, Peep Show being able to figure out simple contrasts, words or visuals, in its cyber-sleep. Not that it would tell anybody anything, being so far away from the focal action in the shot. But if nothing else, the thing might say something about when the picture was taken, like if it was a promotion for one of those TV shows that used to be so popular they broadcast reruns on The Nostalgia Network.

The grid sliced the sign horizontally, almost in half, putting the top half on one block and the bottom half on another. Mike went for the top half first.

Like he figured, Peep Show didn't have to do any heavy lifting on this one. The program easily read the lighter images against the dark backdrop. In about a minute, Mike's screen showed four numbers, 12:31, which for some strange reason registered, him having no clue why, except he knew immediately what he was looking at:

A time and temperature sign, had to be, no different than thousands of others that could be seen at any location in any city in just about any country, anywhere. So while he may have helped Kevin find out when the picture was taken—12:31 in the afternoon—all he'd managed to do from there was narrow the list of possible sites down to the planet.

Not my problem, he thought, printing that image out.

He went to the other half of the sign, the bottom half. Ran the same drill, got four more images: 86 and a degree sign and an F.

Hot in the city.

That registered as well, there being something about that time and that temperature, together.

He printed that out, too, still trying to figure out what it was about 12:31 and 86 degrees F that made an impression on him, where he had seen it before, what significance it had.

Somewhere in the back of his mind, a second picture came into focus.

The time, the temperature, together like that, on a sign, one on top of the other, just like here, just like—

He suddenly shook, involuntarily, thinking No way, man, that was impossible, crazy, but still gluing the printed-out images together, Pain Man first, Blob No. 1, the guy who looked like someone had just knocked the wind out of his sails, then Clump Dude, Blob No. 2, all balled up like that, something coming out of him like a lollipop stick, arrow mark right next to it, running down the forearm, Mike taking it all in, getting the large view, wondering—

"Whoa," he said, the shiver coming back now, flying up his backbone, like an ice water spinal.

He grabbed the top and bottom shots of the time-temperature sign, put them together, staring long and hard at the collective image, now knowing where he'd seen them, knowing the exact day and time and place the shot had been taken, but worse than that, way worse, knowing what was off the frame, what the blobs were pointing at.

The chill in Mike Farmer's backbone went glacier. He picked up his cell phone, started to dial, dropped the thing like it was on fire, remembering cell phones could be monitored, thinking Fool, you need a hard line.

Cruising slowly, quietly, past Trevor and Judy's snore-filled bedroom—why weren't they up, it was a school day, right?—he went downstairs into the den, grabbed the long-corded telephone, dropped into a green upholstered recliner, sitting straight up, though, not reclining. Punched seven numbers.

Ted answered quickly. "This better be Heather Locklear." Sounding more pissed than sleepy.

"Bro, it's me." Whispering. "We gotta talk. You alone?"

"Why would I be asking about Heather Locklear if I was with somebody?"

Mike let it slide, this being no time for chatter. "This dude you turned me on to. This Kevin guy? How well do you know him?"

"Who?"

"That guy you sent to me with the shitty picture."

"I don't know him at all. What's your prob? Why're you whispering?"

"Shuttup, and I'll tell you."

"Well hurry up, man. HBO's showing the only good movie Keanu Reeves ever made."

"*Devil's Advocate?*"

"*Point Break.* Jeez. So wassssssuuuupppp?" Ted sounding like that beer ad, Mike saying nothing for a long while. "Bro?"

Another few seconds passed before Mike Farmer spoke: "I think he's a criminal."

"That's crazy, man. What crime could some old fart like him pull off? Bootlegging Viagra?" More silence, which made Ted all of a sudden think his brother was shook seriously bad. "Bro? What kinda crime you talking about?"

Mike took a deep breath. "Like the crime of the century."

Chapter 25

The ringing phone jolted Kevin from a weird dream about some faceless guy in a gray fedora and long, wrinkled trenchcoat who had tied Taylor to a chair and was about to kill her. There was an instant when for all its surrealism, the images in his head seemed too true, so much so that when he grabbed the line, he felt an odd mix of terror and relief when Taylor's hyper voice shot over the receiver.

"Where are you?" he nearly screamed. "Are you okay?"

"I'm in Maryland," she said, voice puzzled, thinking What's with the panic attack? "I told you."

Kevin took a gulp of air, got in the moment, remembering the message on his machine—

"Hey, you. It's me. Listen, I'm at the airport. You're not gonna believe what I found out. Remember what I showed you on Merke's web page, about all of this, Devereaux and all, about it having something to do with money? It is. I got into a database that tracks non-governmental organizations and their contributions. I think I can actually prove a connection between money that went to him and Worth's death. I found a guy outside of D.C. who says he knows some stuff, so I'm catching the next flight out. I'll call you when I get there. It may be the middle of the night, so don't get mad."

— tried to focus, hearing the TV in the background, *The Today Show*, Tim Russert talking about how the proposed chemical and biological weapons ban would affect the White House, saying it wouldn't just put the president back in office, it would put him in history.

"Kevin? Are you there?"

"Yeah. Yeah." Groggy, still kind of fuzzed-out, thinking about the dream and what if anything it meant, craving coffee and wondering why he was still dressed.

"What's wrong? You sound like you're on drugs."

Things starting to clear up a bit. "Um, no, I was just, uh, I fell asleep watching TV last night, and—"

"You sound guilty. Are you telling me I go out of town for one night, and you're already shacked up with someone else?"

Her voice was playful—if he'd been thinking straight, he'd have heard her smile—but he wasn't thinking straight, so he did what men do best when confronted by a woman, which was stammer and back-pedal. "No, no, no. I was, uh, you know, like I said, I was sleeping, and the call, the phone, it just—"

"Kevin. I was kidding."

"Oh." Feeling equal parts goofy, stupid and embarrassed—and, oddly, warm, her making the comment about 'another woman' and all, the subtext being that she, Taylor, was The Primary. There was a brief silence, Kevin wanting to say something that communicated his feelings, sensing Taylor wanted to hear it, but the moment melted away. It made him feel a little empty. "So you're in Washington?" he asked, changing gears, trying to sound enthused.

"Maryland. Silver Spring. I was at the public library yesterday—have you ever been there?" He said he hadn't, thinking it was an odd question for some reason. "They have this database you can hook on to. It's a list of NGOs that—"

"NGOs?" He leaned against the kitchen wall, slid down into a seated position on the floor.

"Non-governmental organizations. Sorry. I'm a little wired." There's an understatement, Kevin thought, Taylor talking like a tornado, him figuring that was Reporter Speed. "Anyway, you know what they said during Watergate? They said, Follow the Money. That's what Hal Holbrook said in the movie. Follow the Money."

Hal Holbrook being Deep Throat in *All the President's Men.* "I remember. And did you?"

"You bet your ass." Triumphant. "And guess what I found?" Before he could draw the necessary breath to reply, she answered her own question: "Nothing." The way she said it, the word came out like *Eureka!*

Kevin hesitated for a second, thinking he missed something. "I don't get it."

"This guy in Silver Spring, he manages the database I used at the library, right? So I called him, woke his ass up at about 6 this morning, said I was a freelancer working on this story about Devereaux, more fishing than anything else. Okay? So he tells me, he says, I know things. Just like that. *I. Know. Things.*"

Sounded like an out-take from that movie *JFK* to Kevin, but he wasn't about to boot-heel her enthusiasm. "Like what things?"

"Listen to this." Rustling in the background, Taylor pulling out a spiral-topped notebook, he imagined, flipping through the pages, surfing the highlights of her interview. "In 1980, Devereaux creates Americans for America. It's like an advocacy group or something. But as far as I can tell, it was only him. Nobody else." Kevin said he'd heard of it, recalling the meeting with Thomas Cloud, deciding not to break her rhythm by going into that just now. "They raised money to promote democratic ideals, this guy told me, whatever that means. But here's what's interesting: From 1980 to the day Devereaux died, they didn't raise a dime. There's not a single piece of evidence that any money came into the group. No IRS filings at all, ever, either as a not-for-profit or a charity, sole proprietorship, S corporation, anything."

Kevin vaguely recalled something to the same effect on Merke's page. "So?"

"So, get this." She paused, caught her breath, Kevin feeling like she was setting him up for something, which was right. "The guy in Silver Spring also keeps data of corporate contributions, public information stuff, mostly getting it from annual reports, filings, that kind of thing.

He cross-referenced Americans for America with those records, just punched it up on a search field for the hell of it. You'll never guess what he found."

She was right. Kevin didn't have a clue. "What?"

"About $600 million to start with, that's what." Sounding triumphant, but Kevin didn't know why or over what, his silence basically telling her to Go on, and she did. "From 1980 to last year, corporations gave $611 million to Americans for America. And I'm not talking about corner drugstore-type corporations, either. I'm talking about Excelsior Oil, Rodale Technologies, Forrester Chemical. Big, big players."

All of which Kevin found interesting if not especially revealing. "I thought you said this group didn't raise any money—"

"I did, and they didn't, and it gets even better." More shuffling of paper. "Between 1970 and 1980, when Devereaux set up Americans for America, those same companies—there were 14 of them back then— they got more than seven billion in grant money from the government. Think about that: The exact same companies that donated non-existent funds to Devereaux after 1980 got a whole lot of taxpayer money before 1980." Another pause. "Oh, and by the way, the grant money stopped in '80, and since then, they've gotten close to a half *trillion* in federal contracts."

Not being an investigative reporter and not having the universe of knowledge necessary to weave the strands together, Kevin found the whole thing convoluted, making his head feel heavy as a cinderblock and three times as thick. "Look," he said, weary, "I don't know much about how these things work. But it doesn't surprise me that there's money being spent secretly. It's the government. That's their job."

"Oh, that's a great attitude."

Jesus, he thought, not up for an ideological debate. "All I meant was that it could be used for something, I don't know, like research and development. Maybe there was some program, some policy in place that explains everything."

Taylor's momentary detour into reproach ended. "That's what I thought, too. I mean, why all of a sudden do a bunch of companies who've been living off Uncle Sam for 10 years suddenly begin pouring cash into Americans for America? So I started checking, looking at milestone dates, and damned if the two stories didn't intersect in the most unlikely place." He asked where, mostly because he thought it was expected. "Arabaq."

Kevin's mind flashed back to the mini-warehouse and the books he'd stored there, the ones Liz Fletcher had given him, and everything seemed to stop. "What about Arabaq?"

"That was the year, 1980, when General Azid murdered the Royal Family—which the U.S. had been supporting for about a zillion years, its repressive nature notwithstanding—and took over."

"Is that when you were there?" The question just popping out, no warning to either of them.

"No, Kevin. I was there *later*." Her voice flared slightly, like he should have remembered her story a little better, and even so, what did it matter anyway? After a take-five pause, she asked: "Does any of this make any sense to you?"

It happened again, Kevin thinking the question was kind of odd, not because of what she was asking, which was perfectly normal, but the ambiguous way she was asking it, almost like she was pumping him, wanting to know what he knew. He had dealt with journalists before, knew that no matter what they said or how they acted, it never jibed with what they were really thinking, what they really wanted. Experience warned him to tread lightly, but since the other night with Taylor, he wasn't exactly being led around by his experience. Besides, he knew she was after the story, she'd been straight up about it, so there couldn't be any hidden motives or agenda, right? "I don't understand what any of it has to do with Worth."

Taylor upshifted back into Reporter Speed. "Good point." He heard more flipping back and forth of notes, a muffled Oh, shit, I dropped my pen, and then she was back. "Okay. Listen to this time frame: The money from the government started flowing into these companies in January of 1970. So I went back *there* and looked at anything that happened around then, give or take a year, some event that could've started this ball rolling. Guess what I found?" Again, Kevin couldn't, didn't even try, this 20 Questions thing making him way too dizzy. "In 1969, Nixon decided that Uncle Sammy was gonna get out of the chemical weapons business."

Another Eureka moment for her, Kevin still lost as Atlantis. "Okay."

"Fast-forward five years: December 1974, Richard Worth pushes through Senate passage of the Geneva Protocol, which officially puts the U.S. government on record as prohibiting biological and chemical weapons in war. Now fast forward to 1980, Azid murders his way to the top, and out of nowhere this chickenshit little Arab dictatorship ends up with the scariest chemical weapons capability on the globe."

"So what are you saying?"

"I'm saying I'll bet you the national debt the government started bankrolling an illegal chemical weapons operation in 1970 in Arabaq. Some under-the-table rogue deal, like Reagan did in Iran-Contra, channeling the grant money through the companies on that list." Which Kevin thought made some sense, even if didn't explain much of anything. "Then when Azid came in, he took it over. The grant money stops, the contracts go through the stratosphere—got to keep the Corporate Indians on the reservation, you understand—and the companies pony up 600-mill to Devereaux to finance some kind of cover-up. And in the middle of it all, Richard Worth—America's loudest voice in the fight to stop chemical weapons—gets blown away by a nut so predictable he could've come from the remainder bin of Assassins Are Us."

At which point, at least as far as Kevin was concerned, logic took a sharp turn south. "I don't see the connection between—"

"What if Worth found out about the illegal operation? What if they killed him to shut him up?"

"That's crazy."

"Why?" she fired back, almost indignant.

Retreating a bit, not expecting her tone to be so hot. "Because, uh, because, it's not the way things are done. It's not how—"

"Don't be naïve, Kevin. It's exactly how things are done. Every day. You want to know what the U.S. government's greatest accomplishment is? Convincing us we live in a democracy. They do what they want to do, and they make us think it's our choice. And it makes me want to puke, and it should make you wanna puke, too. Because that's *not* what this country is about, and I'll be damned if I'm gonna sit back and let *them* kill good people like Richard Worth because *they* decided it had to be done!"

Kevin wanted to ask who, exactly, *they* were, but sensed that would be like fire-hosing her anger or ardor or passion, whatever that outburst was all about, with premium Exxon. Don't talk unless you can improve the silence, Jon Columbus had often advised, and if there was ever a moment in his brief relationship with Taylor that cried for quiet, this was it.

At the other end of the line, Kevin finally heard a weak little laugh that siphoned some of the tension out of both her voice and the moment. "Sorry. I'm a little fragged. Sometimes when that happens, I forget who I am." A reassuring softness had returned to her voice.

"And who are you?"

"Just a reporter. Looking for a story." He could almost see her shrugging.

"Oh, I think you're a little more than that."

"Do you?" The playfulness back, Keven getting it this time...

•

"Do you?" Trying to make herself sound playful.

"I sure do."

"And what do you think I am?"

"I haven't figured it out yet."

"But it's something good?" Now trying to make herself sound hopeful.

"Oh, yeah. Very good."

"I'm glad. That makes me very happy, Kevin."

"Can I ask you something?"

"Do I have to answer?" Feeling it working on him, men being so, so easy.

"Not if you don't want to."

"Hey, those're the easiest kinds of questions. Fire away."

"When I do figure out who you are, am I going to like her?"

"Do you like her now?" Mixing a touch of anticipation here, some desperation there, a little uncertainty everywhere. Perfect blend.

"Very much."

"Then you're safe, Kevin. You're very, very safe."

"Is that right?"

"Trust me," Taylor Shepard said. "Trust me."

Chapter 26

Ted Farmer looked at the time and temperature image his brother had pasted together, compared it to the image on Mike's computer screen.

Different angle. This one was from ground level, like the shooter was on the street, aiming the camera up, but there was no mistaking what it showed:

12:31. 86 degrees F.

Same time and temperature as in Kevin's photo. Same sign. Had to be.

"Go back to the text," Ted ordered.

Mike, seated at the terminal, put down his bowl of Cocoa Puffs and clicked a left-pointing arrow that said Back. Standing behind him, Ted leaned over his shoulder, peering in to see the one paragraph that returned to the screen under a bold, black headline that read Alternative Theories, reading it out loud:

"Conspiracy theorists have long argued that these two open windows—captured in a home movie taken within seconds of the shooting by an Iowa tourist—provide evidence that there was a second gunman present that day, and that he was perched in a sniper's nest next to the accused killer. These theorists reject the Knight Commission's findings, which were based on ballistics tests, that a single rifle was used in the shooting."

When Ted finished, he began to stroke his wispy tumbleweed chin whiskers, deep in thought. "What are you thinking about, bro?" Mike asked.

"I'm thinking, maybe we're looking at evidence of a second gunman, and maybe we ought to get this Kevin guy over here, pronto. What're you thinking?"

Mike took another spoonful of cereal, used his black, metal-band T-shirt to wipe a drop of milk from the side of his mouth. He turned to Ted, gave him that look, the one that said I am your worldly older brother, the Man With A Plan, and all I need is a few thousand dead presidents to put it in play, get out from under the hideous burden of Trevor and Judy, produce my movie script, take it to Sundance, catch Quentin's attention, party naked with Claire Danes.

Ted had *heard* it all before.

But when Mike said, finally, "I think your pal Kevin is sitting on a pot of gold," it suddenly seemed fresh, like he was *seeing* it for the first time.

•

"Hello, Meredith."

"Why Edward," she said pleasantly, hiding the anxieties and torment of the past few days. "What a nice surprise." Nice and strange because Edward Van Parkes, the food critic whose continuing raves had established the Qaletaqa's four-star status, had never ventured into her office. She stood, and motioned him to take a seat on the chair opposite her desk—it was straight-back and simple, red with thin stripes of arrow-heads—and absently ran a hand through her hair. "Is something wrong?"

Being a fatalist—what choice did she have, life taking the turns it had?—Meredith Whitney Wade spent a large portion of her days and nights wondering when the other shoe was going to drop. Business had been very good for a very long time, thanks in no small part to this tall, graying, 50ish man before her—thin, too, which she found strange for someone who makes a living eating. But it couldn't last. A bad review, a lawsuit, making the wrong person unhappy, any of it could put a Closed sign on the front door. Sometimes she even had dreams about health inspectors strolling into the kitchen, only to be met not by cooks but by chef-hatted rats. Whereupon she usually woke in a sweat, gobbled down whatever pills were by the nightstand at that moment, and drifted back into a troubled sleep.

He smiled. "No, no. Not at all." He was as non-descript as a piece of blank typing paper. That, she'd always thought, was a positive thing: To look like no one and everyone, make no impression, leave no memory. Perfect for a food critic.

"So breakfast was to your liking?"

"Yes, it was." The smile, bland as always.

Meredith got edgy. Usually, a question like that produced an entire menu of questions, Van Parkes asking what she added to the lemon poppy muffins to make them so different from every other one he had ever tasted, or how she managed to keep the homemade blue corn chips so light, or where had she gotten her hands on such a splendid Riesling wine.

Not today, though. No chitchat, professional, casual or otherwise.

This was it, she thought, had to be. Something had gone wrong in the dining room—and with food critics, even the smallest things, the things that would sail right past normal people, could blow up into a nasty review—and Edward was about to trash her. Meredith craved pharmaceutical relief. "Service to your liking?" Trying to control the quiver in her voice.

"Excellent, as always."

Grasping for anything now. "Did you notice we changed the artwork in the restaurant. I found a wonderful Native American painter on the plaza in Sante Fe. Sixth-generation Navajo. Breath-taking talent."

"I'm not really an art aficionado, Meredith." The smile, which as long as she had known him was never really warm, seemed to go dead, and she suddenly understood.

At the flashpoint of recognition, she tried to tell herself it was all in her imagination, or maybe it was the drugs, or stress, or fear, or the fact that she hadn't gotten a decent sleep in weeks, the pills putting her out, but only lightly, never into that deep state necessary to face the morning rested and ready.

It wasn't her imagination, though, or anything else, one look into Edward Van Parkes's lifeless eyes telling her everything she needed to know, also telling her he knew that she knew. "Funny," she said, still trying to play out the string, futile as that was, "I always took you for a man of culture." A tortured smile came to Meredith's face, exiting just as quickly.

"No." He had not moved since sitting down, didn't even shake his head when he said that.

"If you're not a lover of art, then what—"

"Meredith, how difficult is this going to be?" A simple question, simply asked, none of the threat or implied danger she'd always imagined would mark the day that he, or whomever, finally arrived.

"I don't suppose there's anything..." She smiled, sadly. Van Parkes didn't care.

"He wants you back, Meredith. There isn't any *anything* except that."

"And why does he want me back?" She had intended to put some steel, some anger, into her tone, perhaps send Edward Van Parkes a message that the current situation was intolerable, and that no one, no matter who they were or what they did, had any right to impose their misguided, self-interested will on another person.

But Edward Van Parkes just sat there. Blank expression, no distinguishing features, could have been anyone.

Perfect for a food critic.

Even better for a spy.

"Why does he want me back, Edward?" she repeated, wearing her neurosis like a neon necklace, now searching for a cigarette, hands shaking so badly she couldn't light the long table match. Van Parkes pulled out a Zippo, did the honors. Then, for the first time, his expression changed, becoming almost sympathetic.

"Because you're the mother of his child, Meredith," he answered, returning the Zippo to his pants pocket. "Why else?"

•

"Okay, now watch this close."

Kevin was sitting at Mike Farmer's computer terminal, and wasn't real comfortable, what with the defaced Bill Gates and a lot of heavy metal posters staring down on him. On the screen, Mike doubled-clicked on a Statue of Liberty icon that read American Heritage Productions and everything went to black before chaos erupted over the two Boston Acoustic mini-speakers that flanked the Dell monitor. Kevin was impressed at the technology, wondering why a 20-something slacker with no visible means of support had a better system than he did. In the center of the screen, black-and-white video streamed into a 5- by 5-inch square. Dallas police cars, sirens wailing, cut to Bobby Kennedy brushing at his hair, flashing a V for victory sign, encouraging supporters to go to New York and win there, then to a Memphis hotel, and a Maryland shopping center, and then to Richard Francis Worth, smiling out from a *Time* magazine cover. Strained words crackling over walkie-talkies, exchanged by grim-looking men in black glasses and white shirts, cries of "My God, they've killed him!" as people scrambled to protect themselves and their children. All of it finally dissolving into darkness as a solemn-sounding voice filled the speakers with "We conclude there was but a single gunman."

"That's very cool," Ted said. He was standing over Kevin's left shoulder, Mike over the other.

The words **Conspiracy or Case Closed?** came up on the screen.

Not again, Kevin thought, close to being conspiracied-out, Taylor's phone call still not all that far from his thoughts.

Once the title page faded out, an American flag appeared. On each stripe was a single word of text, starting with Lincoln, extending through McKinley, both Kennedys, Malcolm X and Martin Luther King and Wallace. On the eighth stripe was Worth. Mike leaned over, doubled clicked it.

Five images came up on the screen, each promising information about some aspect of the senator's murder: The Knight Commission, The Investigation, Alternative Theories, Visual Documentation and Conclusions. Dragging the cursor to Visual Documentation, Mike pulled up another menu that contained eight items. Five down was a blue line that read, Thompkins Home Video. He doubled-clicked on that.

At the bottom of the screen, a small horizontal time scale appeared. Mike moved the cursor to the Play button and clicked the mouse, the halting video coming into view almost instantly.

This was hardly the dramatic clue Kevin had expected, instead being only eight seconds of hand-held camera images, jittery almost to the point of making everything a blur, that panned up and down the side of a building. After a momentary pause on two open windows about a dozen floors up, the amateur cinematographer lurched his camera left to capture the rooftop of a shorter, squatter building whose roof had—

"Freeze that," Ted ordered, Mike reaching down and hitting the Pause button on command. The image stopped. "According to the way the Knight Commission put things together, this was taken at just about the exact time Worth got it," Ted explained. With a pencil whose yellow paint had been almost totally chewed off, he tapped a portion of the frame containing a sign that clearly read: 12:31 and 86 degrees F.

"Okay." Kevin looked up at each of them, then back at the screen.

Mike dropped the enhanced printout of the time-temperature image onto the keyboard in front of Kevin. "I pulled this from the shot you brought into Ted. It's the lower left-hand corner, you know, where you thought you saw a sign?" Kevin stared at the printout, said nothing. "Well, bud, you were right."

"Righter than you ever thought, man," Ted chimed in.

Kevin asked to see the enhanced version of his entire original photo, part of him, a large part, wanting to ask, Right about what, or Are you telling me that this was the only time in the course of human events when it was 86 degrees at 12:31 in the afternoon somewhere in the world? But the two windows, the front of the building. It all matched. "What does this show?" he asked, looking at the original. "My picture. What, exactly, does it show?"

Mike answered with a question. "What do you know about Worth's assassination?"

"More than I did a week ago."

"Well, I'm a, uh—a buff, I guess. A conspiracy buff. Not a paranoid. No way. I just have, shall we say, a healthy interest in the unexplained." Mike all of a sudden sounding like a flack for some ESP hotline, a far cry from the heavy-metal tech-head Kevin had pegged him to be. "So allow me to elaborate—"

Telling him that the Knight Commission determined Worth had been murdered by a single gunman who was perched in a 12th-floor window of a 43rd Street building opposite *The New York Times* offices. And that it hadn't taken a lot of professional detecting to figure out where the shot had come from, and from whom, as the killer, a right-wing crazy named Rayfield Buskin, was dead in a pool of his own blood, half his head decorating the apartment walls courtesy of a private security man who got so excited he croaked from a heart attack, "which would have really been out there if the dude didn't have a history of pump problems." It was so open and shut that no one bothered to look for anything else. All things being equal, as the saying goes, the simplest explanation is most likely to be the right one. The Knight Commission discovered that Buskin had a longstanding hatred for Worth—threatening letters, stalking, a textbook case—meaning Buskin had to be the killer, and the killshot that took him down had to come from the private cop's rifle, no need to do anything but stamp Investigation Over on this one.

Some of which Kevin knew, some of which he didn't, all of which he didn't care about at the moment, because what he wanted to know, and he said it again, was what the picture showed.

Mike and Ted looked at each other, trying to figure out who was going first, Mike taking the lead at last, him being the conspiracy *buff.*

"Here's what I know," he began, settling his skinny frame onto the desk's edge, looking at Kevin with blue eyes that shocked with their clarity and intelligence. "Your picture, this Frame 214, was taken at just about the exact same time Worth went down. Same place, too. The sign, the buildings, the way the buildings are positioned—next to each other like that—the two open windows. No doubt about it: This is the scene of one heavy-duty crime, historically speaking."

He looked briefly to Ted, who nodded slightly but said nothing, then back to Kevin. "Now, here's what I think:

"I think this guy here"—Mike slid the enhanced images of the two Rorschach tests onto the computer keyboard, pointing to the one on the left, Blob No. 1—"I think he's Buskin. Whoever took this got it the second that security dude greased him. Look at this"—tapping the pencil now on the small gray cloud above the man's head. "I think that's the mush of brain you get when somebody shoots half your skull off. And this here"—pointing first to the left arm, gesturing backward, and then to the right arm, reaching skyward—"this tells me he's just been hit, the force of the bullet, you know, how your arms fly, especially at this angle."

"Where did that shot come from?" Kevin asked, evenly, trying to run all this through his internal bullshit detector, and coming up with something that was half again as confusing.

"This direction," Mike answered, putting the pencil about a foot up and to the right of the Rorschach tests, drawing an invisible line to the blob he said was Buskin. "It's where they said the security dude was. On a 16th floor landing in a building across the street."

"So that part's true?"

"That part," Mike said. "Yeah."

Kevin's stare tracked a path directly backward of the bullet's, moving from the images in front of him up to Mike's eyes. "So what part's not true?"

The Brothers Farmer fidgeted in stereo.

Mike spoke: "Are you, uh, up for a business proposition?"

"Am I up for a *what*?"

"Nothing, man, nothing," Ted broke in. "It's nothing. A bad idea. That's all, nothing but—"

"Bro? It's our movie, dude! Why're you wussing out before we even put the deal before the man?"

"Wait a second, wait a second, wait a second." Kevin had both hands in front of him, palms facing the computer screen, like he stopped halfway when someone screamed Get 'em up. "What's this *deal*? What're you guys talking about?"

Life is a series of moments, Mike believed after he heard Charlie Sheen say it in *Wall Street*, and this is one of them. "Me and my bro here, we got a dream of making a piece of major independent filmed entertainment."

"A movie," Ted translated, willing to jump in now that someone else had tested the water first. "Script is written. We can do it right here in town, using locals, non-union technical people, we'll both direct"—arm flapping back and forth between himself and Mike, meaning the two of them—"and we'll both produce."

"Eighty K," Mike said.

"Hundred, tops," Ted said.

"What does this have to do with me?" Kevin asked.

"Dude, that there piece of film, that Frame 214?" Mike this time, gesturing to the original scan of the photo, turgid and blotted, sitting next to the computer. "It's worth millions. All *we're* asking is to dip our beak in the wishing well, get enough to film my script."

Slowly, what they were suggesting began to sink in, Kevin laughing caustically. "You want me to *sell* it?"

"The tabloids, man," Ted explained, like it was the most logical thing in the world. "*The Globe. Star. Weekly World News.* They'll break the bank for this one."

Mike chimed in: "Truly. Proof of a second gunman in the Worth assassination? That makes the Lee Harvey scenarios look like Sesame Street."

"Where's the proof?" Kevin asked, thinking if this was what they said it was, did he have some obligation to give it to Taylor, forget any thoughts of a fat payday?

"Right there, man!" Mike, jabbing his index finder at Blob No. 2, the balled-up figure who was listening to his arm, the arm with the birth-mark on it, that trombone sticking out and pointed down. "This guy's the real killer. Look: You see any reaction at all to Buskin getting blown away? Any sign he's surprised or scared? It's business as usual, man, another day at the five and dime."

Kevin had to admit the kid had a point.

"Now let's say you're a highly paid professional assassin, okay? You've planned this thing down to the smallest detail. Then, out of nowhere— ba-boom!—your comrade loses his mind when it gets in the path of a totally nastified rapidly moving projectile. So what do you do? Do you just keep on keeping on, thinking, oh, well, this is the life we chose, and we live it and we die it, la di da?" Before Kevin could utter a one-syllable No, Mike had caught his breath and was speeding into the final stretch. "No way, man. You do something. You look over. You get outta the line of fire. You stand up. You run. You do something unexpected because something unexpected happened to you. That's the way the world works. But this guy"—pointing to Blob No. 2 again—"this guy ain't doin' shit. His careful plan is coming apart like a two-dollar suit. What's that tell you?"

"It tells me the second gunman wasn't surprised." Kevin said, his voice hollow. "He knew it was going to happen."

Anticipation blew into the room like a pack of hungry dogs.

Ted and Mike, hoping the guy Kevin would see the beauty of it all, the irony, of using some shit rag like *The Star* to third-party finance a major piece of independent filmed entertainment—

Kevin wondering who else knew about this, and how long it would take that person, whoever it was, to come here and make him, Kevin, disappear, just like what happened to Devereaux, and then thinking maybe he shouldn't tell Taylor for that very reason—

Ted and Mike, imagining what it would be like to tell the parents they weren't wastoids, and that the marathon video viewership that so outraged Trevor was rooted in sound career economics—

Kevin thinking of all the people he'd put at risk, starting to collect the photos and printouts, which was not exactly the response Mike and Ted had expected, saying when he'd swept everything up: "Is this it?"

"Hey, bud, what're you doing?" Mike acting all hurt and betrayed.

"I want everything. My original. Your scans. The enhanced images of these two guys. All of it. Now." He got up, signaling the end to any potential debate.

"No can do, my man," Mike said.

Kevin turned to him, got almost nose to nose. "You wanna know something, *my man*? The person who sent me this? He's dead as Rayfield Buskin. Killed himself a couple days ago after dropping this in the mail with my address on it. Now you tell me something, you being the conspiracy *buff* and all: I get what you say is evidence of the crime of the century, and the guy who sent it to me ends up with a .45 slug through his brain. You call that *fate? Coincidence? Happenstance?* Sorry, I don't think so." Mike's eyes had widened to four lanes. Ted's were at six. "So if I were you, I'd collect every piece of paper I had on this, and

I'd hand it over, and I wouldn't say a word to anyone about it. Because if you do, and they don't kill you, I will. Now give me the pictures."

The neon lights of filmdom started to go down in Mike's eyes. "Okay," was all he could manage, sounding like a scolded puppy.

From down below came a hoarse bellow. "Unemployment line's been open for a couple of hours."

"Thanks for the update, Judy." This time, there wasn't even a sliver of hope in Mike Farmer's voice. Dreams are supposed to die hard, he thought, collecting everything, giving it to Kevin, but this one was going down without a whimper, man, quiet as a Lawrence Welk rerun.

Chapter 27

He was a large man, rumpled, white shirt bulging at the gut, its collar slicing a thin crease into a neck that had more folds than a laundry service. *Large* being the operative word.

"Lucky they didn't cancel this one, too, doncha think? I mean, with the problems they're havin' with the MD-80s and all that."

Naturally, he was sitting in the center seat of U.S. Airways Flight 1625 to Nashville. And, naturally, Maxie was wedged into the window seat, with nowhere to run, nowhere to hide, from this oversized chatterbox. On the aisle, a black kid, maybe 17, was trying to sleep, despite the hip hop music blasting through his blue Panasonic portable stereo. She thought of J.J.

"Lucky," Maxie said, giving Large Man a fleeting look and half-hearted smile before returning to the three sheets of paper she carried in a black leather portfolio. The first was an official-looking letter from the law offices of one Marvin Finn authorizing her to conduct an investigation related to execution of the will of one Darlene Sharpe, deceased. The second was an official request from The County of Mecklenburg, North Carolina, asking that its bearer be granted an opportunity to interview and verify the existence of one Henry Lee Hubbard, who was bequeathed $14,600—after funeral and burial expenses—from the estate of the aforementioned Darlene Sharpe, deceased. The third was a Freedom of Information Request, filed under the name of Marvin Finn, to be used in the event that the first two documents didn't wash.

Which was always possible, being as she forged them herself and neither had so much as a passing acquaintance with legality. Huck was off polishing his pinkie rink on some island that didn't have an extradition agreement with the United States, and while she'd put the address of a mail forwarding service on the county document, the absence of a phone number was likely to raise an eyebrow in certain official circles. Both of which explained the Freedom of Information letter, and the tape recorder in her purse. Experience told her that a bureaucrat would rather do anything than get mixed up in some public records debate. Asking him or her to state on tape "for the record" why they were denying a legally certified "extension of the court" access to free and open documents inevitably produced some irritated huffing and puffing and, ultimately, a "what the hell" approval.

"They say it's rudders, you know. They're canceling flights right and left." Large Man chuckled. "Get it? Right and left? As in rudders?" Laughter seemed to further inflate his round face.

Maxie looked at her watch. Quarter to 12 Eastern time. They had 45 more minutes in the air. Wonderful.

"Is that dangerous?" she asked, suddenly all pie-eyed and concerned.

"Oh, don't you worry, darlin'. That li'l ol' gal at the ticket counter told me we didn't have a thing to be concerned about, 'cause we're on an aircraft that just passed inspection with flying colors." He giggled at his own joke. Again. "Get it? Flying colors?" A heartier laugh. A redder face.

"It sounds dangerous." Trying to look more concerned than creeped-out, reaching for her black leather backpack.

"Well, how 'bout I just entertain you with some stories about work—I sell artificial limbs—and, why, before you know it, we'll be in Music City USA."

"I need comfort." She retrieved a black, leather-bound book from the backpack and set it in her lap, face down.

"I'm here for ya, girl."

Maxie wondered just what this guy was angling for. Did he think all black women were stupid enough to fall for that Benevolent White Protector crap?

She turned the book over, looked at him beatifically. "Spiritual comfort." Large Man's eyes tracked to the gold lettering on the cover, seeing King James Bible, smile freezing in an expression that told Maxie the patron saint that had just occupied his considerable body was edging toward retreat. "Perhaps we could read some Scripture, and pray for a safe arrival?"

Which caused Large Man to throw the Honkie's Here Don't You Worry routine into full reverse. "I'd love to, darlin', but, see, I'm, uh— I'm a Lutheran," like that explained everything, then picking up a copy of the airline magazine, pretending to pore over every page, which she knew was bullshit because it would've made him the first person in recorded history to do it.

"I'll pray for us both, then."

She opened the book, and began to read, shielding the contents from Large Man, not wanting him to know that inside, cut into a thick stack of blank pages, was a copy of *How Stella Got Her Groove Back*. Not that Large Man would have ever noticed, her no longer being there as far as he was concerned, which was okay by Maxie, who closed her eyes in serene repose, silently thanking God for helping her come up with the Bible scam, shuts 'em up every damned time.

•

Why? he thought. Why me?

The question plagued Kevin Columbus as he drove aimlessly around Charlotte. Why would someone send me a picture that, if he was to believe a couple of heavy metal refugees, proved there was a second gunman in Worth's assassination? Made no sense. He was just some guy, some normal guy, no different from anybody else. Except he had a father who may or may not have been his father, a mother whose cryptic words and non-response responses held more secrets than a cancer cell and a life that, in the past few days, was starting to feel like it was written on an Etch-A-Sketch screen. Yeah, right, real normal.

Bolting from the Brothers Farmer, killer images tucked tightly in his hand, Kevin didn't have the thinnest clue as to what he should do next. He stopped at a pay phone, called Maxie, got her machine—"Yo, Maxie McQueen has left the house for a day or two, but you leave a name, and I'll be on the case"—wondered if it had anything to do with Donna Hubbard. Tried to call the girl, got nothing but 26 unanswered rings, so he called Maxie back, and in a voice that didn't even come close to masking his near panic, said they needed to talk as soon as she got the message. Then he checked his home phone, seeing if Taylor had called, which she hadn't. Fished a handful of change from his pocket, tried Arizona, asking a front office clerk if Meredith was around, the clerk apparently knowing his voice by now, not even asking who he was, just saying Mrs. Wade was out of town for an unspecified period. Kevin thinking, again, Thanks, Mom, for being there. Finally pulled into a convenience store, a Circle K, sitting there in the lot watching a couple of skateboarders in long baggy shorts smoke a joint, right out in the open, like So Arrest Me, remembering how much he hated his first draft beer in college because it was bought with a fake ID and all he could think about was getting busted. Times, man, oh how they have changed.

Kevin mentally slapped himself back to the moment. The hell with *times,* now is the only *time* that matters, and you got to start thinking about what to do next, boy, think, think, think.

Okay. Thinking.

Devereaux sends the package. The package has Frame 214. What's that mean? He's either involved or knows something. And what about the frames before and after 214? Where are those? And the photo, the torn photo. Why had Devereaux ripped it, what had he done with the other part, and who if anyone had he sent *it* to? And what about the pictures he'd found in storage, the ones that were ripped just like the one from Switzerland? What did they have to do with anything? And maybe most important of all, why was *he* still alive?

Look, Devereaux was dead, right? And everything pointed to Henry Lee Hubbard being dead—after all, everyone else in the family was, everyone except Donna—

And what was that all about, exactly, everyone dead but her? Even if Rollie Merke was crazier than a dog in a fireplug factory, the fact remained that a lot of people who were interviewed in the Worth shooting were also gone from this world, which would suggest that the conspirators know how to find things out, and how to kill people and get away with it, and were pros at all of the above.

Which brought him back to the original question: Why am I still among the living?

He had no idea, but one thing was certain: Whatever the answer was, it had something to do with Richard Worth getting mowed down in New York, thinking as he pulled out of the Circle K, listening to the giggling potheads, that whoever had the other half of the picture and the rest of the film was neck-deep in the conspiracy.

He drove around for an hour, trying to find someplace to start, finally deciding to forget all this crap about conspiracies, go with the facts, and the only fact he had was that somebody murdered a United States senator on July 6, 1975. Which landed him at the local library, immersed in the "literature" of the senator.

A quick computer check revealed that 18 books had been written about Worth. Kevin didn't know much about the man, other than he was another piece of evidence that unconventional politics and futile ideals too often manifested themselves in an America that ate its own. But who Worth was didn't matter, how and why he died did, so Kevin skipped the books by the senator's wife, his former press secretary, the *Time* writer who'd done the cover piece that started the swell of presidential talk, the two scholarly biographies, the six books about the 1976 presidential election that referenced the assassination, a collection of speeches and a glowing tome by the executive editor of *Newsday*. Instead, he concentrated on the six that dealt with the presumed conspiracy.

The arguments weren't real convincing. No matter how hard the dogged theorists tried, there was just no compelling reason to believe Worth had been murdered in a manner other than The Knight Commission had concluded. Donna Hubbard's family photo was everywhere, of course, paranoid provocateurs arguing that what one termed "multi-directional fingerpointing" demonstrated that shots had to come from more than one point—a conclusion the Commission concurred with: The private security man hired by the campaign was on one side of the street, Buskin on the other. Naturally, the theorists ignored that finding, facts not being great currency in matters like this, and instead created their own, absent evidence, hiding behind the age-old reality that it's impossible to disprove a negative. The Thompkins video, which the Brothers Farmer had shown him, wove itself in and out of the respective narratives, as did the two open windows on the front of the building. One of the books, written by a forensic pathologist who was a vanguard in the Oswald Was A Patsy movement, argued that the angle of impact proved without question that Worth could not have been shot from the window where the Knight Commission placed Rayfield Buskin. He included a set of drawings that purported to show the line of fire, and used what the author called "vector/spatial analysis" to argue that physical science prevented any bullet from Buskin's sniper's nest to travel in a path that would have intersected with the vector where Worth was standing when shot. Not knowing anything about science, Kevin thought the theory made some sense. Until he looked at another book, this one by a writer who'd made millions debunking conspiracy theories, that said *his* computer tests had shown conclusively the bullet that struck Worth could only have come from the window in question.

Great. The conspiracy theorists arguing their "what ifs," mixing an occasional shard of information with unchecked psychosis, the nonbelievers arguing the facts, though reassembling them to reflect their own version of reality, both camps sounding like Congress on a good day, arguing that tax cuts either helped or hurt the poor, that Medicare was either sound or bankrupt, that gun control either protected Americans or endangered them. It all depended on your frame of reference and self-interest, how many sheep you could get to follow or, even better, how many you could disgust into not caring, leaving only the loonies to determine the nation's collective fate.

That pretty much summed up everything written about Worth's killing: Everybody had an agenda, and most of the agenda-setters pursued theirs with foaming-at-the-mouth intensity. And while Kevin couldn't exactly bring himself to accept the nutty positions of the conspiracy school, he didn't find a whole lot of cozy comfort in the neatly tied-up findings of the debunkers, either. Where was the truth? Was it in what you could see and what they told you? Or in what you couldn't see and they never said? Like everything else, he thought, somewhere in the middle, the place where reason had been abandoned and marooned in the name of national leadership, forgive the contradiction in terms.

The library had a copy of the 12-volume Knight Commission Report on CD-ROM, but his keyword search—"Devereaux"—turned up nothing. No real surprise there, although he wondered how the man's name had become written, however lightly, into the conspiracy theories if there was no mention of him in the "official record." Another dozen or so keyword checks—Geneva, Nashville, Swiss Air, terms that might relate to Taylor's story about the gate agent and the man who resembled Jon Columbus—also returned a steady flow of No Matches back to him. Well, sort of.

In the fifth volume of the Knight Commission Report, on Page 779, there was testimony from the LaGuardia gate agent who had provided a description of the man Taylor said was Gary Devereaux, the man Kevin said looked like Jon Columbus. The questioner, Harvard Professor Bartholomew Knight, asked if she had seen anything "out of the ordinary" in the days preceding or following the murder of Senator Worth.

Yes, she replied. Knight asked her to explain. She recalled that a man in his 40's was preparing to board a flight to Geneva when a second man in a suit suddenly stopped him. An agitated discussion followed, the agent related. Knight asked: "Were you able to discern any of what was said?" The gate agent answered No.

That was it.

Kevin stared at the citation on the screen. *That's it? No follow-up questions? From the head of the commission?* It made no sense. None. Jesus, could Knight be involved in the consp—

Whoa, boy, simmer down.

Kevin caught himself in mid-word, telling his jittery psyche to chill, this was no time to start finding a conspirator under every line of the Knight Commission testimony. At the same time, though, the discovery—or non-discovery, if you will—juiced his craving for knowledge. After he'd pulled the CD out of the tray, he went back to the library's research room—all dark wood, and musty with the smell of history, which was strange since it was also where the higher-tech resources were checked in and out—and waited until the woman behind the counter got off the phone. She had a nametag that identified her as Vanessa, a Friend of the Library Volunteer. Vanessa was thin, had straight brown hair and wore a denim smock over a white T shirt, wire-framed glasses and Birkenstock sandals, white socks, all of it shouting Earth Mother, macrobiotic food and NPR to Kevin.

"Can I help you?" she asked, sweetly but not smiling.

"Yeah. How do I go about getting into your databases?"

Vanessa looked at him like he'd asked about getting into something else of hers. "Into my what?"

"Your databases."

She squinted, trying to assimilate the information he'd just transmitted, responding with a slow shake of the head. "No," she answered, uncertain, but still seeming to give it a lot of thought. "We have an extensive *reference* section"—pointing through the glass behind him, to a corner of the second floor that was designated by an overhead sign as being, indeed, Reference—"but that's all."

Kevin wasn't listening. "Maybe I'm using the wrong words. A friend of mine, a reporter, was in here yesterday, and said she used one of your computer databases to get something for a story. I don't know what it's called. I just want to see if there's anything in there I can use."

"Use for what?" Not challenging, just trying to help.

The question stalled him out. "I'm, uh, doing this, something, on, uh, government. Congress. And—"

That seemed to register. "Then you probably want *The Congressional Record*, or *The Congressional Quarterly*. Right?"

He smiled agreeably. "Right. That's exactly it." Anything to get access to the database.

"Just check with the lady at the Reference desk." Again pointing to the corner of the library through the glass behind him.

"But this is the research room, isn't it?"

"Yes."

"What's the difference between this and the reference section?"

"We keep historical documents, primarily."

"On computer?"

"Yes."

"That's what I want, then. I want to look at documents on your computer database."

"We don't have any databases, sir."

"But you just said—"

"We keep material stored on CDs. You look at the CDs on a computer, just as you did with the"—she glanced at the thin square plastic jewel box he'd just handed her, read the label—"Knight

Commission Report. That is the extent of our computer research capabilities at this facility."

Kevin replayed the conversation with Taylor over in his head. It was at the crack of dawn, admittedly, and he wasn't entirely awake, so maybe he had heard her wrong—

No. *They have this database you can hook on to,* was what she said.

"Do you have a CD that includes data on NGOs?" he asked.

Vanessa the Volunteer began to sense the tension in his voice, and the frustration, and took an involuntary step backward. "On what?"

"Non-governmental organizations."

"I'm not sure—"

"They're groups that raise money or advocate positions, but aren't officially part of the government. There was one that she found on your database—"

"Sir, we don't have any databases. I told you." She folded her arms in front of her chest, a defensive posture.

"But my friend—"

"Your friend was mistaken. Now, if you would like to pursue this further, I would thank you to do so with Miss Wormwood in Reference." Vanessa picked up her sweater—an oversized green cardigan—and walked out of the research room, leaving him in a silence pierced only by the throb of a single voice in his head, a voice that kept saying over and over:

I heard her right. I heard her right. I know I heard Taylor right.

•

Hollis Tucker, deputy warden of the Stones River State Prison, was not being very helpful. But what really irritated the absolute hell out of Maxie was that the sonofabitch seemed to be enjoying it.

"Let me get this straight," he said, for what she thought had to be the 10th time. "Your documentation here"—waving the two illegal letters—"says you have the authority to question a Henry Lee Hubbard. I don't contest that authority, Miss McQueen. It's just that the State of Tennessee is not hosting anyone at this facility by that name." He sat back in the high leather chair, resting both hands on a desk whose nicks and scrape marks labeled it Government Surplus, fingers laced. His thick, perfectly parted hair glistened black, like it was spray-painted with enamel, and sat atop a squarish face that was empty of character even when he smiled, like now. "I'm sorry. But I just can't help you."

Maxie took a deep breath, trying to calm down, looked at the woman sitting in the chair next to her, both of them opposite the deputy warden's throne. Tucker's secretary, Ginger. Pretty in a pool hall kind of way, early 30s, reddish hair, pink skirt up to her armpits, slight tear way up on the thigh of her black hose, heels so high they'd give a mountain goat a nose-bleed. "I understand that. But I have reason to believe that this man, Ordell Anthony, and Henry Lee Hubbard may be one and the same."

"And tell me what those reasons are again?" He flicked an invisible something off his suspenders, which were brown and covered with old-time-looking golfers.

She explained, *again,* that she'd been hired by the attorney executing the will of Darlene Sharpe, and that before the disposition could be completed, they had to confirm whether the brother, who had been left some money, was still among the living. Leaving out the part about how she got Ordell's name from a software program she possessed illegally.

"Ordell's got no family, does he, honey?"

Ginger flipped through a thick file, stopping at a page that had been marked with a yellow post-it note. "No, sir. He's an orphan. No kin at all except for a far-removed cousin or great aunt, some such thing."

"See there?" Tucker smiled, throwing his hands up, like What are you gonna do?

Maxie scanned the room. Every wall was about ego. Pictures of Hollis Tucker with Bush. Reagan. Quayle. There was a larger framed photo of the warden and Tennessee's junior U.S. senator, with a thick-lettered, hand-written inscription that read, "To Hollis Tucker, my best campaign manager ever," and another from the governor, "To my dear friend Hollis Tucker, thanks for all your help," and others still, all of them putting out a 150,000-watt signal the man was an All-American political hack.

"Warden, I just need to talk to him. Confirm whether he is or is not the brother, and then I'll be out of your life. It's really just that simple."

"Oh, no, Miss McQueen. You don't understand." His tone had become somber, bordering on dark. "With Ordell Anthony, nothing is that simple." He snapped his fingers. Ginger dutifully handed him the file. Maxie wondered why they didn't try to access the information on the computer that sat inactive on the credenza behind Tucker's desk, thinking probably because the guy didn't know the difference between a megabyte and a spider bite.

"There are few things so complex as to escape my understanding," she replied, adding quickly, so he'd get the point, "meager though that understanding may be," letting him know she had no plans to go gently or quietly.

"Ordell Anthony is crazy as a shithouse rat," Tucker said flatly. He turned quickly to Ginger, saying, "Pardon me, sweetheart," Ginger smiling but not blushing.

Tucker looked back at Maxie, who was neither smiling nor blushing. "Ordell is incarcerated in what we call the CDT. The Corrections Disciplinary Tier, a 100-cell unit within this institution. That is where we house convicts who do not act in a manner consistent with their rehabilitation while among the main population. Their presence in CDT has nothing to do with why they came to us in the first place. It is only because of their actions once they joined us."

Joined us, making it sound like a health club.

"Ordell became a guest of the state when he pleaded guilty to car theft, armed robbery and murder in 1975." Nodding his head now, telling Maxie, See, I told you he was not your typical walk around the yard. "He and another man—a drifter, like Ordell—procured a Ford Falcon from a used car lot, robbed a liquor store over in Brentwood, took booze and money and holed up in a little rat-trap hotel called, uh, called, what the devil is the name of that—"

"The Heart of America Inn," Ginger offered, helpfully.

"Thank you, darlin'. The Heart of America Inn. According to Ordell's confession, the two of them got liquored up pretty good, and this other fellow started to pistol whip the tar out of Ordell. Should've seen the boy's face when we picked him up. So bad you couldn't recognize him. Ordell took all he could take, apparently got him a Colt .45 and emptied its contents into the head and chest of his friend. The state's docs figure it was the beating rendered him crazy as the shithouse rat of which I just spoke."

"*Apparently* got a Colt .45?"

"Never found the weapon. Not that it mattered. He pleaded to murder faster than gossip leaves a beauty parlor." Hollis Tucker poured himself some ice water from the stainless steel service next to his unused computer, offering a sip to Ginger, who politely declined, but not Maxie, who would've told him where to put it anyway.

Maxie wanted to know more about the incident, but knew that those details were beyond the "official" reason for her visit, Tucker not giving her the chance anyway, picking right back up with, "Mr. Anthony came here to CDT in 1988—"

After shoving a nail file into another con's throat, and watching as the blood pumped in and out of the wound to the beat of a dying heart, and repeating, "Bad meanings. Everything has bad meanings." Prison doctors diagnosed him as paranoid—no big surprise there—and he was moved quickly into the solitary confinement of CDT.

His condition seemed to grow worse. He complained of hearing voices, and seeing visions of men in dark suits and dark glasses who hovered over him as he tried to sleep on the concrete slab of a bed molded into the wall of his 8- by 10-foot cell. Whenever the CDT guards would open the sliding steel door that sealed Ordell off from the rest of the world, they were often the target of urine and feces. No visitors, no family, no one to suggest that the guy had a life outside of the joint.

Over time, and courtesy of a boatload of drugs, Ordell seemed to mellow. He quit trying to trash his cell, stopped pounding his head against the concrete floor, ate his breakfast—cream of wheat and orange juice—rather than wearing it. Gradually, he won back some of the perks afforded to other inmates: a Bic pen and composition book, small TV set, paperbacks, exercise time in the yard as opposed to a 15- by 30-foot cage. Taking nothing for granted, the staff monitored him constantly from a master control room that was slightly better equipped than a NATO command post. In 1996, doctors pronounced him fit to return to the general prison population, where he was celled-up with Roscoe Chatham, a bank robber so stupid he got caught 18 minutes after pulling a job because he'd written the demand note on a deposit slip from his own personal checking account. They got along well, sharing cigars that Roscoe's hooker friend Bev would bring by, everything fine—

"Then he just snapped again," Hollis Tucker continued.

"When?"

"Let's see, this is Wednesday. Would've been the first part of last week, I reckon." If the warden had a problem with discussing the case, he didn't show it.

"Anybody know why?"

Tucker shook his head. "No idea. One minute he was fine, and the next minute he was off the deep end."

"Anything happen in between?"

"Apparently he got a phone call, but it was so brief we did not have the opportunity to determine its origin." He reached into his desk drawer and pulled out a tin of Altoid mints, popped two in his mouth.

"The doctors thought he might come out of it, but two days later Roscoe died, and—"

"What happened to Roscoe?" The cellmate's death being an odd coincidence and Maxie not much believing in coincidences, odd or not.

Tucker shook his head dismissively. "Heart attack. Pure and simple. He'd just gotten the weekly cigar ration, and was calmly puffing away when the big one hit. Sad thing, really, and it seemed to just send Ordell deeper into a black tailspin. When he got word, he went back to hearing things no one else heard, and carrying on arguments with people who weren't there. The doctors were still hoping it was temporary, just a relapse. But when the screams picked back up—'Everything has bad meanings, everything has bad meanings'—he got a one-way ticket right back into CDT."

"He is a case, that one," Ginger observed.

"You got that right, girl," Tucker smiled.

"Was there an autopsy on Roscoe?"

"Oh, yes, ma'am," Ginger answered, "there sure was. It confirmed what Holl—I mean, Mister Tucker—it confirmed what he just said."

Maxie resisted the urge to walk all over Ginger's trampy little face with a look that said, I know you're sleeping with the boss, instead turning back to Tucker and asking, "You said he pleaded guilty to the original charge?" He nodded. "And when was that, exactly?"

The deputy warden handed the file back to Ginger, who thumbed agilely through the four inches of paper. "July 12, 1975," she said.

A week after Worth's death. Another coincidence. "You said he was an orphan?" Looking to Ginger now, assuming she was the brains of the outfit. But Tucker answered.

"Far as we can tell. His said his Daddy was in the Army, married a Korean gal he'd"—pausing, cutting a glance at Ginger, measuring his words—"been, uh, with, during the conflict there in 1950, '51."

"Did you ever try to trace them?"

"The parents? Why? They were dead." Said it like her question was the dumbest thing he'd ever heard.

Under different circumstances, Maxie might have jumped down his throat on that. But she let it slide for the moment. "Brothers? Sisters?"

Ginger: "None."

"You know anything about him prior to July 12, 1975? Anything besides his parents being dead? He have a record?"

Tucker said, "Truth be told, we can't find anything about the boy before then."

Maxie couldn't tell if this was true, or he was shining her on. "What do you know about the girl? The one that brought him and the other con, Roscoe, the cigars?"

He shrugged. "Bev? She was just a girl. A hooker. I don't know. Maybe she found it exciting to spend time with a criminal. Some girls do, you know."

"Not this one," Ginger said, making it very clear her excitement was limited to those who walked on the God-fearing side of the law, those or deputy wardens.

Maxie ignored her. "Where is she now?"

"No idea," Tucker said. "She hasn't been here since before Roscoe died."

Coincidence No. 3. The woman who had been dutifully visiting Roscoe Chatham suddenly vanishes after the man dies, doesn't contact anyone here, ask any questions, want to know what happened? "The last time being when she brought the cigars to him and Roscoe?"

"Actually," Ginger said quickly, "it wasn't Bev who brought the cigars this last time."

No. 4. The coincidence forest was getting awfully thick. "Who was it?"

"A friend of hers," Ginger said. "Another, uh, professional woman. Signed in as Regina Hemphill."

"She been back since?"

Hollis Tucker leaned up from his chair and put his clasped hands on the too-neat desk. "You know, Miss McQueen, you're asking a lot of questions that, on the surface, would not seem to have anything to do with the simple disposition of a will." He smiled, letting her know he knew she was up to something.

Maxie didn't give an inch, nor did she feel compelled in the slightest to offer up anything that resembled a legitimate explanation. "Warden, I am an extension of the court in this matter, which as I am sure you know prevents me from sharing any information as to my purposes, all of which are detailed anyway in the documentation I presented you at the beginning of this meeting. Additionally, I am here on official business of the County of Mecklenburg, the State of North Carolina, whose laws I am simply attempting to satisfy by means of this visit." Bureaucratic babble, Maxie knew, but it had the ring of authenticity if not necessarily truth, recited as if by rote in the hate-my-job delivery of a civil servant taught never to deviate from those precise words. "In order for me to complete my constitutional requirements therein, I have to provide as comprehensive a situation analysis as possible. If I do not comply in that regard, another extension of the court will be out here again, going over the same ground. So, please, just one or two more questions, and then we can go about our business."

The last part, a totally bogus threat of a second interview, worked. Whatever Hollis Tucker did to get through the day, this was an irritant he didn't need. "No, Miss McQueen," he said with a see-through smile that did little to hide his annoyance. "She has not been back since."

"Regina hasn't?"

"No."

Maxie thinking That's it, enough, there's something screwy about all this, and Hollis Tucker ain't offering road atlases to the land of understanding. "I need to talk to Mr. Anthony, warden." Maxie's words were measured and even, not trying to open a window to what she was thinking.

Tucker did not waver, but his frustration broke through. "And I'm telling you that Pinkie Anthony is in no condition to be interviewed by you or by anyone else. He is a sick, sick man."

Pinkie. And there, ladies and gentlemen, there you have it.

Maxie silently counted to 10, hoping Tucker would think he was getting the best of her and let his defenses down, not knowing he'd just lost the fight, Maxie needing a second to plot her next step, wanting it to be clear in her own head, making sure she didn't louse it up. "*Pinkie?*" she said finally, narrowing her eyes and smirking, like Give me a break. "This killer nut case about whom you said 'nothing was simple'—this guy's nickname is *Pinkie*? You can't be serious."

"As a snakebite," Ginger confirmed.

"Do I dare ask how that came to be?" Trying to throw the question away, hoping they'd take the bait because it would be tough for her to circle back around to something she'd tossed off with such indifference.

Tucker gobbled it right down. "You know, now that you mention it, we probably could have put this whole thing to rest a half hour ago."

"How's that?" Maxie asked, wary, now not all that sure where this was going.

"By asking you if your client's brother was deformed in any way." A triumphant smile rose like a smug sun on Tucker's face.

"Deformed?" Knowing exactly where they were headed now.

"That's why we call him Pinkie."

"And why is that?" Leading him into a trap of his own making.

"Because of his little finger—"

"Which I'd be willing to bet is chopped off at the middle joint." The trap springing, getting its jaws around Hollis Tucker's smile, ripping it right off his face. "In a boating accident. When he was a kid."

"How'd you know that?" the deputy warden asked, genuinely surprised.

"Because I'm a damned genius, that's why, and I want a sit-down with Ordell Anthony right now or I am gonna make you wish you'd taken your political payoff in some other cushy state job."

Hollis Tucker started to protest. Maxie reached into the leather portfolio and produced the third bogus document—the Freedom of Information request—and slid it in front of Tucker, who no sooner had he blurted out, "What the hell is this?" found a tape recorder under his nose, and heard an angry-sounding black woman barking something about "for the record" why was he refusing to cooperate, and did he understand the consequences of his closed-door policy?

Less than 20 minutes later, Maxie McQueen was sitting in a bare room across a rectangular steel table from Ordell "Pinkie" Anthony, previously known as Henry Lee Hubbard.

Chapter 28

Don't freak out, Kevin told himself, pacing the well-trod L-shaped path in the apartment, front door down mini-hallway and left through the living and dining rooms to the kitchen then back, ignoring himself, still freaking out every step of the way, asking over and over Why? Why had Taylor lied to him?

It was crazy. She was chasing down a story, and while in some perverse way it may have been the story of his life, so what? She didn't have a thing to gain from keeping the truth from him, and even if she did, why yank his chain on something so insignificant—a goddamned database? come on—after she'd gone the whole nine yards on what she'd found in Maryland? *That,* all that stuff about Devereaux and the corporate money and even her theories, cracked as they might be, that all seemed like it was a hell of a lot more important in the overall scheme of things. If this was some kind of hustle, why download the serious info and song-and-dance him on where she'd first found it? And anyway, why not hold back everything, tell him nothing? She had zero to gain from confiding in him, less than zero. They'd intersected because a guy in Florida was dead, which didn't have anything to do with Kevin, so there was nothing evil, nothing preordained about their meeting. It was driven by events, not plots, and had begun with him as a source, not a would-be lover or whatever it was he'd become, and he'd known that from the get-go, and understood it. There was something bigger going on here, maybe, and he was a fringe player. Devereaux, not Kevin Columbus, was central to her story. Her interest in him was only professional, at least to start with, and if for some reason that changed courses, went somewhere else, and she saw something in him, something that could last—

Don't go there, he told himself, dead-ending the back-and-forth in his apartment. Do not go there.

He dropped onto the sofa, holding his head like it was about to explode. It was 3:30 in the afternoon. Maxie was off somewhere, chasing down something. His mother had dropped off the radar screen again, stop the presses. Taylor was in Washington chasing shadows. The only person he'd heard from was that damned Wayne Earl Wiley, asking how the meetings were going, apologizing for the judge not showing up— "Gonna have to dock that ol' boy's pay"—reminding him that time was running out, they needed an answer Monday, the message on his answering machine being, "We're ready to do some bid-ness with you, boy," Wayne Earl saying *with you* like it was *widyuh.*

Kevin thought seriously about the job, more seriously about the money, wondering how much salvation lived inside that stack of hundreds, thinking it had to be a helluva lot more than he was getting anywhere else. He was halfway inclined to just pick up the friggin' phone, call Wiley, say, I'm widya, let's do some bid-ness, quit worrying about what he didn't know, couldn't control, which these days felt like it was pretty much everything. Just do it, man, he goaded himself, staring at the phone in the kitchen, daring himself to dial it, take their money, put himself out of his misery.

Forget all this late-in-life crap about identity and origins, leave it to the gypsies and palmists.

Forget about your old man, who's pushing up carefully manicured grass in Arlington, and even if he wasn't, the sonofabitch should be for running out on him 25 years ago.

Forget about the conspiracies, the paranoid fantasies, that some lying blonde bitch is using to mind-fuck you into collaborating with her.

Just do it, take the money, man, it's a lifeline, a way out of the hole, put this all behind you, where it belongs, burn everything just like

Mother Meredith said, burn it all, like mother like son, take the money, every bit of it, run as far and as fast from everything, all of this, whatever it is, finally deciding the hell with it, they're going to get you one way or another, it's what they're best at, now picking up the phone, dialing, confident he was taking the only option, the only route, then he heard—

"Senator Wiley's office, may I help you?"

— and dropping the phone like it was radioactive, hearing the distant voice on the floor saying Hello, Hello, starting to sweat, looking down at the receiver, more sweat coming, thick enough to surf on, the voice on the line now saying Is someone there? and Kevin not knowing how to answer, thinking this was either the best or the dumbest thing he'd ever done, hearing a click, Wayne Earl's secretary disconnecting, then nothing, Kevin thinking, Saved by the dead air, winner by default: Me.

Whoever that is.

•

Walter Frost loathed this place like death itself.

He loathed the massive lagoon on the first of the hotel lobby's four levels. The construction, all girders and glass. The bar where he now sat, which billed itself as the longest free-standing bar in the country. The little clip-on nametag the bartender wore, Cesar. The three levels of bottles—wines and champagnes and scotches and liqueurs—lit from beneath, 1,400 of them he'd heard, as if that were something to be proud of. The ambiance, which was basically non-existent, a din of chattering conventioneers and salesman that created what to Walter Frost felt like a slaughterhouse, how appropriate for this city of stockyards. The so-called Magnificent Mile, Michigan Avenue below, reeking of commercialism without possessing a shred of the dignity he'd found in Brussels, say, or London. God, and the cigars. Locally made, someone told him, and sold at the bar from a menu, like those ghastly chicken wings. Cigars that to his nose reeked more of the 12-cent variety than the $12 being charged to the gaggle of humanity who descended on this place as if it were a paragon of culture.

He sipped his martini, Bombay Sapphire, looked at two men to his left. Hispanic, drug lords, he imagined, with their gold bracelets and neck chains, shirts open two buttons more than necessary, gaudy wristwatches and hairy chests, both slathering over a couple of women, a blonde and a redhead, plying them with macho posturing and lies.

To his right, smoking a cigarette, was Frost's luncheon companion, a vision in black: Black long-sleeved T-shirt. Loose-fitting black drawstring pants. Black Reeboks. Black baseball cap, Chicago White Sox, pulled down low over a pair of Prada sunglasses so dark the lenses and frames were indistinguishable. Black Nike runner's watch, large, designed for a man. All of it a stark contrast to every other sad sack business person on holiday at the bar, Frost thought, men noteworthy only for their discount-store suits and comb-overs, plain-looking women in dark outfits trying to appear crisp and professional, succeeding only in looking like frumpy grade school teachers from Dayton.

God, how he loathed them, too.

Hiding in plain sight, Frost thought, taking the measure of his companion's black outfit once again, understanding the concept if not necessarily embracing it. He preferred to work with people who blended in better, became Every Man, as it were, like Edward Van Parkes. People who opted for invisibility as opposed to this conscious narcissism, which theorized that any person so devoted to drawing attention to his or herself could never be worthy of so much as a passing glance, and thus work invisibly.

On the other hand, he couldn't argue with results. And no matter what the tactics or strategy, this one had truly delivered. Until recently, anyway.

"Are you sure you wouldn't care for anything to eat, Mr. Frost?" A fork, gesturing to the remains of some designer salad.

Not Walter. *Mr. Frost.* Still calling him that after all these years. On more than a few occasions, he wondered whether it was a title of respect, or just mockery. "No, thank you. I had a late breakfast."

"Don't you love this place?" Knowing full well he didn't, playing with him. "It's so utterly, I don't know, so utterly…American. Just like the town."

Too American, he thought. Which, in the end, was why he so loathed Chicago.

Walter Frost shifted uncomfortably in his barstool. "I'd prefer Le Lion d'Or," he said simply. The bartender, Cesar, wiry and dark, Latin features, with thinning, close-cropped hair, asked if he'd like another martini. Frost nodded, reminding the man, an illegal he'd wager, that it was Sapphire he was drinking.

"Too French for my tastes. Give me a steak at Morton's. There's a Morton's in Washington, isn't there?" Frost nodded. "Red-meat, white potatoes and true blue American food. Nothing like it."

Not necessarily being a good thing, he thought.

A loud laugh to his left. He turned to see one of the Hispanic men whispering something into the blonde's ear while he stroked the back of her white, tight-fitting dress, fiddling suggestively with the zipper at the top. She sipped a screwdriver. Another laugh caused her friend, the red-head—form-fitting jeans, pink top that left her entire back exposed—to turn as well, peering over the broad shoulders of the zipper-fiddler, looking to see what the commotion was all about. She said something in Spanish. The blonde laughed again.

Good Christ, Walter Frost thought, the women are Hispanics, too. Is there a Colombian cartel convention in this godawful metropolis? Are there no Americans anywhere but Washington?

The fresh Sapphire martini arrived, Frost sipping it slowly, eyes grabbing an occasional furtive peek at the black-clad persona to his left, wondering what was going to happen next.

He was a man accustomed to, and secure with, power. Generally, there was little doubt—in his mind, in anyone's mind—that when Walter Frost was in a meeting, Walter Frost was in control. Nothing happened, no decisions were made, no actions were taken, unless he had already decided to do so long before the assembly convened. Frost believed strongly in the perception of democracy, of inviting diverse comments and open, free-flowing discussion. In the end, though, he believed more strongly that too much democracy was a bad thing. The open flow of ideas served only to delay decisions, not inspire them. In a world that needed swift action to prevail over the forces of chaos, a free nation could ill afford the ideological luxury of parsing the concerns of anyone with an opinion.

So it was an established fact that Walter Frost listened, and then did what he thought best. That he had never been elected to anything meant nothing. No one who possessed real power ever had to suffer the whims of the electorate.

Which was why Walter Frost hated these forced meetings, even more than he hated that they were always, God help him, in Chicago:

He was not in control. Yes, he had asked that they get together. And yes, his companion had agreed to join him without hesitation. And yes, he had agreed to come to this town, the center of the Sixpack Universe. And yes, the verbal bow that calling him *Mr. Frost* represented still had the ring of authentic respect. But make no mistake. Walter Frost was at the mercy of someone very unlike those who constituted the American electorate. This was a person whose actions he could direct but whose power he could never overtake.

Such was the case, he always assumed, with people like this, finding odd comfort—or perhaps it was just rationalization, a denial of his own weakness—in the fact that no one ever truly controlled a murderer.

"Would you like some coffee, Mr. Frost?"

He suddenly felt warm, and briefly considered taking off his coat, rejecting the notion for concern it would be seen as a sign of anxiety. "No, thank you."

A moment later, the bartender brought one cup, and a handful of miniature creamer containers, three of which found their way into the coffee.

Frost watched the black liquid spooned into a swirling tan-white. "We have a problem," he said at last.

"Why else would we be here?" Nonchalant, as if it was a given. Two quick sips of the coffee, apparently feeling none of the heat that steamed from its surface.

"The first thing you must understand is that this Kevin fellow is off limits."

"That's fine." A shrug.

Behind the nearly opaque glasses, though, Frost could feel the eyes. Just as he imagined the others must have felt them a quarter century before, in Nashville, in that rat hole of a flophouse—-

"Didn't think you got down into the slime with the rest of us." A vicious stare, complementing a crooked, knowing smile that said You don't got the balls.

"He was your responsibility," Devereaux said.

"And here he is"—gesturing to the quivering man on the unmade bed—"so why don't you just put the gun down, and let's do it, and get outta here."

"You were supposed to eliminate him at the scene." He did not lower the military-issue Colt .45

"How was I supposed to know the private cop wasn't dead?"

"It was your job to know."

"We'd checked him out, we knew he had the bad ticker, he should've—"

"But he wasn't."

"So I hit him with another dose. What's the big deal?"

"The big deal is that the extra seconds allowed your man to escape." A crisp professionalism in the voice.

"This ain't your style. I thought you were the man arranged to have the thing done, not the one who did the thing."

"I arrange that the thing, as you say, is done right."

"So, let's make it right."

"I should be on my way to Geneva right now."

"Who's stopping you? Shoot the guy, and go ski or yodel, whatever it is you planned to do." Not backing down.

"You jeopardized the operation."

There was a silence that to the terrified man on the bed seemed to last for years.

"I have never jeopardized an operation in my entire career." The eyes now filled with a hate darker and deeper than space. "And where there have been lapses, they have been sanitized without disclosure."

"You're not murdering suspected Viet Cong in jungle villages 13,000 miles away. This is America. We have to be better."

"We are. That's why we can do what we do." The eyes now going almost friendly. They could change, just that fast, from one emotion to another, and then another, as if they had neither the ability nor the desire to communicate any single thing for any length of time.

Killer's eyes, revealing everything but honesty.

"You forfeited that right with your incompetence—"

The rage returned. "Don't you fucking—"

"—and leave me no choice—"

"You'll never—"

"—but to terminate you."

"You can't do it." Sneering, getting him in the crosshairs of a stare so filled with derogation and depravity that it was as if pure evil had settled upon them all. "You know why?" The look now dripping with malice. "Because you're a child. A fucking ch—"

At the sound of the gunshots, the man in the bed wet himself, wondering if he was next.

— Walter Frost not knowing exactly what was behind those eyes, but suspecting nothing less than the absolute worst. But it was futile to try and read them, and he knew it. "The detective, however, has become something of a nuisance."

"Yes, she has." A smile. "But I assume CABALGUY is on the case?"

Frost shifted at the mention of his cyber-alter ego. Not his, actually, but the name he'd given the ex-agent and current DDI technician who anonymously passed critical information along to the killer through an unknowing Rollie Merke. "We are attempting to find out where she is at the moment, yes, and what she is doing."

"I could have put her down long before now."

Frost sipped the martini and nodded slightly. "I understand. Our instructions were to keep civilian casualties to a minimum."

"Excluding Agent Addison."

"We had no choice." Another tortured shift on the stool. He added quickly: "It was well-executed, by the way."

"Of course it was. I leave nothing to chance."

Walter Frost paused, taking a moment to beat back the urge not to say *Perhaps if you had been so careful in Alabama, we would not have a dead FBI agent and a curious private eye on our hands.* Instead, he simply nodded. "We don't know what, exactly, this detective will learn. Our man inside could well remain silent, and the curtain may fall quietly and without incident on this little drama."

"Do you really think that, Mr. Frost?"

He shrugged. "His instability may in the end benefit us. He is, after all, a madman."

"Aren't you all?" Another smile.

"You exclude yourself?" Letting his mouth get ahead of his mind. Go lightly, he told himself. Lightly.

The smiled transformed into a wide grin. "Yes, I, do." Then came a laugh, deep and unexpected. "You think I'm the one with the faulty wiring, don't you?" Frost's stare found its way back to the glasses. "You think I'm some kind of freak. Like I'm missing some critical gene, some chromosome, some chemical in the brain. How else do you explain someone like me?"

Frost involuntarily looked around, as if to see who could be listening to their exchange, and what they might think of it. The closest people, the Hispanic quartet to his left, were speaking in hushed tones, lost in their own schemes. One of the women, he noticed, the redhead, had a ring on her thumb.

"Relax, Mr. Frost. People look at us, they assume it's a father and his kid, maybe a student at Northwestern Law, enjoying each other's company over a quiet lunch."

"They can assume what they will. I don't have that luxury."

"What is it that you assume about me?" Leaning on the bar now, face turned to him, chin in hand, sounding almost playful. "Do you think my father molested me as a child? And that in the instant before I pull the trigger, it's him I see, and that my chosen career gives me a chance to extract my revenge over and over and over again?"

Frost took another sip of the martini, dropping his head a bit into his shoulders. He felt like he was being toyed with, and did not appreciate it. "I don't know what you think."

"Then, let me tell you what I feel in the seconds before I"—looking from one side to the other, in pretended conspiracy—"do it." The smile vanished. "I'm scared out of my mind. Nervous as hell. You'd think that after...how many is it now?"

Frost didn't answer. The only ones that mattered to him were the five in Arabaq.

"I don't remember, either, Mr. Frost," both of them knowing it was a lie. "What I remember is the horror. Because you never get used to it. Never." Leaning in closer to him, so he could hear the near-whispered words. "But there always comes a time, one single millisecond, when you know the horror has to be put aside, and you have to do the job. And you don't think of anything else. You just do it." Stretching back into the barstool, looking incredibly at ease, tossing the next comment as simply and comfortably as a parent tossing a ball to a child. "That's why you guys recruited me, wasn't it? Because when Azid's thugs came through the front door, I didn't pause."

Frost nodded slowly. "As I understand it, that's correct."

"I saw what had to be done and did not hesitate to do it. I dropped two of them without even thinking." A deep breath, almost a sigh. "Raymond hesitated. That's why he's dead and I'm not. He had to work himself into that mind-set. Have you seen *The Godfather*?"

The question startled Frost. He nodded fuzzily.

"The scene where Pacino comes out of the bathroom and kills the crooked cop in the Italian restaurant. You can see his emotions all over his face. He stands there, and you're thinking Will He or Won't He? That's what Raymond looked like in the room that day when Azid's gang came. It's what he looked like the instant before they sliced his head off with the Holy Sabre."

Frost's mouth was half-open, somewhere between utter confusion and shock. "*The Godfather*?"

"Oh, yes, Mr. Frost. I rent movies. I like to shop for shoes. I love jewelry. I'll take Michigan Avenue over Fifth Avenue any day of the week. I don't stay in a dark closet, biting the heads off bats. I'm terribly ordinary. I know you don't want to believe I could possibly be sane, or that I'm acting out of choice. You'd much prefer me to be the victim of some insufferable evil, maybe brainwashing or torture. I'm not, though. I'm as normal as anyone else. And that's probably the scariest thing about me. It sure worked with the FBI guy. He paused, too, because he could not believe that a Georgetown law student was about to turn his lights off. You may find that disturbing, Mr. Frost, but given what you pay me to do, it's probably not such a bad trait."

Walter Frost had begun to perspire. He glanced from face to face at the bar, table to table behind him, concerned over eavesdroppers. But the smile was so sweet and the voice so pleasant that they disguised the words completely. He coughed, and cleared his throat of a non-existent obstruction. "Why you do what you do is really none of my concern."

"And you want to know something really weird? I don't know why I do it. Maybe it was the nine months in the Arabaqi desert, learning to shoot and kill, and discovering that, By Gosh, I finally found something I was good at. Maybe it was watching Raymond get decapitated by one of Azid's henchmen who made the fatal mistake of thinking I was just an ornament, along for the thrill. Or the guilt that I shot the two with the guns first, when I should have gone for the one with the sword. Maybe it's the sense of justice I got whenever I put a bullet in the head of one of Azid's children. Hell, Mr. Frost, maybe it *was* because I grew up without a father. I don't know. But let me tell you what I do know. I know that in all that time spent over there, I never slept without a gun in my bed. It gave me more protection than Raymond Trotter ever did. Now you and Freud may think that's got something to do with my desire for a penis, and it may, although I'm not one of those aggressive females who wishes she had her own. I prefer mine attached to a man, and if you have any questions as to that, feel free to contact Kevin Columbus. So once you eliminate the possibility that I'm a lesbian, or a monster, or a debutante who fell for the wrong guy, there's only one explanation left." She leaned over and pecked him lightly on the cheek. "I'm just like you."

Frost recoiled as if stung by hornet.

"Actually," she said, standing up. "I'm better. I'm better because unlike you, I still feel the horror." A smile and a girlish shrug of the shoulders. "But more than that, Mr. Frost, I'm better because I can do something you can't do: I can bring life into this world, and I can nurture that life, and then, if necessary, I can end that life." She removed the White Sox hat, and the blonde hair that fell seemed almost white against the black clothes. "All you can do is end it. And that makes you half the human being I am."

She pulled her hair into a pony tail, and threaded it through the opening in the back of the cap. "And by the way, I told him everything." Said it dismissively, an aside, clearly calculated to unnerve Walter Frost. "About the operation and how it worked, and your little foreign-policy playground, Americans for America. Cute name."

It worked, Frost instantly trying to bottle up the gusher of anxiety and outrage that had suddenly begun to surge in him and was threatening to crack his veneer of self-control. "And why would you do something so stupid as that?"

She leaned into him, whispered: "We're going to have to kill him sooner or later, Mr. Frost. The fact that he now knows your dirty little secrets will prevent any emotional considerations from interfering with the decision-making process when the time comes."

Frost recoiled as if she'd spit fire into his ear. "And you think that was wise?"

A big smile, stop-people-in-the-street beautiful, not a trace of darkness anywhere. "Keeps things interesting, pops," bending over now, kissing him lightly again, this time on the top of his head, smiling like the daughter she wanted people to see, Frost thinking she, too, was reckless, what was it about people like this that made them act with such irresponsibility, especially when so much was at stake?

It was only then that Taylor Shepard took off the midnight black glasses, revealing eyes that were so much like her father's their iciness froze Walter Frost in his chair—

Vaguely hearing her say, "Don't worry—"

The same eyes Gary Devereaux had seen at the instant he understood he was about to die—

"I'll take care of the detective—"

The last eyes that Roscoe Chatham saw before a deadly cigar seared his insides and shut down his heart—

"I'll take care of everything—"

And that Richard Addison stared into, not believing, at the coffee shop—

"Because if there's one thing you need to know—"

Empty eyes.

"It's that you can trust me—"

Dead eyes.

"To do what has to be done."

Killer eyes.

Chapter 29

Maxie knew a loser when she saw one, and the man sitting at the square steel table opposite her was a six-foot mistake piled into a denim jumpsuit.

The interview room was small, no more than 20 by 20. A single light overhead, fluorescent, shaped like an oven burner—round with what looked to be coils—bathed the space with an uncertain glow, as if it was running out of gas. Concrete floor, walls and ceiling, the whole area boxed in save for a shatter-proof window on the heavy steel door, on the other side of which two armed guards stood ready to come crashing in and shoot Henry Lee Hubbard to death if he so much as sneezed wrong. Restrained like he was, though, with leg irons and handcuffs latched to a chain around his waist, Henry Lee didn't look like much of a threat.

"What's this bullshit story about a will?" he asked, not smiling, voice as cracked and dry as an adobe brick. His records said he was 46, but he sounded decades older. Pale, with a week-long growth on his sunken face and arms so thin the veins were grotesquely pronounced, he reminded Maxie of every junkie she'd ever come across.

"Your sister Darlene is dead." Trying to keep everything on an even keel. Hollis Tucker had told her the man was on some mixture of Tegretol for mood disorders; Thorazine, an anti-psychotic, and Verapemil to reduce his violent tendencies. He also said he wasn't exactly sure what chemicals were coursing through Ordell's system at the moment—they still called him Ordell—so Maxie was making damn sure she did everything in her power to avoid knocking this old goat any further out of whack.

His response was unexpected: "I figured. What happened?" Not a touch of nuttiness about him, nor any effort to deny that he was, in fact, Henry Lee Hubbard.

"Automobile accident. She apparently was coming to see you."

Henry Lee closed his eyes tightly, then snapped them open. But there was still no change in his demeanor. He was almost serene, and it didn't strike Maxie that this was the warm-up act for a headlining meltdown. The man appeared truly at peace, far from the portrait Tucker had painted. "You buy that?"

Maxie thought she heard a touch of disdain in his voice, a sense of How could anyone in their right mind possibly believe it was an accident? She didn't take her gaze from him, determined not to back off, not even an inch. "What do you think?"

He twisted his neck back and forth, as if trying to loosen the muscles, and a thin strand of long brown hair fell over one gray eye. He tried to blow it out of the way, without success. "What about Gary? What kind of *accident* killed him?"

Maxie felt her pulse start to climb into a higher gear, thinking of Kevin and Island City and the package. "Gary Devereaux?" Don't get too excited, she warned herself. Stay cool. "How do you know him?"

"He called me." Said it straight out, not a hint of what he was thinking, what might be going on inside his head.

"When?"

"Week ago. Something like that."

"What did you talk about?"

Henry Lee laughed. Again, the response was unexpected. "Old times." Maxie let the silence that followed sit there on the table, hoping the man would get unnerved by the hush and break it on his own. He did, but there was no trace of anxiety when he finally spoke, none of that felon-guilt she'd seen time after time in the police department interrogation rooms. "Gary told me I was the last of a dying breed."

"Why do you think he said that?"

"He knew he was going to die." He stopped, and considered his next words before asking: "When did it happen?"

Maxie wasn't sure how much she wanted to give up at this point in the interview, but instinct warned her not to tell him what she knew, not just yet. "When did what happen?"

Impatience dashed across Henry Lee's face. "I may look stupid, honey, and I ain't the sharpest blade in the kitchen drawer. But we both know why you're here, and it don't have a goddamned thing to do with a will. And as much as I'd like to get outta these things and engage in a little hanky-panky with you, I ain't much in the mood for foreplay at the present time. So why don't you just answer my question, and we'll get wherever we're going a whole hell of a lot faster."

Okay, she thought, some rules were established. "Devereaux killed himself about a week ago."

"Used that Colt, I bet." Another smile, one that looked as if it was built on memory, though not a fond one.

"I don't know. I just know that the official story is he killed himself, and—"

"Kinda like the official story about Darlene being in an automobile accident, right?"

"Yeah." Saying it slowly, wary.

Henry Lee nodded. "I killed her." Which made Maxie sit up a little straighter in the metal folding chair. He noticed. "Don't get your undies in a twist. I killed her the second I made that phone call. Never shoulda done it, but goddammit, with Gary gone, I was afraid they'd come after her, and then Donna, and then me."

"Like they came after the rest of your family?"

He smiled sadly, and shook his head, almost sympathetically. No self-pity, though, more like he felt sorry for Maxie for investing into some grand scheme that, no matter how intriguing, was a crock. "Detective, I wish I could tell you that some big, bad, evil conspiracy was responsible for all the hurt my family has suffered. That kind of explanation would make it easier to accept. But the plain truth is, my family got wiped out by nothing more than bad luck." The smile got sadder. "As the Bible says, Time and chance happeneth to them all."

Although the thought that Henry Lee Hubbard had found God in the pen did not surprise Maxie, she still flinched involuntarily at the biblical reference. Dealing with a nut was one thing, with a religious nut, quite another. He caught her reaction, grinned crookedly. "Don't worry, hon, I'm still a heathen at heart."

She wasn't up for a debate on moral outlook, his, hers or in general. "So they were just a victim of what? Fate?"

"Yep." Now it was Henry Lee's turn to pause, as if wondering how much *he* should give up. "See, they were protected."

Which was about the last thing she expected to hear, so surprising that it took a moment to register, like Henry Lee and suddenly turned into the Easter Bunny and she was trying to figure out what, exactly, was going on. "Protected?" He nodded. "Protected by whom?"

"The government."

Maxie had always thought this case was a crap shoot, long odds made acceptable by the promise of a fat fee check, or at least a plump one, or at least one that had some meat on its bones, when it was over. But when she heard that answer—the *government*, Christ, what did *that* mean?—she felt the odds get smaller, and the risk a whole lot greater. "Protected from what?"

"From being murdered. I cut a deal—"

There he was, cowering on the stained flophouse mattress, weeping from a lack of sleep and too much fear, cold piss gluing the dungarees to his leg. Devereaux was looking down at the floor, where the second man lay dead, blood pouring from wounds that punctured the chest and virtually eliminated the face. Looking up at Henry Lee, he said, "I need you."

"—to keep them all alive."

"What was your part of the deal?" Maxie asked.

"I brought a little something for you," he said, gesturing with his chin toward the left breast pocket of his prison jumpsuit. When Maxie hesitated, he smiled. "It's a picture, detective. What am I gonna do? Pick these with it?" Holding up the chains.

Maxie removed a three-by-five photograph. It was taken in the jungle, Vietnam, she assumed. Two men, shirtless, one covered in camouflage paint, a lot of it black, the other holding an M16 against his thigh. The one with the rifle looked vaguely familiar to her. "Is this you?" she asked, pointing to him.

He shook his head. "The other one." Maxie brought the photo close, as if looking at it from two inches away would somehow reveal something that linked the man in the picture to the man chained before her. There was nothing, though. They were different as a redwood and a toothpick.

"You're telling me *this* is you?" Staring first at Henry Lee and then back at the image on the paper, then up again. Henry Lee nodded. "Sorry, but I don't believe that."

"Look at the right hand."

There it was, clear as could be. Half a little finger. "Son of a bitch," Maxie said.

Henry Lee nodded. "That was my part of the bargain. I had to become someone else."

"How?"

"Gary was a spook. He knew people that could do that sort of thing. Cosmetic surgery." A smile, almost wistful, followed by a tiny, empty laugh. "By the time they finished the operation, my face looked like 40 miles of rough road, I'll tell you that."

Maxie remembering what Hollis Tucker had said, about Henry Lee getting pistol whipped, mangling his face and all. "So the thing about you and the other man, about him beating you—"

"A cover story."

"Why was it necessary? Why'd you have to become somebody else?"

"For insurance," Devereaux said, pointing the .45 at a shaking Henry Lee. "I need you to protect my son. If you don't do this for me, I will shoot you right here, and then systematically murder every member of your family who was with you in New York. If, on the other hand, you agree, I will make certain that they are protected from any recriminations."

"H-h-how can I be sh-sh-sure you'll be alive to p-p-protect them?"

"I've arranged for my own insurance."

"I had to quit being me so I could save them."

"From what?" She asked again, her mental focus split by the nagging familiarity of the guy in the picture, the one with the M16.

"From the government."

Even amid the unfolding mystery, her impatience flared. "Hold on there, bubba. You just said the government was protecting them. Now you're telling me they had to be protected *from* the government?"

"That's right."

Made no sense, none of it. Maxie looked at the second man in the photo, the one who seemed halfway familiar to her. "Who's this other guy?"

"Jut a guy."

"Where is he now?"

Henry Lee said nothing. He just smiled, like she was a prize pupil who had just cracked the math problem. Maxie ignored his silence, reacting more to his satisfied expression, and not reacting real well. "You better start talking to me, man, because I got a feeling you're the one who can string together a whole lot of loose ends."

"Oh," he said, smiling. "I can. I surely can. About Worth. Buskin. Whole lotta good shit."

"But I'm warning you, goddammit, you had better not start spouting a whole lot of crazy shit about how you were in Dallas when Kennedy was shot, or that you're really Raoul, and that you killed Dr. King—and what kind of name is that anyway, Raoul?—or that you were the second gunman in New York when Worth was shot, because I swear to God, if you do, I will rip your lungs out."

"No problem," Henry Lee said simply.

"Good," Maxie answered, calmed down almost immediately by the man's to-the-point acquiescence.

"I wasn't the second gunman when Worth was shot."

"That's the best damned news I've had in weeks."

"I was the third."

Chapter 30

July 1975

Henry Lee Hubbard looked at his watch.

It was 12:16, and he'd been gone for maybe three or four minutes. Too long. The family, down there on the street, would be wondering where he was, why he was spending all this time taking a leak.

No matter. He'd deal with that when the time came.

12:17. Climbing up the stairs to the 16th floor, the stairwell smelling like a cross between paint, pee and Pine Sol, thinking, Would the door to the fire escape be open and would the rifle be there, and most of all would the mug across the street stick his head up in time for him, Henry Lee, to blow it off if he had to, and do it before the guy could shoot Worth like a dog on the street?

12:18. Twelfth floor.

Henry Lee thought briefly about the rest of the security team, where they were deployed, but let it pass. Compartmentalization, they told him. Know your own deal, do your own thing, trust the man next to you to do his even if you can't see him, don't worry about the big picture, don't ask any questions.

Henry Lee was good to go with that. The only question he'd asked was why Worth needed private security, Tim telling him they were like Hell's Angels protecting the Stones at Altamonte. Being a Johnny Cash-Waylon Jennings kind of guy, Henry Lee didn't know what he was talking about, but he was still good to go with things anyway.

12:19. Thirteenth floor.

His deal was this:

On the 16th floor, he'd open the fire escape door onto a metal grid plat-form. The contact would be there. So would a civilian, who'd be the pri-mary, which Henry Lee didn't understand, but it wasn't his job to understand. His job was backup. The guy in the suit fucked up, Henry Lee stepped in. Bang. Done. Go back downstairs, hook up with the family, eat a pretzel, have a hot dog, wait for the money in a week.

Bang. Done.

12:20. Fourteenth floor.

Three months of training, which was a lot of work just to be a backup, the last one out on some godforsaken shooting range, Bumfuck, Texas, tak-ing target practice from a tower-like deal, 16 stories high, just like where he was heading now, except then he was aiming at feed bags piled behind a window in some Hollywood-set-looking building across from him. Right out there in the heart of nowhere, Henry Lee on this cherry-picker, feed bags across the way, three months of shooting, lot of work just to be a backup.

12:21. Fifteenth floor.

Weird as it sounded, though, all that practice for a No. 2 shooter, Tim was right about one thing: After nailing little guys in black pajamas in Laos, torching their villages, shooting their mama-sans and papa-sans and their stinking barnyard animals, this was at least a chance to make it right, whatever it was that needed to be made right. He'd enlisted to fight for his country, and now somebody, he didn't know who, except Tim said it was somebody important, somebody who could make Henry Lee's career, had recruited him and trained him to help protect somebody who bad people were trying to kill. Even if he wasn't the primary, no matter, he was on the team, Team USA, Tim called it, and by God he was ready to lock and load and send this guy Buskin into the great hereafter if he got the chance.

12:22.

He stopped at the landing for just a moment, caught his breath, eyed the yellow-block letters that told him where he was: 16th floor.

"I'm here," Henry Lee Hubbard mumbled to himself. "Everything's A-O-Fuckin'-K."
12:23.
He pushed the metal door open.

•

The best thing about Rayfield Buskin was that nobody had to invent him. He was simply one of the disaffected masses. Every Man in a world coming apart at the seams.

Within a week of his March conversation with Bart Knight, Walter Frost had begun searching the nut job files Worth's office kept. These contained the names and correspondence of anyone who had in any way threatened the senator. While the information was routinely passed on to Capitol security—and, eventually, the Secret Service—Worth's staff maintained its own dossier at the insistence of the senator, who was something of a fatalist and, Frost believed, a willing martyr in waiting.

With the high visibility that accompanied his fight for the chemical weapons ban, Worth had also become a magnet for crazies. Most of them were self-styled America-Firsters, who wrapped their anger over everything from integration to foreign aid in the flag of blind patriotism. Their arguments were decidedly simple: Whatever benefited anyone other than themselves, or recognized any interests other than their own, amounted to high treason. Those who disagreed were traitors.

Because he had a high-level security clearance—and, perhaps more important, because Dan Goggins took a hands-off approach to him, which an easily cowed Senate staff gladly followed—Frost had unlimited access to the nut job files. For the most part, the records gave up the usual suspects: People who thought they shouldn't pay taxes. People who thought blacks should be shipped back to Africa. People who believed the Trilateral Commission and Henry Kissinger really did run the country. People who believed that the liberal agenda was destroying the country, and anyone who advocated or practiced it should be shot.

All of which were categories that fit Rayfield Buskin like a second skin.

Frost first noticed him through a letter written in pencil and dated shortly after Worth had pushed through the chemical weapons treaty the previous December. On lined composition book paper, the writer warned that "you have weakened a great country by removing an important weapon from our arsenal." He continued:

"Thanks to you and your lefty buddies, it will not be long until the mongrel races of the 3rd world will be ahead of us in the production of weapons of mass destruction. To say, as you have, that this treaty is good for America reveals you for the false Christ and false prophet that you truly are. And before the sun shall be darkened, and before the moon shall give no more light, and before the stars shall fall from the sky as the powers of heaven shall be shaken by the actions of you and the other Great Deceivers, I will personally take it upon myself to set your house in order. You have gouged out the eye of America's strength. So, too, shall I gouge out the eye of your pacifism. Vengeance shall be mine."

It was boiler-plate hate rhetoric—big on Biblical references, less so on specifics—but Frost didn't care. His job was to acquire a would-be killer, someone who could be easily and plausibly accepted as the assassin of Richard Francis Worth. Discovering this kind of letter, with its veiled threats and clear allusion to the treaty, was a necessary first step. When Bart Knight agreed—saying, "The question now is can he stand up to scrutiny?"—the process continued.

The "scrutiny" to which Knight referred was a covert investigation of Buskin by intelligence operatives who did not feel bound by the prohibition against domestic CIA actions. And once again, the reality of Rayfield Buskin proved better than any manufactured fiction.

Buskin was, by his own description, an "oddball." The son of an alcoholic father and a mother who freely dispensed sexual favors to the neighbors, he had been in and out of juvenile detention centers from ages 6 to 13. Although there were no signs of neglect or abuse, the boy's records showed without question that he was delusional. Reports from social workers—stolen, photographed and returned by government agents who broke into the Pensacola, Florida, facility where he was treated—stated that Buskin was obsessed with *The Adventures of Ozzie and Harriet,* dreaming of being David Nelson and explaining how, if he really was David, he'd kill Ricky, the little pansy rock star, and the parents, describing the imagined murders in gory detail.

Released into the care of a foster family, Buskin grew into a true loner. He kept to himself, and had virtually no friends in junior high or high school. Over the years, he became known for two things. First, the fact that he always ate lunch alone, as far from his classmates as the cafeteria's layout would allow. And second, because the only conversations he carried on appeared to be with himself. He was often observed walking down the school corridors, grinning and gesturing to a companion that only he could see. Fellow students laughed and made fun of him, but other than noticing, no one really seemed to care. His grades were good, and he managed to hold down a series of typical teen jobs: movie usher, grocery store clerk, dishwasher, yardman.

What Frost found especially appealing about Buskin was that he never seemed to get past his own little world. His isolation only seemed to strengthen with age. He decided not to go to college, instead continuing to live at home with his foster parents. When he finally did move out—at age 22—he rented a one-bedroom apartment in a dilapidated section of town that was transitioning from white middle class to black. Two months later, while Buskin was at work selling paint at a hardware store, the place was broken into and robbed. That episode, more than anything else, turned him into Richard Worth's presumed murderer.

A week after the break-in, Buskin began frequenting a shooting range located just outside of Pensacola on U.S. 29. He bought a pistol, a five-shot Police Bulldog .44 Special, and began taking lessons from the paramilitary-styled instructors at the facility. Meek and deferential at the range, Buskin would go home at night, lock the doors, turn off the lights and wait for any intruders to dare break the threshold of his life. When he was able to place all five bullets into a paper target's kill zone 90 percent of the time, he graduated to rifles, acquiring an Armalite AR-18 after reading that it was what the Los Angeles Police Department used in its 1974 shootout with the Symbionese Liberation Army. In less than three weeks, he had become a marksman.

One day, after a half hour of shooting in which he'd bulls-eyed 11 shots from 50 yards—and five weeks after writing his Armageddon-ish letter to Worth—Buskin was walking to his car in the range's sandy parking lot when he was approached by a slender, good-looking, affable man in a military flight suit. "You're a helluva shot," the man said.

Buskin mumbled something inaudible and opened the hood of the car, a Corvair, to store the rifle, not looking at the man in the flight suit.

"Do much hunting?"

Buskin continued to rummage around in the truck, saying nothing.

The man smiled and squinted into the late spring sun from behind dark aviator glasses. "The reason I ask is that a fella with your kind of skill, well, there are people—important people—willing to pay top dollar for somebody like you." Nothing, not the reference to money or to power or the flattering comment on his skill, produced so much as a twitch of response from Buskin. "Hell, might even make you famous." The man smiled, showing teeth so white he could have brushed with Clorox.

Buskin stopped, didn't move for a couple of seconds. After what seemed to be an inner debate with himself, he began to speak. As he did—and he still didn't look up, instead carrying on a conversation with the hood of the Corvair—the debate became external: "What would you like to be famous for, Ray? Who says I do? Oh, come on, man, what would they say, all those people who laughed at you in school? They don't matter. The hell they don't. They don't matter as much as the jigaboos we're gonna pop. Goddamned spades, I swear, one of 'em ever darkens my doorway again, don't care if they're selling Bibles, and bang-bang-bang, it's off to that big cotton field in the sky. Break into my house, the place where I live. Man has to defend himself. That's what makes this country great and strong. Defense. Any man doesn't believe that, don't matter who he is, got no right to live. Just like all those anti-war Commie-loving liberals. Damned straight. People either want to turn the government over to the Sambos or the Reds. Kill every one of 'em, I say. Lock and load, baby, rock'n'roll, every damned one of them—"

It was a stream of consciousness tirade that was utterly without pretension, a monologue that revealed a mind zigzagging from thought to thought without transition. The man in the flight suit watched in admiration, and just a touch of apprehension, wondering what would happen when this guy's actions started speaking louder than his words.

"—and that day will come, by God, oh yes it will, and when it does, when the day of reckoning arrives, everyone who weakened America will be called upon to answer for their conspiracies, their crimes against democracy, and it will be I who meet them—me!—and those who dare cross my wisdom or question my judgment will pay God's price."

With the speed of and grace of a surgeon's incision, Buskin stood, whirled and leveled a .357 at the man's forehead. "And unless you tell me right this second what it is you're after, the judging's gonna get underway, and you ain't gonna like the sentence, not one little bit."

At that moment, looking into Rayfield Buskin's dark, haunted, remorseless eyes, Jon Columbus knew they had their patsy.

•

In the days that followed, Buskin lived two lives. One as a killer-in-training; the other as a stalker.

The former began as little more than an extended firearms lesson. Working from a sound-proofed basement in New Jersey, he tested an incredible range of rifles, foreign and domestic, most of them classic military sniper weapons, all of them really good. His personal favorite was the Russian Dragunov, which fired 10 rounds at 2,723 feet per second, and had a PSO-1 telescopic sight with range-finding scale. For some reason, though, they decided on a Remington M760 Gamemaster, the kind James Earl Ray used when he shot Martin Luther King. It was truly an American gun, and when employed by someone who knew what he was doing, almost as fast as a semi-automatic.

At some point in early June, the training shifted to a desolate patch of West Texas, a 2,000-acre piece of land owned by Excelsior Oil, or EXCO, that was rimmed by electrified razor wire and patrolled daily by heavily armed guards. There, among the scrawny shrubs, rocks and dirt—on a stage that looked like it had been air-lifted out of Hollywood—Buskin's new employers had constructed a block-long set that included a paved section of road, on either side of which were building fronts made of wood paneling. Day after day, a large cherry-picker lifted Buskin 12 stories above the dry Texas countryside. There, overlooking the strip of pavement below, he would kneel on a six-by-six platform, rest his arms on a 10-inch-thick sill, and point the Gamemaster out of a window-sized hole cut into the front of the model building.

On some days, a black Mercury sedan would drive into view. It contained two human cadavers—one in the front, next to the driver, the other in the back. On those days, Buskin worked on how to fire off a killshot before the targets got out of the car. He would put one bullet in each, and the action would stop while a team of intelligence experts swarmed over the vehicle to examine which way the bodies had fallen. Another round of discussions would follow, and Buskin would get his instructions. Sometimes they told him to aim slightly this way or that; other times, they instructed him on where to place the second shot.

Far more interesting were the days when they didn't use the cadavers, but instead took sawdust dummies and lashed them to poles attached to what looked like square, motorized skateboards. With the sedan already in place, the scarecrow-like targets—remote controlled, all of them— would scoot from what was ostensibly the passenger side doors of the Mercury toward a small flight of steps that led to a door cut into the building front opposite Buskin's sniper's nest. His job, simply enough, was to hit each target twice before they made it to the door. Occasionally, the controllers would challenge him by jerking the remote this way and that, as if the target was trying to avoid his fire. Or maybe they'd just veer the contraption off in some other, unexpected direc- tion. At first, the exercises had the intended effect of surprising Buskin. Combined with the fact that he still wasn't wholly comfortable with the Remington, he couldn't react quickly enough to get the job done. Gradually, though, he got better. By late June, he was scoring hits on eight of every 10 tries. Not perfect by any means, and utterly unaccept- able if the ultimate aim was to remove Richard Worth from the realm of the living.

Which was the plan. And which explained why Rayfield Buskin bitched incessantly when he was arbitrarily plucked from his desert rehearsal hall—just as he had been while testing the guns—and re- inserted into his second life: Worth stalker. "Intelligence," his trainer, a black-ops veteran of the Middle East, told him. "You got to know the target better than the target knows himself."

So Buskin, usually dressed in a bright red shirt, open at the neck, dark slacks, white socks and brown penny loafers, found himself pres- ent at event after event that featured Worth. There were breakfast speeches in Nashua, New Hampshire. Lunches at mom and pop diners in Des Moines, Iowa. Dinners at Democratic Party fundraisers in Bakersfield, California. At each, Worth would hammer home his themes: The world was changing, but it was still a scary place, and the leadership that would take the country through the last quarter of the

20th century had a moral obligation to make it less frightening. Other presumed candidates talked about reducing the nuclear threat, taking a for-or-against position on the Strategic Arms Limitation Treaty that was expected to come to a Senate vote sometime after the 1976 presidential election. Not Worth. He claimed that the true risks facing the civilized world were not ICBMs or long-range bombers or Russian submarines that could hurl nukes at U.S. population centers from beneath the Arctic Circle. No, the real threats were invisible, odorless chemicals that killed from the inside.

"Some people will tell you that we have become too efficient in our choice of weaponry," he said at campaign stop after campaign stop in his still unannounced bid for the White House. "They say because we have perfected a system of annihilation that can be activated by the simple push of a button, we have dehumanized war, and made it easier to conduct. If war were conducted by sane men, I might agree. But the fate of the Earth—our fate, as it were—may well rest in the hands of madmen who will do anything to secure power and stop at nothing to maintain it. Despots and dictators, none serving at the will or choice of the people. Men like this do not abhor armed conflict. They abhor the idea that they cannot enjoy the extraction of pain from an opponent. As such, they do not want to push a button and incinerate millions. That's too easy. Rather, they want to release microscopic weapons of destruction that eat into our lungs, our brains and our flesh, killing us in ways that only the devil can imagine. That, my fellow Americans, is the battle of the future. And we must prevent its occurrence now, or live in its shadow for many, many years."

Worth's mixture of rhetoric, passion and true concern riveted crowds at every event, from mini-rallies at strip shopping centers to tub-thumpings at union halls to quasi-intellectual discourses on college campuses. Audiences—young and old, black and white, male and female—could scarcely take their eyes off this slender, almost boyish-looking figure whose words conveyed a conviction that had all but died in the age of Watergate. So they rarely ever noticed the presence of a man in the red shirt and dark pants; if they did, the Worth '76 button over his shirt pocket identified him as nothing more than another of the growing number of Americans who were climbing aboard the senator's bandwagon. Only later, when news organizations discovered his smiling visage in random photographs of Worth events, would anyone realize that Rayfield Buskin had been following the candidate for months, just waiting for the perfect moment to strike.

If everything went according to plan, and the scenario being played out in the desert set—*sets*, actually, as Henry Lee Hubbard was training 16 miles away, on another EXCO tract—that moment would arrive seconds after Rayfield Buskin was already dead. And no one would know the random photographs were part of a carefully constructed backstory that validated the public's belief that only solitary madmen commit solitary acts of madness.

●

Buskin's shift to training at the Hollywood-like set in June coincided with the strategy Worth had finalized for release of the report Dan Goggins had assembled. A meeting was set with key editors and reporters at *The New York Times* at which the senator planned to brief participants on the findings of his internal probe. "I want it low-key," he told Goggins in finally ordering the session. "Maybe a Sunday."

"Do you want it on the schedule?" Goggins had asked.

"We're meeting with the *press*, Dan," Worth responded with his typical disdain. "How do you propose we keep *that* quiet?"

So on June 1, 1975, when the rolling 45-day schedule came off the typewriter, the meeting became official.

The accelerated timetable raised a lot of concerns. Bart Knight originally feared that the two previous months had not given them ample time to effectively frame Buskin for murder, and that the sudden fast track, even though it allowed for a third, might still be insufficient to create a persona palatable to the media and any potential inquiry. On top of that, Buskin didn't become proficient in the Gamemaster as quickly as they'd have preferred. In an odd way, he was the backup plan as well the patsy. If something went wrong and the initial plan had to be abandoned for any reason, they still had to rely on him to aim and fire with an accuracy that would bring Worth down, or at least slow him, until the second gunman could finish the job.

As it happened, though, 43rd Street where the newspaper was located provided a perfect target of opportunity. Hovering over the urban landscape at the corner of 43rd and 8th Avenue was The Times Square, a turn-of-the-century welfare hotel whose external fire escapes sat on metal grid platforms; the 16th-floor landing offered an unobstructed view of the building across the street, The Carter, where Buskin would be perched in a 12th-floor sniper's nest. When Worth's car pulled in to drop the senator off, Buskin would shoot the man dead somewhere between the automobile and the front door of *The Times*.

That's what Buskin thought, anyway, when he arrived in the city on July 5. What would really happen, what their plan of action specified, was in truth far more complex. So much so, in fact, that when Bart Knight first heard the scenario, he instinctively felt it was *too* complex. Knight was a man who believed in simplicity, because simplicity produced fewer risks. "Why not let this fellow Buskin simply do it, and then eliminate him in the apprehending phase?" he asked.

Because it posed even more risks, he was told. It meant they would have to rely solely on Buskin as a killer. It meant they would have to plot an entirely different murder, made even more difficult by the fact that a suspect could already be in custody, meaning they'd have to get someone inside the NYPD. "Then why not do that?" Knight suggested. "This isn't Dallas and we're not the mob," he was told, followed by a laundry list of answers ranging from problems in bringing another person into the conspiracy this late in the game, to a physical inability to make it happen in such a short time frame. As Knight continued to raise concerns—as much out of a need to war-game the entire plan, look at all contingencies, as anything else—his chief strategist continued to parry them with well-thought-out ease. Eventually, it became clear that the New York location, while not perfect, was the best possible option.

So the focus shifted to the aftermath, which Knight referenced simply by saying, "I assume there will be no lingering problems."

He was told there would be none.

"Explain," Bart Knight said.

They had been through this a thousand times, and both of them knew it. But Knight believed that success lay less in the planning than in the execution. And execution, he said so often, was in the details.

The two principals would go to Switzerland within hours of the incident.

"And the gentlemen on the fire escape?"

Tended to at the site.

"Both of them?"

One by lethal injection, left as evidence, the other by force, deposited in a nearby waste incinerator, reduced to nothing but silent ashes.

"Who will tend to them?"

The handler.

"And what will become of this handler?"

He'll go back into the black hole he came from, to resurface only if and when his services are again required.

"Can he be trusted?"

As much as anyone else. Knight understood the irony of the response, and accepted it.

"And your wife? Does she know?"

Yes, she does, he was told. She will fly to Switzerland to meet us.

"Ostensibly to claim the body?"

Ostensibly.

"And the boy?"

In the years that followed, Bart Knight would recall this moment with utter clarity. It was the instant when he realized that, perhaps, he had made the wrong choice. That it was this man, not the other, in whose hands the fate of the world should be placed. The other one may have had the external attributes that had come to outweigh wisdom, courage, coldness and guile as the requirements of leadership. And his weaknesses of the flesh and the intellect made him more predictable and less independent, and thus easier to manipulate by those in whose hands the true power of government by necessity rested.

This one, though, the chief strategist, he had promise. This was the one who possessed the necessary qualities to inspire men: Conviction. Decisiveness. Cunning. Strength. More than that, this one could set aside self-interest for the good of some larger calling, some perceived greater good. It was an admirable trait in a leader, but a fatal one in a politician.

"Does the boy know?" Knight asked again, when dead silence greeted his initial question.

No, came the simple response.

The voice was devoid of any human emotion. Bart Knight was, once again, impressed by his chief strategist. Knight knew that the wife had come to mean less and less to the man. But the boy, Kevin, the boy was everything. Yet that single word—No—spoke nothing of the pain or sense of imminent loss he must be feeling. It was dead and lifeless, as if the memories of the past dozen years either never existed or had been purged from his brain, and Bart Knight knew exactly what was happening:

While it would be another month or so before events signaled his end, Jon Columbus was already starting to die.

•

"*I'm here,*" *Henry Lee Hubbard mumbled to himself.* "*Everything's A-O-Fuckin'-K.*"

12:23.

He pushed the metal door open, but it didn't budge, not at first.

Locked? How could that be?

He tried again. Nothing.

12:24.

Kick the sonofabitch in, no choice, gotta do what you gotta do.

Henry Lee stepped away from the door, balanced himself against the green iron hand rail, looked down at his feet and wished he'd worn something besides the Converse All-Stars, then thinking he planned for the climb, not for having to knock the door down, remembering something his daddy said: If wishes were fishes, we'd have us a fry.

Gripping the hand rail hard now, tight, getting his leverage, lifting his right leg, raising it as high as he could, bending the knee in close for power, getting set to—

When damned if the thing didn't open all by itself.

Shards of piercing sunlight cut through the murkiness of the stairwell, introducing the shadow of a man silhouetted against the door frame.

Tim.

12:25.

"*Where the fuck've you been, Henry Lee?*" *He said it flat-out, straight and even, not a hint of anger. But the eyes, man. If they'd been M16s, Henry Lee would be KIA right there. That was the thing about Tim. Most people, you listened to what they said, how they said it, for a roadmap into their head. Tim, though, he always sounded in control. Listening to him, you'd never think the man felt a thing. Never heard him laugh or cry. Never heard him sound pitying or concerned. Never happy, sad. Even when he let Henry Lee come home, see his parents, tell them about the trip to New York—even when Henry Lee insisted stubbornly that the whole family got to come along or it was no dice—Tim didn't give up one little bit of what was going on inside.*

But his eyes said he didn't like it. And Tim's view of the world, or of a man, or of a mission, was always communicated not with a loud voice or a friendly smile, but with a pair of eyes that stayed with people like a recurring bad dream.

"I asked you where the fuck you been?" The eyes were not happy.

Henry Lee was about to answer when he saw the body.

12:26.

It was a big guy, thick-set, in a blue suit so dark it might've looked black if they hadn't been outside in the sun. His nose was broad and reddish—a drinker—and he was wearing shades that reminded Henry Lee of the pictures he'd seen of Jack Ruby, the fella who killed Oswald. In fact, the dead man—he thought he was dead, anyway, sure didn't look like he was taking in any air—kind of looked like Ruby.

The body was shoved to one side of the door, like he'd fallen against it and had to be pushed aside so Tim could get the thing open.

12:27.

"Here." Tim handed Henry Lee the rifle.

"Who's that?"

"The primary. He croaked." Explaining all this like it was nothing, standard operating procedure. Henry Lee looked at the guard, then at Tim, then back at the guard. "Guy had a heart attack," Tim said, anticipating the next question before Henry Lee could even get it out.

12:28.

Goddamn, it was hot.

"There he is." Tim pointed across the street, and down.

Two open windows on the 12th floor, on the other side of 43rd Street. In one of them, the one on Henry Lee's right, a man's head came up over the sill, like a chopper on the horizon. A moment later, they saw the barrel of what Tim knew was a Remington Gamemaster.

Henry Lee Hubbard took the rifle, thinking Man I'm gonna be a hero.

That thought of doing something good for his country evaporated as an intense calm came over his entire body. In the next few seconds, he settled into a world of his own, a world empty of anything or anyone. It was the way of the rifleman, of becoming one with the moment, and only the moment, tuning out life and its distractions, tricking the brain into thinking there was nothing more important on the face of this earth than the image being lined up between the crosshairs on the scope.

Across the way, on the 12th floor, the shooter was easing into the same routine. If Henry Lee had been thinking about anything other than nailing the guy, he might've been struck by the fact that in that instant, they were the same person in some weird, screwy way. But he wasn't thinking about any cosmic shit like that, fate and all, he was only thinking about blazing this dude with one, maybe two shots.

Which was exactly what Tim had counted on. Focus. That way, Henry Lee would never know what hit him.

12:29. Tim had a gun, a pistol, silenced. Henry Lee, in a zone, didn't see.

The plan—theirs, not Henry Lee's—was working.

In the window across the way, the guy was a sitting duck. He was wearing a red shirt, like he wanted to get whacked, easy to pick out, easier still to pick off. For all the training of the past few months, and thank God for that, him now being the primary, this really was gonna be like shooting fish in a barrel.

Guy seemed to ease a little forward, anticipation probably. Again, if Henry Lee had been thinking about anything other than rail-splitting this bastard, he'd've figured the target, this fella Worth, was probably on the street below.

What he did notice, though, was the movement. It was bullshit stuff, showed the guy for what he was, a friggin' amateur. Real shooter gets in place, stays there, doesn't so much as breathe.

12:30. Henry Lee blinked, but didn't let his gaze leave the scope, so he still didn't see Tim's pistol, couldn't feel how close it was to his head.

Everything still going according to the plan.

Until the security guard moved.

"Son of a bitch!" Tim blurted.

Breaking Henry Lee's concentration.

"Stay on point, soldier!" Tim ordered. From the corner of his eye, Henry Lee could see his team leader fishing for something in his pocket.

Across the way, the shooter was frozen stiff as a slab of beef in a meat locker, Henry Lee knowing that showtime was near, so he ignored Tim and whatever he was doing, needing to get his own shit back together quick, easing his finger against the trigger, kind of flexing, trying to get back in the groove.

Then he started to fidget, the guy on the 12th floor did.

Henry Lee stayed focused, though, still trying to ignore what was going on behind him, Tim and the security guard, the sounds—like the Jack Ruby guy was groaning, something—setting off alarms like black church bells in his head.

"Soldier," Tim said. "Take him out."

Drawing a deep, unlabored breath, one last hit of calm—

The shooter across the way, leaning even further out the window—

12:31—

Henry Lee wondering what was going on exactly, starting to think maybe there was something he didn't know—

The specially magnified scope showing the target was flexing his hands, too, getting ready—

"Solider," Tim repeated, calmly—

Henry Lee squeezing the trigger, firm and friendly, like he was shaking its hand—

Hearing Tim say "Go"—

Henry Lee's first shot almost lifting the guy up, left arm thrown back behind him, right arm pointed toward the heavens, to God—

Then a second shot, into the head, giving him a brain-blood-bone halo—

Jerking his eye away from the target, knowing the fella on the 12th floor was deader than Buddy Holly—

Hearing a third shot from someplace, not him—

In an instant, seeing all hell breaking loose on the street, two bodies down—

And a fourth, fifth, sixth. Christ, what was happening?

Cutting his eyes back to the 12th floor, to the window next to Buskin's, seeing a second shooter withdraw, drop out of sight, then pop up back up in the other one, Buskin's window, crawling around, just the top of his back showing, doing something that looked like—

Swapping rifles? Sonofa—

— and then being gone, just like that, just that fast.

Now turning, seeing Tim crouched over the security guy, pumping something into him from a long-ass needle, holding a goddamned gun, aiming it at Henry Lee, getting ready to drop him like a bad habit, lowering it for just an instant while he checked the syringe, seeing if it was empty—

Henry Lee, taking the rifle, swinging it like a baseball bat, cracking into Tim's skull, then whirling around with a speed and strength he thought was beyond his ability, hauling ass out the door, down the stairwell, just like that pussy Oswald had to've done, his brain screaming, God oh God what have I done? What the fuck have I done?

Bolting down 43rd Street, and across 8th, toward the Port Authority, thinking only of climbing on a bus, glad he had some leftover cash in his pocket, money Tim had given him, wondering how far it would get him, and if that would ever be far enough.

Chapter 31

"Yo? KC? You still with me?"

When Maxie called and started talking about Nashville and Henry Lee and second and third shooters, Kevin's first thought was This isn't happening, couldn't be, not to people like them. They were too typical, a couple of just-plain-folks who worried about things like car payments and bills and work, getting by as best they could, making it as often as not on hopes and dreams, not because they always believed their own bullshit but because the alternatives basically sucked. And yeah, okay, maybe they had stumbled through life—who hadn't?—but that was part of the Big Overall Plan, except no one ever said the Big Overall Plan included stumbling into conspiracies, too, which produced his second thought, right on top of that, it being, That's all well and good, but welcome to wherever you are. "Yeah, yeah, I'm cool. Really."

"You better be, 'cause this ain't no time to be fading on me, or on this thing, whatever it is, we're up to our asses in. You got to stay in the game."

"No. I'm there. I'm with you."

And he was. Listening to 15 minutes of Maxie's rapid-fire riffing—her not giving him so much as a pause to get a word in about what *he'd* found out, the Brothers Farmer and all—Kevin now felt sharp, strangely on point, like all the weirdness was an upper that had emptied about a million cc's of liquefied jolt into his system.

"Good. Now this guy could be as full of shit as a Christmas turkey. I don't know. He's got more drugs in him than a Colombian crackhouse, and there's nobody at this prison who thinks he has even one or two of his marbles left. So I'm not gonna get too far out on that limb just yet. But where I am gonna go is—"

"I want to know one thing," he interrupted, sharply, breaking into her unpunctuated stream-of-thought monologue, the kind Maxie liked to use to help think through a problem. "Did he say anything about if and where my father fit into all this?"

After hearing Henry Lee's tale minutes before, Maxie wasn't sure of much, but she did know this: Kevin's old man, Devereaux or whoever, dead or alive, was ground-zero on this deal. Beyond that it was any-body's guess. "Your name never came up, neither did your old man's, and I didn't press. But I'd be lying if I told you I thought any of this is accidental."

"Any of what?"

"Whatever's happening to you. I don't believe for a minute that pack-age from Devereaux found its way to you by mistake. Henry Lee says Devereaux shot this guy Tim, blew him away in Nashville, and then agreed to some deal that protects him and his family. *Insurance,* Devereaux said. That's why he didn't grease Henry Lee's punk ass right there. *Insurance.* Then 25 years later, you get this stuff from Devereaux, who says it protected *him* when he was alive and it'll protect *you* when he's dead. So you got everybody looking for some kind of insurance— but the question is against who and what? And that makes me believe that no matter how far removed those two things may be, one has something to do with the other."

Out of nowhere: "The Butterfly Effect."

"The what?" Maxie not sure she heard him right.

"It's a theory that says a butterfly beating its wings in Brazil could cause tornadoes in Texas."

Jesus help us, she groaned inside, maybe his head wasn't in the game, all this philosophical nonsense about bugs and bad weather. "Kevin, I don't need the Dalai Friggin' Lama on this, man, talking deep cosmic shit. I need you, and I need you clear-headed." She waited for a second, standing at a phone booth in the visitor's area of the Stones River State Prison, more than a little jazzed herself, wondering if or when whatever was pinballing around in his brain pan would throw Kevin Columbus into tilt.

"It's something that asks the question of how an event so meaningless, the beating of a butterfly's wings, how could something like that produce such chaos?" Not saying it spacey or zoned-out, more like a straight-out assertion he was putting on the table for discussion.

Which Maxie wasn't real inclined to do, not at the moment. "Why not leave the big thoughts to the big thinkers? You and me, we got other things on our plate."

"I'm serious," his tone confirming that, Maxie rocked a bit because he *did* seem on top of things, all this voodoo babble notwithstanding. "Let's say you're right, about the connections and all, the link between what Henry Lee said and me getting the package from Devereaux. If you are, then something had to happen before Worth was killed, something that at first didn't look like it mattered, or even if it did, nobody ever thought it'd be a big deal down the road."

"Go on." Maxie starting to play along, no idea where he was going, but giving him some room. Besides, wherever it got them was better than standing still, which was more or less their current course setting.

"What if me being born was that thing? What if it was *me* who put all this in play?"

Maxie listened close for any sign of emotional meltdown or pain or sadness, came up empty, thinking Kevin sounded kind of like a cop, free-forming theories with his partner, trying to do a little evidence-weaving. "Which in turn brings us back to your old man."

"Which in turn brings as back to where we started."

"Maybe not." She had that thing in her voice, that thing that said, Let's just take a step or two back, reassess, put what we know through a different grinder, see what comes out. Kevin, running on fumes in the conclusion department, was happy to comply. "I think the first thing we have to ask ourselves is who disappeared at or around the time Worth was killed."

"My father."

"Right, in what, April?" Kevin said yes. "Then there's this guy, this Tim, the one Devereaux eighty-sixed in Nashville. And Buskin. The security guard up on the fire escape with Tim and Henry Lee." She took a beat to see if he was with her, could almost hear him thinking over the line. "Who else?"

"Devereaux?"

"Who himself is now off to the great hereafter, and who we've apparently eliminated as a suspect in the natural father department anyway."

"Henry Lee Hubbard."

"Who for all intents and purposes fell off the face of the earth the day he agreed to become somebody else."

Kevin's irritation blazed for just a second, Maxie taking that as another good sign, his temper coming back. "Then you tell me who's left? Everybody's gone, end of story."

"Not everybody, skippy."

"My father, Tim, Buskin, Henry Lee, the private security guy, who else is there?"

"Think."

It took maybe 10 seconds, but Kevin finally got it. "The second gunman. The guy who Henry Lee says actually killed Worth."

"Give the man a prize."

"You're saying he's my father?"

"I'm not saying anything. I'm not even saying the guy exists. What I *am* saying is that we can, in some way, account for everyone else who was in New York that day. And I'm telling you, if somebody else really did kill Worth, and we find out who did, we'll get the answers to everything, and then—"

"Maxie?"

"—we can start putting—"

"Maxie?"

"—some of the pieces—"

"Maxie?"

"—together. What?"

"What if I told you I think I have proof that Henry Lee's right, that there was a second gunman in New York that day?"

That brought her up short. "The hell're you talking about?"

"That's *my* news, Max."

Her turn to get pissed. "I oughta kick your ass, holding out on me like that. What were you thinking? Oh, I'm sorry, you *weren't* thinking, you couldn't've been because that's the only way to explain why you all of a sudden started acting like a stupid white person, which I know you are, but every once in a while you surprise me, although I got to tell you, Casper, this ain't one of those times. So you best start talkin' and don't leave out any of the juicy stuff, or as God is my witness, I will get very Gothic on your pale ass, we clear?"

She was, Kevin explaining everything be could think of about the images the Brothers Farmer had uncovered, voice getting faster, more wired and excited, like there was some deadline for getting it out, ending with a breathless, "What makes you think he isn't dead, too? The second gunman?"

Maxie didn't have to give that an instant's thought, she was so sure. "Nope."

Kevin heard the certainty in her voice. "Why do you say that?"

"Because whoever the second gunman is, he's the one protecting you." If Kevin was brain-manic by then, her answer hit his hyper-drive button, got him asking all kinds of questions about who and what and why, Maxie trying to answer over him, Kevin not stopping, Maxie finally taking all she was going to take, saying, "Shut the hell up, and listen for one goddamned second," Kevin doing it more because he was out of breath than intimidated. Both paused, gulped some air, Maxie continuing: "Makes me think that if you were as inconsequential as the beating of a butterfly's wings to this person, whoever he is, you'd be as dead as the rest of 'em right now."

Which for some reason brought Wayne Earl Wiley to mind, and what The Legislator of the Goddamned Century must think about Kevin Columbus, that he was just some meaningless loser, utterly without value, an easy mark who they could hustle from here to Pakistan and back because there was no downside to doing it. In Wayne Earl Wiley Land, he didn't matter. "But I'm not dead," he replied, slowly, flash-anger cooling, replaced by something that felt to him, and sounded to Maxie, like newfound purpose. "And as long as I'm not, as long as I'm still here, this isn't over."

Maxie was more or less thinking the same thing. Except she was also wondering how far whoever was protecting the boy would go to pre-serve the secret of what now felt like some really bad truths, and where they'd finally draw the line, and on which side of it she and Kevin would crash-land when it *was* over.

•

Walter Frost was preparing to check out of The Four Seasons when his digital cellular phone rang. It was his Washington office. The secre-tary said they were routing a second call, from suburban D.C., in Virginia, through to him. She began to apologize for the intrusion, but said the caller was very insistent, telling her he'd come upon some mate-rial that was essential to an important case that Frost was preparing. In that it was widely known that Walter Frost practiced power, not law, she assumed it had something to do with politics and promptly called him in Chicago. Don't worry, he told the secretary, who seemed a bit flus-tered by the anonymous caller's demands, she had done the right thing.

In a moment, a voice came over the phone. "Mr. Frost?"

It was his man in Falls Church, at DDI Industries. "Yes?" Walter Frost felt almost instinctively that this was not going to be a good call.

"One of the wires we installed in Nashville, in the prison, after the Florida call?"

Frost closed his eyes wearily. "Yes?"

"Well, sir, it picked up something—"

"Let me call you back on a secure line."

He did, and for the next 12 and a half minutes, Walter Frost listened to the sound of his world begin to come apart. It wasn't the first time one of his creations had been revealed. There had been many others over the years. But because they involved secret people in secret places—people and places that officially did not exist—it was as easy to manipulate their disappearance as it was to create their existence. Sometimes, it was as simple as a shredder. Other times, a winter-night fire fueled by documents whose destruction, rather than their disclo-sure, augured better for the Republic's future. And still others, a well-conceived strategy of disinformation, fed to an ever-hungry, frenzied media pack that delighted in launching the assault before asking about the objective.

Of course, there was also that rare, sad occasion when a death was required. But it was always undertaken someplace else, far-removed, in an alien locale where it could not touch those whose continued liveli-hood demanded it or, more important, where it could not touch Walter Frost. This was the way of the world, the manner in which things were done.

But this time was different. This time, there were no shredders big enough, no fires destructive enough, to help cover up the machinations of the past 25 years. And the story, if it ever did come to light, would produce a scandal for the media that would far outweigh any reporter-source loyalties of decades past. Worse than that, however, there were no exotic locales where the final chapter of this little tale could be written. This was, after all, America, and the problem uniquely American.

When he'd heard the entire tape, he asked his man to replay the last minute or so. As smart as they were and as smart as they'd been—all of them, through all these years—they had never anticipated that the central question of the conspiracy would even be asked, let alone pursued:

"Why do you say that?"

"Because whoever the second gunman is, he's the one who's protecting you."

Some arguing, and then:

"Makes me think if you were as inconsequential as the beating of a butterfly's wings to this person, whoever he is, you'd be as dead as the rest of them right now."

If I truly ruled the world, that would be true, Walter Frost thought after he had given the man in Falls Church explicit instructions on what to do next. In that world, they would simply solve the problem by whatever means or forces were necessary. The only consequence they'd have to consider was detection, which would be little more than a minor irritant. Because in that world, his world, they would control everything, including the channels of distribution. The people would know only what they wanted the people to know, and that would be that. Disclosure would be a moot point.

Walter Frost moved from the window that provided what he felt was an overrated view of an overrated city, and turned to the mirror, checking the knot in his silk tie and absently fiddling with his gold cufflinks, etched with the presidential symbol. Sadly, this wasn't his world alone. He had to share it, and that was the problem. It was a world that invited too many into a process that was better suited for a handful of well-informed, well-intentioned gentlemen who possessed the age and wisdom to do the right thing. Even more sadly, it was becoming less and less his by the day, and that wasn't just because they had the crisis of a millennium on their hands. Rather, Walter Frost had a vague fear that people might soon wake up. That they might somehow feel empowered, and start to think their votes could make something happen in courthouses and state houses, even the White House.

And what then?

Walter Frost looked back out the window, staring down at the people on the street, the shoppers and students and businessmen and families and tourists and conventioneers scampering beneath him along Michigan Avenue. He grimaced. This was, indeed, an American city. God how he loathed it. He couldn't wait to get back to Washington.

•

The Instant Messenger box on Rollie Merke's computer screen read:
CABALGUY: You ready for the big one?
Merke put down the coffee mug that said Y2KAOS, typed in Talk to me, and hit the Send button.
CABALGUY: I have a tip for you.
MERKEYWATERS: What kind of tip?
CABALGUY: Sirhan Sirhan in the fourth at Aqueduct, you fool, what kind do you think?
MERKEYWATERS: You know what I'm interested in: Stink. If that's what you've got, I'm all nose.
CABALGUY: There's been confirmation of a second gunman.
MERKEYWATERS: Go on.
CABALGUY: It came out of Nashville, from a con in prison. He's given the story to a private detective investigating.
MERKEYWATERS: What's he gonna do with it? The detective?
CABALGUY: It's a she.
MERKEYWATERS: She gonna sell it to the tabs?
CABALGUY: Not if you get it out there first. That way, you'll get the scoop, the dailies will pick you up, and the tabs won't have shit.
MERKEYWATERS: What else can you tell me?
CABALGUY: That's all I have right now.
MERKEYWATERS: Hey, wait a second. What about the rest of the story?
CABALGUY: Make it up, Rollie, who cares?

MERKEYWATERS: Let me get this straight: I'm gonna go with a world exclusive that says—

CABALGUY: You're gonna say exactly what I tell you to say. So pay close attention.

•

P.I. In Nashville Uncovers Proof Of Worth Plot;
25-Year-Old Secret Revealed By Convicted Murderer

In her room at The Drake, Taylor Shepard stared at the screen on her laptop. She laughed out loud at the screaming World Exclusive banner, knowing full well the computers at DDI had routed this item to her and her alone, and there wasn't another soul on the earth—other than Merke, who didn't count—who would ever see it.

Without reading the text that sat underneath the screaming head-line—it was all nonsense anyway—she logged off and made the first of two phone calls that would bring this phase of the case to closure. It was to a pager. Less than five minutes later, she got a return call from the Marriott near O'Hare. The pilot told her the jet was fueled and ready. All he had to do was file a quick flight plan.

She told him they were going to Nashville.

He said he'd get right on it, and that if traffic—both on the way to the airport and at O'Hare itself—wasn't too bad, they could be in the air in less than two hours.

She hung up, logged back onto the laptop and made the second call, via modem, to a private number. When the connection was complete, a screen full of gibberish appeared. In the center was a small box that gave no indication as to its purpose. Taylor hit the Enter key on her computer, bringing the laptop's cursor to the box, and typed in four numbers: 7675. Instantly, the gibberish dissolved into English.

In addition to being one of the world's leading manufacturers of computers, Rodale Technologies also held the patent on more than 100 software packages that had been developed for business applications. One was called Guest Host. It was an automated check-in, monitoring and billing program that 97 percent of the hotels and motels in the United States used. Basically, it enabled the establishment in question to track a guest from the day he or she arrived until the minute of departure. An additional feature allowed operators—front desk people, the reservation staff, concierges and the like—to hit a button on their keyboards and find out if the guest had a history with the hotel, including everything from credit card numbers to room and bed-size preferences.

It was pretty standard stuff. Except for the fact that the government of the United States had paid Rodale $1.1 billion to give the Justice Department—the FBI in particular—and the various intelligence agencies unlimited access to the data. With a simple point and click, anyone who knew the pass code, 7576, could go deep into the records of hotels nationwide in search of a suspect, a fleeing felon, a spy, a kidnapper, a lover, anybody.

There wasn't much glitz on the screen, just a lot of information fields, some of which the user had to fill in, some of which were optional.

On the field marked AREA CODE, Taylor typed in 615. In CITY, she entered Nashville, and then selected Tennessee from the drop-down menu that appeared when she double-clicked the STATE button. She left the CHAIN line blank, not having any idea what particular line of hotel she was looking for. Although she had a rough idea of the arrival date, she left that blank as well. In using databases like this, Taylor always opted to keep the initial search broad, not wanting to unnecessarily eliminate anyone or anything too early.

Under GUEST, she typed in the name MCQUEEN. Not knowing whether Maxie was short for Maxine or a nickname, she left both the first name and middle initial spaces blank for the time being. She moved the cursor to a small box that contained the words START SEARCH, clicked and waited.

Taylor loved technology. She loved its cool distance, and the way it lacked humanity while having a personality of its own. Its invisibility appealed to her as well. You could point at a box of wires and chips and connections and whatevers, and you could say Computer, but that was never the whole story. There were things that went on inside it that only a handful of people understood. Functions and actions were undertaken, and decisions made, within the context of a machine that had come to control the world and how we looked at it and experienced it. For the most part, no one had any idea what was going on. Someone had said, This is progress and this is good for you, and people accepted. Taylor Shepard liked that. She admired the fact that there was presumed goodness in something that nobody truly understood.

YOU HAVE 17 MATCHES, the screen flashed.

Taylor scrolled down the list, stopping at name No. 9. It read, M. McQueen. She double-clicked on the Details icon. Seconds later, a full screen of data appeared. Taylor peered closely at the information on the 12-inch monitor. She didn't know the first thing about this private detective, other than she was from North Carolina. The hotel registration listed the guest as being from Charlotte, and the guest's profession as insurance investigator with a company called Piedmont Mutual. The job wasn't exactly right, so she went back and looked at the other 16 names that the computer had turned up. Not one of them came close.

Taylor returned to M. McQueen, insurance investigator. After a moment, she reached for her cell phone and dialed information for Charlotte, asking for a business listing. Piedmont Mutual. The operator quickly informed her that there was no number for a company by that name. Taylor politely thanked the woman, and thought about how Maxie's listing a non-existent employer might cause havoc with the cops who would be investigating her death. Then she decided she didn't much care.

She wrote down the name of the hotel in Nashville and called a private car service to take her to the airport, and the jet that awaited her.

Chapter 32

"Mama, what's the 4-1-1?"

Ah, Maxie thought. The Voice. It was better than any drug, any drink, any high she could imagine. And at that point, sitting alone on a queen-sized bed in a paint-by-numbers hotel adjacent to the Nashville airport—alone save for her own anxieties, which were growing like late afternoon shadows—J.J., even in voice-only, was precisely what her psyche needed. She tried to draw a mental image of her son: Camped out in a big den, maybe playing video games, window opening out onto a backyard that looked more sculpted than mowed, that goddamned trampoline, shooting hoops with that Fat-Ass Speedo—

Enough. "Hey, baby," she said, half-erasing the image, not nearly as successful with the reminder of what it meant. "You doin' okay?"

"I be doin' fine as wine."

"You best be talking English to me, and not that jive crap you pick up from the gangsta wannabes at school." She smiled despite herself.

"Yes, ma'am. How're things out there in Babble-on?" He stretched *things* into two syllables, and adjusted the sound of the vowel: tha-angs.

Which made her smile wilt. "Babylon" was drug-trade talk—Rastafarian for "the outside world"—and that put it about three steps on the wrong side of acceptability, even for a little kid who probably didn't have the first clue what he was saying. "*Babylon*? Where did that come from?"

He let out a cackle. "Me an' my bo-eez, we been doin' some sprayin' and—"

"*Sprayin'*?" Maxie sat straight up in the bed, grabbed the remote and muted *Jeopardy* on the tube.

"Yeah, bay-bee. Crankin'!" Another cackle, like this was great sport. "Sprayin' an' playin' an' ragin' and pagin'!"

Her eyes roamed the room, settling idly on a pale pinkish floral print—Hotel Décor 101—that graced the wall to her left. She didn't know what he was talking about, except for *sprayin'*, which was street slang for nitrous oxide, which didn't please her even a little.

Maxie had a brief talk with her anger, the upshot of which was You Better Calm Down Girl Before Somebody Gets Killed, then leaned against the headboard, took one of the bed pillows in her arms and slowly tried to squeeze the life out of it.

"Mama, you still there?"

"Yeah, baby." Voice taut as a violin string. "Now tell me, what's all this about sprayin' and playin' and ragin' and pagin' and all that noise? What is the 4-1-1 on *that*?"

"Yo. Lissen up!" Maxie shook her head, wondering which was worse: Her kid sounding like a drug dealer or an MTV video jockey, both of them being stones along the path to the end of the world as far as she was concerned. "The bo-ee be strappin', so there gonna be some cappin'!" The cackle grew to a broad laugh.

Strapping? Capping? It sounded as if her little boy was carrying a goddamned gun.

Then she heard three high-pitched beeps, the unmistakable sound of a pager being turned on. "Mama? You hear that? P-Funk here be good to go, an' there ain't gonna be no five-oh in my crib, yo-yo-yo!"

Maxie felt like six sumo wrestlers were standing on her chest. What the *fuck* was going on here? *P-Funk*? That was a street term for synthetic heroin. Five-oh? For crissakes, she thought, *I'm* five-oh. And a beeper? What does an 8-year-old need with a beeper? "When, uh, when did you get that, son?" Usually, Maxie returned J.J.'s street slang when they spoke, thinking it was a way to undermine Carmella, taking the role of the anti-parent, a mother-friend as opposed to just a mother-provider. But this was no time for bonding, clearly, as somebody definitely needed to have a long, stern heart-to-heart with this child.

J.J. told her he had "poached it" the previous day.

Poached it. She rolled her eyes, thinking what the hell am I doing in an airport hotel in Nashville when my son, my sweet little baby boy, is climbing the first wrung up the crime ladder? And Carmella. What in God's name was she doing besides falling asleep at the damned mommy switch?

Chill, girl, she told herself, knowing that rage at Carmella combined with concern over J.J.—concern, hell, she was feeling outright *fear*— knowing that was the kind of mix that could blow up buildings. Reminded herself that kids were impressionable, aped what they saw and heard on the playground, the streets, everywhere. She knew that, knew it probably explained much of what she was hearing. But she also knew that understanding it meant recognizing the role of a parent, the responsibility to provide a better, more desirable place for the child, someplace that was safe, secure and honest, and protected innocent people, everyday people, from the world's unchecked evil.

That's all she'd ever wanted for her kid, all she ever asked for: The chance to be good, and to dream, and to maybe even achieve beyond his own expectations. That was what every parent struggled to provide, wasn't it? Character? The chance for their kids to be whoever or what-ever they could, nudging them here or there to keep their life on course and away from the forces of nature—human nature, externally applied—that took great pleasure in the power to destroy?

Yeah, well, by God, it was time to start nudging.

"Does your Auntie Carmella know about this, uh, pager?" She asked the question evenly, no comment in her voice, wanting her facts lined up all nice and neat before she launched on the Witch.

"Oh, yeah. She not the spoogewank you say she be."

Maxie took a breath so deep it inflated her toes, but the hoped-for calming effect didn't follow. "So she knows about all this?" Trying to be clear about it, real clear.

A great big giggle. "She copped it for me! She da bomb!" Uproarious laughter now, so much so that if Maxie hadn't actually heard the sound of the pager going off, she'd have thought J.J. was pulling her leg.

"Sweetheart, put Auntie Carmella on the phone." Clenched-teeth anger, fighting not to go Chernobyl with the child, it wasn't his fault, he's a little kid, for God's sake, but Carmella on the other hand was theoretically a grown-up, which made her the fairest of game.

"Yo, mama, that ho'—"

"Honey—"

"—be cookin' on high-beams—"

"J.J., please—"

"—in the kitchen, an'—"

"Put that bitch on now!!!"

There was silence, followed by what sounded to Maxie like the phone dropping, followed by what sounded like a little boy, not a juvenile gangster, saying Whoa, shit, mama's mad.

•

Less than 90 minutes after leaving Chicago, a corporate Lear Jet landed at a small executive center airport north of Nashville.

While the sole passenger moved quickly to a waiting car, the pilot spoke briefly to a large woman in a too-tight gray uniform who sat in a glass-cased office inside the facility. He explained that they had official business in the city, and that they expected to be back within two hours. The woman protested, saying the unexpected arrival was going to screw up the early evening schedule because she had a full slate of executives coming in for a conference on trade between the Southeastern United States and Japan.

The pilot said he understood, and apologized again, telling her it was not their intention to cause anyone any undue hardship. She told him that was exactly what they were doing, and added that if they couldn't produce some kind of authorization that gave them the necessary status to keep the plane on the runway—and, not incidentally, to screw up her life for the next few hours—she'd be on the horn to the FAA pronto.

At which point the pilot, who was dressed in a dark neatly tailored suit, reached into his coat pocket and produced a small leather billfold. He opened it and casually showed her the contents. "Is that authorization enough?" he asked, smiling, pleasant, not offering so much as a hint of threat or danger.

She peered into the little carrying case, then up at him, comparing the photo on the identification badge with the man in front of her, the match-up being so perfect the head-shot could have been taken five minutes ago. "Oh, yes, sir. I am sorry, sir." Embarrassed and anxious, clearly worried over the impact that crossing an FBI agent might have on her job.

The man sensed her concern. He told her not to worry about it—"No harm, no foul"—and let the smile get a little broader before walking to the deep blue Crown Victoria, where his partner sat, drumming her fingers on the armrest, ready to get it done.

•

"Is this the kind of parent you plan to be to my son?" Maxie wasn't shouting, not yet anyway.

"I hardly think you are in any position to be commenting on my parenting skills."

"*Parenting skills?* Carmella, you wouldn't know parenting skills if they bit you on the ass. What in God's name were you thinking? A *pager?* Jesus Christ, are you rolling the joints for him, too?"

"What does *that* mean?"

Maxie could see her sister's head going left then right with that retort, a You Better Watch Your Mouth move, looking like Weezie Jefferson when George told her to clean the house or take out the trash. "It means that pagers are the communication of choice for drug dealers, Carmella, and if you'd quit trying to bribe the kid into thinking you'd be a better mother than me, you'd know that."

Still not screaming, but the countdown was on.

"Oh, is that so?" Carmella fired back, with that strutting tone that made Maxie want to find a rusty butter knife, carve the bitch's tongue out. "And I suppose that a mother with tendencies toward drinking and violence would be better for the boy? Is that what I understand you to be saying?"

"What I am saying is that giving him what he wants and giving him what he needs are not the same." She swung her legs around to a sitting position on the edge of the bed, and hung her head low between her knees, like she was getting ready to throw up.

"Well, you just make that case in court, and I'll make mine, and we'll see what the judge has to say."

"Ah, for God's sake, Carmella, did you at least have a talk with him when he asked about the pager?" There was something of a feral plea in Maxie's voice. "Did you at least sit down with him and talk about it?"

The question was as foreign to Carmella as a giraffe in her recently renovated master bath. "Talk to him about what?"

Maxie's head dropped a little further, almost directly between her knees now, a tiny spasm of pain at the base of her back, nice little reminder of the Alabama adventure, Maxie not caring at this particular moment. "Do you ever talk to him about anything? Ask him what his day was like, if he's happy or sad or anything like that?"

"Uh…Of course I do."

It was a lie so obvious, and so obvious to Carmella, that Maxie didn't feel any need to label it as such. "What about school? Do you ever talk to him about school?"

"It's a private school." She said it as if private schools were the answer to all the world's ills. "And just last night, Theo was talking to him about college."

"*College*? He's 8 years old, Carmella. You ought to be talking to him about the things that can keep him from going to college!"

"Like his mother?" That strutting voice again. God, how Maxie wished she was there, face to face with Carmella, so she could enjoy killing her.

"No, Carmella, like drugs."

"It's a pager, Maxine. He wanted a pager because all the other kids have pagers."

"What next? A Tek-9? All the other kids have semi-automatics, you gonna buy him one of those, too?"

"Don't be ridiculous. Those kinds of things don't happen at our school."

Maxie laughed, part frustration, part disbelief that her sister could be so stupid. "Do you really believe that?"

"Of course I do."

"Do you know every kid that walks those hallways? Have you looked in every locker?"

"I don't need to. I trust the system to—"

"To do what, Carmella? To keep my son safe?"

"At least there, and here, he's not around guns, or alcohol, like he is at your home—and I use the term very loosely, Maxine. Jack is far safer here—"

"*Jack*? You call him *Jack*?" Maxie came off the bed like it was that damned trampoline in Carmella's back yard.

"That's his name."

"No, no, no. His name is J.J. *That's* who he is."

"It's who he *was*."

There was a long, pure silence, Maxie holding her breath, trying to ice down the rage, Carmella holder hers, waiting for Maxie to detonate.

When that didn't happen, Carmella's tension only increased. "Take the pager away from him. Please."

"I can't, and I won't, and you need to know—"

"Shuttup and listen to me, Carmella." Maxie's voice seething now, more menace than anger. "Just do this one thing. Take it back. Explain that you understand all the other kids have them, and that right now, they may just seem like harmless toys. And they may be. But they don't stay that way. You tell him that. They don't stay harmless and fun and innocent. They get twisted into something else, something that takes sweet little boys like J.J., honorable boys—good kids, for God's sake!— and turns them into something they were never meant to be."

She dropped back onto the bed, head falling between her knees again, spine hurting a little more, not caring. "He needs somebody to tell him that one thing can lead to another, and then to another, and then before you know it, what was once a very good idea or a very fun idea has suddenly become something dangerous. If that child is going to have a future, or any hope of a future, he has to understand that everything is about everything, and that you just can't isolate one incident, or one stupid little thing like a pager, and pretend that it means nothing. Because it does, Carmella. It has meaning. All of it does. And he needs to know that before the stupid little things start to add up and the world starts to spin in some other direction that none of us—you, me or, most important, J.J—some direction that none of us can stop. Tell me you understand that, Carmella. For heaven's sake, and for J.J.'s, at least tell me you understand that."

Rarely had Maxie ever been this heartfelt, this honest with her sister.

It didn't have a lot of impact.

"Here's what I understand, Maxine Arliss McQueen: I understand that through your choice of careers, to say nothing of your choices in life, you've made a world for yourself that is not a nice place to be. As I said, that choice was yours. But that's your world, not Jack's."

"It's J.J., goddammit!"

"That was another life."

"That's *his* life, and—"

"It's *your* life, Maxine, not his. And to take all the dirt and grime that comes from your life, from the gutters where you earned and continue to earn a living, and to use it to soil me and Jack and my family and my lifestyle—as if to say, it's *our* problem, too—well, I think that is sad. Just sad."

"It *is* your problem, Carmella," Maxie said weakly. "It's everybody's problem."

"It's not Jack's, Maxine. He goes to a private school. We take him there and pick him up every day. We live in a nice neighborhood. There are no guns in this house. No drugs. No filthy books or movies. We don't hit him. Theo works hard to give him the kind of life, and it pains me to say this, Maxine, but to give him the kind of life that you will never be able to provide. Jack is a happy child. What is so wrong with that?" She paused before power-drilling a 10-inch bit straight through Maxie's heart. "Other than the fact he's not happy with you."

Maxie was suddenly too exhausted to fight. "He needs to be protected from the things that can go out of control before we know it."

"Like drinking—"

The exhaustion transmuted into a mad rage.

"—and violence."

Just as quickly, the flaring hate vanished. "Yes," was all Maxie said, recalling The Christening, and how one single episode, fueled by drinking and violence, unexpected, had so thoroughly wrecked everything. "Yes," she said again.

"You're overreacting," Carmella said, stern, chastising, sounding like the mother she was not meant to be.

"Somebody has to. Don't you understand that? Somebody has to."

Carmella had already hung up.

Maxie sat at the edge of the bed, drained, turning the TV sound back on when the screaming of her thoughts got too loud. "Somebody has to," she said again, staring at the screen, the broadcast not even registering. Then she stood and went to take a shower, thinking she should be on her way back home instead of being here, the wrong place at the wrong time.

•

Taylor was dressed just like Rene Russo in that movie with Clint Eastwood, the one where she played a Secret Service agent. Navy pantsuit. White blouse open at the throat. Flat shoes, black. Dark hose. No jewelry. Except for the Czech-made M52 in her purse and the exceedingly well-forged papers identifying her as Special Agent Veronica Simms, she could have been any on-the-make corporate climber, sharking through the waters, looking for another deal.

The driver-pilot had remained in the car downstairs, sitting in the middle of the hotel parking lot. They had decided it would be best if only one of them entered, this being an easy in and out, two players making it more complicated than necessary.

Walking purposefully through the front doors, Taylor didn't so much as glance at the young man at the reception desk. She knew where she was going, didn't need a name or a room number. She did, however, fire a wickedly beautiful smile at three businessmen who looked twice, and then a third time, as she passed on the way to the elevator, feeling them rate her, top to bottom, even after she'd turned into the small alcove and pushed the Up button, knowing she'd scored better than a mere 10.

In a moment, a tinny ring announced the elevator's arrival, and a few seconds later the doors opened onto the third floor, to a long hallway that extended to both her right and left. The gray carpeting was nice if not luxurious, befitting a major chain's discount hotel line, though she couldn't say much for the wallpaper, whose pinkish-striped design seemed a little garish for what was, basically, a one-nighter for traveling businessmen.

Signs directly opposite the elevator advised that odd-numbered rooms, 301 to 349, went left, and their counterparts, 300 to 350, right.

It was quiet, except for the dull crunching of an ice machine.

She turned left, removing the M52 from her purse swiftly and easily as she walked, slinging the bag back over her shoulder when the pistol was clear.

Past Rooms 305, 307, 309.

Reached into the left pocket of her suit coat and pulled out a thin, brushed-steel card, another gift from Rodale, who as part of its hotel package also produced the equipment that created the unmarked swipe cards that replaced room keys. The one Taylor carried had been programmed with an override code that basically tricked the locking devices on the door into thinking it was legitimate. It could get her into any room in four-fifths of the hotels on the planet, and was a lot easier to handle than those decoder boxes used by supposedly well-heeled criminals and the cops who chased them.

Past Rooms 317, 319, 321.

Slowing a bit now, feeling her body start to go taut. Not tension or anxiety. Preparation.

Usually, she had no personal knowledge or involvement with the targets, which was best, as it removed her from the reality of the action, let her exist on some other plane. She'd learned that in Arabaq. There had been some concerns, early, that her rage at Azid might somehow compromise her ability to do the job. Assassination was about efficiency, and the handlers—spies and ex-spies, for the most part—feared that while Taylor clearly had the psychological makeup to kill, she might enjoy murdering Azid's heirs so much it would compromise her effectiveness.

But she had performed, and well. That first time, at The Tombs in El Ashwa's notorious prostitution district, she had sliced into Hakud Azid's throat with professional ease. The only person who ever realized the pleasure she felt from the act had been Hakud himself, the general's son, who laying there on a concrete slab in what had once been a mortuary, pants around his ankles, blood spitting from his throat, him starting to gag on it, saw her smile just before she plunged the blade into his belly, and jerked it up as far as her strength would allow. "For Raymond" was all she said. Hakud's eyes, wide and terrified and uncomprehending, grew even more so as Taylor removed the knife's jagged blade and jammed it through his breastplate, into a heart that would have stopped on its own in a matter of seconds anyway.

That had been revenge. This one, though, it was expedience. And though she might enjoy it, would probably just love to see the riot girl's eyes right before she died, them looking surprised and terrified, just like Hakud's, this was no time for Taylor to amuse herself.

Rooms 331, 333, 335, 337.

She had to get into the zone and stay there. It would take all of about 30 seconds.

Room 339. Taylor stopped, looked both ways, no one down either end of the hallway.

She slid the steel card into the exterior lock, withdrawing it quickly, the small red light on the door handle switching instantly to green, flashing three times. Taylor pulled the latch-knob down carefully, checked the hallway again, still empty, pushed the door open, heard water running, stopping for a second, letting it register.

A shower. Perfect.

On the television, Mary Hart was babbling something about Julia Roberts on the Hollywood news show *Entertainment Tonight*.

Taylor checked the suppressor on the M52, stepped inside.

To her immediate right, a large mirror hung over the sink. There were two cellophane-encased plastic cups, and a brown ice bucket. Opposite was an open closet that contained just one item, a beige-colored suit.

The door to the toilet and bathtub was ajar. Taylor stretched toward its left side, where the knob was, two long, agile steps, like a cat, it taking her just that much time to crack out a plan, a simple one, which went like this: Push the door open, empty all eight rounds into the woman, get out, just that easy.

She took three slow, deep breaths, part of the routine.

Closed her eyes, thought about the gun in her hand, like an extension of her arm, grip at once firm and comfortable.

Every nerve ending on alert, every sense—hearing, seeing, smelling—off the scope, into a place that was beyond the realm of simple human beings.

Time, she told herself. It's time.

Opened her eyes, raised the automatic pistol in her right hand, joining it in one fluid, sweeping motion with her left, stepping through the partly open door—

The shower suddenly getting turned off—

— pivoting left, not even thinking, seeing the dark shape behind the plastic curtain, firing twice, hearing the pooft-pooft sound come out of the suppressor and a micro-instant later the grunting ooomph of a life being deflated.

Seeing the first splash of red against the white tile wall.

Getting off three more rounds before the body ever even hit the tub floor.

More red drizzling down the plastic shower curtain—

Another three into where the upper body was, slicing neat little holes into the curtain.

Turning, not bothering to look.

Not needing to.

Out the door.

Just that easy.

Chapter 33

The knock was half-hearted, unenthusiastic, as if the visitor had come to his apartment in the middle of the night to announce a death in the family. It almost made Kevin's anger, and its sidekick, a feeling of betrayal, go away.

But not quite.

"Why'd you lie to me?" he asked the instant his door opened to reveal Taylor, who was standing, more like sagging, against a peeling faded support column on the front porch.

Her head snapped back slightly, like he'd smacked her with a rotten fish, green eyes getting wide before narrowing into demi-slits and seeming to go gray with rage...

●

...How *dare* you challenge me? her eyes hissed at him.

She wanted to reach into the Kate Spade bag, pull out the freshly reloaded M52 that just hours ago had put down Maxie McQueen and one-way-ticket this little prick off to the great hereafter.

Catching herself, though, warning: Stay in control. Don't show any anger, but don't play nice, either, or cave too fast. Something's going on. Find out what.

"Nice to see you, too." She shoved her way past him, into the hovel, dreaming of the moment when she'd be done with him and all his baggage.

Kevin followed her inside, watching as she flopped into the sofa-bed, now in its sofa mode, still firing away: "Goddammit, Taylor, answer me: Why'd you lie?"

Reminding herself, again, to be calm, let him go, make him a little crazy, see where it leads.

She kicked off her shoes, took leave of the blue coat and jerked the white blouse out of her pants, fished around for a rubber band, pulled the blonde hair back into a pony tail, making no big show of it, letting him know he wasn't getting to her, not at all. "I'm gonna get all this cut off one of these days," she said absently, talking about the hair. "I'm tired of having to deal with it."

Which set him off, as planned. "Yeah, well I'm tired of having to deal with you and your lies!" He was standing over her now, probably thinking he was being menacing or threatening—like he mattered to her anyway, like there was some risk in telling him to go to hell, right—looking more crippled than anything else as far as she was concerned. Her thinking Jesus, a bullet in the head would be a step up for this guy.

"What're you watching?" she asked, still ignoring him, pointing disinterestedly at the color television, TNT airing an old Clint Eastwood western, pre-Dirty Harry.

"A goddamned liar."

Taylor took an exhausted breath, trying to make it look honest. "All right, Kevin," she said, weakly, without emotion. "What's going on?"

"You know exactly what's going on."

He was truly angry, seemed to have located some wellspring of strength or courage or something—determination, that's what it was—which surprised her. There had always been the assumption he'd fall for her, and then benignly follow wherever she led, an attention-starved little puppy dog yip-yip-yipping out everything Taylor needed to know. This sudden hostility, though, it could take them in another direction, make Kevin think he was in charge, which was not a perception she could afford, not now. She needed to reshape the landscape, get back on top.

Taylor frowned, rubbed her forehead, refusing to meet his stare, goading him. "If this has something to do with me being gone for a couple of days—"

"Oh, for crissakes!" Throwing his arms in the air, like I don't believe this. "Is that what you think?"

Both hands on her face now, thumbs under the cheekbones, fingers massaging the temples, deeply, like she was trying to stroke a headache into taking a powder. "Why don't you tell me what I think, Kevin. You seem to know." A pause, setting him up, getting ready to push a whole new set of buttons now. "And listen, if you think I should have asked your permission before leaving, fine, honey, I'm sorry for being so thoughtless, it won't happen again, let me cook you some dinner—"

Screaming now, "This is not about me!!!"

Time to move. Taylor popped up off the sofa like a jack in the box on amphetamines. "Then how about telling me what it is about, Kevin!" Standing right there with him, right in his face, let's-get-ready-to-rumble close. "Because I don't have the first idea!"

He seemed to stagger in place at that, going neither forward nor backward, but not stumbling either, not going down like he should have, instead just staring at her for the longest time, Taylor feeling like his eyes were trying to x-ray her mind, find some deep hidden secret. She gave as good as she got, though, fired the poison eye-darts right back at him, tossing in some anger, a teaspoon of hate and hurt, wanting him to think he'd scored some points, not wanting him to know, not yet, that one way or the other he was going to lose…

●

…Looking at her like that, studying her face, her hair, her lips, Kevin felt his newfound purpose pale against the technicolor images of the other night.

The two of them, talking about lost fathers, Kevin at some point in the evening unable to locate the at-any-cost reporter who'd crashed into his life, instead finding someone not unlike himself, just a person trying to fill in a gap in her existence, and maybe get somewhere better in the process. Someone who'd been given life's operating instructions, except without the warning label, and who was destined or damned, pick one, to go through it on a trial-and-error basis, winning some, losing some, never quite knowing if the most recent battle was just the latest or the last.

Then the hotter images, sex, her naked body, taut, sweaty, an athlete's body, fearless, giving him whatever he wanted and taking nothing from him, nothing but his strength and power, which she sapped up almost as eagerly as he gave—

Telling himself, Stop, hold on, wait, wait, wait, remembering: She lied to you. She said she went to a database at the library, and that database doesn't exist. So the issue on the table is why she manufactured the story, and you can either press that question and risk the other night never going into reruns, or drop it now and wait for the sequel.

Which put that way felt like a no-brainer...

•

...You're mine, Taylor thought, staring right through his eyes, right into his mind, knowing what he was thinking, stepping closer to him, letting him feel her against his body once more, letting him brush up against her warmth, her promise, reminding, teasing, conquering.

She reached for his hand. "Kevin?" He didn't pull away. She lifted it to her lips, kissed it gently, let it rest on her heart, the proposal unstated but clear, very clear, Kevin still not pulling away, just looking at her, not moving.

Oh, yes. You are mine...

•

…His inner voice screaming Don't let go, hang on no matter what, there are explanations, there have to be, she slept with you and told you her secrets and now she's back, doesn't that mean something?

Damned right, the voice said, so don't do anything dumb, but when his outer voice didn't exactly get the message, and Kevin asked, "Why'd you lie to me about the goddamned database?" the only person more surprised than him by the suddenness of the question was Taylor…

•

…The database?

"What are you talking about?" Taylor buying time, scrambling to recall as much as she could about their discussion on the phone that morning, not believing she could have misstepped, or said something so empty-headed it tangled her cover story.

"I'm talking about the database you said you used at the library. Why'd you lie to me about that?" His voice was stronger and clearer than it should have been, throwing her a little more, putting her on the defensive.

The database? One little insignificant bit of information, something of no inportance, no value, and that's why we're here?

Forget what you did or didn't say, she ordered herself, quickly moving to damage control and back to the strategy of not telling him anything. Give him enough rope, enough time, he'll solve the problem for you. "Kevin, I swear, I don't know what you're talking about." Squinting her eyes a little, a slight shake of the head, working him hard, body language saying, I really am lost here.

"You said you went to the library, and used some database they had on CD-ROM."

Let him get mad, give the anger time to settle in, use it against him. "Yeah. So?"

"I was at the library, Taylor, and asked them about it. You know what they said? They said the county library doesn't have that kind of information—"

The *county* library. Thank you, Kevin, she smiled inside, for making it all so easy, thank you very much.

"They told me that—"

"It wasn't the *county* library, Kevin."

His face went blank, and she smiled inside, watching the anger drain away and the certainty veer head-on into a wall of confusion. She was back on top...

•

..."What do you mean?" Kevin felt like someone had surgically removed his focus, replaced it with a smoke implant.

"I didn't go to the *county* library. I went to the library at the *university*."

"Which university?" Challenging her still, but weakly, knowing it was his mistake, rocketing to the wrong conclusion like that.

"UNC-Charlotte. They have the databases on non-governmental organizations."

"But you said, I'm sure, you said the county library." Just standing there, dying.

"Maybe I did. I don't know. Maybe I made a mistake. So what? What's the big deal?" Playing the puzzled victim, trying to understand.

He stared at her, lost again. "The big deal is—"

"What?"

"I don't know what's going on." It was a simple statement that just seemed to spill out. At that moment, Kevin felt like he was in another life, and that he wasn't living it so much as it was collapsing around him. Things that were sure one moment did a 180 the next, the familiar going foreign, the concrete dissolving into a quicksand pit whose inevitability was starting to suffocate him.

"Kevin?"

He stood there, facing her, a missing person in his own home. "What is happening to me?" Not saying it plaintive or pitiful, more like totally bewildered.

"You're just confused. That's all. You're at a strange place right now, and—"

"Oh, there's an understatement."

"Believe me, there's a way out of it. There has to be."

He thought about that. "I'm sorry, but I don't believe you."

"You have to—"

"I don't believe anything. A week ago, maybe. A month ago, probably. Three years ago, absolutely. But you know what? Never again. Because I don't care. I don't care what happens to me, or you or us." He paused, and uttered Us, again, as an aside, a concept he put no credibility in. "There's nothing I can do anymore, Taylor. *They* are in charge of all this. They're making the decisions about what's going to happen to me. Hell, they've apparently been making decisions about my life for 25 years! And I don't know who they are or what they look like, and the truth is, I'm only figuring this out now by accident! If somebody hadn't fucked up and sent me those pictures, they'd still be yanking me around like a puppet, and I'd still be thinking my life was my own, when in fact it's not, never has been, they created it, and I bought into the scam like the blind-fool idiot I am…"

●

…Taylor heard only one word of his tirade:
Pictures.
In that instant, everything changed.

Because she knew that in the next few minutes, maybe hours if she hit the mother lode, she'd find out exactly what he knew, how much he knew and about whom, and with that as a stepping-off point, maybe Mr. Frost would come to his senses, green-light her putting him down, be done with this whole damned thing.

"You're not a fool, Kevin," she began, cautiously, not wanting to go too fast, pushing him to just continue the riff, and not think about what he was doing or saying.

"The hell I'm not." He'd started pacing, back and forth, back and forth, huffing and puffing like a mad bull. Stopping now, approaching her. "None of it's real. Don't you get that?"

"How do you know?" Edging him toward explanation.

"None of it." Ignoring the question. "When my father died. If my father died, whoever he was, if he was my father, shit, I don't know."

Push him, do it gently, but do it. "You don't know that, Kevin—"

"You don't know what I know."

Taylor wanted to just ask him, outright, Then what do you know? but didn't, thinking it was too obvious, deciding to stay low key, lead him in the right direction. Hers. "I know you're confused—"

"Confused, right, let's talk about confused." He disappeared into the kitchen, the silence shattered by slamming drawers and cabinets, returning with something clenched in his fist, something she couldn't see at first, until he thrust it—no, threw it—in her face, and she knew at once her plan had worked, he'd given up his ultimate secret, the one she suspected had kept him alive so far but whose surrender she now guessed changed those dynamics considerably.

"Tell me about it, Kevin," she said, taking his hand once more, guiding him to the sofa, both of them sitting down. "Please."

•

In the blackness, the image returned.

The jungle. Vietnam. The two men. Dressed to kill.

One of them somebody who wasn't really who he was. The other one—

Who was he?

And the picture. Where did it come from, and why was it coming back, now, at a time when darkness was settling over this place, wherever it was, like the black veil of a mourner?

Answer that, take a giant step toward—

Toward what?

It had to come from someplace. The picture. From someone.

A friend? No.

Relative? Hardly.

Just some person, some acquaintance, casual, who'd been showing pictures around, just doing it like a regular person would, saying, Oh, look at my little son, or Oh, look at my little daughter, or This here, it's my wedding picture, or See, here's my mom and—

Understand what he's going through—

Wait a second. Hold on—

Dropped off the face of the earth—

Where was it? Where?!?

Disappeared in Vietnam, too.

Yeah. Heard that one before.

Become somebody else—

Wait. That's not original. Heard it before, too. But where?

The chance to know for sure—

There it is again. The picture. Two guys in the jungle. Neither who they're supposed to be.

— something I have never enjoyed—

Seeing it now. Again. The picture. But for the first time.

— and may never enjoy.

Who disappeared? Who became someone else? Who?

Gee—
Soldier?
— is any—
Lover?
— of this—
Brother?
— starting to sound—
No. Not a soldier or a lover or a brother—
— familiar?
A father.

•

Taylor stared at the torn photo in her hand while Kevin told her everything.

His relationship with Jon Columbus. Going to Washington, for the service at Arlington, after the old man's body was recovered, Kevin for some reason remembering he had a hot dog and pink lemonade at the bus station in Richmond, taking a bus because his grandmother refused to fly. The lost years, ages 12 to 18 or 19, watching his mother go from bottles of liquor to bottles of pills, the day he came home from college to find someone else living in his home. About being a rising corporate star, then a falling corporate star, and how he was trying to get a grip on the chaos that seemed to be coming down on him like hail the size of bowling balls.

Taylor, listening to him intently, throwing in an occasional "Oh, wow" or "That's so sad," sounding concerned but thinking blah blah blah, let's be done with this verbal home movie and get on with the main attraction.

Which, eventually, he did.

The package from Island City. The call from Roper, with the kid-editorial from the Oak Street school paper. The Little Buddy reference in the note, and the story behind that. His trip to Florida, the conversation with Thomas Cloud. The other torn photos he'd found in storage. The strange discussion with his mother. The books Liz Fletcher had given him.

Still, when all was said and done, it didn't sound to her like he knew much of anything. Roper had already put the case to bed, so nothing more was likely to stir there. The Little Buddy thing was a nuisance, but not fatal. Cloud apparently did a decent job of keeping Devereaux a mystery. If the torn pictures were all he had, that was the mother's problem, and she sounded like a basket case, which could explain just about anything that might otherwise make no sense. And even though he hadn't said anything about what the detective was doing in Tennessee, she was dead and so was whatever she'd discovered. Outside of maybe dealing with Donna Hubbard and her brother in the can—neither of whom was that big a deal either—what were Mr. Frost and his crowd worrying about?

"Then there's the photo negative," she heard Kevin say, and just when that started to register with Taylor, her thinking Oh, Jesus, what I don't need is another surprise, not right now, the phone rang.

Chapter 34

"I know it's three in the morning, but don't say a word. Not one damned word."

The up-and-down emotions that had been slapping at Kevin for the past hour were suddenly replaced by yet another wave of profound confusion. He was standing in the dining area, on the phone, facing Taylor, who was still on the sofa, watching him like he was a secret code she was trying to break. He turned away from her, back into the kitchen. "What?"

"That's a word, Kevin. Are you deaf? And don't answer that, either." He said nothing. "Now, tell me you're alone. Tell me that bottle-blonde boy-toy has packed her shit up, and gone off to find Bigfoot or track down rumors that Mickey Mouse is a she-male. Tell me the bitch is anywhere but there, with you, in that gerbil hut you call a house. Tell me that."

His silence was the wrong answer, the disgusted sigh spewing from the other end of the line making that real clear, but the words that followed were colored less with irritation than urgency:

"Okay. Listen to me, Kevin. Listen close and listen good." He nodded, realizing how stupid that was, him being in the middle of a phone conversation with an unseen caller. "She's not who she seems to be."

Unformed words started to surge from his throat, but he swallowed them.

"Now I don't like the bitch, I'll admit that, and I think that even if she was pure as Snow White, she'd still screw you in a flash to get what she wanted. And you'd fall for it. Because you're a man, and that's what men do. I'm saying all this 'cause I want you to know that I know what my prejudices are, okay? I know where I'm coming from, and I am not trying to fool me or you or anyone else into thinking that I'm being objective about this. I'm not. The woman is bad, man. She's cancer on legs. I'm not asking you to agree or disagree with me on that, because it doesn't matter. I'm right. That's all you need to know."

Kevin just stood there, feeling like everything around him was going into a full-tilt boogie.

"Now let me tell you about my dream—"

"Your what?"

"I thought I told you to keep it closed, skippy, didn't I tell you that? And before you go off thinking this is some Dionne Warwick, psychic friends network dial 1-900-Headgame kind of thing, let me assure you of just how wrong that assumption would be. So you would be well-advised not to travel too far down some path you think leads to the Maxie Is Mad destination just because I had a dream—hell, Martin Luther King had a dream, nobody called him nuts—because I am not losing it. You got that?" A half-second. "Don't answer me. Just grunt or sneeze or something."

He responded with a hybrid of non-verbal noises.

"I was dead asleep, man, just dead asleep. And you know how just before you come to, and you see something, and there's a certain weird reality about it?" Kevin said nothing, unsure whether to answer, Maxie pressing on.

"Henry Lee had this picture when we were at the prison. It was him and some other guy, they were in Vietnam, and they were in Total Combat getup, you know? Camos, body paint, large guns, the whole drill." She paused, letting her breath catch up with the story. "He showed it to me to prove he was one of the guys in it. Because I gotta tell you, me and you look like twins compared to Henry Lee now and Henry Lee in the picture. But it was him. He had the chopped-off little finger, just like Donna said. The other guy, his war buddy, his name was

Tim. Tim was the guy Devereaux shot in Nashville when they tracked down Henry Lee, right after Worth was assassinated."

Another pause while she came up for air.

"I was looking at that picture, and the guy, this Tim, he looked familiar to me. Why, I had no idea. He just did. But with all this stuff swirling around in my brain at that moment—Ordell, Henry Lee, the third shooter, all that—I just let it slide, racked it up to paranoia." In the background, Kevin heard what sounded like a public address announcement, Maxie telling him to hang on for a second while she listened, coming back on the line less than thrilled. "Goddamned U.S. Scareways. I got a crisis at home—Carmella's turning J.J. into a serial killer—and I'm stuck at the airport. The very airport, I might add, where I have been stranded since late yesterday when, after discovering my fat-assed sister's plot and prematurely checking out of the hotel, I entertained the hope of getting an earlier flight home. A futile effort, I might add, as it appears the FAA has grounded every MD-80 ever made, leaving me and about 8 million of my closest friends sharing a bed disguised as a gate area."

Kevin thought about asking what the J.J.-Carmella thing was all about, decided it was a bad idea.

"Anyway, in one of the few minutes of sleep I've had the luxury of catching, I saw this picture in my head. It came back to me, for some reason. Like it was trying to tell me something, or remind me of something, or explain something to me, you know? And in my dream, I'm in this room, just a big empty room, and I'm looking at this picture, asking Where? Where have I seen this? And I'm thinking of all the pictures I've seen lately. I'm thinking of all the family shit we got from Donna— mommies and daddies and brothers and sisters and all that. And I'm seeing those pictures in my head, clear as when I was looking at them, but none of them match the one Henry Lee showed me in the prison.

"I try to put it out of my mind. Just get rid of it. Something, though, something won't let me do it. So I sit, alone in this room that's only in my head, my dream, and just stare at the photo, asking myself where have I seen it? I'm concentrating, man, like I never have before, and out of nowhere, in the darkness, comes a light." She paused. Her tone went sour. "A blonde light."

The full-tilt boogie stopped, Kevin going into Red Alert.

"It didn't make everything clear, really. And it just piled a whole lot of hay on top of the stack that's already doing a hell of a job hiding the needle."

He stopped breathing.

"Remember the other night, when we were at your apartment, when I met Miss Melrose Place for the first time, when you and I had words?"

He nodded, this time not caring how ridiculous it might have been.

"She showed us a picture."

Another nod.

"Remember who it was?"

Kevin fought the whole idea of what she was saying.

"And you remember what Donna said about the guy who came home with her brother, right before Worth was shot? She didn't know his last name, just called him Rim Tim Tim?"

Everything getting clearer and more confused at once, Kevin thinking this was more than he could handle.

"What kind of dog was Rin Tin Tin, Kevin?"

Despite himself, and Maxie's warnings, he leaned around the corner and looked back into the living room—

"A German shepherd, Kevin. Get it? German shepherd, Taylor Shepard?"

— closed his eyes, retreated.

"It was her old man in the picture. He was part of the plot. His job was to kill Henry Lee on the fire escape. When that didn't come off as planned, Devereaux killed *him* in Nashville."

Kevin wanted to scream No, but couldn't bring himself to do it. Nothing, it seemed, was beyond possibility anymore, like this was all some American Dream, only in reverse.

"Now, I don't know what's going on with the two of you at the moment. But here's what I do know: You'd better not tell her a damned thing about this—or about anything else you know, because—"

Maxie stopped in mid-sentence, as if the thought had been hit by an asteroid. "Kevin, please tell me you haven't already spilled your innards to this woman. Please tell me. Even if it's a lie, please tell me."

"It's too late," he said.

Man, you could screw up a free lunch, she wanted to tell him, not saying it though, thinking this was not the perfect time to state the obvious. "What have you told her?"

"Uh—"

"Stop me when I'm wrong." She started at the beginning, with everything they knew and had shared, her list unbroken until she arrived at Henry Lee.

"No," he interrupted. "Nothing there."

"Nothing about what I know, anything I found out in Nashville?"

"Nothing."

"How about what those two Wayne's World computer fools told you, about the second shooter and the photos, all that noise?"

"No," he replied quickly, thanking God the call had come when it did. "Nothing there either."

"Well, that's something," Maxie said. "Right?"

"I guess," Kevin agreed, not having the first idea what that *something* was, except thinking that if things kept going the way they were, he couldn't imagine it being anything good.

•

After 15 or so minutes, Taylor's curiosity got the best of her. Once Kevin had disappeared from sight, she had heard only occasional one-syllable words from his end, and that single peek around the corner, then nothing. No sound coming from the kitchen, none at all, making her think maybe he'd passed out or fallen asleep.

When she found him, he was sitting in the middle of the floor, back to the wall, knees up, right hand holding a plastic yogurt cup half full of Irish whiskey. He didn't look angry anymore, or upset, didn't even look exhausted. But he did look somehow changed. There was a sense of solution about him, like he was step away from figuring out the meaning of life, needed one or two more calculations and wisdom would be his.

"Kevin?" she asked, a bit hesitantly, unnerved by his apparent serenity, and not entirely sure which Kevin Columbus might answer, Easy Kevin or Pain in the Ass Kevin.

Neither did. He just took a sip from the yogurt cup, eyes full forward, silent.

"Are you okay?"

A slight, non-committal shrug.

"Who was that on the phone?"

Nothing this time.

"Was it your mom?"

A chuckle, dismal and deep with unstated contempt. "Hardly."

Which caused the high tide of concern to start rising in Taylor, made her reach back into her mind, recalling anyone whose path he'd told her he crossed—Roper, St. Cloud, the real estate woman—giving each name a brief mental look before tossing it at him, making sure she didn't misspeak like she had on the library database.

To every one, he answered with a brief shake of the head, a silent No.

The tide got higher. She needed answers, somehow. "You're beat," she said, soothing, smiling, "so why don't we just go to bed. You can tell me about everything else tomorrow, we'll sort things out, take it nice and slow and easy, get to the bottom—"

"It was nobody," he interrupted. "Just Maxie."

Maxie?

Kevin's eyes were still planted on the kitchen cabinets in front of him, so he didn't see the shock, skepticism, rage and astonishment that were alternately rappelling down Taylor's face, or her hands, both of them clenching into white, bloodless fists.

Maxie?

Impossible.

She caught herself staring at him, quickly breaking the gaze before he could look up and catch her stricken expression, feeling sweat start to bead at the small of her back, thinking, These amateurs are ruining everything!

Taylor's alarm ebbed, panic being counterproductive to shaping a plan, which was what she needed, and this kid, this goddamned *child*, was all she had at the moment. "Maxie," she said at last, with a subtext that added, none too pleasantly, How Utterly Wonderful. "Is she okay?" Once again, making sure she stayed in character, asking the question out of apparent politeness, but wanting him to know she didn't really care if the woman had been hit by a bus.

"She's fine."

The one-syllable answers bothered her, made her think she was losing him and needed to speed things up, mine him for as much as she could before he shut down altogether. "She have anything interesting to offer?"

"No."

Not good enough. "Hey, lemme have a slug of that." Taylor sat down next to him, playfully and suggestively using her hips to nudge him over, give her some room. She took a sip of the whiskey, made a face. "Ugh. I can't drink brown liquor."

"Vodka's in the freezer."

"I'm fine." She shifted a little closer to him, rested her head on his shoulder. "Seriously, is she okay? Maxie, I mean?"

"Yeah. She's fine. She's just been trying to get out of Nashville since yesterday afternoon."

"What's going on in Nashville?"

"Some case. She was gonna stay overnight, but decided to come back early. Apparently there's some problem with the planes, so she's stuck there until the morning."

Decided to come back early?

Goddammit, I should have rechecked the computer program, Taylor screamed at herself, doing it deep down, way externally, careful not to let even a small hint of her self-rage percolate to the surface. "So she's coming back, when, sometime tomorrow?" Working him still, looking for a nugget of gold, the beginning of a plan, any plan.

He nodded. "Something's going on with J.J."

Taylor's invisible radar clicked on. "Who's J.J.?"

"Her little boy." He sighed wearily. "It's a long story. Maxie and her sister went another round yesterday in their ongoing heavyweight fight over J.J."

"What's that all about?"

"Maxie's sister has custody of the boy. He lives with her." Shaking his head, almost sadly. "Like I said, a long story, and not a pretty one."

Long, short, whatever, it was still new information, Taylor processing it as fast as her mental computer would allow. "Where does he live?"

"J.J.? I told you. He lives with Carmella and her husband."

"But where?" Trying to sound like she was halfway interested.

"Oh." Kevin shook his head in what looked to Taylor like a silent apology for being in a fog. "They live here."

"In Charlotte?"

"Yeah."

"I see."

Kevin was saying something about J.J., about what a good kid he was, and all that. But Taylor wasn't listening. She was thinking more about Maxie and how close the riot girl was to wrecking everything, and how something had to be done about her fast. And as Kevin babbled on about how much Maxie loved her kid, and how she'd do anything for him, all that mother-son crap, the first black rays of a plan started to darken Taylor's mind.

Chapter 35

It was shortly after six on Thursday morning, and the sun was only just beginning to bathe Cambridge. Bartholomew Knight, as was customary, had already arrived at his office. But on this day, he'd gotten in much earlier than usual, at precisely 4:45, just as he had promised. Within minutes, a man he had never seen knocked on the door to what Knight's students often called The Dim Den of Brilliance and handed him a small manila envelop. It contained three mini-cassette tapes. For the past 75 or so minutes, Bart Knight had been listening to the conversation between Maxie McQueen and Kevin Columbus over and over again.

When Walter Frost first apprised him of the tapes' existence—or, more importantly, their content—Knight was quick to downplay the significance. They were tending to the detective, and he felt sure the boy could be managed effectively. Frost, uncharacteristically, was less certain. His concerns focused on the growing circle of knowledge. The simple fact that more people were now more aware of what had happened 25 years ago threatened more than just the cover-up. It threatened the pending treaty with Arabaq, and the legacy of this administration. That was true, Knight agreed. Those were legitimate concerns that would play a major role in determining their response to the current crisis. Frost urged quick action: Go to the White House, inform the president, solve the problem. Knight disagreed. He was not about to adopt any strategy in the absence of actually hearing what was being said on the taped conversations. He had learned in the spy business that what you don't see is as important as what you do. The same held true for conversations: what wasn't spoken often communicated more than the words themselves.

And after repeated listenings, everything Bart Knight heard and didn't hear told him that the silent threat these tapes held—

"The second gunman. The guy who Henry Lee says actually killed Worth."

"Give the man a prize."

"You're saying he's my father?"

— put more than just treaties and cover-ups and political legacies at risk. No, the fallout of what they had done a quarter century before now extended beyond the tragic but sometimes necessary act of assassination. Their collective undertaking had put the very government at risk. How ironic: They were on the brink of bringing down the very institution they had been trying to protect.

Bart Knight was not a man who dwelled much in the past, even one as rich as his. He had always believed that the past was prologue and, like Cicero, felt is was best not to go over old ground, but rather to prepare for what was to come. He had done that, too. Every step was calculated to produce yet another step that would inevitably take them to a future of their own shaping. Yes, there was always a nod to days gone. But not much more. If God Himself could not change the past, Knight had always mused, why dwell on it? The best we, any of us, could do was learn from experience, try not to trip over history's wreckage and enjoy what fond memories the passage of time would permit. Then do what you have to do, and get on with it.

Lately, though, Bart Knight felt as if he'd been tripping not only over the wreckage of history, but also its burdens. He had never been especially philosophical. Yet since the slow unraveling of their decades-old cover-up, he had begun to immerse himself in the concept of consequentialism. Not the classic theory, which held that when an individual adopted a set of values, he had a moral responsibility to do whatever was necessary to promote those values. That, after all, was precisely what he, they, had done, wasn't it? They believed in something, something that embodied their values, and pursued it zealously. And if others possessed neither the courage nor the commitment to do likewise, that was not his concern.

But anymore, Knight found himself considering the idea of alternative options, and wondering whether the one they selected back in 1963, the one that more or less started this avalanche of consequences, truly had been the wisest choice. The three of them, sitting in a roadhouse bar just outside of Denver, Knight trying to figure out the best way to protect his investment—

"She's pregnant, Bart."

Knight gazed at him with steel-eyed anger. "How did this happen?"

He laughed. "Well, you take your dick, see, and you put it—"

Bart Knight delivered as vicious a slap as Jon Columbus had ever witnessed. It cracked against the man's face like a whip, forceful enough to produce a trickle of blood from one nostril, which the man wiped away with a white bar napkin. There were a couple of cowboy whoops from a wooden booth behind them, suggesting that this was clearly an establishment where occasional fistfights were as common as the bad draft beer the three of them were sipping. "Jesus, Bart, that's a helluva right."

"Try this," Knight said. Then he delivered an equally sharp slap with his left hand, nearly knocking his target off the bar stool. Jon Columbus started to step in. Knight stopped him by placing a surprisingly gentle hand against his chest, still looking at the third man.

"You're a fool," he said with calm menace. "A reckless fool."

"So we cut it out of her. Big deal." Even in the dark, the red welts on his face were apparent.

"No," Jon Columbus said.

Knight's hateful stare softened into one of admiration as it shifted to Columbus. "I admire your gallantry, Jon," he said evenly. "Would that others among us share that sense of honor."

"Honor, honor. Fuck honor. I knocked her up. We abort the baby. Mission accomplished. I don't understand—"

"No," Jon Columbus repeated. "Meredith won't let that happen."

They both looked at him, clearly surprised. "How do you know this?" Knight asked finally. "You've discussed it with her?"

He nodded. "She came to me when she first started getting sick. I told her to see a doctor."

"I knock her up, and she comes crying to you?"

Knight slapped him again. "How strange, given your reservoir of compassion."

"Hey, I've known her a lot longer than you have, Jon. I was fucking her long before you were."

Knight slapped him again, this time just because he felt like it. He turned back to Jon. "Tell me about this, about your conversations with Meredith."

"Just that she's not going to do it."

"It's not her choice. Tell him, Bart."

"She says if you force her to abort the baby, she's going to your wife—"

"That bitch is threatening me?"

Knight flashed him a look that said another slap was waiting in the wings. "Do you believe her?" he asked Jon Columbus.

"Yeah, Bart. Yeah, I do."

"Just lemme talk to her, I can straighten this whole thing out between us—"

"That's the problem," Jon Columbus said.

"Huh?"

"You've already straightened out something between you. And now, you're going to pay for it."

"You sonofa—"

"Sit down," Bart Knight ordered. "And shut up." He considered the situation for two or three silent, interminable minutes, then asked, "You know her better than any of us, Jon. What do you suggest?"

"Besides castrating him?" Gesturing to the third man.

"Hey, just because you're the one shooting blanks, don't go taking it out on me."

Jon Columbus stared at him for a long, long time, with undisguised hatred, before turning to Knight. "She's going to have the baby. Abortion wouldn't go down real well with her family—"

"Fucking Catholics."

"Next time, try banging an atheist," Jon Columbus fired back.

"Enough," Knight said.

Columbus sipped the watery draft and composed himself. Then he said, simply, "I'll marry her"—

How odd, Bart Knight now mused, that this entire episode had started with an honorable gesture by an honorable man. And what, he wondered, what if Jon Columbus had not been quite so honorable? What if he had not made such an offer? Would they have forced Meredith into an abortion, threatening her with unforeseen consequences if she did not oblige? And what would those consequences have been? Would he, Bart Knight, have actually ordered the murder of a young woman just to protect an asset whose recruitment and rise and future he had shaped from their first discussion at the Air Force Academy in Colorado Springs? And what would have come of his otherwise perfect reputation as a spotter for the CIA when it was learned that he, Bart Knight, had invested so heavily into one so reckless? Would his career have taken the path it had, to this office, at this university, arguably the most prestigious institution in the world? Or would he have been quietly exiled to a small school someplace in Upstate New York, say, where they could keep an eye on him, and make sure that whatever knowledge he possessed remained there, with him?

Or would they have done to him what they had done to so many others, and simply arranged an accident that delivered a swift conclusion to an existence that for all intents and purposes had ended years before, in a cowboy bar, where a man of honor and a man of power dueled over the fate of a woman?

•

Taylor peeked around the corner of the short hallway from Kevin's bedroom-turned-office into the living room. He was still out like a corpse on the sofa, dead from emotional exhaustion, had fallen asleep the second his head hit the pillow, foregoing any suggestion of sex, which was fine with her.

"Look," she said evenly into the cell phone, ducking back into the bedroom-office. "I'll be the first to admit that this is my mistake. I assumed the detective would be where the computer said she was. I shouldn't have done that—"

"How do you plan to rectify your failure?" Walter Frost asked.

Failure. The word like an ice pick to her brain, a concept that, up until recently, had been as unfamiliar to her as Manitoba. But now, after the misplay with Donna Hubbard's sister, and hitting the wrong con in prison, to say nothing of the monumental fuck-up at the hotel in Nashville, she was suddenly vulnerable, and Frost's tone told her as much. It wasn't laced with the usual I Detest You But You Terrify Me that had always underlined their conversations, even the most recent one in Chicago. It was just bland, him treating her like the help, like some cleaning woman who hadn't dusted the blinds. It did not make Taylor Shepard happy. "I'm going to take care of the detective," she said tightly, thinking of B.B. or C.C.—whatever the hell Maxie's kid was called. "And keep in mind that the detective is not *our* problem."

"Is that so?" More of that high-class, holier-than-thou sneer. Jesus, she wanted to go to D.C. now and kill *him.*

Taylor swallowed her anger, this being no time to get mad. She tugged unconsciously at the sleeve of her T-shirt, which had a red-and blue logo of *The Chicago Tribune* stretched across the chest. When

Kevin had commented on it, she delivered a sad, almost rueful "Girl's gotta dream, right?" that dropped his heart to the canvas for a 10 count. "Yes, Walter," she continued, foregoing the usual *Mr. Frost*, letting him chew on that for a second, "it is so. As I said, the detective is *my* problem, and as I have also said, I'll solve it—"

"With better results, I hope."

She turned her head far to the right, then to the left, trying to ease the neck muscles and muffle the percussion section that was full-drumming on her head. Looked at her watch, 6:15 in the morning, way too early for a drink. "Trust me."

"I'll try, but that might be easier—"

"It might be easier, Walter, if I could just go in there and shoot him now and be done with it."

"Out of the question." It was a quick comeback, sharp enough to tell Taylor that the point was non-negotiable.

Still, she tried again: "Weren't you listening to me? He knows a lot. Killing him is the only way we can keep everything under control, where it belongs."

"No."

"Why not?"

"We don't have the authority."

"Then get it."

Walter Frost was silent for a long time, maybe a minute. Taylor knew what was going on, knew it as if she had modemed into his brain, and was listening to the old man's every thought. He was running contingencies. Do I ask for authority, or just let it ride for the time being, or give the go-ahead to do what has to be done? And what are the likely outcomes of each scenario, and how do they affect the bigger picture and, even more important, how do they affect me, my power, my ability to control?

Taylor had to smile. One of the pure joys of what she did was the total lack of middle ground. By the time they, whoever *they* happened to be, came to her, the hand-wringing was over, the decision had been made, someone was going to die. She was merely the instrument. Not that she needed any rationale for what she did, but it was true. Nobody blamed the missile, the bomb or the bullet—and that's exactly what she was—they blamed the people who launched it or dropped it or shot it. That's how she saw it, anyway, and she slept awfully well at night.

"Not now," Frost said at last.

"Then when?" Expecting the answer, but still pushing him, enjoying it, having some fun at the anal-retentive old geezer's expense.

"Perhaps in time."

"How much time?" Really enjoying it now, feeling more in charge, like it was her show, feeling so good that her free hand had found its way to her nipple and was teasing it beneath *The Trib* T-shirt.

"When the moment arrives, if it arrives, you will be among the first to know."

Both nipples hard now, Taylor closing her eyes, licking her upper lip, saying, "Who will be the first?" but keeping it level, not letting Frost in on the secret at her fingertips.

Another pause. Lost in her momentary world, Taylor didn't even try to read Frost's thoughts. When he answered, "That's none of your concern at the moment," she missed the fine thread of warning that held the words together, and instead kept at him.

"Oh, I think it is. I think it's very much my concern." The response arrived a bit too hoarse, too breathy, Taylor warning herself to get control or put your hands back where they belonged, opting for control. After a deep rein-in breath, she continued: "You see, I know just enough to be a risk to you, and to the treaty and to anyone or anything else who has been involved in this *despicable*"—putting the word in bright neon lights, letting him know she, at least, saw the irony—"little endeavor. This seems to me to be an appropriate time to let the girl into the tree house, tell her what all the men are up to."

"Is that a threat?" Frost's voice floated into her ears, airy and detached.

"I mean, I could just push the End button here on my phone, cut you off, go right in the other room and do it."

"You wouldn't dare."

That made her smile. She stroked her nipples a bit more roughly. "You don't think so?"

"No, I don't." Not a moment's hesitation.

The self-caress stopped. Taylor hated anyone assuming what she would or would not do. Fun time was over. Her mood shifted. "Listen to me, and listen carefully: I've got on a T-shirt right now, and nothing else. My nipples are like granite, and I'm so horny I'd straddle a snake if I could get low enough. I have a Czech M52 in my purse and a Ruger Mark II in my suitcase. The Ruger doesn't need a suppressor if you hold it close enough to your target because his body muffles the sound. Great assassin's gun. All of which means I am armed, worked up and want to fuck somebody. So now is not the time to be challenging me. Because if you do, I'll go into that other room, and I will put an all-universe inter-galactic fuck on that boy, and then I'll ventilate his head without so much as a second thought. Think of it as a two-fer, Walter, since I'll be fucking you, too. Are we clear?"

This time Frost did hesitate. It was only momentary, and it did not ease the tension in his voice when he spoke. "Don't kill him. Please."

"Give me a reason not to."

"Because we wouldn't allow it."

"You'd bring him back from the dead? Damn, Walter, you do have some pull." She laughed.

"That I do."

"So let's see: You've got pull. I've got a gun. That means—"

"It means we are looking for a way to bring this to closure as unob-trusively as possible."

"Killing some anonymous kid in North Carolina is hardly going to generate national headlines."

"He's not anonymous." Frost flamed the words back at her, terse, hot and unthinking, and Taylor felt instant regret in his voice. Walter Frost, man of many secrets, had just given up one of the biggest.

"Is that so? Do tell."

"It's not important."

"So you're saying if I do go in there and shoot him, there will be national headlines?"

"Not at all. Even if there were, it wouldn't matter. I don't care about headlines. The masses are not my concern."

"But this kid is."

"Let me put it to you this way: I have an audience of one."

"Are you talking about him? Kevin?"

"Yes and no."

"Don't fuck with me, Walter, or I'll—-"

"Or you'll what?"

His tone was now tundra cold, and twice as lifeless. It was a surprise, coming as suddenly as it did, breaking her rhythm so much that all she could offer was a diluted, "What does that mean?"

"It means, little girl, that you should run along, go and clean up the mess you've made, and leave the larger issues to other people. When you are done, perhaps we will have reached some resolution of this matter."

"What happens if you wait too long?" More a challenge than a question.

"Then you can just pen another one of those ridiculous fictions about the Worth matter you are so good at, which upon publication will once again remind everyone just how absurd any notion of a conspiracy is."

She ignored his shot at the disinformation campaign, which had been her idea—a way to provide cover, get information and generally stay on top of things, while at the same time using Merke's e-zine or The Keyhole to deep-six any thoughts of a real conspiracy. "I'm not in the mood to wait," she replied instead, voice pretending to discover some of its confidence.

"I don't care. The boy stays alive until the decision is made, if it is made, that he shall no longer stay alive. And that decision is not yours."

"Whose is it?"

"As I said, I have an audience of one."

"Well, since my job isn't to satisfy your audience of one—"

"Oh, but it is—"

— which threw her again, this time into silence—

"—and you would be well advised to consider that. Because if you don't, the aforementioned audience of one would not have any qualms about ending your life with the ease and efficiency you demonstrated in ending those of General Azid's children."

By the time she found and formed the words asking what he was talking about, the connection to Washington had long since died.

Chapter 36

Bart Knight had been listening to Walter Frost for 10 minutes now—mostly recounting the discussion with the assassin, that horrid woman, whoever she was—and felt a low storm of depression start to roll in. For 25 years they had managed to cover up a true American murder: The killing of a favorite son. But now, wherever any of them turned, it seemed every artifice they had built was on the brink of exposure. Uncharacteristically, Bart Knight felt powerless to stop what he knew deep in his soul was a pending disaster.

Frost was saying something about the detective in Nashville, but Knight wasn't really listening. This operation, if that was the word, had assumed a life and momentum of its own. From the moment Gary Devereaux mailed his little exit package to Kevin Columbus, control had shifted away from Knight and Frost and a handful of others. No one was in charge now. The truth was, the only way to end it, to regain some power over events, would be to do just exactly what the assassin had urged: Shoot the son, and be done with it, etching one final name on the invisible wall of tribute to the treaty with Arabaq.

Would that ever happen?

Bart Knight couldn't honestly say. But he did believe that President Anderson's administration wanted it both ways—they wanted their treaty, and they wanted the killings to end—and Knight was reasonably certain that both were not within in the realm of possibility. "Closure," the president had said when Azid's intermediaries finally sent word that the general was ready to come to the table. "I want closure. On everything." It was a noble thought, despite coming from a man who had been largely responsible for the near eradication of an entire family, to say nothing of the collateral deaths the operation had caused. But to close the door on the Azid campaign, to really close it, meant permanently tying up a lot of loose ends on the home front. And Kevin Columbus was the loosest of them all.

Frost was now explaining what happened in the Nashville hotel, how the killer had murdered a black, 38-year-old human resources manager from Paramus, New Jersey, while the woman was taking a shower, the unfortunate victim apparently checking in after Miss McQueen had left.

Although the operation was not over, Bart Knight was already performing post-mortems in his own mind. In his days with the Agency, dating back to the OSS, he had always tried to pinpoint the precise moment that events turned. It was an exercise that he felt illuminated failure. And failure, Bart Knight knew, was a far better teacher than success.

So where had it all begun to get away from them?

He broke Frost's near stream-of-consciousness monologue about the cover-up's status to ask the question. When Frost began a litany of possibilities—starting, as might be expected, with Devereaux's package—Knight wished he hadn't raised the issue. Not so much because it invited a long list of missteps, points where events pushed the conspiracy one way when it should have gone in another. No, the problem was that Walter Frost was just dead wrong.

Bart Knight leaned back in his chair, and silently admitted the obvious. They, he, had unwittingly allowed this to happen years before. Maybe it was 1959, at the Air Force Academy, where Knight first noticed a smart, quick-witted, carefree young man in his seminar on Middle East politics. More likely, though, it was two years later, 1961, at a small social gathering in Georgetown—spies, mostly, but one never knew—in a brief conversation with Jonathan Columbus. Yes. That was exactly the moment.

Bart Knight closed his eyes, and watched it play again in the darkness—

"I may have someone for you, Jon."

Although there was expensive caviar on the buffet table and free-flowing champagne courtesy of tuxedoed waiters who seemed to think an empty glass was a felony, Jon Columbus took a long gulp of scotch, washing down a cracker smothered in cream cheese. He wasn't real big on luxury. "Go on."

Knight gestured for Columbus to follow him around the table. Just a couple of friends talking casually amidst the vegetables and dip, pork tenderloin, oysters and little quarter sandwiches on bread without the crusts. "He's a sophomore. Good mind. Bright. Very, very bright."

Columbus touched the table's centerpiece—a pheasant—as if wondering whether it was real. He reached for a carrot stick, swept it through something warm that was in a crock pot, and set it on a crystal plate worth half the GNP of a small Latin American country. "You've just described all of Harvard, Bart. Why is this one different?"

It was an age-old game between spotters and company men. The recruiters touted their finds, the handlers said Prove it. Bart Knight understood this and played his part, knowing—as did Jon Columbus—that the only real game going on at the moment was the two of them standing here, pretending that Knight's power and connections within the intelligence community didn't outrival those of the Air Force officer.

"This one is utterly amoral."

For the first time since they'd been talking, Jon Columbus looked at Knight, and in that moment when their eyes met, it was as if none of Washington's intelligence elite and their subordinates were present. "Tell me about this newfound talent."

A tiny smile of understated victory came to Knight's face. He, too, reached out to touch the pheasant on the buffet table. "Very lifelike."

"This city's full of them."

"Dead, stuffed birds?"

Columbus nodded. "They have another name for them here, though."

"Oh?"

"Senators. Congressmen. Cabinet members. Presidents."

"Taxidermy must be a thriving business."

"We do all right." He grinned, and it rose slowly into a laugh. "We do damned well."

The brief silence that followed was Knight's invitation to speak. He took a small crimson pocket square from his blue blazer, dabbed at his lips. "As I said, this young man is very bright. He knows it, and is not afraid to show it. The odd thing is, I believe he is smarter than even he thinks he is."

"Go on."

"Masterful grasp of international affairs, and a fascination with the Middle East."

"Is he a Jew?"

Knight shook his head, knowing full well that in the WASPy intelligence fraternity, being Jewish was reason for blackballing. "No. And even if he was, he could argue against his Jewishness with the same zeal he could argue for it."

"So he has no principles." Knight and Columbus both knew this was not necessarily a bad thing.

"He is, how shall I say this…flexible."

"Does he have any kind of code—personal, moral, political?"

Knight shrugged slightly. "Not that I am aware of. But he does have the hunger of ambition. And obeys only his appetite."

The mixture of ambition and amorality captured Jon Columbus's interest. Deeply. "Any peculiarities? Does he like little boys, little girls, sheep? Sex with corpses? Liquor problems? Drugs?"

Knight picked through a bowl of mixed nuts, searching for cashews, using the move to cloak his hesitation. He had also prepared himself for this question, too. And while he had decided to just be straight with Jon Columbus, the arrival of the moment seemed to bring all of his options to the mental surface again. In the time it took to fish three whole nuts from the silver serving tray, he rejected them all. "He has an admitted fondness for women."

That broke the spell. Jon Columbus's attention returned to the plates of salads and breads and meats on the long, elegant maple table.

"He also has a steady girlfriend, Jon, a high school sweetheart—"

"Steady? I see. She wearing his ring?" he answered, chuckling derisively, seeming to forget his position in the two-man pecking order.

Knight ignored the slight. "He says he plans to marry her."

"While he parks the pink Caddie up a side street? Come on, Bart. It could compromise him, us and—not to be too melodramatic—the country, too."

Knight nodded slowly. He understood. He was also ready for it. "Remember how we have discussed, through the years, about having our own mole inside our government, Jon? Someone who we owned, who owed their entire career, their life, to us? Someone whose allegiance was only to the intelligence community?"

"A guy with a nomadic pecker ain't that person, Bart."

Knight suddenly clutched Columbus's arm. "In this case, he may be."

It was an uncharacteristic move from this notoriously stand-offish man, and Jon Columbus noticed. He looked at the professor's hand and then into his eyes, which were electric with excitement. "How can you be so sure?"

"He has no values. He has little sense of right and wrong, and has balls you could bowl with—"

"How do you know all that?"

Another smile, this one grim yet at the same time admiring, came to Knight's face. "This is a young man who apparently would prefer to take his exams orally rather than in writing. At the same time, he understood the importance of doing well in the first year at the Academy. So just before finals, when he was a freshman, he broke three fingers on his left hand. The writing hand. Simply pulled them back until they snapped."

"Jesus."

"He took every examination orally, and earned the highest marks in his entire class."

"He sounds like a fucking nut."

"Not at all. He is someone who understands that sometimes, things must be done. Things that, on occasion, can be distasteful."

"He told you all this?" Knight nodded. "What did you say?"

"I said it was foolish, and intellectually dishonest. He laughed at me. He said, 'Unless you know how to fake it, professor, you'll never make it in this life.' I asked him if the pain and potential disfigurement were worth it." Knight shook his head wearily, like a father who just couldn't understand why his son acted the way he did. "It seems that from the day he came on campus, he had immersed himself in medical books, studying the bone structure of the hand, making certain that there were no permanent after-effects."

Jon Columbus flashed a broad smile that began to show some admiration of its own. "He conspired to break his own fingers?"

"No," Bart Knight replied. "He conspired to do what was in his own interests. Breaking his fingers was simply a means to an end." He let that sink in before continuing: "We need people like that, Jon."

"We need patriots."

"We need people we can control. People who, if we want them to be patriots, will be patriots."

"However we define patriotism."

"Yes."

Columbus ate a crab roll in one bite. "The woman thing still bothers me," he said, licking a piece of pastry off his upper lip.

Knight nodded. "I'll talk to him."

"Assuming this makes it through the security maze, what are you suggesting we do for him?"

"Great things, Jon."

"Yeah, right." Columbus made a short masturbation gesture with his right hand. "And what's he gonna do for us?"

A smile the size of a crescent moon lit up Bart Knight's face. "Even greater things."

Greater things, Professor Knight thought, tuning back into Walter Frost's sage-sounding monologue, which had now returned to concerns over whether that horrid woman would arbitrarily kill Kevin Columbus. "If that happens, Bart—"

"It would not be a catastrophe," Knight said quietly.

"I agree," Frost said. "But from the outset, the son has always been out of play. You know that."

"Devereaux changed the rules."

"I still don't like it."

Knight had to smile. "Which part don't you like, Walter? The murder part, or the lack of authorization part?"

"I resent that, Bart."

"Withdrawn, then. With apologies."

"You are as deeply into this as the rest of us. You may not have been there in New York. But you wrote the history of Richard Worth's death. And that makes you as culpable as anyone."

"At least I have the benefit of advancing years, which reduces significantly the likelihood that I will have to suffer through the final chapter of this sordid drama." As if propelled by the thought, he pulled a key ring from his pants pocket—it was silver, with BTK engraved on one side and A True American on the other, a gift from the president—and opened the bottom left drawer on his desk.

"What are you saying, Bart?"

Knight foraged through some folders and a couple of paperback books, trying to find his way to the back of the drawer. "You know precisely what I am saying."

"That this is out of our hands now?"

Ah, there it is. "Indeed." He removed a rectangular wooden case, somewhat surprised to see that even though it had stayed tucked away in that place for years, there was barely a nick on the deep, red-brown wood.

"We can still control the outcome, Bart. Nothing has changed that."

Knight opened the case and smiled, running his hand over its contents, sad and relieved that their efforts had finally come to this. "Everything has changed that."

"What do you think we should do?"

"Get the boy out of circulation."

"You mean kill him?"

Fool. "No. I mean pick him up."

"Kidnap him? We can't do that."

Bart Knight laughed despite himself. "Of course. I forgot our code of moral honor allows murder, but not kidnapping. I must reread the tablets."

"You know what I mean."

"Yes, Walter, I do. You asked me what I thought, and I told you: Send someone to North Carolina to get the boy. Once he is out of the way, and the detective has been dealt with, we will be able to terminate this ruse once and for all."

Over the line, Knight could hear Walter Frost thinking. "I'll take care of it," he said after a few moments, quickly adding: "This doesn't have to end badly."

Bart Knight pulled the small .22 revolver out of the wooden box. "On the contrary, Walter. I'm afraid it does."

Gently replacing the phone in its cradle, Bart Knight said a small prayer to a God he wasn't sure existed and asked for at least some consideration for the good things he'd done in life, mentally starting to tick them off. The list was woefully short for a man of his accomplishments, almost making it easier to place the cold barrel of the pistol into his mouth and pull the trigger.

•

It was 6:52 by the car clock. Life had been stirring in the house across the street for about half an hour.

The day started with a tall, heavy-set man in what looked like a blue terry-cloth robe walking out of the front door and taking three short steps along the sidewalk to retrieve the paper. He stood there for a moment, scanning the front page, then pulling out one of the sections before going back inside.

A kitchen light went on, followed by lights upstairs. Bedrooms, most likely.

A woman, much shorter than the man, slim but starting to thicken courtesy of the good life, was opening and closing the refrigerator doors, the cupboard doors. Cracking eggs and pouring orange juice. Toasting and buttering bread. Three cereal boxes on the table: Frosted Flakes, Wheaties and Special K. A pitcher of milk.

At 7:12, the man appeared again, this time in a dark suit, white shirt and red tie. Power get-up. He looked like a banker.

The man kissed the woman lightly and poured himself a cup of coffee, cutting it with a quick shot from the milk pitcher. She said something to him, and then left the kitchen for a moment. The man sat down, poured himself a bowl of Wheaties and continued reading the paper. In a minute or two, the woman reappeared, shaking her head about something that made the man laugh. She went to the stove to check the eggs, rearranged them with a wooden spoon, took a sip of her own coffee.

It was 7:16.

Two minutes later, a sleepy-looking little boy came into the kitchen. Still dressed in his pajamas—they made him up to be a race car driver—he dropped into a chair opposite the man. The woman kissed him gently on the head, but the boy didn't react. The man acknowledged him without looking up.

At 7:22, the man rose, kissed the boy on the head and the woman on the cheek, and disappeared. Moments later, the garage door opened and a white Volvo station wagon backed out, disappearing around the corner, not giving so much as a second thought to the beige cable television service van parked opposite his suburban house. Never wondering what it was doing there at this hour, or considering whether it might be stolen.

The child finished his Frosted Flakes and eggs at 7:27, and left the kitchen. Fifteen minutes later he was back, dressed in a pair of baggy green jeans and a baseball-looking jersey that had Fubu on the front. A blue and black baseball cap, Carolina Panthers, was turned backward on his head.

The woman fussed with his appearance, turning the hat around, yanking his pants up, but the boy would have none of it. Some kind of debate followed, the woman bending over and shaking her finger in his face like it was some kind of divining rod that would lead him to better behavior.

It didn't work. At 7:45, he simply walked away from her, leaving the house through the front door and waiting on the curb alone. The woman followed, standing in the open door, calling out:

"Jack, didn't you forget something?"

The boy ignored her.

"Didn't you forget to tell mama that you love her?"

A paint-by-numbers smile came to his face. He turned and waved. Maybe he said something, maybe he didn't. If he did, there was no heart in it, because when he turned back around, he pointed a finger at his open mouth, the international kid-symbol of You Make Me Sick.

A blue Chevrolet Suburban pulled up at 7:48. It was already full of what looked like a mobile school district of its own. The boy came around to the driver's side and opened the rear door. As he did, he was talking to himself, saying what halfway sounded like, "It's J.J., you skank, and I don't love you, you ain't my mama."

By 7:50, the Suburban had disappeared.

By 7:51, Taylor Shepard had a plan.

Chapter 37

"You wanna know what I hate, and I mean really hate? Songs about screwing your sister, lubing your truck, loving your dog and putting a job where the sun never shines. So as you can well imagine, any appeal of being stranded in Music City USA is lost on yours truly."

Kevin stood in the kitchen in a pair of running shorts and a gray Nike T-shirt, fragged and cranky, feeling like there was some invisible hand out there, floating around, ready to choke-hold him at any second. Still, he had to smile at Maxie who, current situation aside, had that effect on him.

"They've canceled every flight out of Nashville until sometime in the year 2020," she ranted on, "which means I am stranded on an island of humanity populated by people who, on their best days, could be circus freaks. But enough about me. How are you?"

He poured a cup of coffee, hopped up on the kitchen counter. "Right now, I'm not real sure. Where are you?"

"I told you. Nashville. The airport. And not happy about it."

"I can tell."

"Speaking of which, you don't sound overly pleased to hear my deep, throaty voice. Here they give me a 10-minute calling card, and I decide to grace you with my telephonic presence, and you don't appreciate it not one little bit."

He yawned. "Things, you know. Nothing personal."

"Speaking of things that aren't personal, or maybe just not human, is Blondie still around?"

"No, she—"

"Oh, that's right. Bitch has to be back in the coffin before the sun rises."

"Max, come on—"

"And there better not've been any pillow talk about our little conversation—"

"I'm not that stupid."

"Kevin, you are a man, and men are like tile floors. A woman lays you once, she can walk all over you as long as she wants."

"Nothing happened last night."

"So where is she?" Kevin explaining Taylor had to leave town for a couple of days, Maxie coming back with, "Where'd Elvis show his cracker mug this time?"

Louisiana, apparently, if the note he'd found taped to the refrigerator door that morning was any indication: "K—Sorry to leave so quickly (again!), but my editor emailed me and said to get back to the office ASAP. Needs me to do something about another Elvis sighting (don't say a word!!!) at a Taco Bell outside New Orleans (groan). It'll only be a day or two, and then we'll get back on the case. I'll call soon. Love, Taylor." The crack-of-dawn departure hadn't enthused him much, and the high school girl tone of the note felt a little forced. But hell, he could've woken up to read nothing more than the nutrition information on a bag of bagels, so you take victory however it presents itself, right?

"She didn't say," he lied, not wanting to go there. "Just something about business."

"Yeah, I bet."

"What's that supposed to mean?"

"It means it sounds like you're covering for her bony ass, which is not good, because—and forgive the overused man phrase—you got to keep your eye on the ball and not some blonde's—"

"I get the point."

"Do you? Do you, Kevin? I don't know. Look, I understand this any-port-in-a-storm thing. But my God, why'd you have to pick Key Friggin' West the day before a force five hurricane drops in?"

"Don't worry about me. I'm a big boy." Starting to get tired of this, the Rev. Maxie sermon thing, part of him resenting her for being right, another part resenting her for not understanding, the rest maybe resenting himself for not quite getting it either.

"Listen, you wanna belly-ride the bitch, that's fine—"

"Thanks for your permission." Pretty much snapping, wanting to add, *Even though I didn't ask for it and don't need it or want it,* but having the sense not to.

"Whoa, skippy, let's not get snide. I'm in a terminal full of mutants, and it doesn't appear that U.S. Scareways is doing much to commute my sentence. So I'd be real careful with the tone I adopted. Oh, and did I tell you, I carry a gun?"

The comeback made Kevin smile despite himself, again. "So noted."

"All I'm saying is she wants something." Softening a bit. "You need to keep your eyes open."

"What do I have that she could possibly want?"

Maxie laughed sympathetically, not meaning it, more for effect. "You're beautiful when you're stupid, Kevin, you know that? And this morning, you are positively radiant. That's the point, fool. If you don't know what she's after, you won't know when you've given it up."

"I told you: I didn't give up anything last night. I promise."

"I do believe you, Kevin. You're a good guy. I just worry that sometimes, like most good people, you do dumb things without knowing they're dumb. That's all. I just worry about you."

He started to tell her he appreciated the thought, which was no lie, but a robotic voice interrupted: "You have three minutes."

Which ignited a Maxie rant. "Has civilization come so far that machines do our talking for us? Is there any humanity left in this world? Are there any real people anywhere?"

Kevin let her spout off while he half-watched a breaking news story on CNN, a statement from the president on the proposed treaty with Arabaq. Something about knowing he spoke for all Americans in saying that there was nothing more vital to U.S. security than ending the threat of chemical and biological warfare, vowing to do whatever it took to make the accord a reality, yada yada yada, Kevin thinking about Devereaux's books, Taylor's story of Raymond the Feminist, and about how mondo bizarro it was that history's story line was intersecting with his own.

Maxie still ranting: "All I ask is that when I go to somebody for help, it's a person, you know? A real person, not something somebody's created to make their life a little easier and mine a living hell. Is that too damned much to ask? Huh? Is it?"

Kevin hit the TV mute button, not needing another talking head in a tower of political babble, not even if it was the president. "I don't guess so."

Maxie took a deep breath. "Damn, I feel better. Thanks. Now here's what we're gonna do next."

●

Howard Davis, special agent in charge of the FBI's Charlotte office, had learned long ago not to question directives from Washington. So when the order came down to dispatch two men to an address on the south end of town and position them to acquire the inhabitant "without incident," he assumed that somebody had a reason. Nonetheless, Davis ran a quick computer search to see if the apprehendee in question had a sheet, a record, any kind of personal history that his guys might need to know if and when the call to brace him came. Nothing popped up. Anywhere. Whoever this guy was, he didn't exist as far as law enforcement was concerned. Which made him really good at really bad things. Either that, or really innocent. That's probably why he'd been told to have the agents wait. Washington wanted to be sure that when the force of the United States government swooped down on this individual, it did so with at least a reasonable suspicion and a modicum of propriety.

He briefly weighed contacting the Charlotte-Mecklenburg PD with some made-up story, but decided against it. That was all his career needed, an ill-considered call to some local cowboy who whipped his Johnson out in an ill-considered attempt to impress the Feds, ended up blowing the whole damned show. So he did what they said, dispatched a pair of men to what they reported back was a run-down strip of red-brick apartments. When one of them, Jimmy Galloway, a tough little Irishman who came to the Bureau right out of Fordham Law, asked, "Who is this guy, anyway?" the SAC could only respond:

"It's a secret. And whoever knows ain't telling."

•

Despite agreeing with Bart Knight that bringing the boy in was their best option at the moment, Walter Frost felt an unaccustomed need for some consensus on the decision. Especially since he had no intention, at this point, of telling the president the degree to which the treaty with Arabaq might be jeopardized. So he arranged a conference call on his secure line, setting it up through the technicians at Rodale, who brought an extra layer of high-tech comfort to the process. It was redundant, this backup, totally unnecessary. Frost knew that. But within five days—the following Monday being the target date—the man he more than anyone else had elevated to the presidency was going to earn a place in the pantheon of world peace. There was no such thing as being too safe.

Frost was seated at his desk, which was both massive and immaculate and looked out over K Street, bustling and tree-lined, below. Everyone talked about Washington's glorious views. The White House. The memorials. The Capitol. You can have them, Walter Frost thought. I want to arrive every morning and overlook the true canyons of power, where influence is unfettered by petty jealousies and turf wars. That was his one request upon coming to the law firm. He wanted the partners to build a small balcony outside his office where he could sit and lord over the world beneath him. They had, and Walter Frost did.

Of late, though, he had not spent as much time out there. Beyond that, he'd drawn the vertical blinds on the sliding glass door that opened onto the balcony. Hadn't cracked them in almost a week. Which to all the Frost Watchers in the office meant one of two things: The president's polls were headed south, or Old Walter was up to his neck in some secret dealings on behalf of the White House. One of the downsides to his close relationship with the current administration was that every mood swing, every carefully chosen word—every bowel movement, for goodness sakes—was a barometer of presidential fortunes. Publicly, Frost laughed off the notion as pure nonsense. Privately, he enjoyed the perception it created, but it did require that he live his life with a certain caution that could be both inconvenient and confining.

The phone rang, knocking him from his reverie. He picked up to a Rodale operator, who informed him that all parties were on except the chairman of Helmsford, a medical research facility in Minneapolis. Frost took out a small tablet of notepaper that bore only his monogram, and a $1,400 Krone pen, a special edition honoring Sir Edmund Hillary and those who made it to the top of Mount Everest or died trying. It had been a gift from his colleagues at the firm. In calligraphy, the accompanying card had read: "To Walter, for taking us all to the summit with him." How ironic that after climbing all this way, he now stood barely a step from plunging into the exposed rock and jagged crevices of his own making.

"Good morning," he began, "and thank you for joining me on such short notice. If this was without urgency, I would not be interrupting your day."

Someone, he wasn't sure who and didn't really care anyway, said it was no problem. General concurrence followed.

"Without going into a great deal of detail, we have determined that it may be in the best interest of the operation, the treaty, the president and ourselves to, uh, secure the young man."

There was a moment of silence before an oil company CEO asked, "Why now?"

Frost scanned the bare walls of the gargantuan office as he mulled his response. Except for an oil painting of the Lincoln Memorial that hung next to the door—the closest thing he had to an official "view"—they were all bare. More than one client or associate or colleague had asked why, with all his connections, Walter Frost didn't have at least one vanity wall, stocked with photos of him and leaders from across the world. In a moment of pure ego, he replied, "Because they have pictures of me on theirs." He had been younger then, and more confident that the world would turn out as intended.

In their own way, these men on the conference call—some of them retired, others approaching that age—had been his unseen colleagues for the last quarter of the 20th century. He felt a certain obligation to keep them aware of events, if not altogether informed. It wasn't that he distrusted them. Hadn't they kept the secrets, his and theirs, for 25 years now, and grown obscenely rich for their willingness to conceal the truth? The reason he withheld critical details was because it kept them honest. People close to power want more. Insiders want to be deeper inside. By sustaining a perception that there was always more than meets the eye—and they, in time, would be privy to The Real Story—he kept them on a string. This desire to know, to be truly informed, was a drug more addictive and seductive than any substance ever created by man or nature.

"Events have transpired in the past 24 hours," Frost began, slowly, deliberately, "that pose a more direct threat to the treaty. One of them, related to discoveries made by a private investigator, can be remedied easily." He waited for someone to query him about the remedy, and was thankful that no one did. At this point, they could read between the lines. "The second has to do with the son. We fear he has become…unpredictable."

"What does he know?" This from the head of a chemical manufacturer in rural South Carolina.

"We're not entirely sure. That's one of the reasons we are considering this particular option." Frost drew a vertical line of asterisks on the notepad, invisible footnotes to the conversation.

"How real is the threat, Walter?"

The Krone pen lined a massive question mark. "We're not entirely sure of that either."

"But obviously, you have some concerns." The South Carolinian, again.

Frost smiled weakly. "It's my job to have concerns."

"On a scale of 1 to 10, Walter, with 1 being a precaution and 10 being a disaster, where would you put this strategy?"

"Five."

"That sounds like serious caution." A second oil company chairman, this one from Texas.

"In matters like this, there can be no other kind."

"If I can, Walter, I'd like to ask if this decision has already been made, and you're asking us to rubber-stamp it, or whether you are simply informing us as a courtesy." The Rodale CEO.

Walter Frost smiled, thinking they knew him pretty well. "No decisions have been made," he half-lied, telling himself that if serious concerns arose during the call, they could adjust the strategy-in-waiting. Whether he truly believed that was another matter, though. "This one emerged as the leading near-term option. But being a strong believer in the concept of democracy, I felt it necessary to reach a popular consensus if at all possible."

"Is the president aware of this discussion?"

"No."

"Has he been briefed of the—to use your words, Walter—the urgency of the situation?"

"If your question is whether we have been authorized to take final action on the boy, the answer is in the negative."

That this was, in fact, the question, and that Walter Frost had translated it so easily silenced the line for a few moments. Then the Rodale chairman asked a follow-up that was on everyone's mind: "Will he, Walter? Will he make that authorization if and when the time comes?"

Frost was scribbling idly on the pad now, creating images devoid of logic or sense or clarity. "I don't know."

"With due respect, Walter, we all have a lot to lose if this ends up on the front page of *The Washington Post*."

"I understand."

"So I believe I speak for all of us in saying that if you don't honestly know the answer to the question, we'd sure like to know what you think."

It was a fair request. "I think this president is committed to world peace. I think he is committed to serving a second term. I think he is committed to his legacy, and to his place in history." He took a breath, and tried to drain the bitterness from his voice. "I can think of nothing that he would allow to stand in the way of those objectives, or endanger their collective coming to pass." Another breath. "Nothing, or no one."

As far as the people on the call were concerned, that was the only verification necessary. The Texas oilman spoke for them all: "Hell, then, let's just bring the little bastard in."

It took a moment for everyone to realize what he had said. When they did, a burst of small, knowing laughter danced over the phone lines. Walter Frost did not join in.

•

Howard Davis still had questions about why they were picking up some obscure guy who wasn't so much as a blip on the radar screen, criminal or otherwise. He still didn't ask them, though, didn't even let Washington know he'd run a pro forma check on the name. What he did was contact the two agents who were watching the brick apartment, and give them the Go order. "Nothing bad is to happen," he added. "Do you understand me?"

"Ten-four," Jimmy Galloway replied. When he ended the cell-phone call, he looked over at his partner. "This fella must have something on somebody really important."

The other agent, Paul Benton, who'd been in the office two years longer, shook his head. "Nah. I'll bet you a dollar to a donut he's somebody's kid, and he's screwed something up, and we're gonna snatch him before whatever he did goes totally out of control and the situation gets hot."

Galloway shrugged. "Whatever."

"Happens all the time. I swear, sometimes I feel like we're the Delta Force, and our job is to go in and rescue the rich and famous or their spoiled, silver-spoon-sucking kids from their various fuck-ups."

"Guy's place doesn't look all that Richie Rich to me."

"Looks can be deceiving," Benton said.

"Yeah," Galloway agreed, not real happy about the thought. "Well, fellow D-Boy, what say we bring this little extraction to its appropriate end."

Chapter 38

Kevin had seen Maxie operate her computer often enough in the Finding Your Lost Love gig to know how the thing worked, but it still took him a couple of seconds to master the scanner, Maxie giving instructions over the phone. Turned out not to be all that tough. He slipped the first image—one of the two the Brothers Farmer had pulled from Frame 214, Blob No. 1—into a clear letter-sized vinyl sleeve, fed it through the HP printer-copier-fax-scanner, and watched as it appeared section by section on the screen in front of him. When the thing sent him a mission accomplished message, Maxie told him which directory to save the digitized photo in.

Next, he closed the open window on the computer and got back to the blue-background desktop. "Go to the icon that says Felon Find," she said, telling him it was the lower left-hand corner of the screen, a miniature badge, easy to locate, which it was, Kevin double-clicking, the menu popping right up. On to the male Caucasian database, him watching the computer screen as it tried to match thousands of white-boy features—hair, eyes, glasses, tattoos, nose, lips, chins—to Frame 214, thinking and then asking: "You really think this is going to work?"

Maxie not in the mood. "You got something better to do?"

"No."

"Then shut the hell up before I come through that line and whip you like a rented mule."

"From the sound of things, you might get here quicker doing that than flying." Needling her, not really able to get his arms around the concept that they might find something, but still feeling a little rush of excitement, a tiny shot of *What if?* to his system.

"Tell me about it. I mean, why do I pay tax dollars to the government if they can't make the damned airlines run on time?"

"The government recalled the MD-80s, remember?" Still watching the screen, amazed that there were so many different chins.

"I rest my case." Made no sense, so Kevin dropped it. "Getting anything?"

Noses now, lots of them. "It's taking a long time."

"That's 'cause you're gonna come up with about a trillion matches. If that's Buskin, the guy's been in more papers than Dear Abby."

Finally, the screen stopped spinning images. The results were in, emphasis on the plural: "Seems like we have 2,216 of them," Kevin said.

"Get away from me. I don't care who you are, or who you know, but I'm warning you, I got a gun and a hankering to use it, and as God is my witness, if you don't quit breathing that hot-ass dog breath down my neck, I am gonna kill you so much your mama's gonna die. Now back off!"

"Maxie?" Kevin said.

Returning to him. "I feel like I'm in one of those science fiction movies where all these Planet of the Apes people are trying to steal my shit and I have to beat 'em back with a damned stick." Then to an Ape-in-Waiting: "Get outta my face, man!"

Over the line he heard some muffled sounds that had the ring of a threat, Maxie's manner, especially when she was being harassed by people she saw as cretins—that is, most of the populace—being about as tough to figure out as a *TV Guide* crossword puzzle. "Sorry," she said, back to Kevin again. "There's about 90-11-thousand real unhappy people in this terminal, all of 'em trying to use my pay phone, it appears."

"They'll be ripping your clothes off in a minute."

"I live for that moment." She caught her breath. "All right. How many matches you say you got?" He told her. "Call up the first 25."

They were all wire photos from the Associated Press and United Press International, the same shots, each showing the lopsided face and slightly twisted smile of Rayfield Buskin. "All shooter No. 1," he told her.

"What's the match percentage on each of them?"

He fired through a half dozen of the photos. "Eighty-one percent. All of 'em."

"Forget it. Fifty-five's enough to arrest, 81's money in the bank. The man is as advertised. Let's try the other one."

Kevin slipped the second image, Blob No. 2, into the vinyl sleeve and began the scanning process.

•

The standing rule at DDI Industries was to never leave the phone taps unattended for more than five minutes. Vending machines weren't but a few steps down the hall, and there was a john and a boxy mini-refrigerator right there in the control room. Outside of wanting to do a lap around the building to squelch the boredom, there just wasn't much reason for any of the technicians to leave the cool, dimly lit room. Even if they did, it was generally assumed that a delay of up to five minutes wasn't going to put the fate of Republic—or whatever it was they were watching for—at any risk. They didn't tend to traffic in quick-response scenarios.

Until now, they didn't have to.

•

"I'm sorry, could you repeat that?" Walter Frost felt like his lungs were collapsing.

"We picked something up on North Carolina 2." That was the security code for Kevin Columbus's phone line, the tap installed while he was in Florida.

"When?"

"Uh, a few minutes ago."

"*Exactly* when?"

The DDI technician was starting to thing he'd screwed the moose good, but hell, he'd had to go to the can, stomach virus or maybe that eggplant thing his wife made. And anyway, he was new, and a sub for the regular guy, how was he to know all the friggin' ins and outs, like he was James Friggin' Bond? He took the readout from off the console and looked at the far right-hand column, and then at his watch, quickly calculating the time differential. "Eighteen minutes ago."

Eighteen minutes. My God. "Play it back for me, please."

He put the phone in a cushioned cradle, and hit one of the hundreds of buttons on a rectangular surface that was covered with them.

Walter Frost listened:

"*Now here's what we're gonna do next. You're going to my apartment, and log onto my computer and run Felon Find. You know what I'm talking about?*"

"*Sure. What're we looking for?*"

"*We're gonna shoot those pictures through the scanner, then put 'em through the database and see what pops up.*"

"*Which pictures?*"

"*The ones you told me about. Baskin, whatever his name is—*"

"*Buskin. Rayfield Buskin.*"

"*Whatever. That and the one of the second shooter.*"

There was a brief debate over whether the poor quality of the second image would reveal anything. The boy saying it wouldn't, the detective saying So what?

But that's not what was carving a deep pit into Walter Frost's stomach.

What truly terrified him—and that was the only word to use, *terrify*—was the talk of scanners and images and databases. A sickening possibility began to throb in his head:

They might learn the truth about the second gunman.

Bad as the thought was, it quickly passed. Without saying goodbye to the technician—but not without making a mental note to have the inept bastard fired—he called the FBI director's private number. It rang back to an official-sounding secretary who informed him the director was out of the office.

"You have 30 seconds to find him," Walter Frost said. The half minute that followed would give him time to reconsider the decision he had made the instant he realized they were sending agents to the wrong address, wasting time they didn't have. The same decision that he had avoided making, had refused to make, even under badgering from that hideous woman killer. A decision that circumstances had now robbed of careful consideration. An executive decision without the executive.

A decision that Walter Frost knew full well he could not reverse. Things had gone too far.

He recognized the soft tobacco-road accent of George Bolin, who had been a federal prosecutor in Kentucky before taking over as director of the Bureau. "Walter? What's the problem?"

"That matter you were assisting us with in North Carolina…"

"Yes?"

"The dynamics have changed somewhat."

"Changed, how?"

"The subject is not at the assumed location."

"Where is he?"

"An apartment building in the downtown area." He read off the address from a master list of all the players they had compiled when the crisis first began to unfold.

"So we just go to that location and apprehend him, correct?"

"Some other parameters have changed, too." Bolin said nothing, but his silence trumpeted a growing irritation that this "personal favor" was getting complicated. "He's more of a danger than we thought."

"What does that mean?"

"It means he has stolen some sensitive documents that must be retrieved as part of the operation. I believe they are stored in a computer, but there may well be hard copies in the vicinity of his current work space."

"And would he be inclined to provide us this material upon request?"

Walter Frost closed his eyes. "I think not."

Bolin chose his next words carefully. "You told me earlier to pass along a specific command to the field. Is that command still operative?"

Don't let anything bad happen. That's what he'd said: Don't let anything bad happen. "No. It's not."

"Are there replacement orders?"

"Retrieve the computer and all associated paperwork, photographs and digital images on the premises."

"And the subject?"

"The subject is of purely secondary importance."

Walter Frost felt as if he'd just thrown the switch on his own son.

•

Kevin stared at the screen, the small dose of *What if?* that had been cruising through his system a minute ago now the size of the Queen Mary, him thinking, This cannot possibly be right.

But there it was, right on the screen: Blob No. 2, bad and mushy as it was, had 33 matches.

"Take 'em one by one," Maxie ordered, a careful edge coming to her voice.

"Why not just look at the first few?"

"Because they're listed by date, oldest to newest, not relevance." All business now, Kevin sensing it, doing as told.

He double-clicked on the first entry, got a mugshot of a car thief, Nebraska, June 7, 1973. Feeling his excitement dim for a second, thinking they were just going to end up strolling through a photo gallery of felons, freaks and 15-minutes-of-famers, all of them long since forgotten. Didn't say that to Maxie, of course, taking the wiser route by skipping the editorial comments and simply asking what she thought.

"Run the percentages." He clicked on the appropriate command along the right-hand side of the screen, which said there was a 17 percent chance Blob No. 2 was the grand-theft-auto guy in the picture. "Next," Maxie said.

Felon aside, make room for the freak: A dairy farmer in Vermont who was charged with polygamy, Kevin's interest really starting to flag now, so much so he suggested that a guy with all those wives probably never got out of bed long enough to plot the death of a U.S. senator. "What you think doesn't matter," she answered, no witty comebacks, obviously not sharing his sense of dying expectation. "Run the numbers."

He did. "Six percent."

"Go on to the next one, and keep in mind that if the phrase 'I told you so' leaves your mouth at any time in the next few minutes, it will be the last you ever speak through real teeth and an unwired jaw." Sounding like she meant it.

Once again, Kevin did as ordered, going on to the third photo.

Which stopped him like twin blasts from a shotgun.

Fifteen minutes of fame? Not hardly.

"Max?" he said distantly, getting no response, hearing some background noise that sounded like she was fighting off a coup to recapture the phone, him not paying a lot of attention, just muttering "That's not right" and running the numbers. Pulled a 52 percent match possibility, close but no victory cigar, Kevin refusing to buy it anyway, this being way too off the wall, impossible, had to be some mistake, operator error, something.

On to entries four, five, six. Same except worse, the percentages edging upward, 55, 57, 61, Kevin really not believing it now, thinking Felon

Find was begging for a cyber-lawsuit, false arrest, Johnnie Cochran on the spot, If the program missed, the subject was dissed.

"Max?" Vaguely hearing her far-away voice threaten somebody with something.

He hit the New Search icon on the menu, ran through the process again.

Saw the felon, saw the freak, saw the—

No way.

Except this time not so sure of it, calling up more entries, all 33, getting the felon and the freak, the other 31 having the same ID, Kevin thinking 31 of 33 is a helluva run in anybody's book, especially when the last photo, the most recent one, taken five years ago, especially when there was a 72 percent chance the guy in it was Blob No. 2, who in some other life was secretly known as the second gunman, Richard Worth's real killer.

Kevin's whole body went electric.

"Max," he said for the third time, sounding as scratchy and lost in time as an old .45 record, staring at the screen and trying to sort out what he was seeing, trying to talk his eyes out of what was there, his eyes saying Uh-uh, sorry, what you see is what it is.

"Hang on. I got to kill some bozo with comb-over hair." Sounding like she meant that, too.

"Max. Forget everything else. You have to listen to me. Now."

No Maxie, however, leaving Kevin to sit there alone in his daze, lost in a field of tall grass he'd accidentally fallen into, telling himself, This can't be happening, but knowing that was a lie, too, just like everything else.

•

At just about the time his field people were preparing to call in and bitch about being sent out on a wild goose chase, Howard Davis reached them. "Change of plans, gentlemen."

"Like maybe there'll be somebody behind the next door we knock on," Galloway cracked.

"Out-of-date intel at the source."

"Where to now?" He took down the address. Downtown, right off the interstate, Trade Street exit, gray apartment building, second floor. "Same rules?"

"Not exactly."

The agent reached over and tapped Benton, who was singing along with Tony Bennett on the radio, and motioned him to shut up. "What's changed?"

"The suspect has some—"

"*Suspect*? The guy's a suspect now?"

"He has stolen documents he's not likely to surrender voluntarily." Davis explained the additional need to sweep the apartment for printed materials and confiscate the computer equipment.

"Is this guy just a computer geek, or is there something else you want to tell us?"

The SAC said he had no idea. "All I know is that he's scared the shit out of some powerful people, and that what he's got is more important to them that who he is."

"Which means—"

"Do what you have to do to get the documents."

"And the order about making sure nothing bad happens?"

"There's only one bad thing that can happen, and that's you two coming out of that place with nothing but your dicks in your hands. Are we clear?"

"Crystal," Galloway said, and broke the connection.

●

Telling Maxie what he'd found, it was like Kevin Columbus's world had gone into ultra slow motion. He could hear what she was saying, heard her ordering him Go back to square one, Run the search again, doing what she said, but feeling like everything was being strained through Jell-O, and had become thick and shaky and impossible to get a grip on.

"Kevin, you still there?" Maxie said after the latest search had confirmed the others, 31 out of 33, a .940 average. Kevin said Yeah. "What I was saying, about the second shooter being your father, that was just a theory. You do understand that?" Said he did. "Remember: Even with a 70 percent match, there's still a three in 10 chance the program's wrong." Said he understood that, too. "There's no evidence of anything." Got that as well. "But even if the computer's lost its artificial mind and is taking us down the wrong path, this ain't Chip and Dale time, man. You cannot go squirrelly."

Her voice had somehow gotten sharp and perfect and clear, like she was right there, except the sound felt studio-enhanced or something and he was listening with million-dollar ears that could pick up every little tone. He told her he was okay, or maybe just thought he said it.

"It's got to be the tattoo, Kevin, that's the only explanation, and I bet you can go into any parlor in the world and find the exact same design."

He stared dumbly at the long triangular mark on the right forearm of Blob No. 2, then at the various images Felon Find had retrieved.

The man, smiling at the cameras, arms up in the air, fist clenched in victory, sleeves rolled up to reveal half of an inked dagger on his skin, its point stopping midway between the elbow and wrist.

The man again, shaking hands at a VFW picnic, light-colored polo shirt not hiding anything this time, the veteran smiling, T-shirt pulled back to the shoulder, showing off his own skin job.

The man again, huffing and puffing through a 10-kilometer race, arms pumping, veins throbbing, a dark stain on the light-colored singlet, but not nearly as dark as the fully realized dagger on his arm.

And again, in another photo very reminiscent of the first, the man, sleeves rolled up, arms raised in jubilation. And again, wading through a crowd, reaching out, touching the people. And again, paddling down a river, and again, helping to build a home for the homeless, and again, at a small-town parade, and again playing basketball with a bunch of black kids, and again reading stories to children in a classroom and again and again and again and again until the last one:

The before and after photo, 5-years-old, with a caption that said Skin Fix, the left-hand side showing a close-up of the tattoo, the right-hand side showing how clean and unspoiled the arm looked like when the procedure was done, after some laser process had erased the dagger and, perhaps, finally distanced the man in the pictures from the man who crouched at a 12th-floor window and murdered Richard Worth.

When Kevin finally said, "God, what am I gonna do?" his words and thoughts seemed to fuse at last, like he finally realized this wasn't all just going to go away, he wasn't going to simply wake up and things would be back to normal. This was a situation that required a response.

"Okay, you know all that stuff I just told you, the reassuring stuff about maybe there's some mistake, maybe the computer's wrong, there's no evidence, blah blah blah. Remember that?"

"Yeah."

"Well forget every word of it, get off this phone and get out of there as fast as you can."

"What good is that gonna do?" Sounding like he wanted to stand and fight, Maxie knowing that was maybe the stupidest thing he could do.

"It'll save your skinny white ass to start with."

"You don't really think—"

"I don't know what to think. I only know what I know. And everything I know tells me you'd better take everything and get outta there. Because we got the right goods on the wrong people, and the minute they find that out, whoever or whatever has been protecting you these past two weeks is gonna be rendered inoperative."

"But—"

"Don't 'but' me, Kevin." Voice full of authority now, and tense, none of that mock anger she dispensed like a special edition Maxie Pez machine. "Unless you move, fast, you're dead."

"Max, that's—"

"Which part don't you understand?" Totally pissed now, this fool not getting that she was trying to save his damned life. "The 'move fast' part, or the 'you're dead' part?"

"Shouldn't we take this to the—"

"Who you gonna take it to, Kevin? Huh? There is nobody. The people we'd take it to are the ones who did it. Now go, goddammit! And when you get there, wherever that is, call me at home, leave a message, tell me how to reach you."

Kevin didn't say anything else, ask another question, even acknowledge what she said. Just shot into warp speed, throwing down the phone, picking up all the scans and photos and floppy disks, turning off the computer and hitting No when the screen asked if he wanted to save the search results, bolting out of there, down the wooden stairs to the parking lot, into the Explorer, onto I-77, heading north, no idea where he was going, except thinking he had to make one stop before he got there.

Chapter 39

Great, Cristi Peterson thought. This is just great.

She'd been at the Harris Teeter at Mallard Road and Harris Boulevard. Her husband Ryan, in his typically dimwitted humor, had often asked if they named the road after the store or vice versa. A barrel of yuks, Ryan was. She had popped in for just a second. Had to pick up some toothpaste, a bottle of decent Pinot Grigio—decent for a grocery store, anyway—some low-fat frozen yogurt, sandwich meat for the kids' lunches the next day, some carrots and celery, which she'd drop into their bag and hope they'd eat and not trade off to the granola heads at Hammond Hall, the elite, high-end private school that kept boys and girls safe from the horrors of inner-city education.

Typically, the checker had been slow, which just as typically made Cristi angry. Tapping her Reeboked foot and snorting quietly. Muttering an occasional "Where the hell are the managers" or "I know it's the middle of the day, but come on," always doing it just low enough so that everyone around her got the message without necessarily hearing the words. Silently berating the acne-faced blonde girl at the cash register for being too friendly, taking too much time with an older woman who just wanted to talk, then quickly berating herself for the thought, suddenly feeling warm toward the old lady and the girl. At the register, Cristi actually went so far as to make conversation with the checkout child, asking how she was doing, if they were busy, that kind of thing. The girl, Tabitha was the name on her badge, answered in monotone single syllables, Fine, Yes, not showing the slightest interest in talking to a tall, aerobicized redhead—hair cut like

Jennifer Aniston's on *Friends*—in black designer jeans and a white DKNY tee-shirt.

"Have a nice rest of the day," Cristi smiled when the boy, Will—who, like Tabitha, was dressed in a blue golf shirt and off-white shorts—had finished bagging her groceries. The girl's indifference was now lost on Cristi, who firmly believed you could right a wrong by immediately recognizing what you'd done and moving quickly to correct it. Which explained her sudden pleasantness to Tabitha and the two-dollar tip she slipped into Will's hands, just for bagging her stuff, not even carrying it out, the kid looking at the bills like they were the key to her hotel room.

The gestures made Cristi feel good.

Then she saw the blue Suburban.

The front, specifically. Left-hand side. Flat tire.

Great. This is just great.

"Those little pricks," she hissed, thinking maybe if Tabitha and Will had been a little faster, there might still be enough air in the goddamned tires to drive to the goddamned service station and get the goddamned thing fixed in time to pick the goddamned kids up from goddamned school.

●

"J.J.?"

The boy was standing in front of a somewhat Old South-looking school, trees everywhere, whose administration building—red brick, white trim, proscenium front and three white columns—spread into four large single-story classroom buildings that were connected by covered concrete sidewalks. A gymnasium, newly built from the looks, rose above the low, flat-roofed academic sections. Further back was a large football practice field, the grass worn away in spots to reveal reddish dirt. A line of blocking sleds stood unused beneath one sagging goalpost.

He was in the middle of a clot of kids, all of them trying to look black—the baggy pants, the backward baseball hats, the sports-team jersey shirts, Bulls, White Sox, Panthers—but only one of them pulling it off. That being J.J., because he was the only black kid in the crowd, and one of only a handful at Hammond Hall.

He peered around the shoulder of a pal. Rearranged the hat, tugging it down, making it more snug. "Yo. Who wantsa know?" Trying to sound like a gangsta, instead doing a perfect imitation of a little kid.

"My name is Lisa," the woman said, smiling at his child-toughness. "I work for your father. We've talked on the phone before."

J.J. patted his left pants pocket, like it was a pistol, lifting the Fubu jersey to reveal a blue, transparent beeper. He looked around at his friends, smiling broadly, proudly. "She can find me 24-7."

"Yo, man, you know this hoochie?" one of them asked.

"Shuttup, Gumby, 'fore I open up a can o' ass-whupping on yo ugly face," J.J. fired back, his high-pitched voice sabotaging any potential threat.

"Like to string some tinsel on that bitch," another whispered, loudly. All the boys laughed, one or two doing so exaggeratedly, like it was the funniest thing they'd ever heard.

Lisa nervously straightened out her dark skirt and smoothed the front of her white linen blouse, hands running unwittingly over both breasts. Two of the boys rolled their eyes. One pretended to faint, falling into the arms of his friend.

"Talk to me," J.J. smirked, playing the big dog, wanting his *poss-a* to know why this fly *loxie thang* was gettin' off with his bad ol' self.

"Mrs. Peterson had a flat tire at the market, and can't come pick you up. She tried your mother—"

"The Witch ain't my mama. Maxie's my mama. She my b-girl."

Lisa smiled at that, too. She'd heard the stories. "Mrs. Peterson called your Aunt Carmella, but couldn't reach her. So she got your, uh"—play it right, she counseled herself—"your Uncle Theo, and he asked me to take you home."

"What about my crew?" J.J. asked, still striking the posture, the criminal wannabes thing, the others doing the same, all of them still looking like a poster for Gap Kids.

She shook her head. "I don't know. I think the other mothers are coming for them. Your uncle just asked me to get you."

"Double-J, maybe this knobgobbler'll get your tweeter"—grabbing his crotch—"too."

"Don't be illin', dogg. Show some respect."

Nice, Lisa thought. Maybe the aunt and uncle were doing an okay job with this kid. "J.J.," she continued, "I really have to get back to the bank."

The little boy squinted his eyes. Still trying to look bad. Still not looking like anything else but an 8-year-old. "I don't go nowhere without my *poss-a.*"

"Word," someone said. Three or four heads nodded in silent agreement.

For a second, Lisa was flustered, pushing her hair back behind one ear, fake smile glued onto her mouth, truly at a loss. This wasn't part of the plan. But…

"She be tweakin'," the one J.J. called Gumby laughed. The others joined in.

"Um, I'd be happy to take all of you"—producing a chorus of *damn, sams*—"but the other mothers are coming, and they're expecting you guys to be here."

"I ain't 'fraid o' my mama," Gumby postured.

"You better be thinkin' 'bout that, nig-*gah*, 'cause I seen yo mama, and she ugly as Count Chocula."

"Don't you be dissin' my mama, nig-*gah*, only I can diss my mama."

"I ain't dissin no one, nig-*gah*, I'm just tellin' it like it is." Glancing to Lisa: "Nig-*gah's* mama look like a damned bat, an' I ain't talkin' the Loo-ee-ville Slugger type."

White kids calling each other nig-*gah*, with J.J. standing right there, saying nothing. If Theo heard this, Lisa thought, he'd give the whole Christian school thing some serious reconsideration. Then again, maybe not. "Guys, listen. I really have to get back to the bank. So if anybody wants a lift, climb in—" gesturing to the white Volvo wagon behind her in the circular school driveway—"but we need to get going now. Is that cool?"

"Cool as fool," J.J. said.

Lisa took five long-legged steps to the Volvo and opened the rear door on the passenger side. J.J. followed, stopping before he got in, giving Lisa another bout of heartburn. Please, she thought, let's just go.

"You bluud's comin'?" J.J. called back to his friends.

No one moved. Two of them did some Beastie Boys thing, moving their arms like a Niggah With Attitude, but the message was still the same: Not gonna cross mama, no chance, no way.

J.J. heard it loud and clear, chuckling to himself. "White boys," he said, head shaking like it wasn't their fault, just the way it was.

Lisa got behind the wheel.

"Home, James," the boy said after closing the door.

Lisa fired up the ignition, pulled out of the lot.

J.J. said Home, James again, this time flapping his arm and hand out in front of him, like he was pointing in the general direction of his house.

Lisa turned. She didn't go in that direction.

Chapter 40

For 25 years, Walter Frost had wondered how this moment would manifest itself, what it would look like and feel like: The moment when everything started to spin out of control.

They had managed it so carefully. Hush money in the form of corporate profits. Rigged sole-source contracts to the companies that backed the operation. Strategic eliminations when necessary. And as the stakes got higher, and they all advanced within the hierarchies to which they were bred—politics, business, administration, government, intelligence—the decisions to employ whatever means were necessary became even easier, often undertaken with neither debate nor deferral. At their level of authority, collective as well as individual, nothing mattered except keeping and building upon their power. People could talk about idealism until the end of time, but the sense of doing what's right was little more than a costume that covered the will of power, the need to control. They all understood that, never confusing what they professed to believe with what they truly coveted, knowing that they could mold and shape any outcome to meet any perception. It simplified things considerably.

But now, that beginning-of-the-end moment had arrived, a phone call from George Bolin that left Walter Frost with a crushing sense that somehow, some way, the fabric of the past quarter century was becoming irretrievably frayed.

"There was no sign of him?" Frost asked, for the third time.

"According to our people in the field, he was not on the premises." The FBI director had used the same precise words with each reply. "We confiscated the computer equipment—"

"Were there disks, copies, printouts?"

"No."

"And the computer?"

"It was off when our agents arrived."

In the large, sparsely furnished office, echoes from the drumming of Walter Frost's fingers on his desk echoed off every wall. "Did your agents examine it?" Knowing the answer already.

"Preliminary investigation revealed nothing. It was intact. There was no suggestion that the operator had in any way attempted to destroy or alter the programs or content."

Frost totaled everything in his head, trying to determine what, exactly, the boy knew, if anything. The lack of disks, photos and the like was disconcerting. It had the feel of a clean-up, suggesting that perhaps something had been found and that Kevin had gathered it quickly and left. Which left only the hard drive as a potential source of clues. "Did your agents examine the computer for programs, games, reference materials—anything that might seem out of the ordinary or unusual?" Frost was not entirely sure what answer he was looking for, or what he wanted to hear.

"They did," Bolin said, "and it was pretty much status quo."

"Forgive me, George, but would you define *status quo*?" Impatient, trying to hide it.

The director exhaled just enough to let Walter Frost know he didn't appreciate handling political matters that had nothing to do with his own personal career. For his part, Frost said nothing, sending a message of his own: I don't care. Bolin continued: "There was Windows 95. AOL. An anti-virus program that probably came with the unit because it had never been updated. Microsoft Word. The only thing you wouldn't see on any cheap, typical, out-of-the-box system was a law-enforcement program—"

"Felon Find," Frost interrupted.

Which took the director by surprise. "How did you know that?"

"Tell me how it works." Ignoring the question, not at all concerned that his tone was taking on an undisguised urgency.

Bolin gave him the short version, talking about images, scanners, databases and photo archives. When Frost asked if it was common for a private investigator to possess such technology, the director said it wasn't, because the software is expensive and generally used by local law enforcement. The Bureau, he sniffed, had far superior programs.

"How good is it?" Frost asked curtly, not caring in the least about whose was bigger.

"Can't match ours, like I said—"

"How good is it?" Repeating the question, drilling every word into Bolin's ears, leaving no doubt as to what was important to him at this moment and what wasn't.

"It's all right." Frost could hear the shrug of concession in the man's voice. "Effective more so than not. Depends on the quality of the image being scanned, I suppose."

"You mean the photo."

"The photo. The artist's rendering. Anything you could possibly compare with the features database and then cross-reference with the picture archives."

The photo. That's what they were looking at. Frame 214.

Why in God's name had Devereaux taken it?

"Are you hard of hearing, Walter? I told you: I don't trust the man."

"You made him. You created him. How can you not—"

"Bart Knight recruited him."

"But you said yes."

"I channeled his moral ambivalence in a direction that best suited the national interests."

"So you stand in a hotel room in New York City and photograph him murdering Richard Worth? Jesus, Gary, what if someone saw you, and—"

"Nobody saw me. A little girl told Bart she observed a man looking out a 16th-floor window, wiping his eyes. Bart produced a guy who said he was looking out a 15th-floor window, one down from where Tim and Henry Lee were positioned. Bart took care of it, just like he took care of everything else. The child never appeared before the commission. Her comments vanished from anything resembling the official record."

"But the photos haven't."

"The photos were never part of the official record."

"Does he know about them?"

"Since the 1980 congressional election."

"And that's your assurance? His knowledge that you could destroy him at any point in his career? That's your assurance?"

"No, Walter, it's not my assurance."

"Then what is it?"

"It's my title."

"Your title?"

"Yes. My title to him."

While George Bolin strategized about matters of which he knew nothing, Walter Frost leaned back in his chair, and thought of all the dead—and those who might soon follow—and wondered, What, in the end, had that "title" truly delivered? Certainly it had gained him access to the shadow government that really ran the Republic's affairs. There were few in Washington that were held in the regard typically reserved for Walter Frost, and fewer still whose actual power dwarfed their presumed power. From the larger perspective, they had the treaty with Arabaq, which he was certain would establish their place in the history books and stand as the crowning achievement of this administration.

So in the end, what had actually been delivered to them? They had the power to rule, to control, to manipulate events. They had history, and the ability to write it, rewrite it and shape it in any way they pleased.

They had access, which let them do whatever they wanted, to whomever they wanted, by whatever methods they wanted. In other words, they had it all—everything men like themselves, men of respect and courage and vision, everything they could possibly want in this or any other lifetime. They were not simply leaders. They were rulers, individuals who towered above the simple concept of politics alone because they were accountable to no one, men fortunate enough to live in a country where an unknowing populace gladly ceded them the authority to do what they thought best, never questioning decisions made in the shadows of self-interest.

Goddammit, Walter Frost thought to himself, we've earned the right to dominate, and we will prevail. "Do you have any idea as to the young man's current whereabouts?" he asked Bolin, interrupting a monologue about coastal intercepts, Frost not having a clue what that had to do with anything.

"No," the director answered crisply, knocked back a little because this civilian was ignoring the advice of a trained law enforcement professional.

Frost, still thinking to himself that this boy was not going to rob *us* of what was rightfully *ours*, asking Bolin, telling him: "Cover every means of transportation out of the city—"

"In all directions," the director said, making it a statement and not a suggestion or request for permission.

"Just north." Saying it automatically, still telling himself that after 25 years of service to their own cause, the greater cause, they would not sit back passively, by God, and allow this boy to compromise their legacy, a legacy that was theirs because only they had had the courage to seize it.

"What are you talking about, just north?" Bolin asked, aggravated.

"Check all flights to Washington. Check Hertz, Avis, all of them, for car rentals with drop-offs in Washington—"

"Washington?" Really irritated now. "This guy's running away from the law, and you're telling me he's coming right here, right to the center of our power?"

"Yes." Thinking the only logical place to strike is at the heart, and if Kevin Columbus knew what Frost feared he knew, that is precisely where the boy would aim.

"That's crazy. I have been in criminal justice for 30 years, Walter, and I can tell you without qualification that Washington is the last place a guy like this is gonna run. Especially if he knows the Bureau is after him—"

Which he must, Frost thought. Anyone who possesses a secret knows that forces compelled to protect that secret will inevitably be arrayed against him.

Bolin, still babbling: "I'm telling you, we should stake out every major travel route exiting the Charlotte area, airport, interstates, bus, trains, hell even taxicabs, and do it in every direction. There's no way we can be sure where he is—"

"I'm absolutely sure where he is going, George, and what he is going to do."

"Then why call in the Bureau, you're so wise?" Saying it snide and holier-than-thou.

"You may do as you please, Mr. Director," Frost said, the shortness in his voice hinting strongly this conversation was about to end. "But it will be a waste of manpower and taxpayer dollars." Throwing in that last part, the taxpayer dollars part, as if it gave their plotting some moral underpinning.

"How I deploy my people is my business, Mr. Frost. It's what the president pays me to do."

"Then you should listen to me very closely." Words empty of anything but an implied threat. "This young man is coming to Washington for one reason and one reason alone: To destroy the man who pays you." Which knocked Bolin back into the middle of last week. "And if you are aware of that, and still fail to act in the interests of the man who pays you, history will record this moment as one of utter treason."

"Treason? Jesus, what are you talking about." The director was flailing away in his mind, not used to concepts like treason and assassination—that's what Frost was talking about, right, when he said destroy the man who pays you?—being bandied about in conversation, at least not overt conversation.

"Do what you will, George," Frost said, starting to sign off, "but you would be well-advised to listen to me."

"Is that right?" Trying to stoke the bravado again, getting some smoke but not a lot of fire. "What makes you think you know how this guy ticks, huh? What makes you such an expert, gives you some insight that's deeper than what the best minds in the Bureau know from experience?"

Frost paused, considering an answer, deciding Why Not? and wishing, no matter how far into the abyss they had fallen, wishing he could see Bolin's expression when he said, without emotion, "He's our son," thinking but not adding: He's everyone's son. And no one's son.

Thinking, too: But that doesn't change anything. Because what has to be done has to be done.

●

"No, no, no. It's *you* who doesn't understand. I have to get out of here. Now. This minute."

Maxie had been facing off with the uniformed U.S. Airways representative for 10 minutes and was getting about as far on the ground as she was in the air, which was to say nowhere.

"Ma'am, I'm sorry, we're doing everything we can, it's just—"

"Am I talking in tongues here?" Looking at the woman in the line next to her, one service rep over, tapping her on the shoulder, asking: "What language am I speaking?"

The woman, 50s, very white and elite, looking terrified of any non-white, non-elite who wasn't dressed like a maid, let alone some ghetto-looking rap chick dressed all in black, way too tight, didn't know exactly what to do. So she just muttered, "English?" and closed her eyes, as if hoping it was the right answer and she wouldn't get shot.

"Thank you," Maxie said, smiled, turning back to the airline person. "So I don't understand the problem here. I'm at an airport. I need to fly someplace. You have planes. Why is this so difficult to figure out?"

"We're having equipment problems," the rep said again. Her name was Jenny, kind of pretty and official-looking in her navy blue corporate airline getup. Big hair like a country and western star, which Maxie figured was what she wanted to be, this being Nashville and all.

"So you've said."

Jenny glanced over Maxie's shoulder to the ever-lengthening line of unhappy airline non-passengers. A helpless expression descended on her face, which she no doubt hoped would stir Maxie's sympathies when her eyes fell back on the detective.

Hardly. "Don't you be lookin' at those other people, 'cause those other people aren't your problem at the moment. Maxie McQueen is your problem, and as God is my witness, if you flash me another one of those gimlet-eyed, baby-doe looks I am gonna get drive-by on you. We clear on that?"

The girl nodded, any sign of gimlets or soft furry animals draining from her eyes. "Perhaps you would like to talk to my supervisor?"

"Anything to get this line moving," another happy customer behind them said.

Which was not what Maxie needed to hear. "I'm sorry?" she said, turning slowly, facing the angry hordes. "Was there something someone wanted to say to me?"

Apparently not, as the line got quiet. Five or six people back, a man in jeans and a blue Izod shirt stared at his black tasseled loafers, refusing to meet her gaze, silently pleading guilty to making the inflammatory comment. "I thought not," Maxie said, not necessarily savoring the victory.

She turned back to Jenny. "Listen, honey. I know the skies aren't real friendly today. But you have to understand something: I am having a crisis. I'm not gonna go into it real deep, because then someone—not me, I assure you, but someone—would probably have to kill you." Jenny's eyes got wide as she tried to remind herself what it was about this job that kept her coming in day after day. "I slept in the goddamned airport last night, and even though I just loved the experience—snoozing in a plastic chair, eating food that starving people in Calcutta wouldn't touch, taking in the wonderful aroma of anxiety-drenched travelers—I am not inclined to repeat it."

Jenny saying, "Okay," like she didn't know what else to do.

"So either put me on another plane, give me my money back, get me a bus ticket or a train ticket—hell, put me on an Atlas missile, I don't care—just get me outta here."

"I'm uh, afraid that I'm not, um, authorized to, to, to do that, ma'am." Jenny was stammering now, making Maxie think the girl had skipped the class at Airline Representative School, the one called Angry Customers About To Chew Your Throat Out 101.

"What *are* you authorized to do?" Weary, tired of the battle, starting to settle into the idea of another night at the airport Marriott—except without the Marriott part—and not looking forward to it, especially with Kevin on the run and all this weird conspiracy noise coming down.

Jenny foraged around in her counter drawer, found nothing of any value, then started plumbing the depths of her blue pants pockets, at last pulling out a handful of treasures that she spread before Maxie's eyes like it was a game-winning poker hand.

"Phone cards?"

•

For some reason, Kevin felt the need to flee by bus.

Part of it, he knew, had something to do with the last time he'd Gone Greyhound, when he was 12, a quarter century before, heading to Arlington to watch them plant the guy who he'd loved like a father. In his own way, however strange, he was taking the same trip again, marking the passage from one life to another, from understanding to confusion, from security to loss, from something that was complete to something that was incomplete. When he had climbed onto the bus—he didn't know what time it was or how long it had been since he talked to Maxie, only that it was dark—and dropped into a seat near the back, he recalled the watershed moment when his life changed the first time, when an existence that seemed so full and rich and promising had suddenly felt finished.

"Sweetheart," his mother said. Kevin had been out playing touch football—even though it was baseball season—in an open field next to the woods with a fat black kid and his two brothers, one of whose head was shaped like an egg.

"Yeah?" His jeans were stained with green from the grass.

"Sit down, honey."

He wasn't sure what to think. She looked funny, different, but Kevin couldn't tell if it was anger or pain or worry. "What's wrong?"

She guided him to the dinette in the kitchen, the one where Kevin and his father ate peanut butter and bacon sandwiches, read the sports pages and listened to Cardinals' baseball on KMOX too late into the night. "It's about your dad."

There was silence as Kevin waited for an explanation. He looked into her eyes, trying to see what was behind them, refusing to acknowledge what her somber if puzzling tone was suggesting, daring her to tell him. But she said nothing. She just shook her head slowly, sadly, and all Kevin could say was:

"He said the war was gonna be over soon."

"For people like your father, Kevin, the war is never over."

There was a time when he admired what he mistook for strength from his mother—her ability to hold up in the face of what had to be a shattering personal loss. That was the reason she never cried over Jon Columbus's death, he assumed. Her inner strength. Never cried during that brief discussion, nor at the ceremony at Arlington, nor at any point during the six or eight years that followed, when they spoke occasionally, the years before she went west, marooning him with memories and a hole in his soul the size of Texas. In fact, as he looked back over the years, he often saw that moment, that time in the kitchen, as the only sign of weakness she ever showed. It didn't have anything to do with how she acted, her emotions, anything like that. It was what she didn't say. She never once uttered the words, "Your father is dead."

Kevin hadn't either, because he knew they would unlock his emotions. He just naturally assumed the same was the case with his mother. Besides, if she had the guts not to cry, and that's what it took to keep the dam from bursting, he was going to give it a shot, too.

Except now, sitting alone in the back of a bus that was about two-thirds full, death-gripping a time bomb he wasn't sure when and where to set off, just knowing he had to do something—only now did he see why she never said the words.

Because, like everything else in his life, they weren't true.

•

Maxie was on the third of five phone cards—she'd also managed to get fifty bucks in meal vouchers, but took a pass on the offer for a hotel, saying she'd rather play the long odds of getting on a plane sometime this year—and cursed-worried about Kevin. She hoped to God he hadn't gone bonkers on her, this not being the time for a wig-out. All the boy had to do was listen to her, lay low, stay down, out of sight. No magic to that strategy. Then, when she got back into Charlotte, they'd figure out what to do with what they had, whatever that was.

That bothered her, too—the thing they did or didn't have—and was why, after three phone cards and about 16,000 messages on his machine, half again as many to her number, checking her service, she cursed-worried about Kevin. Worried, because she believed if he thought for a second he had uncovered some long-held secret about his father—the whole Worth thing aside—there was no telling what he'd do. Cursed because if this were *Jeopardy*, the Final Jeopardy Answer would be: He's going to lose it. And the fact that he wasn't home, hadn't called and couldn't be found basically took her anxiety past the ozone layer.

Maxie looked at her watch, which was still on Eastern time. Ten after midnight. All around her, the travel zombies were trancing out, desperately wanting to believe the lying little notices at every gate, the ones that said Delayed, or kept pushing the departure time up 20 minutes whenever the last departure time came and went. They had become like these Stepford Passengers, or maybe inmates at an asylum. All looking dazed, as if the airline, unable to do the job untold thousands were paying it untold millions to do, had drifted into drug therapy, a One Flew Over The Cuckoo's Nest thing, spiking their voucher-bought bottled water with tranquilizers, keeping the patients easily manageable. The ones who weren't stumbling around like some living dead were curled up in seats, looking for one centimeter of comfort, finding none of it. Except for the two kids next to Maxie, blonde, European-looking, wrapped around each other like vines, moving-van backpacks at their feet, sleeping so deeply a nuclear warhead couldn't rouse them. Maxie briefly considered finding her new best friend Jenny, ask if she could get some of what the airline gave *those* guys.

Twelve-fifteen. Kevin should've been somewhere by now, she thought. He should've called. She stretched her black-jeaned legs out, picked up a copy of *Vanity Fair*—big piece on Denzel who she swore would one day be the father of J.J.'s brother—read for a second, put it down, pulled the Raiders hat low, closed her eyes, tried to sleep, no luck, still unable to shake the thought:

He should've been somewhere by now. He should've called.

Twelve eighteen.

Hell with it.

She pulled the fourth phone card from her pocket, walked to a bank of Bell's finest—15, count 'em, 15—the availability of which attested to the fact that the passengers had raised the white flag, given in. Only one of the lines was in use, an airline employee on it, thick-set woman, laughing about something. A quick look around showed mostly airport personnel in the terminal, of the people who were moving anyway, and their ranks were thinning slowly. The bar, ESPN airing a NASCAR event like it was a sport, was the only sign of activity. Maxie would have killed for a drink, but she hated car racing, so that was that. Seeing what looked like a peroxided ex-beauty queen in the corner playing tonsil hockey with a short guy in an Army uniform didn't do a lot for its appeal, either.

She went to the last phone stall in the line, did the card thing and dialed her service, forgetting about calling Kevin, knowing the boy wasn't there, no point in wasting a handful of perfectly good minutes U.S. Scareways mistook for an on-time departure and arrival.

One ring. Two. Three. Four.

Hearing a slight click midway through the fourth, telephone technology assuring her the answering service was going to grab the call, so don't hang up.

Robotic voice thanking her for calling in, Maxie thinking what she always thought when she heard it, that being You'd damned well better be thanking me, all the crap you put on my bill every month.

Hitting the star button on the phone, quickly punching in her number.

The voice telling her, using the key pad, please enter your security code.

She did: 557859, for JJ RULZ, something they'd made up together.

Half expecting to hear that voice again, sounded like it was coming from the daughter of Marilyn Monroe and Hal the computer from 2001, saying There are no new messages in your mailbox.

Almost hanging up, except she heard: You have one new message.

"About damned time," Maxie said.

Doing what the voice said again, punching 1 to listen to whoever had called her.

Waiting to hear Kevin tell her where he was, how to reach him.

Hearing nothing at first, although the line was open, she knew it because there was breathing going on, short and labored, Maxie thinking Oh hell, the boy's done lost it.

Wondering what to do next.

Knowing instantly when she heard the voice, halting, soaked in fear: "Mama. Help me. Please."

•

The other part of the reason Kevin was on a bus was he wanted to see the country, the places that had been forgotten or bypassed. Little towns, mostly, few any bigger than, say, 30,000, maybe 50,000. Being the middle of the night, the bus didn't stop at all of them, but just enough to give him the sense that what he was about to do had some meaning. The people who lived in these places, they never knew how their lives were being shaped. They were good people, honest and hard-working, with a system of values and ethics that in a better world would have been a national treasure. People who knew more about what it was like to be an American than any of the blow-dried millionaires in Congress who railed against the system while profiting from its excesses. People who believed in the flag, and were not embarrassed to sing The National Anthem or America, full-voiced, doing so not because it was fashion or there were votes at stake but because they meant every word of it. People who had been abandoned by those in whom they had placed their trust, their security, their hopes.

People like him.

He felt it in the tiny crossroads communities along State Road 40 out of Charlotte, and on U.S. 64 all the way to Rocky Mount. In the rolling hills, the farm land, the trailers and barns and one-light downtowns. The dilapidated homes and darkened gas stations. The truck stops, with their promise of showers, food, sleep and women, all the necessities.

He felt it going north, up 301, paralleling Interstate 95, seeing some signs of life in Emporia, Virginia, and when they stopped briefly at a Waffle House, bad yellow lighting, grease jockey in the back working the griddle like it was the most important thing in his life, which it was, Kevin's feeling getting routed toward anger, watching the guy, wondering what the hell he'd gotten for his tax dollars, and whatever it was, it wasn't enough.

Anger growing, outside Petersburg, where the bus gassed up and he saw the sign that said they were coming to Richmond, remembering the bus trip 25 years ago, all the time wondering why they couldn't fly, it would have been so much easier, his mother motioning to Grandma sawing logs behind them, then—

"Don't you want to see America?"

— she had asked, Kevin still noticing she hadn't cried, and even at that age, young, not even a teenager, still thinking he owed it to her to be strong, and what a little shit he'd be if he let her down and started bawling. Also thinking it was a funny question.

Kevin, 12, answering:

"No."

Now seeing America for what felt like the first time and feeling sick about it, sick that they'd won, the liars and manipulators, thinking they'd won even back then, because they'd made him blind to all that was, and to all that was coming. He had turned into exactly what they needed, an unknowing accomplice, playing the part like he was born for it, which in a way he was, never letting them down once.

On U.S. 1 now, the sign saying Richmond, 15 miles.

Kevin looked over his sleeping bus-mates, all ages, black and white, men and women, and wondered where they were going, how far they'd come, then thinking he'd been duped just like the rest of them, by public people making private decisions based on personal interests, so it was really, Where are *we* going? How far have *we* come?

Seeing another sign. Richmond, 12 miles.

Recalling an image, him in the bus station there, having to pee so bad he thought he was going to do it right in the gray dress pants his mother had bought at Montgomery Ward, the little boys' room being closed for repairs or something, Kevin looking at a water fountain, wondering if he could—

Strip-mining that image right out of his brain, gone, just like that.

Kevin Columbus was tired of memories. He wanted understanding. He looked at the time-bomb in his lap, the one Liz Fletcher had given him in Island City, the one Gary Devereaux had protected for all these years, the one he'd picked up on the only stop he made after escaping Maxie's apartment, starting his flight from an America he now believed was intent upon succeeding in its lifelong goal of beating him into total submission, pinning him to the mat, never letting him up. Ever.

Richmond, 8 miles.

Too far, he thought. That's how far we've come. Too damned far, and in the wrong direction, recalling again what Jon Columbus had said, about keeping the compass aimed north, straight up, and most important of all, never letting it point west because that was a bad place, explaining to the boy that's why when someone dies the pilots always say He Went West.

Which, Kevin thought, was where they were now.

How? How did we get this far west?

He opened the notebook, and started to read.

Chapter 41

TO: Senator Worth
FR: Daniel R. Goggins
RE: Chemical Weapons Activity In Arabaq
DATE: July 6, 1975

Attached is the background report you requested in re: covert chemical weapon manufacturing activities in the Middle East, Arabaq in particular. This memo shall serve as an executive summary of the report that follows.

In 1953, the United States was facing a dual challenge in Iran. On the one hand, there was reason to believe that the country was drifting toward communism after the rise of a nationalist movement, headed by Muhammad Mussadegh, had successfully diluted the authority of the Shah, Muhammad Reza Pahlevi. On the other, the British, under whose watch the Shah had ruled since 1941, were attempting to protect their interests, primarily the Anglo-Iranian Oil Co. (AIOC), founded in 1901 by a British businessman who in turn received a monopoly in oil production throughout most of the nation. The British owned a significant portion of the company, using it to supply the Royal Navy and paying the Shah production royalties. In 1951, Mussadegh had nationalized AIOC, prompting London to seek compensation, which Mussadegh refused, even in the face of an economically devastating blockade of the country.

The United States, fearing disruption in world oil supplies, to say nothing of Mussadegh's leftist stance, encouraged the British to seek a solution that stopped short of force. After all attempts to ease the situation failed, U.S. officials, notably John Foster Dulles, became more convinced that Western influence in the region was at stake, and they decided to become involved, covertly, through the Central Intelligence Agency. Thus, Operation Ajax was drawn up, with the strategic objective of overthrowing Mussadegh. Under the plan, key groups within the country, including the army, would be mobilized to oust Mussadegh. Although there were indications that, at some level, U.S. decision-makers were uncomfortable with what U.S. Ambassador to Iran Loy Henderson called "this kind of business," there was a consensus that the plan must go forward. The alternatives—an Iran under Russia's thumb, from the American perspective—left no choice.

Within two months, Mussadegh had been overthrown. The belief that Iran's army and its people would rise up against him and in support of the Shah proved amazingly correct. Kermit Roosevelt, the grandson of Theodore Roosevelt and an old hand at covert operations, personally selected Mussadegh's successor as prime minister: General Fazlollah Zahedi. Although Zahedi had been arrested by the British in 1941 on suspicion of being pro-Hitler, London acceded—none too enthusiastically—to Roosevelt's choice. This acceptance ensured that Iran had not simply fallen into the West's orbit, but also that U.S. interests in the country had become paramount.

Despite the success of Operation Ajax, and the establishment of a U.S.-backed government in Iran, some in the intelligence community believed that the situation in the region would remain unstable in both the near and long terms. This was founded on the very theory that had produced the ouster of Mussadegh. It went like this: If the army and the people could be organized and galvanized to rise up and overthrow one leader, they could be organized and galvanized to rise up and overthrow any leader. Given that, the U.S. intelligence community decided to create, in fact, an American protectorate in the region that could be depended upon to preserve and support U.S. interests throughout the

Persian Gulf. This, it was believed, would be an effective buffer against future instability.

As part of a quiet deal with the Shah, the CIA carved out a small, crescent-shaped region along the north end of the Gulf, at the southwest corner of Iran, adjacent to Iraq. Although this new state, Arabaq as it was called, had the appearances of a democracy—including a prime minister and popularly elected legislative body—all power rested primarily in the hands of the Royal Family, which was financially supported by the CIA and through cash payments from U.S. companies that established commercial interests there. The arrangement represented a win-win for all concerned: American companies were making money. The American government had a strong and willing ally in the region. The CIA had a base of operations to conduct activities throughout the Middle East.

In 1969, President Nixon renounced the use of chemical weapons in anticipation of U.S. approval of the Geneva Protocol, and ordered a complete halt to their production. This decision—harshly criticized among CIA hard-liners—came at a time when it had become more and more apparent that the Soviets were engaging in chemical weapons testing, and in some cases actual deployment. With these twin factors in play—the U.S. elimination of chemical weapons and the Russians' growing use of them—the intelligence community found a new purpose for Arabaq: As a beachhead to build a chemical weapons capability that would be a deterrent to that being developed by Moscow.

Since this clearly contravened U.S. policy, the decision was made to undertake the strategy covertly using a blend of government money and private sector resources from companies either with a stake in Arabaq or possessing a unique technical skill necessary to produce chemical weapons. Participating companies received federal funds, disguised as research and development grants, that offset the costs of building, staffing and maintaining the facilities. The list of companies involved reads like a Who's Who of the New York Stock Exchange. From what has been ascertained so far, the amount of taxpayer dollars channeled into these companies for their role has been substantial, well into seven figures.

Direct U.S. involvement appears limited to only a handful of intelligence officials, three in particular: Jonathan Columbus, an Air Force major; Bartholomew Knight, an old Agency hand and spotter for the CIA, now a professor of Middle East studies at Harvard University; and James Anderson, a Knight prodigy who was recruited to The Company out of the Air Force Academy in 1963. In recent years, these three men—and their confederates in the government and the business sector—have effectively built a chemical weapons arsenal that rivals that of the Soviet Union.

Working in conjunction with, and under the protection of, the Royal Family, they have overseen and managed the construction of two facilities: One outside the capital city of El Ashwa, the other 17 miles inland from the Persian Gulf, in the southwestern corner of Arabaq. By 1974, when the U.S. Senate at last ratified the Geneva Protocol, these two sites were creating enough chemical agents to efficiently eliminate the populations of any major metropolitan area in the region. Moreover, a delivery system was in place, through the U.S. presence in Turkey, that would allow chemical weapons to be disbursed in major cities throughout the Soviet Union.

Whether the Soviets were aware of this capability is not known. What is known, however, is that at the time when the United States Senate passed the Geneva Protocol, which prohibited the use of biological and chemical weapons in war, a conspiracy between the intelligence and business communities had secretly created one of the world's deadliest chemical arsenals...

Chapter 42

Kevin Columbus just stood there, watching the soldier.

Mid-20s, probably, maybe a little younger. Standing erect, arrayed in dress blues, eyes focused on 79 tons of Colorado marble, M14 on one shoulder.

A defender. A patriot.

There was a light drizzle, had been since he'd arrived from the bus station, rental car sitting in the lot. Overhead, the skies were gray and ominous, dark at the horizon, looking like they should have been announcing either snow or the end of the world.

Kevin felt something trickle down his back. Sweat, maybe, warm as it was, but more likely rain.

He didn't care, didn't much notice. Too mesmerized, even hypnotized, by the soldier's routine.

Face impassive, not even blinking, like any movement or sneeze or yawn was a crime against the state. Standing at one end of a black rubber mat that stretched before the white sarcophagus, facing east. Counting off 21 seconds in his head, slow, deliberate. Turning, facing north now, silently ticking off another 21 seconds. Then walking exactly 21 steps back across the mat.

Repeating the process. Performance never changing. Expression the same.

Somewhere in the distance, gunfire. Three volleys. A salute.

And a single bugle. Taps.

Above, four jets shattered the serenity, one peeling off in tribute to a passing hero.

Another funeral.

The dress-blued sentry turned, waited 21 seconds, walked the length of the mat, stopped. Kevin wondered what the soldier saw, really saw, when he looked out over this part of the sprawling 600-plus acres, or what he thought about the city below, with its monuments and domes and memorials. Did he believe they were architectural testimonials to greatness? Did he ever wonder what was behind them, the history—true, if there was such a thing, more likely fabricated—that was at their foundation? Did he ever take a moment to think whether anyone down there, making their deals or raising their money or extracting their revenge on someone who dared cross them, did he ever ask if they cared about honor and duty and obligation, the things he, this sentinel of glory, the things he cared about?

Probably not.

What was it Jon Columbus had said? "I'm not paid to think. I'm paid to react."

Like father, like son, Kevin thought, except neither was who they seemed.

Another 21 seconds. Same routine. At every turn, crisply shifting the M14 to the outside shoulder, poised to repel an assault on the Tomb of the Unknown Soldier, the message clear: No one gets by me. No one will threaten the glory of those I protect.

Kevin Columbus stared at the soldier for a bit longer, trying to guess if at any point in the ritual a thought crossed the guard's mind, a question as to who was this lone, lost soul standing in front of the Tomb, denim shirt and jeans getting soaked, no coat, not enough sense to get out of the rain, who was he and why was he staring at America's tribute to honor with the eyes of one who had surrendered so thoroughly to the national deception.

The man conveyed nothing, though. Whatever he thought—about Kevin, about the city below, about the monuments whose meanings were more past than present—all that was secondary to the job he was doing for the country.

Kevin was glad someone still felt that way. "Thank you," he half-said.

The guard didn't respond, just turned and walked 21 steps.

Kevin turned and walked farther.

North along Roosevelt Drive, over to Wilson, oblivious to the lush, damp splendor around him, century-old oaks and immaculate shrubbery and rolling green hillsides, following the winding road to a northeastern corner of Arlington National Cemetery, to the resting place of a soldier who was unknown, it seemed, only to him.

As he made the journey, it all came back to him, in bits and pieces—never the whole picture, never—as real as it was false. Not warm, the memory. Not even a memory, really. More like bile, like this feeling in his stomach that rose to his throat, gagging him, making him want to puke, to rid his body of the lies and deceit that had been growing inside all these years.

No matter what it was, though, and no matter how sick it made him, the image would not stop coming.

The ceremony at Fort Meyer's Old Post Chapel.

The procession. Full military honors. Flag draped over the coffin, caisson, drawn by six horses, three of them riderless, all as black and shiny as the devil's heart.

A band, 15 pieces, playing hymns.

The short trip down Meigs Drive and back up Humphreys Drive. Passing the grave of Abner Doubleday, the general and the inventor of the national pastime, how utterly perfect.

Seeing an old guy, somebody said he was a retired colonel, sitting in a lawn chair by his wife's grave, did it all the time, couple of hours a day, even in the rain. Kevin thinking that was kind of neat when they explained it, his mother dismissing it with a hard look.

Rain coming down, then as now, the more things change the more they stay the same.

Arriving at the hole in Section 1, one of the oldest parts of Arlington, the Officers' Section, beautiful trees and bushes, green and alive even under dead and dismal skies.

The ceremony.

People in uniform, and out. Not a lot of them. Twenty-five, perhaps. Few tears, but a lot of words, kind words, spoken by expert liars.

His mother, dressed in black, taking a white rose and placing it—not gently, more like dropping it—on top of the coffin, starting to bend over, Kevin sure she was going to kiss the dark wood, but Meredith stopping abruptly, standing and sitting back down, not meeting the puzzled eyes of anyone.

Everyone thinking: What is that about? In retrospect, maybe not *every*one.

Twenty-one gun salute, three volleys, seven shots each, the noise causing Kevin to jump every time, the first one making grandma grab her chest, him thinking for an instant, Holy shit, they shot her.

More words from more liars.

Somebody, a general from the looks, lots of ribbons, coming over to Meredith, handing her the flag from Jon Columbus's coffin, saying–– Kevin remembering this like it happened 10 seconds ago—saying: "On behalf of the president of the United States and a grateful nation, please accept this flag in loving memory of one who served so proudly."

Kevin thinking she stared at the flag like it was diseased.

Some woman coming up to where they sat, telling them she represented the Air Force Arlington Ladies, saying, "We express our deepest condolences to you and your loved ones," Kevin giving her a tight smile of thanks, Meredith looking like she wished she had a machine gun.

Overhead, four jets flew by, Kevin wondering what kind they were, F-somethings he imagined, one exiting the formation in respect, letting the world know that a fellow pilot, A Man, had entered the wild blue yonder for eternity, this time for real.

The band again. *Amazing Grace.*

And the single bugler, Taps sounding more forlorn, more painful than it ever did on TV or in the movies.

Everyone starting to move away from the grave site. The band going in another direction, playing hymns Kevin vaguely remembered hearing in church, thinking to himself if this was really about dad, they'd be playing some Buddy Rich.

Music dying down, reduced finally to a single drum counting off a cadence in the distance, a beat that everyone seemed to fall into as they walked off.

Everyone except Kevin, who stayed and watched the casket eased into the wet earth, standing there in Jon Columbus's flight jacket, alone, asking why, why had this happened—

Just as he was doing now, 25 years later, though without the flight jacket, no protection against the rain, against nature, standing, looking at the grave marker, plain and white, the grass thick and neatly trimmed at its base. It was one of thousands of monuments, crosses and stones that stretched over the Arlington grounds, each testifying to the fact that this truly was a nation of good people who lived and died in the belief that America was something—not just a chunk of land, but a concept, an attitude—but something that was worth the sacrifice.

Too bad they all had to perish, Kevin thought. Too bad for all of us.

On the marker, an inscription: "Major Jonathan Alan Columbus. You did your job, and others lived because of it." Kevin remembered seeing it for the first time, and asking his mother why didn't it say Rest In Peace or even Loving Father, which he'd seen on a lot of tombstones. Meredith starting to say something, then not.

Now, of course, now he understood that it was an appropriate omission.

Jon Columbus hadn't rested in peace.

And now he knew that Jon Columbus certainly wasn't his father.

And Kevin Columbus wasn't his—

"Son?"

The voice, unknown to Kevin, froze his mind. For a second, he couldn't even turn to face the speaker, who things being what they were might have been anyone from an Arlington caretaker to another American orphan to some guy with a gun. Given those options, Kevin wasn't real sure which he preferred.

When he turned, though, he found something unexpected:

An older man, into his 70s, it looked like, six feet or better in height, full gray hair sneaking out from under a tweed hat that protected him from the rain, a smile that Kevin felt must have once dazzled but had since become dulled by events. He was wrapped in a black trench coat, the old man was, expensive, with brushed leather lapels. Expensive shoes, too, he imagined, because each was protected by brown rubber covers.

Two other men stood behind him, and to the side. Way back, on the road adjacent to Section 1, a big dark car, not a limo but something just as foreboding.

The old guy reached into one raincoat pocket, produced an envelope. Removed a photo, part of a photo anyway, it was torn, handed it to Kevin.

The other half of the picture he'd received from Gary Devereaux. Switzerland. The unseen man whose arm was around Mother Meredith, the man she was looking at, the man whose image matched those he'd pulled up on Maxie's computer just yesterday.

From the other pocket came a second envelope, which the old man emptied into his hand. Photo negatives. He tried to hand those to Kevin, too.

Kevin waved him off, knowing full well that there was one missing, the one numbered 214.

"I assume you know everything?" the man asked, not looking at him, water starting to cascade off the thin, turned-down brim of his hat.

Kevin, heard himself say, like it was some out-of-body experience, "I don't know what I know anymore, about me, him"—gesturing half-heartedly to the grave—"or anything."

"But you know about these," meaning the negatives, which at the moment seemed more important than the torn photo. Kevin nodded.

A smile, grim and tight and rueful all at once, came to the old guy's face, and he turned slightly to one of the men behind him, shot him a faint nod, and just that quick the two bodyguards or whatever they were had appeared on either side of Kevin, strong arms and vise hands latched onto him, almost lifting him off the ground, felt like he was floating, floating in a dream, a bad dream, right toward the big dark car, which grew larger as they approached it and started to feel suddenly to Kevin like a hearse.

•

Walter Frost didn't follow the two Secret Service agents immediately. He stood instead at the grave, in the rain, thinking about the past.

About Gary Devereaux, Jon Columbus, Darlene Sharpe, Agent Addison, Richard Worth, Dan Goggins, Tim Shepard. And, most recently, about Bart Knight, whose suicide he had learned of late the previous day, the pain rivaling that he felt when cancer stole the last bit of breath from his beloved wife.

All dead. All, in their own ways, victims of empire.

Who, he wondered, would be next?

We shall soon see, he said to himself, turning from the grave that celebrated a hero and a father but held nothing but an empty casket, walking slowly to his waiting car, asking how much further they would have to go to protect the secrets, the rain and gloom making him feel older than he was, and sadder.

•

Maxie was trying to find a zone, needed one bad, needing The Force like Luke Skywalker did just before he atomized the Death Star or whatever it was Darth Vader was cruising the galaxy in. She wanted to get somewhere in her head where she could close her eyes and shut off everything else, kind of go on cruise-control, follow her instincts, trust them to deliver her where she had to be. Clarity was what she needed, an escape from all the fog and storms and shit that had rolled in like a tidal wave the instant she heard J.J.'s cry for help.

Yeah, try finding a zone when some psychotic bitch has your kid, you don't know what she's going to do, and you got no choice but to follow orders, not knowing how the whole thing was going to play out in the end, and not feeling great about the prospects whatever they were.

She thought it would come. The zone. From the second she hot-wired the car in the airport parking lot—no rentals available, and it took her two and a half hours to boost a ride, a Honda Civic in long-term parking, tank full of gas to boot—Maxie figured she had five, six hours to find it, the zone, and crack out a plan from there. It was 441 miles from Nashville to Charlotte, according to the Triple A map in the Honda's glove compartment, interstate pretty much the whole way. Finally out by three, figuring one stop, Asheville, probably, and she'd hit Charlotte by nine at the latest.

All of which had happened, just like it was supposed to.

Except now it was just after nine, she was fighting Friday morning traffic into the city from the north, I-77, buzzed on coffee, and the only zone she'd been able to locate was the one with a sign that flashed How Could You Let This Happen To Your Own Child? in bright red lights.

Jesus, she'd thought over and over again, the whole way, pounding the steering wheel every time she did, what have you done, how could you let it get so far out of hand, just sit back and watch things slip away like sand between your fingers? Making it worse, knowing all the while that if—not if, goddammit, when, *When!*—when they got out of this thing, J.J.'s first driver's license was going to list some yuppie house in the burbs as a permanent address and Maxie would be left standing on the sidewalks, peering through the windows, same as now. Which is just exactly what you deserve, she berated herself, because you've earned your first-class ticket on the Guilt Train, sweetie, and they saved you a primo seat, right up front, right there with all the other glorious fuck-ups.

Longest ride in the world, Nashville to Charlotte had been, especially when terror's riding shotgun—and she was terrified. What scared her now, here, all through the night, was her utter aloneness. Her whole life, Maxie had been able to do the thing, whatever it happened to be, by her own self, alone, not needing to hitch her wagon to anybody, tough enough and strong enough and good enough to fly solo. Never doubted her ability to do just that, either. Never until now, anyway. Because now, she was walking on a real high wire with no net. For all of her Maverick act over the years, Maxie'd always known there were rules—police procedures and the law, and gut feelings that told you just how far you could push both—and that those rules always more or less determined the playing field. Here, though, now, she was making it up as they went along. Her and some sicko holding her kid hostage for some unexplained reason. And there wasn't a thing she, Maxie, could do about it. Nobody she could turn to or plot with, nobody to tell her this was the way it was, and you better deal with it.

All the years, thinking independence was cool, thinking now of all the good it had done: She was by herself. Father gone but not forgotten. Child kidnapped. Good Lord, Maxine Arliss McQueen, she said to herself, hearing Carmella's voice when she did and not able to squeeze the shrill I Told You So tone out of it, what kind of life have you made for yourself?

All these feelings—guilt, rage, pain, fear, frustration—chewed at her like fire ants from the instant she hit I-40 heading east, shifting without warning, too, flip-flopping from one emotion to the next and the next, just like that, snap of a finger, no time to get one out of her system before the next one piled on. Driving through the darkness, white lines on the highway starting to run together, lights from oncoming traffic looking like little stars through her occasional tears before speeding by, leaving only a confused darkness that caused Maxie to pray, over and over, maybe a thousand times, praying all the shit that was stacking up wouldn't suck so much energy out of her she wouldn't know what to do or think when the time came.

Like she had some idea of what had to be done anyway, right?

"It's your son, for God's sakes!" she screamed, so loud it clawed at her throat, made one ear start to ring. Pounding on the wheel again, harder this time, knowing that it was after nine, she was in Charlotte, stuck in traffic, and whatever was going to happen was going to happen soon.

While unintended, the yowl actually did something good.

It was as if someone put a balloon inside of her, like one of those things they use to expand your arteries, and blew it up, and when that happened, everything bad that was kicking around inside Maxie's head, and the fear that was in her heart, it all came blasting out along with the scream.

Calming her, burning off the fog.

Which was fortunate, because timing was everything and at just about the time Maxie was taking her exit off I-77, finally, heading home, her cell phone went off, and before she could do or say anything, she heard Taylor Shepard's voice tell her:

"All right. Here's what you're going to do."

Maxie listening carefully, getting it all down, every detail, but still hearing that voice, that brain-voice, telling herself: I don't care what you think you know, but forget it all and start thinking differently, a lot differently, because this is real girl, real as it gets.

Somewhere in her mind's eye, she saw a green sign, white letters, that directed her, Exit Now for The Zone.

She did, and in that moment, Maxie McQueen knew exactly what she had to do, and did it.

●

Kevin sat in the back of the big dark car, dazed, no longer wondering if they were going to kill him, thinking more about how and where.

Watching as they pulled out of Arlington, passing Memorial Gate and then onto Memorial Drive, heading straight to the Jefferson Memorial. A lot of memorials here. Too many. The Washington Monument off to his right, its height and grandeur shrouded by a hazy mist that hovered over the entire city, clinging to the low building tops like factory smoke.

Veering left there, and then right onto a main drag, Kevin not catching its name, knowing only that they were in The City, downtown, the seat of power and government. Glimpsing the Capitol through windshield wipers that swung back and forth, their rhythmic thwock-thwock-thwock noise lulling him a little, a comfortable backbeat to the story of his death.

The driver acting like he had all the time in the world, not running any lights, not squealing out when the signal went green, just cruising, no big hurry, which made Kevin even more certain they were going to kill him because TV and movie killers always acted normal to avoid police attention. Of course, these guys probably were the government and they'd murdered a lot of people so what did they care about a little police attention anyway, it was just something else to take care of, and they would.

Car smelled nice, new and leathery.

Everything electric, probably, which for a second made Kevin think he could easily pop the auto lock and jump out, but just as quickly thinking they probably had the back seat kid-proofed, these guys being government killers.

Thwock. Thwock. Thwock. Thwock. Thwock.

Another turn. Smack into traffic. Dead stop. One of the guys in the front, not the driver, saying, "Jesus, a half inch of rain and everybody forgets how to drive."

Moving slowly, too slowly, apparently, because the driver cut quickly out of traffic, shooting down one street, named after a state, then going left to parallel the street he'd just gotten off, the sudden haste getting Kevin to think maybe they were going to a meeting, or someone was waiting for them, something like that.

Thwock. Thwock. Thwock. Thwock. Thwock.

The old guy next to him, eyes forward just like the sentry at the Tomb of the Unknown Soldier, saying nothing, probably, Kevin thought, because he was about to kill somebody, even though there wasn't a war and the somebody was an American, reminding himself again that these people were the government, recalling, for no particular reason, that saying, the one that went The only thing certain in life is death and taxes, feeling for some reason that somehow explained everything.

Then finally starting to feel it all slip away, nothing really registering anymore, not when he went through the gate, stopped and got ushered out of the car, someone suddenly materializing with an umbrella to keep him from getting wet, odd being so nice to a dead man walking, and then pushed into an entry on the side of a big building, through a hallway, turning into another hallway, people around him everywhere, the place a nerve center like a hospital or something, down more corridors and then turning sharply into a little office, more like a den or a study really, books on shelves and a small desk with a reading lamp, a small leather sofa against one wall, and then through another door into a larger office, all this feeling more and more like a movie, things registering even less now, although he recognized the man, dimly at first, standing there by his mother—his *mother?*—hand extended, Kevin looking at the hand, the right hand, tracing it with his eyes to the man's face, the man not smiling but looking picture perfect otherwise, a walking photo opportunity, the man's mouth moving, but like everything else, the words not making any sense, Kevin too stunned, looking at his mother—his *mother!*—who was crying softly standing by the desk, the large desk in the odd-shaped office, no corners anywhere, hearing the door close behind him but not looking around, keeping his eyes on the man, the most famous man in the world, the man who refused to withdraw his hand even when Kevin refused to take it, the man who said something else, once again, Kevin hearing the words this time, every one of them, the man, standing on the royal blue rug with the gold presidential seal at its center, the center of the Oval Office, the man who told him:

"I don't know quite what to say, Kevin, except it's good to finally meet my son."

Chapter 43

He'd walked in simply enough, just after 10. Through the North Gate, nobody so much as asking about the contents of the oversized backpack, paying his 32 bucks and pushing on through, just like any other dad off on a family outing at Carowinds, the theme park that sat on the border between North and South Carolina. The state line halved the park, and was officially noted by plaques set into the ground that heralded movies he guessed Paramount—as in the studio, the place being officially called Paramount's Carowinds—had produced. He'd seen three of them: *Grease, Heaven Can Wait* and *Saturday Night Fever.*

He followed the movie plaques beyond a fountain to a small bridge, at the crest of which he politely dismissed a blonde teenaged girl in tan pants and blue Oxford shirt who offered to take his picture. Crossing over, past a cotton candy store to the right and a photo shop to the left, and in front of a Dodge City-looking building whose sign announced itself as The Emporium, he saw a large, roundish cluster of trees rising from an eight-sided brick planter, maybe 12 or 15 feet wide. On the edge that faced back toward the bridge and the gate he'd come through was a memorial of some kind, sitting upright and just inside the planter, mounted into a white slab of rock. On an inset metal plate, coppery-looking words praised the park's creator for having the "vision and determination to make a reality what most people only dream of."

It also said this visionary had died in 1978. Dropping down on the white wooden slat that served as a bench atop the red brick planter walls, he thought it was fortunate that the man was long gone. Because he guessed the reality that would ambush Carowinds in a few minutes wasn't entirely what the guy who created this place had in mind for his family theme park.

Absently, for no other reason than to comfort himself, he unzipped the top of the backpack and reached in.

Felt the steel of the barrel, the wood of the stock, the sleekness of the scope.

Watched the slow trickle of parents and kids, all colors, all ages, pass through the North Gate just like he had. Coming over the bridge toward him, not paying any attention to the movie mementos on the ground. Noticed that too many of the little girls were trying to look older than they really were, the boys looking like boys, which was to say they didn't much care about appearances. And the parents, well, they were just dressed for the heat—and even now, shortly after 10 in the morning, it was already in the mid-80s—cutoffs and linen shorts, tank tops and sleeveless Ts and polos, flat shoes and Nikes, little white socks, hats of every size and description. They all actually looked happy, too, like the sun was bright and the sky was clear and didn't that make everything pretty much right with the world?

Seeing all this but not seeing it, thinking she'd never asked for backup until now, which was why he was here, a sniper in America's playground, not knowing exactly what was going to happen next, except he was going to kill somebody.

He removed his hand from the backpack, zipped it up, felt none of the hoped-for calm. Fastened his eyes on the park entrance a few hundred feet in front of him. Waited.

•

"I'm not sure where to begin," President Jim Anderson said. He was seated on one of two red-striped sofas that faced each other in the Oval Office. Kevin was opposite him. An antique-looking cherrywood coffee table, low and ornately designed, separated them. Meredith sat in a deep gold high-backed chair to Anderson's left, one of a matching set in front of the fireplace where various heads of state were photographed with The Leader of the Free World. To one side was the older man, who had been introduced to Kevin as Walter Frost, leaning on a waist-high cabinet that housed four television screens, three of them dark, CNN showing something about fashion. The only other person in the room was Henry Summer, the president's chief of staff, perched on the front edge of the large mahogany executive desk.

If any of what was going on troubled Anderson, he didn't show it. He wore the navy-almost-black Italian suit, blinding white shirt and burgundy tie like a GQ model. His eyes were clear and blue as an October sky, and surprisingly warm, inviting. Hair, gray but not silver, still a touch of brown, every strand in place, still thick and parted cleanly on the left. Sitting there, he seemed in total control. The same could not be said for Frost, who twitched like a fish on a hook. Summer, short and gaunt with thinning hair and big round glasses that made him look like an owl, sat unmoving, impassive.

Anderson looked to the blue carpet at his feet, rubbing his hands together as if spreading lotion on them, and then to Kevin. "The first thing you have to understand is that at the time, and since then, frankly, we felt that everything was necessary—"

"Mr. President!" Frost and Summer said at once. They exchanged a quick look, both knowing what the other was going to say, Frost quickly deferring.

"Sir, I'm not certain there is a need to stipulate that anything was necessary, because there is no evidence that anything ever occurred." Summer had a surprisingly deep voice for such a little man. When Kevin looked at him, he was struck that the president's desk was clear except for an hourglass and a bust of Thomas Jefferson.

Anderson shook his head slowly. "Is that true"—taking a beat, probably calculated to make everyone in the room wonder whether he was going to say *son*, before ending the question with—"Kevin?"

At that moment, Kevin didn't know what to say. Didn't know much of anything, actually, except he got this sudden, strange feeling that things were back to being real again, that the little "episode" he had suffered during the trip from Arlington to the White House had passed. That sense, once it arrived, reminded him where he was and who he was talking to, and delivered the body-slamming revelation that he was an interloper here, had the power to wreck their public and private lives, something he knew they'd never let happen. For an instant, the daze returned. A tall grandfather clock ticked loudly, the only sound puncturing the room's silence.

Kevin struggled to beam back to the moment. "I, uh, know some things," he said, buying time, trying to slow the discussion down so he could catch up. "I mean, I found some things out, I guess." Shrugged simply. "You know."

"I think that's why we're here," Anderson said. "To find out what you know."

The comment vaporized Kevin's numbness. It wasn't so much that it sounded like a threat—which it no doubt was—as the fact that after all this time, all these years, the man who turned out to be his real father didn't have a goddamned thing to say to him except What Do You Know About What I Did? "I must've missed something," he said, feeling his anxiety burn off with each syllable. "I thought we were here to find out who I am." He looked from Anderson to his mother—whose eyes shone with clarity, what a shock—to the still-fidgeting Frost and stoic Summers, then back to the president.

"You're my son," the president replied, smiling with what the world would see as genuine warmth, Kevin feeling it was nothing more than a Grade A hustle.

"Okay," Kevin said, nodding slowly. "So tell me, what happens now"—taking a beat, his turn to play head games with the audience, making everybody wonder if he was going to say Dad, or Mr. President, or You Asshole, throwing them all for a loop when he said—"Jim?"

Which brought Henry Summer into the act: "It's Mr. President to you."

The comment, more a direct order, crystallized Kevin's anger. The feeling, that feeling he could still be outraged even in this shit stew they were cooking him in, gave him a sense of rebirth, like he had returned from some near-death experience with a new take on his life and on all the people who were trying to steal it or end it or just twist it to their own ends.

But what the comment really did was just totally piss him off, and he let Henry Summer know. "It may be *Mr.* President to you," he said to the chief of staff in a low growl no one in the room expected, then turning to Anderson, and pointedly adding: "But to me, he's nothing more than a common killer."

"That's enough," Summer said, coming off the desk.

"Not until I say it is," Kevin shot back, the words calmer than he was, knowing instinctively he was in over his head, the pawn in a room full of kings, but suddenly not caring.

A little bit of light flickered in Anderson's eyes and then died, like the hold-out bulb in a movie marquee going dark for the last time. Kevin could see it, a look that said this was not going as intended. The president nodded his head slowly. "Okay," he began, not alarmed but not in the same place he'd been seconds before, "I understand where you're coming from—"

"Spare me the I-feel-your-pain crap." Kevin, on a roll, going someplace he couldn't see, the destination not really seeming to matter anymore.

Summer raised his hands in silent outrage. Anderson motioned him to sit down, stay out of it.

"You're aware that Monday afternoon we're signing a treaty with Arabaq that may have the practical effect of banning chemical and biological weapons from the planet?"

"Makes sense," Kevin said, kind of flippant, a kid forgetting his place, or maybe just a madman losing what was left of his mind. "After all, you guys gave Arabaq the capability, and then murdered Richard Worth to hide it."

Even though Anderson had feared Kevin knew the truth, his face still dropped like a runaway elevator. Frost, not twitching anymore, was now massaging his forehead with his left thumb and index finger, as if trying to dig a trench through his skull. Summer looked frozen in place, either because this was the first time he'd heard the accusation or because he had been convinced no one else knew.

"Nothing can get in the way of Monday's ceremony," Anderson said, not fully recovered, but still with a piercing glare that had the power to nail Kevin's confidence to the wall. "Do you understand me? Nothing."

Not taking his gaze off Kevin, who at first didn't meet it but then forced himself, slowly, to give it right back, their eyes remaining locked for a discomforting period of time that caused Walter Frost to finally do what he did best, which was to start the deal-making process.

"Perhaps some accommodation can be reached." He took off his coat, moved from the cabinet to the sofa, next to Anderson, letting Kevin know which side of the coffee table had the true power.

Kevin, every brain cell whispering The Hell With Everything, stared straight through the old man: "Not until I get some answers."

•

He'd been sitting on the lip of the brick planter for about 10 minutes when she arrived. He knew who she was instantly, because she looked like she didn't belong there, didn't want to be there. That, and the fact that she was a good-looking white woman with a little black boy in tow.

The child was well-behaved, he had to say that much. Compliant, not screaming or making a big scene, nothing that would draw any attention to them—other than the occasional glance from an unenlightened few who believed the only proper mixing of black and white was coffee and milk.

He watched as they crossed over the little bridge, and came almost right up to him before veering left, past the Emporium, past a snack place, brown and white, Alpine-looking, that sat under a massive needle thing, the Carolina Skytower, which reached far into the sky and was topped off with an American flag. They drifted in and out of shadows thrown by the sprawling trees just beyond the snack place, stopping abruptly at a souvenir shop, buying post cards, him thinking she was oh so cool, so very good at this. The boy not moving, standing there with her at the cash register, obedient, neither of them realizing that a kid on his best behavior was probably going to stand out more than a screeching little rugrat in this place.

Over hidden speakers, the music from *Star Wars* blared.

Behind him, around him, was a constant din, low and rumbling, punctured by screams of happy terror, coming from the Vortex to his right, the Powderkeg Flume to his left, or any of the other whip-around rides designed to scare their willing passengers into pleasure. Fun-fear in stereo.

The crowd, more moms and dads and sons and daughters, starting to thicken.

She bought three postcards at the souvenir stand, and headed toward an old-time steamship that usually took happy people on a short, circular cruise around an island in the center of the park, except it was closed for repairs. Looking real casual as she passed it, just another snow-white suburban mom out for a day with her little black son.

Checking the backpack again, he got up, followed her.

•

"Fire away," the president agreed.

Smart move, Kevin thought, Anderson giving up nothing, instead inviting Kevin to ask questions that would send everyone a message as to what he did and didn't know. "Start at the beginning," he said, not letting himself get sucked into the ploy.

"The beginning of what?" Henry Summer asked, causing Kevin to think again that Owl Boy here didn't know what was going on.

The president killing off that notion with a curt, "Drop the façade, Henry. He knows."

Kevin looking at the chief of staff: "Yeah, Henry, he knows." Thinking of his own façade, the one he was putting out there now, wondering how long it would last or they would let it last, and what they would do to him when it crumbled, trying to come up with an alternative plan, something besides being cocky, but hitting a dry hole in the strategy department.

Summer threw his hands in the air and made a noise like a broken vacuum cleaner, clanky, mechanical, as if he was sucking air through an iron lung.

Anderson ignored the performance, stayed focused on Kevin. "Meredith, your mother"—talking about her like she wasn't in the room—"and I had an affair in the early 1960's," he began, voice level as an aircraft carrier's deck, no emotion. "It was not something I was proud of then. Nor am I proud of it now."

Kevin looked at his mother. "Is that true?"

She bit her upper lip and blinked her eyes several times, rapidly. Even in her traditional Native American New Age Rich White Western Settler outfit, she looked like the last paleface standing at Little Big Horn. As she struggled for an answer, she seemed to reach into her body for an explanation. The excursion produced nothing of value, though, and she responded with only a weak, "Yes."

"You were the product of that relationship," Anderson said, simply.

The product. Kevin nodded, looked around the room. Caught the portrait of Washington over the fireplace. Noticed how really, really white the molding was in the office, how it seemed to just leap from the pale yellow walls. Saw that the deep blue carpet with the gold presidential seal in the middle really didn't cover the whole floor, leaving a rim of hard wood at its edges. Looking at all the stuff in there—metal cowboy sculptures, antiques, outdoorsy paintings on the wall right next to brightly colored pop art—thinking the politician in Anderson was evident even in his decorations, which sought to be all things to all people. Suddenly wondering about Maxie, where she was, if they knew about her, remembering he'd forgotten to call, smiling inside at the idea of asking Anderson if he could use the phone. "So why didn't you marry her?" he asked at last, not looking at his father, instead staring out the large windows behind the president's desk.

Meredith sat up a little straighter, a weak smile fighting for space on her lips, Kevin shooting her a look that said Not so fast.

"I was married at the time," the president said, all facts, no explanation.

"So you just abandoned her?"

"Yes." All heads turned to Meredith, whose hard, angry response felt to Kevin like the preview for a meltdown. For her part, Meredith focused her rage on Anderson, who silently returned fire with a look of such utter disrespect that it made Kevin actually feel sorry for his mother.

Not removing his stare from her, Anderson said, "This is between Kevin and—"

"Let her talk," Kevin said, still acting like he had the upper hand, which everyone, himself included, knew really wasn't the case.

Meredith took a moment, smoothed her calf-length oatmeal-colored dress, fiddled anxiously with a necklace—a thick sterling silver rope and a cross of inlaid onyx stones—using the time to go back inside of herself, searching for words that had been buried for decades.

She cut her eyes from Anderson to Kevin and back, said nothing.

"Mom?" Kevin urged.

Meredith eased visibly at the sound of that one word, *Mom*, which seemed to both calm and enervate her at once. She quit fussing with her jewelry and her clothes, quit looking like a deer in a trap, quit trying to buy time she couldn't afford. Instead, she spoke directly, deeply, to her son.

"Your father was a wonderful man, Kevin," she began, Anderson shifting imperceptibly at the unanticipated compliment, though still clearly not liking the fact that this was going someplace he wasn't sure of, consuming every syllable like a man hungry for a way out. Turning to Anderson, looking at him with eyes that dreamed of murder, she added: "He was nothing like *this one.*"

Anderson came off of the sofa automatically, just enough to demonstrate that if he and Meredith had been alone, he would have put her lights out. Kevin caught it, felt his body go tight, more out of a fear of the unknown than anything else—what would he do if the man struck his mother, and what would they do to him if he went for The Commander In Chief? But Anderson quickly tamed the reflex, Kevin eased, and Meredith again drew everyone's attention.

"He was wonderful," she repeated, speaking in a clear, confident tone, no hesitation. "And he adored you as if you were his own."

"But I wasn't."

Meredith shook her head sadly. "No. He was, um"—biting her lower lip, trying to be delicate—"incapable."

"Like Gary Devereaux."

She nodded sadly. "They were the same person. Jon turned himself into Gary." Adding almost as an aside: "It was his unique gift, his talent."

Kevin recalled what Maxie told him Henry Lee Hubbard had said in prison—"Gary was a master, could change his whole looks, everything, become somebody else in a day, even less"—and understood at last.

"Gary, I mean Jon, whoever," Meredith laughed absently, hands fluttering in front of her, "he was the only man who had the integrity to do what was right. He wanted to protect my honor."

"He wanted to protect his investment," Anderson retorted, short and crisp.

"He loved me."

"What about you?" Kevin asked Anderson. "Did you love her?"

"He doesn't love anything," Meredith answered coldly, every word thick with loathing. "Anything but himself."

The president's eyes went dead, and his lips twisted into a tight line. Kevin thought he saw a slight head shudder and halfway expected white milky fluids to start oozing out of the man's mouth, like an android whose circuits couldn't take a power surge. It was the expression of someone trying to contain the residual of an internal H-bomb blast, someone not used to being spoken to as if he were a mere mortal. "I was chosen," he said at last, proudly, saying *chosen* like it was a crown. "Bart Knight selected me and brought me to Jon Columbus's attention." Henry Summer started to say something, but stopped quickly. "There was a plan, a plan for me, and if the affair had been exposed, it would have risked that plan."

"God forbid," Kevin said.

"You have to understand: They decided I had what it takes to be a leader." Saying it less like a plea or a request than an order.

"Yeah," Kevin answered, not even taking time to think about it, and certainly not treating it like an executive mandate, "like the ability to walk away from the most important commitment in your life?"

Meredith wondered if he was talking about her.

"You prove my point," Anderson answered, easily. "I couldn't leave my wife."

"You prove mine," Kevin said, just as easily and with even less thought than a moment before. "I was talking about me."

For one brief moment, maybe for the first time in his official career, President Jim Anderson didn't have a comeback. So Kevin filled the silence for him:

"But enough about me. Let's talk about Worth and Arabaq and all the good stuff."

●

Past a pizza place.

Past two kids, teenaged boys, beckoning anyone who was interested to join them for a game of laser tag, a sign sitting there promising "It's a blast."

Through a covered wooden bridge, orange-red sign saying Carolina RFD, faded water wheel to the right, to the left a shooting gallery where happy kids were aiming guns at flowers.

Bright sun overhead, large, thick trees darkening the wide walkways, providing occasional relief from the rising heat.

Crowd starting to grow. More packs of kids, most of them without parents.

More happy-scared yowls from the rumbling roller-coaster-like rides that seemed to be everywhere.

Whoops. Laughter. The sounds of smiles.

Not the little boy, though, white woman toting him just a bit too fast, not yanking him really, more like hurrying him along. No glee there, the kid just trucking on, going with it, not resisting the woman's purposeful march past Harmony Hall, brick and blocky, green and black lights hanging from its burgundy-colored awnings, looking like a Disneyfied version of some Wild West opry house, more like a faded bordello.

She peeled left, suddenly.

Okay, the man thought to himself. Okay.

He followed her for a few more seconds, wondered again why, out of nowhere, after all this time, all these years, all this distance, why she called him for backup.

Then not wondering about it anymore, instead weeding through the crowds, past Top Gun off to his left, the high, swirling ride not looking anything like the jets Tom Cruise flew, not looking like much of anything to him except motion sickness on overhead rails.

Up ahead the Paramount Action FX theatre, sign reading James Bond 007, License to Thrill.

Starting to not pay much attention to everything around him, just making sure she made the turn away from the theatre and toward another sign, which was what happened.

The thing was in play.

Looking quickly in the opposite direction, he saw the other one, dressed all in black, slicing through the crowds like a switchblade on a mission, anyone in the way had best beware.

And he started to run. Away from her.

Looking back only once, just before he rounded the bumper car pavilion, watching as she disappeared under the sign where the blonde woman and the little kid had disappeared a moment ago, the blue and orange sign, faded like a lot of other things in this family paradise, the sign that read:

Millennium Plunge.

Chapter 44

Henry Summer finally shut up. He had been arguing strongly that any questions about Arabaq, especially coming this close to the treaty signing, were affairs of national security and therefore not the province of average people. Anderson listened for maybe 30 seconds, then tersely replied that he was going to explain everything and that if the chief of staff did not like that plan he was free to leave but otherwise had better not say another goddamned word.

Which was when Henry Summer quit talking, silently rejecting the option of walking out, in-the-loop being a far better option than out-of-the-loop, moral implications aside.

Then the president, knowing full well what was about to follow and preferring that not a word of it escape his lips, turned to Walter Frost and invited him to explain. Frost took a deep breath, his jowls rising and falling as he did, and appeared to wince, like a spasm of pain had shot through him. "I assume you've read the notebook?" he asked.

Kevin nodded. "I know that you guys"—meaning Anderson mostly—"set up your own little operation in Arabaq to make chemical weapons, bankrolled by half the stock market. And Worth found out about it and was on his way to *The New York Times* to blow the whistle." He thought briefly of Taylor, wondered if she had any idea how right she'd been.

Frost smiled weakly. "Do I dare ask where it is at the moment?"

In a locker at the bus station, but Kevin wasn't about to give that up. "It's safe."

Anderson started to say something but stopped, instead turning to Frost, the order to continue implicit. "You have to understand the times. The world was an unstable place, economically and militarily. To remain strong, we needed unlimited options. A foothold in Arabaq gave America a vital presence in the Middle East. A chemical weapons capability provided a deterrent against not only the Soviets but against potential madmen and despots in the region."

"As opposed to our own home-grown madmen and despots." Looking squarely at a mute Anderson, his cracked grin almost goading the president to react. Getting no response, Kevin dropped the smile and said, "So you killed Worth to protect the secret."

"Kevin, listen to me," Anderson interjected, causing obvious discomfort to both Frost and Henry Summer. "The country had just come out of Watergate. Confidence in our national institutions was rock bottom. Can you imagine what would have happened if this had become public in that context? Can you even begin to consider the effect on the Republic?"

"Oh, I see," Kevin said, stringing each word out like he was Dr. Watson to Anderson's Sherlock Holmes, and had only just now seen how elementary the whole thing really was. "This is the old, In order to save democracy, we had to destroy democracy argument. Right?" Eyes ricocheting off everyone in the room, Meredith the only one meeting his gaze, looking at him in a blend of amazement and respect, Kevin's glare finally falling on Anderson and showing no inclination to move. "It was you, wasn't it?"

The president returned the stare with unrefined hate, said nothing.

Kevin didn't let up. "Tim Shepard was up on the landing, taking care of the security guard. Henry Lee Hubbard was with him, taking care of Buskin—"

"Gary was up there, too," Anderson said, like that made it all okay.

"Taking pictures, for God's sake," Frost added, shaking his head in utter disbelief.

"He needed a guarantee," Meredith blurted. "Jon, Gary, Jon—shit!—Jon believed absolutely you would kill him and me, and Kevin if you had to, in order to keep everything quiet." Then, straight at Anderson: "He thought you were reckless, and as time went on, unfit for political office, and after you were elected to Congress—"

Kevin, recalling the photos he'd seen on Felon Find, Anderson celebrating his congressional campaign wins—

"—and began to taste the power they had promised you, he became even more convinced of it. Those photos were his insurance. And ours."

Insurance, Kevin thought. Just like he said in the note. Slowly, he began to nod, saying, "Which brings us back to the second gunman, the one he needed insurance from." He looked around, knowing they knew what he was going to say next but wanting to see their faces when they heard the words for what he would've bet the farm was the first time. Coming back to Anderson: "I mean, you killed Worth to cover your ass, sat right there on the 12th floor, in the window next to Buskin, sat there and shot him dead in the street. Hell, after that, killing off an ex-lover and your bastard son ought to be as easy for you as a campaign promise." He'd engaged the full fire of Anderson's unmitigated fury, then tossed lighter fluid on it by adding: "Right, dad?"

Meredith let out an agonized shriek as she took in a lung full of air.

Henry Summer leaned against the president's desk, eyes big and dazed under the giant owl specs, pale as a shut-in.

Anderson said nothing, his wrath evidenced only by two tight fists that pounded a harsh cadence on his knees, right then left, right then left, his gaze unwavering, fixed on Kevin.

Walter Frost closed his eyes, whispered, barely audible, "He didn't kill the senator. I did."

•

Still running, needing a vantage point.

A huge pool off to his right, water as blue as in the movies, giant pink floats bobbing around. Kids in swimsuits everywhere, moms and dads too, the parents lounging on deck chairs, the kind with rubber-plastic strips on them, these having blue ones on the top half, white ones on the bottom.

Big Wave Bay, it was called.

A lot of screaming coming from Big Wave Bay, though not that happy-terrified kind he heard from the rides. This was screaming in a good way, fun-screaming.

It was getting hotter. He felt the sweat coming as he raced past the pool, down the broad whitish path, past some giant purplish thing, some kind of water ride or slide or something, with bright-colored translucent tubes coming out of it, wrapping around each other, looking like a Martian's intestines, then cut around the side of the pastel-colored bath house, fighting past the kids, hearing himself say 'Scuse Me at first, then Comin' Through, then Get Outta My Way, occasionally hearing some indignant park parent telling him to watch what he was doing.

Wrestling with the zipper on the large backpack.

Getting a grip on the rifle—

The sniper's rifle—

Starting to assemble it as best he could on the run—

Not hearing *Star Wars* over the speakers anymore, but the Beach Boys, *Surfin' USA*, racing past more kids having a grand old time splashing around in another pool, this one smaller, with little building-looking things in it, reminding him of monkey bars in a playground, things you could crawl on except they were in water, and people in big round inner tubes kept floating by—

Blitzing past a woman in her 50's sitting alone in a chair that looked as if she'd brought it from home, nearly knocking her over—

By now, seeing where he had to be—

The backpack starting to fall away—

Hearing someone say, Is that a gun he's got? but paying no attention, just heading for the tower, taking long strides, hoping he could kill if he had to, knowing he probably would.

•

Behind closed eyes, Walter Frost remembered:

"Who are we meeting with again?" Senator Worth asked. He sat in the back of the dark sedan with Dan Goggins. Frost was in front, driving.

"Three people," Goggins said. "David Phillip Evans, the national security writer. Shelby Howell, the managing editor for national news. And Arthur Overby, the executive editor."

"What's the format?"

"We tell them what we know."

"That's fine," Worth said, oddly sedate. "You have the notebook?"

Goggins patted a brown leather briefcase, eight or so inches thick. "Right here."

Frost kept his eyes straight ahead.

It was shortly before 12:30, and they'd just turned onto 43rd street. There was little traffic. The car pulled easily to the curb in front of the round globe light that said The Times, any other signage being absolutely unnecessary.

They stopped. No one got out.

"Senator?" Goggins asked after a moment. Getting no answer, he looked at his watch—aware that being late for a meeting with editors of The New York Times on a Sunday was not the best way to genuflect to the press—letting another couple of seconds pass before adding: "Is something wrong?"

In the front seat, Walter Frost felt a slight surge of panic. Something wrong?

Worth removed his glasses, fogged them with hot breath and cleaned the lenses on his blue and red striped tie. "We're about to put the Constitution to its second test in 12 months," he said, voice surprisingly soft. "I'd like to know that we're doing the right thing."

A little late for that, don't you think? Frost screamed in silence.

"If it's what you believe in, senator, then it's the right thing," Goggins answered.

Worth nodded slightly. "I understand that, Dan. But I spent last night wide awake, staring at the ceiling, wondering if what we're doing here today is truly in the country's best interests."

Not knowing what else to say, Goggins could only mutter, "Sir?"

For his part, Frost tried to calculate the impact of second thoughts so late in the game.

Worth slumped deeply into the blue leather car seat. "What I mean, Dan, is this: In having this press briefing, am I doing what's best for me, for my ambitions, or what's best for America? Are my beliefs, the things that drive me, are they superior to the things that drive the people?"

Goggins was dumbfounded. Walter Frost looked in the rear-view mirror, saw total alarm coming from every pore, the horror of knowing that the meeting Goggins had so painstakingly arranged could well come undone because of an 11th hour crisis of confidence, then heard Worth ask: "Are they, Walter?"

The question caught Frost off-guard, causing him to take a moment of what he hoped looked like sage thought but was in fact a chance to get his bearings. "Why do you ask me, senator?" *he replied carefully, like Goggins totally taken aback by a looming change of heart, though for different reasons.* "You know I believe we need a chemical warfare deterrent."

"What if you're right?" *Worth asked, smiling, but not that sneering, cocky grin he dispensed so freely. This one had some depth, like the senator actually understood the irony of the question, and it left Walter Frost with the feeling that his answer would determine whether Richard Worth lived or died.*

Goggins diddled with his bow tie, understanding only from his perspective what hung in the balance.

"I believe you're doing a disservice to the nation," Frost said, finally, deciding to answer honestly, just lay it out there and see what happened. "I believe that if you truly feel this is somehow improper—"

"It's illegal!" Worth erupted, banging the door panel at his right side, the words bursting like mortar shells, showing Frost the senator he had come to know and despise. "It's not improper. It is goddamned illegal! You cannot use the resources of the United States as instruments of your own personal agenda."

"I agree, senator," Walter Frost said calmly. "And I hope you'll think about what you just said."

Then he opened the door and got out, feeling the humid warmth of the early afternoon, a sharp contrast to the air-conditioned chill that Worth always demanded in a car.

From the left side, Goggins did the same. So did Worth, who for all his arrogance was never one for imperial pretensions like having a staffer double as his servant.

Walter Frost looked up.

Saw the two windows open, side by side, on the 12th floor to their left.

Saw the landing on the 16th floor to their right, a man with a rifle kneeling, knowing it wasn't the security guard he'd convinced Goggins needed to be hired, but Henry Lee Hubbard, army marksman.

Glanced down from the buildings to the street.

Saw a couple with a cheap-looking camera, taking home movies.

Just past them, a man with what was probably a basic Kodak, aiming up the street toward Times Square.

The little gaggle of country hicks across the street, bumpkins in the city, Henry Lee's family.

Then hearing, from some distant place, hearing Richard Worth call out, "You're right, Walter," the senator then turning to Goggins, saying, "Call it off, Dan," stopping right there, right on the steps in front of The Times building, Goggins starting to protest.

Then thinking about the abort signal, a simple stretch, left arm straight up, visual instructions to stop the plan if something went wrong, which following the senator's sudden reversal was exactly what was happening—

Thinking about it, but doing nothing.

Once second passed, then two, Frost feeling each of them tick by with the slowness of a Russian winter—

Worth standing there, still—

Three seconds—

Talking or arguing with Goggins, Walter Frost not knowing which, thinking only of raising his left arm, stretching it, ending the plot—

Four seconds—

Neither Worth nor Goggins moving, Frost starting to give the signal, arm feeling heavy as doom, refusing to cooperate—

Five seconds—

Arm starting to raise, Frost unaccountably worried that he might not get it up in time, starting to panic, hearing himself say, Senator! watching as Worth turned to him, a look of respect mutating into the truest smile Frost had ever seen—

Six seconds—

Worth giving him a short nod of the head, a gesture of concession and maybe thanks, that look and smile and nod—

Frost hearing car backfires, and then two muffled thuds and accompanying grunts as the bullets ripped into Worth, dropping him to the pavement, a third shot tearing away the top of his skull.

Dan Goggins, frozen in fear and confusion, opening his mouth, trying to scream, but unable to make a sound, like it was all a dream he couldn't escape, two more car backfires, dead before he hit the scorching sidewalk.

Walter Frost, dropping to the pavement, crawling to Goggins, retrieving the briefcase, the one with the report, hoping the shooters knew he was one of them, ripping the knees of his suit pants open, tearing a seam under the left arm of his coat, even at that moment knowing full well that last image of Richard Worth—that look, that nod, that smile—would haunt him forever, and then silently praying that maybe the snipers wouldn't know who he was, and just go ahead and end the misery he knew would walk with him from this moment forward.

●

"Mama!"

Maxie saw them on the wooden landing of The Millennium Plunge, a massive roller-coaster that sat on the south edge of Carowinds. The loading platform was covered in an open white structure, no sides, roof held up by a dozen or so thick wood columns, a waist-high safety fence trimmed in pale blue framing the entire landing.

She raced up the matching walkway, inclined, white and blue and fenced, and then right, and then left into the winding waiting line that fed into the platform, 12 turnstiles, each an entry to the ride—

"Mama!"

Pushing unsuspecting moms and dads and kids out of the way, hearing Hey, Watch It, but not listening, charging forward.

A deep, scratchy, amplified voice, coming from the operator inside a glass-encased control room:

"Is everybody ready?"

Lots of other voices, mostly children, screaming happy-scared, in unison: "Yeeeaaahhhh!"

Not the kid in the third car from the back, though, not J.J, who was scared-screaming, "Mama!"

Some grinding. A jerk, and a short lunge forward. The ride starting.

Maxie charging now, hard, onto the platform, seeing the massive roller-coaster start to leave, thinking No Way, Uh-Uh, climbing up on the first turnstile, leaping to the next, parallel to the ride, trying to keep her balance, trying to keep up.

"Are you sure?" The voice in the control room roared over the growing rumble of the roller-coaster as it slowly pulled out.

Maxie, still turnstile-hopping, nobody happy at her rudeness, more Heys and Watch Its, her paying no attention.

"I'm gonna give you one last chance," the voice roared, getting even louder.

Lots of high-pitched Nooooooooos.

Five more turnstiles, the ride getting ahead of her, Maxie ordering herself to forget about falling, you make it or you don't.

"Well then—"

Getting to the last one, wishing she had a moment to steady herself, knowing she didn't, leaping, sprawling—

"If you're really sure—"

And finally crashing onto the top of the last car, screaming at two teenagers, "Get out, Get Out!" neither of them moving, one saying Fuck you, both of them wriggling out from under the metal safety bar at the first sight of her gun, jumping over the side, maybe a five-foot drop into soft grass, yelling about some crazy nigger bitch.

Maxie feeling the thing starting to pick up speed under her, scrambling to get into the safety bar that was already locked in place—thinking in that instant it wasn't tight enough, and what if J.J. wasn't secure?—managing to pour herself under it after a few frantic seconds.

J.J. in front of her, two cars ahead.

And Taylor.

The guy in the glass booth screaming, "Then get ready to take The! Millennium! Pluuuuuuunnnnnngggggge!!!"

•

"Everyone was responsible, Walter," Jim Anderson said, having no idea what Frost was thinking or saying, not caring, cutting him off when the advisor started to explain. Kevin thinking how the president had still avoided any direct self-incrimination.

"We had to protect the national interest, son." Saying *son* not like they were related, but like a college professor, lecturing. Not that it mattered. "The Russians and their surrogates were making this stuff, chemical weapons, making it up like it was moonshine, and then just handing it over to crazed Middle Eastern rulers." His tone went from urgent to disdainful. "Meanwhile, back at the ranch, we're legislating our own weakness. Good God, what were men of honor supposed to do, Kevin?"

"I don't know," he replied after a second, voice thick with mockery. "Pretending this is a banana republic and murdering the opposition seems like a swell idea to me."

"What about Arabaq?" Anderson fired back, deftly not answering the question but instead turning it in another direction. "Five years later, this thug Azid takes over, murders the Royal Family and about 300,000 other 'traitors.' Let's talk about banana republics." He turned back to Frost, a clear signal that if the explanation was going to continue, it would not come from the president.

Frost sighed deeply. Kevin could almost see the burden of the past 25 years perched on his shoulders, eating away at his soul like a vulture. "Azid seized our production facilities," he began, slowly, adding almost as an afterthought: "No one got out alive." Rubbing his hands together, speaking to them and not to Kevin or Anderson. "Although we knew he did not have the technical capabilities to resume the work immediately, we felt it was just a matter of time." He shrugged. "Soviet technicians. Iraqis. Arab extremists. Whomever. Someone was going to get in there and figure out how we were doing it, and eventually turn the whole operation against us."

"Which was not acceptable," Anderson chimed in, Kevin smiling at the man's seeming instinct for finding the perfect opportunity for a patriotic statement, even when he was up to his eyeballs in lies.

"No," Frost continued, still staring at his agitated hands, "it wasn't."

"The national interest was at stake, Kevin," Anderson said firmly.

Meredith snorted. "There you go again." She appeared to be gaining courage as the truth tumbled out. The president looked at her harshly. She returned his stare without backing down.

"So we simply changed the parameters of our, uh, operation," Frost explained, ignoring any dynamic in the room. His voice shrugged. "We became an assassination team."

Kevin looked at Henry Summer, still wondering if the chief of staff had any idea what he had gotten into, or whether he thought this was just part of power's baggage, something you stepped over on the climb to the top. The man's face revealed nothing, no shame or regret or anger or amazement, nothing. He sat on the edge of the president's desk like a wax dummy.

"The companies who had invested in the facility, who had supported and staffed it, well, they had a great deal to lose if we were exposed," Frost said, his voice as devoid of feeling as Summer's face was. "They provided funds to the intelligence community, through an organization that Gary created, Americans for America, which in turn recruited and managed numerous international assassins on assignment in Arabaq."

"Azid's still alive," Kevin said, "which doesn't say a whole lot for the expertise of your mercenaries."

"We would never kill a foreign leader," Anderson blurted, again finding the perfect moment for an All-American sound bite, but this time not seeing the irony in his remark.

Kevin did see it. "As opposed to one of our own," he said, not even trying to hide the disgust.

Anderson slumped back in the sofa. Kevin could almost see the struggle going on inside the president, and Anderson's battle to prevent himself from ordering the summary execution of this smart-ass critic, blood or no blood.

"Azid was never the target," Frost said. "Not directly."

"So who was?" Kevin asked.

"His sons. In Arabaqi society, the male offspring are revered. If a woman bears a daughter before she bears a son, the child is, well—"

"Murdered," Kevin answered, remembering Raymond Trotter, thinking ever-so-briefly of Taylor, again.

Frost nodded. "Azid had 12 sons. Beginning in the early 1980s, we began to systematically eliminate every one of them. We hoped that after the first two or three, we could prevail upon the general to come to his senses, and perhaps enter into some kind of arrangement with the West in which production of these weapons would cease." He paused, shook his head. "But he just kept making more."

"And you just kept killing his sons."

"He was single-handedly destabilizing the entire region," Anderson said, like he was answering a reporter's question at a press conference, all formal and condescending. "Our economic and diplomatic well-being was at stake. We could not sit back idly while this murdering dictator threatened our future, the future of our children."

Which made Kevin laugh out loud, the comment about *future of our children.*

"Over the next 18 or 19 years, we killed 11 of them," Frost continued. "When only one remained, Azid came to the table, begging, pleading, asking us not to take his sole surviving boy."

Kevin thought about saying something like How Touching, but instead asked Anderson: "How many of them notched *your* belt?"

"I was in Congress at the time."

"So you were killing the American future instead of—"

"Remember who you are talking to, my friend," Henry Summer warned. "That is the president of the United States, and no one talks to the president in that tone."

"Maybe someone should start," Kevin retorted, almost automatically, as if it was the most logical comeback in the world.

Frost's silence suggested that maybe, just maybe, he agreed. But all he said was, "It was my operation."

"Ever the loyal soldier," Meredith muttered, shaking her head, like You Poor Foolish Old Man.

"How come it took you so long to kill them all?" Kevin asked.

"We're not barbarians," Frost smiled, sadly, finally looking up at Kevin like this was an acceptable moment to make eye contact. "We wanted them to mature, to allow Azid the opportunity to enjoy them. This government does not murder children."

"How gallant," Kevin said, repulsed and not bothering to hide it.

"We had no choice," Frost said.

"That's bullshit. You always have a choice."

"That's correct," the president said suddenly, like this was his cue to re-enter the conversation, leaning forward in the sofa, elbows resting on his knees, eyes going from Kevin to Meredith and back, as if neither Frost nor Summer were even in the same time zone. "There was a choice, and it was made." Still not implicating himself in the decision, still being smart and artful. "Whether it was right, whether it was wrong, we could debate that for eternity and never reach a consensus. It doesn't matter anyway, Kevin. It's past. Gone. History."

"Then what does matter?"

"You," the president said simply.

"Kinda late to be putting on the Dad Suit, isn't it?"

Anderson smiled. It was the smile of a gambler, someone who held a poor hand but was a good bluffer, who for safety sake had a pistol under the table, ready to dead-bang his adversary, just to be sure that he still took home all the chips in the end.

The president ignored Kevin's comment. "The way I see it," he replied instead, "you have two choices." Pausing for effect before adding: "And the question is, are you going to make the right one or the wrong one?"

Chapter 45

He'd made his way to the Tidal Wave, a water slide adjacent to The Millennium Plunge where children rode bright yellow floats through more giant intestine-looking tubes, these being green, before splashing down into a pool below, part of a complex called Carolinas' Ramblin' River.

Bolting up the bluish-purple stairs, the gun in clear view now, people scattering against the turquoise banisters like ten-pins. Reaching the first landing of the Wave's squat tower, finally getting the rifle together, taking in a full, clear view of the roller-coaster's entire route:

It swung left out of the loading platform, slowly at first, then going up and down three ever-heightening humps, climbing and falling, gaining speed for a long, torturous rise 750 feet in the air and then a swift return to earth, another sharp left at the bottom, swinging up maybe three stories from there and angling inward, whipping down through a final left and up and down two more humps before dropping into a low, flat route, slowing back into the gate.

He saw it instantly, the place where the killshot had to be delivered:

The top, as the roller-coaster crawled to its apex, in the moment when he knew it would slow, coming to an almost complete stop before reaching the peak, passing the point of no return, beginning its terrifying plunge down the other side.

He tucked himself into a corner, leaning against the sun-bleached yellow railing for support, holding the stock against his shoulder, hearing the screams that had gone from fun and frolicking to fearful and frantic.

Tuning it all out. Not thinking about what would happen when the panicked masses notified park security there was a crazy man with a gun on the water slide. Knowing there was a pistol in the backpack for just that reason.

Concentrating, focusing, thinking only: Take 'em out when they're at the top, and then, Don't choke, because there won't be a second chance.

He watched the train of white cars, a strip of checkerboard patterns lining the sides of each one, pull out of the gate. His eyes captured the last three. The two women and the son. There was a moment when he wasn't sure he could do it. The moment passed quickly. He aimed the rifle.

•

Maxie saw Taylor's gun as they gained speed and headed toward the first rise.

"Get down!" she screamed to the people in the car in front of her, a young mother and her little boy, the child dressed in denim shorts and a Jeff Gordon NASCAR T-shirt.

The mother apparently didn't hear, or was frozen in terror at the prospect of the pending 750-foot drop. The boy, however, did, turning to Maxie, and when he did the coast-to-coast smile on his face melted into horror, his young voice hollering out, "Mom, she's got a gun!" His mother swung the top of her body around, saw Maxie and her gun, swung back and saw Taylor with hers, and started to cry.

"Get your stupid white ass down!" Maxie shouted.

The mother yanked the boy into her lap and angled her body on top of his.

Then it was just the three of them. Maxie in the last car. Taylor in the third to last car, J.J. seated, eyes glued to Maxie.

The ride slowed as it took the first rise. As it did, Taylor screamed over her shoulder:

"You got a choice, mom, and not a lot of time to make it."

•

"In two days, Azid will be in Washington to sign what may well be the most important treaty of our time," Anderson was saying. "It will potentially eliminate the threat of chemical and biological warfare in the world." He added, as if in justification, "It is exactly what Senator Worth was trying to do 25 years ago."

"I bet he's smiling in that big cloakroom in the sky as we speak," Kevin said offhandedly, still wondering where the president was going with this talk about choices.

Anderson ignored the sarcasm. "You have the power, right here, right now, to destroy that treaty. I know that. We all"—sweeping his arm inclusively to the others in the room—"know that. You simply have to pick up the phone, call *The New York Times*, just like Worth was going to do, tell them what you know, and the treaty will be dead." He paused, added dramatically: "Of course, so will my presidency. And America's standing in the world. Indeed, the fate of the Republic may well reside in your hands as we speak." Another brief hesitation. "That's one choice, and I know it would make you feel awfully good, getting back at me, and your mother, and revealing all the lies and betrayal and deceit of the past 25 years." He smiled slightly. "In an odd way, you'd be doing the right thing. Richard Worth was murdered. The Constitution was circumvented. Azid's family was virtually wiped out. I don't think that anyone could argue, all things being equal, that the people don't have a right to know those things. In an ideal world, the government doesn't kill or break laws, and if it does, exposure is the ultimate price. But in a free society, it must be paid."

"I appreciate the civics lesson. On the other hand—"

"Yes," the president interrupted, "there is another hand. Another choice."

"Which is?"

"Say nothing. Do nothing. We'll take care of you, protect you, for the rest of your life."

Kevin began to blink his eyes rapidly, it total disbelief. "Wait, wait, wait, wait, wait." Put his hands up, palms out, like Stay Away From Me. "You want to make a *deal*? You're offering me what—money? power?— in exchange for my silence?"

Anderson and Frost looked squarely at Meredith, eyes telling her to speak up, explain to the boy how they'd bought her silence with thousands in cash, month after month, and turned an intelligence operative into a freelance writer whose glowing reviews transformed her obscure bed-and-breakfast into a worldwide tourist destination. Meredith's hands, which just moments before had been still and steady, were suddenly seized with tremors and her expression looked as if she was begging for a quick end, anything that prevented her from having to answer the question.

But she did, and when she did it surprised them all: "It's no way to live, Kevin. Owing them. It's no way to live at all."

The president stood as if he was going to slap her. Frost, in an action so swift and natural Kevin thought this scene must have been played out before, probably many times with many people, gripped Anderson's wrist just as it balled into a fist, then gradually and forcefully eased him back onto the sofa.

"What the president is asking," Frost began, again keeping the chief executive from reducing himself to horse trader, "is what will it take for you to protect the interests of the country."

His outrage was so thorough that Kevin could do nothing, say nothing, muttering only, "What?" voice sounding small and hollow, like a baby echo.

Anderson picked up the discussion. "That's the choice, son. Destroy me, my presidency and America's reputation because it's what *you* want to do, because it's what makes *you* feel good, because it's in *your* best interests." He shrugged nonchalantly. "Or do what's right for your country."

Kevin felt the room begin to shift under and around him, heard himself say things like Perpetuate the crime, Justify murder, Extend the cover-up, none of it sounding real, then feeling like he was losing it right there, about to tumble into the hole they'd dug for him, thinking it would almost be a good thing if he fell in, never to be seen or heard from again, liking the idea of an easy way out until Anderson snapped him back to his senses with—

"You or the country, Kevin. The high road or the low road. That's the choice."

Then at that moment thinking about that damned Wayne Earl Wiley, and his offer, which wasn't all that different from what Anderson was putting on the table, wondering to himself what it was about people who had power that made them think the rest of us could be so easily manipulated with a kind word, a false promise, a veiled threat or a stack of cash. People whose moral compass was pointed far, far west, away from everything right and good, but who still played the ethics card, thinking we didn't have the guts to trump them. Did they think we were all that weak and stupid?

Anderson apparently did. He said it again:

"You or the country, Kevin. The high road or the low road."

"And I suppose you guys think you've taken the high road?"

Henry Summer said, "We're less than 48 hours from eliminating the greatest threat of the new century."

Anderson nodded. "You have to agree, Kevin. That is the high road."

Kevin considered the president's words, which were confident, like the man knew what the answer was going to be. "Maybe you are on the high road," he began, watching as Anderson, Frost and Summer all visibly relaxed. "But if that's the high road, guys, you've all been going the wrong way."

Anderson's head snapped up sharply at the unexpected comeback, the confusion turning him uncharacteristically quiet.

Kevin didn't wait for a response. He simply added: "I want two things."

There was silence. Finally, Anderson ventured forth, hesitantly. "All right. Tell us what they are."

●

Taylor looked over her shoulder, blonde hair blowing like she was two inches from an industrial high-speed fan, as The Millennium Plunge swept down from the top of the first hump, heading for No. 2 and the eventual 750-foot drop. Although the roller-coaster rattled and shook like a small earthquake on wheels, she never took the gun off J.J., who never took his terrified eyes off Maxie.

"In about 15 seconds," she yelled, loud above the growing din of the ride, twisting her body to face Maxie, "we're gonna start to take the last big drop"—meaning they'd hit the ride's crest, 750 feet high. "When we get there, you're either gonna jump off, or I'm gonna shoot the kid."

J.J.'s eyes got big as a pizza plate. But he didn't cry, didn't even look confused, and the fear seemed to drain from his face. He just flashed Maxie a look, a look that said he knew, just *knew*, she'd figure something out.

"Why?" Maxie screaming to Taylor so the wind wouldn't blow the question away, eyes never leaving J.J., her look saying, You're doing good little man, just hang tough, this will all work out. Hoping she was actor enough to make him believe the fiction.

After they began the quick climb to the second hump, Maxie took advantage of the slowdown, trying to find some balance with her free hand, the one not holding the gun on Taylor. Underneath her, the metallic, industrial-sounding creaks of the roller-coaster broadcast its labor.

"Because I can, and I will, and I don't care," Taylor screamed back, a sick smile coming to her face. "And because you made me look bad."

J.J.'s eyes flashed to Taylor, like What are you talking about? Then back to Maxie, like What are you going to do, mama?

They hit the top of the second hump.

Speed increasing as they flew down, wind turbulence too, Maxie feeling like about 3 Gs were smacking into her face, eyes starting to water, not good, can't shoot what you can't see, and By God, Taylor Shepard was going down one way or another.

The people in the cars in front of them laughed and shrieked with glee, unaware.

The couple between them, mother protecting child, neither looking up.

Maxie wondering what the hell Taylor was talking about. Making her *look* bad?

Momentum took over, sweeping the roller-coaster up the third hump with almost no loss of speed. Maxie felt her bones vibrating. She tried to speak. Nothing came out. Her chest felt heavy, like someone was standing on it, jumping on it, crushing her lungs.

Top of the third hump.

The growing fun-fear thick among the other riders as they saw what awaited them on the other side of the rainbow-shaped steel rise.

Careening down now, the car rattling, shaking, Maxie thinking her teeth were coming out they were bouncing around so much.

In the cars ahead of them, children threw their arms into the air. Lots of Whees and happy screams.

Not from J.J., though, who just hung onto the rail, eyes pasted to Maxie's face, Maxie thinking again they were showing way too much confidence in her at this moment. "You need to know something," she screamed, louder than ever, not sure the words were making it the six or so feet from her mouth to Taylor's ears.

"What's that?" Taylor shouted back, gun still on J.J.

For reasons she could not have explained, Maxie struggled to stand up. "Nothing bad is going to happen to that child today."

Taylor laughed. "Looks to me like something already has."

They were roaring along the flat approach to the final tower, Taylor's back to the Plunge, hair flaring straight toward Maxie, blonde strands harsh and horizontal in the furious air, like icicles hanging sideways from her skull.

J.J. looking at his mother, hoping for a word, a gesture he could hang his hopes on, Maxie trying to give it to him with, "There's no way in the world I'm gonna let you harm my son." Looking to J.J., see if maybe it made him feel better.

The boy smiled, slightly, and nodded even more slightly, like he and his mother had a secret code and they'd just connected.

Approaching the big drop, barely slowing, Maxie hanging onto the metal support bar in the car like it was her escape valve, except there was nowhere to go. She tried to stabilize her footing, wishing she could crouch down low, get out of the wind resistance, anything that would take some of the risk out of the next few seconds, risk that grew about 1000 percent when Taylor put the barrel of her pistol flat against J.J.'s left temple and said, "I'm a hell of a lot more accurate at this distance than you are at that one." Meaning that even if Maxie fired first, she was as likely to miss as hit, the roller-coaster shaking her like she was some black Raggedy Ann, and when Taylor, crazy as she was, when Taylor fired she wouldn't miss, and then what would be the point of living after that?

"You're not gonna take my son," she said.

"You know something I don't know?" Taylor screamed back.

Then J.J. did the damndest thing. He winked at his mother. And in that shared moment, he looked just like his father, his long-gone father, and that thought triggered something in Maxie's head, an idea, a strategy even, and she looked at Taylor and it got even clearer, and when they hit the base of the 750-foot rise, Maxie said, "Yeah," looking at J.J., passing along her own secret visual code, one that said, Sit tight, kid, I may have a plan after all, screaming to Taylor: "As a matter of fact I do."

The roller coaster began the slow climb to the final plunge.

•

He didn't hear anything.

Not the happy cries of kids swimming. Not the Beach Boys over the sound system. Not the splashing from pools and water slides beneath him, over his shoulder. Not the low grumbles from all the other rides that were throwing families into every possible state of physical disarray, or the joyous whoops from the riders who in the back of their minds were really wondering if this was the time when everything was going to come off track.

Tracing the roller-coaster's final climb up the high, broad infrastructure of crisscrossing support girders through his sniper rifle's scope, he watched the two women, trying not to think of anything but killing one of them.

Lost in the moment, like he should be, like he had to be.

Not hearing the shouts of Up There and There He Is.

Or noticing the uniformed men, service revolvers drawn, racing past the Splash Factory.

Tuning it all out.

In his own little world, waiting for it to take the last big plunge.

•

"There's a lot of political problems with that," Henry Summer said, arms folded, shaking his head in doubt, still stitched to the edge of Anderson's desk.

Kevin looked at him, flashed a warped smile. "More than, say, head-lines about assassinations and cover-ups?"

"Arlington Cemetery is a sacred place," Summer tried to explain. "It's for heroes and warriors. Men who served their country and died for it."

"Are you saying my father wasn't a hero?" Kevin fired back, not up for a speech. "He died for what he thought was right"—aiming eye-razors at Anderson now—"not for what he thought was popular."

Frost, who had been silent to this point, happy to let the chief of staff try to finesse the subject, attempted to explain. "I think what Henry is saying is that exhuming one casket and replacing it—"

"I'm not talking about digging up anything. Leave the empty casket where it is. But I want that headstone to read Gary Devereaux, and I want my father buried someplace else in Arlington under his own name."

Frost tried again, clearly not feeling the urgency of his, or this, argu-ment. "I just don't think—"

"I don't think it's an option," Meredith said.

All eyes went to Anderson, who did not hesitate. "Done."

Summer wouldn't let go. "Sir, surely you know the can of worms—"

"Done," the president repeated, with a forceful impatience designed to remind Summer who was really in charge.

"If it makes you feel any better, Henry," Kevin added quickly and with a healthy dose of utter disrespect for Summer, "I don't want him buried with full military honors. The irony would be a little too much to handle."

Summer chewed on his lower lip, remaining silent.

"You said you had two requests," Anderson continued—

"Demands."

The president smile tightly. "Two *demands*. What's the second one?"

Kevin sat back in the sofa, crossed his legs, looking more at ease than he had any right to be. "I look at it this way, Jim." Pausing, giving the *Jim* its full run. "You really screwed up our family. I mean, you just took a wrecking ball to it. And what's even worse, you never took responsibility for any of it. You never did the right thing. Not once. Which probably explains your attraction to politics."

"You don't think this treaty—"

"I'm not talking about the goddamned treaty! I'm not talking about history or your legacy or your presidential library! Because outside of you and anyone who has anything to gain personally from those things, no one cares. Do you understand me? No. One. Cares. The only thing that matters is who you are and what you are, and there's nothing in this world that can change that. Nothing. This is life, *dad*, remember? And in life, there are no re-election campaigns, no chances for an image overhaul."

"I don't need a lecture from you on public service."

"Well you sure as hell need it from someone, because when you say 'public service' all I hear is What's In It For Me."

"I resent that."

"Yeah, well, I resent not knowing who I was all these years. And I resent being fatherless. And I resent not having somebody to turn to when I needed to talk, when I needed a friend, somebody to listen to me and advise me and tell what was right and wrong. But most of all, I resent spending my entire goddamned life in love with a memory that wasn't even true when it was real!"

Meredith stifled a sob.

Kevin felt the emotion of everything—the loss of his father, the discovery of his father, the lies behind both—begin to build from his feet, coursing its way from the very depth of his soul, racing like a thoroughbred to his heart then roaring to his brain, where the anger and sadness erupted into words whose calm quiet hid the rage that burned in every centimeter of his being.

"So don't talk to me about *resent*," he said, slowly, voice beginning to tremble, tears lining up behind his eyes. "You *resent* a bad newspaper story. You *resent* a friend who voted against you. You *resent* an ex-staffer who wrote a tell-all book. I'm your fucking son!" He tried to beat back a sob. "And I'm here to tell you that however you twist history, whatever hoops you make it jump through"—tears coming now, freely, Kevin pointing a shaking finger at Anderson—"I want you to know that you failed as a man." A deep, tortured sniffle. "You took something of unspeakable value and corrupted it. And I'm not just talking as a son, here. I'm talking as an American citizen."

He wiped his nose, rubbed his eyes, took a deep breath, basically recomposed. It took about a minute before the smart-ass worked its way back into his body. He looked at Anderson with a perverse grin that said he knew something he wasn't telling, and said: "But don't worry, dad. I am going to give you a second chance to atone for all those sins of the father."

●

"Is that right?" Taylor screamed as the ride crawled up the steep incline to the peak of The Millennium Plunge, though she didn't have to, the only real sound being the clatter of straining metal as the roller-coaster rose, the happy riders all silenced by what was about to happen. "Tell me what you know." Looking back over her shoulder toward the top, maybe 50 feet from the summit. "But be quick about it. Not a lot of time for chitchat."

Maxie felt a moment of self-doubt, a sense that her entire life had come to this point, and the only thing she had to show for it was the little kid in front of her—who at this instant had more confidence in her than she did—and a half-baked plan that could come apart in a second if she was wrong about its potential impact. For the first time, she took her gaze from J.J. and concentrated solely on Taylor, staring deeply into the woman's eyes, dead-looking like a shark's, wondering what it was that drove her, and how much of what she passed off as the story of her life was true.

Deciding it didn't matter, they were moments away from starting the Plunge, with no time for second guesses and half as much for second chances.

Always introduce a surprise at the end, she knew from her interrogation days, then strike the moment they realize you know more than you're letting on.

Now looking at J.J.

At the mother and child in front of them, shaking and crying.

At Taylor.

Climbing.

Thirty feet away.

Maxie saying, "I found your father."

●

Through the scope, he saw the blonde go suddenly still, frozen, like she was inexplicably straightened by a confusion deeper than the mysteries of life.

For one second, maybe less, the pistol eased from the little boy's head.

He waited for the other one to do something, to aim and fire, but nothing happened. Nothing except one of them looked to be handing something over to the other.

He steadied himself against the rail, rifle snug against his left shoulder, odd for a right-hander to shoot that way, and prayed that the wrong one wouldn't get into his line of fire during the exchange.

Got her in the cross hairs.

Ignored the pounding of feet up the steps of the tower, accompanied by calls of Police Police.

Took a deep breath.

Aimed.

●

The revelation had its intended effect, totally disorienting Taylor. And while she had pulled the gun slightly away from J.J.'s head, it was still too close, and Maxie knew she wasn't home, not yet.

"He was part of the conspiracy that killed Worth."

Taylor's head began to jerk, slightly at first then seeming to warm up and exploding into a violent tic. "That's not not not possible." Less of a scream than a wounded yelp, the uncomprehending cry of a wounded animal.

Fifteen feet to go, Maxie thinking maybe that was enough time if she moved fast to get the photo, reaching into her back jeans pocket, not being able to pull it out on first try, damned tight-ass pants. "One of the gunmen gave me his picture," she yelled. "At a prison in Nashville."

The words Prison In Nashville took on a meaning to her that Maxie didn't understand, a meaning that seemed to make everything she was saying true in Taylor's mind.

"Where where where where is he?" Eyes fluttering like she was in rapture, almost rolling back in her head, making her every movement even more unpredictable.

Five feet and rising slowly.

Time to end it all. Maxie took a deep breath of her own.

"He's dead, Taylor. A man named Walter Frost killed him in Nashville."

From deep inside of her, a wail dense with pain blew out of Taylor's mouth, and her entire body started twisting in place, as if it was on fire, but not before she managed a second long, low, wild moan, "Nooooooooooooo!!!" and put the pistol back at J.J.'s temple, threw her head back, like a drug-besotted shaman in some tribal ritual.

Maxie raised her pistol, knowing from the moment she did it would be seconds too late.

J.J. just looked at her, like everything was still going to be okay.

Right at the top.

From behind Maxie, somewhere, a crack.

Taylor's weird body language going mute for a fraction of a second before the side of her head disappeared into a mist of spray, red and white and gray, and she toppled over the side, taking a 750-foot plunge without the benefit of a roller-coaster.

J.J. screaming now, "Mamamamamamamamama!"

Maxie reaching across to him, over the weeping mother and terrified son, grabbing for her little boy, the love and light of her life, hanging on tight as the Millennium Plunge began.

●

"Police! Drop the gun and put your hands over your head!"

"Don't shoot don't shoot don't shoot!"

"Then drop it!"

He already had, already had his hands in the air, didn't want to give them a reason to take him down, black man with a rifle, it'd be way too easy.

They cuffed him, threw him harshly into the corner of the landing. From the ground below, there was some light applause.

The lead cop, decked out in full Kevlar, spun him around, bringing them face to face, his expression only a fraction as surprised as his voice when he blurted, "Holy fucking mother."

Three others behind him, them in Kevlar, too, getting to the landing, seeing the same thing, looks just as confused, just as shocked.

The lead man finally saying, "Jesus Christ, Carl, I hope you got some explanation for all this."

Carl Grigsby, detective, Charlotte-Mecklenburg PD, hoped he did too.

●

"I'm not sure we can do that," Anderson said after hearing Kevin's second demand.

"Seems pretty simple to me. You make a phone call to one of your cronies, some guy who gave you the maximum allowable limit and raised 100 times as much, tell him what you want, and it's a done deal."

The president shook his head. "You really think that's what government is all about? Money?"

Kevin smiled. "No, but you do." Summer started another one of his Defend The Integrity of the Office speeches, but didn't get the first word out before Kevin asked. "What time is the news conference Monday when you announce the treaty?"

"Two p.m.," Summer said.

"Courts open an nine, should give you all sorts of time."

"Kevin, we have a Constitution—"

"No, *we* have a Constitution, *Mr.* President," tapping a finger on his own chest, meaning We The People. "*You* have a problem."

"I can't just intrude into another branch of government like—"

"Yeah, you can. And if I haven't heard by noon on Monday that the aforementioned intrusion has taken place, I'll be burning up the fax to *The New York Times*, and your little treaty announcement will take a back seat to an even bigger story." He stood. "And God forbid the masses should ever see how the wizard behind the curtain is jerking their strings."

Anderson rose as well, planting a firm grip on Kevin's forearm. "What you're asking me to do is an abuse of power, son."

Kevin just stared at him for a long time before dissolving into a long, hysterical, exhausted laugh. "Whereas murdering somebody's just a mere crime against people," he said, finally, through the gasps, moving toward a door that he assumed took him anyplace out of Washington. "Jeez, you guys need a reality check bad."

As Kevin walked out, Henry Summer said something about following him, not letting him get away, trying to do something, but if Kevin noticed or heard, he didn't respond. When the president took his final shot, though, he did.

"You know," Anderson said, "there are a lot of people out there who would be proud to say their father is the president."

Which stopped Kevin halfway through his exit. He didn't turn back to him, any of them. Instead, he just stood there and said, "Name one."

He waited for an answer. When none came, he laughed again. Then he was gone.

Chapter 46

The stack of money was still there, had gotten a little thicker even.

"Padded it just a tad," Wayne Earl Wiley confirmed, leaning back in his man-in-charge chair, grinning, eyes twinkling like a couple of black Christmas lights. "Bit of interest money. Didn't want our newest partner-to-be to suffer none just because he took a rational, logical approach to the decision-making process. Hell, that's the way I legislate." He laughed.

"Let me get something straight," Kevin said, gaze not moving from the money.

Wayne Earl Wiley, Everybody's Favorite Senator, Legislator of the Century, Just the Best Human Being in the History of the World, stuck his thumbs in his brown leather suspenders, showed some serious teeth, smelling blood. "Anything you want to know, son. Anything at all."

"Don't call me son." It was a reflex answer, summoned without benefit of forethought or calculation, and brought Wiley up short. Apparently, members of the unwashed masses did not talk to important, powerful lawmakers this way.

"No need to get all pissy," he said after a moment, still smiling but meaning it even less. "We're all friends here." Not meaning that in the slightest. "Right?" Kevin shrugged, fired back a smile of his own that matched Wiley's note for note in its complete lack of honesty. "Now, what was it you wanted to get straight with me?" Making it sound like a challenge.

Kevin rubbed his chin lightly, as if deep in thought. "You know what you said a second ago, that bit about you taking a rational, logical approach to legislating?"

Wiley nodded. "Only way to conduct the people's business." Still saying *bid*-ness, Kevin wondering did they think that was cool, pronouncing it that way.

"Well, I just wanted to know if you pocketed the money before or after taking that rational, logical approach?"

The senator's face went from its usual pale, fleshy pink to stoplight red. He leaned up on his desk, an intimidation move. "I don't think I follow you." Working hard at not losing it.

Drifting into his best lost-but-not-really mode, brows furrowed, eyes narrowed, hands extended in a help-me-out-on-this gesture, voice sounding slightly confused but only slightly, Kevin said, "I'm just trying to get the process clear in my head." Looking up at him now, catching his gaze, not even trying to avoid the poison arrows Wiley's eyes were Robin Hooding at him. "Do you take your payoffs before or after you decide? I mean, do you go up to someone before a bill is introduced and say, Give me cash and I'll help you? Or do you wait until after , and go to the people it'll screw and say, Pay Me to fight it or I'll find someone on the other side who'll pay me to support it?"

Which basically caused Wayne Earl Wiley to tumble out of character for just a second, anger more explicit now thanks to a sudden tic that briefly kidnapped his right eye. He leaned further over the desk, burying his head into his shoulders, arms straight, hands bent out at the wrists, palms open, at about a 45-degree angle, like he was saying, Son, you are about this far from gettin' your ass whipped. "You got any idea who you are fuckin' with?"

"Yeah. I can read the walls in here."

"Truth be told, I'd've been hard-pressed to say you had enough sense to read, what with all this trash you're talkin' this morning. I mean, what have I done to earn this kind of treatment? Beau LaLonde, a fella you used to work for—"

"He worked for me," Kevin corrected, feeling small for making the comment, but feeling he had to do it anyway.

Not that it mattered to Wiley. "Beau comes to me, says you could use a little help. I got the stroke to do it, so I tried to help. What's so damned wrong with—"

"Beau came to you because he thought I was an easy mark."

"Hey, there's nothing wrong with taking a little handout."

"I know that. Look at you."

The thought that he'd just, basically, been accused of accepting bribes did not sit well with Wayne Earl Wiley. His eyes contracted into near slits, his mouth—the smile long gone—stretched tight as a rubber band. "I guess Beau was wrong about you."

Kevin shook his head. "No, actually, Beau was pretty much on target. I could use a little help, and God knows, I could sure use it from people such as yourself, senator. People who matter." A beat. "People with stroke."

The sudden change, from accuser to flatterer, clearly threw Wiley, who was not used to conversations whose direction he didn't control. "So you're sayin' you want to do business?" *Bid*-ness.

Kevin shook his head slowly, again looking confused, but not feeling it, not for the first time in a long time. "I don't know what I'm saying. I mean, here you are telling me to take your money. But the only reason I can find for doing that is my own personal greed. Do I need it? Damned right I do. Do I want it?" He smiled, nodded. "Man, if you only knew. But the thing is, and maybe this is what I'm saying, the thing I keep asking myself is this: What if I take your money, and the people in that little town get sick, or maybe even die? They're in your district, senator. They voted for you and they trusted you, and you're selling them out."

Wiley got indignant. "I am doin' no such thing. I am a pro-business legislator who believes strongly in my responsibility to give all sides of an issue, any issue, a fair hearing." Like Kevin was part of a sting operation, and that little speech was for the benefit of the Feds monitoring the wire.

"I understand that," Kevin replied, nodding. "I even admire it at some level. The concept, anyway. But the fact remains, you know and I know that those people will never get a fair hearing because they don't have the power to scare you or the money to buy you. And the sad truth is, it's in my best interests to be with you on this because you're probably my only hope to get back in the game." He paused. "I'm just like them. Those people with the poisoned water. The only difference is, you're giving me a chance to save myself."

Another confused look crept onto Wiley's face, one that said For crissakes, quit jabbering like a drunken granny and say if you're gonna take the money or not.

"When we first met, senator, you told me I could do what's right for me and forget about everything else, or I could worry about the good of everyone. Remember?" He looked to Wiley like he wanted an answer, which he did, although not necessarily from this man. "And when I think of it like that, it's the best argument in the world for taking your money. You know why?" Wiley just shook his head, like Kevin was from Pluto. "Because it's not my job to look out for the good of everyone. It's yours."

"And my record speaks loud and clear in that regard, thank you very much."

Kevin stood. "So I am gonna take your money, senator, and I'm gonna do what makes me feel, I don't know—not right or good, necessarily. Maybe just better."

Nervous laugh from the Legislator of the Century. "That sounds kinda like you're gonna take my money, give it to all those folks out there in the country with water problems."

"I'm no saint," Kevin said, shaking his head, "and I'm not a fool. I do that, and God knows what'll happen to me. What you'd do to me." He shrugged. "Man's got to eat, right?"

Wiley nodded. "That he does."

"So I'm going to take your money, senator, and do what good I can for me." He reached down and plucked a single $100 bill from the top of the stack, left the rest untouched, started to leave.

"Hey," Wiley called out, laughing in confusion, "didn't you forget something?"

An image flashed into Kevin's mind, and he returned to a thoroughly befuddled Wayne Earl Wiley, liking the image a lot. "In fact I did, senator. Thanks."

He picked up another $100 and turned to leave again.

"You know," Wiley called out before Kevin was out the door, "I wouldn't be discussing our business with anybody else. People might get the wrong idea."

"Relax, senator, I'm not going to drop a dime on you." Not turning around, not giving Wiley the respect of a face-to-face response. "I can't change how the system works, and my guess is that even if you went down, someone else would pop up to take your place, and nothing would be any different." Now he turned. "But I won't let you beat me. Not any more. That may not be the same as winning, I'll admit. But it's better than giving in."

"Damn, you sound like you're gonna go out, get a gun and start shooting people." Which Wiley, thinking this boy had lost his mind, did not believe was beyond the realm of possibility.

But Kevin just laughed at the thought. "Senator, let me tell you something. I know first-hand that doesn't work. Trust me." He left.

Outside, rain clouds were carpet-bombing the streets below. Naturally, Kevin was without an umbrella, which for an odd reason didn't bother him. Shrinks might say that after all the insanity of the past two weeks, he needed a kind of ritual cleansing, a baptism into the world—a new world, a different world—that now awaited him. But that was psycho-bullshit, and Kevin knew the truth was a whole lot simpler: Wayne Earl Wiley made him want to take a shower.

By the dumpster on the sidewalk, the same homeless guy Kevin had seen when he first met with Wiley was looking at his reflection in a compact disc. The man appeared lost in the image, running his free hand through long, wet, stringy hair like he was preparing for a close-up, repeating over and over, "You good-looking SOB, don't you ever die," the voice strong and without pretense, like he believed, really believed, his own words. A white mini-van flew by, tossing a cascade of water over his already soaked pant legs, him not caring much at all.

"Hey," Kevin called, gently.

The guy froze, snapped his head around, death grip on the CD. "I found this, it's mine, didn't take it from anybody."

Rain was still pounding down, as if God was trying to get back at them for some unknown sin. But neither tried to duck under an awning, or into a doorway or alley. Just a couple of homeless pals, having a discussion over a big green garbage can in a thunderstorm, accepting the nature of things and dealing with it the best they could. "I have something for you," Kevin said, spitting rainwater off his lips as he spoke.

"Yeah?" The homeless man was wary.

Kevin nodded, reached into his pocket. "Yeah." He pulled out one of the $100 bills he'd taken from Wayne Earl Wiley—the one he'd gone back for, actually—and handed it the guy. "Here."

The man looked at the money, watched the rain drip from his forehead onto the bill, then up at Kevin. "What do I have to do for this?" he asked finally, the rusting gears in his head clanging as he tried to balance his desire for the cash with whatever burden it imposed. "I don't do no kinky shit. I'm a moral, upright man."

"I know that," Kevin nodded, seeing the grubby dignity and respecting it. "You don't have to do anything."

Which both reassured and puzzled the man. "Ain't no free lunches in this world, man, 'specially when a C-note's involved." He squinted with suspicion. "You're not with the government are you, paying me to be in some experiment, something where they take your mind, rearrange the brain cells, make you believe everything they say?"

Kevin laughed. "Just take the money."

"Because I don't work for the government, won't work for the government, uh-uh, no how no way, and I know they're after me, know they're after me, know they're after me, but I ain't goin', not without a fight, not me."

"That's why I'm giving it to you." Kevin took the hundred back, folded it in half, slipped it into the man's soggy shirt pocket. "To help you fight."

"They'll win if you let 'em, win if you let 'em, win if you let 'em."

"I know."

Neither moved for a second, the homeless guy scratching at the growth on his face before finally putting out his hand and saying, "I'm Harold. Who're you?"

Kevin took his hand, gripped it firmly, feeling an odd shot of strength from the connection. But he didn't answer, just shrugged and smiled and said, "Gotta run, Harold." Which he did.

Standing on the street corner, waiting for the light to turn, he heard that sand-papery voice behind him, Harold's, calling out through the rain, "It's the beginning, you know. Of the millennium. We didn't miss our chance. That's what I decided when I woke up at the shelter this morning. Just felt something good was gonna happen, and it was gonna be this day, this day, this day, felt it right down to my bones, down to my bones, knew good things were gonna start today."

Kevin looked at his watch, 11:05, and no word from Washington, turned to Harold and shook his head. "I don't know, man. It's still too early to say for sure."

•

Standing in the checkout line at the Wal-Mart superstore, Kevin was thinking about his conversation with Ty Roper, the Island City detective. Remembering the cop say that if he was ever banging around on the makeshift drum kit Kevin and his father had rigged, and remembered anything important, to let him know. Him telling Roper he didn't have the set anymore, that he put away childish things, Roper saying, "Maybe you ought to think about rebuilding it, you know? Help you remember things."

Kevin answering, "I remember things just fine, detective. Just fine."

Which was true then, less so now.

The middle-aged woman at the register finished ringing up the cheese grater, the pie plates, a large wooden picture frame that he'd stretch a piece of canvas over, some kid's plastic drumsticks and a round, two-foot-wide white Naugahyde ottoman. Came to $55.17. Kevin gave her the other $100 bill he'd taken from Wayne Earl Wiley. He bagged everything himself, tossing it in the shopping cart with the ottoman and heading to the parking lot. When the checkout woman chased him down outside, saying he'd forgotten his change, he smiled slightly and told her to keep it, buy something nice for her kids. As he pulled out of the lot and into traffic, Kevin could still see her image in the rear-view mirror, just standing there, stunned at the gesture.

He checked his watch again, 11:51. It was time.

There was a Kinko's just up from the Wal-Mart. The document itself, the backgrounder that Worth had originally planned to leave with *The Times*, ran 71 pages. He first thought about sending it in parts, from three or four different locations, like he was going to disguise his whereabouts. Cloak-and-dagger stuff, except it didn't matter, because the White House knew who he was and where he was, and if they couldn't put their finger on him exactly, they'd figure out a way to find him. So now the plan was to just fax it all from one place, suck up the $15 or $20 in charges, call it his donation to good government.

He slowly pulled the Explorer into the Kinko's lot, careful to avoid a rain-filled hole in the macadam that could've swallowed a small house. Funny, but there hadn't been a doubt in his mind that he'd go through with the threat, and even now, at the proverbial point of no return, he didn't feel anything resembling a second thought knocking on the door of his self-preservation. He had asked them to do something, they hadn't come through, a deal was a deal.

As he reached for the blue notebook, Kevin's cell phone rang. He felt no anxiety, no relief, no tension, nothing, because they'd numbed him to the after-effects of what he was about to do. Whatever happened, happened, and the only thing he thought about as he answered the call was who would be at the other end of the line.

And for all the possible suspects who might've delivered whatever news awaited, the last messenger he expected was Maxie.

"What do you know about things?" she asked, not bothering to say Hello, How are you, Why haven't you called in the past couple of days, Where have you been.

"A lot more than I did two weeks ago," he said. "Or maybe a lot less. I'm not sure which. By the way, nice to hear from you."

"I've been rather busy, junior. Don't you read the papers?"

He had, saw the stories about how an off-duty cop, acting on a tip, had taken out a kidnaper on a fun family ride, Kevin thinking it would be in everybody's best interest if he just stayed out of it. "Yeah."

Maxie paused. "She was nuts, you know." Talking about Taylor, which he expected. "I wish I could tell you I was sorry for what happened, that I know you got to be hurting—"

"I'm not." And mostly, he wasn't. There was some pain, sure, but it came from a lot of places, most of them far deeper than Taylor Shepard. "You saved your son, Max. Nothing else in this world matters after that."

"Bitch was about to blow my little boy's head off, man. There's not a night gonna go by I won't pray she'll somehow come back, so I can kill her all over."

"I don't blame you." He didn't, either. Kevin only had some vague suspicions as to Taylor's role in all this, none of them mattering now, him not really interested in dissecting some *Fatal Attraction* thing at the moment. He was just glad to still be among the living, to have survived a dance with the demons.

"Just so we understand each other," Maxie said. Kevin replied that they did. "Good. Now that we've dispensed with the nicey-nice, let's get back to the question of the moment: What do you know about things?"

Kevin not sure how to play this, what to say or not say, certain only that he had to keep her on the sidelines as best he could. "You mean the things about Worth and the president and all that?"

"No. But if you want to start there, I'm happy to go along."

"And if I don't?"

She paused, Kevin hearing her take a deep breath at the other end, bracing himself for a Mad Maxie moment, surprised, even shocked, when all she said was, "As long as you're comfortable with that, and you're safe, I don't much care. Are you?"

"Hang on." It was just about noon. Kevin gathered the notebook, got out of the car, ran quickly through the hammering rain into the Kinko's, cell phone in hand. He asked the college girl at the counter where the fax machine was. She pointed to a small island that stood against one wall.

"Now what was it you said?" Kevin asked, removing the pages from the three-ring binder, setting them on the table next to the fax. Behind him, the incessant chatter of warp-speed copying machines filled the large open room.

"I asked if you were safe."

"No, I meant before, when you asked something about knowing things."

"Yeah," Maxie said, letting him off the hook but only for a second, "like how the law works."

"I know it rarely works, and when it does, it's not for people like you and me."

"That's what I thought, too, man. Then this morning, my lawyer calls."

Kevin stopped taking the pages from the notebook. "Your lawyer?"

"Uh-huh. I'm getting J.J. back. For good. Carmella and Theo dropped their custody action."

Son of a bitch, he thought. They came through. "That's great, Max. Just wonderful."

"Gets even better."

Which blindsided Kevin. His demand to Anderson had been simple: Get Maxie's child back to her permanently. There was nothing he asked for on top of that, so what was she talking about, something *even better*? "What happened?"

"His father came home, too."

"Oh, yeah?" Genuinely surprised.

"Uh-huh. Well, actually, he never left. He's been here the whole time. I've been kinda holding out on you, man. But don't feel like the Lone Ranger, 'cause I've been doing it to everyone."

At which point Kevin was thinking about Carowinds and J.J. and Taylor, and how it all made perfect sense. "Carl Grigsby," he said.

"The very same."

"But isn't he married?" Starting to put the document back in the notebook, wondering what he'd do with it now, deciding to delay that decision, at least for the moment.

"I didn't say he was the *perfect* father," she laughed. "Just the father. Which given everything that's been pouring down on us lately, that's probably good enough."

Couldn't argue with that. "He gonna leave his wife? What's the deal?"

"The deal, skippy, is to take it one step at a time. All he's done is to acknowledge that J.J. is his. Told his wife—Muffie or Trixie or some other name that's better fit for a poodle than a human, not that she qualifies—explained everything. So now we wait."

"Wait for what?"

"What happens next."

"Any idea what that's going to be?"

"Not a clue. But you know something? That's okay, too. Because my kid is back, and so's his father—sort of—and while a week ago everything looked like it was pretty much going to hell, today we seem to have climbed our way up to purgatory. Who knows, maybe we'll get out of this thing yet." Kevin said he understood. Perfectly. "So what do you think happened, I mean, with the custody case?"

Everything was packed up, the pages back in the notebook, Kevin heading to the car, getting soaked, not caring. He briefly considered telling her the story, at least about his deal with Anderson, but decided against it. Her world had taken a turn for the better, no point screwing that up. "Who knows?" he said, settling in behind the wheel, dripping. "Maybe you got friends in high places." Trying to sound jokey but not really pulling it off, the comment probably being a little too close to the truth, at least the way he saw it.

"Or maybe *you* do," was all she said, four words, but enough to let him know she was on to him. "And for the record, if that happens to be the case, I just wanted to say thanks."

"Don't thank me," he answered, a bit too fast and defensively. "I'm just a rat in somebody else's cage."

She laughed. "No, man, what you are is a fox in a hen house. A big *white* hen house."

That shook him a bit. "Max, listen, whatever you know or think you know, please don't say—"

"I don't. I won't. See you in the funny papers." She broke the connection without another word, both of them knowing that any further discussion was unnecessary.

Stopping the car in his driveway a few minutes later, Kevin stole a quick look at the notebook, thought about Maxie and J.J., silently thanking anyone who would listen that it had worked out, that he didn't have to reveal the document, in some strange, perverted way appreciating the fact that Anderson had come through, and everything could stay secret. Maybe it wasn't the best outcome, maybe not the worst, and maybe it still left way too many unanswered questions about how he'd gotten to this place, and what tomorrow held, and every day after that. Didn't matter. Because even with the doubts and the mysteries and the lies, the strange thing was he really *did* feel safe. For how long was anybody's guess. But at least for the moment. The world being what it was, that was enough.

Not up for any more deep thoughts, he quickly stashed them someplace in the back of his mind and got out of the car, oblivious to the rain, grabbed the stuff from Wal-Mart and headed toward the apartment. There would be time enough to sort things out, decide what they meant, if anything. And when that time came, he'd be ready. Right now, though, right now there was a drum set that needed rebuilding. Memories, too.

About the Author

Doug Williams is the principal of Lone Star Writers Group, a business communications and writing training firm headquartered in Houston, Texas.

9 780595 158645